Clive Cussler

Clive Cussler grew up in Alhambra, California, and attended Pasadena City College before joining the Air Force. He went on to a successful advertising career, winning many national honours for his copywriting. Now a full-time bestselling author, he has also explored the deserts of the American Southwest in search of lost gold mines, dived in isolated lakes in the Rocky Mountains looking for lost aircraft and hunted under the sea for shipwrecks of historic significance, discovering and identifying more than sixty. Like his hero, Dirk Pitt, he is also an avid enthusiast of classic cars. He is married with three children, and divides his time between Colorado and Arizona.

For automatic updates on Clive Cussler visit HarperCollins.co.uk and register for Author Tracker.

CLIVE CUSSLER

INCA GOLD

HarperCollins*Publishers*

HarperCollins*Publishers*
77–85 Fulham Palace Road,
Hammersmith, London W6 8JB

www.harpercollins.co.uk

This paperback edition 2005
1

First published in Great Britain
by HarperCollins*Publishers* 1994

ISBN 978-0-00-788847-4

Set in Meridien

Printed and bound in Great Britain by
Clays Limited, St Ives plc

In memory of
Dr Harold Edgerton
Bob Hesse
Eric Schonstedt
and
Peter Throckmorton
loved and respected by everyone
whose lives they touched

In 1997 the United States, the only nation in the world still adhering to a non-decimal standard of measurement, finally converted to the metric system – a compelling necessity if the nation wanted to be competitive in the international trade arena.

The Mysterious Intruders

INCA SEAGOING VESSEL

They came from the south with the morning sun, shimmering like ghosts in a desert mirage as they slipped across the sun-sparkled water. The rectangular cotton sails on the flotilla of rafts sagged lifelessly under a placid azure sky. No commands were spoken as the crews dipped and pulled their paddles in eerie silence. Overhead, a hawk swooped and soared as if guiding the steersmen towards a barren island that rose from the centre of the inland sea.

The rafts were constructed of reed bundles bound and turned up at both ends. Six of these bundles made up one hull, which was keeled and beamed with bamboo. The raised prow and stern were shaped like serpents with dog heads, their jaws tilted towards the sky as if baying at the moon.

The lord in command of the fleet sat on a thronelike chair perched on the pointed bow of the lead raft. He wore a cotton tunic adorned with turquoise platelets and a wool mantle of multicolored embroidery. His head was covered with a plumed helmet and a face mask of gold. Ear ornaments, a massive necklace, and arm bracelets also gleamed yellow under the sun. Even his shoes were fashioned from gold. What made the sight even more astonishing was that the crew members were adorned no less magnificently.

Along the shoreline of the fertile land surrounding the sea, the local native society watched in fear and wonder as the foreign fleet intruded into their waters. There were no attempts at defending their territory against invaders. They were simple hunters and foragers who trapped rabbits, caught fish, and harvested a few seeded plants and nuts. Theirs was an archaic culture, curiously unlike their neighbours to the east and south who built widespread empires. They lived and died without ever constructing massive temples to a race of gods and now watched in fascination at the display of wealth and power that moved across the water. As one mind they saw the fleet as a miraculous appearance of warrior gods from the spirit world.

The mysterious strangers took no notice of the people crowding the shore and continued paddling towards their destination. They were on a sanctified mission and ignored all distractions. They propelled their craft impassively, not one head turned to acknowledge their stunned audience.

They headed straight for the steep, rock-blanketed slopes of a small mountain making up an island that rose 200 metres (656 feet) from the surface of the sea. It was uninhabited and mostly barren of plant life. To the local people who lived on the mainland it was known as the dead giant because the crest of the long, low mountain resembled the body of a woman lying in wakeless sleep. The sun added to the illusion by giving it a glow of unearthly radiance.

Soon the lustrously attired crewmen grounded their rafts on a small pebble-strewn beach that opened into a narrow canyon. They lowered their sails, woven with huge figures of supernatural animals, symbols that added to the hushed fear and reverence of the native onlookers, and began unloading large reed baskets and ceramic jars on to the beach.

Throughout the long day, the cargo was stacked in an immense but orderly pile. In the evening, as the sun fell to the west, all view of the island from the shore was cut off. Only the faint flicker of lights could be seen through the darkness. But in the dawn of the new day, the fleet was still snug on shore and the great mound of cargo was unmoved.

On top of the island mountain much labour was being expended by stone workers assaulting a huge rock. Over the next six days and nights, using bronze bars and chisels, they laboriously pecked and hammered the stone until it slowly took on the shape of a fierce, winged jaguar with the head of a serpent. When the final cutting and grinding were finished, the grotesque beast appeared to leap from the great rock it was carved upon. During the sculpting process the cargo of baskets and jars was slowly removed until there was no longer any trace.

Then one morning the inhabitants looked across the water at the island and found it empty of life. The enigmatic people from the south, along with their fleet of rafts, had disappeared, having sailed away under cover of darkness. Only the imposing stone jaguar/serpent, its teeth curved in a bed of bared fangs and with slitted eyes surveying the vast terrain of endless hills beyond the small sea, remained to mark their passage.

Curiosity quickly outweighed fear. The next afternoon, four men from the main village along the coast of the inland sea, their courage boosted by a potent native brew, pushed off in a dugout canoe and paddled across the water to the island to investigate. After landing on the little beach, they were observed entering the narrow canyon leading inside the mountain. All day and into the next their friends and relatives anxiously awaited their return. But the men were never seen again. Even their canoe vanished.

The primitive fear of the local people increased when a great storm suddenly swept the small sea and turned it into a raging tempest. The sun blinked out as the sky went blacker than anyone could ever remember. The frightening darkness was accompanied by a terrible wind that shrieked and churned the sea to froth and devastated the coastal villages. It was as though a war of the heavens had erupted. The violence lashed the shoreline with unbeliev-able fury. The natives were certain the gods of the sky and darkness were led by the jaguar/serpent to punish them for their intrusion. They whispered of a curse against those who dared trespass on the island.

Then as abruptly as it came, the storm passed over the horizon and the wind died to a baffling stillness. The brilliance of the sun burst on to a sea as calm as before. Then gulls appeared and wheeled in a circle above an object that had been washed on to the sandy beach of the eastern seashore. When the people saw the unmoving form lying in the tide line, they approached warily and stopped, then cautiously moved forward and peered down to examine it. They gasped as they realized it was the dead body of one of the strangers from the south. He wore only an ornate, embroidered tunic. All trace of golden face mask, helmet, and bracelets was gone.

Those present at the macabre scene stared in shock at the appearance of the corpse. Unlike the dark-skinned natives with their jet black hair, the dead man had white skin and blond hair. His eyes were staring sightless and blue. If standing, he would have stood a good half-head taller than the astonished people studying him.

Trembling with fear, they tenderly carried him to a canoe and gently lowered him inside. Then two of the bravest men were chosen to transport the body to the island. Upon reaching the beach they quickly laid him on the sand and paddled furiously back to shore. Years after those who witnessed the remarkable event had died, the bleached skeleton could still be observed partly embedded in the sand as a morbid warning to stay off the island.

It was whispered the golden warriors' guardian, the winged jaguar/serpent, had devoured the inquisitive men who trespassed its sanctuary, and no one ever again dared risk its wrath by setting foot on the island. There was an eerie quality, almost a ghostliness about the island. It became a sacred place that was only mentioned in hushed voices and never visited.

Who were the warriors in gold and where did they come from? Why had they sailed into the inland sea and what did they do there? The witnesses had to accept what they had seen; no explanation was possible. Without knowledge the myths were born. Legends were created and nurtured when the surrounding land was shaken by an immense earthquake that destroyed the shoreline villages. When, after five days, the tremors finally died away, the great inland sea had vanished, leaving only a thick ring of shells on what was once a shoreline.

The mysterious intruders soon wove their way into religious tradition and became gods. Through time, stories of their sudden manifestation and disappearance grew and then eventually faded until they were but a bit of vague supernatural folklore handed down from generation to generation, by a people who lived in a haunted land where unexplained phenomena hovered like smoke over a campfire.

Cataclysm

Captain Juan de Anton, a brooding man with Castilian green eyes and a precisely trimmed black beard, peered through his spyglass at the strange ship following in his wake and raised his eyebrows in mild surprise. A chance encounter, he wondered, or a planned interception?

On the final lap of a voyage from Callao de Lima, de Anton had not expected to meet other treasure galleons bound for Panama, where the king's wealth would be packed aboard mules for a journey across the isthmus, and then shipped over the Atlantic to the coffers of Seville. He perceived a trace of French design in the hull and rigging of the stranger trailing his wake a league and a half astern. If he had been sailing the Caribbean trade routes to Spain de Anton would have shunned contact with other ships, but his suspicions cooled slightly when he spied an enormous flag streaming from a tall staff on the stern. Like his own ensign, snapping tautly in the wind, it sported a white background with the rampant red cross of sixteenth-century Spain. Still, he felt a trifle uneasy.

De Anton turned to his second-in-command and chief pilot, Luis Torres. 'What do you make of her, Luis?'

Torres, a tall, clean-shaven Galician, shrugged. 'Too small for a bullion galleon. I judge her to be a wine merchantman out of Valparaiso heading for port in Panama the same as we.'

'You do not think there is a possibility she might be an enemy of Spain?'

'Impossible. No enemy ships have ever dared attempt the passage through the treacherous labyrinth of the Magellan Strait around South America.'

Reassured, de Anton nodded. 'Since we have no fear of them being French or English, let us put about and greet them.'

Torres gave the order to the steersman, who sighted his course across the gun deck from under a raised trunk on the deck above. He manhandled a vertical pole that pivoted on a long shaft that turned the rudder. The *Nuestra Señora de la Concepción*, the largest and most regal of the Pacific armada treasure galleons, leaned on to her port side and came around on a reverse course to the southwest. Her nine sails filled from a swift, easterly offshore breeze that pushed her 570-ton bulk through the rolling swells at a comfortable five knots.

Despite her majestic lines and the ornate carvings and colourful art designs painted on the sides of her high stern and forecastle, the galleon was a tough customer. Extremely rugged and seaworthy, she was the workhorse of the oceangoing vessels of her time. And if need be, she could slug it out with the best privateers a marauding sea nation could throw at her to defend the precious treasure in her cargo holds.

To the casual eye, the treasure galleon looked to be a threatening warship bristling with armament, but surveyed from the inside she could not conceal her true purpose as a merchant ship. Her gun decks held ports for nearly fifty four-pound cannon. But lulled by the Spanish belief that the South Seas were their private pond, and the knowledge that none of their ships had ever been attacked or captured by a foreign raider, the *Concepción* was lightly armed with only two guns to reduce her tonnage so she could carry heavier cargo.

Now feeling that his ship was in no danger, Captain de Anton casually sat on a small stool and resumed peering through his spyglass at the rapidly approaching ship. It never occurred to him to alert his crew for battle just to be on the safe side.

He had no certain foreknowledge, not even a vague premonition that the ship he had turned to meet was the *Golden Hind*, captained by England's indefatigable seadog, Francis Drake, who stood on his quarterdeck and calmly stared back at de Anton through a telescope, with the cold eye of a shark following a trail of blood.

'Damned considerate of him to come about and meet us,' muttered Drake, a beady-eyed gamecock of a man with dark red curly hair complemented by a light sandy beard that tapered to a sharp point under a long swooping moustache.

'The very least he could do after we've chased his wake for the past two weeks,' replied Thomas Cuttill, sailing master of the *Golden Hind*.

'Aye, but she's a prize worth chasing.'

Already laden with gold and silver bullion, a small chest of precious stones, and valuable linens and silks after capturing a score of Spanish ships since becoming the first English vessel to sail into the Pacific, the *Golden Hind*, formerly named the *Pelican*, pounded through the waves like a beagle after a fox. She was a stout and sturdy vessel with an overall length of about 31 metres (102 feet) and a displacement tonnage of 140. She was a good sailor and answered the helm well. Her hull and masts were far from new, but, after a lengthy refit at Plymouth, she had been made ready for a voyage that was to take her 55,000 kilometres (over 34,000 miles) around the world in thirty-five months, in one of the greatest sea epics of all time.

'Do you wish to cut across her bow and rake the Spanish jackals?' Cuttill inquired.

Drake dropped his long telescope, shook his head, and smiled broadly. 'The better part of courtesy would be to trim sail and greet them like proper gentlemen.'

Cuttill stared uncomprehending at his audacious commander. 'But suppose they've put about to give battle?'

'Not damned likely her captain has a notion as to who we are.'

'She's twice our size,' Cuttill persisted.

'According to the sailors we captured at Callao de Lima, the *Concepción* carries only two guns. The *Hind* boasts eighteen.'

'Spaniards!' Cuttill spat. 'They lie worse than the Irish.'

Drake pointed at the unsuspecting ship approaching bow on. 'Spanish ship captains run rather than fight,' he reminded his feisty subordinate.

'Then why not stand off and blast her into submission?'

'Not wise to fire our guns and run the risk of sinking her with all her loot.' Drake clapped a hand on Cuttill's shoulder. 'Not to fear, Thomas. If I scheme a crafty plan, we'll save our powder and rely on stout Englishmen who are spoiling for a good fight.'

Cuttill nodded in understanding. 'You mean to grapple and board her then?'

Drake nodded. 'We'll be on her decks before her crew can prime a musket. They don't know it yet, but they're sailing into a trap of their own making.'

Slightly after three in the afternoon, the *Nuestra Señora de la Concepción* came about on a parallel course to the northwest again and ranged towards the *Golden Hind*'s port quarter. Torres climbed the ladder to his ship's forecastle and shouted across the water.

'What ship are you?'

Numa de Silva, a Portuguese pilot Drake had appropriated after capturing de Silva's ship off Brazil, replied in Spanish, '*San Pedro de Paula* out of Valparaiso.' The name of a vessel Drake had seized three weeks earlier.

Except for a few crew members who were dressed as Spanish sailors, Drake had hidden the mass of his men below decks and armed them with protective coats of mail and an arsenal of pikes, pistols, muskets, and cutlasses. Grappling hooks attached to stout ropes were stowed along the bulwarks on the top deck. Crossbowmen were secretly stationed in the fighting tops above the mainyards of the masts. Drake forbade firearms in the fighting tops where musket fire could easily ignite the sails into sheets of flame. The mainsails were hauled up and furled to give the bowmen an unobscured line of vision. Only then did he relax and patiently wait for the moment to attack. The fact that his Englishmen numbered eighty-eight against the Spanish crew of nearly two hundred bothered him not at all. It was not the first time nor the last he would ignore superior odds. His renowned fight against the Spanish Armada in the English Channel was yet to come.

From his view, de Anton saw no unusual activity on the decks of the seemingly friendly and businesslike ship. The crew looked to be going about their duties without undue curiosity towards the *Concepción*. The captain, he observed, leaned casually against the railing of the quarterdeck and saluted de Anton. The newcomer seemed deceptively innocent as it unobtrusively angled closer to the big treasure galleon.

When the gap between the two ships had narrowed to 30 metres (97 feet), Drake gave an almost imperceptible nod, and his ship's finest sharpshooter, who lay concealed on the gun deck, fired his musket and struck the *Concepción*'s steersman in the chest. In unison the crossbowmen in the fighting tops began picking off the Spaniards manning the sails. Then, with the galleon losing control of its steerageway, Drake ordered his helmsman to run the *Hind* alongside the bigger vessel's high sloping hull.

As the ships crushed together and their beams and planking groaned in protest, Drake roared out, 'Win her for good Queen Bess and England, my boys!'

Grappling hooks soared across the railings, clattered and caught on the *Concepción*'s bulwarks and rigging, binding the two vessels together in a death grip. Drake's crew poured on to the galleon's deck, screaming like banshees. His bandsmen added to the terror by beating on drums and blaring away on trumpets. Musket balls and arrows showered the dumbfounded Spanish crew as they stood frozen in shock.

It was over minutes after it began. A third of the galleon's crew fell dead or wounded without firing a shot in their defence. Stunned by confusion and fear they dropped to their knees in submission as Drake's crew of boarders brushed them aside and charged below decks.

Drake rushed up to Captain de Anton, pistol in one hand, cutlass in the other. 'Yield in the name of Her Majesty Queen Elizabeth of England!' he bellowed above the din.

Dazed and incredulous, de Anton surrendered his ship. 'I yield,' he shouted back. 'Take mercy on my crew.'

'I do not deal in atrocities,' Drake informed him.

As the English took control of the galleon, the dead were thrown overboard and the surviving crew and their wounded were confined in a hold. Captain de Anton and his officers were escorted across a plank laid between the two ships on to the deck of the *Golden Hind*. Then, with the characteristic courtesy that Drake always displayed towards his captives, he gave Captain de Anton a personally guided tour of the *Golden Hind*. Afterwards he treated all the galleon's officers to a gala dinner, complete with musicians playing stringed instruments, solid silver tableware, and the finest of recently liberated Spanish wines.

Even while they were dining, Drake's crewmen turned the ships to the west and sailed beyond Spanish sea-lanes. The following morning they heaved to, trimming the sails so that the ship's speed fell off but they maintained enough headway to keep the bows up to the seas. The next four days were spent transferring the fantastic treasure trove from the cargo holds of the *Concepción* to the *Golden Hind*. The vast plunder included thirteen chests of royal silver plate and coins, eighty pounds of gold, twenty-six tons of silver bullion, hundreds of boxes containing pearls and jewels, mostly emeralds, and a great quantity of food stores such as fruits and sugar. The catch was to be the richest prize taken by a privateer for several decades.

There was also a hold full of precious and exotic Inca artifacts that were being transported to Madrid for the personal pleasure of His Catholic Majesty, Philip II, the King of Spain. Drake studied the artifacts with great astonishment. He had never seen anything like them. Reams of intricately embroidered Andean textiles filled one section of the hold from deck to ceiling. Hundreds of crates contained intricately sculpted stone and ceramic figures mingled with highly crafted masterpieces of carved jade, superb mosaics of turquoise and shell, all plundered from sacred religious temples of the Andean civilizations overrun by Francisco Pizarro and succeeding armies of gold-hungry conquistadors. It was a glimpse of magnificent artistry that Drake never dreamed existed. Oddly, the item that interested him most was not a masterwork of three-dimensional art inlaid with precious stones but rather a simple box carved from jade with the mask of a man for a lid. The masked lid sealed so perfectly the interior was nearly airtight. Inside was a multicolored tangle of long cords of different thicknesses with over a hundred knots.

Drake took the box back to his cabin and spent the better part of a day studying the intricate display of cords tied to lesser cords in vibrantly dyed colours with the knots tied at strategic intervals. A gifted navigator and an amateur artist, Drake realized that it was either a mathematical instrument or a method of recording dates as a calendar. Intrigued by the enigma, he tried unsuccessfully to determine the meaning behind the coloured strands and the different disposition of the knots. The solution was as obscure to him as to a native trying to interpret latitude and longitude on a navigational chart.

Drake finally gave up and wrapped the jade box in linen. Then he called for Cuttill.

'The Spaniard rides higher in the water with most of her riches relieved,' Cuttill announced jovially as he entered the captain's cabin.

'You have not touched the artworks?' Drake asked.

'As you ordered, they remain in the galleon's hold.'

Drake rose from his worktable and walked over to the large window and stared at the *Concepción*. The galleon's sides were still wet several feet above her present waterline. 'The art treasures were meant for King Philip,' he said. 'Better they should go to England and be presented to Queen Bess.'

'The *Hind* is already dangerously overladen,' Cuttill protested. 'By the time another five tons are loaded aboard, the sea will be lapping at our lower gunports, and she won't answer the helm. She'll founder sure as heaven if we take her back through the tempest of Magellan Strait.'

'I don't intend to return through the strait,' said Drake. 'My plan is to head north in search of a northwest passage to England. If that is not successful, I'll follow in Magellan's wake across the Pacific and around Africa.'

'The *Hind* will never see England, not with her cargo holds busting their seams.'

'We'll jettison the bulk of the silver on Cano Island off Ecuador, where we can salvage it on a later voyage. The art goods will remain on the *Concepción*.'

'But what of your plan to give them to the queen?'

'That still stands,' Drake assured him. 'You, Thomas, will take ten men from the *Hind* and sail the galleon to Plymouth.'

Cuttill spread his hands in anguish. 'I can't possibly sail a vessel her size with only ten men, not through heavy seas.'

Drake walked back to his worktable and tapped a pair of brass dividers on a circle marked on a chart. 'On charts I found in Captain de Anton's cabin I've indicated a small bay on the coast north of here that should be free of

Spaniards. You will sail there and cast off the Spanish officers and all wounded crewmen. Impress twenty of the remaining able-bodied seamen to man the vessel. I'll see you're supplied with more than enough weapons to preserve command and prevent any attempt to wrest control of the ship.'

Cuttill knew it was useless to object. Debating with a stubborn man like Drake was a lost cause. He accepted his assignment with a resigned shrug. 'I will, of course, do as you command.'

Drake's face was confident, his eyes warm. 'If anyone can sail a Spanish galleon up to the dock at Plymouth, Thomas, you can. I suspect you'll knock the eyes out of the queen's head when you present her with your cargo.'

'I would rather leave that piece of work to you, Captain.'

Drake gave Cuttill a friendly pat on one shoulder. 'Not to fear, my old friend. I'm ordering you to be standing dockside with a wench on each arm, waiting to greet me when the *Hind* arrives home.'

At sunrise the following morning Cuttill ordered the crewmen to cast off the lines binding the two ships. Safely tucked under one arm was the linen-wrapped box that Drake had directed him to personally give to the queen. He carried it to the captain's cabin and locked it inside a cabinet in the captain's quarters. Then he returned to deck and took command of the *Nuestra Señora de la Concepción* as she drifted away from the *Golden Hind*. Sails were set under a dazzling crimson sun the superstitious crews on both ships solemnly described as red as a bleeding heart. To their primitive way of thinking it was considered a bad omen.

Drake and Cuttill exchanged final waves as the *Golden Hind* set a course to the northeast. Cuttill watched the smaller ship until she was hull down over the horizon. He did not share Drake's confidence. A deep feeling of foreboding settled in the pit of his stomach.

Several days later, after dumping many tons of silver ingots and coins off Cano Island to lighten her draft, the sturdy *Hind* and the intrepid Drake sailed north ... to what would be known more than two centuries later as Vancouver Island ... before turning west across the Pacific on their epic voyage.

Far to the south the *Concepción* tacked and headed due east, making landfall and reaching the bay marked on the Spanish chart by Drake sometime late the next evening. The anchor was dropped and the watch lights set.

Daylight brought the sun shining down over the Andes as Cuttill and his crew discovered a large native village of more than a thousand inhabitants, surrounded by a large bay. Without wasting time, he ordered his men to begin ferrying the Spanish officers and their wounded to shore. Twenty of the best seamen among the survivors were offered ten times their Spanish pay to help sail the galleon to England where they were promised to be set free upon landing. All twenty gladly signed on.

Cuttill was standing on the gun deck overseeing the landing operation just after midday when the ship began to vibrate as though a giant hand were rocking it. Everyone immediately stared at the long streamlike ensigns tied to the top of the masts. But only the ends of their tails fluttered under a slight whisper of wind. Then every eye turned to shore where a great cloud of dust rose from the base of the Andes and appeared to be moving towards the sea. A frightening thundering sound increased to deafening proportions along with a tremendous convulsion of the earth. As the crew gawked in stunned fascination, the hills east of the village seemed to rise and fall like breakers rolling on a shallow shore.

The dust cloud descended on the village and swallowed it. Above the uproar came the screams and cries of the villagers and the crashing sounds of their rock and adobe mud houses as they shook apart and crumbled into ruin.

None of the crew had ever experienced an earthquake, and few were even aware of such a phenomenon. Half the Protestant English and every one of the Catholic Spaniards on the galleon dropped to their knees and began praying fervently to God for deliverance.

In minutes the dust cloud passed over the ship and dispersed out to sea. They all stared uncomprehendingly at what had been a thriving village bustling with activity. Now it was nothing but flattened ruins. Cries came from those trapped under the debris. A later estimate would show that fewer than fifty of the local inhabitants survived. The Spaniards on shore ran up and down the beach in panic, shouting and begging to be brought back to the ship. Collecting his senses, Cuttill ignored the pleas, ran to the railing and scanned the surrounding sea. Beyond showing a mild chop, the water appeared indifferent to the nightmare tragedy in the village.

Suddenly desperate to escape the cataclysm on shore, Cuttill began shouting orders to get the galleon underway. The Spanish prisoners cooperated wholeheartedly, working alongside the English to unfurl the sails and pull in the anchor. Meanwhile, the survivors from the village crowded the beach, imploring the galleon's crew to return and help them rescue their relatives from the shattered wreckage and carry them aboard the ship to safety. The seamen turned deaf ears to the pleas, concerned only with their own preservation.

Suddenly, another earthquake shook the land, accompanied by an even more thunderous roar. The terrain began to undulate as if some monster were shaking a giant carpet. This time the sea slowly rolled back, stranding the *Concepción* and exposing the floor of the sea. The seamen, none of whom knew how to swim, possessed an unnatural fear of what was under the water. Now they stared wonderingly at the sight of thousands of fish flipping about like wingless birds amid the rocks and corals where they had been left high and dry by the retreating sea.

Sharks, squid, and a rainbow of tropical fish all mingled together in their death throes.

A constant flow of tremors moved the earth as the submarine quake caused crustal fracturing, collapsing the seafloor and creating a vast depression. Then it was the sea's turn to go crazy as it swept in from all sides to fill the hole. The water piled up in a gigantic countersurge with incredible speed. Millions of tons of pure destruction rose higher and higher until its crest reached 40 metres (157 feet) high, a phenomenon that would later become known as a tsunami.

There was no time for the helpless men to clutch a solid object for support, no time for the devout to pray. Paralysed and speechless in fear of the green and froth-white mountain of water rising before their eyes, they could only stand and watch it rush towards them with the ungodly sounds of a thousand hells. Only Cuttill had the presence of mind to run under the protecting deck over the tiller and wrap his limbs around its long wooden shaft.

Bow on to the colossal wall of water, the *Concepción* arched and soared vertically towards the curling crest. Moments later she was engulfed in a boiling turbulence as nature ran berserk.

Now that the mighty torrent had the *Concepción* in its grasp, it hurled the galleon towards the devastated shore at tremendous speed. Most of the crew on the open decks were snatched away and never seen again. The poor souls on the beach and those struggling to free themselves from the wreckage of the village were inundated as if a sudden gush of water had rushed over an ants' nest. One second they were there, the next they were gone, mere bits and pieces of smashed debris being hurled towards the Andes.

Buried under the towering mass of water for what seemed an incredible length of time, Cuttill held his breath until his lungs turned to fire and gripped the tiller as if he were a mutated branch that had grown from it. Then, with every one of her beams howling and creaking at their joints, the tough old ship battled her way back to the surface.

How long she was swept through the swirling vortex, Cuttill could not remember. The violent surge totally erased what was left of the village. The few drenched men who somehow remained alive on the battered *Concepción* were even further terrorized by the sight of centuries-dead mummies of the ancient Incas rising to the surface and surrounding the ship. Torn by the wave from their graves in some long-forgotten burial ground, the amazingly well-preserved bodies of the dead stared sightlessly at the horrified sailors, who were certain they were being cursed by creatures of the devil.

Cuttill attempted to move the tiller as if steering the ship. His was a useless gesture as the rudder had been ripped off its pintles soon after the wave struck. He clung tenaciously to life, his fear heightened by the mummies that swirled around the galleon.

The worst was far from over. The mad swirl of the tidal current caused a vortex that spun the galleon with such force the masts went crashing over the sides and the two guns broke their lashings and tumbled about the deck in a wild dance of destruction. One by one the fear-crazed seamen were swept away by the gyrating avalanche of water until only Cuttill was left. The enormous surge smashed and ravaged its way 8 kilometres (5 miles) inland, uprooting and shredding trees until over 100 square kilometres (62 square miles) were utterly devastated. Massive boulders were scattered ahead of the wave's force like small pebbles thrown by a boy's sling. Then at last, as the leviathan of death met the foothills of the Andes it began to lose momentum. Its fury spent, it lapped at the foot of the mountains and finally began to recede with a great sucking sound, leaving in its wake a swath of destruction unknown in recorded history.

Cuttill felt the galleon become motionless. He stared across the gun deck covered with fallen rigging and timbers, unable to see another living soul. For nearly an hour he huddled under the tiller, fearing a return of the murderous wave, but the ship remained still and silent. Slowly, stiffly, he made his way to the top of the quarter-deck and surveyed the scene of devastation.

Astoundingly, the *Concepción* sat upright, high and dry in a flattened jungle. He judged her to be almost three leagues from the nearest water. Her survival was due to her rugged construction and the fact she was sailing into the wave when it struck. If she had been sailing away the watery force would have smashed into her high sterncastle and ripped her to kindling. She had endured, but she was a wreck that would never feel the sea beneath her keel again.

Far in the distance, the village had disappeared. All that remained was a wide beach of sand swept free of wreckage. It was as if a thousand people and their homes had never existed. Corpses littered the drenched jungle. To Cuttill they seemed to be scattered everywhere, in some places over 3 metres deep (10 feet). Many were hanging grotesquely in the twisted branches of the trees. Most had been battered into almost unrecognizable shapes.

Cuttill could not believe he was the only human to survive the cataclysm, and yet he failed to see another living soul. He thanked God for his deliverance and prayed for guidance. Then he took stock of his situation. Stranded fourteen thousand nautical miles from England, deep in a part of the world controlled by the Spanish, who would gladly torture and execute a hated English pirate should they lay hands on him, his odds of living a long life were slim indeed. Cuttill saw absolutely no hope of returning home by sea. He decided his only course, one with little probability of success, was to trek over the Andes and work east. Once he reached the Brazilian coast there was always the possibility of meeting up with an English marauder that was raiding Portuguese shipping.

The following morning he made a litter for his sea chest

and filled it with food and water from the ship's galley, bedding, two pistols, a pound of gunpowder, a supply of shot, flint, and steel, a sack of tobacco, a knife, and a Spanish Bible. Then with nothing else but the clothes on his back, Cuttill set off with his litter for the mists hovering over the peaks of the Andes, taking one final look at the forlorn *Concepción* and wondering if perhaps the gods of the Incas were somehow responsible for the catastrophe.

Now they had their sacred relics back, he thought, and they were damned welcome to them. The antique jade box with its strange lid came to mind, and he did not envy the next men who came to steal it.

Drake returned triumphantly to England, arriving at Plymouth on September 26, 1580, with the *Golden Hind*'s holds bulging with spoils. But he found no sign of Thomas Cuttill and the *Nuestra Señora de la Concepción*. His backers received a 4700 per cent profit on their investment and the queen's share became the foundation for future British expansion. During a lavish party on board the *Hind* at Greenwich, Queen Elizabeth conferred knighthood on Drake.

The second ship to circumnavigate the world was made a tourist attraction. For three generations she remained on view until finally she either rotted away or burned to the waterline. History doesn't know for certain how it happened, but the *Golden Hind* vanished into the water of the Thames.

Sir Francis Drake continued his exploits for another sixteen years. On a later voyage, he seized the city ports of Santo Domingo and Cartagena and became Her Majesty's Admiral-of-the-Seas. He also served as mayor of Plymouth and a member of Parliament. And then there was his bold attack on the great Spanish Armada in 1588. His end came during an expedition to plunder ports and shipping on the Spanish Main in 1596. After succumbing to dysentery he was sealed in a lead coffin and dropped in the sea near Portobelo, Panama.

Before his death, hardly a day passed when Drake didn't puzzle over the disappearance of the *Concepción* and the enigma of the mysterious jade box and its knotted cords.

PART ONE

Bones and Thrones

1

The skeleton reclined in the sediment of the deep pool as if resting on a soft mattress, the cold unwinking eye sockets of the skull staring upward through the liquid gloom towards the surface 36 metres (120 feet) away. There was a horrible vindictive grin set in the teeth as a small water snake thrust its evil head from under the rib cage, and then slithered away, leaving a tiny cloud of silt to smudge its trail. One arm was held in an upright position by an elbow imbedded in the muck, the bony fingers of the hand as if beckoning the unwary.

From the bottom of the pool to the sun above, the water gradually lightened from a dismal grey-brown to a pea-soup green from the pond scum that flourished under the tropical heat. The circular rim stretched 30 metres (98 feet) across and the sheer walls dropped 15 metres (49 feet) to the water. Once in, there was no way a human or animal could escape without help from above.

There was an ugliness about the deep limestone sink-hole, or cenote as it was technically called, a repugnant menace that animals sensed, refusing to approach within fifty metres of its perimeter. A grim sense of death hung about the place, and rightly so. The place was more than a sacred well where men, women, and children had been thrown alive into the dark waters as sacrifices during times of drought and harsh storms. Ancient legends and myths called it a house of evil gods where strange and unspeakable events occurred. There were also tales of rare artifacts, handcrafted and sculpted, along with jade, gold, and precious gemstones, that were said to have been cast into the forbidding pool to appease the evil gods who were inflicting bad weather. In 1964 two divers entered the depths of the sinkhole and never returned. No attempt had been made to recover their bodies.

The sinkhole's early history began in the Cambrian era when the region was part of an ancient sea. Through the following geological eras, thousands of generations of shellfish and coral lived and died, their skeletal carcasses forming an enormous mass of lime and sand that compressed into a limestone and dolomite layer two kilometres thick. Then, beginning sixty-five million years ago, an intense earth uplifting occurred that raised the Andes Mountains to their present height. As the rain ran down from the mountains it formed a great underground water table that slowly began dissolving the limestone. Where it collected and pooled, the water ate upward until the land surface collapsed and created the sinkhole.

In the damp air above the jungle surrounding the cavity, an Andean condor banked in great lazy circles, one emotionless eye fastened on a group of people working around the edge of the cenote. Its long, broad wings, measuring 3 metres (10 feet) arched stiff to catch the air currents. The huge black bird, with its white ruff and bald pinkish head, soared effortlessly as it studied the movement below. Finally, satisfied that no meal was in the offing, the vulture ascended to a greater height for distant observation and drifted eastward in search of carrion.

A great deal of unresolved controversy had surrounded the sacred pool, and now archaeologists had finally gathered to dive and retrieve artifacts from its enigmatic depths. The ancient site was located on a western slope beneath a high ridge of the Peruvian Andes near a great ruined city. The nearby stone structures had been part of a vast confederation of city-states, known as the Chachapoyas, that was conquered by the renowned Inca empire around A.D. 1480.

The Chachapoyan confederation encompassed almost 400 square kilometres (250 square miles). Its metropolitan spread of farms, temples, and fortresses now lie in mostly unexplored heavily forested mountains. The ruins of this great civilization indicated an incredibly mysterious blend of cultures and origins that were mostly unknown. The Chachapoyan rulers or council of elders, their architects, priests, soldiers, and ordinary working people in the cities and on the farms left virtually no record of their lives. And archaeologists had yet to fathom their government bureaucracy, justice system, and religious practices.

As she stared down at the stagnant water through big, wide, hazel eyes under raised dark brows, Dr Shannon Kelsey was too excited to feel the cold touch of fear. A very attractive woman when dressed and made up, she possessed a rather cool and aloof self-sufficiency that most men found irritating, particularly so since she could gaze into their eyes with a teasing boldness. Her hair was straight and soft blond and tied in a ponytail by a red bandanna, and the abundance of skin that showed on her face, arms, and legs was richly tanned. The inside of her one-piece black Lycra swim suit was nicely filled by an hourglass figure with an extra twenty minutes thrown in for good measure, and when she moved it was with the fluid grace of a Balinese dancer.

In her late thirties, Dr Kelsey had enjoyed a ten-year fascination with the Chachapoyan cultures. She had explored and surveyed important archaeological sites on five previous expeditions, clearing the invading plant growth from a number of the major buildings and temples of the region's ancient cities. As a respected archaeologist of Andes culture, following in the footsteps of a glorious past was her great passion. To work where an enigmatic and obscure people had flourished and died was a dream made possible by a grant from the Archaeology Department of Arizona State University.

'Useless to carry a video camera unless the visibility opens up below the first two metres,' said Miles Rodgers, the photographer who was filming the project.

'Then shoot stills,' Shannon said firmly. 'I want every dive recorded whether we can see past our noses or not.'

A year shy of forty and sporting luxuriant black hair and a beard, Rodgers was an old pro at underwater photography. He was in demand by all the major science and travel publications to shoot below-the-sea photos of fish and coral reefs. His extraordinary pictures of World War II shipwrecks in the South Pacific and ancient submerged seaports throughout the Mediterranean had won him numerous awards and the respect of his peers.

A tall, slender man in his sixties, with a silver grey beard that covered half his face, held up Shannon's air tank so she could slip her arms through the straps of the backpack. 'I wish you'd put a hold on this until we've finished constructing the dive raft.'

'That's two days away. By doing a preliminary survey now we can get a head start.'

'Then at least wait for the rest of the dive team to arrive from the university. If you and Miles get into trouble, we have no backup.'

'Not to worry,' Shannon said gamely. 'Miles and I will only do a bounce dive to test depth and water conditions. We won't run our dive time past thirty minutes.'

'And no deeper than fifteen metres,' the older man cautioned her.

Shannon smiled at her colleague, Dr Steve Miller from the University of Pennsylvania. 'And if we haven't touched bottom at fifteen metres?'

'We've got five weeks. No need to get antsy and risk an accident.' Miller's voice was quiet and deep, but there was a noticeable trace of concern in it. One of the leading anthropologists of his time, he had devoted the last thirty years to unravelling the mysteries of the cultures that had evolved in the upper regions of the Andes and spilled down to the jungles of the Amazon. 'Play it safe, make a study of water conditions and the geology of the pool walls, then get back to the surface.'

Shannon nodded and spat into her face mask, smearing the saliva around the inside of the lens to keep it from misting. Next she rinsed the mask from a canteen of water. After adjusting her buoyancy compensator and cinching her weight belt, she and Rodgers made a final check of each other's equipment. Satisfied everything was in place and their digital dive computers properly programmed, Shannon smiled at Miller.

'See you soon, Doc. Keep a martini on ice.'

The anthropologist looped under their arms a wide strap that was attached to long nylon lines, gripped tightly by a team of ten Peruvian graduate students of the university's archaeology programme, who had volunteered to join the project. 'Lower away, kids,' Miller ordered the six boys and four girls.

Hand over hand the lines were paid out as the divers began their descent into the ominous pool below. Shannon and Rodgers extended their legs and used the tips of their dive fins as bumpers to keep from scraping against the rough limestone walls. They could clearly see the coating of slime covering the surface of the water. It looked as viscous and about as inviting as a tub of green mucus. The aroma of decay and stagnation was overwhelming. To Shannon the thrill of the unknown abruptly changed to a feeling of deep apprehension.

When they were within I metre (about 3 feet) of the surface, they both inserted their air regulator mouthpieces between their teeth and signalled to the anxious faces staring from above. Then Shannon and Miles slipped out of their harnesses and dropped out of sight into the odious slime.

Miller nervously paced the rim of the sinkhole, glancing at his watch every other minute while the students peered in fascination at the green slime below. Fifteen minutes passed with no sign of the divers. Suddenly, the exhaust bubbles from their air regulators disappeared. Frantically Miller ran along the edge of the well. Had they found a cave and entered it? He waited ten minutes, then ran over to a nearby tent and rushed inside. Almost feverishly he picked up a portable radio and began hailing the project's headquarters and supply unit in the small town of Chachapoyas, 90 kilometres (56 miles) to the south. The voice of Juan Chaco, inspector general of Peruvian archaeology and director of the Museo de la Nación in Lima, answered almost immediately.

'Juan here. That you, Doc? What can I do for you?'

'Dr Kelsey and Miles Rodgers insisted on making a preliminary dive into the sacrificial well,' replied Miller. 'I think we may have an emergency.'

'They went into that cesspool without waiting for the dive team from the university?' Chaco asked in a strangely indifferent tone.

'I tried to talk them out of it.'

'When did they enter the water?'

Miller checked his watch again. 'Twenty-seven minutes ago.'

'How long did they plan to stay down?'

'They planned to resurface after thirty minutes.'

'It's still early.' Chaco sighed. 'So what's the problem?'

'We've seen no sign of their air bubbles for the last ten minutes.'

Chaco caught his breath, closed his eyes for a second. 'Doesn't sound good, my friend. This is not what we planned.'

'Can you send the dive team ahead by helicopter?' asked Miller.

'Not possible,' Chaco replied helplessly. 'They're still in transit from Miami. Their plane isn't scheduled to land in Lima for another four hours.'

'We can't afford government meddling. Certainly not now. Can you arrange to have a dive rescue team rushed to the sinkhole?'

'The nearest naval facility is at Trujillo. I'll alert the base commander and go from there.'

'Good luck to you, Juan. I'll stand by the radio at this end.'

'Keep me informed of any new developments.'

'I will, I promise you,' Miller said grimly.

'My friend?'

'Yes?'

'They'll come through,' offered Chaco in a hollow tone. 'Rodgers is a master diver. He doesn't make mistakes.'

Miller said nothing. There was nothing more to say. He broke contact with Chaco and hurried back to the silent group of students, who were staring down into the sinkhole with dread.

In Chachapoyas, Chaco pulled out a handkerchief and mopped his face. He was a man of order. Unforeseen obstacles or problems irritated him. If the two stupid Americans drowned themselves, there would be a government enquiry. Despite Chaco's influence, the Peruvian news media were bound to make an overblown incident out of it. The consequences might very well prove to be nothing less than disastrous.

'All we need now,' he muttered to himself, 'are two dead archaeologists in the pool.'

Then with shaking hands he gripped the radio transmitter and began sending out an urgent call for help.

2

One hour and forty-five minutes had passed since Shannon and Miles had entered the sacrificial pool. Any attempt at rescue now seemed an empty gesture. Nothing could save Shannon and Miles now. They had to be dead, their air used up long ago. Two more victims added to the countless number who had disappeared into the morbid waters through the centuries.

In a voice frantic with desperation, Chaco had informed him that the Peruvian navy was caught unprepared for an emergency. Their water escape and recovery team was on a training mission far to the south of Peru near the Chilean border. It was impossible for them to airlift the dive team and their equipment to the sinkhole before sundown. Chaco helplessly shared Miller's anxiety over the slow response time. But this was South America and speed was seldom a priority.

One of the female students heard it first. She cupped her hands to her ears and turned back and forth like a radar antenna. 'A helicopter!' she announced excitedly, pointing in a westerly direction through the tops of the trees.

In an expectant hush everyone around the rim of the pool listened. The faint thumping sound of a rotor blade beating the air came towards them, growing louder with each passing moment. A minute later a turquoise helicopter with the letters NUMA painted on its sides swept into view.

Where had it come from? Miller wondered, his spirits rising. It obviously didn't have the markings of the Peruvian navy. It had to be a civilian craft.

The tops of the surrounding trees were whipped into a frenzy as the helicopter began its descent into a small clearing beside the sinkhole. The landing skids were still in the air when the fuselage door opened and a tall man with wavy black hair made an agile leap to the ground. He was dressed in a thin, shorty wet suit for diving in warm waters. Ignoring the younger people, he walked directly up to the anthropologist.

'Dr Miller?'

'Yes, I'm Miller.'

The stranger, a warm smile arched across his face, shoved out a calloused hand. 'I'm sorry we couldn't have arrived sooner.'

'Who *are* you?'

'My name is Dirk Pitt.'

'You're American,' Miller stated, staring into a craggy face with eyes that seemed to smile.

'Special Projects Director for the US National Underwater and Marine Agency. As I understand it, two of your divers are missing in an underwater cave.'

'A sinkhole,' Miller corrected him. 'Dr Shannon Kelsey and Miles Rodgers entered the water almost two hours ago and have failed to resurface.'

Pitt walked over to the edge of the pool, stared down at the stagnant water, and quickly determined that diving conditions were rotten. The pool went from slime green at the outer edges to pitch black in the centre, giving the impression of great depth. There was nothing to indicate that the operation would prove to be anything more than a body recovery. 'Not too inviting,' he mused.

'Where did you come from?' queried Miller.

'NUMA is conducting an underwater geological survey off the coast due west of here. The Peruvian naval headquarters radioed a request to send divers on a rescue mission and we responded. Apparently we're the first to arrive on-site.'

'How can oceanographic scientists carry out a rescue

and recovery operation in a hellhole?' Miller snapped, becoming suddenly angry.

'Our research ship contained the necessary diving equipment,' Pitt explained unemotionally. 'I'm not a scientist but a marine engineer. I've only had a few training sessions in underwater recovery, but I'm a reasonably good diver.'

Before a discouraged Miller could reply, the helicopter's engine died as the rotor blades slowly swung to a stop, and a short man with the broad shoulders and barrel chest of a dock worker squeezed through the exit door and approached. He looked the complete opposite of the tall, lean Pitt.

'My friend and associate, Al Giordino,' Pitt said, introducing him.

Giordino nodded under a mass of dark, curly hair and said simply, 'Hello.'

Miller looked behind them through the windshield of the aircraft, and seeing the interior held no other passengers, groaned in despair. 'Two of you, only two of you. My God, it will take at least a dozen men to bring them out.'

Pitt wasn't the least bit annoyed by Miller's outburst. He stared at the anthropologist with tolerant understanding through deep green opaline eyes that seemed to possess a mesmeric quality. 'Trust me, Doc,' he said in a tone that stopped any further argument. 'Al and I can do the job.'

Within minutes, after a brief planning session, Pitt was ready to be lowered into the pool. He was wearing a full EX0-26 face mask from Diving Systems International with an exothermic air regulator good for polluted water applications. The earphone sockets were connected to an MK1-DCI Ocean Technology Systems diver radio. He carried twin 100-cubic-foot air tanks on his back and wore a buoyancy compensator with an array of instruments indicating depth, air pressure, and compass direction. As he geared up, Giordino connected a thick nylon Kermantle communications and safety line to Pitt's earphone and an emergency release buckle on a strap cinched around Pitt's waist. The remainder of the safety line wound around a large reel mounted inside the helicopter and connected to an outside amplifier. After a final check of Pitt's equipment, Giordino patted him on the head and spoke into the communication system's microphone.

'Looking good. Do you read?'

'As though you were inside my head,' Pitt answered, his voice audible to everyone through an amplifier. 'How about me?'

Giordino nodded. 'Clear and distinct. I'll monitor your decompression schedule and dive time from here.'

'Understood.'

'I'm counting on you to give me a running account of your situation and depth.'

Pitt wrapped the safety line around one arm and gripped it with both hands. He gave Giordino a wink from behind the lens of the face mask. 'Okay, let's open the show.'

Giordino motioned to four of Miller's students who began unwinding the reel. Unlike Shannon and Miles who bounced their way down along the sinkhole walls, Giordino had strung the nylon line over the end of a dead tree trunk that hung 2 metres (over 6 feet) beyond the edge of the vertical precipice, allowing Pitt to drop without scraping against the limestone.

For a man who was conceivably sending his friend to an untimely death, Miller thought, Giordino appeared incredibly calm and efficient. He did not know Pitt and Giordino, had never heard of the legendary pair. He could not know they were extraordinary men with almost twenty years of adventuring under the seas who had developed an unerring sense for assessing the odds of survival. He could only stand by in frustration at what he was certain was an exercise in futility. He leaned over the brink and watched intently as Pitt neared the green surface scum of the water.

'How's it look?' asked Giordino over the phone.

'Like my grandmother's split pea soup,' replied Pitt.

'I don't advise sampling it.'

'The thought never entered my mind.'

No further words were spoken as Pitt's feet entered the liquid slime. When it closed over his head, Giordino slackened the safety line to give him freedom of movement. The water temperature was only about ten degrees cooler than the average hot tub. Pitt began breathing through his regulator, rolled over, kicked his fins, and dived down into the murky world of death. The increasing water pressure squeezed his ear drums and he snorted inside his mask to equalize the force. He switched on a Birns Oceanographics Snooper light, but the hand-held beam could barely penetrate the gloom.

Then, abruptly, he passed through the dense murk into a yawning chasm of crystal clear water. Instead of the light beam reflecting off the algae into his face, it suddenly shot into the distance. The instant transformation below the layer of slime stunned him for a moment. He felt as if he were swimming in air. 'I have clear visibility at a depth of four metres,' he reported topside.

'Any sign of the other divers?'

Pitt slowly swam in a 360-degree circle. 'No, nothing.'

'Can you make out details of the bottom?'

'Fairly well,' replied Pitt. 'The water is transparent as glass but quite dark. The scum on the surface cuts the sunlight on the bottom by seventy per cent. It's a bit dark around the walls so I'll have to swim a search pattern so I won't miss the bodies.'

'Do you have enough slack on the safety line?'

'Maintain a slight tension so it won't hinder my movement as I go deeper.'

For the next twelve minutes Pitt circled the steep walls of the sinkhole, probing every cavity, descending as if revolving around a giant corkscrew. The limestone, laid down hundreds of millions of years earlier, was mineral-stained with strange, abstract images. He planed horizontally and swam in languid slow motion, sweeping the beam of light back and forth in front of him. The illusion of soaring over a bottomless pit was overwhelming.

Finally, he levelled out over the floor of the sacrificial pool. No firm sand or plant life, just one uneven patch of ugly brown silt broken by clusters of greyish rock. 'I have the bottom at slightly over thirty-six metres. Still no sign of Kelsey or Rodgers.'

Far above the pool, Miller gave Giordino a dazed look. 'They *must* be down there. Impossible for them to simply vanish.'

Far below, Pitt kicked slowly across the bottom, careful to stay a good metre above the rocks and especially the silt, which might billow into a blinding cloud and reduce his visibility to zero within seconds. Once disturbed, silt could remain suspended for several hours before settling back to the bottom. He gave an involuntary shudder. The water had turned uncomfortably cold as he passed into a cool layer suspended beneath the warmer water above. He slowed and drifted, adding enough lift from his compensator for slight buoyancy, achieving a slight head-down, fins-up swimming position.

Cautiously, he reached down and gently sank his hands into the brown muck. They touched bedrock before the silt rose to his wrists. Pitt thought it strange the silt was so shallow. After countless centuries of erosion from the walls and runoff from the ground above, the rocky subsurface should have been covered with a layer at least 2 metres (over 6 feet) deep. He went motionless and floated over what looked like a field of bleached white tree limbs sprouting from the mud. Gripping one that was gnarled with small protrusions, he eased it out of the bed of silt. He found himself staring at a spinal column from an ancient sacrificial victim.

Giordino's voice broke through his earphones. 'Speak to me.'

'Depth thirty-seven metres,' Pitt answered as he flung aside the spinal column. 'The floor of the pool is a bone yard. There must be two hundred skeletons scattered around down here.'

'Still no sign of bodies?'

'Not yet.'

Pitt began to feel an icy finger trail up the nape of his neck as he spotted a skeleton with a bony hand pointing into the gloom. Beside the rib cage was a rusty breastplate, while the skull was still encased in what he guessed was a sixteenth-century Spanish helmet.

Pitt reported the sighting to Giordino. 'Tell Doc Miller I've found a long-dead Spaniard complete with helmet and breastplate down here.' Then, as if drawn by an unseen force, his eyes followed in the direction a curled finger of the hand pointed.

There was another body, one that had died more recently. It appeared to be a male with the legs drawn up and the head tilted back. Decomposition had not had time to fully break down the flesh. The corpse was still in a state of saponification, where the meaty tissue and organs had turned into a firm soaplike substance.

The expensive hiking boots, a red silk scarf knotted around the neck, and a Navaho silver belt buckle inlaid with turquoise stones made it easy for Pitt to recognize someone who was not a local peasant. Whoever he was, he was not young. Strands of long silver hair and beard swayed with the current from Pitt's movements. A wide gash in the neck also showed how he had died.

A thick gold ring with a large yellow stone flashed under the beam of the dive light. The thought occurred to Pitt that the ring might come in handy for identifying the body. Fighting the bile rising in his throat, he easily pulled the ring over the knuckle of the dead man's rotting finger while half expecting a shadowy form to appear and accuse him of acting like a ghoul. Disagreeable as the job was, he swished the ring through the silt to clean off any remnant of its former owner, and then slipped it on to one of his own fingers so he wouldn't lose it.

'I have another one,' he notified Giordino.

'One of the divers or an old Spaniard?'

'Neither. This one looks to be a few months to a year old.'

'Do you want to retrieve it?' asked Giordino.

'Not yet. We'll wait until after we find Doc Miller's people — ' Pitt suddenly broke off as he was struck by an enormous force of water that surged into the pool from an unseen passage on the opposite wall and churned up the silt like dust whirling around a tornado. He would have tumbled out of control like a leaf in the wind by the unexpected energy of the turbulence but for his safety line. As it was he barely kept a firm grip on his dive light.

'That was a hell of a jerk,' said Giordino with concern. 'What's going on?'

'I've been struck by a powerful surge from nowhere,' Pitt replied, relaxing and allowing himself to go with the flow. 'That explains why the silt layer is so shallow. It's periodically swept away by the turbulence.'

'Probably fed by an underground water system that builds up pressure and releases it as a surge across the floor of the sinkhole,' Giordino speculated. 'Shall we pull you out?'

'No, leave me be. Visibility is nil, but I don't seem to be in any immediate danger. Slowly release the safety line and let's see where the current carries me. There must be an outlet somewhere.'

'Too dangerous. You might get hung up and trapped.'

'Not if I keep from entangling my safety line,' Pitt said easily.

On the surface, Giordino studied his watch. 'You've been down sixteen minutes. How's your air?'

Pitt held his pressure gauge in front of his face mask. He could barely read the needle through the maelstrom of silt. 'Good for another twenty minutes.'

51

'I'll give you ten. After that, at your present depth, you'll be looking at decompression stops.'

'You're the boss,' Pitt came back agreeably.

'What's your situation?'

'Feels like I'm being pulled into a narrow tunnel feet first. I can touch the walls closing around me. Lucky I have a safety line. Impossible to swim against the surge.'

Giordino turned to Miller. 'Sounds as if he may have a lead on what happened to your divers.'

Miller shook his head in anger. 'I warned them. They could have avoided this tragedy by keeping their dive in shallow depths.'

Pitt felt as though he was being sucked through the narrow slot for an hour when it was only twenty seconds. The silt cloud had faded slightly, most of it remaining in the deep pool behind. He began to see his surroundings more clearly. His compass showed he was being carried in a southeasterly direction. Then the walls suddenly opened out into one enormous, flooded room. To his right and below he caught the momentary flash of something glinting in the murk. Something metallic vaguely reflecting the silt-dimmed beam of his dive light. It was an abandoned air tank. Nearby was a second one. He swam over and peered at their pressure gauges. The needles were pegged on empty. He angled his dive light around in a circle, expecting to see dead bodies floating in the darkness like phantom demons.

The cool bottom water had drained away a measure of Pitt's strength and he could feel his motions becoming sluggish. Although Giordino's voice still came through the earphones as clearly as if Pitt was standing next to him, the words seemed less distinct. Pitt switched his mind off automatic and put it on full control, sending out instructions to check data gauges, safety line, and buoyancy compensator as if there were another Pitt inside his head.

He mentally sharpened his senses and forced himself to be alert. If the bodies were swept into a side passage, he thought, he could easily pass them by and never notice. But a quick search turned up nothing but a pair of discarded swim fins. Pitt aimed the dive light upward and saw the reflective glitter of surface water that indicated the upper dome of the chamber contained an air pocket.

He also glimpsed a pair of white feet.

3

Trapped far from the outside world in a prison of perpetual silence, breathing in a small pocket of air millions of years old and lying smothered in total blackness deep under the earth is too alien, too terrible to imagine. The horror of dying under such terrifying conditions can provide nightmares on a par with being locked in a closet full of snakes.

After initial panic had passed and a small degree of rationality was retrieved, any hope that Shannon and Rodgers had of surviving vanished when the air in their tanks became exhausted and the final spark of life in the batteries of their dive lights gave out. The air in the small pocket soon became foul and stale from their own breathing. Dazed and lightheaded from lack of oxygen, they knew their suffering would only end when the watery chamber became their tomb.

The underground current had sucked them into the cavern after Shannon had excitedly dived to the bottom of the sinkhole after glimpsing the field of bones. Rodgers had faithfully followed and exhausted himself in a frantic effort to escape the surge. The last of their air had been used up in a vain attempt to find another passage leading out of the chamber. There was no exit, no escape. They could only drift in the blackness, held afloat by their buoyancy compensators, and wait to die.

Rodgers, for all his guts, was in a bad way, and Shannon was just hanging on by a thread when suddenly she noticed a flickering light in the forbidding water below. Then it became a bright, yellow beam stabbing the blackness in her direction. Was her numbed mind playing tricks? Did she dare entertain a glimmer of hope?

'They've found us,' she finally gasped as the light moved towards her.

Rodgers, his face etched and grey with fatigue and despair, stared blankly down at the approaching light beam without reaction. The lack of breathable air and the crushing blackness had left him in a near comatose state. His eyes were open and he was still breathing, and, incredibly, he still tightly grasped his camera. He felt a vague awareness that he was entering the tunnel of light described by people who returned from death.

Shannon felt a hand grab her foot, and then a head popped out of the water less than an arm's length away. The dive light was beamed into her eyes, momentarily blinding her. Then it moved on to Rodgers's face. Instantly recognizing who was the worse off, Pitt reached under one arm and took hold of an auxiliary air regulator that was connected to the dual valve manifold of his air tanks. He quickly slipped the mouthpiece of the regulator between Rodgers's lips. Then he passed Shannon a reserve pony bottle and air regulator that was attached to his waist belt.

Several deep breaths later, the revival in mood and physical well-being was nothing short of miraculous. Shannon gave Pitt a big bear hug as a renewed Rodgers pumped his hand so vigorously he nearly sprained Pitt's wrist. There were moments of speechless joy as all three were swept away in a euphoria of relief and excitement.

Only when Pitt realized that Giordino was shouting through his earphones, demanding a situation report, did he announce, 'Tell Doc Miller I've found his lost lambs. They are alive, repeat, they are alive and well.'

'You have them?' Giordino burst through Pitt's earphones. 'They're not dead?'

'A little pale around the gills but otherwise in good shape.'

'How is it possible?' muttered a disbelieving Miller.

Giordino nodded. 'The Doc wants to know how they stayed alive.'

'The current swept them into a chamber with an air pocket in its dome. Lucky I arrived when I did. They were minutes away from using up the oxygen.'

The crowd grouped around the amplifier was stunned by the announcement. But as the news sank in, relief spread across every face, and the ancient stone city echoed with cheers and applause. Miller turned away as if wiping tears from his eyes while Giordino smiled and smiled.

Down in the chamber Pitt motioned that he could not remove his full face mask and converse. He indicated they would have to communicate through hand signals. Shannon and Rodgers nodded, and then Pitt began to describe visually the procedure for their escape.

Since the lost divers had dropped all of their useless dive gear, except for face masks and buoyancy compensators, Pitt felt confident the three of them could be pulled back through the narrow shaft against the current and into the main pool by his phone and safety line without complications. According to the manufacturers' specs, the nylon line and phone cable could support up to almost six thousand pounds.

He signalled Shannon to wrap one leg and one arm around the line and lead off, breathing through her pony bottle. Rodgers would repeat the step and follow, with Pitt bringing up the rear close enough for the spare regulator to reach Rodgers's mouth. When Pitt was sure they were stable and breathing easy, he alerted Giordino.

'We're positioned and ready for escape.'

Giordino paused and stared at the young archaeology students, their hands gripping the safety line, poised as if ready for a tug-of-war. He studied their impatient expressions and quickly realized he would have to keep their enthusiasm and excitement in check or they might haul the divers through the rock passageway like so much meat through a jagged pipe. 'Stand by. Give me your depth.'

'I read slightly over seventeen metres. Much higher than

56

the bottom of the sinkhole. We were sucked into a passage that sloped upward for twenty metres.'

'You're borderline,' Giordino informed him, 'but the others have exceeded their time and pressure limits. I'll compute and advise you of decompression stops.'

'Don't make them too long. Once the pony bottle is empty, it won't take long for the three of us to use up what air I have left in my twin tanks.'

'Perish the thought. If I don't hold these kids by the collar, they'll jerk you out of there so fast you'll feel like you were fired from a cannonball.'

'Try to keep it civilized.'

Giordino held up his hand as a signal for the students to begin pulling. 'Here we go.'

'Bring on the jugglers and the clowns,' Pitt answered in good humour.

The safety line became taut and the long, slow haul began. The rush of the surge through the shaft was matched by the gurgling of their exhaust bubbles from the air regulators. With nothing to do now but grip the line, Pitt relaxed and went limp, allowing his body to be drawn against the flow of the underground current that gushed through the narrow slot like air through a venturi tube. The lighter silt-clouded water in the pool at the end of the passage seemed miles away. Time had no meaning, and he felt as if he'd been immersed for an age. Only Giordino's steady voice helped Pitt keep his grip on reality.

'Cry out if we haul too fast,' ordered Giordino.

'Looking good,' Pitt replied, hearing his air tanks grinding against the ceiling of the shaft.

'What is your estimate of the current's rate of speed?'

'Close to eight knots.'

'Small wonder your bodies are causing severe resistance. I've got ten kids up here, pulling their hearts out.'

'Six more metres and we're out of here,' Pitt informed him.

And then a minute, probably a minute and a half,

struggling to hold on to the safety line as they were buffeted by the diminishing force of the torrent, and they broke free of the shaft into the cloud of silt swirling around the floor of the sacrificial pool. Another minute and they were pulled upward and clear from the drag of the current and into transparent, unclouded water. Pitt looked up, saw the light filtering through the green slime, and felt a wondrous sense of relief.

Giordino knew they were free of the suction when the tension on the safety line suddenly diminished. He ordered a halt to the ascent operation as he rechecked his decompression data on a laptop computer. One stop of eight minutes would take Pitt out of any danger of decompression sickness, but the archaeology project divers would need stops of far longer duration. They had been down over two hours at depths ranging from 17 to 37 metres (67 to 122 feet). They would require at least two stops lasting over an hour. How much air was left in Pitt's tanks to sustain them? That was the life-or-death dilemma. Enough for ten minutes? Fifteen? Twenty?

At sea level, or one atmosphere, the normal human body contains about one litre of dissolved nitrogen. Breathing larger quantities of air under the pressure of water depth increases the absorption of nitrogen to two litres at two atmospheres (10 metres, or 30 feet of water depth), three litres at three atmospheres (30 metres, or 90 feet), and so on. During diving the excess nitrogen is rapidly dissolved in the blood, carried throughout the body, and stored in the tissues. When a diver begins to ascend, the situation is reversed, only this time far more slowly. As the water pressure decreases, the overabundance of nitrogen travels to the lungs and is eliminated by respiration. If the diver rises too quickly, normal breathing can't cope and bubbles of nitrogen form in the blood, body tissue, and joints, causing decompression sickness, better known as the bends, a condition that has crippled or killed thousands of divers over the past century.

Finally, Giordino set aside the computer and called Pitt. 'Dirk?'

'I hear you.'

'Bad news. There isn't enough air left in your tanks for the lady and her friend to make the necessary decompression stops.'

'Tell me something I don't know,' Pitt came back. 'What about backup tanks in the chopper?'

'No such luck,' moaned Giordino. 'In our rush to leave the ship the crew threw on an air compressor but forgot to load extra air tanks.'

Pitt stared through his face mask at Rodgers, still clutching his camera and shooting pictures. The photographer gave him a thumbs up sign as though he'd just cleared the pool table at the neighbourhood saloon. Pitt's gaze moved to Shannon. Her hazel eyes stared back at him through her face mask, wide and content as if she thought the nightmare was over and her hero was going to sweep her off to his castle. She had not realized the worst was far from over. For the first time he noticed that she had blond hair, and Pitt found himself wondering what she looked like in only her swim suit without the diving equipment.

The daydream was over almost as soon as it was begun. His mind came back on an even keel and he spoke into his face mask receiver. 'Al, you said the compressor is on board the chopper.'

'I did.'

'Send down the tool kit. You'll find it in the storage locker of the chopper.'

'Make sense,' Giordino urged.

'The manifold valves on my air tanks,' Pitt explained hastily. 'They're the new prototypes NUMA is testing. I can shut off one independently of the other and then remove it from the manifold without expelling air from the opposite tank.'

'I read you, pal,' said an enlightened Giordino. 'You disconnect one of your twin tanks and breathe off the other. I pull up the empty and refill it with the compressor. Then we repeat the process until we satisfy the decompression schedule.'

'A glittering concept, don't you think?' asked Pitt with dark sarcasm.

'Fundamental at best,' grunted Giordino, artfully concealing his elation. 'Hang at six-point-five metres for seventeen minutes. I'll send the tool kit down to you on the safety line. I just hope your plan works.'

'Never a doubt.' Pitt's confidence seemed genuine. 'When I step on to firm ground again, I'll expect a Dixieland band playing "Waiting for the Robert E. Lee."'

'Spare me,' Giordino groaned.

As he ran towards the helicopter, he was confronted by Miller.

'Why did you stop?' the anthropologist demanded. 'Good God, man, what are you waiting for? Pull them up!'

Giordino fixed the anthropologist with an icy stare. 'Pull them to the surface now and they die.'

Miller looked blank. 'Die?'

'The bends, Doc, ever hear of it?'

A look of understanding crossed Miller's face, and he slowly nodded. 'I'm sorry. Please forgive an excitable old bone monger. I won't trouble you again.'

Giordino smiled sympathetically. He continued to the helicopter and climbed inside, never suspecting that Miller's words were as prophetic as a lead dime.

The tool kit, consisting of several metric wrenches, a pair of pliers, two screwdrivers, and a geologist's hammer with a small pick on one end, was tied loosely to the safety line by a bowline knot and lowered by a small cord. Once the tools were in Pitt's hands he gripped the air tank pack between his knees. Next he adroitly shut off one valve and unthreaded it from the manifold with a wrench. When one air tank came free, he attached it to the cord.

'Cargo up,' Pitt announced.

In less than four minutes, the tank was raised by willing hands on the secondary cord, connected to the throbbing gas-engine compressor and taking on purified air. Giordino was cursing, sweet talking, and begging the compressor to pump 3500 pounds of air per square inch into the 100-cubic-foot steel tank in record time. The needle on the pressure gauge was just shy of 1800 pounds when Pitt warned him that Shannon's pony bottle was dry and his lone tank had only 400 pounds left. With three of them sucking on one tank, that did not leave a comfortable safety margin. Giordino cut off the compressor when the pressure reached 2500 and wasted no time in sending the tank back down into the sinkhole. The process was repeated three more times after Pitt and the other divers moved to their next decompression stop at three metres, which meant they had to endure several minutes in the slime. The whole procedure went off without a hitch.

Giordino allowed an ample safety margin. He let nearly forty minutes pass before he pronounced it safe for Shannon and Rodgers to surface and be lifted to the brink of the sacrificial pool. It was a measure of his complete confidence in his friend that Pitt didn't even bother to question the accuracy of Giordino's calculations. Ladies went first as Pitt encircled Shannon's waist with the strap and buckle that was attached to the safety and communications line. He waved to the faces peering over the edge and Shannon was on her way to dry land.

Rodgers was next. His utter exhaustion after his narrow brush with death was forgotten at the sheer exhilaration of being lifted out of the godforsaken pool of death and slime, never, he swore, to return. A gnawing hunger and a great thirst mushroomed inside him. He remembered a bottle of vodka that he kept in his tent and he began to think of reaching for it as though it were the holy grail. He was high enough now to see the faces of Dr Miller and the Peruvian archaeology students. He had never been as happy to see anyone in his life. He was too overjoyed to notice that none of them was smiling.

Then, as he was hoisted over the edge of the sinkhole, he saw to his astonishment and horror a sight that was completely unexpected.

Dr Miller, Shannon, and the Peruvian university students stepped back once Rodgers was on solid ground. As soon as he had unbuckled the safety line he saw that they all stood sombrely with their hands clasped behind their necks.

There were six in all, Chinese-manufactured Type 56-1 assault rifles gripped ominously by six pairs of steady hands. The six men were strung out in a rough semicircle around the archaeologists, small, blank-faced, silent men dressed in wool ponchos, sandals, and felt hats. Their furtive dark eyes darted from the captured group to Rodgers.

To Shannon, these men were not simple hill-folk bandits supplementing their meagre incomes by robbing visitors of food and material goods that could be hawked in public markets, they had to be hardened killers of the *Sendero Luminoso* ('Shining Path'), a Maoist revolutionary group that had terrorized Peru since 1981 by murdering thousands of innocent victims, including political leaders, policemen, and army soldiers. She was suddenly gripped by terror. The Shining Path killers were notorious for attaching explosives to their victims and blasting them to pieces.

After their founder and leader, Abimael Guzman, was captured in September 1992, the guerrilla movement had split into unorganized splinter groups that carried out haphazard car bombings and assassinations by blood-crazed death squads that achieved nothing for the people of Peru but tragedy and grief. The guerrillas stood around their captives, alert and watchful, with sadistic anticipation in their eyes.

One of them, an older man with an immense sweeping

moustache, motioned for Rodgers to join the other captives. 'Are there more people down there?' he asked in English with the barest trace of a Spanish accent.

Miller hesitated and cast a side glance at Giordino.

Giordino nodded at Rodgers. 'That man is the last,' he snapped in a tone filled with defiance. 'He and the lady were the only divers.'

The rebel guerrilla gazed at Giordino through lifeless, carbon black eyes. Then he stepped to the sheer drop of the sacrificial pool and peered downward. He saw a head floating in the middle of green slime. 'That is good,' he said in a sinister tone.

He picked up the safety line that descended into the water, took a machete from his belt and brought it down in a deft swing, severing the line from the reel. Then the expressionless face smiled a morbid smile as he casually held the end of the line over the edge for a moment before dropping it into the unescapable sinkhole.

4

Pitt felt like the chump in a Laurel and Hardy movie who yells to be saved from drowning and is thrown both ends of a rope. Holding up the severed end of the safety and communications line, he stared at it, incredulous. Besides having his means of escape dropped around his head, he had lost all contact with Giordino. He floated in the slime in total ignorance of the hostile events occurring above the sinkhole. He unbuckled the head straps holding the full face mask securely around his head, pulled it off, and stared up at the rim expectantly. Nobody stared back.

Pitt was half a second away from shouting for help when a roaring blast of gunfire reverberated around the limestone walls of the sinkhole for a solid sixty seconds. The acoustics of the stone amplified the sound deafeningly. Then, as abruptly as the automatic weapons' fire cut the quiet jungle, the harsh clatter faded and all went strangely silent. Pitt's thoughts were hurtling around in an unbreakable circle. To say he was mystified was a vast understatement. What was happening up there? Who was doing the shooting, and at whom? He became increasingly apprehensive with each passing moment. He had to get out of this death pit. But how? He didn't need a manual on mountain climbing to tell him it was impossible to climb the sheer ninety-degree walls without proper equipment or help from above.

Giordino would never have deserted him, he thought bleakly. Never — unless his friend was injured or unconscious. He didn't allow himself to dwell on the unthinkable possibility that Giordino was dead. Heartsick and mad from the desperation welling up inside him, Pitt shouted to the open sky, his voice echoing in the deep chamber. His only answer was a deathly stillness. He couldn't conceive why any of this was happening. It was becoming increasingly obvious that he would have to climb out alone. He looked up at the sky. There was less than two hours of daylight left. If he was to save himself, he had to start now. But what of the unseen intruders with guns? The nagging question was would they wait until he was as exposed as a fly on a windowpane before they blew him away? Or did they figure he was as good as dead? He decided not to wait to find out. Nothing short of the threat of being thrown in molten lava could keep him in that hot, scummy-layered water through the night.

He floated on his back and examined the walls that seemed to reach to a passing cloud, and tried to recall what he'd read about limestone in what seemed a centuries-old geology course in college. *Limestone: a sedimentary rock composed of calcium carbonate, a sort of blend of crystalline calcite and carbonate mud, produced by lime-secreting organisms from ancient coral reefs. Limestones vary in texture and colour.* Not bad, Pitt thought, for a student who pulled a B— in the course. His old teacher would be proud of him.

He was lucky he wasn't facing granite or basalt. The limestone was pockmarked with small hollow cavities and lined with tiny edges. He swam around the circular walls until he was under a small outcropping that protruded from the side about halfway to the top. He removed his air tank pack and the rest of his diving gear, except for the accessory belt, and let it drop to the floor of the sinkhole. All he kept were the pliers and the geologist's pick hammer from the tool kit. If for some unfathomable reason his best friend and the archaeologists above the ledge had been killed or wounded, and Pitt had been left to die in the sacrificial pool with only the ghosts of previous victims for company, he was damned well going to find out why.

First, he pulled a dive knife from a sheath strapped to his leg and cut off two lengths of safety line. He tied one section of the line tightly to the narrow section of the pick hammer's handle close to the head so it wouldn't slip over the wider base. Then he tied a step-in loop at the free end of the line.

Next he rigged a hook from the buckle of his accessory belt, bending it with the pliers until it resembled a C. He then fastened the second section of line to the hook with another step-in loop. When he was finished, he had functional, though rudimentary, climbing tools.

Now came the tough part.

Pitt's climbing technique was not exactly that of a veteran mountaineer. The sad truth was that he had never climbed any mountain except on a beaten trail by foot. What little he'd seen of experts scaling vertical rock walls came from public service television or magazine articles. Water was *his* element. His only contact with mountains was an occasional ski trip to Breckenridge, Colorado. He didn't know a piton (a metal spike with a ring in one end) from a carabiner (an oblong metal ring with a springloaded closing latch that hooks the climbing rope to the piton). He vaguely knew rappelling had something to do with descending a rope that wrapped under a thigh, across the body, and over the opposite shoulder.

There wasn't an expert climber in the business who would have given five hundred to one odds Pitt could make it to the top. The problem with the odds was that Pitt was too stubborn to even consider them. The old diehard Pitt came back on balance. His mind felt clear and sharp as a needle. He knew his life, and perhaps the lives of the others, hung on an unravelling thread. Cold, self-possessed inner resolve took hold as it had so many times in the past.

With a commitment bred of desperation, he reached up and stuck the belt hook into a small protruding edge of limestone. He then stepped into the loop, grasped the upper end of the line and pulled himself out of the water.

Now he lifted the hammer as high as he could reach, slightly off to one side, and rapped the pick end of the hammer into a limestone pocket. Then he placed his free foot in the loop and pulled himself to a higher stance up the limestone wall.

Crude by professional standards, Pitt mused, but it worked. He repeated the process, first with the C hook, then with the pick hammer, moving up the steep wall with his arms and legs articulating like a spider. It was exhausting effort even for a man in good physical condition. The sun had vanished below the tops of the trees as if jerked to the west by a string when Pitt finally climbed on to the small outcropping halfway up the steep wall. Still no sign from anyone above.

He clung there, thankful for the resting place, even though it was barely large enough to sit one of his buttocks on. Breathing heavily, he rested until his aching muscles stopped protesting. He could not believe the climb had taken so much out of him. An expert who knew all the tricks, he presumed, wouldn't even be breathing hard. He sat there hugging the sheer side of the sinkhole wall for almost ten minutes. He felt like sitting there for another hour, but time was passing. The surrounding jungle was quickly turning dark once the sun was gone.

Pitt studied the crude climbing tool that had taken him this far. The hammer was as good as new, but the C hook was beginning to straighten from the constant strain of supporting the dead weight of a human body. He took a minute to recurl the hook by beating it against the limestone with his pick hammer.

He had expected the darkness to shroud his vision, forcing him to scale the limestone by feel only. But a strange light was forming below him. He turned and stared down into the water.

The pool was emitting an eerie phosphorescent green light. No chemist, Pitt could only assume the strange emission was caused by some sort of chemical reaction from the decaying slime. Thankful for the illumination, however dim, he continued his gruelling climb upward.

The last 3 metres (10 feet) were the worst. So near, yet so far. The brink of the sinkhole seemed close enough to touch with his outstretched fingertips. Three metres, no more. Just ten feet. It might as well have been the summit of Mount Everest. A high school track star could have done it in his sleep. But not Pitt. A few months on the low side of forty, he felt like a tired old man.

His body was hard and lean, he watched his diet and exercised just enough to maintain a steady weight. There were the scars from numerous injuries, including gunshot wounds, but all the joints still functioned in a reasonably satisfactory manner. He'd given up smoking years ago, but still indulged himself occasionally with a glass of good wine or a tequila on the rocks with lime. His tastes had changed through the years from Cutty Sark scotch to Bombay gin to Sauza Commemorativo tequila. If asked why, he had no answer. He met each day as if life-was-a-game and games-were-life, and the reasons for doing certain things were hermetically sealed and buried inside his head.

Then, when he was within reach of the sinkhole's edge, he dropped the loop attached to the C hook. One moment stiffening fingers were tugging it from the limestone, the next it was falling towards the water where it entered the weirdly glowing algae layer with hardly a splash to mark its entry. In combination with the pick hammer, he began using the pockets of limestone as toe- and handholds. Near the top he swung the hammer in a circle above his head and hurled it over the edge of the sinkhole in an attempt to implant the pick end into soft soil.

It took four tries before the sharp point dug in and remained firm. With the final reserve of his strength, he took the line in both hands and pulled his body up until he could see flat ground before him in the growing darkness. He lay quiet and studied his surroundings. The dank rain forest seemed to close in around him. It was dark now and the only light came from the few stars and a crescent moon that breached the scattered clouds and the intertwined branches of the crowded trees. The dim light that filtered down illuminated the ancient ruins with a ghostly quality that was equalled by the sinister, claustrophobic effect of the invading walls of the forest. The eerie scene was enhanced by the almost complete silence. Pitt half expected to see weird stirring and hear ominous rustling in the darkness, but he saw no lights or moving shadows nor heard voices. The only sound came from the faint splatter of a sudden light rain on the leaves.

Enough laziness, he told himself. Get on, get moving, find out what happened to Giordino and the others. Time is slipping away. Only your first ordeal is over. That was physical, now you have to use your brain. He moved away from the sinkhole as fleetingly as a phantom.

The campsite was deserted. The tents he'd observed before being lowered into the sacrificial well were intact and empty. No signs of carnage, no indications of death. He approached the clearing where Giordino had landed the NUMA helicopter. It was riddled from bow to tail by bullets. Using it to fly for help was a dashed hope. No amount of repair would put it in the sky again.

The shattered rotor blades hung down like distorted arms twisted at the elbow. A colony of termites couldn't have done a better job on a decaying tree stump. Pitt sniffed the aroma of aviation fuel and thought it incredible the fuel tanks had failed to explode. It was too painfully obvious that a group of bandits or rebels had attacked the camp and blasted the craft into scrap.

His fears lessened considerably at discovering the gun-fire he'd heard in the sinkhole was directed against the helicopter and not human flesh. His boss at NUMA's national headquarters in Washington, DC, Admiral James

Sandecker, wouldn't take kindly to the write-off of one of the agency's fleet of aircraft, but Pitt had braved the feisty little seadog's wrath on numerous occasions and lived to tell about it. Not that it mattered what Sandecker would say now. Giordino and the archaeology project people were gone, taken captive by some force unknown to him.

He pushed aside the entry door that sagged drunkenly on one hinge and entered, making his way to the cockpit. He groped under the pilot's seat until he found a long pocket and retrieved a flashlight. The battery case felt undamaged. He held his breath and flicked on the switch. The beam flashed on and lit up the cockpit.

'Score one for the home team,' he muttered to himself.

Pitt carefully made his way into the cargo compartment. The hurricane of shells had torn it into a jagged mess, but nothing seemed vandalized or removed. He found his nylon carry bag and pulled out the contents. His shirt and sneakers had escaped unscathed but a bullet had pierced the knee of his pants and caused irreparable damage to his brief boxer shorts. Removing the shorty wet suit, he found a towel and gave his body a vigorous rubdown to remove the sinkhole's slime from his skin. After pulling on his clothes and sneakers, he then rummaged around until he came upon the box lunches packed by the chef on board their research ship. His box was splattered against a bulkhead, but Giordino's had survived intact. Pitt wolfed down a peanut butter sandwich and a dill pickle and drained a can of root beer. Now, he felt almost human again.

Back in the cockpit, he unlatched a panel door to a small compartment and pulled out a leather holster containing an old .45-calibre automatic Colt pistol. His father, Senator George Pitt, had carried it from Normandy to the Elbe River during World War II and then presented it to Dirk when he graduated from the Air Force Academy. The weapon had saved Pitt's life at least twice in the ensuing seventeen years. Though the blueing was pretty well worn

70

away, it was lovingly maintained and functioned even more smoothly than when new. Pitt noted with no small displeasure that a stray bullet had gouged the leather holster and creased one of the grips. He ran his belt through the loops of the holster and buckled it around his waist along with the sheath of the dive knife.

He fashioned a small shade to contain the beam of the flashlight and searched the campsite. Unlike the helicopter, there was no sign of gunfire except spent shells on the ground, but the tents had been ransacked and any useful equipment or supplies that could be carried away were gone. A quick survey of the soft ground showed what direction the exodus had taken. A path that had been hacked out by machetes angled off through the dense thickets before vanishing in the darkness.

The forest looked forbidding and impenetrable. This was not an expedition he would have ever considered or undertaken in daylight, much less nighttime. He was at the mercy of the insects and animals that found humans fair game in the rain forest. With no small concern the subject of snakes came to mind. He recalled hearing of boa constrictors and anacondas reaching lengths of 24 metres (80 feet). But it was the deadly poisonous snakes like the bushmaster, the cascabel, or the nasty fer-de-lance, or lancehead, that caused Pitt a high degree of trepidation. Low sneakers and light fabric pants offered no protection against a viper with a mean streak.

Beneath great stone faces staring menacingly down at him from the walls of the ruined city, Pitt set off at a steady pace, following the trail of footprints under the narrow beam of the flashlight. He wished he had a plan, but he was operating in the unknown. His chances of dashing through a murderous jungle and rescuing the hostages from any number of hard-bitten bandits or revolutionaries were plain hopeless. Failure seemed inevitable. But any thought of sitting around and doing nothing, or trying somehow to save himself, never entered his mind.

Pitt smiled at the stone faces of long-forgotten gods that stared back in the beam of the flashlight. He turned and took a last look at the unearthly green glow coming from the bottom of the sinkhole. Then he entered the jungle.

Within four paces the thick foliage swallowed him as if he'd never been.

5

Soaked by a constant drizzle, the prisoners were herded through a moss-blanketed forest until the trail ended at a deep ravine. Their captors drove them across a fallen log that served as a bridge to the other side where they followed the remains of an ancient stone road that wound up the mountains. The leader of the terrorist band set a fast pace, and Doc Miller was particularly hard-pressed to keep up. His clothes were so wet it was impossible to tell where the sweat left off and the damp from the rain began. The guards prodded him unmercifully with the muzzles of their guns whenever he dropped back. Giordino stepped beside the old man, propped one of Miller's arms over his shoulder, and helped him along, seeming oblivious to the pummelling provided by the sadistic guards against his defenceless back and shoulders.

'Keep that damned gun off him,' Shannon snapped at the bandit in Spanish. She took Miller's other arm and hung it around her neck so that both she and Giordino could support the older man. The bandit replied by kicking her viciously in the buttocks. She staggered forward, grey-faced, her lips tight in pain, but she regained her balance and gave the bandit a withering stare.

Giordino found himself smiling at Shannon, wondering at her spirit and grit and untiring fortitude. She still had on her swim suit under a sleeveless cotton blouse the guerrillas had allowed her to retrieve from her tent, along with a pair of hiking boots. He was also conscious of an overwhelming sense of ineffectiveness, his inability to save this woman from harm and degradation. And there was also a feeling of cowardice for deserting his old friend without a fight. He'd thought of snatching a guard's gun at least twenty times since being forced away from the sinkhole. But that would only have got him killed and solved nothing. As long as he somehow stayed alive there was a chance. Giordino cursed each step that took him farther and farther away from saving Pitt.

For hours they fought for breath in the thin Andes air as they struggled to an altitude of 3400 metres (11,000 feet). Everyone suffered from the cold. Although it soared under a blazing sun during the day, the temperature dropped to near freezing in the early hours of morning. Dawn found them still ascending along an ancient avenue of ruined white limestone buildings, high walls, and agricultural terraced hills that Shannon never dreamed existed. None of the structures looked as though they were built to the same specifications. Some were oval, some circular, very few were rectangular. They appeared oddly different from the other ancient structures she had studied. Was this all part of the Chachapoya confederation, she wondered, or another kingdom, another society? As the stone road followed along raised walls that reached almost into the mists rolling in from the mountain peaks above, she was astounded by the thousands of stone carvings of a very different ornamentation than she had ever seen. Great dragonlike birds and serpent-shaped fish mingled with stylized panthers and monkeys. The chiselled reliefs seemed oddly similar to Egyptian hieroglyphics except that they were more abstract. That unknown ancient peoples had inhabited the great plateau and ridges of the Peruvian Andes and constructed cities of such immense proportions came as a thrilling surprise to Shannon. She had not expected to find a culture so architecturally advanced that it erected structures on top of mountains as elaborate or extensive as any in the known ancient world. She would have given the Dodge Viper that she bought with her grandfather's inheritance to have lingered long enough to study these extraordinary ruins, but whenever she paused, she was roughly shoved forward.

The sun was showing when the bedraggled party emerged from a narrow pass into a small valley with mountains soaring on all sides. Though the rain thankfully had stopped, they all looked like rats who had barely escaped drowning. They saw ahead a lofty stone block building rising a good twelve storeys high. Unlike the Mayan pyramids of Mexico, this structure·had a rounder, more conical shape that was cut off at the top. It had ornate heads of animals and birds carved into the walls. Shannon recognized it as a ceremonial temple of the dead. The rear of the structure merged into a steep sandstone cliff honeycombed with thousands of burial caves, all with ornate exterior doorways facing on to a sheer drop. An edifice on the top of the building, flanked with two large sculptures of a feathered jaguar with wings, she tentatively identified as a palace of the death gods. It was sitting in a small city with over a hundred buildings painstakingly constructed and lavishly decorated. The variety of architecture was astonishing. Some structures were built on top of high towers surrounded by graceful balconies. Most were completely circular while others sat on rectangular bases.

Shannon was speechless. For a few moments the immensity of the sight overwhelmed her. The identity of the great complex of structures became immediately apparent. If what she saw before her was to be believed, the Shining Path terrorists had discovered an incredible lost city. One that archaeologists, herself included, doubted existed, that treasure seekers had searched for but never found through four centuries of exploration – the lost City of the Dead, whose mythical riches went beyond those in the Valley of the Kings in ancient Egypt.

Shannon gripped Rodgers tightly about one arm. 'The lost Pueblo de los Muertos,' she whispered.

'The lost what?' he asked blankly.

'No talking,' snapped one of the terrorists, jamming the butt of his automatic rifle in Rodgers's side just above the kidneys.

Rodgers gave a stifled gasp. He staggered and almost went down, but Shannon bravely held him on his feet, tensed for a blow that mercifully never came.

After a short walk over a broad stone street, they approached the circular structure that towered over the surrounding ceremonial complex like a Gothic cathedral over a medieval city. They toiled up several flights of an extraordinary switchback stairway decorated with mosaics of winged humans set in stone, designs Shannon had never seen before. On the upper landing, beyond a great arched entrance, they entered a high-ceilinged room with geometric motifs cut into the stone walls. The centre of the floor was crammed with intricately carved stone sculptures of every size and description. Ceramic effigy jars and elegant ornately painted vessels were stacked in chambers leading off the main room. One of these chambers was piled high with beautifully preserved textiles in every imaginable design and colour.

The archaeologists were stunned to see such an extensive cache of artifacts. To them it was like entering King Tut's tomb in Egypt's Valley of the Kings before the treasures were removed by famed archaeologist Howard Carter and put on display in the national museum in Cairo.

There was little time to study the treasure trove of artifacts. The terrorists quickly led the Peruvian students down an interior stairway and imprisoned them in a cell deep beneath the upper temple. Giordino and the rest were roughly thrown into a side room and guarded by two surly rebels who eyed them like exterminators contemplating a spider's nest. Everyone except Giordino sank gratefully to the hard, cold floor, fatigue etched in their drawn faces.

Giordino pounded his fist against the stone wall in frustration. During the forced march, he had watched intently for a chance to fade into the jungle and make his way back to the sinkhole, but with at least three guards taking turns training their automatic weapons at his back with cold steadiness the entire trip, the opportunity for escape never materialized. He didn't need any convincing that they were old hands at rounding up hostages and driving them through rugged terrain. Any hope of reaching Pitt now was slim indeed. During the march he had smothered his characteristic defiance and acted meek and subjugated. Except for a doughty display of concern for Doc Miller, he did nothing to invite a torrent of bullets to the gut. He had to stay alive. In his mind, if he died, Pitt died.

If Giordino had the slightest notion that Pitt had climbed out of the sinkhole and was pounding over the old stone trail only thirty minutes behind, then he might have felt the urge to attend church at his earliest opportunity. Or at the very least, he might have given the idea brief consideration.

With the flashlight carefully hooded to prevent being seen by the terrorists, and its beam angled down at the indentations in the compost covering the soft earth that travelled into the darkness, Pitt plunged through the rain forest. He ignored the rain with utter indifference. He moved with the determination of a man outside himself. Time meant nothing, not once did he glance at the luminous dial of his watch. The trek through the rain forest in the dead of night became a blur in his mind. Only when the morning sky began to brighten and he could put away the flashlight did his spirits take a turn for the better.

When he began his pursuit, the terrorists had more than a three-hour start. But he had closed the gap, walking at a steady gait when the trail ran steeply upward, jogging on the rare stretches where it levelled briefly. He never broke his stride, never once stopped to rest. His heart was beginning to pound under the strain, but his legs still pumped away without any muscle pain or tightness.

When he came on the ancient stone road and the going became easier, he actually increased his pace. Thoughts of the unseen horrors of the jungle had been cast aside, and throughout that seemingly perpetual night, all fear and apprehension became strangely remote.

He paid scant notice to the immense stone structures along the long avenue. He rushed on, now in daylight and on open ground, making little or no attempt at concealment. Only when he reached the pass into the valley did he slow down and stop, surveying the landscape ahead. He spotted the huge temple against the steep cliff approximately a half kilometre (a third of a mile) distant. One tiny figure sat at the top of the long stairway, hunched over with his back against a wide archway. There was no doubt in Pitt's mind this was where the terrorists had taken their hostages. The narrow pass was the only way in and out of the steep-walled valley. The fear and anxiety that he might stumble across the bodies of Giordino and the archaeologists were swept away in a wave of relief. The hunt was ended; now the quarry, who did not yet know they were quarry, had to be quietly cancelled out one by one until the odds became manageable.

He moved in closer, using the fallen walls of old residential homes around the temple as cover. He crouched and ran soundlessly from one shelter to the next until he crawled behind a large stone figure displaying a phallic design. He paused and stared up at the entrance to the temple. The long stairway leading to the entrance presented a formidable obstacle. Unless he somehow possessed the power of invisibility, Pitt would be shot down before he was a quarter of the way up the steps. Any attempt in broad daylight was suicidal. No way in, he thought bitterly. Flanking the staircase was out of the question. The temple's side walls were too sheer and too smooth. The stones were laid with such precision a knife blade could not fit between the cracks.

Then providence laid a benevolent hand on his

shoulder. The problem of creeping up the stairs unseen was erased when Pitt observed that the terrorist who was guarding the entrance to the temple had fallen hard asleep from the effects of the exhausting march through the jungle mountains. Inhaling and exhaling a deep breath, Pitt stealthily crept towards the stairway.

Tupac Amaru was a smooth but dangerous character, and he looked it. Having taken the name of the last king of the Incas to be tortured and killed by the Spanish, he was short, narrow-shouldered, with a vacant, brown face devoid of expression: he looked as though he never learned how to express the least hint of compassion. Unlike most of the hill-country people whose broad faces were smooth and hairless, Amaru wore a huge moustache and long sideburns that stretched from a thick mass of straight hair that was as black as his empty eyes. When the narrow, bloodless lips arched in a slight smile, which was rare, they revealed a set of teeth that would make an orthodontist proud. His men, conversely, often grinned diabolically through jagged and uneven coca-stained bicuspids.

Amaru had cut a swath of death and destruction throughout the jungle hill country of Amazonas, a department in northeastern Peru that had more than its share of poverty, terrorism, sickness, and bureaucratic corruption. His band of cutthroats was responsible for the disappearance of several explorers, government archaeologists, and army patrols that had entered the region and were never seen again. He was not the revolutionary he seemed. Amaru couldn't have cared less about revolution or improving the lot of the abysmally poor Indians of the Peruvian hinterlands, most of whom worked tiny plots to eke out a bare existence. Amaru had other reasons for controlling the region and keeping the superstitious natives under his domination.

He stood in the doorway of the chamber, staring stonily

at the three men and one woman before him as if for the first time, relishing the defeat in their eyes, the weariness in their bodies, exactly the state he wanted them.

'I regret the inconvenience,' he said, speaking for the first time since the abduction. 'It is good that you offered no resistance or you would have surely been shot.'

'You speak pretty good English for a highlands guerrilla,' Rodgers acknowledged, 'Mr – ?'

'Tupac Amaru. I attended the University of Texas at Austin.'

'What hath Texas wrought,' Giordino mumbled under his breath.

'Why have you kidnapped us?' Shannon whispered in a voice hushed with fear and fatigue.

'For ransom, what else?' replied Amaru. 'The Peruvian government will pay well for the return of such respected American scientists, not to mention their brilliant archaeology students, many of whom have rich and respected parents. The money will help us continue our fight against repression of the masses.'

'Spoken like a Communist milking a dead cow,' muttered Giordino.

'The old Russian version may well be history, but the philosophy of Mao Tse-tung lives on,' Amaru explained patiently.

'It lives on, all right,' Doc Miller sneered. 'Billions of dollars in economic damage. Twenty-six thousand Peruvians dead, most of the victims the very peasants whose rights you claim to be fighting for – ' His words were cut off by a rifle butt that was jammed into his lower back near the kidney. Miller sagged to the stone floor like a bag of potatoes, his face twisted in pain.

'You're hardly in a position to question my dedication to the cause,' Amaru said coldly.

Giordino knelt beside the old man and cradled his head. He looked up at the terrorist leader with scorn. 'You don't take criticism very well, do you?'

Giordino was prepared to ward off a blow to his exposed head, but before the guard could raise his rifle butt again, Shannon stepped between them.

She glared at Amaru, the pale fear in her face replaced with red anger. 'You're a fraud,' Shannon stated firmly.

Amaru looked at her with a bemused expression. 'And what brings you to that curious conclusion, Dr Kelsey?'

'You know my name?'

'My agent in the United States alerted me of your latest project to explore the mountains before you and your friends left the airport in Phoenix, Arizona.'

'Informant, you mean.'

Amaru shrugged. 'Semantics mean little.'

'A fraud and a charlatan,' Shannon continued. 'You and your men aren't Shining Path revolutionaries. Far from it. You're nothing more than *huaqueros*, thieving tomb robbers.'

'She's right,' Rodgers said, backing her up. 'You wouldn't have time to chase around the countryside blowing up power lines and police stations and still accumulate the vast cache of artifacts inside this temple. It's obvious; you're running an elaborate artifact theft ring that has to be a full-time operation.'

Amaru looked at his prisoners in mocking speculation. 'Since the fact must be patently apparent to everyone in the room, I won't bother to deny it.'

A few seconds passed in silence, then Doc Miller rose unsteadily to his feet and stared Amaru directly in the eye. 'You thieving scum,' he rasped. 'Pillager, ravager of antiquities. If it was in my power, I'd have you and your band of looters shot down like – '

Miller broke off suddenly as Amaru, his features utterly lacking the least display of emotion and his black eyes venting evil, removed a Heckler & Koch nine-millimetre automatic from a hip holster. With the paralysing inevitability of a dream, he calmly, precisely, shot Doc Miller in the chest. The reverberating blast echoed through the temple, deafening all ears. One shot was all that was required. Doc Miller jerked backward against the stone wall for one shocking moment, and then dropped forward on to his stomach without a sound, hands and arms twisted oddly beneath his chest as a pool of red oozed across the floor.

The captives all reflected different reactions. Rodgers stood like a statue frozen in time, eyes wide with shock and disbelief, while Shannon instinctively screamed. No stranger to violent death, Giordino clenched his hands at his sides. The ice-cold indifference of the murderous act filled him with a savage rage that was tempered only by maddening helplessness. There was no doubt in his mind, in anybody's mind, that Amaru intended to kill them all. With nothing to lose, Giordino tensed to leap at the killer and tear out his throat before he received the inevitable bullet through the head.

'Do not try it,' said Amaru, reading Giordino's thoughts, aiming the muzzle of the automatic between the eyes that burned with hate. He inclined his head towards the guards, who stood with guns level and ready, and gave them orders in Spanish. Then he stepped aside as one of the guards grabbed Miller around the ankles, and dragged his body out of sight into the main room of the temple, leaving a trail of blood across the stone floor.

Shannon's scream had given way to uncontrollable sobbing as she stared with bleak, unwavering eyes at the bloody streak on the floor. She sagged to her knees in shock and buried her face in her hands. 'He couldn't harm you. How could you shoot down a kindly old man?'

Giordino stared at Amaru. 'For him, it was easy.'

Amaru's flat, cold eyes crawled to Giordino's face. 'You would do well to keep your mouth closed, little man. The good doctor was supposed to be a lesson that apparently you did not comprehend.'

No one took notice of the return of the guard who had dragged away Miller's body. No one except Giordino. He caught the hat pulled down over the eyes, the hands concealed within the poncho. He flicked a glance at the second guard who slouched casually against the doorway, his gun now slung loosely over one shoulder, the muzzle pointing at no one in particular. Only two metres separated them. Giordino figured he could be all over the guard before he knew what hit him. But there was still the Heckler & Koch tightly gripped in Amaru's hand.

When Giordino spoke, his voice wore a cold edge. 'You are going to die, Amaru. You are surely going to die as violently as all the innocent people you've murdered in cold blood.'

Amaru didn't catch the millimetric curl of Giordino's lips, the slight squint of the eyes. His expression turned curious, then the teeth flashed and he laughed. 'So? You think I'm going to die, do you? Will you be my executioner? Or will the proud young lady do me the honour?'

He leaned down and savagely jerked Shannon to her feet, took hold of her flowing ponytail, and viciously pulled her head backward until she was staring from wide, terrified eyes into his leering face. 'I promise that after a few hours in my bed you'll crawl to obey my commands.'

'Oh, God, no,' Shannon moaned.

'I take great pleasure in raping women, listening as they scream and beg – '

A brawny arm tightened around his throat and choked off his words. 'This is for all the women you made suffer,' said Pitt, a macabre look in his intense green eyes, as he cast aside the poncho, jammed the barrel of the .45 Colt down the front of Amaru's pants, and pulled the trigger.

6

For the second time the small confines of the room echoed with the deafening sound of gunfire. Giordino hurled himself forward, his head and shoulder driving into the startled guard, crushing him against the hard wall, causing an explosive gasp of pain. He caught the distorted look of horror and agony on Amaru's face, the bulging eyes, his mouth open in a silent scream, a fleeting glimpse of the Heckler & Koch flying through the air as his hands clutched the mushrooming red stain in his groin. And then Giordino punched the guard in the teeth and tore the automatic rifle from his hands in almost the same movement. He swung around in a crouched firing position, muzzle aimed through the doorway.

This time Shannon didn't scream. Instead, she crawled into a corner of the room and sat motionless, like a waxen effigy of herself, staring dumbly at Amaru's blood splattered over her bare arms and legs. If she had been terrified earlier, she was now merely numb with shock. Then she stared up at Pitt, lips taut, face pale, specks of blood in her blond hair.

Rodgers was staring at Pitt too, with an expression of astonishment. Somehow he knew, recognized the eyes, the animal-like movements. 'You're the diver trom the cave,' he said dazedly.

Pitt nodded. 'One and the same.'

'You're supposed to be back in the well,' Shannon murmured in a trembling voice.

'Sir Edmund Hillary has nothing on me.' Pitt grinned slyly. 'I scramble up and down the walls of sinkholes like a human fly.' He shoved a horrified Amaru to the floor as if the terrorist were a drunk on a sidewalk and placed a hand on Giordino's shoulder. 'You can relax, Al. The other guards have seen the light of decency and virtue.'

Giordino, with a smile as wide as an open drawbridge, laid aside the automatic rifle and embraced Pitt. 'God, I never thought I'd see your gargoyle face again.'

'The things you put me through. A damned shame. I can't go away for half an hour without you involving me in a local crime wave.'

'Why the delay?' asked Giordino, not to be outdone. 'We expected you hours ago.'

'I missed my bus. Which reminds me, where is my Dixieland band?'

'They don't play sinkholes. Seriously, how in hell did you climb a sheer wall and trail us through the jungle?'

'Not exactly a fun-filled feat, believe me. I'll tell you over a beer another time.'

'And the guards, what happened to the other four guards?'

Pitt gave a negligent shrug. 'Their attention wandered and they all met with unfortunate accidents, mostly concussions or possible skull fractures.' Then his face turned grim. 'I ran into one pulling Doc Miller's body through the main entrance. Who carried out the execution?'

Giordino nodded at Amaru. 'Our friend here shot him in the heart for no good reason. He's also the guy who dropped the safety line down around your head.'

'Then I won't bother myself with remorse,' Pitt said, staring down at Amaru, who was clutching his groin and moaning in agony, fearful of looking to ascertain the damage. 'Kind of makes me warm all over knowing that his sex life just went dysfunctional. Does he have a name?'

'Calls himself Tupac Amaru,' answered Shannon. 'The name of the last Inca king. Probably took it to impress the hill people.'

'The Peruvian students,' Giordino said, remembering.

'They were herded down a stairway underneath the temple.'

'I've already released them. Brave kids. By now they should have the guerrillas tied up and neatly packaged until the government authorities arrive.'

'Not guerrillas, and hardly dedicated revolutionaries. More like professional artifact looters masquerading as Shining Path terrorists. They pillage precious antiquities to sell through international underground markets.'

'Amaru is only the base of a totem pole,' added Rodgers. 'His clients are the distributors who make the bulk of the profits.'

'They have good taste,' observed Pitt. 'From what I glimpsed, there must be enough prime merchandise stashed here to satisfy half the museums and private collectors in the world.'

Shannon hesitated a moment, then stepped up to Pitt, put her hands around his neck, pulled his head down and kissed him lightly on the lips. 'You saved our lives. Thank you.'

'Not once but twice,' Rodgers added, pumping Pitt's hand while Shannon still clung to him.

'A lot of luck was involved,' Pitt said with uncharacteristic embarrassment. Despite the damp, stringy hair, the lack of makeup, the dirty and torn blouse over the black swim suit, and the incongruous hiking boots, he still saw a sensual lustiness about her.

'Thank God you got here when you did,' said Shannon with a shiver.

'I deeply regret I was too late to save Doc Miller.'

'Where have they taken him?' asked Rodgers.

'I stopped the scum who was disposing of the body just outside the temple entrance. Doc is lying on the landing above the steps.'

Giordino gazed at Pitt, inspecting him from head to toe, observing the multitude of cuts and scratches on his friend's face and arms from his race through the jungle in the dark, seeing a man who was all but dead on his feet. 'You look like you just finished a triathlon and then fell on a roll of barbed wire. As your resident medicine man, I recommend a few hours' rest before we hike back to the sinkhole campsite.'

'I look worse than I feel,' Pitt said cheerfully. 'Time enough for a snooze later. First things first. Me, I don't have the slightest inclination to play Tarzan again. I'm taking the next flight out of here.'

'Madness,' muttered Giordino half in jest. 'A few hours in the jungle and he goes flaky.'

'Do you really think we can fly out of here?' inquired Shannon sceptically.

'Absolutely,' Pitt said. 'In fact I guarantee it.'

Rodgers stared at him. 'Only a helicopter could come in and out of the valley.'

Pitt grinned. 'I wouldn't have it any other way. How else do you think Amaru, or whatever his name is, transports his stolen goods to a coastal port for shipment out of the country? That calls for a communications system, so there must be a radio around we can appropriate to send out a call for help.'

Giordino gave an approving nod. 'Makes sense, providing we can find it. A portable radio could be hidden anywhere in one of the surrounding ruins. We could spend days looking for it.'

Pitt stared down at Amaru, his face expressionless. 'He knows where it is.'

Amaru fought off the pain and stared back at Pitt with black malignant eyes. 'We have no radio,' he hissed through clenched teeth.

'Forgive me if I don't take you at your word. Where do you keep it?'

'I will tell you nothing.' Amaru's mouth twisted as he spoke.

'Would you rather die?' Pitt queried drily.

'You would do me a service by killing me.'

Pitt's green eyes were as cold as a lake above timberline. 'How many women have you raped and murdered?'

Amaru's expression was contemptuous. 'So numerous I've lost count.'

'You want me to fly into a rage and blow you away, is that it?'

'Why don't you ask how many children I've slaughtered?'

'You're only kidding yourself.' Pitt took the Colt .45 and placed the muzzle against the side of Amaru's face. 'Kill you? I fail to see the percentage in that. One shot through both eyes would be more appropriate. You'll still live, but along with your other recent impairment you'll also be blind.'

Amaru put on a show of arrogance, but there was unmistakable fear in his dead eyes, and there was a noticeable trembling of his lips. 'You're bluffing.'

'After the eyes, then the kneecaps,' Pitt described conversationally. 'Perhaps the ears next, or better yet the nose. If I were you, I'd quit while I was ahead.'

Seeing that Pitt was stone-cold serious, and realizing he was at a dead end, Amaru caved in. 'You'll find what you're looking for inside a round building fifty metres west of the temple. There is a monkey carved above the doorway.'

Pitt turned to Giordino. 'Take one of the students with you to translate. Contact the nearest Peruvian authorities. Give our location and report our situation. Then request they send in an army unit. There may be more of these characters lurking in the ruins.'

Giordino looked thoughtfully at Amaru. 'If I send a Mayday over an open frequency, this homicidal maniac's pals in Lima might very well pick it up and send in a force of goons ahead of the army.'

'Trusting the army can be touch-and-go,' added Shannon. 'One or more of their high-ranking officers could be in on this.'

'Graft,' Pitt stated philosophically, 'makes the world go round.'

Rodgers nodded. 'Shannon's right. This is tomb robbery on a grand scale. The profits could easily match the take of any top drug smuggling operation. Whoever the mastermind is, he couldn't conduct business without paying off government officials.'

'We can use our own frequency and contact Juan,' suggested Shannon.

'Juan?'

'Juan Chaco, the Peruvian government coordinator for our project. He's in charge of our supply headquarters at the nearest city.'

'Can he be trusted?'

'I believe so,' Shannon replied without hesitation. 'Juan is one of the most respected archaeologists in South America, and a leading scholar on Andean cultures. He's also the government watchdog on illegal diggings and smuggling of antiquities.'

'Sounds like our man,' Pitt said to Giordino. 'Find the radio, call him up and ask for a chopper to airlift us the hell back to our ship.'

'I'll go with you and notify Juan of Doc's murder,' offered Shannon. 'I'd also like a closer look at the structures around the temple.'

'Take along weapons and keep a sharp eye,' Pitt warned them.

'What about Doc's body?' asked Rodgers. 'We can't leave him lying around like a road kill.'

'I agree,' said Pitt. 'Bring him inside the temple out of the sun and wrap him in some blankets until he can be airlifted to the nearest coroner.'

'Leave him to me,' Rodgers said angrily. 'It's the least I can do for a good man.'

Amaru grinned hideously, actually grinned through his agony. 'Fools, crazy fools,' he sneered. 'You'll never leave the Pueblo de los Muertos alive.'

'Pueblo de los Muertos means city of the dead,' Shannon translated.

The others glanced in disgust at Amaru. To them he seemed like an impotent rattlesnake too injured to coil and strike. But Pitt still saw him as dangerous and was not about to make the fatal mistake of underestimating him. He didn't care for the eerie expression of confidence in Amaru's eyes.

As soon as the others hurried out of the room, Pitt knelt beside Amaru. 'You act pretty sure of yourself for a man in your position.'

'The last laugh will be mine.' Amaru's face contorted in a sudden spasm of pain. 'You have blundered into the path of powerful men. Their wrath will be terrible.'

Pitt smiled indifferently. 'I ve blundered up against powerful men before.'

'By lifting a tiny piece of the curtain you have endangered the *Solpemachaco*. They will do whatever necessary to prevent exposure, even if it means the elimination of an entire province.'

'Not exactly a sweet-tempered group you're associated with. What do you call them again?'

Amaru went silent. He was becoming weak from shock and the loss of blood. Slowly, with much difficulty, he lifted a hand and pointed a finger at Pitt. 'You are cursed. Your bones will rest with the Chachapoyas forever.' Then, his eyes went unfocused, closed, and he fainted.

Pitt stared at Shannon. 'Who are the Chachapoyas?'

'Known as the Cloud People,' Shannon explained. 'They were a pre-Inca culture that flourished high in the Andes from A.D. 800 to 1480, when they were conquered by the Incas. It was the Chachapoyas who built this elaborate necropolis for the dead.'

Pitt rose to his feet, removed the guard's felt hat from his head and dropped it on Amaru's chest. He turned and walked into the main chamber of the temple and spent the next few minutes examining the incredible cache of

Chachapoyan artifacts. He was admiring a large clay mummy case when Rodgers rushed up, looking disturbed.

'Where did you say you left Doc Miller?' Rodgers asked, half out of breath.

'On the landing above the exterior steps.'

'You'd better show me.'

Pitt followed Rodgers outside the arched entrance. He stopped and stared down at a bloodstain on the stone landing, then looked up questioningly. 'Who moved the body?'

'If you don't know,' said an equally mystified Rodgers, 'I certainly don't.'

'Did you look around the base of the temple? Maybe he fell — '

'I sent four of the archaeology students down to search. They found no sign of the Doc.'

'Could any of the students have moved him?'

'I checked. They're all as bewildered as we are.'

'Dead bodies do not get up and walk off,' said Pitt flatly.

Rodgers looked around the outside of the temple, then gave a shrug. 'It looks as if this one did.'

7

The air conditioner whirred and circulated cool dry air inside the long motor home that served as the archaeology project's headquarters in Chachapoya. And the man reclining on a leather sofa was a great deal less fatigued than the men and women in the City of the Dead. Juan Chaco rested languidly while maintaining a firm grip on his well-iced gin and tonic. But he sat up in full wakefulness almost instantly when a voice came over the radio speaker mounted on a wall behind the driver's compartment.

'Saint John calling Saint Peter.' The voice came sharp and distinct. 'Saint John calling Saint Peter. Are you there?'

Chaco moved quickly across the interior of the plush motor home and pressed the transmit button on the radio. 'I am here and listening.'

'Turn on the recorder. I don't have time to repeat myself or explain the situation in detail.'

Chaco acknowledged and switched on a cassette recorder. 'Ready to receive.'

'Amaru and his followers were overpowered and taken prisoner. They are now being held under guard by the archaeologists. Amaru was shot and may be badly wounded.'

Chaco's face suddenly turned grim. 'How is this possible?'

'One of the men from NUMA, who responded to your distress call, somehow escaped from the sinkhole and pursued Amaru and his captives to the valley temple where he managed to subdue our overpaid cutthroats one by one.'

'What sort of devil could do all this?'

'A very dangerous and resourceful devil.'

'Are you safe?'

'For the moment.'

'Then our plan to frighten the archaeologists from our collection grounds has failed.'

'Miserably,' replied the caller. 'Once Dr Kelsey saw the artifacts awaiting shipment, she guessed the setup.'

'What of Miller?'

'They suspect nothing.'

'At least something went right,' said Chaco.

'If you send in a force before they leave the valley,' explained the familiar voice, 'we can still salvage the operation.'

'It was not our intention to harm our Peruvian students,' said Chaco. 'The repercussions from my countrymen would spell the end to any further business between us.'

'Too late, my friend. Now that they realize their ordeal was caused by a looting syndicate instead of Shining Path terrorists, they can't be allowed to reveal what they've seen. We have no choice but to eliminate them.'

'None of this would have occurred if you had prevented Dr Kelsey and Miles Rodgers from diving in the sacred well.'

'Short of committing murder in front of the students, there was no stopping them.'

'Sending out the rescue call was a mistake.'

'Not if we wished to avoid serious enquiry by your government officials. Their drownings would have appeared suspicious if the correct rescue measures hadn't been taken. We cannot afford to expose the *Solpemachaco* to public scrutiny. Besides, how could we know that NUMA would respond from out of nowhere?'

'True, an event that was inconceivable at the time.'

As Chaco spoke, his empty eyes gazed at a small stone statue of a winged jaguar that was dug up in the valley of the dead. Finally he said quietly, 'I'll arrange for our hired mercenaries from the Peruvian army to drop in the Pueblo de los Muertos by helicopter within two hours.'

'Do you have confidence in the commanding officer to do the job?'

Chaco smiled to himself. 'If I can't trust my own brother, who can I trust?'

'I never believed in resurrection of mere mortals.' Pitt stood gazing down at the pool of crimson on the landing above the near-vertical stairway leading to the floor of the valley. 'But this is as good an example as I've ever seen.'

'He was dead,' Rodgers said emphatically. 'I was standing as close to him as I am to you when Amaru put a bullet through his heart. Blood was everywhere. You saw him lying here. There can be no doubt in your mind Doc was a corpse.'

'I didn't take the time to do a postmortem examination.'

'Okay, but how do you explain the trail of blood from the interior chamber where Doc was shot? There must be a gallon of it spread from here to there.'

'Closer to a pint,' said Pitt thoughtfully. 'You exaggerate.'

'How long would you guess the body rested here from the time you knocked out the guard and then released the students who arrived and tied him up?' asked Rodgers.

'Four, maybe five minutes at the outside.'

'And within that time a sixty-seven-year-old dead man bounds down two hundred tiny, narrow, niched steps laid on a seventy-five-degree angle. Steps that can't be taken more than one at a time without falling, and then he vanishes without shedding another drop of blood.' Rodgers shook his head. 'Houdini would have flushed with envy.'

'Are you sure it was Doc Miller?' Pitt asked pensively.

'Of course it was Doc,' Rodgers said incredulously. 'Who else do you think it was?'

'How long have you known him?'

'By reputation, at least fifteen years. Personally, I only

met him five days ago.' Rodgers stared at Pitt as if he were a madman. 'Look, you're fishing in empty waters. Doc is one of the world's leading anthropologists. He is to ancient American culture what Leakey is to African prehistory. His face has graced a hundred articles in dozens of magazines from the *Smithsonian* to the *National Geographic*. He has narrated and appeared in any number of public service television documentaries on early man. Doc was no recluse, he loved publicity. He was easily recognizable.'

'Just fishing,' Pitt said in a patient explaining tone. 'Nothing like a wild plot to stir the mind – '

He broke off as Shannon and Giordino sprinted into view around the circular base of the temple. Even at this height above the ground he could see they appeared agitated. He waited until Giordino was halfway up the stairs before he shouted.

'Don't tell me, somebody beat you to the radio and smashed it.'

Giordino paused, leaning against the sheer stairway. 'Wrong,' he shouted back. 'It was gone. Snatched by person or persons unknown.'

By the time Shannon and Giordino reached the top of the stairs they were both panting from the exertion and glistening with sweat. Shannon daintily patted her face with a soft tissue all women seem to produce at the most crucial times. Giordino merely rubbed an already damp sleeve across his forehead.

'Whoever built this thing,' he said between breaths, 'should have installed an elevator.'

'Did you find the tomb with the radio?' Pitt asked.

Giordino nodded. 'We found it all right. No cheapskates, these guys. The tomb was furnished right out of Abercrombie & Fitch. The best outdoor paraphernalia money can buy. There was even a portable generator providing power to a refrigerator.'

'Empty?' Pitt guessed.

Giordino nodded. 'The rat who made off with the radio

took the time to smash nearly four sixpacks of perfectly good Coors beer.'

'Coors in Peru?' Rodgers asked dubiously.

'I can show you the labels on the broken bottles,' moaned Giordino. 'Someone wanted us to go thirsty.'

'No fear of that with a jungle just beyond the pass,' Pitt said with a slight smile.

Giordino stared at Pitt, but there was no return smile. 'So how do we call in the marines?'

Pitt shrugged. 'With the tomb robbers' radio missing, and the one in our helicopter looking like a lump of Swiss cheese – ' he broke off and turned to Rodgers. 'What about your communications at the sinkhole site?'

The photographer shook his head. 'One of Amaru's men shot our radio to junk the same as yours.'

'Don't tell me,' Shannon said resignedly, 'we have to trudge thirty kilometres back through the forest primeval to the project site at the sinkhole, and then another ninety kilometres to Chachapoya?'

'Maybe Chaco will become worried when he realizes all contact is lost with the project and sends in a search party to investigate,' Rodgers said hopefully.

'Even if they traced us to the City of the Dead,' Pitt said slowly, 'they'd arrive too late. All they'd find would be dead bodies scattered around the ruins.'

Everyone glanced at him in puzzled curiosity.

'Amaru claimed we have upset the applecart of powerful men,' Pitt continued by way of explanation, 'and that they would never allow us to leave this valley alive for fear that we would expose their artifact theft operation.'

'But if they intended to kill us,' Shannon said uncertainly, 'why bring us here? They could have just as well shot everyone and thrown our remains into the sinkhole.'

'In order for them to make it look like a Shining Path raid, they may have had it in their mind to play the hostage for ransom game. If the Peruvian government, your university officials in the States, or the families of the archaeological students had paid enormous sums for your release, all the better. They'd have simply considered the ransom money as a bonus to the profits of their illegal smuggling and murdered all of you anyway.'

'Who are these people?' Shannon asked sharply.

'Amaru referred to them as the *Solpemachaco*, whatever that translates into.'

'*Solpemachaco*,' Shannon echoed. 'A combination Medusa/dragon myth from the local ancients. Folklore passed down through the centuries describes *Solpemachaco* as an evil serpent with seven heads who lives in a cave. One myth claims he lives here in the Pueblo de los Muertos.'

Giordino yawned indifferently. 'Sounds like a bad screenplay starring another monster from the bowels of the earth.'

'More likely a clever play on words,' said Pitt. 'A metaphor as a code name for an international looting organization with a vast reach into the underground antiquities market.'

'The serpent's seven heads could represent the master-minds behind the organization,' suggested Shannon.

'Or seven different bases of operation,' added Rodgers.

'Now that we've cleared up that mystery,' Giordino said wryly, 'why don't we clear the hell out of here and head for the sinkhole before the Sioux and Cheyenne come charging through the pass?'

'Because they'd be waiting when we got there,' said Pitt. 'Methinks we should stay put.'

'You really believe they'll send men to kill us?' Shannon said, her expression more angry than fearful.

Pitt nodded. 'I'd bet my pension on it. Whoever made off with the radio most certainly tattled on us. I judge his pals will soar into the valley like maddened hornets in . . .' he paused to glance at his watch before continuing, '. . . about an hour and a half. After that, they'll shoot down anyone who vaguely resembles an archaeologist.'

'Not what I call a cheery thought,' she murmured.

'With six automatic rifles and Dirk's handgun I reckon we might discourage a first-rate gang of two dozen cutthroats for all of ten minutes,' muttered Giordino gloomily.

'We can't stay here and fight armed criminals,' Rodgers protested. 'We'd all be slaughtered.'

'And there are the lives of those kids to consider,' said Shannon, suddenly looking a little pale.

'Before we're swept up in an orgy of pessimism,' said Pitt briskly, as if he hadn't a care in the world, 'I suggest we round up everyone and evacuate the temple.'

'Then what?' demanded Rodgers.

'First, we look around for Amaru's landing site.'

'For what purpose?'

Giordino rolled his eyes. 'I know that look. He's hatching another Machiavellian scheme.'

'Nothing too contrived,' Pitt said patiently. 'I figure that after the bushwhackers land and begin chasing around the ruins searching for us, we'll borrow their helicopter and fly off to the nearest four-star hotel and a refreshing bath.'

There was a moment of incredulous stillness. They all stared at Pitt as if he'd just stepped out of a Martian space capsule. Giordino was the first to break the stunned silence.

'See,' he said with a wide grin. 'I told you so.'

8

Pitt's estimate of an hour and a half was shy by only ten minutes. The stillness of the valley was broken by the throb of rotor blades whipping the air as two Peruvian military helicopters flew over the crest of a saddle between mountain peaks and circled the ancient buildings. After a cursory reconnaissance of the area, they descended in a clearing amid the ruins less than 100 metres (328 feet) from the front of the conical temple structure. The troops spilled out rapidly through the rear clamshell doors under the beating rotor blades and lined up at rigid attention as though they were standing for inspection.

These were no ordinary soldiers dedicated to preserving the peace of their nation. They were mercenary misfits who hired themselves out to the highest bidder. At the direction of the officer in charge, a captain incongruously attired in full dress uniform, the two platoons of thirty men each were formed into one closely packed battle line led by two lieutenants. Satisfied the line was straight, the captain raised a swagger stick above his head and motioned for the officers under his command to launch the assault on the temple. Then he climbed a low wall to direct the one-sided battle from what he thought was a safe viewpoint.

The captain shouted encouragement to his men, urging them to bravely charge up the steps of the temple. His voice echoed because of the hard acoustics of the ruins. But he broke off and uttered a strange *awking* sound that became a fit of gagging pain. For a brief instant he stiffened, his face twisted in incomprehension, then he folded forward and pitched off the wall, landing with a loud crack on the back of his head.

A short, dumpy lieutenant in baggy combat fatigues rushed over and knelt beside the fallen captain, looked up at the funeral palace in dazed understanding, opened his mouth to shout an order, then crumpled over the body beneath him, the sharp crack of a Type 56-1 rifle the last thing he heard before death swept over him.

From the landing on the upper level of the temple, flat on his stomach behind a small barricade of stones, Pitt stared down at the line of confused troops through the sights of the rifle and fired another four rounds into their ranks, picking off the only remaining officer. There was no look of surprise or fear on Pitt's face at seeing the overwhelming mercenary force, only a set look of determination in the deep green eyes. By resisting he was providing a diversion to save the lives of thirteen innocent people. Merely firing over the troops' heads to momentarily slow the assault was a futile waste of time. These men had come to kill all witnesses to a criminal operation. Kill or be killed was a cliche, but it held true. These men would give no quarter.

Pitt was not a pitiless man; his eyes were neither steel hard nor ice cold. For him there was no enjoyment in killing a complete stranger. His biggest regret was that the faceless men responsible for the crimes were not in his sights.

Cautiously, he pulled the assault rifle back from the tight peephole between the stones and surveyed the ground below. The Peruvian mercenaries had fanned out behind the stone ruins. A few scattered shots were fired upward at the temple, chipping the stone carvings before ricocheting and whining off into the cliff of tombs behind. These were hardened, disciplined fighting men who recovered quickly under pressure. Killing their officers had stalled but not stopped them. The sergeants had taken command and were concentrating on a tactic to eliminate this unexpected resistance.

Pitt ducked back behind the stone barricade as a torrent

100

of automatic weapons fire peppered the outside columns, sending chips of stone flying in all directions. This came as no surprise to him. The Peruvians were laying down a covering fire as they crouched and dashed from ruin to ruin, moving ever closer to the base of the stairs leading up the rounded front of the temple. Pitt moved sideways like a crab and edged into the shelter of the death palace before rising to his feet and running to the rear wall. He cast a wary eye out an arched window.

Knowing that the round walls of the temple were too smooth to scale for an attack and too steep for the defenders to escape, none of the soldiers had circled around to the rear. Pitt could easily predict that they were gambling their entire force on a frontal assault up the stairway. What he hadn't foreseen was that they were going to reduce a lot of the palace of the dead on top of the temple to rubble before charging up the stairway.

Pitt scurried back to the barricade and let loose a long burst from the Chinese automatic rifle until the final shell spat across the stone floor. He rolled to one side and was in the act of inserting another long, curved ammo stick in the gun's magazine when he heard a *whoosh*, and a forty-millimetre rocket from a People's Republic of China Type 69 launcher sailed up and burst against one side of the temple 8 metres (26 feet) behind Pitt. It detonated with a thunderous explosion that hurled stone like shrapnel and tore a huge hole in the wall. Within seconds the ancient shrine to the death gods was clogged with debris and the evil stench of high explosives .

There was a loud ringing in Pitt's ears, the reverberating roar of the detonation, the pounding of his own heart. He was momentarily blinded and his nose and throat were immediately filled with dust. He frantically rubbed his eyes clear and gazed down at the surrounding ruins. He was just in time to see the black smoke cloud and bright flash produced by the rocket's booster. He ducked with his hands over his head as another rocket slammed into the ancient stone and exploded with a deafening roar. The vicious blow pelted Pitt with flying rubble and the concussion knocked the breath out of him.

For a moment he lay motionless, almost lifeless. Then he struggled painfully to his hands and knees, coughing dust, seized the rifle, and crawled back into the interior of the palace. He took a last look at the mountain of precious artifacts and paid a final call on Amaru.

The grave looter had regained consciousness and glared at Pitt, his hands clutching his groin, now clotted with dried blood, the murderous face masked in hate. There was a strange coldness about him now, an utter indifference to the pain. He radiated evil.

'Your friends have a destructive nature,' said Pitt, as another rocket struck the temple.

'You are trapped,' Amaru rasped in a low tone.

'Thanks to your staged murder of Dr Miller's imposter. He made off with your radio and called in reinforcements.'

'Your time to die has arrived, Yankee pig.'

'Yankee pig,' Pitt repeated. 'I haven't been called that in ages.'

'You will suffer as you have made me suffer.'

'Sorry, I have other plans.'

Amaru tried to rise up on an elbow and say something, but Pitt was gone.

He rushed to the rear opening again. A mattress and pair of knives he had scrounged from living quarters inside the cliff tomb discovered by Giordino and Shannon sat beside the window. He laid the mattress over the lower sill, then lifted his legs outside and sat on it. He cast aside the rifle, gripped the knives in outstretched hands, and glanced apprehensively at the ground 20 metres (65 feet) below. He recalled an occasion when he bungee-jumped into a canyon on Vancouver Island in British Columbia. Leaping into space, he mused, went against all human nature. Any hesitation or second thoughts abruptly ended when a fourth rocket smashed into the temple. He dug the heels of his sneakers into the steep slope and jammed the knife blades into the stone blocks for brakes. Without a backward glance, he launched himself over the side, and slid down the wall, using the mattress as a toboggan/sled.

Giordino, with Shannon and the students trailing behind him and Rodgers bringing up the rear, cautiously climbed a stairway from an underground tomb where they had been hiding when the helicopters landed. Giordino paused, raised his head slightly over a fallen stone wall, and scanned the landscape. The helicopters were sitting only 50 metres (164 feet) away, engines idling, the two-man flight crews calmly sitting in their cockpits watching the assault on the temple.

Shannon moved beside Giordino and looked over the wall just in time to see a rocket bring down the arched entrance of the upper palace. 'They'll destroy the artifacts,' she said in grief.

'No concern over Dirk?' Giordino spared her a brief glance. 'He's only risking his life for us, fighting off an army of mercenaries so we can steal a helicopter.'

She sighed. 'It pains any archaeologist to see precious antiquities lost forever.'

'Better yesterday's junk than us.'

'I'm sorry, I want him to escape as much as you. But it all seems so impossible.'

'I've known the guy since we were kids.' Giordino smiled. 'Believe me, he never passed up an opportunity to play Horatius at the bridge.' He studied the two helicopters that sat in the clearing in a slightly staggered formation.

He selected the one in the rear as a prime candidate for escape. It was only a few metres from a narrow ravine they could move in without being seen, and more important, it was out of easy view of the crew seated in the forward craft. 'Pass the word,' he ordered over the sounds of battle, 'we're going to hijack the second chopper in line.'

*

103

Pitt shot uncontrollably down the side of the temple, like a plummeting boulder on a path that took him between the stone animal heads protruding from the convex sloping walls with only centimetres to spare. His hands gripped the knife handles like vices, and he pushed with all the strength in his sinewy arms as the braking blades began to throw out sparks of protest from the friction of steel against hard stone. The rear edges of the rubber heels on his sneakers were being ground smooth by the rough surface of the wall. And yet he accelerated with dismaying speed. His two greatest fears were falling forward and tumbling headfirst like a cannon ball into the ground or striking with such force that he broke a leg. Either calamity and he was finished, dead meat for the Peruvians who wouldn't treat him kindly for killing their officers.

Still fighting grimly but hopelessly to arrest his velocity, Pitt flexed his legs a split second before he struck the ground with appalling force. He let loose of the knives on impact as his feet drove into the ooze of rain-soaked soil. Using his momentum, he rolled over on one shoulder and tumbled twice as required in a hard parachute landing. He lay in the mud for a few moments, thankful he hadn't landed on a rock, before rising experimentally to his feet and checking for damage.

One ankle slightly sprained, but still in working condition, a few abrasions on his hands, and an aching shoulder appeared to be the only damage. The damp earth had saved him from serious injury. The faithful mattress was in shreds. He took a deep breath, happy at still being intact. Having no time to waste, Pitt broke into a run, keeping as much of the ruins as possible between him and the troops massing for an assault up the temple stairs.

Giordino could only hope that Pitt had survived the rockets and somehow made it safely down the wall of the temple without being spotted and shot. It seemed an impossible act, Giordino thought. Pitt was seemingly indestructible, but the old faceless man with the scythe catches up to us all. That he might catch up with Pitt was a prospect Giordino could not accept. It was inconceivable to him that Pitt could die anywhere but in bed with a beautiful woman or in a nursing home for aged divers.

Giordino crouched and ran into a blind position behind the trailing helicopter as a squad of troops began charging up the precipitous temple steps. The reserve squad remained below while pouring a covering storm of rifle fire at the now shattered palace of the dead.

Every one of the Peruvians had his attention focused on the attack. No one saw Giordino, clutching an automatic rifle, steal around the tail boom of the helicopter and enter through the rear clamshell doors. He hurried inside and dropped flat, his eyes taking in the empty troop carrier and cargo compartment and the two pilots in the cockpit with their backs turned to him, intently watching the one-sided battle.

With practised stealth Giordino moved with incredible quickness for a man built like a compact bulldozer. The pilots did not hear him or feel his presence as he came up behind their seats. Giordino reversed the rifle and clubbed the copilot on the back of the neck. The pilot heard the thud and twisted around in his seat, staring briefly at Giordino more from curiosity than dread. Before he could blink an eye, Giordino rammed the butt of the steel folding rifle stock against the pilot's forehead.

Quickly he dragged the unconscious pilots to the doorway and dumped them on the ground. He frantically waved to Shannon, Rodgers, and the students, who were hiding in the ravine. 'Hurry!' he shouted, 'for God's sake hurry!'

His words carried clearly above the sounds of the fighting. The archaeologists needed no further urging. They broke from cover and dashed through the open door into the helicopter in seconds. Giordino had already returned to the cockpit and was hurriedly scanning the instruments and the console between the pilots' seats to familiarize himself with the controls.

'Are we all here?' he asked Shannon as she slipped into the copilot's seat beside him.

'All but Pitt.'

He did not reply, but glanced out the window. The troops on the stairway, becoming more courageous at encountering no defensive fire, surged on to the landing and inside the fallen palace of the dead. Only seconds were left before the attackers realized they'd been had.

Giordino turned his attention back to the controls. The helicopter was an old Russian-built Mi-8 assault transport, designated a Hip-C by NATO during the cold war years. A rather ancient, ugly craft, thought Giordino, with twin 1500-horsepower engines that could carry four crew and thirty passengers. Since the engines were already turning, Giordino placed his right hand on the throttles.

'You heard me?' said Shannon nervously. 'Your friend isn't with us.'

'I heard.' With a total absence of emotion, Giordino increased power.

Pitt crouched behind a stone building and peered around a corner, hearing the growing whine of the turboshaft engines and seeing the five-bladed main rotor slowly increase its revolutions. An hour previously, it had taken no little persuasion for him to convince Giordino that he must take off whether Pitt arrived or not. The life of one man was not worth the death of thirteen others. Though only 30 metres (98 feet) of open ground, completely devoid of any brush or cover, separated Pitt from the helicopter, it seemed more like a mile and a half.

There was no longer any need for caution. He had to make a run for it. He leaned down and gave his bad ankle a fast massage to knead out a growing tenseness. He felt little pain, but it was beginning to tighten up and grow numb. No time left if he wanted to save himself. He plunged forward like a sprinter and raced into the open.

The rotors were beating the ground into dust when Giordino lifted the old Hip-C into a hover. He gave one fast scan of the instrument panel to see if it showed any red lights and tried to sense any strange noises or weird vibrations. Nothing seemed wrong, as the weary engines of an aircraft badly overdue for an overhaul responded in a businesslike manner as he dipped the nose and increased power.

In the main compartment, the students and Rodgers saw Pitt launch his dash towards the gaping clamshell doors. They all began shouting encouragement as he pounded over the soft ground. Their shouts turned urgent as a sergeant happened to glance away from the battle scene and saw Pitt chasing after the rising helicopter. He immediately shouted for the men of the reserve squad who were still waiting for the order to advance up the stairway.

The sergeant's shouts – they were almost screams – carried over the last echoes of the firing from atop the temple. 'They're escaping! Shoot, for the love of Jesus, shoot them!'

The troops did not respond as ordered. Pitt was in a direct line of fire with the helicopter. To fire at him meant riddling their own aircraft. They hesitated, unsure of following the frantic sergeant's commands. Only one man lifted his rifle and fired.

Pitt ignored the bullet that cut a crease in his right thigh. He had other priorities than feeling pain. And then he was under the long tail boom and in the shadow of the clamshell doors, and Rodgers and the Peruvian young people were on their stomachs, leaning out, reaching out to him in the opening between the doors. The helicopter shuddered as it was buffeted by its own downdraught and lurched backward. Pitt extended his arms and jumped.

Giordino bent the helicopter into a hard turn, putting the rotor blades dangerously close to a grove of trees. A bullet shattered his side window and sprayed a shower of silvery fragments across the cockpit, cutting a small gash across his nose. Another round plunked into the rear frame of his seat, missing his spinal cord by a whisker. The helicopter took several more hits before he yanked it over the grove and below the far side, out of the line of fire from the Peruvian assault force.

Soon out of range, he went into a left climbing turn until he had enough altitude to pass over the mountains. At almost 4000 metres (13,000 feet) he had expected to find barren, rocky slopes above a timberline, but was mildly surprised to find the peaks so heavily forested. Once clear of the valley, he set a course to the west. Only then did he turn to Shannon. 'You all right?'

'They were trying to kill us,' she said mechanically.

'Must not like gringos,' Giordino replied, surveying Shannon for damage. Seeing no signs of punctures or blood, he refocused on flying the aircraft and pulled the lever that closed the clamshell doors. Only then did he shout over his shoulder into the main cabin. 'Anyone hit back there?'

'Just little old me.'

Giordino and Shannon twisted in their seats in unison at recognizing the voice. Pitt. A rather exhausted and mud-encrusted Pitt, it was true, a Pitt with one leg seeping blood through a hastily tied bandanna. But a Pitt as indefatigable as ever leaned through the cabin door with a devilish smirk on his face.

A vast wave of relief swept over Giordino, and he flashed a smile.

'You almost missed your bus again.'

'And you still owe me a Dixieland band.'

Shannon smiled, knelt in her seat facing backward, threw her arms around Pitt and gave him a big hug. 'I was afraid you wouldn't make it.'

'I damn near didn't.'

She looked down and her smile faded. 'You're bleeding.'

'A parting shot from the soldiers just before Rodgers and the students pulled me on board. Bless their hearts.'

'We've got to get you to a hospital. It looks serious.'

'Not unless they were using bullets dipped in hemlock,' Pitt said facetiously.

'You should get off that leg. Take my seat.'

Pitt eased Shannon around and pressed her back into the copilot's seat. 'Stay put, I'll sit in coach with the rest of the peasants.' He paused and looked around the control cabin. 'This is a real antique.'

'She shakes, rattles, and rolls,' said Giordino, 'but she hangs in the air.'

Pitt leaned over Giordino's shoulder and examined the instrument panel, his eyes coming to rest on the fuel gauges. He reached over and tapped the instrument glass. Both needles quivered just below the three-quarter mark. 'How far do you figure she'll take us?'

'Fuel range should be in the neighbourhood of three hundred and fifty kilometres. If a bullet didn't bite a hole in one of the tanks, I'd guess she'll carry us about two hundred and eighty.'

'Must be a chart of the area around somewhere and a pair of dividers.'

Shannon found a navigation kit in a pocket beside her seat and passed it to Pitt. He removed a chart and unfolded it against her back. Using the dividers, careful not to stick the points through the chart paper and stab her, Pitt laid out a course to the Peruvian coast.

'I estimate roughly three hundred kilometres to the *Deep Fathom*.'

'What's *Deep Fathom*?' asked Shannon.

'Our research ship.'

'Surely you don't intend to land at sea when one of Peru's largest cities is much closer?'

'She means the international airport at Trujillo,' explained Giordino.

'The *Solpemachaco* has too many friends to suit me,' said Pitt. 'Friends who have enough clout to order in a regiment of mercenaries at a moment's notice. Once they spread the word we stole a helicopter and sent the pride of their military to a graveyard, our lives won't be worth the spare tyre inside the trunk of an Edsel. We'll be safer on board an American ship outside their offshore limit until we can arrange for our US Embassy staff to make a full report to honest officials in the Peruvian government.'

'I see your point,' agreed Shannon. 'But don't overlook the archaeology students. They know the whole story. Their parents are very influential and will see that a true account of their abduction and the pillaging of national treasures hits the news media.'

'You're assuming, of course,' Giordino said matter-of-factly, 'that a Peruvian posse won't cut us off at any one of twenty passes between here and the sea.'

'On the contrary,' replied Pitt. 'I'm counting on it. Care to bet the other assault helicopter isn't chasing our tail rotor as we speak?'

'So we hug the ground and dodge sheep and cows until we cross over water,' acknowledged Giordino.

'Precisely. Cuddling with low clouds won't hurt matters either.'

'Forgetting a little something, aren't you?' said Shannon wearily, as though reminding a husband who neglected to carry out the trash. 'If my math is correct, our fuel tanks will run dry twenty kilometres short of your ship. I hope you aren't proposing we swim the rest of the way.'

'We solve that insignificant problem,' said Pitt calmly, 'by calling up the ship and arranging for it to run full speed on a converging course.'

'Every klick helps,' said Giordino, 'but we'll still be cutting it a mite fine.'

'Survival is guaranteed,' Pitt said confidently. 'This aircraft carries life vests for everyone on board plus two life rafts, I know, I checked when I walked through the main cabin.' He paused, turned, and looked back. Rodgers was checking to see all the students had their shoulder harnesses on properly.

'Our pursuers will be on to us the instant you make contact with your vessel,' Shannon persisted bleakly. 'They'll know exactly where to intercept and shoot us down.'

'Not,' Pitt replied loftily, 'if I play my cards right.'

Setting the office chair to almost a full reclining position, communications technician Jim Stucky settled in comfortably and began reading a paperback mystery novel by Wick Downing. He had finally got used to the thump that reverberated throughout the hull of the NUMA oceanographic ship, *Deep Fathom*, every time the sonar unit bounced a signal off the seafloor of the Peru Basin. Boredom had set in soon after the vessel began endlessly cruising back and forth charting the geology 2500 fathoms below the ship's keel. Stucky was in the middle of the chapter where a woman's body is found floating inside a waterbed when Pitt's voice crackled over the speaker.

'NUMA calling *Deep Fathom*. You awake, Stucky?'

Stucky jerked erect and pressed the transmit button. 'This is *Deep Fathom*. I read you, NUMA. Please stand by.' While Pitt waited, Stucky alerted his skipper over the ship's speaker system.

Captain Frank Stewart hurried from the bridge into the communications cabin. 'Did I hear you correctly? You're in contact with Pitt and Giordino?'

Stucky nodded. 'Pitt is standing by.'

Stewart picked up the microphone. 'Dirk, this is Frank Stewart.'

'Good to hear your beer-soaked voice again, Frank.'

'What have you guys been up to? Admiral Sandecker has been erupting like a volcano the past twenty-four hours, demanding to know your status.'

'Believe me, Frank, it hasn't been a good day.'

'What is your present position?'

'Somewhere over the Andes in an antique Peruvian military chopper.'

'What happened to our NUMA helicopter?' Stewart demanded.

'The Red Baron shot it down,' said Pitt hastily. 'That's not important. Listen to me carefully. We took bullet strikes in our fuel tanks. We can't stay in the air for more than a half hour. Please meet and pick us up in the town square of Chiclayo. You'll find it on your charts of the Peruvian mainland. Use our NUMA backup copter.'

Stewart looked down at Stucky. Both men exchanged puzzled glances. Stewart pressed the transmit button again. 'Please repeat. I don't read you clearly.'

'We are required to land in Chiclayo due to loss of fuel. Rendezvous with us in the survey helicopter and transport us back to the ship. Besides Giordino and me, there are twelve passengers.'

Stewart looked dazed. 'What in hell is going on? He and Giordino flew off the ship with our only bird. And now they're flying a military aircraft that's been shot up with twelve people on board. What's this baloney about a backup chopper?'

'Stand by,' Stewart transmitted to Pitt. Then he reached out and picked up the ship's phone and buzzed the bridge. 'Find a map of Peru in the chart room and bring it to communications right away.'

'You think Pitt has fallen off his pogo stick?' asked Stucky.

'Not in a thousand years,' answered Stewart. 'Those guys are in trouble and Pitt's laying a red herring to mislead eavesdroppers.' A crewman brought the map, and

Stewart stretched it flat on a desk. 'Their rescue mission took them on a course almost due east of here. Chiclayo is a good seventy-five kilometres southwest of his flight path.'

'Now that we've established his con job,' said Stucky, 'what's Pitt's game plan?'

'We'll soon find out.' Stewart picked up the microphone and transmitted. 'NUMA, are you still with us?'

'Still here, pal,' came Pitt's imperturbable voice.

'I will fly the spare copter to Chiclayo and pick up you and your passengers myself. Do you copy?'

'Much appreciated, skipper. Always happy to see you never do things *halfway*. Have a beer waiting when I arrive.'

'Will do,' answered Stewart.

'And put on some speed will you?' said Pitt. 'I need a bath real bad. See you soon.'

Stucky stared at Stewart and laughed. 'Since when did you learn to fly a helicopter?'

Stewart laughed back. 'Only in my dreams.'

'Do you mind telling me what I missed?'

'In a second.' Stewart picked up the ship's phone again and snapped out orders. 'Pull in the sonar's sensor and set a new course on zero-nine-zero degrees. Soon as the sensor is secured, give me full speed. And no excuses from the chief engineer that his precious engines have to be coddled. I want every revolution.' He hung up the phone with a thoughtful expression. 'Where were we? Oh yes, you don't know the score.'

'Is it some sort of riddle?' Stucky muttered.

'Not at all. Obvious to me. Pitt and Giordino don't have enough fuel to reach the ship, so we're going to put on all speed and meet them approximately halfway between here and the shore, hopefully before they're forced to ditch in water infested with sharks.'

113

9

Giordino whipped along, a bare 10 metres (33 feet) above the tops of the trees at only 144 kilometres (90 miles) an hour. The twenty-year-old helicopter was capable of flying almost another 100 kilometres faster, but he reduced speed to conserve what little fuel he had left after passing over the mountains. Only one more range of foothills and a narrow coastal plain separated the aircraft from the sea. Every third minute he glanced warily at the fuel gauges. The needles were edging uncomfortably close to the red. His eyes returned to the green foliage rushing past below. The forest was thick and the clearings were scattered with large boulders. It was a decidedly unfriendly place to force-land a helicopter.

Pitt had limped back into the cargo compartment and begun passing out the life vests. Shannon followed, firmly took the vests out of his hands, and handed them to Rodgers.

'No, you don't,' she said firmly, pushing Pitt into a canvas seat mounted along the bulkhead of the fuselage. She nodded at the loosely knotted, blood-soaked bandanna around his leg. 'You sit down and stay put.'

She found a first aid kit in a metal locker and knelt in front of him. Without the slightest sign of nervous stress, she cut off Pitt's pant leg, cleaned the wound, and competently sewed the eight stitches to close the wound before wrapping a bandage around it.

'Nice job,' said Pitt admiringly. 'You missed your calling as an angel of mercy.'

'You were lucky.' She snapped the lid on the first aid kit. 'The bullet merely sliced the skin.'

114

'Why do I feel as though you've acted on *General Hospital*?'

Shannon smiled. 'I was raised on a farm with five brothers who were always discovering new ways to injure themselves.'

'What turned you to archaeology?'

'There was an old Indian burial mound in one corner of our wheat field. I used to dig around it for arrowheads. For a book report in high school, I found a text on the excavation of the Hopewell Indian culture burial mounds in southern Ohio. Inspired, I began digging into the site on our farm. After finding several pieces of pottery and four skeletons, I was hooked. Hardly a professional dig, mind you. I learned how to excavate properly in college and became fascinated with cultural development in the central Andes, and made up my mind to specialize in that area.'

Pitt looked at her silently for a moment. 'When did you first meet Doc Miller?'

'Only briefly about six years ago when I was working on my doctorate. I attended a lecture he gave on the Inca highway network that ran from the Colombian-Ecuador border almost five thousand kilometres to central Chile. It was his work that inspired me to focus my studies on Andean culture. I've been coming down here ever since.'

'Then you didn't really know him very well?' Pitt questioned.

Shannon shook her head. 'Like most archaeologists, we concentrated on our own pet projects. We corresponded occasionally and exchanged data. About six months ago, I invited him to come along on this expedition to supervise the Peruvian university student volunteers. He was between projects and accepted. Then he kindly offered to fly down from the States five weeks early to begin preparations, arranging permits from the Peruvians, setting up the logistics for equipment and supplies, that sort of thing. Juan Chaco and he worked closely together.'

'When you arrived, did you notice anything different about him?'

A curious look appeared in Shannon's eyes. 'What an odd question.'

'His looks, his actions,' Pitt persisted.

She thought a moment. 'Since Phoenix, he had grown a beard and lost about fifteen pounds, but now that I think of it, he rarely removed his sunglasses.'

'Any change in his voice?'

She shrugged. 'A little deeper perhaps. I thought he had a cold.'

'Did you notice whether he wore a ring? One with a large amber setting?'

Her eyes narrowed. 'A sixty-million-year-old piece of yellow amber with the fossil of a primitive ant in the centre? Doc was proud of that ring. I remember him wearing it during the Inca road survey, but it wasn't on his hand at the sacred well. When I asked him why it was missing, he said the ring became loose on his finger after his weight loss and he left it home to be resized. How do you know about Doc's ring?'

Pitt had been wearing the amber ring he had taken from the corpse at the bottom of the sacred well with the setting unseen under his finger. He slipped it off and handed it to Shannon without speaking.

She held it up to the light from a round window, staring in amazement at the tiny ancient insect imbedded in the amber. 'Where . . .?' her voice trailed off.

'Whoever posed as Doc murdered him and took his place. You accepted the imposter because there was no reason not to. The possibility of foul play never entered your mind. The killer's only mistake was forgetting to remove the ring when he threw Doc's body into the sinkhole.'

'You're saying Doc was murdered before I left the States?' she stated in bewilderment.

'Only a day or two after he arrived at the campsite,' Pitt

116

explained. 'Judging from the condition of the body, he must have been under water for more than a month.'

'Strange that Miles and I missed seeing him.'

'Not so strange. You descended directly in front of the passage to the adjoining cavern and were sucked in almost immediately. I reached the bottom on the opposite side and was able to swim a search grid, looking for what I thought would be two fresh bodies before the surge caught me. Instead, I found Doc's remains and the bones of a sixteenth century Spanish soldier.'

'So Doc really was murdered,' she said as a look of horror dawned on her face. 'Juan Chaco *must* have known, because he was the liaison for our project and was working with Doc before we arrived. Is it possible he was involved?'

Pitt nodded. 'Up to his eyeballs. If you were smuggling ancient treasures, where could you find a better informant and front man than an internationally respected archaeological expert and government official?'

'Then who was the imposter?'

'Another agent of the *Solpemachaco*. A canny operator who staged a masterful performance of his death, with Amaru's help. Perhaps he's one of the men at the top of the organization who doesn't mind getting his hands dirty. We may never know.'

'If he murdered Doc, he deserves to be hanged,' Shannon said, her hazel eyes glinting with anger.

'At least we'll be able to nail Juan Chaco to the door of a Peruvian courthouse — ' Pitt suddenly tensed and swung towards the cockpit as Giordino threw the helicopter in a steeply banked circle. 'What's up?'

'A gut feeling,' Giordino answered. 'I decided to run a three-sixty to check our tail. Good thing I'm sensitive to vibes. We've got company.'

Pitt pushed himself to his feet, returned to the cockpit and, favouring his leg, eased into the copilot's seat. 'Bandits or good guys?' he asked.

'Our pals who dropped in on us at the temple didn't fall for your artful dodge to Chiclayo.' Without taking his hands from the controls, Giordino nodded out of the windshield to his left at a helicopter crossing a low ridge of mountains to the east.

'They must have guessed our course and overhauled us after you reduced speed to conserve fuel,' Pitt surmised.

'No racks mounting air-to-air rockets,' observed Giordino. 'They'll have to shoot us down with rifles – '

A burst of flame and a puff of smoke erupted from the open forward passenger door of the pursuing aircraft, and a rocket soared through the sky, passing so close to the nose of the helicopter Pitt and Giordino felt they could have reached out the side windows and touched it.

'Correction,' Pitt called. 'A forty-millimetre rocket launcher. The same one they used against the temple.'

Giordino slammed the collective pitch into an abrupt ascent and shoved the throttles to their stops in an attempt to throw off the launcher team's aim. 'Grab your rifle and keep them busy until I can reach those low clouds along the coast.'

'Tough luck!' Pitt shouted over the shrill whine of the engines. 'I tossed it away, and my Colt is empty. Any of you carry a gun on board?'

Giordino made an imperceptible nod as he hurled the chopper in another violent manoeuvre. 'I can't speak for the rest of them. You'll find mine wedged in a corner behind the cabin bulkhead.'

Pitt took a radio headset that was hanging on the arm of his seat and clamped it over his ears. Then he struggled out of his seat and clutched both sides of the open cockpit door with his hands to stay on his feet during a sharp turn. He plugged the lead from the headset into a socket mounted on the bulkhead and hailed Giordino. 'Put on your headset so we can coordinate our defence.'

Giordino didn't answer as he mashed down on the left pedal and skidded the craft around in a flat turn. As if he were juggling, he balanced his movements with the controls while slipping the headset over his ears. He winced and involuntarily ducked as another rocket tore through the air less than a metre under the belly of the helicopter and exploded in an orange burst of flame against the palisade of a low mountain.

Grabbing whatever handhold was within reach, Pitt staggered to the side passenger door, undogged the latches, and slid the door back until it was wide open. Shannon, her face showing more concern than fear, crawled across the floor with a cargo rope and wrapped one end around Pitt's waist as he was reaching for the automatic rifle Giordino had used to knock out the Peruvian pilots. Then she tied the opposite end to a longitudinal strut.

'Now you won't fall out,' she exclaimed.

Pitt smiled. 'I don't deserve you.' Then he was lying flat on his stomach aiming the rifle out the door. 'I'm ready, Al. Give me a clear shot.'

Giordino fought to twist the helicopter so that Pitt would face the blind side of the attackers. Because the passenger doors were positioned on the same side of both helicopters, the Peruvian pilot was faced with the same dilemma. He might have risked opening the clamshell doors in the aft end to allow the mercenary rifleman to blast away with an open line of fire, but that would have slowed his airspeed and made control of the chopper unwieldy. Like old propeller-driven warbirds tangling in a dogfight, the pilots manoeuvred for an advantage, hurling their aircraft around the sky in a series of acrobatics never intended by their designers.

His opponent knew his stuff, thought Giordino, with the respect of one professional for another. Outgunned by the military mercenaries, he felt like a mouse tormented by a cat before becoming a quick snack. His eyes darted from the instruments to his nemesis, then down at the ground to make certain he didn't pile into a low ridge or a tree. He yanked back the collective and broadened the pitch of the rotor blades to increase their bite in the damp air. The chopper shot upward in a manoeuvre matched by the other pilot. But then Giordino pushed the nose down and mashed his foot on the right rudder pedal, accelerating and throwing the craft on its side under his attacker and giving Pitt a straight shot.

'Now!' he yelled in his microphone.

Pitt didn't aim at the pilots in the cockpit, he sighted at the engine hump below the rotor and squeezed the trigger. The gun spat twice and went silent.

'What's wrong?' inquired Giordino. 'No gunfire. I run interference to the goal line and you fumble the ball.'

'This gun had only two rounds in it,' Pitt snapped back.

'When I took it off one of Amaru's gunmen, I didn't stop to count the shells.'

Furious with frustration, Pitt jerked out the clip and saw it was empty. 'Did any of you bring a gun on board?' he shouted to Rodgers and the petrified students.

Rodgers, tightly strapped in a seat with legs braced against a bulkhead to avoid being bounced around by Giordino's violent tactics, spread his hands. 'We left them behind when we made a break for the ship.'

At that instant a rocket burst through a port window, flamed across the width of the fuselage, and exited through the opposite side of the helicopter without bursting or injuring anyone. Designed to detonate after striking armoured vehicles or fortified bunkers, the rocket failed to explode after striking thin aluminium and plastic. If one hits the turbines, Pitt thought uneasily, it's all over. He stared wildly about the cabin, saw that they had all released their shoulder harnesses and lay huddled on the floor under the seats as if the canvas webbing and small tubular supports could stop a forty-millimetre tank-killing rocket. He cursed as the wildly swaying aircraft threw him against the door frame.

Shannon saw the furious look on Pitt's face, the despair

as he flung the empty rifle out the open door. And yet she stared at him with absolute faith in her eyes. She had come to know him well enough in the past twenty-four hours to know he was not a man who would willingly accept defeat.

Pitt caught the look and it infuriated him. 'What do you expect me to do,' he demanded, 'leap across space and brain them with the jawbone of an ass? Or maybe they'll go away if I throw rocks at them — ' Pitt broke off as his eyes fell on one of the life rafts. He broke into a wild grin. 'Al, you hear me?'

'I'm a little busy to take calls,' Giordino answered tensely.

'Lay this antique on her port side and fly above them.'

'Whatever you're concocting, make it quick before they put a rocket up our nose or we run out of fuel.'

'Back by popular demand,' Pitt said, becoming his old cheerful self again, 'Mandrake Pitt and his death-defying magic act.' He unsnapped the buckles on the tie-down straps holding one of the life rafts to the floor. The fluorescent orange raft was labelled Twenty-Man Flotation Unit, in English, and weighed over 45 kilograms (100 pounds). Leaning out the door secured by the rope Shannon had tied around his waist, both legs and feet spread and set, he hoisted the uninflated life raft on to his shoulder and waited.

Giordino was tiring. Helicopters require constant hands-on concentration just to stay in the air, because they are made up of a thousand opposing forces that want nothing to do with each other. The general rule of thumb is that most pilots fly solo for an hour. After that, they turn control over to their backup or copilot. Giordino had been behind the controls for an hour and a half, was denied sleep for the past thirty-six hours, and now the strain of throwing the aircraft all over the sky was rapidly draining what strength he had in reserve. For almost six minutes, an eternity in a dogfight, he had prevented his adversary from gaining a brief advantage for a clear shot from the men manning the rocket launcher.

The other craft passed directly across Giordino's vulnerable glass-enclosed cockpit. For a brief instant in time he could clearly see the Peruvian pilot. The face under the combat flight helmet flashed a set of white teeth and waved. 'The bastard is laughing at me,' Giordino blurted in fury.

'What did you say?' came Pitt.

'Those fornicating baboons think this is funny,' Giordino said savagely. He knew what he had to do. He had noticed an almost indiscernible quirk to the enemy pilot's flying technique. When he bent left there was no hesitation, but he was a fraction of a second slow in banking right. Giordino feinted left and abruptly threw the nose skyward and curled right. The other pilot caught the feint and promptly went left but reacted too slowly to Giordino's wild ascending turn and twist in the opposite direction. Before he could counter, Giordino had hurled his machine around and over the attacker.

Pitt's opportunity came in just the blink of an eye, but his timing was right on the money. Lifting the life raft above his head with both hands as easily as if it were a sofa pillow, he thrust it out the open door as the Peruvian chopper whipped beneath him. The orange bundle dropped with the impetus of a bowling ball and smashed through one of the gyrating rotor blades 2 metres (about 6 feet) from the tip. The blade shattered into metallic slivers that spiralled outward from the centrifugal force. Now unbalanced, the remaining four blades whirled in ever-increasing vibration until they broke away from the rotor hub in a rain of small pieces.

The big helicopter seemed to hang poised for a moment before it yawed in circles and angled nose-first towards the ground at 190 kilometres (118 miles) an hour. Pitt hung out the door and watched, fascinated, as the Peruvian craft bored through the trees and crashed into a low hill only a few metres below the summit. He stared at the glinting shreds of metal that flew off into the branches of the trees. The big injured bird came to rest on its right side, a crumpled lump of twisted metal. And then it was lost in a huge fireball that erupted and wrapped it in flames and black smoke.

Giordino eased back on the throttles and made a slow circular pass over the column of smoke, but neither he nor Pitt saw any evidence of life. 'This has to be the first time in history an aircraft was knocked out of the sky by a life raft,' said Giordino.

'Improvisation.' Pitt laughed softly, bowing to Shannon, Rodgers, and the students who were all applauding with rejuvenated spirits. 'Improvisation.' Then he added, 'Fine piece of flying, Al. None of us would be breathing but for you.'

'Ain't it the truth, ain't it the truth,' said Giordino, turning the nose of the craft towards the west and reducing the throttle settings to conserve fuel.

Pitt pulled the passenger door closed, redogged the latches, untied Shannon's line from around his waist, and returned to the cockpit. 'How does our fuel look?'

'Fuel, what fuel?'

Pitt gazed over Giordino's shoulder at the gauges. Both showed flickering red warning lights. He could also see the drawn look of fatigue on his friend's face. 'Take a break and let me spell you at the controls.'

'I got us this far. I'll take us what little distance we have left before the tanks run dry.'

Pitt did not waste his breath in debate. He never ceased to marvel at Giordino's intrepid calm, his glacial fortitude; he could have searched the world and never found another friend like the tough burly Italian. 'Okay, you take her in. I'll sit this one out and pray for a tailwind.'

A few minutes later they crossed over the shoreline and headed out to sea. A resort with attractive lawns and a large swimming pool encircled a small cove with a white sand beach. The sunbathing tourists looked up at the low-flying helicopter and waved. With nothing better to do, Pitt waved back.

Pitt returned to the cargo cabin and approached Rodgers. 'We've got to dump as much weight as possible, except for survival equipment like the life vests and the remaining raft. Everything else goes, excess clothing, tools, hardware, seats, anything that isn't welded or bolted down.'

Everyone pitched in and passed whatever objects they could find to Pitt, who heaved them out the passenger door. When the cabin was bare the chopper was lighter by almost 136 kilograms (300 pounds). Before he closed the door again, Pitt looked aft. Thankfully, he didn't see any pursuing aircraft. He was certain the Peruvian pilot had radioed the sighting and his intention to attack, blowing Pitt's Chiclayo smokescreen. But he doubted the *Solpemachaco* would suspect the loss of their mercenary soldiers and helicopter for at least another ten minutes. And if they belatedly totalled the score, and whistled up a Peruvian Air Force fighter jet to intercept, then it would be too late. Any attack on an unarmed American research ship would stir up serious diplomatic repercussions between the United States government and Peru, a situation the struggling South American nation could ill afford. Pitt was on safe ground in assuming that no local bureaucrat or military officer would risk political disaster regardless of any under-the-table payoff by the *Solpemachaco*.

Pitt limped back to the cockpit, slid into the copilot's seat, and picked up the radio microphone. He brushed aside all caution as he pressed the transmit button. To hell with any bought-and-paid-for *Solpemachaco* cronies who were monitoring the airwaves, he thought.

'NUMA calling *Deep Fathom*. Talk to me, Stucky.'

'Come in, NUMA. This is *Deep Fathom*. What is your position?'

'My, what big eyes you have, and how your voice has changed, Grandma.'

'Say again, NUMA.'

'Not even a credible effort.' Pitt laughed. 'Rich Little you ain't.' He looked over at Giordino. 'We've got a comic impersonator on our party line.'

'I think you better give him our position,' Giordino said with more than a trace of cynicism in his voice.

'Right you are.' Pitt nodded. '*Deep Fathom*, this is NUMA. Our position is just south of the Magic Castle between Jungleland and the Pirates of the Caribbean.'

'Please repeat your position,' came the voice of the flustered mercenary who had broken in on Pitt's call to Stucky.

'What's this, a radio commercial for Disneyland?' Stucky's familiar voice popped over the speaker.

'Well, well, the genuine article. What took you so long to answer, Stucky?'

'I was listening to what my alter ego had to say. You guys landed in Chiclayo yet?'

'We were sidetracked and decided to head home,' said Pitt. 'Is the skipper handy?'

'He's on the bridge playing Captain Bligh, lashing the crew in an attempt to set a speed record. Another knot and our rivets will start falling out.'

'We do not have a visual on you. Do you have us on radar?'

'Affirmative,' answered Stucky. 'Change your heading to two-seven-two magnetic. That will put us on a converging course.'

'Altering course to two-seven-two,' Giordino acknowledged.

'How far to rendezvous?' Pitt asked Stucky.

'The skipper makes it about sixty kilometres.'

'They should be in sight soon.' Pitt looked over at Giordino. 'What do you think?'

Giordino stared woefully at the fuel gauges, then at the instrument panel clock. The dial read 10:47 A.M. He couldn't believe so much had happened in so little time since he and Pitt had responded to the rescue appeal by the imposter of Doc Miller. He swore it took three years off his life expectancy.

'I'm milking her for every litre of fuel at an airspeed of only forty klicks an hour,' he said finally. 'A slight tailwind off the shore helps, but I estimate we have only another fifteen or twenty minutes of flight time left. Your guess is as good as mine.'

'Let us hope the gauges read on the low side,' said Pitt. 'Hello, Stucky.'

'I'm here.'

'You'd better prepare for a water rescue. All predictions point to a wet landing.'

'I'll pass the word to the skipper. Alert me when you ditch.'

'You'll be the first to know.'

'Good luck.'

The helicopter droned over the tops of the rolling swells. Pitt and Giordino spoke very little. Their ears were tuned to the sound of the turbines, as if expecting them to abruptly go silent at any moment. They instinctively tensed when the fuel warning alarm whooped through the cockpit.

'So much for the reserves,' said Pitt. 'Now we're flying on fumes.'

He looked down at the deep cobalt blue of the water only 10 metres (33 feet) beneath the belly of the chopper. The sea looked reasonably smooth. He figured wave height from trough to crest was less than a metre. The water looked warm and inviting. A power-off landing did not appear to be too rough, and the old Mi-8 should float for a good sixty seconds if Giordino didn't burst the seams when he dropped her in.

Pitt called Shannon to the cockpit. She appeared in the doorway, looked down at him, and smiled faintly. 'Is your ship in sight?'

'Just over the horizon, I should think. But not close

enough to reach with the fuel that's left. Tell everybody to prepare for a water landing.'

'Then we *do* have to swim the rest of the way,' she said cynically.

'A mere technicality,' said Pitt. 'Have Rodgers move the life raft close to the passenger door and be ready to heave it in the water as soon as we ditch. And impress upon him the importance of pulling the inflation cord *after* the raft is safely through the door. I for one do not want to get my feet wet.'

Giordino pointed dead ahead. 'The *Deep Fathom*.'

Pitt nodded as he squinted at the dark tiny speck on the horizon. He spoke into the radio mike. 'We have you on visual, Stucky.'

'Come to the party,' answered Stucky. 'We'll open the bar early just for you.'

'Heaven forbid,' said Pitt, elaborately sarcastic. 'I don't imagine the admiral will take kindly to that suggestion.'

Their employer, chief director of the National Underwater and Marine Agency, Admiral James Sandecker, had a regulation etched in stone banning all alcoholic spirits from NUMA vessels. A vegetarian and a fitness nut, Sandecker thought he was adding years to the hired help's life span. As with prohibition in the nineteen twenties, men who seldom touched the stuff began smuggling cases of beer on board or buying it in foreign ports.

'Would you prefer a hearty glass of Ovaltine?' retorted Stucky.

'Only if you mix it with carrot juice and alfalfa sprouts – '

'We just lost an engine,' announced Giordino conversationally.

Pitt's eyes darted to the instruments. Across the board, the needles of the gauges monitoring the port turbine were flickering back to their stops. He turned and looked up at Shannon. 'Warn everyone that we'll impact the water on the starboard side of the aircraft.'

127

Shannon looked confused. 'Why not land vertically?'

'If we go in bottom first, the rotor blades settle, strike the water, and shatter on a level with the fuselage. The whirling fragments can easily penetrate the cabin's skin, especially the cockpit, resulting in the loss of our intrepid pilot's head. Coming down on the side throws the shattered blades out and away from us.'

'Why the starboard side?'

'I don't have chalk and a blackboard,' snapped Pitt in exasperation. 'So you'll die happy, it has to do with the directional rotation of the rotor blades and the fact the exit door is on the port side.'

Enlightened, Shannon nodded. 'Understood.'

'Immediately after impact,' Pitt continued, 'get the students out the door before this thing sinks. Now get to your seat and buckle up.' Then he slapped Giordino on the shoulder. 'Take her in while you still have power,' he said as he snapped on his safety harness.

Giordino needed no coaxing. Before he lost his remaining engine, he pulled back on the collective pitch and pulled back the throttle on his one operating engine. As the helicopter lost its forward motion from a height of 3 metres above the sea, he leaned it gently on to the starboard side. The rotor blades smacked the water and snapped off in a cloud of debris and spray as the craft settled in the restless waves with the awkward poise of a pregnant albatross. The impact came with the jolt of a speeding car hitting a sharp dip in the road. Giordino shut down the one engine and was pleasantly surprised to find the old Mi-8, Hip-C floating drunkenly in the sea as if she belonged there.

'End of the line!' Pitt boomed. 'Everyone the hell out!'

The gentle lapping of the waves against the fuselage came as a pleasant contrast to the fading whine of the engines and thump of the rotor blades. The pungent salt air filled the stuffy interior of the compartment when Rodgers slid open the passenger door and dropped the collapsible twenty-person life raft into the water. He was extra careful not to pull the inflation cord too soon and was relieved to hear the hiss of compressed air and see the raft puff out safely beyond the door. In a few moments it was bobbing alongside the helicopter, its mooring line tightly clutched in Rodgers's hand.

'Out you go,' Rodgers yelled, herding the young Peruvian archaeology students through the door and into the raft.

Pitt released his safety harness and hurried into the rear cabin. Shannon and Rodgers had the evacuation running smoothly. All but three of the students had climbed into the raft. A quick examination of the aircraft made it clear she couldn't stay afloat for long. The clamshell doors were buckled from the impact just enough to allow water to surge in around the seams. Already the floor of the fuselage was beginning to slant towards the rear, and the waves were sloshing over the sill of the open passenger door.

'We haven't much time,' he said, helping Shannon into the raft. Rodgers went next and then he turned to Giordino. 'Your turn, Al.'

Giordino would have none of it. 'Tradition of the sea. All walking wounded go first.'

Before Pitt could protest, Giordino shoved him out the door, and then followed as the water swept over his ankles. Breaking out the raft's paddles, they pushed clear of the helicopter as its long tail boom dipped into the waves. Then a large swell surged through the open passenger door and the helicopter slipped backward into the uncaring sea. She disappeared with a faint gurgle and a few ripples, her shattered rotor blades being the last to go, the stumps slowly rotating from the force of the current as if she were descending to the seafloor under her own power. The water surged through her open door and she plunged under the waves to a final landing on the seafloor.

No one spoke. They all seemed saddened to see the

helicopter go. It was as if they all suffered a personal loss. Pitt and Giordino were at home on the water. The others, suddenly finding themselves floating on a vast sea, felt an awful sense of emptiness coupled with the dread of helplessness. The latter feeling was particularly enhanced when a shark's fin abruptly broke the water and ominously began circling the raft.

'All your fault,' Giordino said to Pitt in mock exasperation. 'He's homed in on the scent of blood from your leg wound.'

Pitt peered into the transparent water, studying the sleek shape as it passed under the raft, recognizing the horizontal stabilizerlike head with the eyes mounted like aircraft wing lights on the tips. 'A hammerhead. No more than two and a half metres long. I shall ignore him.'

Shannon gave a shudder and moved closer to Pitt and clutched his arm. 'What if he decides to take a bite out of the raft and we sink?'

Pitt shrugged. 'Sharks seldom find life rafts appetizing.'

'He invited his pals for dinner,' said Giordino, pointing to two more fins cutting the water.

Pitt could see the beginnings of panic on the faces of the young students. He nestled into a comfortable position on the bottom of the raft, elevated his feet on the upper float, and closed his eyes. 'Nothing like a restful nap under a warm sun on a calm sea. Wake me when the ship arrives.'

Shannon stared at him in disbelief. 'He must be mad.'

Giordino quickly sized up Pitt's scheme and settled in. 'That makes two of us.'

No one knew quite how to react. Every pair of eyes in the raft swivelled from the seemingly dozing men from NUMA to the circling sharks and back again. The panic slowly subsided to uneasy apprehension while the minutes crawled by as if they were each an hour long.

Other sharks joined the predinner party, but all hearts began filling with newfound hope as the *Deep Fathom* hove into view, her bows carving the water in a spray of foam.

No one on board knew the old workhorse of NUMA's oceanographic fleet could drive so hard. Down in the engine room the chief engineer, August Burley, a powerfully built man with a portly stomach, walked the catwalk between the ship's big diesels, closely observing the needles on the rpm gauges, which were hard in the red, and listening for any signs of metal fatigue from the overstressed engines. On the bridge, Captain Frank Stewart gazed through binoculars at the tiny splash of orange against the blue sea.

'We'll come right up on them at half speed before reversing the engines,' he said to the helmsman.

'You don't want to stop and drift up to them, Captain?' asked the blond, ponytailed man at the wheel.

'They're surrounded by a school of sharks,' said Stewart. 'We can't waste time with caution.' He stepped over and spoke into the ship's speaker system. 'We'll approach the survivors on the port side. All available hands prepare to bring them aboard.'

It was a neat bit of seamanship. Stewart stopped the ship within 2 metres of the life raft with only a slight wash. Several crewmen stared down and waved, leaning far over the railing and bulwark to shout greetings. The boarding ladder had been lowered and a crewman stood on the lower platform with a boat hook. He extended it, the end was grabbed by Giordino, and the raft was pulled in alongside the platform.

The sharks were forgotten and everyone began smiling and laughing with unabashed happiness at having survived death without major injuries at least four times since being taken hostage. Shannon stared up at the towering hull of the research ship, took in the ungainly superstructure and derricks, and turned to Pitt with a shrewd twinkle in her eyes.

'You promised us a four-star hotel and a refreshing bath. Certainly not a rusty old work boat.'

Pitt laughed. 'A rose by any other name. Any port in a

storm. So you share my attractive, but homespun state-room. As a gentleman, I'll give you the lower berth while I suffer the indignity of the upper.'

Shannon looked at him with amusement. 'Taking a lot for granted, aren't you?'

As Pitt relaxed and kept a paternal eye on the occupants of the raft, who were climbing the ladder one after the other, he smiled fiendishly at Shannon and murmured, 'Okay, we'll keep a low profile. You can have the upper and I'll take the lower.'

10

Juan Chaco's world had cracked and crumbled to dust around him. The disaster in the Valley of Viracocha was far worse than anything he could have imagined. His brother had been the first to be killed, the artifact smuggling operation was in shambles, and once the American archaeologist, Shannon Kelsey, and the university students told their story to the news media and government security officials, he would be thrown out of the Department of Archaeology in disgrace. Far worse, there was every possibility he would be arrested, tried for selling his nation's historical heritage, and sentenced to a very long jail term.

He was a man racked with anxiety as he stood beside the motor home in Chachapoya and watched the tilt-rotor aircraft come to a near halt in the air as the twin outboard engines on the end of the wings swivelled from forward flight to vertical. The black, unmarked craft hovered for a few moments before the pilot gently settled the extended landing wheels on the ground.

A heavily bearded man in dirty rumpled shorts and a khaki shirt with an immense bloodstain in its centre exited the nine-passenger cabin and stepped to the ground. He looked neither right nor left, the expression on his face set and grim. Without a word of greeting, he walked past Chaco and entered the motor home. Like a chastised collie, Chaco followed him inside.

Cyrus Sarason, the impersonator of Dr Steven Miller, sat heavily behind Chaco's desk and stared icily. 'You've heard?'

Chaco nodded without questioning the bloodstain on Sarason's shirt. He knew the blood represented a fake gunshot wound. 'I received a full report from one of my brother's fellow officers.'

'Then you know Dr Kelsey and the university students slipped through our fingers and were rescued by an American oceanographic research ship.'

'Yes, I am aware of our failure.'

'I'm sorry about your brother,' Sarason said without emotion.

'I can't believe he's gone,' muttered Chaco, strangely unmoved. 'His death doesn't seem possible. The elimination of the archaeologists should have been a simple affair.'

'To say your people bungled the job is an understatement,' said Sarason. 'I warned you those two divers from NUMA were dangerous.'

'My brother did not expect organized resistance by an army.'

'An army of one man,' Sarason said acidly. 'I observed the action from a tomb. A lone sniper atop the temple killed the officers and held off two squads of your intrepid mercenaries, while his companion overpowered the pilots and commandeered their helicopter. Your brother paid dearly for his overconfidence and stupidity.'

'How could a pair of divers and a juvenile group of archaeologists scourge a highly trained security force?' Chaco asked in bewilderment.

'If we knew the answer to that question, we might learn how they knocked the pursuing helicopter out of the air.'

Chaco stared at him. 'They can still be stopped.'

'Forget it. I'm not about to compound the disaster by destroying a US government ship and all on board. The damage is already done. According to my sources in Lima, full exposure, including Miller's murder, was communicated to President Fujimori's office by Dr Kelsey soon after she boarded the ship. By this evening, the story will be broadcast all over the country. The Chachapoyan end of our operation is a washout.'

'We can still bring the artifacts out of the valley.' The

recent demise of Chaco's brother had not fully pushed aside his greed.

Sarason nodded. 'I'm ahead of you. A team is on its way to remove whatever pieces survived the rocket attack launched by those idiots under your brother's command. It's a miracle we still have something to show for our efforts.'

'I believe there is a good possibility a clue to the Drake *quipu* may still be found in the City of the Dead.'

'The Drake *quipu*.' Sarason repeated the words with a faraway look in his eyes. Then he shrugged. 'Our organization is already working on another angle for the treasure.'

'What of Amaru? Is he still alive?'

'Unfortunately, yes. He'll live the rest of his days as a eunuch.'

'Too bad. He was a loyal follower.'

Sarason sneered. 'Loyal to whoever paid him best. Tupac Amaru is a sociopathic killer of the highest order. When I ordered him to abduct Miller and hold him prisoner until we concluded the operation, he put a bullet in the good doctor's heart and threw him in the damned sinkhole. The man has the mind of a rabid dog.'

'He may still prove useful,' said Chaco slowly.

'Useful, how?'

'If I know his mind, he'll swear vengeance on those responsible for his newly acquired handicap. It might be wise to unleash him on Dr Kelsey and the diver called Pitt to prevent them from being used by international customs investigators as informants.'

'We'd be skating on thin ice if we turned a crazy man like him loose. But I'll keep your suggestion in mind.'

Chaco went on. 'What plans do the *Solpemachaco* have for me? I am finished here. Now that my countrymen will know I have betrayed their trust with regard to our historical treasures, I could spend the rest of my life in one of our filthy prisons.'

'A foregone conclusion.' Sarason shrugged. 'My sources

also revealed that the local police have been ordered to pick you up. They should arrive within the hour.'

Chaco looked at Sarason for a long moment, then said slowly: 'I am a scholar and a scientist, not a hardened criminal. There is no telling how much I might reveal during lengthy interrogation, perhaps even torture.'

Sarason suppressed a smile at the veiled threat. 'You are a valuable asset we cannot afford to lose. Your expertise and knowledge of ancient Andean cultures is second to none. Arrangements are being made for you to take over our collection facilities in Panama. There you will direct the identification, cataloguing, and restoration operations on all artifacts we either purchase from the local *huaqueros* or acquire under the guise of academic archaeological projects throughout South America.'

Chaco suddenly looked wolfish. 'I'm flattered. Of course I accept. Such an important position must pay well.'

'You will receive two per cent of the price the artifacts bring at our auction houses in New York and Europe.'

Chaco was too far down the rungs of the organizational ladder to be privy to the inner secrets of the *Solpemachaco*, but he well knew the network, and its profits were vast. 'I will need help getting out of the country.'

'Not to worry,' said Sarason. 'You'll accompany me.' He nodded out a window at the ominous black aircraft sitting outside the motor home, the big three-bladed rotors slowly beating the air at idle. 'In that aircraft we can be in Bogota, Colombia, within four hours.'

Chaco couldn't believe his luck. One minute he was a step away from disgrace and prison for defrauding his government, the next he was on his way to becoming an extremely wealthy man. The memory of his sibling was rapidly fading; they were only half-brothers and had never been close anyway. While Sarason patiently waited, Chaco quickly gathered some personal items and stuffed them in a suitcase. Then the two men walked out to the aircraft together.

Juan Chaco never lived to see Bogota, Colombia. Farmers tilling a field of sweet potatoes near an isolated village in Ecuador paused to look up in the sky at the strange droning sound of the tilt-rotor as it passed overhead 500 metres (1600 feet) above the ground. Suddenly, in what seemed a horror fantasy, they caught sight of the body of a man dropping away from the aircraft. The farmers could also clearly see that the unfortunate man was alive. He frantically kicked his legs and clawed madly at the air as if he could somehow slow his plunging descent.

Chaco struck the ground in the middle of a small corral occupied by a scrawny cow, missing the startled animal by only 2 metres. The farmers came running from their field and stood around the crushed body that was embedded nearly half a metre into the soil. Simple countryfolk, they did not send a runner to the nearest police station over 60 kilometres (37 miles) to the west. Instead, they reverently lifted the broken remains of the mysterious man who had dropped from the sky and buried him in a small graveyard beside the ruins of an old church, unlamented and unknown, but embellished in myth for generations yet to come.

11

The top of Shannon's head was wrapped turban-style with a towel, her hair still wet after a hot blissful bath in the captain's cabin. She had allowed the Peruvian female students to go first before luxuriating in the steaming water while sipping wine and eating a chicken sandwich thoughtfully provided by Pitt from the ship's galley. Her skin glowed all over and smelled of lavender soap after washing the sweat and grime out of her pores and the jungle mud from under her nails. One of the shorter crewmen, who was close to her size, lent her a pair of coveralls; the only female crewmember, a marine geologist, had used most of her wardrobe to reclothe the Peruvian girls. As soon as Shannon was dressed she promptly threw the swim suit and the dirty blouse in a trash container. They held memories she'd just as soon forget.

After drying and brushing out her hair, she sneaked a bit of Captain Stewart's aftershave lotion. Why is it, she wondered, men never use talcum powder after they shower? She was just tying her long hair in a braid when Pitt knocked on the door. They stood there for a moment staring at each other before breaking into laughter.

'I hardly recognized you,' she said, taking in clean and shaven Pitt wearing a brightly flowered Hawaiian aloha shirt and light tan slacks. He was not what you'd call devilishly good-looking, she thought, but any flaws in his craggy face were more than offset by a masculine magnetism she found hard to resist. He was even more tanned than she was, and his black, wavy hair was a perfect match for the incredibly green eyes.

'We don't exactly look like the same two people,' he said with an engaging smile. 'How about a tour of the ship before dinner?'

'I'd like that.' Then she gave him an appraising look. 'I thought I was supposed to bunk down in your cabin. Now I find out the captain has generously offered me his.'

Pitt shrugged. 'The luck of the draw, I guess.'

'You're a fraud, Dirk Pitt. You're not the lecher you make yourself out to be.'

'I've always believed intimacy should be drifted into gradually.'

She suddenly felt uneasy. It was as though his piercing eyes could read her mind. He seemed to sense there was someone else. She forced a smile and wrapped her arm around his. 'Where shall we begin?'

'You're speaking of the tour, of course.'

'What else?'

The *Deep Fathom* was a state-of-the-art scientific work boat, and she looked it. Her official designation was Super-Seismic Vessel. She was primarily designed for deep ocean geophysical research, but she could also undertake a myriad of other subsea activities. Her giant stern and side cranes, with their huge winches, could be adapted to operate every conceivable underwater function, from mining excavation to deep water salvage and manned and unmanned submersible launch and recovery.

The ship's hull was painted in NUMA's traditional turquoise with a white superstructure and azure blue cranes. From bow to stern she stretched the length of a football field, berthing up to thirty-five scientists and twenty crew. Although she didn't look it from the outside, her interior living quarters were as plush as most luxurious passenger liners. Admiral James Sandecker, with rare insight given to few bureaucrats, knew his people could perform more efficiently if treated accordingly, and the *Deep Fathom* reflected his conviction. Her dining room was fitted out like a fine restaurant and the galley was run by a first-rate chef.

Pitt led Shannon up to the navigation bridge. 'Our brain centre,' he pointed out, sweeping one hand around a vast room filled with digital arrays, computers, and video monitors mounted on a long console that ran the full width of the bridge beneath a massive expanse of windows. 'Most everything on the ship is controlled from here, except the operation of deep water equipment. That takes place in compartments containing electronics designed for specialized deep sea projects.'

Shannon stared at the gleaming chrome, the colourful images on the monitors, the panoramic view of the sea around the bows. It all seemed as impressive and modern as a futuristic video parlour. 'Where is the helm?' she asked.

'The old-fashioned wheel went out with the *Queen Mary*,' answered Pitt. He showed her the console for the ship's automated control, a panel with levers and a remote control unit that could be mounted on the bridge wings. 'Navigation is now carried out by computers. The captain can even con the ship by voice command.'

'For someone who digs up old potsherds, I had no idea ships were so advanced.'

'After lagging as a stepchild for forty years, marine science and technology have finally been recognized by government and private business as the emerging industry of the future.'

'You never fully explained what you're doing in the waters off Peru.'

'We're probing the seas in search of new drugs,' he answered.

'Drugs, as in take two plankton and call me in the morning?'

Pitt smiled and nodded. 'It's entirely within the realm of possibility your doctor may someday actually prescribe such a remedy.'

'So the hunt for new drugs has gone underwater.'

'A necessity. We've already found and processed over ninety per cent of all the land organisms that provide sources of medicine to treat diseases. Aspirin and quinine come from the bark of trees. Chemicals contained in everything from snake venom to secretion from frogs to lymph from pigs' glands are used in drug compounds. But marine creatures and the microorganisms that dwell in the depths have been an untapped source, and might well be the hope of curing every affliction, including the common cold, cancer, or AIDS.'

'But surely you can't simply go out and bring back a boatload of microbes for processing at a laboratory for distribution to your friendly pharmacy?'

'Not as farfetched as you might think,' he said. 'Any one of a hundred organisms that live in a drop of water can be cultivated, harvested, and rendered into medicines. Jellyfish, an invertebrate animal called a bryozoan, certain sponges, and several corals are currently being developed into anticancer medicines, anti-inflammatory agents for arthritis pain, and drugs that suppress organ rejection after transplant surgery. The test results on a chemical isolated from kelp look especially encouraging in combating a drug-resistant strain of tuberculosis.'

'Just where in the ocean are you looking for these wonder drugs?' asked Shannon.

'This expedition is concentrating on a ridge of chimney-like vents where hot magma from within the earth's mantle comes in contact with cold seawater and spews through a series of cracks before spreading across the bottom. You might call it a deep-ocean hot spring. Various minerals are deposited over a wide area – copper, zinc, iron, along with water heavy in hydrogen sulphide. Incredibly, vast colonies of giant clams, mussels, huge tube worms, and bacteria that utilize the sulphur compounds to synthesize sugars live and thrive in this dark and toxic environment. It is this remarkable species of sea life that we're collecting with submersibles for laboratory testing and clinical trials back in the States.'

'Are there many scientists working on these miracle cures?'

Pitt shook his head. 'Around the world, maybe fifty or sixty. Marine medical research is still in its infancy.'

'How long before we see the drugs on the market?'

'The regulatory obstacles are staggering. Doctors won't be prescribing many of these medications for another ten years.'

Shannon walked over to an array of monitors that filled an entire panel of one bulkhead. 'This looks impressive.'

'Our secondary mission is to map the seafloor wherever the ship sails.'

'What are the monitors showing?'

'You're looking at the bottom of the sea in a myriad of shapes and images,' Pitt explained. 'Our long-range, low-resolution side-scan sonar system can record a swath in three-dimensional colour up to fifty kilometres wide.'

Shannon stared at the incredible display of ravines and mountains thousands of metres below the ship. 'I never thought I'd be able to observe the land beneath the sea this clearly. It's like staring out the window of an airliner over the Rocky Mountains.'

'With computer enhancement it becomes even sharper.'

'Romance of the seven seas,' she waxed philosophically. 'You're like the early explorers who charted new worlds.'

Pitt laughed. 'High tech takes away any hint of the romance.'

They left the bridge, and he showed her through the ship's laboratory where a team of chemists and marine biologists were fussing over a dozen glass tanks teeming with a hundred different denizens from the deep, studying data from computer monitors, and examining micro-organisms under microscopes.

'After retrieval from the bottom,' said Pitt, 'this is where the first step in the quest for new drugs begins.'

'What is your part in all of this?' Shannon asked.

'Al Giordino and I operate the robotic vehicles that probe the seafloor for promising organism sites. When we think we've located a prime location, we go down in a submersible to collect the specimens.'

She sighed. 'Your field is far more exotic than mine.'

Pitt shook his head. 'I disagree. Searching into the origins of our ancestors can be pretty exotic in its own right. If we feel no attraction for the past, why do millions of us pay homage to ancient Egypt, Rome, and Athens every year? Why do we wander over the battlefields of Gettysburg and Waterloo or stand on the cliffs and look down on the beaches of Normandy? Because we have to look back into history to see ourselves.'

Shannon stood silently. She had expected a certain coldness from a man whom she had watched kill without apparent remorse. She was surprised at the depth of his words, at his easy way of expressing ideas.

He spoke of the sea, of shipwrecks, and of lost treasure. She described the great archaeological mysteries waiting to be solved. There was mutual delight in this exchange, yet there was still an indefinable gap between them. Neither felt strongly attracted to the other.

They had strolled out on deck and were leaning over the railing, watching the white foam thrown from the *Deep Fathom*'s bow slide past the hull and merge with the froth from the wake, when skipper Frank Stewart appeared.

'It's official,' he said in his soft Alabama drawl, 'we've been ordered to transport the Peruvian young people and Dr Kelsey to Lima's port city of Callao.'

'You were in communication with Admiral Sandecker?' inquired Pitt.

Stewart shook his head. 'His director of operations, Rudi Gunn.'

'After we set everyone on shore, I assume we sail back on-site and continue with the project?'

'The crew and I do. You and Al have been ordered to return to the sacred well and retrieve Dr Miller's body.'

Pitt looked at Stewart as if he were a psychiatrist contemplating a mental case. 'Why us? Why not the Peruvian police?'

Stewart shrugged. 'When I protested that the two of you were vital to the specimen collection operation, Gunn said he was flying in your replacements from NUMA's research lab in Key West. That's all he would say.'

Pitt swung a hand towards the empty helicopter landing pad. 'Did you inform Rudi that Al and I are not exactly popular with the local natives and that we're fresh out of aircraft?'

'No to the former.' Stewart grinned. 'Yes to the latter. American embassy officials are making arrangements for you to charter a commercial helicopter in Lima.'

'This makes about as much sense as ordering a peanut butter sandwich in a French restaurant.'

'If you have a complaint, I suggest you take it up with Gunn personally when he meets us on the dock in Callao.'

Pitt's eyes narrowed. 'Sandecker's right-hand man flies over sixty-five hundred kilometres from Washington to oversee a body recovery? What gives?'

'More than meets the eye, obviously,' said Stewart. He turned and looked at Shannon. 'Gunn also relayed a message to you from a David Gaskill. He said you'd recall the name.'

She seemed to stare at the deck in thought for a moment. 'Yes, I remember, he's an undercover agent with the US Customs Service who specializes in the illicit smuggling of antiquities.'

Stewart continued, 'Gaskill said to tell you he thinks he's traced the Golden Body Suit of Tiapollo to a private collector in Chicago.'

Shannon's heart fluttered and she gripped the handrail until her knuckles turned ivory.

'Good news?' asked Pitt.

She opened her mouth, but no sound came out. She looked stunned.

Pitt put his arm around her waist to support her. 'Are you all right?'

'The Golden Body Suit of Tiapollo,' she murmured reverently, 'was lost to the world in a daring robbery at the Museo Nacional de Antropologia in Seville in 1922. There isn't an archaeologist alive who wouldn't sign away his or her pension to study it.'

'What exactly makes it so special?' asked Stewart.

'It is considered the most prized artifact to ever come out of South America because of its historic significance,' Shannon lectured, as if entranced. 'The gold casing covered the mummy of a great Chachapoyan general known as Naymlap, from the toes to the top of the head. The Spanish conquerors discovered Naymlap's tomb in 1547 in a city called Tiapollo high in the mountains. The event was recorded in two early documents but today Tiapollo's precise location is unknown. I've only seen old black-and-white photos of the suit, but you could tell that the intricately hammered metalwork was breathtaking. The iconography, the traditional images, and the designs on the exterior were lavishly sophisticated and formed a pictorial record of a legendary event.'

'Picture writing, as in Egyptian hieroglyphics?' asked Pitt.

'Very similar.'

'What we might call an illustrated comic strip,' added Giordino as he stepped out on deck.

Shannon laughed. 'Only without the panels. The panels were never fully deciphered. The obscure references seem to indicate a long journey by boat to a place somewhere beyond the empire of the Aztecs.'

'For what purpose?' asked Stewart.

'To hide a vast royal treasure that belonged to Huascar, an Inca king who was captured in battle and murdered by his brother Atahualpa, who was in turn executed by the

Spanish conqueror Francisco Pizarro. Huascar possessed a sacred gold chain that was two hundred and fourteen metres long. One report given to the Spaniards by Incas claimed that two hundred men could scarcely lift it.'

'Roughly figuring that each man hoisted sixty per cent of his weight,' mused Giordino, 'you're talking over nine thousand kilograms or twenty thousand pounds of gold. Multiply that by twelve troy ounces . . .'

'And you get two hundred and forty thousand ounces,' Pitt helped out. Giordino's calculating expression suddenly crumbled into blank astonishment. 'Oh my God. On today's gold market that works out to well over a hundred million dollars.'

'That can't be right,' scoffed Stewart.

'Compute it for yourself,' muttered Giordino, still stupefied.

Stewart did, and his face went as blank as Giordino's. 'Mother of heaven, he's right.'

Shannon nodded. 'That's just the price of the gold. As an artifact it is priceless.'

'The Spanish never got their hands on it?' Pitt asked Shannon.

'No, along with a vast hoard of other royal wealth, the chain disappeared. You've probably all heard the story of how Huascar's brother Atahualpa tried to buy his freedom from Pizarro and his conquistadors by offering to fill a room that measured seven metres in length by five metres wide with gold. Atahualpa stood on his tiptoes, reached up and drew a line around the room that was almost three metres from the floor, the height to which the gold would top out. Another smaller room nearby was to be filled with silver twice over.'

'Has to be a world's record for ransom,' mused Stewart.

'According to the legend,' Shannon continued, 'Atahualpa seized massive numbers of golden objects from palaces, religious temples, and public buildings. But the supply was coming up short, so he went after his brother's treasures. Huascar's agents warned him of the situation, and he conspired to have his kingdom's treasures spirited away before Atahualpa and Pizarro could get their hands on them. Guarded by loyal Chachapoyan warriors, commanded by General Naymlap, untold tons of gold and silver objects, along with the chain, were secretly transported by a huge human train to the coast, where they were loaded on board a fleet of reed and balsa rafts that sailed toward an unknown destination far to the north.'

'Is there any factual basis to the story?' Pitt asked.

'Between the years 1546 and 1568, a Jesuit historian and translator, Bishop Juan de Avila, recorded many mythical accounts of early Peruvian cultures. While attempting to convert the Chachapoyan people to Christianity, he was told four different stories about a great treasure belonging to the Inca kingdom that their ancestors helped carry across the sea to an island far beyond the land of the Aztecs, where it was buried. Supposedly it is guarded by a winged jaguar until the day the Incas return and retake their kingdom in Peru.'

'There must be a hundred coastal islands between here and California,' said Stewart.

Shannon followed Pitt's gaze down to the restless sea. 'There is, or I should say was, another source of the legend.'

'All right,' said Pitt, 'let's hear it.'

'When the Bishop was questioning the Cloud People, as the Chachapoyans were called, one of the tales centred on a jade box containing a detailed chronicle of the voyage.'

'An animal skin painted with symbolic pictographs?'

'No, a *quipu*,' Shannon replied softly.

Stewart tilted his head quizzically. 'A what?'

'*Quipu*, an Inca system for working out mathematical problems and for record keeping. Quite ingenious, really. It was a kind of ancient computer using coloured strands of string or hemp with knots placed at different intervals. The various colour-coded strands signified different things

– blue for religion, red for the king, grey for places and cities, green for people, and so forth. A yellow thread could indicate gold while a white one referred to silver. The placement of knots signified numbers, such as the passage of time. In the hands of a *quipu-mayoc*, a secretary or clerk, the possibilities of creating everything from records of events to warehouse inventories were endless. Unfortunately, most all the *quipus*, one of the most detailed statistical records of a people's history ever kept, were destroyed during the Spanish conquest and the oppression that followed.'

Pitt said, 'And this stringed instrument, if you'll forgive the pun, was used to give an account of the voyage, including time, distances, and location?'

'That was the idea,' Shannon agreed.

'Any clues as to whatever became of the jade box?'

'One story claims the Spaniards found the box with its *quipu* and not knowing its value, sent it to Spain. But during shipment aboard a treasure galleon bound for Panama, the box, along with a cargo of precious artifacts and a great treasure of gold and silver, was captured by the English sea hawk, Sir Francis Drake.'

Pitt turned and regarded her as he might a classic automobile he'd never seen before. 'The Chachapoyan treasure map went to England?'

Shannon gave a helpless shrug. 'Drake never mentioned the jade box or its contents when he reached England after his epic voyage around the world. Since then, the map has become known as the Drake *quipu*, but it was never seen again.'

'A hell of a tale,' Pitt muttered quietly. His eyes seemed to turn dreamlike as his mind visualized something beyond the horizon. 'But the best part is yet to come.'

Shannon and Stewart both stared at him. Pitt's gaze turned skyward as a sea gull circled the ship and then winged towards land. There was a look of utter certainty in his eyes as he faced them again, a crooked smile curving his lips, the wavy strands of his ebony hair restless in the breeze.

'Why do you say that?' Shannon asked hesitantly.

'Because I'm going to find the jade box.'

'You're putting us on.' Stewart laughed.

'Not in the least.' The distant expression on Pitt's craggy face had changed to staunch resolve.

For a moment Shannon was stunned. The sudden change from his previous mocking scepticism was totally unexpected. 'You sound like you're on the lunatic fringe.'

Pitt tilted his head back and laughed heartily. 'That's the best part about being crazy. You see things nobody else can see.'

12

St Julien Perlmutter was a classic gourmand and bon vivant. Excessively fond of fine food and drink, he revelled in sociable tastes, possessing an incredible file of recipes from the renowned chefs of the world and a cellar with more than 4000 bottles of vintage wine. A host with an admirable reputation for throwing gourmet dinners at elegant restaurants, he paid a heavy price. St Julien Perlmutter weighed in at close to 181 kilograms (400 pounds). Scoffing at physical workouts and diet foods, his fondest wish was to enter the great beyond while savouring a 100-year-old brandy after a sumptuous meal.

Besides eating, his other burning passion was ships and shipwrecks. He had accumulated what was acknowledged by archival experts as the world's most complete collection of literature and records on historic ships. Maritime museums around the world counted the days until overindulgence did him in, so they could pounce like vultures and absorb the collection into their own libraries.

There was a reason Perlmutter always entertained in restaurants instead of at his spacious carriage house in Georgetown outside the nation's capital. A gigantic mass of books was stacked on the floor, on sagging shelves, and in every nook and cranny of his bedroom, the living and dining rooms, and even in the kitchen cabinets. They were piled head-high beside the commode in his bathroom and were scattered like chaff on the king-size waterbed. Archival experts would have required a full year to sort out and catalogue the thousands of books stuffed in the carriage house. But not Perlmutter. He knew precisely where any particular volume was stashed and could pick it out within seconds.

He was dressed in his standard uniform of the day, purple pyjamas under a red and gold paisley robe, standing in front of a mirror salvaged from a stateroom on the *Lusitania*, trimming a magnificent grey beard, when his private line gave off a ring like a ship's bell.

'St Julien Perlmutter here. State your business in a brief manner.'

'Hello, you old derelict.'

'Dirk!' he boomed, recognizing the voice, his blue eyes twinkling from a round crimson face. 'Where's that recipe for apricot sautéed prawns you promised me?'

'In an envelope on my desk. I forgot to mail it to you before I left the country. My apologies.'

'Where are you calling from?'

'A ship off the coast of Peru.'

'I'm afraid to ask what you're doing down there.'

'A long story.'

'Aren't they all?'

'I need a favour.'

Perlmutter sighed. 'What ship is it this time?'

'The *Golden Hind*.'

'Francis Drake's *Golden Hind*?'

'The same.'

'*Sic parvis magna*,' Perlmutter quoted. 'Great things have small beginnings. That was Drake's motto. Did you know that?'

'Somehow it escaped me,' Pitt admitted. 'Drake captured a Spanish galleon — '

'The *Nuestra Señora de la Concepción*,' Perlmutter interrupted. 'Captained by Juan de Anton, bound for Panama City from Callao de Lima with a cargo of bullion and precious Inca artifacts. As I recall, it was in March of 1578.'

There was a moment of silence at the other end of the line. 'Why is it when I talk to you, Julien, you always

151

make me feel as if you took away my bicycle?'

'I thought you'd like a bit of knowledge to cheer you up.' Perlmutter laughed. 'What precisely do you wish to know?'

'When Drake seized the *Concepción*, how did he handle the cargo?'

'The event was quite well recorded. He loaded the gold and silver bullion, including a hoard of precious gems and pearls, on board the *Golden Hind*. The amount was enormous. His ship was dangerously overloaded, so he dumped several tons of the silver into the water by Cano Island off the coast of Ecuador before continuing on his voyage around the world.'

'What about the Inca treasures?'

'They were left in the cargo holds of the *Concepción*. Drake then put a prize crew on board to sail her back through the Magellan Strait and across the Atlantic to England.'

'Did the galleon reach port?'

'No,' answered Perlmutter thoughtfully. 'It went missing and was presumed lost with all hands.'

'I'm sorry to hear that,' said Pitt, disappointment in his voice. 'I had hopes it might have somehow survived.'

'Come to think of it,' recalled Perlmutter, 'a myth did arise concerning the *Concepción*'s disappearance.'

'What was the gist of it?'

'A fanciful story, little more than rumour, said the galleon was caught in a tidal wave that carried it far inland. Never verified or documented, of course.'

'Do you have a source for the rumour?'

'Further research will be needed to verify details, but if my memory serves me correctly, the tale came from a mad Englishman the Portuguese reported finding in a village along the Amazon River. Sorry, that's about all I can give you on the spur of the moment.'

'I'd be grateful if you dug a little deeper,' said Pitt.

'I can give you the dimensions and tonnage of the

Concepción, how much sail she carried, when and where she was built. But a crazy person wandering around a rain forest calls for a source outside my collection.'

'If anyone can track down a sea mystery, you can.'

'I have an utter lack of willpower when it comes to delving into one of your enigmas, especially after we found old Abe Lincoln on a Confederate ironclad in the middle of the Sahara Desert together.'

'I leave it to you, Julien.'

'Ironclads in a desert, Noah's Ark on a mountain, Spanish galleons in a jungle. Why don't ships stay on the sea where they belong?'

'That's why you and I are incurable lost shipwreck hunters,' said Pitt cheerfully.

'What's your interest in this one?' Perlmutter asked warily.

'A jade box containing a knotted cord that gives directions to an immense Inca treasure.'

Perlmutter mulled over Pitt's brief answer for several seconds before he finally said,

'Well, I guess that's as good a reason as any.'

Hiram Yaeger looked as if he should have been pushing a shopping cart full of shabby belongings down a back alley. He was attired in a Levi's jacket and pants, his long blond hair tied in a loose ponytail, and his boyish face half-hidden by a scraggly beard. The only shopping cart Yaeger ever pushed, however, was down the delicatessen aisle of a supermarket. A stranger would have been hard-pressed to imagine him living in a fashionable residential area of Maryland with a lovely artist wife and two pretty, smart teenage girls in private school, and driving a top-of-the-line BMW.

Nor would someone who didn't know him guess that he was chief of NUMA's communications and information network. Admiral Sandecker had pirated him away from a Silicon Valley computer corporation to build a vast data library, containing every book, article, or thesis, scientific or historical, fact or theory, ever known to be written about the sea. What St Julien Perlmutter's archive was to ships, Yaeger's was to oceanography and the growing field of undersea sciences.

He was sitting at his own private terminal in a small side office of the computer data complex that took up the entire tenth floor of the NUMA building when his phone buzzed. Without taking his eyes from a monitor that showed how ocean currents affected the climate around Australia, he picked up the receiver.

'Greetings from the brain trust,' he answered casually.

'You wouldn't know grey matter if it splashed on your shoe,' came the voice of an old friend.

'Good to hear from you, Mr Special Projects Director. The office topic of the day says you're enjoying a fun-filled holiday in sunny South America.'

'You heard wrong, pal.'

'Are you calling from the *Deep Fathom*?'

'Yes, Al and I are back on board after a little excursion into the jungle.'

'What can I do for you?'

'Delve into your data bank and see if you can find any record of a tidal wave that struck the shoreline between Lima, Peru, and Panama City sometime in March of 1578.'

Yaeger sighed. 'Why don't you also ask me to find the temperature and humidity on the day of creation?'

'Just the general area where the wave struck will do, thank you.'

'Any record of such an event would likely be in old weather and maritime records I gleaned from Spanish archives in Seville. Another remote possibility would be the local inhabitants, who might have handed down legends of such an event. The Incas were good at recording social and religious occasions on textiles or pottery.'

'Not a good lead,' Pitt said doubtfully. 'The Inca empire was smashed by the Spanish conquest nearly forty years earlier. Whatever records they made in recalling the news of the day were scattered and lost.'

'Most tidal waves that come inland are caused by seafloor movement. Maybe I can piece together known geological events of that era.'

'Give it your best try.'

'How soon do you need it?'

'Unless the admiral has you on a priority project, drop everything else and go.'

'All right,' said Yaeger, eager for the challenge. 'I'll see what I can come up with.'

'Thanks, Hiram. I owe you.'

'About a hundred times over.'

'And don't mention this to Sandecker,' said Pitt.

'I thought it sounded like another one of your shady schemes. Mind telling me what this is all about?'

'I'm looking for a lost Spanish galleon in a jungle.'

'But of course, what else?' Yaeger said with routine resignation. He had learned long before never to anticipate Pitt.

'I'm hoping you can find me a ballpark to search.'

'As a matter of fact, through clean living and moral thinking, I can already narrow your field of search by a wide margin.'

'What do you know that I don't?'

Yaeger smiled to himself. 'The lowlands between the west flank of the Andes and the coast of Peru have an average temperature of eighteen degrees Celsius or sixty-five degrees Fahrenheit and an annual rainfall that would hardly fill a shot glass, making it one of the world's coldest and driest low altitude deserts. No jungle for a ship to get lost in there.'

'So what's your hot spot?' asked Pitt.

'Ecuador. The coastal region is tropical all the way to Panama.'

'A precision display of deductive reasoning. You're okay, Hiram. I don't care what your ex-wives say about you.'

'A mere trifle. I'll have something for you in twenty-four hours.'

'I'll be in touch.'

As soon as he put down the phone, Yaeger began assembling his thoughts. He never failed to find the novelty of a shipwreck search stimulating. The areas he planned to investigate were neatly filed in the computer of his mind. During his years with NUMA, he had discovered that Dirk Pitt didn't walk through life like other men. Simply working with Pitt and supplying data information had been one long, intrigue-filled, vicarious adventure, and Yaeger took pride in the fact that he had never fumbled the ball that was passed to him.

13

As Pitt was making plans to search for a landlocked Spanish galleon, Adolphus Rummel, a noted collector of South American antiquities, stepped out of the elevator into his plush penthouse apartment twenty floors above Lake Shore Drive in Chicago. A short, stringy man with a shaven head and an enormous walrus moustache, Rummel was in his midseventies and looked more like a Sherlock Holmes villain than the owner of six huge auto salvage yards.

Like many of his extremely wealthy peers who compulsively amassed priceless collections of antiquities from the black market with no questions asked, Rummel was unmarried and reclusive. No one was ever allowed to view his pre-Columbian artifacts. Only his accountant and attorney were aware of their existence, but they had no idea of how extensive his inventory was.

In the nineteen fifties German-born Rummel smuggled a cache of Nazi ceremonial objects across the Mexican border. The contraband included presentation daggers and knights-cross medals awarded to Germany's greatest World War II heroes, as well as a number of historic documents signed by Adolph Hitler and his maniacal cronies. Selling his hoard to collectors of Nazi artifacts at premium prices, Rummel took the profits and launched an auto junkyard that he built into a scrap metal empire, netting him nearly 250 million dollars over forty years.

After a business trip to Peru in 1974, he developed an interest in ancient South American art and began buying from dealers, honest or criminal. Source did not matter to him. Corruption was as common as rain in a jungle among the brotherhood of artifact finders and sellers throughout Central and South America. Rummel gave no thought to whether his acquired pieces were legally excavated but sold out the back door, or stolen from a museum. They were for his satisfaction and enjoyment, and his alone.

He walked past the Italian marble walls of his foyer and approached a large mirror with a thick gilded frame covered with naked cherubs entwined around a continuous grapevine. Twisting the head of a cherub in one corner, Rummel sprang the catch that unlatched the mirror, revealing a concealed doorway. Behind the mirror a stairway led down into eight spacious rooms lined with shelves and filled with tables supporting at least thirty glass cases packed with more than two thousand ancient pre-Columbian artifacts. Reverently, as if walking down the aisle of a church towards the altar, he moved about the gallery, cherishing the beauty and craftsmanship of his private hoard. It was a ritual he performed every evening before going to bed, almost as if he were a father looking in on his sleeping children.

Rummel's pilgrimage finally ended at the side of a large glass case that was the centerpiece of the gallery. It held the crowning treasure of his collection. Gleaming under halogen spotlights, the Golden Body Suit of Tiapollo lay in splendour, arms and legs outstretched, the mask sparkling with emeralds in the eye sockets. The magnificent brilliance of the artistry never failed to move Rummel.

Knowing full well it had been stolen from the national anthropological museum in Seville, Spain, seventy-six years previously, Rummel did not hesitate to pay one million two hundred thousand dollars in cash when he was approached by a group of men who claimed to be connected to the Mafia but were in reality members of a clandestine underground syndicate that specialized in the theft of precious art objects. Where they had come upon the golden suit, Rummel had no idea. He could only assume they had either stolen it themselves or bought it from the collector who had dealt with the original thieves.

Having had his nightly gratification, Rummel turned off the lights, returned upstairs to the foyer, and closed the mirror. Moving behind a wet bar designed around a two-thousand-year-old Roman sarcophagus, he half-filled a small snifter from a bottle of brandy and retired to his bedroom to read before falling asleep.

In another apartment directly level and across the street from Rummel's building, United States Customs Agent David Gaskill sat and peered through a pair of high-powered binoculars mounted on a tripod as the artifacts collector prepared for bed. Another agent might have been bored after nearly a week of stake out, but not Gaskill. An eighteen-year veteran of the Customs Service, Gaskill looked more like a football coach than a special government agent, a look he cultivated for his work. His grey hair was curly and combed back. An African American, his skin was more doeskin brown than dark coffee, and his eyes were a strange mixture of mahogany and green. His massive bulldog head seemed to grow out of his shoulders on a stunted, tree-trunk neck. A huge mountain of a man, he was once an all-star linebacker for the University of Southern California. He had worked hard to lose his South Carolina drawl and spoke with practised diction, occasionally being mistaken for a former British citizen from the Bahamas.

Gaskill had been fascinated by pre-Columbian art ever since a field trip to the Yucatan Peninsula during school. When stationed in Washington, DC, he had handled dozens of investigations involving looted artifacts from the Anasazi and Hohokam cultures of the American Southwest desert. He was working on a case involving the smuggling of carved Mayan stone panels when he received a tip that was passed along to him by Chicago police from a cleaning woman. She had accidentally discovered photographs protruding from a drawer in Rummel's penthouse of what she believed to be a man's body covered in gold. Thinking that someone might have been murdered, she stole a photo and turned it over to the police. A detective who had worked on art fraud cases recognized the golden object as an antiquity and called Gaskill.

Rummel's name had always been high on the Custom Service's list of people who collected ancient art without concern about where it came from, but there was never any evidence of illegal dealings, nor did Gaskill have a clue where Rummel kept his hoard. The special agent, who possessed the expertise of an antiquities scholar, immediately recognized the photo supplied by the cleaning lady as the long-lost Golden Body Suit of Tiapollo.

He set up an immediate round-the-clock surveillance of Rummel's penthouse and had the old man tailed from the time he left the building until he returned. But six days of tight scrutiny had turned up no indication of where Rummel's collection was hidden. The suspect never varied his routine. After leaving for his office at the lower end of Michigan Avenue, where he'd spend four hours, sifting through his investments, it was lunch at a rundown cafe where he always ordered bean soup and a salad. The rest of the afternoon was spent prowling antique stores and art galleries. Then dinner at a quiet German restaurant, after which he would take in a movie or a play. He usually arrived home at eleven-thirty. The routine never varied.

'Doesn't he ever get tired of drinking the same rotgut in bed?' muttered Special Agent Winfried Pottle. 'Speaking for myself, I'd prefer the waiting arms of a beautiful woman oozing supple elegance and wearing a little something black and flimsy.'

Gaskill pulled back from the binoculars and made a dour face at his second-in-command of the surveillance team. Unlike Gaskill in his Levis and USC football jacket, Pottle was a slim, handsome man with sharp features and soft red hair, who dressed in three-piece suits complete with pocket watch and chain. 'After seeing a few of the women you date, I'd have to say that was wishful thinking.'

Pottle nodded at Rummel's penthouse. 'At least give me credit for not leading a regimented existence.'

'I shudder to think how you'd behave if you had his money.'

'If I had invested a king's ransom in stolen Indian art, I doubt if I could do as good a job of hiding it.'

'Rummel has to conceal it somewhere,' said Gaskill with a slight trace of discouragement. 'His reputation as a buyer of hot goods with a colourful history comes from too many sources in the antiquities market not to be genuine. Makes no sense for a man to build a world-class collection of ancient artifacts and then never go near it. I've yet to hear of a collector, whether he goes in for stamps, coins, or baseball cards, who didn't study and fondle them at every opportunity. Wealthy art junkies who pay big bucks for stolen Rembrandts and van Goghs are known to sit all alone in hidden vaults, gazing at them for hours on end. I know some of these guys, who started with nothing, got rich and then lusted to collect objects only they could possess. Many of them abandoned families or gladly suffered divorce because their craving became an obsession. That's why someone as addicted to pre-Columbian art as Rummel could never ignore a hoard that's probably more valuable than any in the finest museums in the world.'

'Did you ever consider the possibility that our sources might be wrong or highly exaggerated?' asked Pottle gloomily. 'The cleaning lady who claimed she found the photograph of the gold suit is a confirmed alcoholic.'

Gaskill slowly shook his head. 'Rummel's got it stashed somewhere. I'm convinced.'

Pottle stared across at Rummel's apartment as the lights blinked out. 'If you're right, and if I were Rummel, I'd take it to bed with me.'

'Sure you would – ' Gaskill stopped abruptly as Pottle's wit triggered a thought. 'Your perverted mind just made a good point.'

'It did?' muttered a confused Pottle.

'What rooms do not have windows in the penthouse? The ones we can't observe?'

Pottle looked down at the carpet in thought for a moment. 'According to the floor plan, two bathrooms, a pantry, the short hall between the master and guest bedrooms, and the closets.'

'We're missing something.'

'Missing what? Rummel seldom remembers to draw his curtains. We can watch ninety per cent of his movements once he steps off the elevator. No way he could store a ton of art treasures in a couple of bathtubs and a closet.'

'True, but where does he spend the thirty or forty minutes from the time he exits the lobby and steps into the elevator until he sets foot in his living room? Certainly not in the foyer.'

'Maybe he sits on the john.'

'Nobody is that regular.' Gaskill stood and walked over to a coffee table and spread out a set of blueprints of Rummel's penthouse obtained from the building's developer. He studied them for what had to be the fiftieth time. 'The artifacts *have* to be in the building.'

'We've checked every apartment from the main floor to the roof,' said Pottle. 'They're all leased by live-in tenants.'

'What about the one directly below Rummel?' asked Gaskill.

Pottle thumbed through a sheaf of computer papers. 'Sidney Kammer and wife, Candy. He's one of those high-level corporate attorneys who saves his clients from paying a bushel of taxes.'

Gaskill looked at Pottle. 'When was the last time Kammer and his wife made an appearance?'

Pottle scanned the log they maintained of residents who entered and left the building during the surveillance. 'No sign of them. They're no-shows.'

'I bet if we checked it out, the Kammers live in a house

162

somewhere in a plush suburb and never set foot in their apartment.'

'They could be on vacation.'

The voice of agent Beverly Swain broke over Gaskill's portable radio. 'I have a large moving van backing into the basement of the building.'

'Are you manning the front security desk or checking out the basement?' asked Gaskill.

'Still in the lobby, walking my post in a military manner,' Swain answered pertly. A smart little blonde, and a California beach girl before joining Customs, she was the best undercover agent Gaskill had on his team and the only one inside Rummel's building. 'If you think I'm bored with watching TV monitors depicting basements, elevators, and hallways, and on my way out the door for a flight to Tahiti, you're half right.'

'Save your money,' replied Pottle. 'Tahiti is nothing but tall palms and exotic beaches. You can get that in Florida.'

'Run tape on the front entrance,' ordered Gaskill. 'Then trot down to the basement and question the movers. Find out if they're moving someone in or out of the building, what apartment, and why they're working at this ungodly hour.'

'On my way,' Swain answered through a yawn.

'I hope she doesn't meet up with a monster,' said Pottle.

'What monster?' asked Gaskill with raised eyebrows.

'You know, in all those stupid horror movies, a woman alone in a house hears a strange noise in the cellar. Then she investigates by going down the stairs without turning on the lights or holding a kitchen knife for protection.'

'Typical lousy Hollywood direction.' Gaskill shrugged. 'Not to worry about Bev. The basement is lit like Las Vegas Boulevard and she's packing a nine-millimetre Colt Combat Commander. Pity the poor monster who comes on to her.'

Now that Rummel's penthouse was dark, Gaskill took a

few minutes away from the binoculars to knock off half a dozen glazed doughnuts and down a thermos bottle of cold milk. He was sadly contemplating the empty doughnut box when Swain reported in.

'The movers are unloading furniture for an apartment on the nineteenth floor. They're ticked off at working so late but are being well paid for overtime. They can't say why the client is in such a rush, only that it must be one of those last-minute corporate transfers.'

'Any possibility they're smuggling artifacts into Rummel's place?'

'They opened the door of the van for me. It's packed with art deco style furniture.'

'Okay, monitor their movements every few minutes.'

Pottle scribbled on a notepad and hung up a wall phone in the kitchen. When he returned to Gaskill's position at the window, he had a cagey grin on his face. 'I bow to your intuition. Sidney Kammer's home address is in Lake Forest.'

'I'll bet you Kammer's biggest client turns out to be Adolphus Rummel,' Gaskill ventured.

'And for the bongo drums and a year's supply of Kitty Litter, tell me who Kammer leases his apartment to.'

'Got to be Adolphus Rummel.'

Pottle looked pleased with himself. 'I think we can safely shout *Eureka*.'

Gaskill stared across the street through an open curtain into Rummel's living room, suddenly knowing his secret. His dark eyes deepened as he spoke. 'A hidden stairway leading from the foyer,' he said, carefully choosing his words as if describing a screenplay he was about to write. 'Rummel walks off the elevator, opens a hidden door to a stairway and descends to the apartment below his penthouse, where he spends forty-five minutes gloating over his private store of treasures. Then he returns upstairs, pours his brandy, and sleeps the sleep of a satisfied man. Strange, but I can't help envying him.'

Pottle had to reach up to pound Gaskill on the shoulder. 'Congratulations, Dave. Nothing left now but to obtain a search warrant and conduct a raid on Rummel's penthouse.'

Gaskill shook his head. 'A warrant, yes. A raid by an army of agents, no. Rummel has powerful friends in Chicago. We can't afford a big commotion that could result in a media barrage of criticism or a nasty lawsuit. Particularly if I've made a bad call. A quiet little search by you and me and Bev Swain will accomplish whatever it takes to ferret out Rummel's artifact collection.'

Pottle slipped on a trench coat, a never-ending source of friendly ridicule by fellow agents, and headed for the door. 'Judge Aldrich is a light sleeper. I'll roust him out of bed and be back with the paperwork before the sun comes up.'

'Make it sooner.' Gaskill smiled wryly. 'I'm itching with anticipation.'

After Pottle left, Gaskill called up Swain. 'Give me a status report on the movers.'

In the lobby of Rummel's apartment building, Bev Swain sat behind the security desk and stared up at an array of four monitors. She watched as the furniture haulers moved out of camera range. Pressing the buttons on a remote switch, she went from camera to camera, mounted at strategic areas inside the building. She found the movers coming out of the freight elevator on the nineteenth floor.

'So far they've brought up a couch, two upholstered chairs with end tables, and what looks like boxed crates of household goods, dishes, kitchen and bathroom accessories, clothing. You know, stuff like that.'

'Do they return anything to the truck?'

'Only empty boxes.'

'We think we've figured where Rummel stashes his artifacts. Pottle's gone for a warrant. We'll go in as soon as he returns.'

'That's good news,' Swain said with a sigh. 'I've almost forgotten what the world looks like outside this damn lobby.'

Gaskill laughed. 'It hasn't improved. Sit tight on your trim little bottom for a few more hours.'

'I may take that statement as sexual harassment,' said Swain primly.

'Merely words of praise, Agent Swain,' Gaskill said wearily, 'words of praise.'

A beautiful day dawned, crisp and cool, with only a whisper of breeze coming off Lake Michigan. The *Farmer's Almanac* had predicted an Indian summer for the Great Lakes region. Gaskill hoped so. A warmer than normal fall meant a few extra days of fishing on the Wisconsin lake beside his getaway cabin. He led a lonely private life since his wife of twenty years died from a heart attack brought on by an iron overload disease known as hemochromatosis. His work had become his love, and he used his leisure time comfortably settled in a Boston Whaler outboard boat, planning his investigations and analysing data as he cast for pike and bass.

As he stood next to Pottle and Swain in the elevator rising to Rummel's penthouse, Gaskill skimmed the wording of the warrant for the third time. The judge had allowed a search of Rummel's penthouse, but not Kammer's apartment on the floor below, because he failed to see just cause. A minor inconvenience. Instead of going directly into what Gaskill was certain were the rooms that held the artifacts, they would have to find a hidden access and come down from the top.

Suddenly he was thinking a strange thought: what if the collector had been sold fakes and forged artworks? Rummel would not be the first greedy collector who had been sold a bill of goods in his unbridled lust to acquire art from any source, legal or not. He swept away the pessimistic thought and basked in a glow of fulfilment. The culmination of long hours of unflagging effort was only minutes away.

Swain had punched in the security code that allowed the elevator to rise beyond the residents' apartments and open directly into Rummel's penthouse. The doors parted and they stepped on to the marble floor of the foyer, unannounced. Out of habit, Gaskill lightly fingered his shoulder-holstered nine-millimetre automatic. Pottle found the button to a speaker box on a credenza and pressed it. A loud buzzer was heard throughout the penthouse.

After a short pause, a voice fogged with sleep answered. 'Who's there?'

'Mr Rummel,' said Pottle into the speaker. 'Will you please come to the elevator?'

'You'd better leave. I'm calling security.'

'Don't bother. We're federal agents. Please comply and we'll explain our presence.'

Swain watched the floor lights over the elevator flicker as it automatically descended. 'That's why I'd never lease a penthouse,' she said in mock seriousness. 'Intruders can rig your private elevator easier than stealing a Mercedes-Benz.'

Rummel appeared in pyjamas, slippers, and an old-fashioned chenille robe. The material of the robe reminded Gaskill of a bedspread he'd slept on as a young boy in his grandmother's house. 'My name is David Gaskill. I'm a special agent with the United States Customs Service. I have an authorized federal court warrant to search the premises.'

Rummel indifferently slipped on a pair of rimless glasses and began reading the warrant as if it were the morning newspaper. Up close, he looked a good ten years younger than seventy-six. And although he had just come out of bed, he appeared alert and quite meticulous.

Impatient, Gaskill moved around him. 'Pardon me.'

Rummel peered up. 'Look through my rooms all you want. I have nothing to hide.'

The wealthy scrap dealer appeared anything but rude and irritable. He seemed to take the intrusion in good grace with a show of cooperation.

Gaskill knew it was nothing but an act. 'We're only interested in your foyer.'

He had briefed Swain and Pottle on what to search for and they immediately set to work. Every crack and seam was closely examined. But it was the mirror that intrigued Swain. As a woman she was instinctively drawn to it. Gazing into the reflective backing, she found it free of even the tiniest imperfection. The glass was bevelled around the edges with etchings of flowers in the corners. Her best guess was that it was eighteenth century. She could not help but wonder about all the other people who had stood in front of it over the past three hundred years and stared at their reflections. Their images were still there. She could sense them.

Next she studied the intricately sculptured frame, crowded with cherubs overlaid in gold. Keenly observant, she noticed the tiny seam on the neck of one cherub. The gilt around the edges looked worn from friction. Swain gently grasped the head and tried to turn it clockwise. It remained stationary. She tried the opposite direction, and the head rotated until it was facing backward. There was a noticeable *click*, and one side of the mirror came ajar and stopped a few centimetres from the wall.

She peered through the crack down the hidden stairwell and said, 'Good call, boss.'

Rummel paled as Gaskill silently swung the mirror wide open. He smiled broadly as he was swept by a wave of satisfaction. This was what Gaskill liked best about his job, the game of wits culminating in ultimate triumph over his antagonist.

'Will you please lead the way, Mr Rummel?'

'The apartment below belongs to my attorney, Sidney Kammer,' said Rummel, a shrewd gleam forming in his eyes. 'Your warrant only authorizes you to search my penthouse.'

Gaskill groped about in his coat pocket for a moment before extracting a small box containing a bass plug, a fishing lure he had purchased the day before. He extended his hand and dropped the box down the stairs. 'Forgive my clumsiness. I hope Mr Kammer doesn't mind if I retrieve my property.'

'That's trespassing!' Rummel blurted.

There was no reply. Followed by Pottle, the burly Customs agent was already descending the stairway, pausing only to retrieve his bass plug box. What he saw upon reaching the floor below took his breath away.

Magnificent pre-Columbian artworks filled room after room of the apartment. Glass-enclosed Incan textiles hung from the ceilings. One entire room was devoted solely to ceremonial masks. Another held religious altars and burial urns. Others were filled with ornate headdresses, elaborately painted ceramics, and exotic sculptures. All doors in the apartment had been removed for easier access, the kitchen and bathrooms stripped of their sinks, cupboards and accessories to provide more space for the immense collection. Gaskill and Pottle stood overwhelmed by the spectacular array of antiquities. The quantity went far beyond what they expected.

After the initial amazement faded, Gaskill rushed from room to room, searching for the pièce de résistance of the collection. What he found was a shattered, empty glass case in the centre of a room. Disillusionment flooded over him.

'Mr Rummel!' he shouted. 'Come here!'

Escorted by Swain, a thoroughly defeated and distraught Rummel shuffled slowly into the exhibition room. He froze in sudden horror as though one of the Inca battle lances on the wall had pierced his stomach. 'It's gone!' he gasped. 'The Golden Body Suit of Tiapollo is gone.'

Gaskill's face went tight and cold. The floor around the

empty display case was flanked by a pile of furniture consisting of a couch, end tables, and two chairs. He looked from Pottle to Swain. 'The movers,' he rasped in a tone barely audible. 'They've stolen the suit from right under our noses.'

'They left the building over an hour ago,' said Swain tonelessly.

Pottle looked dazed. 'Too late to mount a search. They've already stashed the suit by now.' Then he added, 'If it isn't on an aeroplane flying out of the country.'

Gaskill sank into one of the chairs. 'To have come so close,' he murmured vacantly. 'God forbid the suit won't be lost for another seventy-six years.'

PART TWO

In Search of the *Concepción*

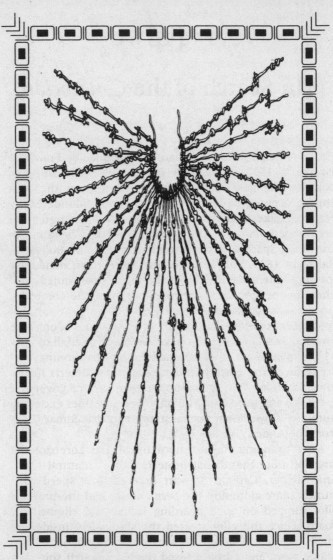

THE DRAKE *QUIPU*

14

Peru's principal seaport, Callao, was founded by Francisco Pizarro in 1537 and quickly became the main shipping port for the gold and silver plundered from the Inca empire. Appropriately, the port itself was plundered by Francis Drake forty-one years later. Spain's conquest of Peru ended almost at the spot where it had begun. The last of the Spanish forces surrendered to Simon Bolivar at Callao in 1825, and Peru became a sovereign nation for the first time since the fall of the Incas. Now joined with Lima as one sprawling metropolitan area, the combined cities host a population of nearly 6.5 million.

Situated on the west bank of the Andes along the lowlands, Callao and Lima have an annual rainfall of only 41 millimetres (1.5 inches), making the surrounding land area one of the earth's chilliest and driest deserts in the lower latitudes. Winter fog supports thin ground cover and mesquite and little else. The only water, besides excessive humidity, flows down several streams and the Rimac River from the Andes.

After rounding the northern tip of San Lorenzo, the large offshore island that protects Callao's natural maritime shelter, Captain Stewart ordered slow speed as a launch came alongside the *Deep Fathom* and the harbour pilot jumped on to a boarding ladder and climbed on board. Once the pilot steered the ship safely inside the main channel, Captain Stewart took command of the bridge again and adroitly eased the big research ship to a stop beside the dock of the main passenger terminal. Under his watchful eye the mooring lines were slipped over big, rusty bollards. Then he shut down his automatic control system, rang his chief engineer, and told him that he was through with the engines.

Everyone lining the ship's rail was surprised to see over a thousand people jamming the dock. Along with an armed military security force and a large contingent of police, TV news cameras and press photographers quickly began jockeying for position as the gangway was lowered. Beyond the news media stood a group of smiling government officials, and behind them the happily waving parents of the archaeology students.

'Still no Dixieland band playing "Waiting for the Robert E. Lee,"' Pitt said, feigning a disappointed tone.

'Nothing like a cheering populace to snap one out of depression,' said Giordino, gazing at the unexpected reception.

'I never expected so grand a turnout,' murmured Shannon in awe. 'I can't believe word spread so fast.'

Miles Rodgers lifted one of three cameras hung around his neck and began shooting. 'Looks to me like half the Peruvian government turned out.'

The dock was filled with an air of excitement. Small children were waving Peruvian and American flags. A roar came from the crowd as the archaeology students climbed out on the bridge wing and began waving and shouting as they recognized their parents. Only Stewart looked uneasy.

'My God, I hope they all don't expect to storm aboard my ship.'

'Too many boarders to repel.' Giordino shrugged. 'Better to haul down your flag and plead for mercy.'

'I told you my students came from influential families,' said Shannon happily.

Unnoticed by the crowd, a small man wearing glasses and carrying a briefcase expertly squeezed through the milling throng and slipped around the cordon of security guards. He bounded up the still-lowering gangway before anyone could stop him and leapt on to the deck with the elated expression of a running back who has just crossed a goal line. He approached Pitt and Giordino and grinned.

'Why is it prudence and discretion are beyond your talents?'

'We try not to fly in the face of public opinion,' Pitt said before smiling broadly and embracing the little man. 'Good to see you, Rudi.'

'Seems we can't get away from you,' said Giordino warmly.

Rudi Gunn, the deputy director of NUMA, shook Stewart's hand and was introduced to Shannon and Rodgers. 'Will you excuse me if I borrow these two rogues before the welcoming ceremonies?' he asked graciously.

Without waiting for an answer, he stepped through a hatch and walked down an alleyway with ease. Gunn had helped design the *Deep Fathom* and was very familiar with the ship's deck layout. He stopped before the doorway to the conference room, opened it and entered. He went directly to the head of a long table and fished through his briefcase for a yellow legal pad filled with notations as Pitt and Giordino settled into a pair of leather chairs.

Though Giordino and Gunn were both short, they were as unalike as a gibbon and a bulldog. While Gunn was as slight as a girl, Giordino was a huge walking muscle. They also differed in brain power. Giordino was shrewd and street smart. Gunn was sheer genius. Number one in his class at the Naval Academy, and a former navy commander who could easily have ascended to a top staff job in the Navy Department, he preferred the underwater science of NUMA to the science of warfare. Extremely nearsighted, he peered through heavy hornrimmed glasses, but never missed the slightest movement within two hundred yards.

Pitt was the first to speak. 'Why the frenzy to send Al and me back to that rotten sinkhole to retrieve a body?'

'The request came from US Customs. They made an urgent appeal to Admiral Sandecker to borrow his best men.'

'And that includes you.'

'I could have begged off, claiming my present projects would grind to a stop without my presence. The admiral would not have hesitated to send someone else. But a canary let slip your little unauthorized mission to find a lost galleon in the wilds of Ecuador.'

'Hiram Yaeger,' Pitt supplied. 'I should have remembered you two are as close as Frank and Jesse James.'

'I couldn't resist dumping the routine of Washington to mix a little business with adventure, so I volunteered for the dirty job of briefing and joining you on the Customs project.'

'You mean you sold Sandecker a bill of goods and skipped town?' said Pitt.

'Mercifully for everyone involved, he doesn't know about the hunt for the galleon. At least not yet.'

'He's not an easy man to fool,' said Giordino seriously.

'Not for very long,' added Pitt. 'He's probably already on to you.

Gunn waved a hand indifferently. 'You two are on safe ground. Better me than some poor fool unfamiliar with your escapades. Anyone else in the NUMA bureaucracy might overestimate your abilities.'

Giordino made a surly face. 'And we call him a friend?'

'What can NUMA do for Customs that's so special?' asked Pitt.

Gunn spread a sheaf of papers on the table. 'The issue is complex but involves the plunder of ancient art.'

'Isn't that a little out of our line? Our business is underwater exploration and research.'

'Destruction for the purpose of looting underwater archaeological sites *is* our business,' Gunn stated earnestly.

'Where does recovering Dr Miller's body enter the picture?'

'Only the first step of our cooperation with Customs. The murder of a world-renowned anthropologist is the bedrock of their case. They suspect the killer is a high-level member of an international looting syndicate, and they need proof for an indictment. They also hope to use the killer as a key to unlock the door leading to the masterminds of the entire theft and smuggling operation. As for the sacred well, Customs and Peruvian authorities believe a vast cache of artifacts was raised from the bottom and has already been shipped to black-market receiving stations around the world. Miller discovered the theft and was terminated to shut him up. They want us, you and Al in particular, to search the floor of the well for evidence.'

'And our plan to explore for the lost galleon?'

'Complete the job on the well, and I'll authorize a small budget out of NUMA to fund your search. That's all I can promise.'

'And if the admiral shoots you down?' asked Giordino.

Gunn shrugged. 'He's my boss as well as yours. I'm an old navy man. I follow orders.'

'I'm old air force,' Pitt replied. 'I question them.'

'Worry about it when the time comes,' said Giordino. 'Let's get the sinkhole probe out of the way.'

Pitt took a deep breath and relaxed in his chair. 'Might as well do something useful while Yaeger and Perlmutter conduct their research. They should have some solid leads by the time we stumble out of the jungle.'

'There is one more request from the Customs agents,' said Gunn.

'What the hell else do they have on their want list?' demanded Pitt roughly. 'A dive orgy for souvenirs thrown off cruise ships by tourists afraid of Customs inspectors?'

'Nothing so mundane,' Gunn explained patiently. 'They also insist that you return to the Pueblo de los Muertos.'

'They must think artifacts sitting in the rain qualify as underwater stolen goods,' Giordino said with acidic humour.

'The Customs people are in dire need of an inventory.'

'Of the artifacts in the temple?' Pitt asked incredulously. 'Do they expect an indexed catalogue? There must be close to a thousand items stacked inside whatever is left of the temple after the mercenaries finished blowing it all to hell. They need archaeologists to sort through the hoard, not marine engineers.'

'The Peruvian Investigative Police have investigated and reported that most of the artifacts were removed from the temple soon after you escaped,' explained Gunn. 'International Customs agents need descriptions so they can identify the artifacts should they begin to show up at antique auctions, or in private collections, galleries, and museums in affluent first world countries. They hope that a return trip to the scene of the crime will jog your memories.'

'Events were moving too fast for a quick tally.'

Gunn nodded in understanding. 'But certain objects must have stuck in your mind, especially the outstanding pieces. What about you, Al?'

'I was busy prowling the ruins for a radio,' said Giordino. 'I didn't have time to examine the stuff.'

Pitt held his hands to his head and massaged his temples. 'I might be able to recall fifteen or twenty items that stood out.'

'Can you sketch them?'

'I'm a miserable artist, but I think I can draw reasonably accurate pictures. No need to visit the place again. I can just as well illustrate what I remember while lounging by a swimming pool at a resort hotel.'

'Sounds sensible to me,' Giordino said cheerfully.

'No,' Gunn said, 'it's not sensible. Your job goes much deeper. As much as it turns my stomach, you two middle-aged delinquents are Peruvian national heroes. Not only

178

are you in demand with the Customs Service, the State Department wants a piece of you.'

Giordino stared at Pitt. 'One more manifestation of Giordino's list of laws. Any man who volunteers for a rescue mission becomes a victim.'

'What does the State Department have to do with us making a round trip to the temple?' Pitt demanded.

'Since the South American Free Trade Treaty, the petroleum and mining industries have been denationalized. Several American companies are currently completing negotiations to help Peru better exploit its natural resources. The country desperately needs foreign investment, and the money is ready to pour in. The catch is that labour unions and the opposition parties of the legislature are against foreign involvement in their economy. By saving the lives of sons and daughters of the local VIPs, you and Al indirectly influenced a number of votes.'

'All right, so we give a speech at the local Elks Club and accept a certificate of merit.'

'Fine as far as it goes,' said Gunn. 'But State Department experts and the Congressional Committee on Latin American Affairs think you both should hang around and make the dirty Yankees look good by helping to halt the looting of Peru's cultural heritage.'

'In other words, our esteemed government wants to milk our benevolent image for all it's worth,' said Pitt stonily.

'Something along those lines.'

'And Sandecker agreed to it.'

'Goes without saying,' Gunn assured him. 'The admiral never misses a chance to stroke Congress if it can lead to more funding for NUMA's future operations.'

'Who is going in with us?'

'Dr Alberto Ortiz from the National Institute of Culture in Chiclayo will supervise the archaeological team. He'll be assisted by Dr Kelsey.'

'Without reliable protection we'll be asking for trouble.'

'The Peruvians have assured us they will send in a highly trained security force to control the valley.'

'But are they trustworthy? I don't want an encore by an army of rogue mercenaries.'

'Nor me,' Giordino agreed firmly.

Gunn made a helpless gesture. 'I can only pass on what I was told.'

'We'll need better equipment than what we took in on our last trip.'

'Give me a list and I'll handle the logistics.'

Pitt turned to Giordino. 'Do you get the distinct impression we've been had?'

'As near as I can tell,' said the stocky Italian, 'this makes about four hundred and thirty-seven times.'

Pitt did not look forward to a repeat dive in the sinkhole. There was a haunted aura about it, something evil in its depths. The yawning cavity gaped in his mind as though it were the mouth of the devil. The imagery was so irrational that he tried to erase it from his mind, but the vision would not go away. It clung like the vague memory of a repugnant nightmare.

15

Two days later, at about eight in the morning, preparations were completed for the dive to retrieve Doc Miller's body from the sacred well. As Pitt stared down at the surface slime of the sinkhole, all his apprehension evaporated. The loathsome cavity still looked as menacing as when he had first encountered it, but he had survived its deadly surge, climbed its sheer walls. Now that he knew its hidden secrets, it no longer held any threat. The first hurried, planned-on-the-spot rescue was quickly forgotten. This was now a state-of-the-art project.

True to his word, Gunn had chartered two helicopters and scrounged the necessary gear for the job. One whole day was spent ferrying Dr Kelsey and Miles Rodgers, the dive crew, and their equipment to the site and reestablishing the destroyed camp. Gunn was not known for running sloppy operations. There was no deadline, and he took the time to plan every step with precision. Nothing was left to chance.

A fifty-man contingent from Peru's élite special security unit was already in place when Gunn's first helicopter landed. To the taller North Americans the South American men seemed small in stature. They had an almost gentle look on their faces, but they were a tough lot, hardened by years of fighting Shining Path guerrillas in the heavily forested mountain country and barren coastal deserts. They quickly set up defences around the camp and sent patrols into the surrounding jungle.

'Wish I was going with you,' said Shannon from behind Pitt.

He turned and smiled. 'I can't imagine why. Retrieving

181

a human body that's been decomposing in tropically heated soup is not what I call a fun experience.'

'Sorry, I didn't mean to sound cold-hearted.' There was little expression of sorrow in her eyes. 'I had the deepest admiration for Doc. But the archaeologist in me wants desperately to explore the bottom of the sacred pool.'

'Don't get your hopes up of finding a treasure in antiquities,' Pitt consoled her. 'You'd be disappointed. All I saw was an acre of silt with an old Spaniard growing out of it.'

'At least allow Miles to dive with you and make a photo record.'

'Why the rush?'

'During the recovery, you and Al might disturb the bottom and move artifacts from their original positions.'

Pitt gazed at her through disbelieving eyes. 'You consider that more important than showing respect for Doc Miller?'

'Doc is dead,' she said matter-of-factly. 'Archaeology is an exacting science that deals with dead things. Doc taught that better than anyone. The slightest disturbance could alter significant findings.'

Pitt began to see a side of Shannon that was all business. 'After Al and I bring up Miller's remains, you and your Miles can dive and retrieve artifacts to your heart's content. But mind you don't get sucked into the side cavern again.'

'Once is enough,' she said with a tight smile. Then her expression turned to one of concern. 'Be careful and don't take chances.'

Then she kissed him lightly on the cheek, turned and hurried off towards her tent.

Dropping into the water went smoothly, thanks to a small crane and a motorized winch operated under the watchful eye of Rudi Gunn. When Pitt was about a metre above the water, he released the safety catch holding him on the end of the cable running to the winch. The upper, slime-laden level of the water was as tepid as expected but he did not recall it smelling quite so pungent. He floated lazily on his back, waiting for the cable to return topside before lowering Giordino.

Pitt's full face mask was connected to a communications and safety line while Giordino dived free and unencumbered, relying on hand signals from Pitt for instructions. As soon as his diving buddy slid into the muck beside him, Pitt motioned downward, and they rolled forward and dived into the depths of the sinkhole. They stayed close to avoid becoming separated and losing sight of one another in the dismal murk before reaching the incredibly clear water 4 metres (13 feet) below the surface of the pool. The greyish brown of the bottom silt and rocks materialized out of the gloom and came up to meet them. They levelled off at 2 metres (6 feet), and Pitt made a motion to stop all movement. Carefully, so he didn't stir up a cloud of silt, he removed a stainless steel shaft that was attached to a reel of nylon cord and shoved it into a pocket of silt.

'How are you doing?' Gunn's voice came over the earphones inside Pitt's face mask.

'We've reached bottom and are beginning a circular search for the body,' Pitt replied as he began unwinding the line.

Pitt obtained bearings from his compass and began sweeping around the shaft that protruded from the silt, enlarging the search pattern while unreeling the line, as if following the path of a pinwheel. He slowly swam above the muck, scanning from side to side with Giordino following slightly to the side and rear of Pitt's fins. In the transparent liquid void they soon spotted the saponified remains of Doc Miller.

In the few days since he had seen the body it had changed for the worse. Tiny pieces were missing from the exposed skin areas. Pitt was at a loss to explain this until he glimpsed a strange brightly speckled fish with luminous

183

scales dart in and begin nibbling one of Doc's eyes. He brushed away the carnivorous fish, the size of a small trout, and wondered how it came to be stranded in a deep pool in the middle of a jungle.

He gave a hand signal to Giordino who removed a rubberized body bag from a pack that was strapped to his chest above his weight belt. A decomposing body cannot be smelled under water. That's what they say. Perhaps it was in their minds, but the smell of death seemed to flow through their breathing regulators as if their air tanks were contaminated with it. An impossibility, to be sure, but tell that to rescue teams who have seen the horror of long-immersed dead.

They wasted no time in examining the body but moved as fast as their hands would let them, pulling the body bag over the corpse while trying not to stir up a cloud of silt. The silt did not cooperate, billowing up in a dense cloud, cutting off all visibility. They worked blind, carefully zipping up the bag, making sure no flesh protruded from the seam. When the grisly job was completed, Pitt reported to Gunn.

'We have the body contained and are on our way up.'

'Acknowledged,' Gunn replied. 'We will lower a sling with a stretcher.'

Pitt grabbed Giordino's arm through the silt cloud, signalling for a mutual ascent. They began raising the remains of Doc Miller to the sunlight. After reaching the surface, they gently eased the body on to the stretcher and secured it with buckled straps. Then Pitt advised Gunn.

'Ready for lift.'

As Pitt watched the stretcher rise towards the rim of the sinkhole, he sadly wished he had known the genuine Steve Miller instead of the imposter. The esteemed anthropologist had been murdered without knowing why. No hint was given by the scum that cut his throat. He never knew that his death was an unnecessary act by a sociopathic killer. He was simply a cast-off pawn in the high-stakes game of stolen art and antiquities.

There was nothing more to be done. Their part of the body retrieval operation was finished. Pitt and Giordino could only float and wait for the winch to lower the cable again. Giordino looked over at Pitt expectantly and removed the breathing regulator from his mouth.

We still have plenty of air, he wrote on a communications board. *Why not poke around while we're waiting for the next elevator?*

To Pitt the suggestion struck a harmonious chord. Unable to remove his head mask and speak, he replied on his own communications board: *Stay close to me and grab hold if struck by surge.* Then he gestured downward. Giordino nodded and faithfully swam alongside as they jackknifed and kicked once more towards the floor of the sinkhole.

The puzzle in Pitt's mind was the lack of artifacts in the silt. Bones, yes, there was an overabundance. But after probing the sinkhole's floor for half an hour, they found no sign of ancient artifacts. Nothing except the armour on the intact skeleton he had discovered on his first dive, and the dive gear Pitt had cast off before his climb out of the well. Two minutes was all it took to relocate the site. The bony hand was still raised, one finger pointing in the direction where Miller had lain.

Pitt slowly drifted around the armour-encased Spaniard, examining every detail, occasionally glancing up and around the dim reaches of the sinkhole, alert to any disturbance in the silt that signalled the approach of the mysterious surge. He felt his every movement was followed from deep within the empty eye sockets of the skull. The teeth seemed frozen in a mocking grin, taunting and baiting him at the same time. The sunlight from above filtered through the slime and painted the bones a ghostly shade of green.

Giordino floated nearby, observing Pitt with detached curiosity. He had no clue to what captivated his friend. The old bones held little fascination for Giordino. The remains of a five-hundred-year-old Spaniard conjured up nothing in his imagination, except possibly the eruption that would occur when Shannon Kelsey discovered that her precious archaeological site had been disturbed before she could investigate it.

No such thoughts ran through Pitt's mind. He was beginning to sense that the skeleton did not belong here. He rubbed a finger lightly over the breastplate. A thin smudge of rust came away, revealing smooth, unpitted, uncorroded metal beneath. The leather straps that held the armour against the chest were incredibly well preserved. And so were the fasteners that joined the straps. They had the appearance of metal buckles on old shoes that had sat inside a trunk in an attic for one or two generations.

He swam a few metres away from the skeleton and pulled a bone out of the silt, a tibia by the shape of it. He returned and held it against the Spaniard's protruding forearm and hand. The bone from the silt was much rougher and pitted as well as more deeply stained from the minerals in the water. The bony structure of the skeleton was smooth in comparison. Next he studied the teeth, which were in remarkably good condition. Pitt found caps on two molars, not gold but silver. Pitt was no expert on sixteenth-century dentistry, but he knew that Europeans didn't even begin to fill cavities and cap teeth until the late eighteenth century.

'Rudi?'

'I'm listening,' answered Gunn.

'Please send down a line. I want to lift something.'

'A line with a small weight attached to the end is on the way.'

'Try to drop it where you see our bubbles.'

'Will do.' There was a pause, and then Gunn's voice came back over Pitt's earphones with a slight edge to it. 'Your archaeologist lady is raising hell. She says you can't touch anything down there.'

'Pretend she's in Moline, Illinois, and drop the line.'

Gunn replied nervously. 'She's making a terrible scene up here.'

'Either drop the line or throw her over the edge,' Pitt snapped obstinately.

'Stand by.'

Moments later a small steel hook attached to a nylon line materialized through the green void and landed in the silt two metres away. Giordino effortlessly swam over, snagged the line with one hand, and returned. Then, with the finesse of a pickpocket delicately lifting a wallet, Pitt very carefully wrapped the loose end of the line around a strap holding the breastplate to the skeleton and cinched it with the hook. He stared at Giordino and made the thumbs-up gesture. Giordino nodded and was mildly surprised when Pitt released the line, allowing it to slacken and leaving the skeleton where it lay.

They took turns being lifted out of the sinkhole. As the crane raised him by his safety line, Pitt looked down and vowed he would never again enter that odious slough. At the rim, Gunn was there to help swing him on to firm ground and remove his full face mask.

'Thank God, you're back,' he said. 'That madwoman threatened to shoot off my testicles.'

Giordino laughed. 'She learned that from Pitt. Just be thankful your name isn't Amaru.'

'What . . . what was that?'

'Another story,' said Pitt, inhaling the humid mountain air and enjoying every second of it.

He was struggling out of his dive suit when Shannon stormed up to him like a wild grizzly who has had her cubs stolen. 'I warned you not to disturb any artifacts,' she said firmly.

Pitt looked at her for a long moment, his green eyes strangely soft and understanding. 'There is nothing left to touch,' he said finally. 'Somebody beat you to it. Any artifacts that were in your sacred pool a month ago are gone. Only the bones of animals and sacrificial victims are left scattered on the bottom.'

Her face turned incredulous and the hazel eyes flew very wide. 'Are you certain?'

'Would you like proof?'

'We have our own equipment. I'll dive into the pool and see for myself.'

'Not necessary,' he advised.

She turned and called to Miles Rodgers. 'Let's get suited up.'

'You begin probing around in the silt and you will surely die,' Pitt said, with all the emotion of a professor lecturing to a physics class.

Maybe Shannon wasn't listening to Pitt, but Rodgers was. 'I think we had better listen to what Dirk is saying.'

'I don't wish to sound nasty, but he lacks the necessary credentials to make a case.'

'What if he's right?' Rodgers asked innocently.

'I've waited a long time to explore and survey the bottom of the pool. You and I came within minutes of losing our lives trying to unlock its secrets. I can't believe there isn't a time capsule of valuable antiquities down there.'

Pitt took the line leading down into the water and held it loosely in his hand. 'Here is the verification. Pull on this line and I guarantee you'll change your mind.'

'You attached the other end?' she challenged him. 'To what?'

'A set of bones masquerading as a Spanish conquistador.'

'You're beyond belief,' she said helplessly.

It was a long time since a woman had stared at him like that. 'Do you think I'm a head case? Do you think I enjoy this? I damn well don't enjoy spending my time saving your backside. Okay, you want to die and be buried in a thousand bits and pieces, enjoy the trip.'

Uncertainty crept into her expression. 'You're not making sense.'

'Perhaps a little demonstration is in order.' Pitt gently pulled in the line until it became taut. Then he gave it a hard jerk.

For a moment nothing happened. Then a rumbling came from the bottom of the well, swelling in volume, sending tremors through the limestone walls. The violence of the explosion was electrifying. The underwater blast came like the eruption of a huge depth charge as a seething column of white froth and green slime burst out of the sinkhole, splattering everyone and everything standing within 20 metres (66 feet) of the edge. The thunder of the explosion rolled over the jungle as the spray fell back into the sinkhole, leaving a heavy mist that swirled into the sky and temporarily blocked out the sun.

16

Shannon stood half-drenched and stared down into her beloved sacred well as if she couldn't make up her mind whether or not to be sick. Everyone around the edge stood like statues suddenly frozen in shock. Only Pitt looked as though he'd witnessed an everyday event.

Fading incomprehension and the tentative beginnings of understanding appeared in Shannon's eyes. 'How in God's name did you know . . .'

'That there was a booby trap?' Pitt finished. 'No great deduction. Whoever buried a good forty-five kilograms of high explosive under the skeleton made two major mistakes. One, why clean out every antiquity but the most obvious? And two, the bones couldn't have been more than fifty years old and the armour hasn't rusted enough to have been underwater for four centuries.'

'Who would have done such a thing?' asked Rodgers dazedly.

'The same man who murdered Doc Miller,' answered Pitt.

'The imposter?'

'More likely Amaru. The man who took Miller's place didn't want to risk exposure and investigation by Peruvian authorities, not before they cleaned out the City of the Dead. The *Solpemachaco* had robbed the sacrificial well of its artifacts long before you arrived. That's why the imposter sent out a call for help when you and Shannon vanished in the sinkhole. It was all part of the plot to make your deaths look like an accident. Although he felt reasonably sure that you'd be sucked into the adjoining cavern by the underwater surge before you could fully search the bottom and realize all artifacts had been removed, he hedged his bets by lowering the phony conquistador into position purely as a red herring to blow you to pieces in the event the surge didn't carry you away.'

Shannon's eyes took on a saddened and disillusioned look. 'Then all antiquities from the sacred well are gone.'

'You can take a small measure of cheer in knowing they were removed and not destroyed,' said Pitt.

'They'll turn up,' said Giordino consolingly. 'They can't remain hidden away in some rich guy's collection forever.'

'You don't understand the discipline of archaeology,' Shannon said dully. 'No scholar can study the artifacts, classify or trace them without knowing their exact site of origin. Now we can learn nothing of the people who once lived here and built the city. A vast archive, a time capsule of scientific information, has been irretrievably lost.'

'I'm sorry all your hopes and efforts have come to grief,' Pitt said sincerely.

'Grief, yes,' she said, thoroughly defeated now. 'More like a tragedy.'

Rudi Gunn walked back from the helicopter that was transporting Miller's body to the morgue in Lima. 'Sorry to interrupt,' he said to Pitt. 'Our job is finished here. I suggest we pack up the helicopter, lift off, and rendezvous with Dr Ortiz at the City of the Dead.'

Pitt nodded and turned to Shannon. 'Well, shall we move on to the next disaster your antiquity looters have left us?'

Dr Alberto Ortiz was a lean, wiry old bird in his early seventies. He stood off to one side of the helicopter landing site dressed in a white duck shirt and matching pants. A long, flowing, white moustache drooped across his face making him look like a wanted poster for an ageing Mexican *bandido*. If inconsistency was his trademark, it was demonstrated by a wide-brimmed panama hat sporting a colourful band, a pair of expensive designer sandals, and a tall iced drink in one hand. A Hollywood casting director searching for someone to play a beachcomber in a South Seas epic would easily have decided that Dr Ortiz fit the role to perfection. He was not what the NUMA men had pictured as Peru's most renowned expert on ancient culture.

He came smiling to greet the newcomers, drink in left hand, right extended for shaking. 'You're early,' he said warmly in almost perfect English. 'I didn't expect you for another two or three days.'

'Dr Kelsey's project was cut short unexpectedly,' said Pitt, grasping a strong, callused hand.

'Is she with you?' asked Ortiz, peering around Pitt's broad shoulders.

'She'll be here first thing in the morning. Something about using the afternoon to photograph the carvings on an altar stone beside the well.' Pitt turned and made the introductions. 'I'm Dirk Pitt and this is Rudi Gunn and Al Giordino. We're with the National Underwater and Marine Agency.'

'A great pleasure to meet you gentlemen. I'm grateful for the opportunity to thank you in person for saving the lives of our young people.'

'Always a joy to play the palace again,' said Giordino, looking up at the battle-scarred temple.

Ortiz laughed at the distinct lack of enthusiasm. 'I don't imagine you enjoyed your last visit.'

'The audience didn't throw roses, that's for sure.'

'Where would you like us to set up our tents, Doctor?' Gunn inquired.

'Nothing of the sort,' Ortiz said, his teeth flashing beneath the moustache. 'My men have cleaned up a tomb that belonged to a rich merchant. Plenty of room, and it's dry during a rain. Not a four-star hotel, of course, but you should find it comfortable.'

'I hope the original owner isn't still in residence,' Pitt said cautiously.

'No, no, not at all,' replied Ortiz, mistakenly taking him seriously. 'The looters cleaned out the bones and any remains in their frantic search for artifacts.'

'We could bed down in the structure used by the looters for their headquarters,' suggested Giordino, angling for more deluxe accommodations.

'Sorry, my staff and I have already claimed it as our base of operations.'

Giordino offered Gunn a sour expression. 'I told you to call ahead for reservations.'

'Come along, gentlemen,' said Ortiz cheerfully. 'I'll give you a guided tour of the Pueblo de los Muertos on our way to your quarters.'

'The inhabitants must have taken a page from the elephants,' said Giordino.

Ortiz laughed. 'No, no, the Chachapoyas didn't come here to die. This was a sacred burial place that they believed was a way station on their journey to the next life.'

'No one lived here?' asked Gunn.

'Only priests and the workers who built the funeral houses. It was off limits to everyone else.'

'They must have had a thriving business,' Pitt said, staring at the maze of crypts spread throughout the valley and the honeycomb of tombs in the soaring cliffs.

'The Chachapoyan culture was highly stratified but it did not have a royal élite like the Inca,' explained Ortiz. 'Learned elders and military captains ruled the various cities in the confederation. They and the wealthy traders could afford to erect elaborate mausoleums to rest between lives. The poor were put in adobe, human-shaped funeral statues.'

Gunn gave the archaeologist a curious look. 'The dead were inserted into statues?'

'Yes, the body of the deceased was placed in a crouched position, knees tucked under the chin. Then a cone of sticks was placed around the body as a cagelike support.

Next, wet adobe was plastered around the support, forming a casing around the body. The final step was to sculpt a face and head on top that vaguely resembled the person inside. When the funeral receptacle was dry, the mourners inserted it into a previously dug niche or handy crevice in the face of the cliff.'

'The local mortician must have been a popular guy,' observed Giordino.

'Until I study the city in greater detail,' said Ortiz, 'I'd estimate that it was under continual construction and expansion as a cemetery between A.D. 1200 and A.D. 1500 before it was abandoned. Probably sometime after the Spanish conquest.'

'Did the Inca bury their dead here after they subdued the Chachapoyas?' asked Gunn.

'Not to any great extent. I've found only a few tombs that indicate later Inca design and architecture.'

Ortiz led them along an ancient avenue made from stones worn smooth by the elements. He stepped inside a bottle-shaped funeral monument constructed of flat stones and decorated with rows of diamond-style motifs intermingled with zigzag designs. The workmanship was precise, with refined attention to detail, and the architecture was magnificent. The monument was topped by a narrow, circular dome 10 metres high (33 feet). The entrance was also formed in the shape of a bottle and was a tight fit, allowing only one man to squeeze through at a time. Steps rose from the street to the exterior threshold outside, and then dropped to the floor inside. The interior funeral chamber had a heavy, damp, musty smell that hit like a punch on the nose. Pitt sensed a haunting grandeur and the ghostly presence of the people who performed the final ceremony and closed the crypt for what they thought would be eternity, never envisaging that it would become a shelter for living men not born for another five hundred years.

The stone floor and the burial niches were empty of

funerary objects and swept clean. Curious, smiling faces of carved stone, the size of a serving platter, beamed midway around a corbelled ceiling that stepped up and out from the vertical walls. Hammocks had been strung from sculpted snake heads protruding from the lower walls with wide eyes and open, fanged mouths. Ortiz's workers had also spread straw mats on the floor. Even a small mirror hung from a nail driven into a tight seam between the rows of the masonry.

'I judge it was built about 1380,' said Ortiz. 'A fine example of Chachapoyan architecture. All the comforts of home except a bath. There is, however, a mountain stream about fifty metres to the south. As for your other personal needs, I'm sure you'll make do.'

'Thank you, Dr Ortiz,' said Gunn. 'You're most considerate.'

'Please, it's Alberto,' he replied raising a bushy white eyebrow. 'Dinner at eighteen hundred hours at my place.' He gave Giordino a benevolent stare. 'I believe you know how to find your way about the city.'

'I've taken the tour,' Giordino acknowledged.

An invigorating bath in the icy water of the stream to wash off the day's sweat, a shave, a change into warmer clothes to ward off the cold of the Andes night air, and the men from NUMA trooped through the City of the Dead towards the Peruvian cultural authority's command post. Ortiz greeted them at the entrance and introduced four of his assistants from the National Institute of Culture in Chiclayo, none of whom spoke English.

'A drink before dinner, gentlemen? I have gin, vodka, scotch, and *pisco*, a native white brandy.'

'You came well prepared,' observed Gunn.

Oritz laughed. 'Just because we're working in difficult areas of the country does not mean we can't provide a few creature comforts.'

'I'll try your local brandy,' said Pitt.

Giordino and Gunn were not as adventurous and stuck with scotch on the rocks. After he did the honours, Ortiz gestured for them to sit in old-fashioned canvas lawn chairs.

'How badly were the artifacts damaged during the rocket attack?' asked Pitt, launching the conversation.

'What few objects the looters left behind were badly crushed by falling masonry. Most of it is shattered beyond restoration, I'm afraid.'

'You found nothing worth saving?'

'A thorough job.' Ortiz shook his head sadly. 'Amazing how they worked so fast to excavate the ruins of the temple, remove the salvageable and undamaged antiquities, and escape with a good four tons of the stuff before we could arrive and catch them in the act. What the early Spanish treasure hunters and their sanctimonious missionary padres didn't plunder from the Inca cities and send back to Seville, the damned *huaqueros* have found and sold. They steal antiquities faster than an army of ants can strip a forest.'

'*Huaqueros?*' questioned Gunn.

'The local term for robbers of ancient graves,' explained Giordino.

Pitt stared at him curiously. 'Where did you learn that?'

Giordino shrugged. 'You hang around archaeologists, you're bound to pick up a few expressions.'

'It is hard to entirely fault the *huaqueros*,' said Ortiz. 'The poor farmers of the high country suffer from terrorism, inflation, and corruption that rob them of what little they can take from the earth. The wholesale looting of archaeological sites and the selling of artifacts by these people enable them to purchase a few small comforts to ease their dreadful poverty.'

'Then there is the good with the bad,' observed Gunn.

'Unfortunately, they leave nothing but a few scraps of bone and broken pottery for scientists like me to study. Entire buildings – temples and palaces – are gutted and demolished for their architectural ornamentation, the carvings sold for outrageously low prices. Nothing is spared. The stones from the walls are taken away and used as cheap building materials. Much of the architectural beauty of these ancient cultures has been destroyed and lost forever.'

'I gather it's a family operation,' said Pitt.

'Yes, the search for underground tombs has been carried on from one generation to another for hundreds of years. Fathers, brothers, uncles, and cousins all work together. It has become a custom, a tradition. Entire communities band together to dig for ancient treasures.'

'Tombs being their primary target,' Gunn presumed.

'That is where most of the ancient treasures are hidden. The riches of most ancient empires were buried with their rulers and the wealthy.'

'Big believers in you *can* take it with you,' said Giordino.

'From the Neanderthals to the Egyptians to the Incas,' Ortiz continued, 'they all believed in a continued life in the great beyond. Not reincarnation, mind you. But life as they lived on earth. So they believed in taking their most prized possessions with them into the grave. Many kings and emperors also took along their favourite wives, officials, soldiers, servants, and prized animals as well as treasure. Grave robbing is as old as prostitution.'

'A pity US leaders don't follow in their footsteps,' said Giordino sardonically. 'Just think, when a President dies, he could order that he be buried with the entire Congress and half the bureaucracy.'

Pitt laughed. 'A ritual most American citizens would applaud.'

'Many of my countrymen feel the same about our government,' Ortiz agreed.

Gunn asked, 'How do they locate the graves?'

'The poorer *huaqueros* search with picks and shovels and long metal rods to probe for buried tombs. The well-funded theft and smuggling organizations, on the other hand, use modern, expensive metal detectors and low-level radar instruments.'

'Have you crossed paths with the *Solpemachaco* in the past?' asked Pitt.

'At four other historical sites.' Ortiz spat on the ground. 'I was always too late. They're like a stench with an unknown source. The organization exists, that much is certain. I have seen the tragic results of their pillage. But I have yet to find hard evidence leading to the bastards who make the payoffs to the *huaqueros* and then smuggle our cultural heritage into an international underground market.'

'Your police and security forces can't put a stop to the flow of stolen treasures?' asked Gunn.

'Stopping the *huaqueros* is like trying to catch mercury in your hands,' answered Ortiz. 'The profit is too enormous and there are too many of them. As you have found out for yourselves, any number of our military and government officials can be bought.'

'You have a tough job, Alberto,' Pitt sympathized. 'I don't envy you.'

'And a thankless one,' Ortiz said solemnly. 'To the poor hill people, I am the enemy. And the wealthy families avoid me like the plague because they collect thousands of precious artifacts for themselves.'

'Sounds as if you're in a no-win situation.'

'Quite true. My colleagues from other cultural schools and museums around the country are in a race to discover the great treasure sites, but we always lose to the *huaqueros*.'

'Don't you receive help from your government?' asked Giordino.

'Obtaining funding from the government or private sources for archaeology projects is an uphill battle. A pity, but it seems no one wants to invest in history.'

The conversation drifted to other subjects after one of Ortiz's assistants announced that dinner was ready. Two courses consisted of a pungent beef stew accompanied by bowls of locally grown parched corn and beans. The only touches of more refined dining came from an excellent Peruvian red wine and a fruit salad. Dessert consisted of mangos with syrup.

As they gathered around a warm campfire, Pitt asked Ortiz, 'Do you think Tupac Amaru and his men have totally stripped the City of the Dead, or are there tombs and buildings that are still undiscovered?'

Ortiz suddenly beamed like a strobe light. 'The *huaqueros* and their *Solpemachaco* bosses were here only long enough to loot the obvious, the artifacts easily found on the surface. It will take years to conduct a thorough archaeological excavation of the Pueblo de los Muertos. I fervently believe the bulk of the treasures have yet to be found.'

Now that Ortiz was in a happy mood, his stomach warmed by numerous glasses of white brandy, Pitt circled around from left field. 'Tell me, Alberto, are you an expert on legends dealing with lost Inca treasure after the Spanish came?'

Ortiz lit a long, narrow cigar and puffed until the end turned red and smoke curled into the dank and increasingly cold night air. 'I only know of a few. Tales of lost Inca treasure might not be found in abundant lots if my ancestral cultures had made detailed accounts of their everyday existence. But unlike the Mayans and Aztecs of Mexico, the cultures of Peru did not leave behind an abundance of hicroglyphic symbols. They never devised an alphabet or ideographic system of communication. Except for a scattering of designs on buildings, ceramic pots, and textiles, the records of their lives and legends are few.'

'I was thinking of the lost treasure of Huascar,' said Pitt. 'You've heard of that one?'

'Dr Kelsey recounted it. She described an immense golden chain that sounded a bit farfetched.'

Ortiz nodded. 'That part of the legend happens to be

true. The great Inca king, Huayna Capac, decreed that a huge gold chain be cast in honour of the birth of his son, Huascar. Many years later, after Huascar succeeded his father as king, he ordered the royal treasure to be smuggled from the Inca capital at Cuzco and hidden to keep it out of the hands of his brother Atahualpa, who later usurped the kingdom after a lengthy civil war. The vast hoard, besides the golden chain, included life-size statues, thrones, sun discs, and every insect and animal known to the Incas, all sculpted in gold and silver and set with precious gems.'

'I've never heard of a treasure that grand,' said Gunn.

'The Incas had so much gold they couldn't understand why the Spanish were so fanatical for it. The craze became part of the El Dorado fable. The Spanish died by the thousands searching for the treasure. The Germans and the English, who included Sir Walter Raleigh, all scoured the mountains and jungles, but none ever found it.'

'As I understand it,' said Pitt, 'the chain and the other art treasures were eventually transported to a land beyond the Aztecs and buried.'

Ortiz nodded. 'So the story goes. Whether it was actually taken north by a fleet of ships has never been verified. It was reasonably proven, however, that the hoard was protected by Chachapoyan warriors who formed the royal guard for Inca kings after their confederation was conquered by Huayna Capac in 1480.'

'What is the history of the Chachapoyas?' asked Gunn.

'Their name means Cloud People,' replied Ortiz. 'And their history has yet to be written. Their cities, as you well know from recent experience, are buried in one of the most impenetrable jungles of the world. As of this date, archaeologists have neither the funds nor the means to conduct extensive surveys and excavations on Chachapoyan ruins.'

'So they remain an enigma,' said Pitt.

'In more ways than one. The Chachapoya people,

according to the Incas, were fair-skinned, with blue and green eyes. The women were said to be very beautiful and became highly prized by both the Incas and the Spanish. They were also quite tall. An Italian explorer found a skeleton in a Chachapoyan tomb that was well over two metres.'

Pitt was intrigued. 'Close to seven feet?'

'Easily,' Ortiz answered.

'Any possibility they might have been descendants of early explorers from the Old World, perhaps the Vikings who might have sailed across the Atlantic, up the Amazon, and settled in the Andes?'

'Theories of early transoceanic migration to South America across both the Atlantic and the Pacific have always abounded,' answered Ortiz. 'The fancy term for pre-Columbian travel to and from other continents is *diffusionism*. An interesting concept, not well accepted but not entirely ignored either.'

'Is there evidence?' asked Giordino.

'Mostly circumstantial. Ancient pottery found in Ecuador that has the same designs as the Ainu culture of northern Japan. The Spanish, as well as Columbus, reported seeing white men sailing large ships off Venezuela. The Portuguese found a tribe in Bolivia whose beards were more magnificent than the Europeans', contrary to the fact that most Indians lacked abundant facial hair. Reports of divers and fishermen finding Roman or Grecian amphorae in the waters off Brazil come up routinely.'

'The giant stone heads from the Olmec culture of Mexico show definite features of black Africans,' said Pitt, 'while any number of carved stone faces throughout the Mesoamerican cultures have Oriental characteristics.'

Ortiz nodded in agreement. 'The serpent heads that decorate many of the Mayan pyramids and temples are the spitting image of dragon heads carved in Japan and China.'

'But is there hands-on proof?' asked Gunn.

'No objects that can be conclusively proven as manufactured in Europe have yet been found.'

'The sceptics have a strong case in the lack of pottery lathes or wheeled vehicles,' Gunn added.

'True,' agreed Ortiz. 'The Mayans did adopt the wheel for children's toys but never for practical use. Not surprising when you consider they had no beasts of burden until the Spanish introduced the horse and oxen.'

'But you would think they could have found a purpose for the wheel, say for hauling construction materials,' Gunn persisted.

'History tells us that the Chinese developed the wheelbarrow six hundred years before it found its way to Europe,' Ortiz countered.

Pitt downed the last of his brandy. 'It doesn't seem possible an advanced civilization existed in such a remote region without some kind of outside influence.'

'The people living in the mountains today, descendants of the Chachapoyas, many of them still fair-skinned with blue and green eyes, speak of a godlike man who appeared among their ancestors from the eastern sea many centuries ago. He taught them building principles, the science of the stars, and the ways of religion.'

'He must have forgotten to teach them how to write,' quipped Giordino.

'Another nail in the coffin of pre-Columbian contact,' said Gunn.

'This holy man had thick white hair and a flowing beard,' Ortiz continued. 'He was extremely tall, wore a long white robe, and preached goodness and charity towards all. The rest of the story is too close to that of Jesus to be taken literally – the natives must have introduced events from Christ's life into the ancient story after they were converted to Christianity. He travelled the land, healing the sick, making the blind see again, working all sorts of miracles. He even walked on water. The people raised temples to him and carved his likeness in wood and stone. None of these portraits, I might add, has ever been found. Almost verbatim, the same myth has come down through the ages from the early Mexican cultures in the form of Quetzalcoatl, the ancient god of old Mexico.'

'Do you believe any part of the legend?' asked Pitt.

Ortiz shook his head. 'Not until I excavate something substantial that I can positively authenticate. We may, however, have some answers quite soon. One of your universities in the United States is currently running DNA tests on Chachapoyan remains removed from tombs. If successful, they will be able to confirm whether the Chachapoyas came from Europe or evolved independently.'

'What about Huascar's treasure?' said Pitt, bringing the conversation back on track.

'A discovery that would stun the world,' Ortiz answered. 'I'd like to think the hoard still exists in some forgotten cave in Mexico.' Then he exhaled a cloud of cigar smoke and stared at the evening stars. 'The chain would be a fabulous discovery. But for an archaeologist, the great finds would be the huge solid gold sun disc and the royal golden mummies that vanished along with the chain.'

'Golden mummies,' echoed Gunn. 'Did the Incas preserve their dead like the Egyptians?'

'The preservation process was not nearly as complex as that practised by the Egyptians,' explained Ortiz. 'But the bodies of the supreme rulers, or Sapa Incas as they were called, were encased in gold and became cult objects in the people's religious practices. The mummies of the dead kings lived in their own palaces, were frequently reclothed with fresh wardrobes, served sumptuous feasts, and maintained harems of the most beautiful women. Chosen as attendants, I might add, not to indulge in necrophilia.'

Giordino stared over the shadows of the city. 'Sounds like a waste of taxpayers' money.'

'A large body of priests supervised the upkeep,' Ortiz

continued, 'acquiring a lucrative interest in keeping the dead kings happy. The mummies were often carried around the country in great splendour, as if they were still heads of state. Needless to say, this absurd love affair with the dead caused a great drain on Inca financial resources, helping immeasurably to topple the empire during the Spanish invasion.'

Pitt zipped his leather jacket against the cold and said, 'While on board our ship, Dr Kelsey received a message concerning a stolen suit of gold that was traced to a collector in Chicago.'

Ortiz looked thoughtful and nodded. 'Yes, the Golden Body Suit of Tiapollo. It covered the mummy of a great general called Naymlap who was the right-hand adviser to an early Inca king. Before leaving Lima, I heard that American Customs agents had tracked it down, only to lose it again.'

'Lose it?' For some reason Pitt didn't feel vastly surprised.

'The director of our National Cultural Ministry was about to board a plane to the United States to lay claim to the mummy and the body suit when he was informed that your Customs agents were too late. Thieves made off with it while they had the owner under surveillance.'

'Dr Kelsey said that images engraved on the suit depicted the voyage of the fleet that carried the treasure to Mexico.'

'Only a few of the images were deciphered. Modern scholars never had a chance to study the suit properly before it was stolen from its case in the museum in Seville.'

'It's conceivable,' suggested Pitt, 'that whoever grabbed the suit this time is on the trail of the golden chain.'

'A credible conclusion,' Ortiz agreed.

'Then the thieves have an inside track,' said Giordino.

'Unless someone else discovers the Drake *quipu*,' Pitt said slowly, 'and gets there first.'

'Ah yes, the infamous jade box,' Ortiz sighed sceptically. 'A fanciful tale that has refused to die. So you also know about the legendary rope trick giving directions to the golden chain?'

'You sound dubious,' said Pitt.

'No hardcore evidence. All reports are too flimsy to take seriously.'

'You could write a thick book about the superstitions and legends that were proved to be true.'

'I am a scientist and a pragmatist,' said Ortiz. 'If such a *quipu* exists, I would have to hold it in my own hands, and even then I wouldn't be fully convinced of its authenticity.'

'Would you think me mad if I told you I was going to hunt for it?' asked Pitt.

'No madder than the thousands of men throughout history who have chased over the horizon after a nebulous dream.' Ortiz paused, flicked the ash from his cigar, and then stared heavily at Pitt through sombre eyes. 'Be forewarned. The one who finds it, if it really exists, will be rewarded with success and then doomed to failure.'

Pitt stared back. 'Why doomed to failure?'

'An *amauta*, an educated Inca who could understand the text, and a *quipu-mayoc*, a clerk who recorded on the device, can't help you.'

'What are you telling me?'

'Simply put, Mr Pitt. The last people who could have read and translated the Drake *quipu* for you have been dead for over four hundred years.'

17

In a remote, barren part of the Southwest desert, a few kilometres east of Douglas, Arizona, and only 75 metres (246 feet) from the border between Mexico and the United States, the hacienda *La princesa* loomed like a Moorish castle at an oasis. It was named by the original owner, Don Antonio Diaz, in honour of his wife, Sophia Magdalena, who died during childbirth and was entombed in an ornate, baroque crypt that stood enclosed within a high-walled garden. Diaz, a peon who became a miner, struck it rich and took an immense amount of silver out of the nearby Huachuca Mountains.

The huge feudal estate rested on lands that were originally granted to Diaz by General, later President of Mexico, Antonio Lopez de Santa Ana, for helping to finance the despot's campaigns to subdue Texas and later launch a war against the United States. This was a disaster that Santa Ana compounded by selling the Mesilla Valley in southern Arizona to the United States, a transaction known as the Gadsden Purchase. The border shift left Diaz's hacienda in a new country a stone's throw from the old.

The hacienda was passed down through the Diaz family until 1978, when the last surviving member, Maria Estala, sold it to a rich financier shortly before she died at ninety-four. The new owner, Joseph Zolar, made no mystery of the fact that he acquired the hacienda as a retreat for entertaining celebrities, high government officials, and wealthy business leaders on a lavish scale. Zolar's hacienda quickly became known as the San Simeon of Arizona. His high-profile guests were flown or bused to the estate and his parties were dutifully reported in all the gossip columns and photographed for the slick magazines around the country.

An antiquarian and fanatical art collector, Zolar had amassed a vast accumulation of art objects and antiques, both good and bad. But every piece was certified by experts and government agents as having been legally sold from the country of origin and imported with the proper papers. He paid his taxes, his business dealings were aboveboard, and he never allowed his guests to bring drugs into his home. No scandal had ever stained Joseph Zolar.

He stood on a roof terrace amid a forest of potted plants and watched as a private jet touched down on the estate runway that stretched across the desert floor. The jet was painted a golden tan with a bright purple stripe running along its fuselage. Yellow letters on the stripe read *Zolar International*. He watched as a man casually dressed in a flowered sport shirt and khaki shorts left the aircraft and settled in the seat of a waiting golf cart.

The eyes below Zolar's surgically tightened lids glittered like grey crystal. The pinched, constantly flushed face complemented the thin, receding, brushed-back hair that was as dull red as Mexican saltillo tile. He was somewhere in his late fifties, with a face that was fathomless, a face that had rarely been out of an executive office or a boardroom, a face that was tempered by hard decisions and cold from issuing death warrants when he felt they were required. The body was small but hunched over like a vulture about to take wing. Dressed in a black silk jumpsuit, he wore the indifferent look of a Nazi concentration camp officer who considered death about as interesting as rain.

Zolar waited at the top of the stairs as his guest climbed towards the terrace. They greeted each other warmly and embraced. 'Good to see you in one piece, Cyrus.'

Sarason grinned. 'You don't know how close you came to losing a brother.'

'Come along, I've held lunch for you.' Zolar led Sarason

through the maze of potted plants to a lavishly set table beneath a palapa roof of palm fronds. 'I've selected an excellent chardonnay and my chef has prepared a delicious braised pork loin.'

'Someday I'm going to pirate him away from you,' said Sarason.

'Fat chance.' Zolar laughed. 'I've spoiled him. He enjoys too many perks to jump ship.'

'I envy your lifestyle.'

'And I yours. You've never lost your spirit of adventure. Always skirting death and capture by police in some desert or jungle when you could conduct business out of a luxurious corporate office and delegate the dirty work to others.'

'A nine-to-five existence was never in my blood,' said Sarason. 'I find wallowing in dirty dealings an exciting challenge. You should join me sometime.'

'No, thank you. I prefer the comforts of civilization.'

Sarason noticed a table with what looked like four weathered tree limbs about one metre in length lying across its surface. Intrigued, he walked over and studied them more closely. He recognized them as sun-bleached roots of cottonwood trees that had grown naturally into grotesque human-shaped figures, complete with torsos, arms and legs, and rounded heads. Faces were crudely carved in the heads and painted with childlike features. 'New acquisitions?' he asked.

'Very rare religious ceremonial idols belonging to an obscure tribe of Indians,' answered Zolar.

'How did you come by them?'

'A pair of illegal artifact hunters found them in an ancient stone dwelling they discovered under the over-hang of a cliff.'

'Are they authentic?'

'Yes, indeed.' Zolar took one of the idols and stood it on its feet. 'To the Montolos, who live in the Sonoran Desert near the Colorado River, the idols represent the gods of the sun, moon, earth, and life-giving water. They were carved centuries ago and used in special ceremonies to mark the transition of boys and girls into young adulthood. The rite is full of mysticism and staged every two years. These idols are the very core of the Montolo religion.'

'What do you estimate they're worth?'

'Possibly two hundred thousand dollars to the right collector.'

'That much?'

Zolar nodded. 'Providing the buyer doesn't know about the curse that stalks those who possess them.'

Sarason laughed. 'There is always a curse.'

Zolar shrugged. 'Who can say? I do have it on good authority that the two thieves have suffered a run of bad luck. One was killed in an auto accident and the other has contracted some sort of incurable disease.'

'And you believe that hokum?'

'I only believe in the finer things of life,' said Zolar, taking his brother by the arm. 'Come along. Lunch awaits.'

After the wine was poured by a serving lady, they clinked glasses and Zolar nodded at Sarason. 'So, brother, tell me about Peru.'

It always amused Sarason that their father had insisted on his sons and daughters adopting and legalizing different surnames. As the oldest, only Zolar bore the family name. The far-flung international trade empire that the senior Zolar had amassed before he died was divided equally between his five sons and two daughters. Each had become a corporate executive officer of either an art and antique gallery, an auction house, or an import/export firm. The family's seemingly separate operations were in reality one entity, a jointly owned conglomerate secretly known as the *Solpemachaco*. Unknown and unregistered with any international government financial agencies or stock markets, its managing director was Joseph Zolar in his role as family elder.

'Nothing short of a miracle that I was able to save most of the artifacts and successfully smuggle them out of the country after the blunders committed by our ignorant rabble. Not to mention the intrusion by members of our own government.'

'US Customs or drug agents?' asked Zolar.

'Neither. Two engineers from the National Underwater and Marine Agency. They showed up out of nowhere when Juan Chaco sent out a distress call after Dr Kelsey and her photographer became trapped in the sacred well.'

'How did they cause problems?'

Sarason related the entire story from the murder of the true Dr Miller by Amaru to the escape of Pitt and the others from the Valley of the Viracocha to the death of Juan Chaco. He finished by giving a rough tally of the artifacts he had salvaged from the valley, and how he arranged to have the cache transported to Callao, then smuggled out of Peru in a secret cargo compartment inside an oil tanker owned by a subsidiary of Zolar International. It was one of two such ships used for the express purpose of slipping looted and stolen art in and out of foreign countries while transporting small shipments of crude oil.

Zolar stared into the desert without seeing it. 'The *Aztec Star*. She is scheduled to reach San Francisco in four days.'

'That puts her in brother Charles's sphere of activity.'

'Yes, Charles has arranged for your shipment to be transported to our distribution centre in Galveston where he will see to the restoration of the artifacts.' Zolar held his glass up to be refilled. 'How is the wine?'

'A classic,' answered Sarason, 'but a bit dry for my taste.'

'Perhaps you'd prefer a sauvignon blanc from Touraine. It has a pleasing fruitiness with a scent of herbs.'

'I never acquired your taste for fine wines, brother. I'll settle for a beer.'

Zolar did not have to instruct his serving lady. She

quietly left them and returned in minutes with an iced glass and a bottle of Coors beer.

'A pity about Chaco,' said Zolar. 'He was a loyal associate.'

'I had no choice. He was running scared after the fiasco in the Valley of Viracocha and made subtle threats to unveil the *Solpemachaco*. It would not have been wise to allow him to fall into the hands of the Peruvian Investigative Police.'

'I trust your decisions, as I always have. But there is still Tupac Amaru. What is his situation?'

'He should have died,' replied Sarason. 'Yet when I returned to the temple after the attack of our gun-happy mercenaries, I found him buried under a pile of rubble and still breathing. As soon as the artifacts were cleared out and loaded aboard three additional military helicopters, whose flight crews I was forced to buy off at a premium, I paid the local *huaqueros* to carry him to their village for care. He should be back on his feet in a few days.'

'You might have been wise to remove Amaru too.'

'I considered it. But he knows nothing that could lead international investigators to our doorstep.'

'Would you like another serving of pork?'

'Yes, please.'

'Still, I don't like having a mad dog loose around the house.'

'Not to worry. Oddly, it was Chaco who gave me the idea of keeping Amaru on the payroll.'

'Why, so he can murder little old ladies whenever the mood strikes him?'

'Nothing so ludicrous.' Sarason smiled. 'The man may well prove to be a valuable asset.'

'You mean as a hired killer?'

'I prefer to think of him as someone who eliminates obstacles. Let's face it, brother. I can't continue eliminating our enemies by myself without risk of eventual discovery

211

and capture. The family should consider itself fortunate that I am the only one who has the capacity to kill if necessary. Amaru makes an ideal executioner. He enjoys it.'

'Just be sure you keep him on a strong leash when he's out of his cage.'

'Not to worry,' said Sarason firmly. Then he changed the subject. 'Any buyers in mind for our Chachapoyan merchandise?'

'A drug dealer by the name of Pedro Vincente,' replied Zolar. 'He hungers after anything that's pre-Columbian. He also pays a cash premium since it's a way for him to launder his drug profits.'

'And you take the cash and use it to finance our underground art and artifact operations.'

'An equitable arrangement for all concerned.'

'How soon before you make the sale?'

'I'll set up a meeting with Vincente right after Marta has your shipment cleaned up and ready for display. You should have your share of the profits within ten days.'

Sarason nodded and gazed at the bubbles in his beer. 'I think you see through me, Joseph. I'm seriously considering retiring from the family business while I'm still healthy.'

Zolar looked at him with a shifty grin. 'You do and you'll be throwing away two hundred million dollars.'

'What are you talking about?'

'Your share of the treasure.'

Sarason paused with a forkful of pork in front of his mouth. 'What treasure?'

'You're the last of the family to learn what ultimate prize is within our grasp.'

'I don't follow you.'

'The object that will lead us to Huascar's treasure.' Zolar looked at him slyly for a moment, then smiled. 'We have the Golden Body Suit of Tiapollo.'

The fork dropped to the plate as Sarason stared in total

incredulity. 'You found Naymlap's mummy encased in his suit of gold? It is actually in your hands?'

'Our hands, little brother. One evening, while searching through our father's old business records, I came upon a ledger itemizing his clandestine transactions. It was he who masterminded the mummy's theft from the museum in Spain.'

'The old fox, he never said a word.'

'He considered it the highlight of his plundering career, but too hot a subject to reveal to his own family.'

'How did you track it down?'

'Father recorded the sale to a wealthy Sicilian mafioso. I sent our brother Charles to investigate, not expecting him to learn anything from a trail over seventy years old. Charles found the late mobster's villa and met with the son, who said his father had kept the mummy and its suit hidden away until he died in 1984 at the ripe old age of ninety-seven. The son then sold the mummy on the black market through his relatives in New York. The buyer was a rich junk dealer in Chicago by the name of Rummel.'

'I'm surprised the son spoke to Charles. Mafia families are not noted for revealing their involvement with stolen goods.'

'He not only spoke,' said Zolar, 'but received our brother like a long-lost relative and cooperated wholeheartedly by providing the name of the Chicago purchaser.'

'I underestimated Charles,' Sarason said, finishing off his final morsel of braised pork. 'I wasn't aware of his talent for obtaining information.'

'A cash payment of three million dollars helped immeasurably.'

Sarason frowned. 'A bit generous, weren't we? The suit can't be worth more than half that much to a collector with deep pockets who has to keep it hidden.'

'Not at all. A cheap investment if the engraved images on the suit lead us to Huascar's golden chain.'

'The ultimate prize,' Sarason repeated his brother's

phrase. 'No single treasure in world history can match its value.'

'Dessert?' Zolar asked. 'A slice of chocolate apricot torte?'

'A very small slice and coffee, strong,' answered Sarason. 'How much extra did it cost to buy the suit from the junk dealer?'

Zolar nodded, and again his serving lady silently complied. 'Not a cent. We stole it. As luck would have it, our brother Samuel in New York had sold Rummel most of his collection of illegal pre-Columbian antiquities and knew the location of the concealed gallery that held the suit. He and Charles worked together on the theft.'

'I still can't believe it's in our hands.'

'A near thing too. Charles and Sam barely smuggled it from Rummel's penthouse before Customs agents stormed the place.'

'Do you think they were tipped off?'

Zolar shook his head. 'Not by anyone on our end. Our brothers got away clean.'

'Where did they take it?' asked Sarason.

Zolar smiled, but not with his eyes. 'Nowhere. The mummy is still in the building. They rented an apartment six floors below Rummel and hid it there until we can safely move it to Galveston for a proper examination. Both Rummel and the Customs agents think it was already smuggled out of the building by a moving van.'

'A nice touch. But what happens now? The images engraved in the gold body casing have to be deciphered. Not a simple exercise.'

'I've hired the finest authorities on Inca art to decode and interpret the glyphs. A husband and wife team. He's an anthropologist and she's an archaeologist who excels as a decoding analyst with computers.'

'I should have known you'd cover every base,' said Sarason, stirring his coffee. 'But we'd better hope their version of the text is correct, or we'll be spending a lot of time and money chasing up and down Mexico after ghosts.'

'Time is on our side,' Zolar assured him confidentially. 'Who but us could possibly have a clue to the treasure's burial site?'

18

After a fruitless excursion to the archives of the Library of Congress, where he had hoped to find documentary evidence leading to the *Concepción*'s ultimate fate, Julien Perlmutter sat in the vast reading room. He closed a copy of the diary kept by Francis Drake and later presented to Queen Elizabeth, describing his epic voyage. The diary, lost for centuries, had only recently been discovered in the dusty basement of the royal archives in England.

He leaned his great bulk back in the chair and sighed. The diary added little to what he already knew. Drake had sent the *Concepción* back to England under the command of the *Golden Hind*'s sailing master, Thomas Cuttill. The galleon was never seen again and was presumed lost at sea with all hands.

Beyond that, the only mention of the fate of the *Concepción* was unverified. It came from a book Perlmutter could recall reading on the Amazon River, published in 1939 by journalist/explorer Nicholas Bender, who followed the routes of the early explorers in search of El Dorado. Perlmutter called up the book from the library staff and reexamined it. In the Note section there was a short reference to a 1594 Portuguese survey expedition that had come upon an Englishman living with a tribe of local inhabitants beside the river. The Englishman claimed that he had served under the English sea dog, Francis Drake, who placed him in command of a Spanish treasure galleon that was swept into a jungle by an immense tidal wave. The Portuguese thought the man quite mad and continued on their mission, leaving him in the village where they found him.

Perlmutter made a note of the publisher. Then he signed the Drake diary and Bender's book back to the library staff and caught a taxi home. He felt discouraged, but it was not the first time he had failed to run down a clue to a historical puzzle from the twenty-five million books and forty million manuscripts in the library. The key to unlocking the mystery of the *Concepción*, if there was one, had to be buried somewhere else.

Perlmutter sat in the backseat of the cab and stared out the window at the passing automobiles and buildings without seeing them. He knew from experience that each research project moved at a pace all its own. Some threw out the key answers with a shower of fireworks. Others entangled themselves in an endless maze of dead ends and slowly died without a solution. The *Concepción* enigma was different. It appeared as a shadow that eluded his grip. Did Nicholas Bender quote a genuine source, or did he embellish a myth as so many nonfiction authors were prone to do?

The question was still goading his mind when he walked into the clutter that was his office. A ship's clock on the mantel read three thirty-five in the afternoon. Still plenty of time to make calls before most businesses closed. He settled into a handsome leather swivel chair behind his desk and punched in the number for New York City information. The operator gave him the number of Bender's publishing house almost before he finished asking for it. Then Perlmutter poured a snifter of Napoleon brandy and waited for his call to go through. No doubt one more wasted effort, he thought. Bender was probably dead by now and so was his editor.

'Falkner and Massey,' answered a female voice heavy with the city's distinct accent.

'I'd like to talk to the editor of Nicholas Bender, please.'

'Nicholas Bender?'

'He's one of your authors.'

'I'm sorry, sir, I don't know the name.'

'Mr Bender wrote nonfiction adventure books a long time ago. Perhaps someone who has been on your staff for a number of years might recall him?'

'I'll direct you to Mr Adams, our senior editor. He's been with the company longer than anyone I know.'

'Thank you.'

There was a good thirty-second pause, and then a man answered. 'Frank Adams here.'

'Mr Adams, my name is St Julien Perlmutter.'

'A pleasure, Mr Perlmutter. I've heard of you. You're down in Washington, I believe.'

'Yes, I live in the capital.'

'Keep us in mind should you decide to publish a book on maritime history.'

'I've yet to finish any book I started.' Perlmutter laughed. 'We'll both grow old waiting for a completed manuscript from me.'

'At seventy-four, I'm already old,' said Adams congenially.

'The very reason I rang you,' said Perlmutter. 'Do you recall a Nicholas Bender?'

'I do indeed. He was somewhat of a soldier of fortune in his youth. We've published quite a few of the books he wrote describing his travels in the days before globetrotting was discovered by the middle class.'

'I'm trying to trace the source of a reference he made in a book called *On the Trail of El Dorado*.'

'That's ancient history. We must have published that book back in the early forties.'

'Nineteen thirty-nine to be exact.'

'How can I help you?'

'I was hoping Bender might have donated his notes and manuscripts to a university archive. I'd like to study them.'

'I really don't know what he did with his material,' said Adams. 'I'll have to ask him.'

'He's still alive?' Perlmutter asked in surprise.

'Oh dear me, yes. I had dinner with him not more than three months ago.'

'He must be in his nineties.'

'Nicholas is eighty-four. I believe he was just twenty-five when he wrote *On the Trail of El Dorado*. That was only the second of twenty-six books we published for him. The last was in 1978, a book on hiking in the Yukon.'

'Does Mr Bender still have all his mental faculties?'

'He does indeed. Nicholas is as sharp as an icepick despite his poor health.'

'May I have a number where I can reach him?'

'I doubt whether he'll take any calls from strangers. Since his wife died, Nicholas has become somewhat of a recluse. He lives on a small farm in Vermont, sadly waiting to die.'

'I don't mean to sound heartless,' said Perlmutter. 'But it is most urgent that I speak to him.'

'Since you're a respected authority on maritime lore and a renowned gourmand, I'm sure he wouldn't mind talking to you. But first, let me pave the way just to play safe. What is your number should he wish to call you direct?'

Perlmutter gave Adams the phone number for the line he used only for close friends. 'Thank you, Mr Adams. If I ever do write a manuscript on shipwrecks, you'll be the first editor to read it.'

He hung up, ambled into his kitchen, opened the refrigerator, expertly shucked a dozen Gulf oysters, poured a few drops of Tabasco and sherry vinegar into the open shells, and downed them accompanied by a bottle of Anchor Steam beer. His timing was perfect. He had no sooner polished off the oysters and dropped the empty bottle in a trash compactor when the phone rang.

'Julien Perlmutter here.'

'Hello,' replied a remarkably deep voice. 'This is Nicholas Bender. Frank Adams said you wished to speak to me.'

'Yes, sir, thank you. I didn't expect you to call me so soon.'

'Always delighted to talk to someone who has read my books,' said Bender cheerfully. 'Not many of you left.'

'The book I found of interest was *On the Trail of El Dorado*.'

'Yes, yes, I nearly died ten times during that trek through hell.'

'You made a reference to a Portuguese survey mission that found a crewman of Sir Francis Drake living among the natives along the Amazon River.'

'Thomas Cuttill,' Bender replied without the slightest hesitation. 'I recall including the event in my book, yes.'

'I wonder if you could refer me to the source of your information,' said Perlmutter, his hopes rising with Bender's quick recollection.

'If I may ask, Mr Perlmutter, what exactly is it you are pursuing?'

'I'm researching the history of a Spanish treasure galleon captured by Drake. Most reports put the ship lost at sea on its way back to England. But according to your account of Thomas Cuttill, it was carried into a rain forest on the crest of a tidal wave.'

'That's quite true,' replied Bender. 'I'd have looked for her myself if I had thought there was the slightest chance of finding anything. But the jungle where she disappeared is so thick you'd literally have to stumble and fall on the wreck before you'd see it.'

'You're that positive the Portuguese account of finding Cuttill is not just a fabrication or a myth?'

'It is historical fact. There is no doubt about that.'

'How can you be so sure?'

'I own the source.'

Perlmutter was momentarily confused. 'I'm sorry, Mr Bender. I miss your point.'

'The point is, Mr Perlmutter, I have in my possession the journal of Thomas Cuttill.'

'The hell you say?' Perlmutter blurted.

'Indeed,' Bender answered triumphantly. 'Cuttill gave it to the leader of the Portuguese survey party with the request that it be sent to London. The Portuguese, however, turned it over to the viceroy at Macapa. He included it with dispatches he forwarded to Lisbon, where it passed through any number of hands before ending up in an antique bookstore, where I bought it for the equivalent of thirty-six dollars. That was a lot of money back in 1937, at least to a lad of twenty-three who was wandering the globe on a shoestring.'

'The journal must be worth considerably more than thirty-six dollars today.'

'I'm sure of it. A dealer once offered me ten thousand for it.'

'You turned him down?'

'I've never sold mementoes of my journeys so someone else could profit.'

'May I fly up to Vermont and read the journal?' asked Perlmutter cautiously.

'I'm afraid not.'

Perlmutter paused as he wondered how to persuade Bender to allow him to examine Cuttill's journal. 'May I ask why?'

'I'm a sick old man,' Bender replied, 'whose heart refuses to stop.'

'You certainly don't sound ill.'

'You should see me. The diseases I picked up during my travels have returned to ravage what's left of my body. I am not a pretty sight, so I rarely entertain visitors. But I'll tell you what I'll do, Mr Perlmutter. I'll send you the book as a gift.'

'My God, sir, you don't have to – '

'No, no, I insist. Frank Adams told me about your magnificent library on ships. I'd rather someone like you, who can appreciate the journal, possess it rather than a collector who simply puts it on a shelf to impress his friends.'

'That's very kind of you,' said Perlmutter sincerely. 'I'm truly grateful for your kind generosity.'

'Take it and enjoy,' Bender said graciously. 'I assume you'd like to study the journal as soon as possible.'

'I don't want to inconvenience you.'

'Not at all, I'll send it Federal Express so you'll have it in your hands first thing tomorrow.'

'Thank you, Mr Bender. Thank you very much. I'll treat the journal with every bit of the respect it deserves.'

'Good. I hope you find what you're looking for.'

'So do I,' said Perlmutter, his confidence soaring over the breakthrough. 'Believe me, so do I.'

At twenty minutes after ten o'clock the next morning, Perlmutter threw open the door before the Federal Express driver could punch the doorbell button. 'You must be expecting this, Mr Perlmutter,' said the young black-haired man, wearing glasses and a friendly smile.

'Like a child waiting for Santa,' Perlmutter laughed, signing for the reinforced envelope.

He hurried into his study, pulling the tab and opening the envelope as he walked. He sat at his desk, slipped on his glasses, and held the journal of Thomas Cuttill in his hands as if it were the Holy Grail. The cover was the skin of some unidentifiable animal and the pages were yellowed parchment in a state of excellent preservation. The ink was brown, probably a concoction Cuttill had managed to brew from the root of some tree. There were no more than twenty pages. The entries were written in the quaint Elizabethan prose of the day. The handwriting seemed laboured, with any number of misspellings, indicating a man who was reasonably well educated for the times. The first entry was dated March 1578, but was written much later:

Mine strange historie of the passte sexteen yeares, by Thomas Cuttill, formerly of Devonshire.

It was the account of a shipwrecked sailor, cast away after barely surviving the sea's violent fury, only to endure incredible hardships in a savage land in his unsuccessful attempt to return home. As he read the passages, beginning with Cuttill's departure from England with Drake, Perlmutter noted that it was written in a more honest style than narratives of later centuries, which were littered with sermons, romantic exaggerations, and clichés. Cuttill's persistence, his will to survive, and his ingenuity in overcoming terrible obstacles without once begging for the help of God made a profound impression on Perlmutter. Cuttill was a man he would like to have known.

After finding himself the only survivor on the galleon after the tidal wave carried it far inland, Cuttill chose the unknown horrors of the mountains and jungle rather than capture and torture by the avenging Spanish, who were mad as wasps at the audacious capture of their treasure galleon by the hated Englishman, Drake. All Cuttill knew was that the Atlantic Ocean lay somewhere far to the east. How far, he could not even guess. Reaching the sea, and then somehow finding a friendly ship that might carry him back to England would be nothing short of a miracle. But it was the only path open to him.

On the western slopes of the Andes the Spanish had already created colonies of large estates, now worked by the once-proud Incas, who were enslaved and greatly reduced in numbers by inhumane treatment and infection from measles and smallpox. Cuttill crept through the estates under cover of darkness, stealing food at every opportunity. After two months of travelling a few short kilometres each night to elude the Spanish and remain out of sight of any Indians who might give him away, he crossed over the continental divide of the Andes, through the isolated valleys, and descended into the green hell of the Amazon River Basin .

From that point on, Cuttill's life became even more of a

nightmare. He struggled through unending swamps up to his waist, fought his way through forests so thick every metre of growth had to be cut away with his knife. Swarms of insects, snakes, and alligators were a constant peril, the snakes often attacking without warning. He suffered from dysentery and fever but still struggled on, often covering only 100 metres (328 feet) during daylight. After several months, he stumbled into a village of hostile natives, who immediately tied him with ropes and kept him imprisoned as a slave for five years.

Cuttill finally managed to escape by stealing a dugout canoe and paddling down the Amazon River at night under a waning moon. Contracting malaria, he came within an inch of dying, but as he drifted unconscious in his canoe he was found by a tribe of long-haired women who nursed him back to health. It was the same tribe of women the Spanish explorer Francisco de Orellana had discovered during his futile search for El Dorado. He named the river Amazonas in honour of the Amazon warriors of Greek legend because the native women could draw a bow with any man.

Cuttill introduced a number of labour-saving devices to the women and the few men who lived with them. He built a potter's wheel and taught them how to make huge intricate bowls and water vessels. He constructed wheelbarrows and waterwheels for irrigation, and showed them how to use pulleys to lift heavy weights. Soon looked upon as a god, Cuttill made an enjoyable life among the tribe. He took three of the most attractive women as wives and quickly produced several children.

His desire to see home again slowly dimmed. A bachelor when he left England, he was sure there would be no relatives or old shipmates left to greet his return. And then there was the possibility that Drake, a stern disciplinarian, would demand punishment for losing the *Concepción*.

No longer physically capable of suffering the deprivations and hardships of a long journey, Cuttill reluctantly decided to spend the remaining years of his life on the banks of the Amazon. When the Portuguese survey party passed through, he gave them his journal, requesting that it be somehow sent to England and placed in the hands of Francis Drake.

After Perlmutter finished reading the journal, he leaned back in his swivel chair, removed his glasses and rubbed his eyes. Any doubts he might have had in the back of his mind about the authenticity of the journal had quickly evaporated. The writing on the parchment showed strong, bold strokes, hardly the work of a madman who was sick and dying. Cuttill's descriptions did not seem fabricated or embellished. Perlmutter felt certain the experiences and hardships suffered by Francis Drake's sailing master truly occurred, and that the account was honestly set down by someone who lived what he wrote.

Perlmutter went back to the heart of his quest, Cuttill's brief mention of the treasures left on board the *Concepción* by Drake. He resettled his glasses on his imposing red nose and turned to the final entry of the narrative:

Me mind is as set as a stout ship before a narth winde. I shalle not retarn to mye homelande. I feare Captaan Drake was maddened for me not bringen the achant tresures and the jaade boxe withe the notted stringe to England soos it cud be preezentid to guude Queen Bess. I left it withe the wraaked ship. I shalle be baryed heer among the peapol who have becume my famly. Writen bye the hande of Thomas Cuttill, sailing mastere of the Golden Hinde *this unknown day in the yeare 1594*

Perlmutter slowly looked up and stared at a seventeenth-century Spanish painting on his wall, depicting a fleet of Spanish galleons sailing across a sea under the golden orange glow of a setting sun. He had found it in a bazaar in Segovia and took it home for a tenth of its real value. He gently closed the fragile journal, lifted his bulk from the chair and began to pace around the room, hands clasped behind his back.

A crewman of Francis Drake *had* truly lived and died somewhere along the Amazon River. A Spanish galleon was thrown into a coastal jungle by an immense tidal wave. And a jade box containing a knotted cord *did* exist at one time. Could it still lie amid the rotting timbers of the galleon, buried deep in a rain forest? A four-hundred-year-old mystery had suddenly surfaced from the shadows of time and revealed an enticing clue. Perlmutter was pleased with his successful investigative effort, but he well knew that confirmation of the myth was merely the first enticing step in a hunt for treasure.

The next trick, and the most perplexing one, was to narrow the theatre of search to as small a stage as possible.

19

Hiram Yaeger adored his big supercomputer as much as he did his wife and children, perhaps more; he could seldom tear himself away from the images he projected on his giant monitor to go home to his family. Computers were his life from the first time he looked at the screen on a monitor and typed out a command. The love affair never cooled. If anything it grew more passionate with the passing years, especially after he constructed a monster unit of his own design for NUMA's vast oceans data centre. The incredible display of information-gathering power at his beck and call never ceased to astound him. He caressed the keyboard with his fingers as though it were a living entity, his excitement blossoming whenever bits and pieces of data began coming together to form a solution.

Yaeger was hooked into a vast high-speed computing network with the capacity to transfer enormous amounts of digital data between libraries, newspaper morgues, research laboratories, universities, and historic archives anywhere in the world. The 'data superhighway,' as it was called, could transmit billions of bits of information in the blink of a cursor. By tapping into the gigabit network, Yaeger began retrieving and assembling enough data to enable him to lay out a search grid with a 60 per cent probability factor of containing the four-century-old land-locked galleon.

He was so deeply involved with the search for the *Nuestra Señora de la Concepción* that he did not notice nor hear Admiral James Sandecker step into his sanctum sanctorum and sit down in a chair behind him.

The founder and first director of NUMA was small in

stature but filled with enough testosterone to fuel the offensive line of the Dallas Cowboys. A trim fifty-eight, and a fitness addict, he ran five miles every morning from his apartment to the imposing glass building that housed two of the five thousand engineers, scientists, and other employees that formed NUMA, the undersea counterpart of the space agency NASA. His head was covered by straight flaming red hair, greying at the temples and parted in the middle, while his chin bristled with a magnificent Vandyke beard. Despite his addiction to health and nutrition, he was never without a huge cigar made from tobacco personally selected and rolled for him by the owner of a plantation in Jamaica.

Under his direction NUMA had taken the field of oceanography and made it as popular as space science. His persuasive pleas to Congress for funding, supported by twenty top universities with schools in the marine sciences and a host of large corporations investing in underwater projects, had enabled NUMA to take great strides in deep sea geology and mining, marine archaeology, biological studies of sea life, and studies of the effects of oceans on the earth's climate. One of his greatest contributions, perhaps, was supporting Hiram Yaeger's huge computer network, the finest and largest archive of ocean sciences in the world.

Sandecker was not universally admired by all of Washington's bureaucracy, but he was respected as a hard-driving, dedicated, and honest man, and his relationship with the man in the Oval Office of the White House was warm and friendly.

'Making any progress?' he asked Yaeger.

'Sorry, Admiral.' Yaeger spoke without turning around. 'I didn't see you come in. I was in the midst of collecting data on the water currents off Ecuador.'

'Don't stroke me, Hiram,' Sandecker said, with the look of a ferret on a hunt. 'I know what you're up to.'

'Sir?'

'You're searching for a stretch of coastline where a tidal wave struck in 1578.'

'A tidal wave?'

'Yes, you know, a big wall of water that barrelled in from the sea and carried a Spanish galleon over a beach and into a jungle.' The admiral puffed out a cloud of noxious smoke and went on. 'I wasn't aware that I had authorized a treasure hunt on NUMA's time and budget.'

Yaeger paused and swivelled around in his chair. 'You know?'

'The word is *knew*. Right from the beginning.'

'Do you know what you are, Admiral?'

'A canny old bastard who can read minds,' he said with some satisfaction.

'Did your Ouija board also tell you the tidal wave and the galleon are little more than folklore?'

'If anyone can smell fact from fiction, it's our friend Dirk Pitt,' Sandecker said inflexibly. 'Now what have you dug up?'

Yaeger smiled wanly and answered. 'I began by dipping into various Geographic Information Systems to determine a logical site for a ship to remain hidden in a jungle over four centuries somewhere between Lima and Panama City. Thanks to global positioning satellites, we can look at details of Central and South America that were never mapped before. Maps showing tropical rain forests that grow along the coastline were studied first. I quickly dismissed Peru because its coastal regions are deserts with little or no vegetation. That still left over a thousand kilometres of forested shore along northern Ecuador and almost all of Colombia. Again, I was able to eliminate about forty per cent of the coastline with geology too steep or unfavourable for a wave with enough mass and momentum to carry a five-hundred-and-seventy-ton ship any distance overland. Then I knocked off another twenty per cent for open grassland areas without thick trees or other foliage that could hide the remains of a ship.'

'That still leaves Pitt with a search area four hundred kilometres in length.'

'Nature can drastically alter the environment in five hundred years,' said Yaeger. 'By starting with antique maps drawn by the early Spaniards, and examining records of changes that occurred in the geology and landscape, I was able to decrease the length of the search grid another hundred and fifty kilometres.'

'How did you compare the modern terrain with the old?'

'With three-dimensional overlays,' replied Yaeger. 'By either reducing or increasing the scale of the old charts to match the latest satellite maps, and then overlaying one upon the other, any variations of the coastal jungles since the galleon vanished became readily apparent. I found that much of the heavily forested coastal jungles had been cut down over the centuries for farmland.'

'Not enough,' Sandecker said irritably, 'not nearly enough. You'll have to whittle the grid down to no more than twenty kilometres if you want to give Pitt a fighting chance of finding the wreck.'

'Bear with me, Admiral,' said Yaeger patiently. 'The next step was to conduct a search through historical archives for recorded tidal waves that struck the Pacific coastline of South America in the sixteenth century. Fortunately, the occasions were well documented by the Spanish during the conquest. I found four. Two in Chile in 1562 and 1575. Peru suffered them in 1570 and again in 1578, the year Drake captured the galleon.'

'Where did the latter strike?' Sandecker asked.

'The only account comes from the log of a Spanish supply ship on its way to Callao. It passed over a "crazy sea" that swept inland towards Bahía de Caráquez in Ecuador. Bahia, of course, means *bay*.'

' "Crazy sea" is a good description of water turmoil above an earthquake on the seafloor. No doubt a seismic wave generated by a movement of the fault that parallels the west coast of the entire South American continent.'

'The captain also noted that on the return voyage, a village that sat at the mouth of a river running into the bay had vanished.'

'There is no question of the date?'

'Right on the money. The tropical rain forest to the east appears to be impenetrable.'

'Okay, we have a ballpark. The next question is, what was the wave length?'

'A tidal wave, or tsunami, can have a length of two hundred kilometres or more,' said Yaeger.

Sandecker considered this. 'How wide is the Bay of Caráquez?'

Yaeger called up a map on his monitor. 'The entrance is narrow, no more than four or five kilometres.'

'And you say the captain of the supply ship logged a missing village by a river?'

'Yes, sir, that was his description.'

'How does the contour of the bay today differ from that period?'

'The outer bay has changed very little,' answered Yaeger, after bringing up a program that depicted the old Spanish charts and the satellite map in different colours as he overlaid them on the screen. 'The inner bay has moved about a kilometre towards the sea due to silt buildup from the Chone River.'

Sandecker stared at the screen for a long moment, then said slowly, 'Can your electronic contraption do a simulation of the tidal wave sweeping the galleon on to shore?'

Yaeger nodded. 'Yes, but there are a number of factors to consider.'

'Such as?'

'What was the height of the wave and how fast was it travelling.'

'It would have to be at least thirty metres high and travelling at better than a hundred and fifty kilometres an hour to carry a five-hundred-and-seventy-ton ship so far into the jungle that she has never been found.'

'Okay, let's see what I can do with digital imagery.'

Yaeger typed a series of commands on his keyboard and sat back, staring at the monitor for several seconds, examining the image he produced on the screen. Then he used a special function control to fine-tune the graphics until he could generate a realistic and dramatic simulation of a tidal wave crossing an imaginary shoreline. 'There you have it,' he announced. 'Virtual reality configuration.'

'Now generate a ship,' ordered Sandecker.

Yaeger was not an expert on the construction of sixteenth-century galleons, but he produced a respectable image of one rolling slowly on the waves that was equal to a projector displaying moving graphics at sixty frames per second. The galleon appeared so realistic any unsuspecting soul who walked into the room would have thought they were watching a movie.

'How does it look, Admiral?'

'Hard to believe a machine can create something so lifelike,' said Sandecker, visibly impressed.

'You should see the latest computer-generated movies featuring the long-gone old stars with the new. I've watched the video of *Arizona Sunset* at least a dozen times.'

'Who plays the leads?'

'Humphrey Bogart, Lionel Barrymore, Marilyn Monroe, Julia Roberts, and Tom Cruise. It's so real, you'd swear they all acted together on the set.'

Sandecker laid his hand on Yaeger's shoulder. 'Let's see if you can make a reasonably accurate documentary.'

Yaeger did his magic on the computer, and the two men watched, fascinated, as the monitor displayed a sea so blue and distinct it was like looking through a window at the real thing. Then slowly, the water began convulsing into a wave that rolled away from the land, stranding the galleon on the seabed, as dry as if it were a toy boat on the blanket of a boy's bed. Then the computer visualized the wave rushing back towards shore, rising higher and higher, then cresting and engulfing the ship under a rolling mass of froth, sand, and water, hurling it towards land at an incredible speed, until finally the ship stopped and settled as the wave smoothed out and died.

'Five kilometres,' murmured Yaeger. 'She looks to be approximately five kilometres from the coast.'

'No wonder she was lost and forgotten,' said Sandecker. 'I suggest you contact Pitt and make arrangements to fax your computer's grid coordinates.'

Yaeger gave Sandecker a queer look indeed. 'Are you authorizing the search, Admiral?'

Sandecker feigned a look of surprise as he rose and walked towards the door. Just before exiting, he turned and grinned impishly 'I can't very well authorize what could turn out to be a wild goose chase, now can I?'

'You think that's what we're looking at, a wild goose chase?'

Sandecker shrugged. 'You've done your magic. If the ship truly rests in a jungle and not on the bottom of the sea, then the burden falls on Pitt and Giordino to go in that hell on earth and find her.'

20

Giordino contemplated the dried red stain on the stone floor of the temple. 'No sign of Amaru in the rubble,' he said with an utter lack of emotion.

'I wonder how far he got?' Miles Rodgers asked no one in particular. He and Shannon had arrived from the sacred well an hour before noon on a helicopter piloted by Giordino.

'His mercenary buddies must have carried him off,' Pitt surmised.

'Knowing a sadist like Amaru might still be alive,' said Rodgers, 'is enough to cause nightmares.'

Giordino gave a mechanical shrug. 'Even if he survived the rocket attack, he'd have died from loss of blood.'

Pitt turned and stared at Shannon, who was directing a team of archaeologists and a small army of workers. They were numbering the shattered blocks of stone from the temple in preparation for a restoration project. She seemed to have discovered something in the debris and was bending down for a closer examination. 'A man like Amaru doesn't die easily. I don't think we've heard the last of him.'

'A grim prospect,' said Rodgers, 'made worse by the latest news from Lima.'

Pitt raised an eyebrow. 'I didn't know we received CNN this deep in the Andes.'

'We do now. The helicopter that landed about an hour ago belonged to the Peruvian News Bureau. It brought in a team of television reporters and a mountain of equipment. The City of the Dead has become international news.'

'So what did they have to report?' pressed Giordino.

'The military and police have admitted their failure to capture the army renegade mercenaries who flew into the valley to slit our throats and remove the artifacts. Nor have investigators tracked down any of Amaru's grave looters.'

Pitt smiled at Rodgers. 'Not exactly the sort of report that will look good on their résumés.'

'The government tried to save face by handing out a story that the thieves dumped the artifacts over the mountains and are now hiding out in the Amazon forests of Brazil.'

'Never happened,' said Pitt. 'Otherwise why would US Customs insist we provide them with an inventory of the artifacts? They know better. No, the loot is not scattered on a mountaintop. If I read the brains behind the *Solpe-machaco* correctly, they're not the kind to panic and run. Their informants in the military alerted them every step of the way, from the minute an assault force was assembled and launched to capture them. They would have also learned the flight plan of the assault transports, and then plotted a safe route to avoid them. After quickly loading the artifacts, they flew to a prearranged rendezvous at an airstrip or seaport where the stolen riches were either transferred aboard a jetliner or a cargo ship. I doubt whether Peru will ever see its historical treasures again.'

'A nice tight scenario,' said Rodgers thoughtfully. 'But aren't you forgetting the bad guys only had one helicopter after we stole their backup?'

'And we knocked that one into a mountain,' added Giordino.

'I think if we knew the full truth, the gang of second-rate killers ordered in by the boss who impersonated Doc Miller was followed later by a couple of heavy-lift helicopter transports, probably the old model Boeing Chinooks that were sold around the world. They can lift almost fifty troops or twenty tons of cargo. Enough mercenaries were left on the ground to stow the artifacts. They made their getaway in plenty of time after our escape and before we alerted the Peruvian government, who took their time in mounting an aerial posse.'

Rodgers stared at Pitt with renewed admiration. Only Giordino was not impressed. He knew from long years of experience that Pitt was one of that rare breed who could stand back and analyse events as they occurred, down to the finest details. It was a gift with which few men and women are born. Just as the greatest mathematicians and physicists compute incredibly intricate formulas on a level incomprehensible to people with no head for figures, so Pitt operated on a deductive level incomprehensible to all but a few of the top criminal investigators in the world. Giordino often found it maddening that while he was attempting to explain something to Pitt, the mesmeric green eyes would focus on some unseen object in the distance and he would know that Pitt was concentrating on something.

While Rodgers was pondering Pitt's reconstruction of events, trying to find a flaw, the big man from NUMA turned his attention to Shannon.

She was on her hands and knees on the temple floor with a soft-bristled paintbrush, gently clearing away dust and tiny bits of rubble from a burial garment. The textile was woven from wool and adorned with multicoloured embroidery in the design of a laughing monkey with hideous, grinning teeth and coiled snakes for arms and legs.

'What the well-dressed Chachapoyan wore?' he asked.

'No, it's Inca.' Shannon did not turn and look up at him but remained absorbed in her work.

'They did beautiful work,' Pitt observed.

'The Inca and their ancestors were the finest dyers and weavers in the world. Their fabric weaving techniques are too complicated and time-consuming to be copied today. They are still unrivalled in interlocking tapestry construction. The finest tapestry weavers of Renaissance Europe used eighty-five threads per inch. The early Peruvians used up to five hundred threads per inch. Small wonder the Spanish mistakenly thought the finer Inca textiles were silk.'

'Maybe this isn't a good time for pursuing the arts, but I thought you'd like to know that Al and I have finished sketching the artifacts we caught sight of before the roof fell in.'

'Give them to Dr Ortiz. He's most interested in what was stolen.'

Then lost in her project, she turned back to the excavation.

An hour later, Gunn found Pitt standing beside Ortiz, who was directing several workers in scraping vegetation from a large sculpture of what appeared to be a winged jaguar with a serpent's head. The menacing jaws were spread wide, revealing a set of frightening curved fangs. The massive body and wings were sculpted into the doorway of a huge burial house. The only entrance was the gaping mouth, which was large enough for a man to crawl into. From the feet to the tip of the raised wings, the stone beast stood over 6 metres high (20 feet).

'Not something you'd want to meet some night in a dark alley,' said Gunn.

Dr Ortiz turned and waved a greeting. 'The largest Chachapoyan sculpture yet found. I judge it dates somewhere between A.D. 1200 and 1300.

'Does it have a name?' asked Pitt.

'*Demonio del Muertos,*' answered Ortiz. 'The demon of the dead, a Chachapoyan god who was the focus of a protective rite connected with the cult of the underworld. Part jaguar, part condor, part snake, he sank his fangs into whoever disturbed the dead and then dragged them into the black depths of the earth.'

'He wasn't exactly pretty,' said Gunn.

'The demon wasn't meant to be. Effigies ranged in size

from one like this to those no larger than a human hand, depending on the deceased's wealth and status. I imagine we'll find them in almost every tomb and grave in the valley.'

'Wasn't the god of the ancient Mexicans some kind of serpent?' asked Gunn.

'Yes, Quetzalcoatl, a feathered serpent who was the most important deity of Mesoamerica, beginning with the Olmecs in 900 B.C. and ending with the Aztecs during the Spanish conquest. The Inca also had sculptures of serpents, but no direct connection has yet been made.'

Ortiz turned away as a labourer motioned for him to examine a small figurine he had excavated next to the sculpture. Gunn took Pitt by the arm and led him over to a low stone wall where they sat down.

'A courier from the US Embassy flew in from Lima on the last supply copter,' he said, removing a folder from his briefcase, 'and dropped off a packet that was faxed from Washington.'

'From Yaeger?' Pitt asked anxiously.

'Both Yaeger and your friend Perlmutter.'

'Did they strike pay dirt?'

'Read for yourself,' said Gunn. 'Julien Perlmutter found an account by a survivor of the galleon being swept into the jungle by a tidal wave.'

'So far so good.'

'It gets better. The account mentions a jade box containing knotted cords. Apparently the box still rests in the rotting timbers of the galleon.'

Pitt's eyes lit up like beacons. 'The Drake *quipu*.'

'It appears the myth has substance,' Gunn said with a broad smile.

'And Yaeger?' Pitt asked as he began sifting through the papers.

'His computer analysed the existing data and came up with grid coordinates that put the galleon within a ten-square-kilometre ballpark.'

'Far smaller than I expected.'

'I'd say our prospects of finding the galleon and the jade box just improved by a good fifty per cent.'

'Make that thirty per cent,' said Pitt, holding up a sheet from Perlmutter giving the known data on the construction, fittings, and cargo of the *Nuestra Señora de la Concepción*. 'Except for four anchors that were probably carried away during the impact of the tidal wave, the magnetic signature of any iron on board would be too faint to be detected by a magnetometer more than a stone's throw away.'

'An EG&G Geometrics G-813G could pick up a small iron mass from a fair distance.'

'You're reading my thoughts. Frank Stewart has a unit on board the *Deep Fathom*.'

'We'll need a helicopter to tow the sensor over the top of the rain forest,' said Gunn.

'That's your department,' Pitt said to him. 'Who do you know in Ecuador?'

Gunn thought a moment, and then his lips creased in a grin. 'It just so happens the managing director of the Corporación Estatal Petrolera Ecuatoriana, the state oil company, is indebted to NUMA for steering his company on to significant deposits of natural gas in the Gulf of Guayaquil.'

'Then they owe us big, enough to lend us a bird.'

'You could safely say that, yes.'

'How much time will you need to put the bite on them?'

Gunn held up his wrist and peered through his glasses at the dial of his trusty old Timex. 'Give me twenty minutes to call and make a deal. Afterward, I'll inform Stewart that we'll drop in and pick up the magnetometer. Then I'll contact Yaeger and reconfirm his data.'

Pitt stared blankly at him. 'Washington isn't exactly around the corner. Are you making conference calls with smoke signals or mirrors?'

Gunn reached into his pocket and held up what looked

like a small, portable telephone. 'The Iridium, built by Motorola. Digital, wireless, you can call anywhere in the world with it.'

'I'm familiar with the system,' Pitt acknowledged. 'Works off a satellite enhancement network. Where did you steal a unit?'

Gunn glanced furtively around the ruins. 'Bite your tongue. This is merely a temporary appropriation from the Peruvian television crew.'

Pitt gazed fondly at his little bespectacled friend with deep admiration and wonder. It was a rare event when shy Gunn slipped out of his academic shell to perform a sneaky deed. 'You're okay, Rudi, I don't care what the celebrity gossip columns say about you.'

In terms of artifacts and treasures, the looters had barely scratched the surface in the City of the Dead. They had concentrated on the royal tombs near the temple, but thanks to Pitt's intrusion, they did not have time to do extensive excavation on most of the surrounding tombs. Many of them contained the remains of high officials of the Chachapoya confederation. Ortiz and his team of archaeologists also found what appeared to be untouched burial houses of eight noblemen. Ortiz was overjoyed when he discovered the royal coffins were in pristine condition and had never been opened.

'We will need ten years, maybe twenty, to conduct a full excavation of the valley,' said Ortiz during the customary after-dinner conversation. 'No discovery in the Americas can touch this one for the sheer number of antiquities. We have to go slow. Not even the seed of a flower or one bead of a necklace can be overlooked. We must miss nothing, because we have an unparalleled opportunity to gain a new understanding of the Chachapoyan culture.'

'You have your work cut out for you,' said Pitt. 'I only hope none of the Chachapoya treasures are stolen during shipment to your national museum.'

'Any loss between here and Lima is the least of my worries,' replied Ortiz. 'Almost as many artifacts are stolen from our museums as from the original tombs.'

'Don't you have tight security to protect your country's valuable objects?' asked Rodgers.

'Of course, but professional art thieves are very shrewd. They often switch a genuine artifact with a skilfully done forgery. Months, sometimes years, can go by before the crime is discovered.'

'Only three weeks ago,' said Shannon, 'the National Heritage Museum in Guatemala reported the theft of pre-Columbian Mayan art objects with an estimated value of eight million dollars. The thieves were dressed as guards and carried off the treasures during viewing hours as if they were simply moving them from one wing to another. No one thought to question them.'

'My favourite,' said Ortiz without smiling, 'was the theft of forty-five twelfth-century Shang dynasty drinking vessels from a museum in Beijing. The thieves carefully disassembled the glass cases and rearranged the remaining pieces to create the illusion that nothing was missing. Three months passed before the curator noticed the pieces were missing and realized they'd been stolen.'

Gunn held up his glasses and checked for smudges. 'I had no idea art theft was such a widespread crime.'

Ortiz nodded. 'In Peru, major art and antiquity collections are stolen as often as banks are robbed. What is even more tragic is that the thieves are getting bolder. They have no hesitation in kidnapping a collector for ransom. The ransom is, of course, his art objects. In many cases, they simply murder a collector before looting his house.'

'You were lucky only a fraction of the art treasures were plundered from the City of the Dead before the looters were stopped,' said Pitt.

'Lucky indeed. But tragically the choice items have already made their way out of the country.'

'A wonder the city wasn't discovered by the *huaqueros*

long before now,' said Shannon, deliberately avoiding any eye contact with Pitt.

'Pueblo de los Muertos sits in this isolated valley ninety kilometres from the nearest village,' replied Ortiz. 'Travelling in here is a major ordeal, especially by foot. The native population had no reason to struggle seven or eight days through a jungle to search for something they thought existed only in legends from their dim past. When Hiram Bingham discovered Machu Picchu on a mountaintop the local inhabitants had never ventured there. And though it would not deter a hardened *huaquero*, descendants of the Chachapoya still believe that all ruins across the mountains in the great forests to the east are protected by a demon god like the one we found this afternoon. They're deathly afraid to go near them.'

Shannon nodded. 'Many still swear that anyone who finds and enters the City of the Dead will be turned to stone.'

'Ah yes,' Giordino murmured, 'the old, cursed be you who disturb my bones, routine.'

'Since none of us feels any stiffening of the joints,' said Ortiz jovially, 'I must assume the evil spirits that frequent the ruins have lost their spell.'

'Too bad it didn't work against Amaru and his looters,' said Pitt.

Rodgers moved behind Shannon and placed a possessive hand on the nape of her neck. 'I understand you're all bidding us goodbye in the morning.'

Shannon looked surprised and made no attempt to remove Rodgers' hand. 'Is that true?' she said looking at Pitt. 'You're leaving?'

Gunn answered before Pitt. 'Yes, we're flying back to our ship before heading north into Ecuador.'

'You're not going to search in Equador for the galleon we discussed on the *Deep Fathom*?' Shannon asked.

'Can you think of a better place?'

'Why Ecuador?' she persisted.

'Al enjoys the climate,' Pitt said, clapping Giordino on the back.

Giordino nodded. 'I hear the girls are pretty and wild with lust.'

Shannon stared at Pitt with a look of interest. 'And you?'

'Me?' Pitt murmured innocently. 'I'm going for the fishing.'

21

'You sure can pick 'em,' said FBI Chief of Interstate Stolen Art, Francis Ragsdale, as he eased into the vinyl seat of a booth in a nineteen-fifties-style chrome diner. He studied the selections on the coin-operated music unit that was wired to a Wurlitzer jukebox. 'Stan Kenton, Charlie Barnett, Stan Getz. Who ever heard of these guys?'

'Only people who appreciate good music,' Gaskill replied sourly to the younger man. He settled his bulk, which filled two-thirds of the seat on his side of the booth.

Ragsdale shrugged. 'Before my time.' To him, at thirty-four, the great musicians of an earlier era were only vague names mentioned occasionally by his parents. 'Come here often?'

Gaskill nodded. 'The food really sticks to your ribs.'

'Hardly an epicurean recommendation.' Clean-shaven, with black wavy hair and a reasonably well-exercised body, Ragsdale had the handsome face, pleasant grey eyes, and bland expression of a soap opera actor automatically reacting to his counterpart's dialogue. A good investigator, he took his job seriously, maintaining the image of the bureau by dressing in a dark business suit that gave him the appearance of a successful Wall Street broker.

With a professional eye for detail, he examined the linoleum floor, the round stools at the counter, the period napkin holders and art deco salt and pepper shakers that were parked beside a bottle of Heinz ketchup and a jar of French's mustard. His expression reflected urbane distaste. He would unquestionably have preferred a more trendy restaurant in midtown Chicago.

'Quaint place. Hermetically sealed within the Twilight Zone.'

'Atmosphere is half the enjoyment,' said Gaskill resignedly.

'Why is it when I pay, we eat in a class establishment, but when it's your turn we wind up in a geriatric beanery?'

'It's knowing I always get a good table.'

'What about the food?'

Gaskill smiled. 'Best place I know to eat good chicken.'

Ragsdale gave him a look just shy of nausea and ignored the menu, mimeographed entrées between sheets of plastic. 'I'll throw caution to the winds and risk botulism with a bowl of soup and a cup of coffee.'

'Congratulations on solving the Fairchild Museum theft in Scarsdale. I hear you recovered twenty missing Sung dynasty jade carvings.'

'Twenty-two. I've got to admit I passed over the least obvious suspect until I drew blanks on all the probables. The seventy-two-year-old director of security. Who would have figured him? He worked at the museum for close to thirty-two years. A record as clean as a surgeon's scrubbed hands. The curator refused to believe it until the old guy broke down and confessed. He had removed the carved figurines one at a time over a period of four years, returning after closing hours, shutting down the alarm system, picking the locks on the cases and lowering the carvings into the bushes beside the building from a bathroom window. He replaced the stolen carvings in the cases with less valuable pieces stored in a basement vault. The catalogue labels were also altered. He even managed to reset the raised stands in their exact positions without leaving telltale dust-free spots on the floor of the cases. Museum officials were more than impressed with his display technique.'

The waitress, the archetype of all those who wait on counters and tables in small-town cafés or truck stop restaurants, pencil in funny little cap, jaws furiously grinding gum, and surgical stockings hiding varicose veins, came over, pencil stub poised above a small green pad.

'Dare I ask what your soup of the day is?' inquired Ragsdale loftily.

'Curried lentil with ham and apple.'

Ragsdale did a double take. 'Did I hear you correctly?'

'Want me to repeat it?'

'No, no, the curried lentil soup will be fine.'

The waitress wagged her pencil at Gaskill. 'I know what you want.' She yelled their orders to an unseen chef in the kitchen in a voice mixed with ground glass and river gravel.

'After thirty-two years,' asked Gaskill, continuing the conversation, 'what triggered the museum's security chief to go on a burglary binge?'

'A passion for exotic art,' answered Ragsdale. 'The old guy loved to touch and fondle the figurines when no one was around, but then a new curator made him take a cut in pay as an austerity measure just when he expected a raise. This made him mad and triggered his desire to possess the jade from the exhibits. It seemed from the first the theft could only have been pulled off by a first-rate team of professionals or someone from the inside. I narrowed it down to the senior security director and obtained a warrant to search his house. It was all there on his fireplace mantel, every missing piece, as if they were bowling trophies.'

'Working on a new case?' asked Gaskill.

'Just had one laid in my lap.'

'Another museum theft?'

Ragsdale shook his head. 'Private collection. The owner went to Europe for nine months. When he returned home, his walls were bare. Eight watercolours by Diego Rivera, the Mexican painter and muralist.'

'I've seen the murals he did for the Detroit Institute of Art.'

246

'Insurance company adjusters are foaming at the mouth. It seems the watercolours were insured for forty million dollars.'

'We may have to exchange notes on this one.'

Ragsdale looked at him. 'You think Customs might be interested?'

'A thin possibility we have a connecting case.'

'Always glad to have a helping hand.'

'I saw photos of what may be your Rivera watercolours in an old box of Stolen Art Bulletins my sister cleaned out of an old house she bought. I'll know when I compare them with your list. If there is a connection, four of your watercolours were reported missing from the University of Mexico in 1923. If they were smuggled into the United States, that makes it a Customs case.'

'That's ancient history.'

'Not for stolen art,' Gaskill corrected him. 'Eight months later, six Renoirs and four Gauguins vanished from the Louvre in Paris during an exhibition.'

'I gather you're alluding to that old master art thief, what was his name?'

'The Spectre,' replied Gaskill.

'Our illustrious predecessors in the Justice Department never caught him, did they?'

'Never even made an ID.'

'You think he had a hand in the original theft of the Riveras?'

'Why not? The Spectre was to art theft what Raffles was to diamond thefts. And just as melodramatic. He pulled off at least ten of the greatest art heists in history. A vain guy, he always left his trademark behind.'

'I seem to recall reading about a white glove,' said Ragsdale.

'That was Raffles. The Spectre left a small calendar at the scene of his crimes, with the date of his next theft circled.'

'Give the man credit. He was a cocky bastard.'

A large, oval plate of what looked like chicken on a bed of rice arrived. Gaskill was also served an appetizing salad on the side. Ragsdale sombrely examined the contents of his bowl and looked up at the waitress.

'I don't suppose this greasy spoon serves anything but beer in cans.'

The grizzled waitress looked down at him and smiled like an old prostitute. 'Honey, we got beer in bottles and we got wine. What'll it be?'

'A bottle of your best burgundy.'

'I'll check with the wine steward.' She winked through one heavily mascaraed eye before waddling back to the kitchen.

'I forgot to mention the friendly service.' Gaskill smiled.

Ragsdale warily dipped a spoon into his soup, suspicion lining his face. He slowly sipped the contents of his spoon as if judging a wine tasting. Then he looked across the booth with widening eyes. 'Good heavens. Sherry and pearl onions, garlic cloves, rosemary, and three different kinds of mushrooms. This is delicious.' He peered at Gaskill's plate. 'What did you order, chicken?'

Gaskill tilted his plate so Ragsdale could see it. 'You're close. The house speciality. Broiled marinated quail on a bed of bulgur with currants, scallions, purée of roasted carrots, and leeks with ginger.'

Ragsdale looked as if his wife had presented him with triplets. 'You conned me.'

Gaskill appeared hurt. 'I thought you wanted a good place to eat.'

'This is fantastic. But where are the crowds? They should be lined up outside.'

'The owner and chef, who by the way used to be at the Ritz in London, closes his kitchen on Mondays.'

'But why did he open just for us?' Ragsdale asked in awe.

'I recovered his collection of medieval cooking utensils after they were stolen from his former house in England and smuggled into Miami.'

The waitress returned and thrust a bottle in front of Ragsdale's face so he could read the label. 'Here you go, honey, Chateau Chantilly 1878. You got good taste, but are you man enough to pay eight thousand bucks for the bottle?'

Ragsdale stared at the dusty bottle and faded label and went absolutely numb with surprise. 'No, no, a good California cabernet will be fine,' he choked out.

'Tell you what, honey. How about a nice medium-weight Bordeaux, a 1988 vintage. Say around thirty bucks.'

Ragsdale nodded in dumb assent. 'I don't believe this.'

'I think what really appeals to me about the place,' said Gaskill, pausing to savour a bit of quail, 'is its incongruity. Who would ever expect to find gourmet food and wine like this in a diner?'

'It's a world apart all right.'

'To get back to our conversation,' said Gaskill, daintily removing a bone from the quail with his massive hands. 'I almost laid my hands on another of the Spectre's acquisitions.'

'Yes, I heard about your blown stakeout,' Ragsdale muttered, having a difficult time bringing his mind back on track. 'A Peruvian mummy covered in gold, wasn't it?'

'The Golden Body Suit of Tiapollo.'

'Where did you go wrong?'

'Bad timing more than anything. While we were keeping an eye on the owner's penthouse, a gang of thieves acting as furniture movers snatched the mummy from an apartment on a lower floor where it was hidden along with a huge cache of other art and artifacts, all with shady histories.'

'This soup is outstanding,' Ragsdale said, trying to get the waitress's attention. 'I'd better take another look at the menu and order an entrée. Have you made up a catalogue yet?'

'End of the week. I suspect there may be between thirty

and forty items on your FBI wish list of stolen art in my suspect's underground collection.'

The waitress wandered over with the wine and Ragsdale ordered seared salmon with sweet corn, shiitake mushrooms, and spinach. 'Good choice, honey,' she drawled as she opened the bottle.

Ragsdale shook his head in wonderment before turning his attention back to Gaskill. 'What's the name of the collector who squirrelled away the hot art?'

'His name is Adolphus Rummel, a wealthy scrap dealer out of Chicago. His name ring a bell?'

'No, but then I've never met a big-time underground buyer and collector who held open house. Any chance Rummel will talk?'

'No way,' said Gaskill regretfully. 'He's already hired Jacob Morganthaler and is suing to get his confiscated art objects back.'

'Jury-rig Jake,' Ragsdale said disgustedly. 'Friend and champion of indicted black market art dealers and collectors.'

'With his acquittal record, we should consider ourselves lucky he doesn't defend murderers and drug dealers.'

'Any leads on who stole the golden body suit?'

'None. A clean job. If I didn't know better, I'd say the Spectre did it.'

'Not unless he came back from the dead. He'd have to be well over ninety years old.'

Gaskill held up his glass, and Ragsdale poured the wine. 'Suppose he had a son, or established a dynasty who carried on the family tradition?'

'That's a thought. Except that no calendars with circled dates have been left at art robberies for over fifty years.'

'They could have branched out into smuggling and forgeries and dropped the cornball theatrics. Today's professionals know that modern investigative technology could easily comb enough evidence out of those hokey calendars to put a collar on them.'

'Maybe.' Ragsdale paused as the waitress brought his salmon. He sniffed the aroma and gazed in delight at the presentation. 'I hope it tastes as good as it looks.'

'Guaranteed, honey,' the old waitress cackled, 'or your money back.'

Ragsdale drained his wine and poured another glass. 'I can hear your mind clicking from here. Where are you headed?'

'Whoever committed the robbery didn't do it to gain a higher price from another black market collector,' Gaskill replied. 'I did some research on the golden body suit encasing the mummy. Reportedly, it was covered with engraved hieroglyphs, illustrating a long voyage by a fleet of Inca ships carrying a vast treasure, including a huge golden chain. I believe the thieves took it so they can trace a path to the mother lode.'

'Does the suit tell what happened to the treasure?'

'Legend says it was buried on an island of an inland sea. How's your salmon?'

'The best I've ever eaten,' said Ragsdale happily. 'And believe you me, that's a compliment. So where do you go from here?'

'The engravings on the suit have to be translated. The Inca did not have a method of writing or illustrating events like the Mayans, but photographs of the suit taken before its earlier theft from Spain show definite indications of a pictorial graphic system. The thieves will need the services of an expert to decode these glyphs. Interpretation of ancient pictographs is not exactly an overcrowded field.'

'So you're going to chase down whoever gets the job?'

'Hardly a major effort. There are only five leading specialists. Two of them are a husband and wife team by the name of Moore. They're considered the best in the field.'

'You've done your homework.'

Gaskill shrugged. 'The greed of the thieves is the only lead I've got.'

'If you require the services of the bureau,' Ragsdale said, 'you have only to call me.'

'I appreciate that, Francis, thank you.'

'There's one other thing.'

'Yes?'

'Can you introduce me to the chef? I'd like an inside track on a table for Saturday night.'

22

After a short layover at the Lima airport to pick up the EG&G magnetometer that was flown in from the *Deep Fathom* by a US Embassy helicopter, Pitt, Giordino, and Gunn boarded a commercial flight to Quito, the capital of Ecuador. It was after two o'clock in the morning when they landed in the middle of a thunderstorm. As soon as they stepped through the gate they were met by a representative of the state oil company, who was acting on behalf of the managing director Gunn had negotiated with for a helicopter. He quickly herded them into a limousine that drove to the opposite side of the field, followed by a small van carrying their luggage and electronic equipment. The two-vehicle convoy stopped in front of a fully serviced McDonnell Douglas Explorer helicopter. As they exited the limo, Rudi Gunn turned to express his appreciation, but the oil company official had rolled up the window and ordered the driver to move on.

'Makes one want to lead a clean life,' Giordino muttered at the efficiency of it all.

'They owed us bigger than I thought,' said Pitt, ignoring the downpour and staring blissfully at the big, red, twin-engined helicopter with no tail rotor.

'Is it a good aircraft?' asked Gunn naively.

'Only the finest rotorcraft in the sky today,' replied Pitt. 'Stable, reliable, and smooth as oil on water. Costs about two point seven-five million. We couldn't have asked for a better machine to conduct a search and survey project from the air.'

'How far to the Bay of Caráquez?'

'About two hundred and ten kilometres. We can make

it in less than an hour with this machine.'

'I hope you don't plan to fly over strange terrain in the dark during a tropical storm,' Gunn said uneasily, holding a newspaper over his head as a shield against the rain.

Pitt shook his head. 'No, we'll wait for first light.'

Giordino nodded towards the helicopter. 'If I know only one thing, it's not to take a shower with my clothes on. I recommend we throw our baggage and electronic gear on board and get a few hours sleep before dawn.'

'That's the best idea I've heard all day,' Pitt agreed heartily.

Once their equipment was stowed, Giordino and Gunn reclined the backrests of two passenger seats and fell asleep within minutes. Pitt sat in the pilot's seat under a small lamp and studied the data accumulated by Perlmutter and Yaeger. He was too excited to be tired, certainly not on the eve of a shipwreck search. Most men turn from Jekyll to Hyde whenever the thought of a treasure hunt floods their brain. But Pitt's stimulant was not greed but the challenge of entering the unknown to pursue a trail laid down by adventurous men like him, who lived and died in another era, men who left a mystery for later generations to unravel.

What kind of men walked the decks of sixteenth-century ships, he wondered. Besides the lure of adventure and the remote prospect of riches, what possessed them to sail on voyages sometimes lasting three or more years on ships not much larger than a modest suburban, two-storey house? Out of sight of land for months at a time, their teeth falling out from the ravages of scurvy, the crews were decimated by malnutrition and disease. Many were the voyages completed by only ship's officers, who had survived on more abundant rations than the common seamen. Of the eighty-eight men on board the *Golden Hind* when Drake battled through the Strait of Magellan into the Pacific, only fifty-six were left when he entered Plymouth Harbour.

Pitt turned his attention to the *Nuestra Señora de la Concepción*. Perlmutter had included illustrations and cut-away plans of a typical Spanish treasure galleon that sailed the seas during the sixteenth and seventeenth centuries. Pitt's primary interest was in the amount of iron that was on board for the magnetometer to detect. Perlmutter was certain the two cannon she reportedly carried were bronze and would not register on an instrument that measures the intensity of the magnetic field produced by an iron mass.

The galleon carried four anchors. Their shanks, arms, and flukes were cast from iron, but their stocks were wood and they were secured to hemp lines, not chains. If she had been riding on two anchors, the force of the wave, suddenly striking the ship and hurling it ashore, would have probably snapped the lines. That left a small chance her two spare anchors might have survived intact and still be somewhere in the wreckage.

He totalled up the rest of the iron that might have been on board. The fittings, ship's hardware, the big gudgeons and pintles that held the rudder and allowed it to turn. The trusses (iron brackets that helped support the yards or spars), any shackles or grappling irons. The cook's kettle, carpenter's tools, maybe a keg of nails, small firearms, swords, and pikes. Shot for the cannon.

It was an exercise in the dark. Pitt was hardly an authority on sixteenth-century sailing ships. He could only rely on Perlmutter's best guess as to the total iron mass on board the *Concepción*. The best estimate ran between one and three tons. Enough, Pitt fervently hoped, for the magnetometer to detect the galleon's anomaly from 50 to 75 metres in the air.

Anything less, and they'd stand about as much chance of locating the galleon as they would of finding a floating bottle with a message in the middle of the South Pacific.

It was about five in the morning, with a light blue sky turning orange over the mountains to the east, as Pitt swung the McDonnell Douglas Explorer helicopter over the waters of the Bay of Caráquez. Fishing boats were leaving the bay and heading out to sea for the day's catch. The crewmen paused as they readied their nets, looked up at the low-flying aircraft and waved. Pitt waved back as the shadow of the Explorer flickered over the little fishing fleet and darted towards the coastline. The dark, radiant blue of deep water soon altered to a turquoise green streaked by long lines of breaking surf that materialized as the seafloor rose to meet the sandy beach.

The long arms of the bay circled and stopped short of each other at the entrance to the Chone River. Giordino, who was sitting in the copilot's seat, pointed down to the right at a small town with tiny streets and colourfully painted boats drawn up on the beach. The town was surrounded by numerous farms no larger than three or four acres, with little whitewashed adobe houses next to corrals holding goats and a few cows. Pitt followed the river upstream for two kilometres where it foamed white with rapids. Then suddenly the dense rain forest rose like an impenetrable wall and stretched eastward as far as they could see. Except for the river, no opening beneath the trees could be seen.

'We're approaching the lower half of our grid,' Pitt said over his shoulder to Gunn, who was hunched over the proton magnetometer.

'Circle around for a couple of minutes while I set up the system,' Gunn replied. 'Al, can you drop the tow bird for me?'

'As you wish.' Giordino nodded, moving from his seat to the rear of the cabin.

Pitt said, 'I'll head towards the starting point for our first run and hang around until you're ready.'

Giordino lifted the sensor. It was shaped like an air-to-air missile. He lowered it through a floor hatch of the helicopter. Then he unreeled the sensor on its umbilical cable. 'Tow bird out about thirty metres,' he announced.

'I'm picking up interference from the helicopter,' said Gunn. 'Give me another twenty metres.'

Giordino complied. 'How's that?'

'Good. Now hold on while I set the digital and analogue recorders.'

'What about the camera and data acquisition systems?'

'Them too.'

'No need to hurry,' said Pitt. 'I'm still programming my grid lane data into the satellite navigation computer.'

'First time with a Geometrics G-813G?' Giordino asked Gunn.

Gunn nodded. 'I've used the model G-801 for marine and ocean survey, but this is my introduction to the aerial unit.'

'Dirk and I used a G-813G to locate a Chinese airliner that crashed off Japan last year. Worked like a woman of virtue – sensitive, reliable, never drifted, and required no calibration adjustments. Obviously, my ideal for a mate.'

Gunn looked at him strangely. 'You have odd taste when it comes to women.'

'He has this thing for robots,' Pitt joked.

'Say no more,' Giordino said pretentiously. 'Say no more.'

'I'm told this model is good for accurate data on small anomalies,' said Gunn, suddenly serious. 'If she won't lead us to the *Concepción*, nothing will.'

Giordino returned to the copilot's seat, settled in and stared down at the unbroken carpet of green no more than 200 metres (656 feet) below. There wasn't a piece of ground showing anywhere. 'I don't think I'd like to spend my holidays here.'

'Not many people do,' said Pitt. 'According to Julien Perlmutter, a check of local historical archives came up with the rumour that the local farmers shun the area. Julien said Cuttill's journal mentioned that mummies of long-dead Inca were torn from graveyards by the tidal wave before being swept into the jungle. The natives are highly superstitious, and they believe the spirits of their ancestors still drift through the jungle in search of their original graves.'

'You can run your first lane,' declared Gunn. 'All systems are up and tuned.'

'How far from the coast are we going to start mowing the lawn?' Giordino asked, referring to the seventy-five-metre-wide grid lanes they planned to cover.

'We'll begin at the three-kilometre mark and run parallel to the shore,' answered Pitt, 'running lanes north and south as we work inland.'

'Length of lanes?' inquired Gunn, peering at the stylus marking the graph paper and the numbers blinking on his digital readout window.

'Two kilometres at a speed of twenty knots.'

'We can run much faster,' said Gunn. 'The mag system has a very fast cycle rate. It can easily read an anomaly at a hundred knots.'

'We'll take it nice and slow,' Pitt said firmly. 'If we don't fly directly over the target, any magnetic field we hope to find won't make much of an impression on your gamma readings.'

'And if we don't pick up an anomaly, we increase the perimeters of the grid.'

'Right. We'll conduct a textbook search. We've done it more times than I care to count.' Then Pitt glanced over at Giordino. 'Al, you mind our altitude while I concentrate on our lane coordinates.'

Giordino nodded. 'I'll keep the tow bird as low as I can without losing it in the branches of a tree.'

The sun was up now and the sky was clear of all but a few small, wispy clouds. Pitt took a final look at the instruments and then nodded. 'Okay, guys, let's find ourselves a shipwreck.'

Back and forth over the thick jungle they flew, the air-conditioning system keeping the hot, humid atmosphere outside the aircraft's aluminium skin. The day wore on and by noon they had achieved nothing. The magnetometer failed to register so much as a tick. To someone who had never searched for an unseen object, it might have seemed discouraging, but Pitt, Giordino, and Gunn took it in stride. They had all known shipwreck or lost aircraft hunts that had lasted as long as six weeks without the slightest sign of success.

Pitt was also a stickler for the game plan. He knew from experience that impatience and deviation from the computed search lanes usually spelled disaster for a project. Rather than begin in the middle of the grid and work out, he preferred to start at the outer edge and work in. Too often a target was discovered where it was not supposed to be. He also found it expedient to eliminate the open, dry areas so no time was wasted rerunning the search lanes.

'How much have we covered?' asked Gunn for the first time since the search began.

'Two kilometres into the grid,' Pitt answered. 'We're only now coming into Yaeger's prime target area.'

'Then we're about to run parallel lines five kilometres from the 1578 shoreline.'

'Yes, the distance the wave carried the galleon, as indicated by Yaeger's computer program.'

'Three hours of fuel left,' said Giordino, tapping the two fuel gauges. He showed no sign of fatigue or boredom; if anything he seemed to be enjoying himself.

Pitt pulled a board with a chart clipped to it from a side pocket of his seat and studied it no more than five seconds. 'The port city of Manta is only fifty-five klicks away. They have a good-sized airport where we can refuel.'

'Speaking of refuelling,' said Gunn, 'I'm starved.' Since he was the only one with free hands, he passed around sandwiches and coffee, thoughtfully provided by the oil company's helicopter service crew.

'Weird tasting cheese,' muttered Giordino, examining the inside of his sandwich with a cynical eye.

Gunn grinned. 'Beggars can't be choosers.'

Two hours and fifteen minutes later they had travelled the twenty-eight lanes it took to cover kilometres five and six. They definitely had a problem now as they were beyond Yaeger's estimated target site. None of them believed a tidal wave could carry a 570-ton ship more than 5 kilometres (3 miles) over land from the sea. Certainly not a wave with a crest less than 30 metres (90 feet) high. Their confidence ebbed as they worked farther out of the prime search area.

'Beginning the first lane of the seven-kilometre mark,' announced Pitt.

'Too far, way too far,' Giordino muttered.

'I agree,' said Gunn. 'We either missed her, or she lies off the north and south perimeters of our grid. No sense in wasting time in this area.'

'We'll finish kilometre seven,' Pitt said, his eyes locked on the navigational instrument displaying his coordinates.

Gunn and Giordino knew better than to debate the matter. They were well aware that when Pitt's mind was set there was no moving him. He stubbornly felt the possibility of finding the old Spanish ship was promising despite the density of the jungle growth and the passage of four centuries. Giordino vigilantly kept the helicopter just high enough for the sensor to skim the tops of the trees while Gunn stared at the recording paper and digital readings. They were beginning to feel they had not been dealt a lucky hand and steeled themselves for a long and arduous search.

Fortunately, the weather held in their favour. The sky remained clear with an occasional cloud drifting far above them, and the wind stayed steady from the west at only five knots. The monotony was as unchanging as the weather. The forest below unfurled as though it were a continous sea of algae. No human lived down there. Sunless days without end. The constant damp, warm climate caused the flowers to bloom, the leaves to fall, and the fruits to grow and ripen all through the year. Rare was the spot where sun reached through the branches of the trees and plants to touch the ground.

'Mark it!' Gunn burst abruptly.

Pitt responded by copying the navigation coordinates. 'Do you have a target?'

'I recorded a slight bump on my instruments. Nothing big, but definitely an anomaly.'

'Shall we turn back?' asked Giordino.

Pitt shook his head. 'Let's finish the lane and see if we pick up a stronger reading on the next heading.'

No one spoke as they completed the lane, made a complete 180-degree turn and headed back on a reverse course 75 metres (246 feet) farther to the east. Pitt and Giordino could not resist stealing a glance downward at the rain forest, hoping to spot a sign of the wreck, but knowing it was next to impossible to see through the thick foliage. It was a wilderness truly terrible in its monotonous beauty.

'Coming opposite the mark,' Pitt alerted them. 'Now passing.'

The sensor, trailing on an arc behind the helicopter, lagged slightly before crossing the site of Gunn's anomaly reading. 'Here she comes!' he said excitedly. 'Looking good. The numbers are climbing. Come on, sweetheart, give with the big gamma readings.'

Pitt and Giordino leaned out their windows and stared down, but saw only a dense canopy of tall trees rising in tiered galleries. It required no imagination to see the rain forest was a forbidding and dangerous place. It looked quiet and deadly. They could only guess at what perils lurked in the menacing shadows.

'We have a hard target,' said Gunn. 'Not a solid mass, but scattered readings, the kind of display I would expect from bits and pieces of iron dispersed around a wrecked ship.'

Pitt wore a big smile as he reached over and lightly punched Giordino on the shoulder. 'Never a doubt.'

Giordino grinned back. 'That was one hell of a wave to have carried the ship seven kilometres inland.'

'She must have crested close to fifty metres,' Pitt calculated.

'Can you bring us around on an east/west course so we can bisect the anomaly?' asked Gunn.

'At your command.' Pitt banked the Explorer around to the west in a tight turn that lightened Gunn's stomach. After flying half a kilometre, he sideslipped and set his coordinates to pass over the target from the new direction. This time the readings showed a slight increase and held for a longer duration.

'I think we passed over her from bow to stern,' said Gunn. 'This must be the place.'

'This must be the place,' Giordino repeated happily.

Pitt hovered as Gunn gave bearing commands while they probed for the highest readings from the magneto-meter which would show the Explorer was directly over the wreck site. 'Bring her twenty metres to starboard. Now thirty metres astern. Too far. Ten metres ahead. Hold it. That's it. We can drop a rock on her.'

Giordino pulled the ring on a small canister and casually tossed it out his side window. It fell through the leaves and disappeared. A few seconds later a cloud of orange smoke began to rise above the trees. 'X marks the spot,' he said happily. 'I can't say I look forward to the hike.'

Pitt looked at him. 'Who said anything about walking seven kilometres through that botanical nightmare?'

Giordino gave him a quizzical stare in return. 'How else do you expect to reach the wreck?'

'This marvel of aircraft technology has a winch. You can lower me through the trees.'

Giordino peered at the thick mantle of the rain forest. 'You'd get hung up in the trees. We'd never be able to hoist you out again.'

'Not to worry. I checked the tool locker beneath the floor before we left Quito. Someone thoughtfully provided a machete. I can hang from a harness and hack my way down and up again.'

'Won't work,' said Giordino with a trace of concern in his voice. 'We don't have enough fuel to hang around while you play Jungle Jim and still reach the airport in Manta.'

'I don't expect you to wait at the kerb. Once I'm on the ground, you head for Manta. After you refuel, you come back and pick me up.'

'You might have to wander around before you find the wreck. No way you can be spotted from the air. How will we know exactly where to lower the harness?'

'I'll take a couple of smoke canisters with me and set them off when I hear you return.'

The expression in Giordino's eyes was anything but cheerful. 'I don't suppose I can talk you out of this craziness.'

'No, I don't suppose you can.'

Ten minutes later Pitt was secure in a safety harness connected to a cable leading to a winch mounted on the roof of the helicopter's cabin. While Giordino hovered the craft just above the top of the trees, Gunn operated the controls to the winch.

'Don't forget to bring back a bottle of champagne so we can celebrate,' Pitt shouted as he stepped through the open door of the ship and hung suspended.

'We should be back in two hours,' Gunn yelled back over the sound of the rotors and the engine exhaust. He pushed the descent button and Pitt dropped below the skids of the helicopter and soon disappeared into the dense vegetation as if he had jumped into a green ocean.

23

As he hung supported by his safety harness, machete gripped in his right hand, a portable radio in his left, Pitt felt almost as if he were once again dropping into the green slime of the sacrificial well. He could not tell for certain how high he was above the ground, but he estimated the distance from the roof of the forest to its floor to be at least 50 metres (164 feet).

Seen from the air, the rain forest looked like a chaotic mass of struggling plant growth. The trunks of the taller trees were crowded with dense layers of shorter growth, each seeking its share of sunlight. The twigs and leaves nearest the sun danced under the downdraught provided by the helicopter's rotor, giving them the appearance of a restless, undulating ocean.

Pitt held an arm over his eyes as he slowly descended through the first tier of the green canopy, narrowly brushing past the limbs of a high mahogany tree that was sprouting clusters of small white flowers. He used his feet to spring without difficulty out of the way of the thicker branches. A draft of rising steam, caused by the sun's heat, wafted up from the still unseen ground. After the air-conditioned cabin of the helicopter, it didn't take long for sweat to flow from every pore. As he frantically pushed aside a branch that was rising between his legs, he frightened a pair of spider monkeys that leapt chattering around to the other side of the tree.

'You say something?' asked Gunn over the radio.

'I flushed a pair of monkeys during their siesta,' Pitt replied.

'Do you want me to slow you down?'

'No, this is fine. I've passed through the first layer of trees. Now it looks like I'm coming down through what I'd guess is laurel.'

'Yell if you want me to move you around,' said Giordino over the cockpit radio.

'Maintain your position,' Pitt directed. 'Shifting around might snag the descent cable and leave me hanging up here till I'm an old man.'

Pitt entered a thicker maze of branches and quickly managed to cut a tunnel with his machete without having to order Gunn to reduce his rate of descent. He was invading a world seldom seen, a world filled with beauty and danger. Immense climbing plants, desperate for light, crawled straight up the taller trees, some clutching their hosts with tendrils and hooks while others twined upward towards the light like corkscrews. Moss draped the trees in great sheets, reminding him of cobwebs in a crypt from a horror movie. But there was beauty too. Vast garlands of orchids circled their way towards the sky as if they were strings of lights on a Christmas tree.

'Can you see the ground?' asked Gunn.

'Not yet. I still have to move through a small tree that looks like some sort of palm with wild peaches growing on it. After that, I have to dodge a snarl of hanging vines.'

'I believe they're called lianas.'

'Botany wasn't one of my better subjects.'

'You could grab one and play Tarzan,' said Gunn, injecting some humour into a potentially dangerous situation.

'Only if I saw Jane – '

Gunn tensed at Pitt's sudden pause. 'What is it? Are you okay?'

When Pitt answered, his voice was barely louder than a whisper. 'I almost grabbed what I took to be a thick vine. But it was a snake the size of a drainpipe with a mouth like an alligator.'

'What colour?'

'Black with yellowish brown spots.'

'A boa constrictor,' explained Gunn. 'He might give you a big hug, but he's not poisonous. Pet him on the head for me.'

'Like hell,' Pitt snorted. 'If he so much as looks cross-eyed at me, he meets Madame LaFarge.'

'Who?'

'My machete.'

'What else do you see?'

'Several magnificent butterflies, a number of insects that look like they belong on an alien planet, and a parrot too shy to ask for a cracker. You wouldn't believe the size of the flowers growing out of nooks in the trees. There are violets the size of my head.'

Conversation dropped off as Pitt chopped his way through a low tree with dense branches. He was sweating like a prizefighter in the last round of a championship match, and his clothes were soaked through from the heavy moisture clinging to the leaves of the trees. As he raised the machete, his arm brushed a vine armoured with thorns that shredded his shirt sleeve and sliced his forearm as neatly as claws on a cat. Luckily, the cuts were not deep or painful, and he disregarded them.

'Stop the winch,' he said as he felt firm ground beneath his feet. 'I'm down.'

'Any sign of the galleon?' Gunn asked anxiously.

Pitt did not immediately answer. He tucked the machete under his arm and turned a complete circle, unclipping the safety harness as he surveyed his surroundings. It was like being at the bottom of a leafy ocean. There was scarcely any light, and what little was available had the same eerie quality a diver would experience at 60 metres (196 feet) beneath the surface of the sea. The dense vegetation blotted out most of the colour spectrum from the little sunlight that reached him, leaving only green and blue mixed with grey.

He was pleasantly surprised to find the rain forest was

not impassable at ground level. Except for a soft carpet of decomposing leaves and twigs, the floor beneath the canopy of trees was comparatively free of growth, with none of the heaps of mouldering vegetation he had expected. Now that he was standing in the sunless depths he could easily understand why plant life that grew close to the ground was scarce.

'I see nothing that resembles the hull of a ship,' he said. 'No ribs, no beams, no keel.'

'A bust,' said Gunn, the disillusionment coming through in his voice. 'The mag must have read a natural iron deposit.'

'No,' Pitt replied, striving to keep his voice calm, 'I can't say that.'

'What are you telling us?'

'Only that the fungi, insects, and bacteria that call this place home have made a meal out of every organic component of the ship. Not too surprising when you figure that they had four hundred years to devour it down to the keel.'

Gunn went silent, not quite comprehending. Then it struck him like a lightning bolt.

'Oh, my God!' he yelped. 'We found it. You're actually standing on the wreck of the galleon.'

'Dead centre.'

'You say all sign of the hull is gone?' Giordino cut in.

'All that remains is covered by moss and humus, but I think I can make out some ceramic pots, a few scattered cannon shot, one anchor, and a small pile of ballast stones. The site reads like an old campsite with trees growing through the middle of it.'

'Shall we hang around?' asked Giordino.

'No, get your tails to Manta and refuel. I'll poke around for the jade box until you get back.'

'Can we drop you anything?'

'I shouldn't need anything but the machete.'

'You still have the smoke canisters?' Giordino asked.

'Two of them clipped to my belt.'

'Set one off soon as you hear us return.'

'Never fear,' Pitt said blithely. 'I'm not about to try walking out of here.'

'See you in two hours,' said Gunn, his spirits brimming.

'Try to be on time.'

In a different circumstance, at a different time, Pitt might have experienced a fit of depression as the sound of the McDonnell Douglas Explorer died away, leaving behind the heavy atmosphere of the rain forest. But he was energized at knowing that somewhere within a short distance of where he was standing, buried in the ancient pile of debris, was the key to a vast treasure. He did not throw himself into a frenzy of wild digging. Instead, he slowly walked through the scattered remains of the *Concepción* and studied her final position and configuration. He could almost trace the original outline by the shape of the broken mounds of debris.

The shaft and one fluke of an anchor that protruded from the humus beneath the more recently fallen leaves indicated the location of the bow. He did not think that sailing master Thomas Cuttill would store the jade box in the cargo hold. The fact that Drake intended it as a gift to the queen suggested that he kept it near him, probably in the great cabin in the stern occupied by the captain of the ship.

As Pitt walked through the debris field, clearing away small areas with the machete, he found relics of the crew but no bones. Most of them had been swept off the ship by the tidal wave. He spied pairs of mouldy leather shoes, hardened bone handles on knives whose blades had rusted away, ceramic eating bowls, and a still blackened iron cooking pot. Dread grew inside him as he realized the meagreness of the debris. He began to fear the wreck might have already been found and looted. He removed a plastic packet from inside his shirt, opened one end and pulled out the illustrations and cutaway plans of a standard treasure galleon Perlmutter had faxed. Using the plans as a guide, he carefully measured off his steps until he estimated he was in the area of the hold where the valuable cargo would have been stored.

Pitt went to work clearing what he thought was a heavy layer of compost. It proved to be only 10 centimetres (4 inches) thick. He had only to brush away the decomposing leaves with his hands to reveal several beautifully carved stone heads and full figures of various sizes. He guessed they were religious animal gods. A sigh of relief escaped his lips at discovering that the wreck of the galleon was untouched.

Scraping away a length of rotting vine that had fallen from the trees far above, he discovered twelve more carvings, three that were life-size. In the ghostly light their green coating of mould made them look like corpses arising from the grave. A clutter of clay pots and effigies had not fared as well after the damp of four centuries. Those that were relatively intact crumbled when touched. Of the textiles that had been part of the original treasure trove, all had rotted into a few swatches of black mould.

Pitt eagerly dug deeper, ignoring torn fingernails and the slime that smeared his hands. He found a cache of jade, elegantly ornate and painstakingly carved. There were so many pieces he soon lost count. They were mingled with mosaics made of mother-of-pearl and turquoise. Pitt paused and wiped the sweat from his face with his forearm. This bonanza was bound to open a can of worms, he reflected. He could already envision the legal battles and diplomatic machinations that would occur between Ecuadorian archaeologists and government officials, who would claim the artifacts belonged to them by right of possession, and their counterparts in Peru, who would claim the trove as their original property. Whatever the legal entanglements, the one certainty was that none of the masterworks of Inca art would end up on a shelf in Pitt's home.

He glanced at his watch. Over an hour had passed since he dropped through the trees. He left the mass of jumbled antiquities and continued moving towards what had once been the captain's cabin on the stern of the galleon. He was swinging the blade of the machete back and forth to sweep the dead vegetation away from a debris mound when the blade suddenly clanged on a solid metal object. Kicking the leaves to the side he found that he had stumbled on one of the ship's two cannons. The bronze barrel had long since been coated by a thick green patina and the muzzle was filled with compost accumulated through the centuries.

Pitt could no longer tell where his perspiration left off and the humid moisture from the forest began. It was like working in a steam bath, with the added annoyance of tiny gnatlike insects that swarmed around his unprotected head and face. Fallen vines wrapped around his ankles, and twice he slipped on the wet plant growth and fell. A layer of clay soil and decayed leaves adhered to his body, giving him the look of some swamp creature from a haunted bog. The steamy atmosphere was slowly sapping his strength, and he fought back an overwhelming urge to lie down on a soft pile of leaves and take a nap, an urge that abruptly vanished at the repulsive sight of a bushmaster slithering across a nearby heap of ballast stones. The largest poisonous snake in the Americas, 3 metres (10 feet) long, pink and tan with dark diamond-shaped blotches, the notorious pit viper was extremely lethal. Pitt gave it a wide berth and kept a wary eye for its relatives.

He knew he was in the right area when he uncovered the big pintles and gudgeons, now badly rusted, that once held and pivoted the rudder. His foot accidentally kicked something buried in the ground, an unidentifiable circular band of ornate iron. When he bent down for a closer inspection he saw shards of glass. He checked Perlmutter's illustrations and recognized the object as the stern running light. The rudder fittings and the lamp told him that he

270

was standing over what had been the captain's cabin. Now his search for the jade box began in earnest.

In forty minutes of searching on his hands and knees, he found an inkwell, two goblets, and the remains of several oil lamps. Without stopping to rest, he carefully brushed away a small heap of leaves and found himself looking into a green eye that stared back through the dank humus. He wiped his wet hands on his pants, took a bandanna from his pocket, and lightly cleaned the features around the eye. A human face became visible, one that had been artistically carved with great care from a solid piece of jade. Pitt held his breath.

Keeping his enthusiasm in check, he painstakingly dug four small trenches around the unblinking face, deep enough to see that it was the lid to a box about the size of a twelve-volt car battery. When the box was totally uncovered, he lifted it from the moist soil where it had rested since 1578 and set it between his legs.

Pitt sat in wondrous awe for the better part of ten minutes, afraid to prise off the lid and find nothing but damp rot inside. With great trepidation he took a small Swiss army knife from one pocket, swung out the thinnest blade and began to jimmy the lid. The box was so tightly sealed he had to constantly shift the knife blade around the box, prising each side a fraction of a millimetre before moving on to the next. Twice he paused to wipe away the sweat that trickled into his eyes. Finally, the lid popped free. Then, irreverently, he clenched the face by the nose, lifted the lid and peeked inside.

The interior of the box was lined with cedar and contained what looked to him to be a folded mass of multicoloured knotted string. Several of the strands had faded but they were intact and their colours could still be distinguished. Pitt couldn't believe the remarkable state of preservation, until he closely studied the antiquity and realized it was made, not from cotton or wool, but twisted coils of tinted metal.

'That's it!' he shouted, startling a tree full of macaws, who winged into the depths of the rain forest amid a chorus of shrieking chatter. 'The Drake *quipu*.'

Clutching the box with the tenacity of an Ebenezer Scrooge refusing to donate to a Christmas charity, Pitt found a reasonably dry fallen tree to sit on. He stared into the jade face and wondered if the *quipu*'s secret could somehow be unriddled. According to Dr Ortiz, the last person who might have read the knotted strands had died four hundred years ago. He fervently hoped that Yaeger's state-of-the-art computer could cut through time and solve the mystery.

He was still sitting there amid the ghosts of the English and Spanish seamen, oblivious to a swarm of biting insects, the stabbing pain from his gashed arm, and the clammy dampness, when the returning helicopter came within earshot from somewhere in the shrouded sky.

24

A small van, marked with the name of a well-known express package company, drove up a ramp and stopped at the shipping and receiving door of a sizable one-storey concrete building. The structure covered one city block of a huge warehouse complex near Galveston, Texas. There was no company sign on the roof or walls. The only evidence that it was occupied came from a small brass plaque beside the door that read Logan Storage Company. It was just after six o'clock in the evening. Too late for employees to be working on the job but still early enough not to arouse the suspicion of the patrolling security guards.

Without exiting the van, the driver punched in a code on a remote control box that deactivated the security alarm and raised the big door. As it rose to the ceiling, it revealed the interior of a vast storehouse filled to the roof support girders with seemingly endless racks packed with furniture and ordinary household goods. There was no hint of life anywhere on the spacious concrete floor. Now assured that all employees had left for home, the driver moved the van inside and waited for the door to close. Then he drove on to a platform scale large enough to hold an eighteen-wheel truck and trailer.

He stepped from the vehicle and walked over to a small instrument panel on a pedestal and pressed a code into a switch labelled Engage weigh-in. The platform vibrated and then began to sink beneath the floor, revealing itself to be a huge freight elevator. After it settled on to the basement floor, the driver eased the van into a large tunnel while behind him the elevator automatically returned to the upper storage floor.

The tunnel stretched for nearly a full kilometre before ending deep beneath the main floor of another huge warehouse. Here in a vast subterranean complex the Zolar family conducted their criminal operations, while operating as a legitimate business on the main floor.

On the honest business level, regular employees entered a glass entrance to administration offices that ran along one entire wall of the building. The rest of the spacious floor housed thousands of valuable paintings, sculptures, and a great variety of antiques. All had impeccably bona fide origins and were legally purchased and sold on the open market. A separate department at the rear housed the preservation department, where a small team of master craftsmen worked to restore damaged art and ancient artifacts to their original splendour. None of the employees of Zolar International or Logan Storage Company, even those with twenty years of service or more, remotely suspected the great clandestine operation that took place beneath their feet.

The driver exited the tunnel and entered an enormous sprawling secret sub-basement whose interior floor space was even larger than the main surface level 20 metres (66 feet) above. About two-thirds of the area was devoted to the accumulation, storage, and eventual sale of stolen and smuggled artworks. The remaining third was set aside for the Zolar family's thriving artifact forgery and fabrication programme. This subterranean level was known only to the immediate members of the Zolar family, a few loyal copartners in the operation, and the original construction crew, who were brought in from Russia and then returned when the subterranean rooms were completed, so no outsiders could reveal the facility's existence.

The driver slipped from behind the steering wheel, walked around to the rear of the van and pulled a long metal cylinder from inside that was attached to a cart whose wheels automatically unfolded once it was pulled free, like an ambulance gurney. When all four wheels

274

were extended, he rolled the cart and cylinder across the huge basement towards a closed room.

As he pushed, the van driver stared at his reflection in the polished metal of the cylinder. He was of average height with a well-rounded stomach. He looked heavier than his actual weight because of a tight-fitting pair of white coveralls. His medium brown hair was clipped short in a military crew cut, and his cheeks and chin were closely shaven. He found it amusing that his shamrock green eyes took on a silver tint from the aluminium container. Now deceptively dreamy, they could turn as hard as flint when he was angry or tense. A police detective, good at providing accurate descriptions, would have described Charles Zolar, legal name Charles Oxley, as a con man who did not look like a con man.

His brothers, Joseph Zolar and Cyrus Sarason, opened the door and stepped from the room to affectionately embrace him.

'Congratulations,' said Sarason, 'a remarkable triumph of subterfuge.'

Zolar nodded. 'Our father couldn't have planned a smoother theft. You've done the family proud.'

'Praise indeed,' Oxley said, smiling. 'You don't know how happy I am to finally deliver the mummy to a safe place.'

'Are you certain no one saw you remove it from Rummel's building or followed you across the country?' asked Sarason.

Oxley stared at him. 'You insult my capabilities, brother. I took all the required precautions and drove to Galveston during daylight business hours over secondary roads. I was especially careful not to break any traffic laws. Trust me when I say I wasn't followed.'

'Pay no heed to Cyrus,' said Zolar, smiling. 'He tends to be paranoid when it comes to covering our tracks.'

'We've come too far to make a mistake now,' Sarason said in a low voice.

Oxley peered behind his brothers into the reaches of the vast storage room. 'Are the glyph experts here?'

Sarason nodded. 'A professor of anthropology from Harvard, who has made pre-Columbian ideographic symbols his life's work, and his wife, who handles the computer end of their decoding program. Henry and Micki Moore.'

'Do they know where they are?'

Zolar shook his head. 'They've been wearing blindfolds and listening to cassette players ever since our agents picked them up in a limo at their condo in Boston. After they were airborne in a chartered jet, the pilot was instructed to circle around for two hours before flying to Galveston. They were brought here from the airport in a soundproof delivery truck. It's safe to say they haven't seen or heard a thing.'

'So for all they know, they're in a research laboratory somewhere in California or Oregon?'

'That's the impression laid on them during the flight,' replied Sarason.

'They must have asked questions?'

'At first,' answered Zolar. 'But when our agents informed them they would receive two hundred and fifty thousand dollars in cash for decoding an artifact, the Moores promised their full cooperation. They also promised to keep their lips sealed.'

'And you trust them?' Oxley asked dubiously.

Sarason smiled malevolently. 'Of course not.'

Oxley didn't have to read minds to know that Henry and Micki Moore would soon be names on a tombstone. 'No sense in wasting more time, brothers,' he said. 'Where do you want General Naymlap's mummy?'

Sarason gestured towards one section of the underground facility. 'We've partitioned a special room. I'll show you the way while brother Joseph escorts our experts.' He hesitated, pulled three black ski masks from his coat pocket and flipped one to Oxley. 'Put that on, we don't want them to see our faces.'

'Why bother? They won't live to identify us.'

'To intimidate them.'

'A little extreme, but I guess you have a point.'

While Zolar guided the Moores to the enclosed room, Oxley and Sarason carefully removed the golden mummy from the container and laid it on a table covered with several layers of velvet padding. The room had been furnished with a small kitchen, beds, and a bathroom. A large desk was set with note and sketch pads and several magnifying glasses with varied degrees of magnification. There was also a computer terminal with a laser printer loaded with the proper software. An array of overhead spotlights was positioned to accent the images engraved on the golden body suit.

When the Moores entered the room, their headsets and blindfolds were removed.

'I trust you were not too uncomfortable,' said Zolar courteously.

The Moores blinked under the bright lights and rubbed their eyes. Henry Moore looked and acted the role of an Ivy League professor. He was ageing gracefully with a slim body, a full head of shaggy grey hair, and the complexion of a teenage boy. Dressed in a tweed jacket with leather patches on the sleeves, he wore his school tie knotted under the collar of a dark green cotton shirt. As an added touch he sported a small white carnation in his lapel.

Micki Moore was a good fifteen years younger than her husband. Like him, she had a slender figure, almost as thin as the seventies era fashion model she had once been. Her skin was on the dark side and the high, rounded cheekbones suggested American Indian genes somewhere in her ancestry. She was a goodlooking woman, beautifully poised, with an elegance and regal bearing that made her stand out at university cocktail and dinner parties. Her grey eyes focused and then darted from one masked brother to another before coming to rest on the Golden Body Suit of Tiapollo.

'A truly magnificent piece of work,' she said softly. 'You never fully described what it was you wanted my husband and me to decipher.'

'We apologize for the melodramatic precautions,' Zolar said sincerely. 'But as you can see, this Inca artifact is priceless, and until it is fully examined by experts such as you, we do not wish word of its existence to reach certain people who might attempt to steal it.'

Henry Moore ignored the brothers and rushed to the table. He took a pair of reading glasses from a case in his breast pocket, slid them over his nose and peered closely at the glyphs on one arm of the suit. 'Remarkable detail,' he said admiringly. 'Except for textiles and a few pieces of pottery, this is the most extensive display of iconography I've ever seen produced on any object from the Late Horizon era.'

'Do you see any problem in deciphering the images?' asked Zolar.

'It will be a labour of love,' said Moore, without taking his eyes from the golden suit. 'But Rome wasn't built in a day. It will be a slow process.'

Sarason was impatient. 'We need answers as soon as possible.'

'You can't rush me,' Moore said indignantly. 'Not if you want an accurate version of what the images tell us.'

'He's right,' said Oxley. 'We can't afford faulty data.'

'The Moores are being well paid for their efforts,' Sarason said sternly. 'Misinterpretations will cancel all payment.'

Anger rising, Moore snapped, 'Misinterpretations indeed! You're lucky my wife and I accepted your proposal. One look at what's on the table, and we're aware of the reasons behind your juvenile hocus-pocus games. Running around with masks over your faces as if you were holding up a bank. Total and utter nonsense.'

'What are you saying?' Sarason demanded.

'Any historian worth his salt knows the Golden Body

Suit of Tiapollo was stolen from Spain in the nineteen twenties and never recovered.'

'How do you know this isn't another one that was recently discovered?'

Moore pointed to the first image of a panel that travelled from the left shoulder to the hand. 'The symbol of a great warrior, a Chachapoyan general known as Naymlap who served the great Inca ruler Huascar. Legend claims he stood as high as any modern star basketball player and had blond hair, blue eyes, and fair skin. Judging from the size of the golden suit and my knowledge of its history, there is no doubt that this is Naymlap's mummy.'

Sarason moved close to the anthropologist. 'You and your wife just do your job, no mistakes, no more lectures.'

Zolar quickly stepped in to defuse what was rapidly developing into a nasty confrontation. 'Please excuse my associate, Dr Moore. I apologize for his rude behaviour, but I think you understand that we're all a little excited about finding the golden suit. You're quite right. This is Naymlap's mummy.'

'How did you come by it?' asked Moore.

'I can't say, but I will promise you that it is going back to Spain as soon as it has been fully studied by experts such as you and your wife.'

A canny smile curled Moore's lips. 'Very scrupulous of you, whatever your name is, to send it back to its rightful owners. But not before my wife and I decode the instructions leading to Huascar's treasure.'

Oxley muttered something unintelligible under his breath as Sarason stepped towards Moore. But Zolar stretched out an arm and held him back. 'You see through our masquerade.'

'I do.'

'Shall I assume you wish to make a counterproposal, Dr Moore?'

Moore glanced at his wife. She looked strangely withdrawn. Then he turned to Zolar. 'If our expertise leads you to the treasure, I don't think a twenty per cent share is out of line.'

The brothers stared at one another for several moments, considering. Oxley and Zolar couldn't see Sarason's face behind the ski mask but they could see their brother's eyes blaze with fury.

Zolar nodded. 'Considering the potential for incredible riches, I do believe Dr Moore is being quite generous.'

'I agree,' said Oxley. 'All things considered, the good professor's offer is not exorbitant.' He held out his hand. 'You and Mrs Moore have a deal. If we find the treasure, your share is twenty per cent.'

Moore shook hands. He turned to his wife and smiled as if blissfully unaware of their death sentence. 'Well, my dear, shall we get to work?'

PART THREE

The Demon of Death

CERRO EL CAPIROTE

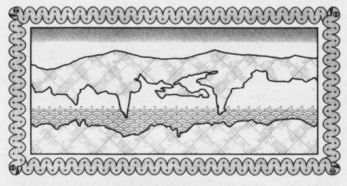

CROSS-SECTION OF UNDERGROUND RIVER

25

She was waiting at the kerb outside the terminal, her windblown cinnamon hair glistening under the morning sun, when Pitt walked out of the baggage area of Dulles airport. Congresswoman Loren Smith lifted the sunglasses that hid her incredible violet eyes, rose from behind the wheel, and perched on top of the car seat. She waved, her hands covered with supple leather driving gloves.

A tall woman with an exquisitely proportioned Sharon Stone body, she was wearing red leather pants and jacket over a black turtleneck sweater. Everyone within twenty metres, male and female, openly stared at her as she sat on top of the bright, fire engine red, 1953 Allard J2X sports car. She and the car were both classic works of stylish elegance, and they made a perfect match.

She threw Pitt a seductive look and said, 'Hi, sailor, need a ride?'

He set his bag and a large metal case containing the jade box on the sidewalk, leaned over the low-slung body of the Allard and gave Loren a hard, quick kiss on the mouth. 'You stole one of my cars.'

'That's the thanks I get for playing hooky from a committee hearing to meet you at the airport?'

Pitt stared down at the Spartan vehicle that had won eight of the nine sports car races it had entered forty-five years earlier. There was not enough room for the two jof them and his baggage in the small seating area, and the car had no trunk. 'Where am I supposed to put my bags?'

She reached down on the passenger's seat and handed him a pair of bungee cords. 'I came prepared. You can tie down your baggage on the trunk rack.'

Pitt shook his head in wonderment. Loren was as bright and perceptive as they come. A five-term congresswoman from the state of Colorado, she was respected by her colleagues for her grasp of difficult issues and her uncanny gift for coming up with solid solutions. Vivacious and outgoing in the halls of Congress, Loren was a private woman, seldom showing up at dinner parties and political functions, preferring to stay close to her townhouse in Alexandria, studying her aides' recommendations on bills coming up for a vote and responding to her constituents' mail. Her only social interest outside her work was her sporadic affair with Pitt.

'Where's Al and Rudi?' she asked, a look of tender concern in her eyes at seeing his unshaven face, haggard from exhaustion.

'On the next flight. They had a little business to clear up and return some equipment we borrowed.'

After cinching his bags on a chrome rack mounted on the rear deck of the Allard, he opened the tiny passenger door, slid his long legs under the low dashboard and stretched them out to the firewall. 'Dare I trust you to drive me home?'

Loren threw him a wily smile, nodded politely to the airport policeman who was motioning her to move on, shifted the Allard's three-speed gearbox into first gear, and mashed down the accelerator. The big Cadillac V-8 engine responded with a mighty roar, and the car leapt forward, rear tires screeching and smoking on the asphalt pavement. Pitt shrugged helplessly at the policeman as they whipped past him, furiously groping for the buckle of his seat belt.

'This is hardly conduct becoming a representative of the people,' he yelled above the thunder of the exhaust.

'Who's to know?' She laughed. 'The car is registered in your name.'

Several times during the wild ride over the open highway from Dulles to the city, Loren swept the tachometer needle into the red. Pitt took a fatalistic view. If he was going to die at the hands of this madwoman, there was little else he could do but sit back and enjoy the ride. In reality, he had complete confidence in her driving skills. They had both driven the Allard in vintage sports car races, he in the men's events, she in the women's. He relaxed, zipped up his windbreaker and breathed in the brisk fall air that rushed over and around the little twin windscreens mounted on the cowling.

Loren slipped the Allard through the traffic with the ease of quicksilver running downhill through a maze. She soon pulled up in front of the old metal aircraft hangar, on the far end of Washington's international airport, that Pitt called home.

The structure had been built during the late nineteen-thirties as a maintenance facility for early commercial airliners. In 1980, it was condemned and scheduled for demolition, but Pitt took pity on the deserted and forlorn structure and purchased it. Then he talked the local heritage preservation committee into having it placed on the National Register of Historic Landmarks. Afterward, except for remodelling the former upstairs offices into an apartment, he restored the hangar to its original condition.

Pitt never felt the urge to invest his savings and a substantial inheritance from his grandfather into stocks, bonds, and real estate. Instead, he chose antique and classic automobiles, and souvenirs large and small collected during his global adventures as special projects director for NUMA.

The ground floor of the old hangar was filled with nearly thirty old cars, from a 1932 Stutz towncar and French

Avions Voisin sedan to a huge 1951 Daimler convertible, the youngest car in the collection. An early Ford Trimotor aircraft sat in one corner, its corrugated aluminium wing sheltering a World War II Messerschmitt ME 262 jet fighter. Along the far wall, an early Pullman railroad car, with Manhattan Limited lettered on the sides, rested on a short length of steel track. But perhaps the strangest item was an old Victorian claw-footed bathtub with an outboard motor clamped to the back. The bathtub, like the other collectibles inside the hangar, had its own unique story.

Loren stopped beside a small receiver mounted on a post. Pitt whistled the first few bars of 'Yankee Doodle' and sound recognition software electronically shut down the security system and opened a big drive-through door. Loren eased the Allard inside and turned off the ignition.

'There you are,' she announced proudly. 'Home in one piece.'

'With a new speed record from Dulles to Washington that will stand for decades,' he said drily.

'Don't be such an old grunt. You're lucky I picked you up.'

'Why are you so good to me?' he asked affectionately.

'Considering all the abuse you heap on me, I really don't know.'

'Abuse? Show me your black-and-blue marks.'

'As a matter of fact – ' Loren slipped down her leather pants to reveal a large bruise on one thigh.

'Don't look at me,' he said, knowing full well he wasn't the culprit.

'It's your fault.'

'I'll have you know I haven't socked a girl since Gretchen Snodgrass smeared paste on my chair in kindergarten.'

'I got this from a collision with a bumper on one of your old relics.'

Pitt laughed. 'You should be more careful.'

'Come upstairs,' she ordered, wiggling her pants back up. 'I've planned a gourmet brunch in honour of your homecoming.'

Pitt undid the cords to his baggage and dutifully followed Loren upstairs, enjoying the fluid movement of the tightly bound package inside the leather pants. True to her word, she had laid out a lavish setting on the formal table in his dining room. Pitt was starved and his anticipation was heightened by the appetizing aromas drifting from the kitchen.

'How long?' he asked.

'Just time enough for you to get out of your grimy duds and shower,' she answered.

He needed no further encouragement. He quickly stripped off his clothes and stepped into the shower, reclining on the tile floor with his feet propped on one wall as steaming hot water splashed on the opposite side. He almost drifted off to sleep, but roused himself after ten minutes and soaped up before rinsing off. After shaving and drying his hair, he slipped into a silk paisley robe Loren had given him for Christmas.

When he entered the kitchen, she came over and gave him a long kiss. 'Ummm, you smell good, you shaved.'

He saw that the metal case containing the jade box had been opened. 'And you've been snooping.'

'As a congresswoman I have certain inalienable rights,' she said, handing him a glass of champagne. 'A beautiful work of art. What is it?'

'It,' he answered, 'is a pre-Columbian antiquity that contains the directions to hidden riches worth so much money it would take you and your buddies in Congress all of two days to spend it.'

She looked at him suspiciously. 'You must be joking. That would be over a billion dollars.'

'I never joke about lost treasure.'

She turned and retrieved two dishes of huevos rancheros with chorizo and refried beans heavy on the salsa from the oven and placed them on the table. 'Tell me about it while we eat.'

Between mouthfuls, as he ravenously attacked Loren's Mexican brunch, Pitt began with his arrival at the sacrificial well and told her what happened up to his discovery of the jade box and the *quipu* in the Ecuadorian rain forest. He rounded out his narrative with the myths, the precious few facts, and finished with broad speculation.

Loren listened without interrupting until Pitt finished, then said, 'Northern Mexico, you think?'

'Only a guess until the *quipu* is deciphered.'

'How is that possible if, as you say, the knowledge about the knots died with the last Inca?'

'I'm banking on Hiram Yaeger's computer to come up with the key.'

'A wild shot in the dark at best,' she said, sipping her champagne.

'Our only prospect, but a damned good one.' Pitt rose, pulled open the dining room curtains and gazed at an airliner that was lifting off the end of a runway, then sat down again. 'Time is our real problem. The thieves who stole the Golden Body Suit of Tiapollo before Customs agents could seize it have a head start.'

'Won't they be delayed too?' asked Loren.

'Because they have to translate the images on the suit? A good authority on Inca textile designs and ideographic symbols on pottery should be able to interpret the images on the suit.'

Loren came around the table and sat in Pitt's lap. 'So it's developing into a race for the treasure.'

Pitt slipped his arms around her waist and gave her a tight squeeze. 'Things seem to be shaping up that way.'

'Just be careful,' she said, running her hands under his robe. 'I have a feeling your competitors are not nice people.'

26

Early the next morning, a half hour ahead of the morning traffic rush, Pitt dropped Loren off at her townhouse and drove to the NUMA headquarters building. Not about to risk damage to the Allard by the crazy drivers of the nation's capital, he drove an ageing but pristine 1984 Jeep Grand Wagoneer that he had modified by installing a Rodeck 500-horsepower V-8 engine taken from a hot rod wrecked at a national drag race meet. The driver of a Ferrari or Lamborghini who might have stopped beside him at a red light would never suspect that Pitt could blow their doors off from zero to a hundred miles an hour before their superior gear ratios and wind dynamics gave them the edge.

He slipped the Jeep into his parking space beneath the tall, green-glassed tower that housed NUMA's offices and took the elevator up to Yaeger's computer floor, the carrying handle of the metal case containing the jade box gripped tightly in his right hand. When he stepped into a private conference room he found Admiral Sandecker, Giordino, and Gunn already waiting for him. He set the case on the floor and shook hands.

'I apologize for being late.'

'You're not late.' Admiral James Sandecker spoke in a sharp tone that could slice a frozen pork roast. 'We're all early. In suspense and full of anticipation about the map, or whatever you call it.'

'*Quipu*,' explained Pitt patiently. 'An Inca recording device.'

'I'm told the thing is supposed to lead to a great treasure. Is that true?'

'I wasn't aware of your interest,' Pitt said, with the hint of a smile.

'When you take matters into your own hands on agency time and money, all behind my back I might add, I'm giving heavy thought to placing an advertisement in the help wanted section for a new projects director.'

'Purely an oversight, sir,' said Pitt, exercising considerable willpower to keep a straight face. 'I had every intention of sending you a full report.'

'If I believed that,' Sandecker snorted, 'I'd buy stock in a buggy whip factory.'

A knock came on the door and a bald-headed, cadaverous man with a great scraggly Wyatt Earp moustache stepped into the room. He was wearing a crisp, white lab coat. Sandecker acknowledged him with a slight nod and turned to the others.

'I believe you all know Dr Bill Straight,' he said.

Pitt extended his hand. 'Of course. Bill heads up the marine artifact preservation department. We've worked on several projects together.'

'My staff is still buried under the two truckloads of antiquities from the Byzantine cargo vessel you and Al found imbedded in the ice on Greenland a few years ago.'

'All I remember about that project,' said Giordino, 'is that I didn't thaw out for three months.'

'Why don't you show us what you've got?' said Sandecker, unable to suppress his impatience.

'Yes, by all means,' said Yaeger, polishing one lens of his granny spectacles. 'Let's have a look at it.'

Pitt opened the case, gently removed the jade box, and placed it on the conference table. Giordino and Gunn had already seen it during the flight from the rain forest to Quito, and they stood back while Sandecker, Yaeger, and Straight moved in for a close look.

'Masterfully carved,' said Sandecker, admiring the intricate features of the face on the lid.

'A most distinctive design,' observed Straight. 'The

serene expression, the soft look of the eyes definitely have an Asian quality about them. Almost a direct association with statuary art from the Cahola dynasty of southern India.'

'Now that you mention it,' said Yaeger, 'the face does have a remarkable resemblance to most sculptures of Buddha.'

'How is it possible for two unrelated cultures to carve similar likenesses from the same type of stone?' asked Sandecker.

'Pre-Columbian contact by a transpacific crossing?' speculated Pitt.

Straight shook his head. 'Until someone discovers an ancient artifact in this hemisphere that is absolutely proven to have come from either Asia or Europe, all similarities have to be classed as sheer coincidence. No more.'

'Likewise, no early Mayan or Andean art has ever shown up in excavations of ancient cities around the Mediterranean or the Far East,' said Gunn.

Straight lightly ran his fingertips over the green jade. 'Still, this face presents an enigma. Unlike the Maya and the ancient Chinese, the Inca did not prize jade. They preferred gold to adorn their kings and gods, living or dead, believing it represented the sun that gave fertility to the soil and warmth to all life.'

'Let's open it and get to that thing inside,' ordered Sandecker.

Straight nodded at Pitt. 'I'll let you do the honours.'

Without a word, Pitt inserted a thin metal shaft under the lid of the box and carefully prised it open.

There it was. The *quipu*, lying as it had in the cedar-lined box for centuries. They stared curiously at it for almost a minute, wondering if its riddle could be solved.

Straight zipped open a small leather pouch. Neatly arrayed inside was a set of tools, several different-sized tweezers, small calipers, and a row of what looked like the picks that dentists use for cleaning teeth. He pulled on a pair of soft white gloves and selected a pair of tweezers and one of the picks. Then he reached in the box and began probing the *quipu*, delicately testing the strands to see if they could be separated without breaking.

As if he were a surgeon lecturing to a group of interns over a cadaver, he began explaining the examination process. 'Not as brittle nor as fragile as I expected. The *quipu* is made from different metals, mostly copper, some silver, one or two gold. Looks like they were hand-formed into wire and then wound into tiny coiledlike cables, some thicker than others, with varied numbers of strands and colours. The cables still retain a measure of tensile strength and a surprising degree of resilience. There appear to be a total of thirty-one cables of various lengths, each with a series of incredibly small knots spaced at irregular intervals. Most of the cables are individually tinted, but a few are identical in colour. The longer cables are linked to subordinates that act as modifying clauses, similar to the diagram of a sentence in an English class. This is definitely a sophisticated message that cries out to be unravelled.'

'Amen,' muttered Giordino.

Straight paused and turned to the admiral. 'With your permission, sir, I will remove the *quipu* from its resting place.'

'What you're saying is that I'm responsible in the event you break the damn thing,' Sandecker scowled.

'Well, sir . . .'

'Go ahead, man, get with it. I can't stand around here all day staring at some smelly old relic.'

'Nothing like the aroma of rotting mulch to put one on edge,' said Pitt drolly.

Sandecker fixed him with a sour stare. 'We can dispense with the humour.'

'The sooner we unsnarl this thing,' said Yaeger anxiously, 'the sooner I can create a decoding program.'

Straight flexed his gloved fingers like a piano player

292

about to assault Franz Liszt's Hungarian Rhapsody Number Two. Then he took a deep breath and slowly reached into the box. He slipped a curved probe very carefully under several cables of the *quipu* and gently raised them a fraction of a centimetre. 'Score one for our side,' he sighed thankfully. 'After lying in the box for centuries, the coils have not fused together or stuck to the wood. They pull free quite effortlessly.'

'They appear to have survived the ravages of time extremely well,' observed Pitt.

After examining the *quipu* from every angle, Straight then slipped two large tweezers under it from opposite sides. He hesitated as if bolstering his confidence, then began raising the *quipu* from its resting place. No one spoke, all held their breath until Straight laid the multi-coloured cables on a sheet of glass. Setting aside the tweezers in favour of the dental picks, he meticulously unfolded the cables one by one until they were all spread flat like a fan.

'There it is, gentlemen,' he sighed with relief. 'Now we have to soak the strands in a very mild cleaning solution to remove stains and corrosion. This process will then be followed by a chemical preservation procedure in our lab.'

'How long before you can return it to Yaeger for study?' asked Sandecker.

Straight shrugged. 'Six months, maybe a year.'

'You've got two hours,' said Sandecker without batting an eye.

'Impossible. The metal coils lasted as long as they did because they were sealed in a box that was almost airtight. Now that they're fully exposed to air they'll quickly begin to disintegrate.'

'Certainly not the ones spun from gold,' said Pitt.

'No, gold is practically indestructible, but we don't know the exact mineral content of the other tinted coils. The copper, for instance, may have an alloy that crumbles from

293

oxidation. Without careful preservation techniques they might decay, causing the colours to fade to the point of becoming unreadable.'

'Determining the colour key is vital to deciphering the quipu,' Gunn added.

The mood in the room had suddenly turned sour. Only Yaeger seemed immune. He wore a canny smile on his face as he gazed at Straight.

'Give me thirty minutes for my scanning equipment to measure the distances between the knots and fully record the configuration, and you can keep the thing in your lab until you're old and grey.'

'That's all the time you'll need?' Sandecker asked incredulously .

'My computers can generate three-dimensional digital images, enhanced to reveal the strands as vividly as they were when created four hundred years ago.'

'Ah, but it soothes the savage beast,' Giordino waxed poetically, 'to live in a modern world.'

Yaeger's scan of the Drake quipu took closer to an hour and a half, but when he was finished the graphics made it look better than when it was brand new. Four hours later he made his first breakthrough in deciphering its message. 'Incredible how something so simple can be so complex,' he said, gazing at the vividly coloured simulation of the cables that fanned out across a large monitor.

'Sort of like an abacus,' said Giordino, straddling a chair in Yaeger's computer sanctuary and leaning over the backrest. Only he and Pitt had remained with Yaeger. Straight had returned to his lab with the quipu while Sandecker and Gunn went off to a Senate committee hearing on a new underwater mining project.

'Far more complicated.' Pitt was leaning over Yaeger's shoulder, studying the image on the monitor. 'The abacus is basically a mathematical device. The quipu, on the other hand, is a much more subtle instrument. Each colour, coil thickness, placement and type of knot, and the tufted ends, all have significance. Fortunately, the Inca numerical system used a base of ten just like ours.'

'Go to the head of the class.' Yaeger nodded. 'This one, besides numerically recording quantities and distances, also recorded a historical event. I'm still groping around in the dark, but, for example . . .' He paused to type in a series of instructions on his keyboard. Three of the *quipu's* coils appeared to detach themselves from the main collar and were enlarged across the screen. 'My analysis proves pretty conclusively that the brown, blue, and yellow coils indicate the passage of time over distance. The numerous smaller orange knots that are evenly spaced on all three coils symbolize the sun or the length of a day.'

'What brought you to that conclusion?'

'The key was the occasional interspacing of large white knots.'

'Between the orange ones?'

'Right. The computer and I discovered that they coincide perfectly with phases of the moon. As soon as I can calculate astronomical moon cycles during the fifteen hundreds, I can zero in on approximate dates.'

'Good thinking,' said Pitt with mounting optimism. 'You're on to something.'

'The next step is to determine what each cable was designed to illustrate. As it turns out, the Incas were also masters of simplicity. According to the computer's analysis, the green coil represents land and the blue one the sea. The yellow remains inconclusive.'

'So how do you read it?' asked Giordino.

Yaeger punched two keys and sat back. 'Twenty-four days of travel over land. Eighty-six by sea. Twelve days in the yellow, whatever that stands for.'

'The time spent at their destination,' Pitt ventured.

Yaeger nodded in agreement. 'That figures. The yellow coil might denote a barren land.'

'Or a desert,' said Giordino.

'Or a desert,' Pitt repeated. 'A good bet if we're looking at the coast of northern Mexico '

'On the opposite side of the *quipu*,' Yaeger continued, 'we find cables matching the same blue and green colours, but with a different number of knots. This suggests, to the computer, the time spent on the return trip. Judging by the additions and shorter spacing between knots, I'd say they had a difficult and stormy voyage home.'

'It doesn't look to me as if you're groping in the dark,' said Pitt. 'I'd say you have a pretty good grasp of it.'

Yaeger smiled. 'Flattery is always gratefully accepted. I only hope I don't fall into the trap of inventing too much of the analysis as I go.'

The prospect did not sit well with Pitt. 'No fiction, Hiram. Keep it straight.'

'I understand. You want a healthy baby with ten fingers and ten toes.'

'Preferably one holding a sign that says "dig here,"' Pitt said in a cold, flat voice that almost curled Yaeger's hair, 'or we'll find ourselves staring down a dry hole.'

27

High on the funnel-shaped peak of a solitary mountain that rises like a graveyard monument in the middle of a sandy desert there is an immense stone demon.

It has stood there, legs tensed as if ready to spring, since prehistoric times, its claws dug into the massive basalt rock from which it was carved. In the desert tapestry at its feet ghosts of the ancients mingle with the ghosts from the present. Vultures soar over it, jackrabbits leap between its legs, lizards scurry over its giant paws.

From its pedestal on the summit, the beast's snakelike eyes command a panoramic vista of sand dunes, rocky hills and mountains, and the shimmering Colorado River that divides into streams across its silted delta before merging with the Sea of Cortez.

Exposed to the elements on the top of the mountain, which is said to be mystic and enchanted, much of the intricate detail of the sculpture has been worn away. The body appears to be that of a jaguar or a huge cat with wings and a serpent's head. One wing still protrudes above a shoulder, but the other has long since fallen on the hard, rocky surface beside the beast and shattered. Vandals have also taken their toll, chipping away the teeth from the gaping jaws and digging their names and initials on the flanks and chest.

Weighing several tons and standing as high as a bull elephant, the winged jaguar with the serpent's head is one of only four known sculptures produced by unknown cultures before the appearance of the Spanish missionaries in the early fifteen hundreds. The other three are static crouching lions in a national park in New Mexico that were far more primitive in their workmanship.

Archaeologists who had scaled the steep cliffs were mystified as to its past. They had no way of guessing its age or who carved the beast from one enormous outcropping of rock. The style and design were far different from any known artifacts of the prehistoric cultures of the American Southwest. Many theories were created, and many opinions offered, but the enigma of the sculpture's significance remained shrouded in its past.

It was said that the ancient people feared the awesome stone beast, believing it to be a guardian of the underworld, but presentday elders of the Cahuilla, Quechan, and Montolo tribes that live in the area cannot recall any significant religious traditions or detailed rituals that pertain to the sculpture. No oral history had been passed down, so they simply created their own myth on the ashes of a forgotten past. They invented a supernatural monster that all dead people must pass on their journey to the great beyond. If they led bad lives, the stone beast came to life. It snatched them in its mouth, chewed them with its fangs, and spat them out as maimed and disfigured ghosts doomed to walk the earth forever as malignant spirits. Only those good of heart and mind were allowed to proceed unmolested into the afterworld.

Many of the living made the difficult climb up the sharp walls of the mountain to lay gifts of hand-modelled clay dolls, and ancient seashells etched with the figures of animals, at the feet of the sculpture as tribute, a bribe to ease the way when their time came. Bereaved family members often stood on the desert floor far below the menacing sculpture and sent an emissary to the top while they prayed for the beast to grant their loved one safe passage.

Billy Yuma had no fear of the stone demon as he sat in his pickup truck under the shadow of the mountain and gazed up at the forbidding sculpture far above him. He was hopeful his parents and his friends who had died had been allowed to freely pass the guardian of the dead. They were good people who had harmed no one. But it was his brother, the black sheep of the family, who beat his wife and children and died an alcoholic, that Billy feared had become an evil ghost.

Like most Native Americans of the desert, Billy lived in the constant presence of the hideously deformed spirits who wandered aimlessly and did malicious things. He knew his brother's spirit could rise at any moment and throw dirt on him or tear his clothes, even haunt his dreams with horrible visions of the restless dead. But Billy's greatest worry was that his brother might bring illness or injury to his wife and children.

He had seen his brother three times. Once as a whirlwind that left behind a trail of choking dust, next as a wavering light spinning around a mesquite, and finally as a shaft of lightning that struck his truck. These were ominous signs. Billy and his tribe's medicine man had huddled around an open fire to discuss a way to combat his brother's ghost. If not stopped, the apparition could pose an eternal threat to Billy's family and his future descendants.

Everything was tried, and nothing worked. The tribe's old shaman prescribed eating a mixture of cactus buds and herbs as a measure of protection while fasting for ten days alone in the desert. A cure that failed miserably. Near-starvation induced Billy to see his brother's apparition on a regular basis and hear eerie wails during the lonely nights. Powerful rituals such as ceremonial chanting were tried, but nothing appeased the brother's evil spirit, and his manifestations became more violent.

Billy was not the only one of his tribe with problems. Ever since the tribe's most sacred and secret religious objects were found missing from their hiding place in an isolated ruin belonging to their ancestors, whole villages had suffered ill fortune. Poor crops, contagious sickness among the children, unseasonably hot and dry weather. Fights broke out when men became drunk, and some were killed. But by far the worst calamity was the sudden increase of ghost sickness. People who had never before seen or heard an evil spirit began describing haunted visitations. Ghosts of early Montolos suddenly appeared during their dreams, often materializing in broad daylight. Almost everyone, including young children, claimed to have seen supernatural phantoms.

The theft of the wooden idols that represented the sun, moon, earth, and water shattered the Montolos' religious society. The anguish of not having their presence during the initiation ceremony for entering adulthood devastated the tribe's young sons and daughters. Without the carved deities the centuries-old rituals could not be performed, leaving the young ones in adolescent limbo. Without the sacred religious objects, all worship ceased. To them it was the same as if the world's Christians, Muslims, and Jews woke up one morning and suddenly found that the entire city of Jerusalem had been torn from the earth and carried into deep space. To non-Indians it was a simple case of theft, but to a Montolo it amounted to blasphemy that bordered on atrocity.

Around fires in the underground ceremonial structures, the old religion's priests whispered of how they could hear the mournful pleading of the idols on nocturnal winds, pleading to be returned to the safety of their hiding place.

Billy Yuma was desperate. The medicine man had given him instructions while reading the embers of a dying fire. To send his brother's ghost back to the underworld and save his family from further disaster, Billy had to find the lost idols and return them to their sacred hiding place in the ancient ruins of his ancestors. In a desperate attempt to end the hauntings and avoid more ill fortune he decided to fight evil with evil. He resolved to climb the mountain, confront the demon, and pray for its help in returning the precious idols.

He was no longer a young man, and the ascent would be perilous without the equipment used by modern rock climbers. But he had set himself to the task and was not about to back down. Too many of his people were counting on him.

About a third of the way up the south wall his heart hammered against his ribs and his lungs ached from the gruelling effort. He could have stopped to rest and catch his breath, but he pushed on, determined to reach the peak without pause. He turned and gazed down only once, checking his Ford pickup truck parked at the base of the mountain. It looked like a toy he could reach down and snatch up with one hand. He looked back at the cliff face. It was changing colours under the setting sun, from amber to tile red.

Billy regretted not starting out earlier in the day, but he had chores to complete, and the sun was high when he drove to the mountain and began his ascent. Now the orange ball was creeping below the ridge of the Sierra de Juarez mountains to the west. The climb was more difficult than he had imagined and was taking far longer. He tilted his head, shaded his eyes against the brightness of the sky, and squinted up towards the cone top of the mountain. He still had 85 metres (278 feet) to go, and full darkness was only a half hour away. The prospect of spending the night with the great stone beast filled him with foreboding, but it would have been suicidal to attempt the descent in the dark.

Billy was a small man of fifty-five. But a life spent ranching in the harsh climate of the Sonora Desert had made him as hard and tough as an old cast-iron frying pan. Perhaps his joints were not as flexible as they were the day he won a bronco riding contest in Tucson, nor did he move with the agility of the boy who was once the fastest cross-country runner in the tribe, nor did he have the stamina, but he was still as tough as an ageing mountain goat.

The whites of his eyes were yellowed and the rims reddened from ignoring the onslaught of the desert sun all his life and never wearing sunglasses. He had a round brown face with a strong jaw, straggly grey eyebrows, and thick black hair – the kind of face that seemed expressionless but revealed deep character and an insight into nature rarely understood by anyone who was not a Native American.

A shadow and a cold breeze suddenly passed over him. He shuddered from the unexpected chill. Was it a spirit? Where did they come from, he wondered. Could it be his brother was trying to make him fall to the rocks far below? Maybe the great stone beast knew he was approaching and was issuing a warning. Beset with foreboding, Billy kept on climbing, teeth clenched, staring only at the vertical rock before his eyes.

Fortunately, others who went before him had chiselled foot- and handholds on the steeper face of the wall near the summit. He could see they were very old by the rounded smoothness of their edges. Within 50 metres (164 feet) of his goal, he entered a rock chimney that had split away from the wall, leaving a trail of loose and shattered stone inside a wide crack that slanted a little more gently and made the climb a fraction less tiring.

At last, just as his muscles were tightening and he was losing all feeling in his legs, the rock wall gave way to an easy incline, and he crawled on to the open surface of the peak. He rose to his feet as the final light of day faded, breathing deeply, inhaling the cool, pure air of the desert. He rubbed his hands on the legs of his pants to remove the dirt and grit and stared at the shadow of the demon looming in the growing darkness. Though it was carved from the rock of the mountain, Billy swore that it glowed. He was tired and sore, but strangely he felt no fear of the timeworn effigy, despite the tales about how the restless spirits who were denied entry into the afterworld walked the haunted mountain.

He saw no sign of fearsome creatures lurking in the dark. Except for the jaguar with the serpent's head, the mountain was empty. Billy spoke out.

'I have come.'

There was no answer. The only sounds came from the wind and the beat from the wings of a hawk. No eerie cries from the tormented souls of the underworld.

'I have climbed the enchanted mountain to pray to you,' he said.

Still no sign or reply, but a chill went up his spine as he felt a presence. He heard voices speaking in a strange tongue. None of the words were familiar. Then he saw shadowy figures take shape.

The people were visible but transparent. They appeared to be moving about the mesa, taking no notice of Billy, walking around and through him as if it were he who did not exist. Their clothes were unfamiliar, not the brief cotton loincloths or rabbit-skin cloaks of his ancestors. These people were dressed as gods. Golden helmets adorned with brilliantly coloured birds' feathers covered most of the phantoms' heads, while those who went bareheaded wore their hair in strange distinctive fashions. Their bodies were clothed with textiles Billy had never seen. The knotted mantles that draped over their shoulders and the tunics worn underneath were decorated with incredibly ornate and beautiful designs.

After a long minute the strange people seemed to dissolve and their voices ceased. Billy stood as still and silent as the rock beneath his feet. Who were these strange people who paraded before his eyes? Was this an open door to the spirit world, he wondered.

He moved closer to the stone monster, reached out a trembling hand and touched its flank. The ancient rock felt disturbingly hotter than it should have been from the day's heat. Then, incredibly, an eye seemed to pop open on the serpent's face, an eye with an unearthly light behind it.

Terror stirred through Billy's mind, but he was determined not to flinch. Later, he would be accused of an overactive imagination. But he swore a thousand times before his own death many years later that he had seen the demon stare at him from a sparkling eye. He summoned up his courage, dropped to his knees and spread out his hands. Then he began to pray. He prayed to the stone effigy through most of the night before falling into a trancelike sleep.

In the morning, as the sun rose and painted the clouds with a burst of gold, Billy Yuma awoke and looked around. He found himself lying across the front seat of his Ford pickup truck on the floor of the desert, far below the silent beast of the mountain that stared sightlessly across the dry waste.

28

Joseph Zolar stood at the head of the golden suit, watching Henry and Micki Moore huddle over the computer and laser printer. After four days of round-the-clock study, they had reduced the images from symbols to descriptive words and concise phrases.

There was a fascination about the way they snatched up the sheets as they rolled out on to the printer's tray, excitedly analysing their conclusions as a wall clock ticked off the remaining minutes of their lives. They went about their business as if the men behind the ski masks did not exist.

Henry laboured in focused dedication. His world existed in just one narrow hall of academia. Like most university professors of anthropology and archaeology, he laboured for prestige, because financial wealth eluded him. He had pieced together potsherds and had written a prodigious number of books that few read and even fewer paid good money to own. Published with small print runs, all his works ended up gathering dust in the basements of college libraries. Ironically, the fame and the honours that he foresaw would be heaped upon him as the interpreter, and perhaps discoverer, of Huascar's treasure meant more to him than mere monetary returns.

At first the Zolars found Micki Moore sexually appealing. But soon her indifference towards them became irritating. It was obvious that she loved her husband and had little interest in anyone else. They lived and worked together in a world of their own making.

Joseph Zolar would suffer little remorse over their termination. He had dealt with disgusting and despicable sellers and collectors over the years, and hardened criminals as well, but these two people were an enigma to him. He no longer cared what form of execution his brothers had in mind for them. All that mattered now was that the Moores come up with concise and accurate directions to Huascar's golden chain.

Wearing the ski masks had been a waste of time, but they kept them on during the entire time they were in the Moores' presence. It was obvious the Moores did not intimidate easily.

Zolar looked at Henry Moore and attempted a smile. It wasn't very successful. 'Have you finished decoding the symbols?' he asked hopefully.

Moore winked foxlike at his wife and gave her a smug grin before turning to Zolar. 'We are finished. The story we have deciphered is one of great drama and human endurance. Our unravelling of the images and successful translation greatly expands the current knowledge of the Chachapoyas. And it will rewrite every text ever written on the Inca.'

'So much for modesty,' said Sarason sarcastically.

'Do you know precisely where the treasure is buried?' Charles Oxley asked.

Henry Moore shrugged. 'I can't say precisely.'

Sarason moved forward, tight-lipped and angry. 'I'd like to ask if our illustrious code breakers have the slightest idea in hell what they're doing?'

'What do you want?' Moore stated coldly. 'An arrow that points to X marks the spot.'

'Yes, dammit, that's exactly what we want!'

Zolar smiled condescendingly. 'Let's get down to the hard facts, Dr Moore. What can you tell us?'

'You'll be happy to learn,' Micki Moore answered for her husband, 'that, incredible as it sounds, the golden chain is only a small part of the treasure's stockpile. The inventory my husband and I have deciphered records at least another forty or more tons of ceremonial ornaments and vessels, headdresses, breastplates, necklaces, and solid gold and silver objects that each took ten men to carry. There were also massive bundles of sacred textiles, at least twenty golden-cased mummies, and over fifty ceramic pots filled with precious gems. If given more time we can give you a complete breakdown.'

Zolar, Sarason, and Oxley stared at Micki, their eyes unblinking through the masks, their expressions of insatiable greed well hidden. For several moments there wasn't a sound except their breathing and the whir of the printer. Even for men used to dealing in million-dollar sums, the extent of Huascar's golden wealth went far beyond their wildest imaginings.

'You paint a glowing picture,' said Zolar finally. 'But do the symbols on the mummy's case tell us where the treasure is buried?'

'It's not buried in the strict sense of the word,' said Henry Moore.

He stared at Zolar, waiting for him to react to his statement. Zolar stood there impassively.

'According to the narrative engraved on the suit,' Moore explained, 'the hoard was secreted in a cavern on a river – '

Sarason's eyes flashed with sudden disappointment. 'Any cavern by a well-travelled river would have been discovered long before now, and the treasure removed.'

Oxley shook his head. 'It's not likely a golden chain that took two hundred men to lift could have vanished a second time.'

'Nor an inventory as vast as the Moores describe,' added Zolar. 'As an acknowledged expert on Inca antiquities I'd be aware of any artifacts identified as belonging to Huascar that have made their way on to the market. No one who discovered such a cache could keep it secret.'

'Maybe we've placed too much trust in the good doctor and his wife,' said Sarason. 'How do we know they're not leading us down the garden path?'

'Who are you to talk about trust?' Moore said quietly. 'You lock my wife and me inside this concrete dungeon without windows for four days, and you don't trust us? You people must enjoy childish games.'

'You have no grounds for complaint,' Oxley told him. 'You and Mrs Moore are being paid extremely well.'

Moore gave Oxley an impassive look. 'As I was about to say, after the Incas and their Chachapoyan guards deposited Huascar's vast store of treasure in the cavern, they covered the entrance to a long passageway that led to it. Then they blended the soil and rocks to make it look natural and planted native plants over the area to make certain the passage to the cavern was never found again.'

'Is there a description of the terrain around the entrance to the cavern?' Zolar asked.

'Only that it is on a rounded peak of a steep-sided island in an inland sea.'

'Wait a moment,' snapped Oxley. 'You said the cavern was near a river.'

Moore shook his head. 'If you had listened, you'd have heard me say, the cavern was *on* a river.'

Sarason stared angrily at Moore. 'What ridiculous myth are you handing us? A cavern on a river on an island in an inland sea? Took a wrong turn in your translation, didn't you, Doc?'

'There is no mistake,' said Moore firmly. 'Our analysis is correct.'

'The use of the word *river* could be purely symbolic,' suggested Micki Moore.

'So could the island,' Sarason retorted.

'Perhaps you'd get a better perspective if you heard our entire interpretation,' offered Henry Moore.

'Please spare us the details,' said Zolar. 'We're already familiar with how Huascar smuggled his kingdom's treasury from under the collective noses of his brother Atahualpa and Francisco Pizarro. Our only interest is the

308

direction General Naymlap sailed the treasure fleet and the exact location where he hid the hoard.'

The Moores exchanged glances. Micki gave Henry an affirmative nod, and he turned to Zolar. 'All right, since we're partners.' He paused to scan a page rolled out by the printer. 'The pictographs on the suit tell us that the treasure was carried to a coastal port and loaded on a great number of ships. The voyage north lasted a total of eighty-six days. The final twelve days were spent sailing across an inland sea until they came to a small island with high, steep walls that rose out of the water like a great stone temple. There, the Incas beached their ships, unloaded the treasure and carried it down a passageway to a cavern deep inside the island. At this point, however you interpret it, the glyphs claim the gold hoard was stashed beside the banks of a river.'

Oxley unrolled a map of the Western Hemisphere and traced the sea route from Peru past Central America and along the Pacific coast of Mexico. 'The inland sea must be the Gulf of California.'

'Better known as the Sea of Cortez,' added Moore.

Sarason also studied the map. 'I agree. From the tip of Baja to Peru it's all open water.'

'What about islands?' asked Zolar.

'At least two dozen, maybe more,' replied Oxley. 'It would take years to search them all.'

Sarason picked up and read the final page of the Moores' translation of the glyphs. Then he stared coldly at Henry Moore. 'You're holding out, my friend. The images on the golden suit have to give exact guidelines to finding the treasure. No map worth the paper it's printed on stops short of pinning down the final step-by-step instructions.'

Zolar carefully examined Moore's expression. 'Is this true, Doctor, that you and your wife have not provided us with a full solution to the riddle?'

'Micki and I have decoded all there is to decode. There is no more.'

'You're lying,' said Zolar evenly.

'Of course he's lying,' Sarason snapped. 'Any moron can see that he and his wife have held back the vital clues.'

'Not a sound course, doctor. You and Mrs Moore would be wise to abide by our agreement.'

Moore shrugged. 'I'm not such a fool as you think,' he said. 'The fact that you still refuse to identify yourselves tells me the three of you don't have the slightest intention of carrying out our bargain. What guarantee do I have that you'll hold up your end? Nobody, not even our friends and relatives, knows where we were taken. Bringing us here wearing blindfolds and holding us virtual prisoners is nothing less than abduction. What were you going to do once the full instructions for finding Huascar's treasure were in your hands? Blindfold us again and fly us home? I don't think so. My guess is Micki and I were going to quietly disappear and become a folder in a missing persons file. You tell me, am I wrong?'

If Moore wasn't such an intelligent man, Zolar would have laughed. But the anthropologist had seen through their plan and called their hand. 'All right, Doctor, what will it take for you to release the data?'

'Fifty per cent of the trove when we find it.'

That pushed Sarason over the edge. 'The bastard, he's holding us up.' He walked over to Moore, lifted him off his feet and slammed him against the wall. 'So much for your demands,' he shouted. 'We're not taking any more of your crap. Tell us what we want to know or I'll beat it out of you. And believe you me, I'd take great joy in seeing you bleed.'

Micki Moore stood there, as calm as if she was standing over a stove in a kitchen. Her uncanny coolness did not seem logical to Zolar. Any other wife would have demonstrated fear at a violent threat towards her husband.

Incredibly, Moore smiled. 'Do it! Break my legs, kill me. And you'll never find Huascar's golden chain in a thousand years.'

'He's right, you know,' said Zolar, quietly gazing at Micki.

'When I'm finished with him, he won't be fit for dog food,' Sarason said as he pulled back his fist.

'Hold on!' Oxley's voice stopped him. 'For efficiency's sake, better that you take your wrath out on Mrs Moore. No man enjoys watching his wife ravished.'

Slowly, Sarason let Moore down and turned to Micki, his face taking on the expression of a pillaging Hun. 'Persuading Mrs Moore to cooperate will be a pleasure.'

'You're wasting your time,' said Moore. 'I did not allow my wife to work on the final translation with me. She has no idea of the key to the treasure's location.'

'The hell you say?'

'He's telling the truth,' Micki said, unruffled. 'Henry wouldn't allow me to see the end results.'

'We're still left with a winning hand,' said Sarason coldly.

'Understood,' said Oxley. 'You work over Mrs Moore as proposed until *he* cooperates,'

'Either way, we get answers.'

Zolar stared at Moore. 'Well, Doctor, it's your call.'

Moore looked at them in cold calculation. 'Do with her what you will. It won't make any difference.'

A strange silence came over the Zolar brothers. Sarason, the grittiest of them all, stood open-mouthed, disbelieving. What sort of man could calmly, without the slightest hint of shame or fear, toss his wife to the wolves?

'You can stand by while your wife is beaten and raped and murdered, and not say one word to stop it?' Zolar asked, studying Moore's reaction.

Moore's expression remained unchanged. 'Barbaric stupidity will gain you nothing.'

'He's bluffing.' Moore needed an acid bath after the look Sarason gave him. 'He'll crumble as soon as he hears her scream.'

Zolar shook his head. 'I don't think so.'

'I agree,' said Oxley. 'We've underestimated his monumental greed and his ruthless mania for becoming a big star in the academic world. Am I right, Doctor?'

Moore was unmoved by their contempt. Then he said, 'Fifty per cent of something beats a hundred per cent of nothing, gentlemen.'

Zolar glanced at his brothers. Oxley gave a barely perceptible nod. Sarason clenched his fists so tightly they went ivory – he turned away but the expression on his face gave every indication of wanting to tear Moore's lungs out.

'I think we can avoid further threats and settle this in an orderly manner,' said Zolar. 'Before we can agree to your increased demands, I must have your complete assurance you can guide us to the treasure.'

'I have deciphered the description of the landmark that leads to the entrance of the cavern,' said Moore, speaking slowly and distinctly. 'There is no probability of error. I know the dimensions and its shape. I can recognize it from the air.'

His confident assertion was met with silence. Zolar walked over to the golden mummy and looked down at the glyphs etched in the gold covering. 'Thirty per cent. You'll have to make do with that.'

'Forty or nothing.' Moore said resolutely.

'Do you want it in writing?'

'Would it stand up in a court of law?'

'Probably not.'

'Then we'll just have to take each other at our word.' Moore turned to his wife. 'Sorry, my dear, I hope you didn't find this too upsetting. But you must understand. Some things are more important than marriage vows.'

What a strange woman, Zolar thought. She should have looked frightened and humiliated, but she showed no indication of it. 'It's settled then,' he said. 'Since we're now working partners, I see no need to continue wearing our ski masks.' He pulled it over his head and ran his hands through his hair. 'Everyone try to get a good night's sleep. You will all fly to Guaymas, Mexico, on our company jet first thing in the morning.'

'Why Guaymas?' asked Micki Moore.

'Two reasons. It's centrally located in the Gulf, and a good friend and client has an open invitation for my use of his hacienda just north of the port. The estate has a private airstrip, which makes it an ideal headquarters for conducting the search.'

'Aren't you coming?' asked Oxley.

'I'll meet you in two days. I have a business meeting in Wichita, Kansas.'

Zolar turned to Sarason, leery that his brother might launch another rampage against Moore. But he need not have worried.

Sarason's face had a ghoulish grin. His brothers could not see inside his mind, see that he was happily imagining what Tupac Amaru would do to Henry Moore after the treasure was discovered.

29

'Brunhilda has gone as far as she can go,' said Yaeger, referring to his beloved computer terminal. 'Together, we've painstakingly pieced together about ninety per cent of the stringed codes. But there are a few permutations we haven't figured out – '

'Permutations?' muttered Pitt, sitting across from Yaeger in the conference room.

'The different arrangements in lineal order and colour of the *quipu*'s coiled wire cables.'

Pitt shrugged and looked around the room. Four other men were there: Admiral Sandecker, Al Giordino, Rudi Gunn, and Hiram Yaeger. Everyone's attention was focused on Yaeger, who looked like a coyote who had bayed nonstop all night at a full moon.

'I really must work on my vocabulary,' Pitt murmured. He slouched into a comfortable position and stared at the computer genius who stood behind a podium under a large wall screen.

'As I was about to explain,' Yaeger continued, 'a few of the knots and coils are indecipherable. After applying the most sophisticated and advanced information and data analysis techniques known to man, the best I can offer is a rough account of the story.'

'Even a mastermind like you?' asked Gunn, smiling.

'Even Einstein. If he'd unearthed an Inca Rosetta Stone or a sixteenth-century how-to book on the art of creating your very own *quipu*, he'd have worked in a vacuum too.'

'If you're going to tell us the show ends with no grand climax,' said Giordino, 'I'm going to lunch.'

'Drake's *quipu* is a complex representation of numerical

314

data,' Yaeger pushed on, undaunted by Giordino's sarcasm, 'but it's not strong on blow-by-blow descriptions of events. You can't narrate visual action and drama with strategically placed knots on a few coils of coloured wire. The *quipu* can only offer sketchy accounts of the people who walked on and off this particular stage of history.'

'You've made your point,' said Sandecker, waving one of his bulbous cigars. 'Now why don't you tell us what you sifted from the maze?'

Yaeger nodded and lowered the conference room lights. He switched on a slide projector that threw an early Spanish map of the coast of North and South America on the wall screen. He picked up a metal pointer that telescoped like an automobile radio aerial and casually aimed it in the general direction of the map.

'Without a long-winded history lesson, I'll just say that after Huascar, the legitimate heir to the Inca throne, was defeated and overthrown by his bastard half-brother, Atahualpa, in 1533, he ordered his kingdom's treasury and other royal riches to be hidden high in the Andes. A wise move, as it turned out. During his imprisonment, Huascar suffered great humiliation and grief. All his friends and kinsmen were executed, and his wives and children were hanged. Then to add insult to injury, the Spanish picked that particular moment to invade the Inca empire. In a situation similar to Cortez in Mexico, Francisco Pizarro's timing couldn't have been more perfect. With the Inca armies divided by factions and decimated by civil war, the disorder played right into his hands. After Pizarroi's small force of soldiers and adventurers slaughtered a few thousand of Atahualpa's imperial retainers and bureaucrats in the square at the ancient city of Caxanarca, he won the Inca empire on a technical foul.'

'Strange that the Inca simply didn't attack and overwhelm the Spanish,' said Gunn. 'They must have outnumbered Pizarro's troops by a hundred to one.'

'Closer to a thousand to one,' said Yaeger. 'But again, as

with Cortez and the Aztecs, the sight of fierce bearded men wearing iron clothes no arrow or rock could penetrate, riding ironclad horses, previously unknown to the Incas, while slashing with swords and shooting matchlock guns and cannons, was too much for them. Thoroughly demoralized, Atahualpa's generals failed to take the initiative by ordering determined mass attacks.'

'What of Huascar's armies?' asked Pitt. 'Surely they were still in the field.'

'Yes, but they were leaderless.' Yaeger nodded. 'History can only look back on a what-if situation. What if the two Inca kings had buried the hatchet and merged their two armies in a do-or-die campaign to rid the empire of the dreaded foreigners? An interesting hypothesis. With the defeat of the Spanish, God only knows where the political boundaries and governments of South America might be today.'

'They'd certainly be speaking a language other than Spanish,' commented Giordino.

'Where was Huascar during Atahualpa's confrontation with Pizarro?' asked Sandecker, finally lighting his cigar.

'Imprisoned in Cuzco, the capital city of the empire, twelve hundred kilometres south of Caxanarca.'

Without looking up from the notations he was making on a legal pad, Pitt asked, 'What happened next?'

'To buy his liberty, Atahualpa contracted with Pizarro to cram a room with gold as high as he could reach,' answered Yaeger. 'A room, I might add, slightly larger than this one.'

'Did he fulfil the contract?'

'He did. But Atahualpa was afraid that Huascar might offer Pizarro more gold, silver, and gems than he could. So he ordered that his brother be put to death, which was carried out by drowning, but not before Huascar ordered the royal treasures to be hidden.'

Sandecker stared at Yaeger through a cloud of blue smoke. 'With the king dead, who carried out his wish?'

'A general called Naymlap,' replied Yaeger. He paused and used the pointer to trace a red line on the map that ran from the Andes down to the coast. 'He was not of royal Inca blood, but rather a Chachapoyan warrior who rose through the ranks to become Huascar's most trusted adviser. It was Naymlap who organized the movement of the treasury down from the mountains to the seashore, where he had assembled a fleet of fifty-five ships. Then, according to the *quipu*, after a journey of twenty-four days, it took another eighteen days just to load the immense treasure on board.'

'I had no idea the Incas were seafaring people,' said Gunn.

'So were the Mayans, and like the Phoenicians, Greeks, and Romans before them, the Incas were coastal sailors. They were not afraid of open water, but they wisely beached their boats on moonless nights and during stormy weather. They navigated by the sun and stars and sailed with prevailing winds and currents up and down the shoreline, conducting trade with the Mesoamericans in Panama and perhaps beyond. An Inca legend tells of an early king who heard a tale about an island rich in gold and intelligent people, that lay far out beyond the horizon of the sea. With loot and slaves in mind, he built and rigged a fleet of ships, and then sailed off with a company of his soldiers acting as marines to what is thought to be the Galapagos Islands. Nine months later he returned with scores of black prisoners and much gold.'

'The Galapagos?' wondered Pitt.

'As good a guess as any.'

'Do we have any records of their ship construction?' Sandecker queried.

'Bartolome Ruiz, Pizarro's pilot, saw large rafts equipped with masts and great square cotton sails. Other Spanish seamen reported sailing past rafts with hulls of balsa wood, bamboo and reed, carrying sixty people and forty or more large crates of trade goods. Besides sails, the rafts were also propelled by teams of paddlers. Designs found on pre-Columbian clay pottery show two-decker boats sporting raised stem and sternposts with carved serpent heads similar to the dragons gracing Viking longships.'

'So there is no doubt they could have transported tons of gold and silver long distances across the sea?'

'No doubt at all, Admiral.' Yaeger tapped the pointer on another line that traced the voyage of Naymlap's treasure fleet. 'From point of departure, north to their destination, the voyage took eighty-six days. No short cruise for primitive ships.'

'Any chance they might have headed south?' asked Giordino.

Yaeger shook his head. 'My computer discovered that one coil of knots represented the four basic points of direction, with the knot for north at the top and the knot for south at the bottom. East and west were represented by subordinate strands.'

'And their final landfall?' Pitt prodded.

'The tricky part. Never having the opportunity to clock a balsa raft under sail over a measured nautical mile, estimating the fleet's speed through water was strictly guesswork. I won't go into it now, you can read my full report later. But Brunhilda, in calculating the length of the voyage, did a masterful job of projecting the currents and wind during 1533.'

Pitt put his hands behind his head and leaned his chair back on two legs. 'Let me guess. They came ashore somewhere in the upper reaches of the Sea of Cortez, also known as the Gulf of California, a vast cleft of water separating the Mexican mainland from Baja California.'

'On an island as you and I already discussed,' Yaeger added. 'It took the crews of the ships twelve days to stash the treasure in a cave, a large one according to the dimensions recorded on the *quipu*. An opening, which I translated as being a tunnel, runs from the highest point of the island down to the treasure cave.'

'You can conclude all this from a series of knots?' asked Sandecker, incredulous.

Yaeger nodded. 'And much more. A crimson strand represented Huascar, a black knot the day of his execution at the order of Atahualpa, whose attached strand was purple. General Naymlap's is a dark turquoise. Brunhilda and I can also give you a complete tally of the hoard. Believe me when I say the bulk sum is far and away more than what has been salvaged from sunken treasure ships during the last hundred years.'

Sandecker looked sceptical. 'I hope you're including the *Atocha*, the *Edinburgh*, and the *Central America* in that claim.'

'And many more.' Yaeger smiled confidently.

Gunn looked puzzled. 'An island, you say, somewhere in the Sea of Cortez?'

'So where exactly is the treasure?' said Giordino, cutting to the heart of the lecture.

'Besides in a cavern on an island in the Sea of Cortez,' summed up Sandecker.

'Sung to the tune of "My Darlin' Clementine",' Pitt jested.

'Looks to me,' Giordino sighed, 'like we've got a hell of a lot of islands to consider. The Gulf is loaded with them.'

'We don't have to concern ourselves with any island below the twenty-eighth parallel.' Yaeger circled a section of the map with his pointer. 'As Dirk guessed, I figure Naymlap's fleet sailed into the Gulf's upper reaches.'

Giordino was ever the pragmatist. 'You still haven't told us where to dig.'

'On an island that rises out of the water like a pinnacle, or as Brunhilda's translation of the *quipu* suggests, the Temple of the Sun at Cuzco.' Yaeger threw on an enlarged slide of the sea between Baja California and the mainland of Mexico on the screen. 'A factor that narrows the search zone considerably.'

Pitt leaned forward, studying the chart on the screen.

'The central islands of Ángel de la Guarda and Tiburón stretch between forty and sixty kilometres. They each have several prominent pinnaclelike peaks. You'll have to cut it even closer, Hiram.'

'Any chance Brunhilda missed something?' asked Gunn.

'Or drew the wrong meaning from the knots?' said Giordino, casually pulling one of Sandecker's specially made cigars from his breast pocket and igniting the end.

The admiral glared, but said nothing. He had long ago given up trying to figure out how Giordino got them, certainly not from his private stock. Sandecker kept a tight inventory of his humidor.

'I admit to a knowledge gap,' Yaeger conceded. 'As I said earlier, the computer and I decoded ninety per cent of the *quipu*'s coils and knots. The other ten per cent defies clear meaning. Two coils threw us off the mark. One made a vague reference to what Brunhilda interpreted as some kind of god or demon carved from stone. The second made no geological sense. Something about a river running through the treasure cave.'

Gunn tapped his ballpoint pen on the table. 'I've never heard of a river running under an island.'

'I haven't either,' agreed Yaeger. 'That's why I hesitated to mention it.'

'Must be seepage from the water in the Gulf,' said Pitt.

Gunn nodded. 'The only logical answer.'

Pitt looked up at Yaeger. 'You couldn't find any reference to landmarks?'

'Sorry, I struck out. For a while there I entertained hopes the demon god might hold a key to the location of the cave,' answered Yaeger. 'The knots on that particular coil seemed to signify a measurement of distance. I have the impression it indicates a number of paces inside a tunnel leading from the demon to the cave. But the copper strands had deteriorated, and Brunhilda couldn't reconstruct a coherent meaning.'

'What sort of demon?' asked Sandecker.

'I don't have the slightest idea.'

'A signpost leading to the treasure maybe?' mused Gunn.

'Or a sinister deity to scare off thieves,' suggested Pitt.

Sandecker rapped his cigar on the lip of a glass cup, knocking off a long ash. 'A sound theory if the elements and vandals haven't taken their toll over four hundred years, leaving a sculpture that can't be distinguished from an ordinary rock.'

'To sum up,' said Pitt, 'we're searching for a steep outcropping of rock or pinnacle on an island in the Sea of Cortez with a stone carving of a demon on top of it.'

'A generalization,' Yaeger said, sitting down at the table. 'But that pretty well summarizes what I could glean out of the *quipu*.'

Gunn removed his glasses, held them up to the light and checked for smudges. 'Any hope at all that Bill Straight can restore the deteriorated coils?'

'I'll ask him to begin work on them,' answered Yaeger.

'He'll be diligently labouring over them within the hour,' Sandecker assured him.

'If Straight's conservation experts can reconstruct enough of the knots and strands for Brunhilda to analyse, I think I can promise to add enough data to put you within spitting distance of the tunnel leading to the treasure cave.'

'You'd better,' Pitt advised, 'because I have ambitions in life other than going around Mexico digging empty holes.'

Gunn turned towards Sandecker. 'Well, what do you say, Admiral? Is it a go?'

The feisty little chief of NUMA stared at the map on the screen. Finally, he sighed and muttered, 'I want a proposal detailing the search project and its cost when I walk in my office tomorrow morning. Consider yourselves on paid vacation for the next three weeks. And not a word outside this room. If the news media get wind that NUMA is conducting a treasure hunt, I'll catch all kinds of hell from Congress.'

'And if we find Huascar's treasure?' asked Pitt.

'Then we'll all be impoverished heros.'

Yaeger missed the point. 'Impoverished?'

'What the admiral is implying,' said Pitt, 'is that the finders will not be the keepers.'

Sandecker nodded. 'Cry a river, gentlemen, but if you are successful in finding the hoard, every troy ounce of it will probably be turned over to the government of Peru.'

Pitt and Giordino exchanged knowing grins, each reading the other's mind, but it was Giordino who spoke first.

'I'm beginning to think there is a lesson somewhere in all this.'

Sandecker looked at him uneasily. 'What lesson is that?'

Giordino studied his cigar as he answered. 'The treasure would probably be better off if we left it where it is.'

30

Gaskill lay stretched out in bed, a cold cup of coffee and a dish with a half-eaten bologna sandwich beside him on the bedstand. The blanket warming his huge bulk was strewn with typewritten pages. He raised the cup and sipped the coffee before reading the next page of a book-length manuscript. The title was *The Thief Who Was Never Caught*. It was a nonfiction account of the search for the Spectre, written by a retired Scotland Yard inspector by the name of Nathan Pembroke. The inspector spent nearly five decades digging through international police archives, tracking down every lead, regardless of its reliability, in his relentless hunt.

Pembroke, hearing of Gaskill's interest in the elusive art thief from the nineteen twenties and thirties, sent him the yellowed, dog-eared pages of the manuscript he had painstakingly compiled, one that had been rejected by over thirty editors in as many years. Gaskill could not put it down. He was totally absorbed in the masterful investigative work by Pembroke, who was now in his late eighties. The Englishman had been the lead investigator on the Spectre's last known heist, which took place in London in 1939. The stolen art consisted of a Joshua Reynolds, a pair of Constables, and three Turners. Like all the other brilliantly executed thefts by the Spectre, the case was never solved and none of the art was recovered. Pembroke, stubbornly insisting there was no such thing as a perfect crime, became obsessed with discovering the Spectre's identity.

For half a century his obsession never dimmed, and he refused to give up the chase. Only a few months before his health failed, and he was forced to enter a nursing home, did he make a breakthrough that enabled him to write *the end* to his superbly narrated account.

A great pity, Gaskill thought, that no editor thought it worth publishing. He could think of at least ten famous art thefts that might have been solved if *The Thief Who Was Never Caught* had been printed and distributed.

Gaskill finished the last page an hour before dawn. He lay back on his pillow staring at the ceiling, fitting the pieces into neat little slots, until the sun's rays crept above the windowsill of his bedroom in the town of Cicero just outside Chicago. Suddenly, he felt as if a logjam had broken free and was rushing into open water.

Gaskill smiled like a man who held a winning lottery ticket as he reached for the phone. He dialled a number from memory and fluffed the pillows so he could sit up while waiting for an answer.

A very sleepy voice croaked, 'Francis Ragsdale here.'

'Gaskill.'

'Jesus, Dave. Why so early?'

'Who's that?' came the slurred voice of Ragsdale's wife over the receiver.

'Dave Gaskill.'

'Doesn't he know it's Sunday?'

'Sorry to wake you,' said Gaskill, 'but I have good news that couldn't wait.'

'All right,' Ragsdale mumbled through a yawn. 'Let's hear it.'

'I can tell you the name of the Spectre.'

'Who?'

'Our favourite art thief.' Ragsdale came fully awake. 'The Spectre? You made an ID.?'

'Not me. A retired inspector from Scotland Yard.'

'A limey made him?'

'He spent a lifetime writing an entire book on the Spectre. Some of it's conjecture, but he's compiled some pretty convincing evidence.'

'What does he have?'

Gaskill cleared his throat for effect. 'The name of the greatest art thief in history was Mansfield Zolar.'

'Say again?'

'Mansfield Zolar. Mean anything to you?'

'You're running me around the park.'

'Swear on my badge.'

'I'm afraid to ask – '

'Don't bother,' Gaskill interrupted. 'I know what you're thinking. He was the father.'

'Good lord, Zolar International. This is like finding the last piece of a jigsaw puzzle that fell on matching carpet. The Zolars, or whatever cockamamie names they call themselves. It all begins to fit.'

'Like bread crumbs to the front door.'

'You were right during lunch the other day. The Spectre *did* sire a dynasty of rotten apples who carried on the tradition.'

'We've had Zolar International under surveillance on at least four occasions that I can recall, but it always came up clean. I never guessed a connection to the legendary Spectre.'

'Same with the bureau,' said Ragsdale. 'We've always suspected they were behind just about every seven-figure art and artifact theft that goes down, but we've been unable to find enough evidence to indict any one of them.'

'You have my sympathy. No evidence of stolen goods, no search warrant or arrest.'

'Little short of a miracle how an underground business as vast as the Zolars' can operate on such a widespread scale and never leave a clue.'

'They don't make mistakes,' said Gaskill.

'Have you tried to get an undercover agent inside?' asked Ragsdale.

'Twice. They were wise almost immediately. If I wasn't certain my people are solid, I'd have sworn they were tipped off.'

'We've never been able to penetrate them either. And the collectors who buy the hot art are just as tight-lipped and cautious.'

'And yet we both know the Zolars launder stolen artifacts like drug dealers launder money.'

Ragsdale was silent for a few moments. Finally he said, 'I think it's about time we stop meeting for lunch to exchange notes and start working together on a full-time basis.'

'I like your style,' Gaskill acknowledged. 'I'll start the ball rolling on my end by submitting a proposal for a joint task force to my superior as soon as I hit the office.'

'I'll do likewise on my end.'

'Why don't we set up a combined meeting with our teams, say Thursday morning?'

'Sounds like a winner,' agreed Ragsdale.

'That should give us time to lay the initial groundwork.'

'Speaking of the Spectre, did you track down the stolen Diego Riveras? You mentioned over lunch that you might have a lead on them.'

'Still working on the case,' Gaskill replied. 'But it's beginning to look like the Riveras went to Japan and ended up in a private collection.'

'What do you want to bet the Zolars set up the buy?'

'If they did, there will be no trail. They use too many front organizations and intermediaries to handle the sale. We're talking the superstars of crime. Since old Mansfield Zolar pulled off his first heist, no one in the family has ever been touched by you, by me, by any other law enforcement agency in the world. They've never seen the inside of a courtroom. They're so lily white it's disgusting.'

'We'll take them down this time,' Ragsdale said encouragingly.

'They're not the type to make mistakes we can use to our advantage,' said Gaskill.

'Maybe, maybe not. But I've always had the feeling that

an outsider, someone not directly connected with you, me, or the Zolars, will come along and short-circuit their system.'

'Whoever he is, I hope he shows up quick. I'd hate to see the Zolars retire to Brazil before we can drop the axe on their necks.'

'Now that we know Papa was the founder of the operation, and how he operated, we'll have a better idea of what to look for.'

'Before we ring off,' said Ragsdale, 'tell me, did you ever tie an expert translator to the golden mummy suit that slipped through your hands?'

Gaskill winced. He didn't like to be reminded. 'All known experts on such glyphs have been accounted for except two. A pair of anthropologists from Harvard, Dr Henry Moore and his wife. They've dropped from sight. None of their fellow professors or neighbours have a clue to their whereabouts.'

Ragsdale laughed. 'Be nice to catch them playing cosy with one of the Zolars.'

'I'm working on it.'

'Good luck.'

'Talk to you soon,' said Gaskill.

'I'll call you later this morning.'

'Make it this afternoon. I have an interrogation beginning at nine o'clock.'

'Better yet,' said Ragsdale, 'you call me when you have something in the works for a joint conference.'

'I'll do that.'

Gaskill hung up smiling. He had no intention of going into the office this morning. Getting agency sanction for a joint task force with the FBI would be more complicated on Ragsdale's end than Gaskill's. After reading all night, he was going to enjoy a nice, mind-settling sleep.

He loved it when a case that died from lack of evidence one minute abruptly popped back to life again. He began to see things more clearly. It was a nice feeling to be in control. Motivation stimulated by incentive was a wonderful thing.

Where had he heard that, he wondered. A Dale Carnegie class? A Customs Service policy instructor? Before it came back to him, he was sound asleep.

31

Pedro Vincente set down his beautifully restored DC-3 transport on to the runway of the airport at Harlingen, Texas. He taxied the fifty-five-year-old aircraft down to the front of the US Customs Service hangar and shut down the two 1200-horsepower, Pratt & Whitney engines.

Two uniformed Customs agents were waiting when Vincente opened the passenger door and stepped to the ground. The taller of the two, with red hair mussed by a breeze and a face full of freckles, held a clipboard above his eyes to shield them from the bright Texas sun. The other was holding a beagle by a leash.

'Mr Vincente?' the agent asked politely. 'Pedro Vincente?'

'Yes, I'm Vincente.'

'We appreciate your alerting us of your arrival into the United States.'

'Always happy to cooperate with your government,' Vincente said. He would have offered to shake hands, but he knew from previous border crossings the agents steered clear of bodily contact. He handed the redheaded agent a copy of his flight plan.

The agent slipped the paper on to his clipboard and examined the entries while his partner lifted the beagle into the aircraft to sniff for drugs. 'Your departure point was Nicoya, Costa Rica?'

'That is correct.'

'And your destination is Wichita, Kansas?'

'My ex-wife and my children live there.'

'And the purpose of your visit?'

Vincente shrugged. 'I fly from my home once a month

329

to see my children. I'll be flying home the day after tomorrow.'

'Your occupation is "farmer"?'

'Yes, I grow coffee beans.'

'I hope that's all you grow,' said the agent with a tight-lipped grin.

'Coffee is the only crop I need to make a comfortable living,' said Vincente indignantly.

'May I see your passport, please?'

The routine never varied. Though Vincente often drew the same two agents, they always acted as if he were a tourist on his first visit to the States. The agent eyeballed the photo inside, comparing the straight, slicked-back black hair, partridge brown eyes, smooth olive complexion, and sharp nose. The height and weight showed a short man on the thin side whose age was forty-four.

Vincente was a fastidious dresser. His clothes looked as if they came right out of GQ – designer shirt, slacks, and green alpaca sport coat with a silk bandanna tied around his neck. The Customs agent thought he looked like a fancy mambo dancer.

Finally the agent finished his appraisal of the passport and smiled officially. 'Would you mind waiting in our office, Mr Vincente, while we search your aircraft? I believe you're familiar with the procedure.'

'Of course.' He held up a pair of Spanish magazines. 'I always come prepared to spend some time.'

The agent stared admiringly at the DC-3. 'It's a pleasure to examine such a great old aircraft. I bet she flies as good as she looks.'

'She began life as a commercial airliner for TWA shortly before the war. I found her hauling cargo for a mining company in Guatemala. Bought her on the spot and spent a goodly sum having her restored.'

He was halfway to the office when he suddenly turned and shouted to the agent, 'May I borrow your phone to

330

call the fuel truck? I don't have enough in my tanks to make Wichita.'

'Sure, just check with the agent behind the desk.'

An hour later, Vincente was winging across Texas on his way to Wichita. Beside him in the copilot's seat were four briefcases stuffed with over six million dollars, smuggled on board just prior to takeoff by one of the two men who drove the refuelling truck.

After a thorough search of the plane, and not finding the slightest trace of drugs or other illegal contraband, the Customs agents concluded Vincente was clean. They had investigated him years before and were satisfied he was a respected Costa Rican businessman who made a vast fortune growing coffee beans. It was true that Pedro Vincente owned the second largest coffee plantation in Costa Rica. It was also true he had amassed ten times what his coffee plantation made him as he was also the genius behind a highly successful drug smuggling operation known as Julio Juan Carlos.

Like the Zolars and their criminal empire, Vincente directed his smuggling operation from a distance. Day-to-day activities were left to his lieutenants, none of whom had a clue to his real identity.

Vincente actually had a former wife who was living with his four children on a large farm outside of Wichita. The farm was a gift from him after she begged for a divorce. An airstrip was built on the farm so he could fly in and out from Costa Rica to visit the children while purchasing stolen art and illegal antiquities from the Zolar family. Customs and Drug Enforcement agents were more concerned about what came into the country rather than what went out.

It was late afternoon when Vincente touched down on the narrow strip in the middle of a corn field. A golden-tan jet aircraft with a purple stripe running along its side was parked at one end. A large blue tent with an awning extending from the front had been erected beside the jet. A man in a white linen suit was seated under the awning beside a table set with a picnic lunch. Vincente waved from the cockpit, quickly ran through his postflight checklist, and exited the DC-3. He carried three of the briefcases, leaving one behind.

The man sitting at the table rose from his chair, came forward and embraced Vincente. 'Pedro, always a delight to see you.'

'Joseph, old friend, you don't know how much I look forward to our little encounters.'

'Believe me when I say I'd rather deal with an honourable man like you than all my other clients put together.'

Vincente grinned. 'Fattening the lamb with flattery before the slaughter?'

Zolar laughed easily. 'No, no, not until we've had a few glasses of good champagne to make you mellow.'

Vincente followed Joseph Zolar under the awning and sat down as a young Latin American serving girl poured the champagne and offered hors d'oeuvres. 'Have you brought choice merchandise for me?'

'Here's to a mutual transaction that profits good friends,' Zolar said as they clinked glasses. Then he nodded. 'I have personally selected for your consideration the rarest of rare artifacts from the Incas of Peru. I've also brought extremely valuable religious objects from American Southwest Indians. I guarantee objects that have just arrived from the Andes will lift your matchless collection of pre-Columbian art above that of any museum in the world.'

'I'm anxious to see them.'

'My staff has them displayed inside the tent for your pleasure,' said Zolar.

People who begin to collect scarce and uncommon objects soon become addicts, enslaved by their need to acquire and accumulate what no one else can own. Pedro Vincente was one of the brotherhood who was driven constantly to expand his collection, one that few people knew existed. He was also one of the lucky ones who possessed secret, untaxed funds that could be laundered to satisfy his craving.

Vincente had purchased 70 per cent of his cherished collectibles from Zolar over twenty years. It did not bother him in the least that he often paid five or ten times the true value of the objects, especially since most of them were stolen goods. The relationship was advantageous to both. Vincente laundered his drug money, and Zolar used the cash to secretly purchase and expand his ever-increasing inventory of illegal art.

'What makes the Andean artifacts so valuable?' asked Vincente, as they finished off a second glass of champagne.

'They are Chachapoyan.'

'I've never seen Chachapoyan artwork.'

'Few have,' replied Zolar. 'What you are about to view was recently excavated from the lost City of the Dead high in the Andes.'

'I hope you're not about to show me a few potsherds and burial urns,' said Vincente, his anticipation beginning to dwindle. 'No authentic Chachapoyan artifacts have ever come on the market.'

Zolar swept back the tent flap with a dramatic flourish. 'Feast your eyes on the greatest collection of Chachapoyan art ever assembled.'

In his unbridled excitement, Vincente did not notice a small glass case on a stand in one corner of the tent. He walked directly to three long tables with black velvet coverings set up in the shape of a horseshoe. One side table held only textiles, the other ceramics. The centre table was set up like an exhibit in a Fifth Avenue jewellery store. The extensive array of precious handcrafted splendour stunned Vincente. He had never seen so many pre-Columbian antiquities so rich in rarity and beauty displayed in one place.

'This is unbelievable!' he gasped. 'You have truly out-done yourself.'

'No dealer anywhere has ever had his hands on such masterworks.'

Vincente went from piece to piece, touching and examining each with a critical eye. Just to feel the embroidered textiles and gold ornaments with their gemstones took Vincente's breath away. It seemed utterly incongruous that such a hoard of wealth was sitting in a corn field in Kansas. At last he finally murmured in awe, 'So this is Chachapoyan art.'

'Every piece original and fully authenticated.'

'These treasures all came from graves?'

'Yes, tombs of royalty and the wealthy.'

'Magnificent.'

'See anything you like?' Zolar asked facetiously.

'Is there more?' asked Vincente as the excitement wore off and he began to turn his mind towards acquisition.

'What you see is everything I have that is Chachapoyan.'

'You're not holding back any major pieces?'

'Absolutely not,' Zolar said with righteous resentment. 'You have first crack at the entire collection. I will not sell it piecemeal. I don't have to tell you, my friend, there are five other collectors waiting in the wings for such an opportunity.'

'I'll give you four million dollars for the lot.'

'I appreciate the richness of your initial offer. But you know me well enough to understand I never haggle. There is one price, and one price only.'

'Which is?'

'Six million.'

Vincente cleared several artifacts, making an open space on one table. He opened the briefcases side by side, one at a time. All were filled with closely packed stacks of high denomination bills. 'I only brought five million.'

Zolar was not fooled for an instant. 'A great pity I have to pass. I can't think of anyone I'd rather have sold the collection to.'

'But I am your best customer,' complained Vincente.

'I can't deny that,' said Zolar. 'We are like brothers. I am the only man who knows of your secret activities, and you are the only one outside my family who knows mine. Why do you put me through this ordeal every time we deal? You should know better by now.'

Suddenly Vincente laughed and gave a typically Latin shrug. 'What is the use? You know I have more money than I can ever spend. Having the artifacts in my possession makes me a happy man. Forgive my bargaining habits. Paying retail was never a tradition in my family.'

'Your reserve supply of cash is still in your aircraft, of course.'

Without a word, Vincente exited the tent and returned in a few minutes with the fourth briefcase. He set it beside the others and opened it. 'Six million, five hundred thousand. You said you have some rare religious objects from the American Southwest. Are they included too?'

'For the extra five hundred thousand you can have them,' answered Zolar. 'You'll find the Indian religious idols under the glass case in the corner.'

Vincente walked over and removed the glass dust cover. He stared at the strangely shaped gnarled figures. These were no ordinary ceremonial idols. Although they looked as if they had been carved and painted by a young child, he was aware of their significance from long experience of collecting objects from the American Southwest.

'Hopi?' he asked.

'No, Montolo. Very old. Very important in their ceremonial rituals.'

Vincente reached down and began to pick one up for a closer look. His heart skipped the next three beats and he felt an icy shroud fall over him. The fingers of his hand did not feel as if they came in contact with the hardened root of a long-dead cottonwood tree. The idol felt more like the soft flesh of a woman's arm. Vincente could have sworn he heard it utter an audible moan.

'Did you hear that?' he asked, thrusting the idol back in the case as if it had burned his hand.

Zolar peered at him questioningly. 'I didn't hear anything.'

Vincente looked like a man having a nightmare. 'Please, my friend, let us finish our business, and then you must leave. I do not want these idols on my property.'

'Does that mean you don't wish to buy them?' Zolar asked, surprised.

'No, no. Spirits are alive in those idols. I can feel their presence.'

'Superstitious nonsense.'

Vincente grasped Zolar by the shoulders, his eyes pleading. 'Destroy them,' he begged. 'Destroy them or they will surely destroy you.'

32

Under an Indian summer sun, two hundred prime examples of automotive builders' art sat on the green grass of East Potomac Park and glittered like spangles under a theatrical spotlight.

Staged for people who appreciated the timeless beauty and exacting craftsmanship of coach-built automobiles, and those who simply had a love affair with old cars, the annual Capital Concours de Beaux Moteurcar was primarily a benefit to raise money for child abuse treatment centres around metropolitan Washington. During the weekend the event was held, fifty thousand enthusiastic old-car buffs swarmed into the park to gaze lovingly at the Duesenbergs, Auburns, Cords, Bugattis, and Packards, products of automakers long since gone.

The atmosphere was heavy with nostalgia. The crowds that strolled the exhibit area and admired the immaculate design and flawless detailing could but wonder about an era and lifestyle when the well-to-do ordered a chassis and engine from a factory and then had the body custom-built to their own particular tastes. The younger onlookers dreamed of owning an exotic car someday while those over the age of sixty-five fondly recalled seeing them driven through the towns and cities of their youth.

The cars were classified by year, body style, and country of origin. Trophies were awarded to the best of their class and plaques to the runners-up. 'Best of show' was the most coveted award. A few of the wealthier owners spent hundreds of thousands of dollars restoring their pride and joy to a level of perfection far beyond the car's original condition on the day it rolled out of the factory.

Unlike the more conservatively dressed owners of other cars, Pitt sat in an old-fashioned canvas lawn chair wearing a flowered Hawaiian aloha shirt, white shorts, and sandals. Behind him stood a gleaming, dark blue 1936 Pierce Arrow berline (sedan body with a divider window) that was hitched to a 1936 Pierce Arrow Travelodge house trailer painted a matching colour.

In between answering questions from passersby about the car and trailer, he had his nose buried in a thick boater's guide to the Sea of Cortez. Occasionally he jotted notes on a long pad of legal notepaper, yellow with blue-ruled lines. None of the islands listed and illustrated in the guide matched the steeply sided slopes of the monolithic outcropping that Yaeger had gleaned out of the Drake *quipu*. Only a few showed sheer walls. A number of them inclined sharply from the surrounding water, but instead of rising in the shape of a Chinese hat or a Mexican sombrero, they flattened out into mesas.

Giordino, wearing baggy khaki shorts that dropped to just above his knees and a T-shirt advertising Alkali Sam's Tequila, approached the Pierce Arrow through the crowd. He was accompanied by Loren, who looked sensational in a turquoise jumpsuit. She was carrying a picnic basket while Giordino balanced an ice chest on one shoulder.

'I hope you're hungry,' she said brightly to Pitt. 'We bought half ownership in a delicatessen.'

'What she really means,' Giordino sighed as he set the ice chest on the grass, 'is we loaded up only enough food to feed a crew of lumberjacks.'

Pitt rolled forward out of the lawn chair and stared at a sentence printed across Giordino's shirt. 'What does that say about Alkali Sam's Tequila?'

'If your eyes are still open,' Giordino recited, 'it ain't Alkali Sam's.'

Pitt laughed and pointed towards the open door of the sixty-two-year-old house trailer. 'Why don't we step into my mobile palace and get out of the sun?'

Giordino hoisted the ice chest, carried it inside, and set it on a kitchen counter. Loren followed and began spreading the contents of the picnic basket across the table of a booth that could be made into a bed. 'For something built during the Depression,' she said, gazing at the wooden interior with leaded glass windows in the cupboards, 'it looks surprisingly modern.'

'Pierce Arrow was ahead of its time,' Pitt explained. 'They went into the travel trailer business to supplement dwindling profits from the sales of their cars. After two years, they quit. The Depression killed them. They manufactured three models, one longer and one shorter than this one. Except for updating the stove and the refrigerator, I restored it to original condition.'

'I've got Corona, Coors, or Cheurlin,' said Giordino. 'Name your poison.'

'What kind of beer is Cheurlin?' asked Loren.

'Domaine Cheurlin Extra Dry is a brand name for a bubbly. I bought it in Elephant Butte.'

'A champagne from where?'

'New Mexico,' Pitt answered. 'An excellent sparkling wine. Al and I stumbled on to the winery during a canoe trip down the Rio Grande.'

'Okay.' Loren smiled, holding up a flute-stemmed glass. 'Fill it up.'

Pitt smiled and nodded at the glass. 'You cheated. You came prepared.'

'I've hung around you long enough to know your solemn secret.' She fetched a second glass and passed it to him. 'For a price I won't tell the world the big, dauntless daredevil of the dismal depths prefers champagne over beer.'

'I drink them both,' Pitt protested.

'If she tells the boys down at the local saloon,' said Giordino in a serious tone, 'you'll be laughed out of town.'

'What is it going to cost me?' Pitt asked, acting subdued.

Loren gave him a very sexy look indeed. 'We'll negotiate that little matter later tonight.'

Giordino nodded at the open Sea of Cortez boating book. 'Find any likely prospects?'

'Out of nearly a hundred islands in and around the Gulf that rise at least fifty metres above the sea, I've narrowed it down to two probables and four possibles. The rest don't fit the geological pattern.'

'All in the northern end?'

Pitt nodded. 'I didn't consider any below the twenty-eighth parallel.'

'Can I see where you're going to search?' asked Loren, as she laid out a variety of cold cuts, cheeses, smoked fish, a loaf of sourdough bread, coleslaw, and down-home potato salad.

Pitt walked to a closet, pulled out a long roll of paper and spread it on the kitchen counter. 'An enhanced picture of the Gulf. I've circled the islands that come closest to matching Yaeger's translation of the *quipu*.'

Loren and Giordino put down their drinks and examined the photo, taken from a geophysical orbiting satellite, that revealed the upper reaches of the Sea of Cortez in astonishing detail. Pitt handed Loren a large magnifying glass.

'The definition is unbelievable,' said Loren, peering through the glass at the tiny islands.

'See anything resembling a rock that doesn't look natural?' asked Giordino.

'The enhancement is good, but not that good,' answered Pitt.

Loren hovered over the islands Pitt had circled. Then she looked up at him. 'I assume you intend to make an aerial survey of the most promising sites?'

'The next step in the process of elimination.'

'By plane?'

'Helicopter.'

'Looks to me like a pretty large area to cover by helicopter,' said Loren. 'What do you use for a base?'

'An old ferryboat.'

'A ferry?' Loren said, surprised.

'Actually a car/passenger ferry that originally plied San Francisco Bay until 1957. She was later sold and used until 1962 by the Mexicans from Guaymas across the Gulf to Santa Rosalía. Then she was taken out of service. Rudi Gunn chartered her for a song.'

'We have the admiral to thank,' Giordino grunted. 'He's tighter than the lid on a rusty pickle jar.'

'1962?' Loren muttered, shaking her head. 'That was thirty-six years ago. She's either a derelict by now or in a museum.'

'According to Rudi she's still used as a work boat,' said Pitt, 'and has a top deck large enough to accommodate a helicopter. He assures me that she'll make a good platform to launch reconnaissance flights.'

'When search operations cease with daylight,' Giordino continued to explain, 'the ferry will cruise overnight to the next range of islands on Dirk's survey list. This approach will save us a considerable amount of flight time.'

Loren handed Pitt a plate and silverware. 'Sounds like you've got everything pretty well under control. What happens when you find what looks like a promising treasure site?'

'We'll worry about putting together an excavation operation after we study the geology of the island,' Pitt answered.

'Help yourself to the feast,' said Loren.

Giordino wasted no time. He began building a sandwich of monumental proportions. 'You lay out a good spread, lady.'

'Beats slaving over a hot stove.' Loren laughed. 'What about permits? You can't go running around digging for treasure in Mexico without permission from government authorities.'

Pitt laid a hefty portion of mortadella on a slice of sourdough bread. 'Admiral Sandecker thought it best to wait. We don't want to advertise our objective. If word got out that we had a line on the biggest bonanza in history, a thousand treasure hunters would descend on us like locusts. Mexican officials would throw us out of the country in a mad grab to keep the hoard for their own government. And Congress would give NUMA hell for spending American tax dollars on a treasure hunt in another country. No, the quieter, the better.'

'We can't afford to be shot down before we've had half a chance of making the find,' said Giordino in an unusual display of seriousness.

Loren was silent while she ladled a spoonful of potato salad on to her plate, then asked, 'Why don't you have someone on your team as insurance in the event local Mexican officials become suspicious and start asking questions?'

Pitt looked at her. 'You mean a public relations expert?'

'No, a bona fide, card-carrying member of the United States Congress.'

Pitt stared into those sensual violet eyes. 'You?'

'Why not? The Speaker of the House has called for a recess next week. My aides can cover for me. I'd love to get out of Washington for a few days and see a piece of Mexico.'

'Frankly,' said Giordino, 'I think it's a stellar concept.' He gave Loren a wink and a toothy smile. 'Dirk is always more congenial when you're around.'

Pitt put his arm around Loren. 'If something should go wrong, if this thing blows up in our faces while we're in foreign territory and you're along for the ride, the scandal could ruin your political career.

She looked across the table at him brazenly. 'So the voters throw me out on the streets. Then I'd have no choice but to marry *you*.'

'A fate worse than listening to a presidential speech,' said Giordino, 'but a good idea just the same.'

'Somehow I can't picture us walking down the aisle of the Washington Cathedral,' Pitt said thoughtfully, 'and then setting up housekeeping in some brick townhouse in Georgetown.'

Loren had hoped for a different reaction, but she knew that Pitt was no ordinary man. She recalled their first meeting at a lawn party nearly ten years before given by some forgotten former secretary of environment. There was a magnetism that had drawn her to him. He was not handsome in the movie star sense, but there was a masculine, no-nonsense air about him that awakened a desire she hadn't experienced with other men. He was tall and lean. That helped. As a congresswoman she had known many wealthy and powerful men, several of them devilishly good-looking. But here was a man who wore the reputation of an adventurer comfortably and cared nothing for power or fame. And rightly so. He was the genuine article.

There were no strings attached to their off-and-on ten-year affair. He had known other women, she had known other men, and yet their bond still held firm. Any thought of marriage had seemed remote. Each was already married to his or her job. But the years had mellowed their relationship, and as a woman Loren knew her biological clock did not have too many ticks left if she wished to have children.

'It doesn't have to be like that,' she said finally.

He sensed her feeling. 'No,' he said affectionately, 'we can make several major improvements.'

She gave him a peculiar look. 'Are you proposing to me?'

A quiet look deepened his green eyes. 'Let's just say I was making a suggestion about things to come.'

33

'Can you put us closer to the dominant peak?' Sarason asked his brother Charles Oxley, who was at the controls of a small amphibious flying boat. 'The crest of the lower one is too sharp for our requirements.'

'Do you see something?'

Sarason peered through binoculars out a side window of the aircraft. 'The island has definite possibilities, but it would help if I knew what sort of landmark to look for.'

Oxley banked the twin turboprop-engined Baffin CZ-410 for a better view of Isla Danzante, a steep-sided, 5-square-kilometre (3-square-mile) rock formation that jutted 400 metres (1312 feet) above the Sea of Cortez just south of the popular resort town of Loreto. 'Has the right look about it,' he commented, staring down. Two small beaches to land boats. The slopes are honeycombed with small caves. What do you say, brother?'

Sarason turned and looked at the man in the rear passenger seat. 'I say the esteemed Professor Moore is still holding out on us.'

'You'll be alerted to the proper site when I see it,' Moore said curtly.

'I say we throw the little bastard out the hatch and watch him try to fly,' Sarason snapped harshly.

Moore crossed his arms smugly. 'You do, and you'll never find the treasure.'

'I'm getting damned sick of hearing that.'

'What about Isla Danzante?' asked Oxley. 'Has it got the right features?'

Moore snatched the binoculars from Sarason without asking and peered at the broken terrain running across the ridge of the island. After a few moments, he handed them back and relaxed in his seat with an iced shaker of martinis. 'Not the one we're looking for,' he proclaimed regally.

Sarason clasped his hands tightly to prevent them from strangling Moore. After a few moments, he regained a degree of composure and turned the page of the same boater's guide that was being used by Pitt. 'Next search point is Isla Carmen. Size, one hundred and fifty square kilometres. Length, thirty kilometres. Has several peaks rising over three hundred metres.'

'That's a pass,' announced Moore. 'Far too large.'

'Your speedy response is duly noted,' Sarason muttered sarcastically. 'After that we have Isla Cholla, a small flat-topped rock with a light tower and a few fishing huts.'

'Skip that one too,' said Moore.

'Okay, next up is Isla San Ildefonso, six miles offshore east of San Sebastian.'

'Size?'

'About two and a half square kilometres. No beaches.'

'There has to be a beach,' said Moore, taking another slug from his martini shaker. He swallowed the last few drops and his face took on an expression of deprivation. 'The Incas could not have landed and unloaded their rafts without a beach.'

'After San Ildefonso we come to Bahía Coyote,' said Sarason. 'There we'll have a choice of six islands that are little more than huge rocks rising from the sea.'

Oxley eased the Baffin amphibian into a slow climb until he reached 700 metres (about 2300 feet). Then he set a course due north. Twenty-five minutes later the bay and the long peninsula that shield it from the Gulf came into view. Oxley descended and began circling the small rocky islands scattered around the entrance to the bay.

'Isla Guapa and Isla Bargo are possibilities,' observed Sarason. 'They both rise sharply from the water and have small but open summits.'

Moore squirmed sideways in his seat and peered down. 'They don't look promising to me – ' He stopped talking and grabbed Sarason's binoculars again. 'That island down there.'

'Which one?' queried Sarason irritably. 'There are six of them.'

'The one that looks like a floating duck looking backward.'

'Isla Bargo. Fits the profile. Steep walls on three sides, rounded crest. There is also a small beach in the crook of the neck.'

'That's it,' Moore said excitedly. 'That must be it.'

Oxley was sceptical. 'How can you be so sure?'

A curious look crossed Moore's face for a fleeting instant. 'A gut feeling, nothing more.'

Sarason snatched back the glasses and studied the island. 'There, on the crown. It looks like something carved in the rock.'

'Don't pay any attention to that,' said Moore, wiping a trickle of sweat from his forehead. 'It doesn't mean a thing.'

Sarason was no fool. Could it be a signpost cut by the Incas to mark the passageway to the treasure, he wondered in silence.

Moore sank back in his seat and said nothing.

'I'll land and taxi to that little beach,' said Oxley. 'From the air, at least, it looks like a relatively easy climb to the summit.'

Sarason nodded. 'Take her down.'

Oxley made two passes over the water off the island's beach, making certain there were no underwater reefs or rocks that could tear out the bottom of the aircraft. He came into the wind and settled the plane on the blue sea, striking the light swells and riding them like a speedboat across a choppy lake. The propellers flashed in the sun as they whipped sheets of spray over the wing.

The plane quickly slowed from the drag of the water as

346

Oxley eased back on the throttles, keeping just enough power to move the plane towards the beach. Forty-six metres (151 feet) from shore, he extended the wheels into the water. The tyres soon touched and gripped the sandy shelf that sloped towards the island. Two minutes later the plane rose from a low surf and rolled on to the beach like a dripping duck.

Two fishermen wandered over from a small driftwood shack and gawked at the aircraft as Oxley turned off the ignition switches and the propellers swung to a stop. The passenger door opened and Sarason stepped down to the white sand beach, followed by Moore and finally Oxley, who locked and secured the door and cargo hatch. As an added security measure, Sarason generously paid the fishermen to guard the plane. Then they set off on a scarcely defined footpath leading to the top of the island.

At first the trail was an easy hike but then it angled more steeply the closer they came to the summit. Gulls soared over them, squawking and staring down at the sweating humans through indifferent beady eyes. Their flight was majestic as they steered by the feathers in their tails, wings outstretched and motionless to catch the warm updraughts. One particularly curious bird swooped over Moore and splattered his shoulder.

The anthropologist, appearing to suffer from the effects of alcohol and exertion, stared dumbly at his stained shirt, too tired to curse. Sarason, a wide grin on his face, saluted the gull and climbed over a large rock blocking the trail. Then the blue sea came into view and he looked across the channel to the white sand beach of Playa el Coyote and the Sierra el Cardonal mountains beyond.

Moore had stopped, gasping for air, sweat flowing freely. He looked on the verge of collapse when Oxley grabbed his hand and heaved him on to the flat top of the summit.

'Didn't anybody ever tell you booze and rock climbing don't mix?'

Moore ignored him. Then suddenly, the exhaustion

washed away and he stiffened. His eyes squinted in drunken concentration. He brushed Oxley aside and stumbled towards a rock the size of a small automobile that was crudely carved in the shape of some animal. Like a drunk who had witnessed a vision, he staggered around the rock sculpture, his hands fluttering over the rough, uneven surface.

'A dog,' he gasped between laboured breaths, 'it's only a stupid dog.'

'Wrong,' said Sarason. 'A coyote. The namesake of the bay. Superstitious fishermen carved it as a symbol to protect their crews and boats when they go to sea.'

'Why should an old rock carving interest you?' asked Oxley.

'As an anthropologist, primitive sculptures can be a great source of knowledge.'

Sarason was watching Moore, and for once his eyes were no longer filled with distaste. There was no question in his mind that the drunken professor had given away the key to the treasure's location.

He could kill Moore now, Sarason thought icily. Throw the little man over the edge of the island's west palisade into the surf that crashed on the rocks far below. And who would care? The body would probably drift out with the tide and become shark food. Any investigation by local Mexican authorities was doubtful.

'You realize, of course, that we no longer require your services, don't you, Henry?' It was the first time Sarason had uttered Moore's given name, and there was an unpleasant familiarity about it.

Moore shook his head and spoke with an icy composure that seemed unnatural under the circumstances. 'You'll never do it without me.'

'A pathetic bluff,' Sarason sneered. 'Now that we know we're searching for an island with a sculpture, an ancient one I presume, what more can you possibly contribute to the search?'

Moore's drunkenness had seemingly melted away, and he abruptly appeared as sober as a judge. 'A rock sculpture is only the first of several benchmarks the Incas erected. They all have to be interpreted.'

Sarason smiled. It was a cold and evil smile. 'You wouldn't lie to me now, would you, Henry? You wouldn't deceive my brother and me into thinking Isla Bargo isn't the treasure site so you can return later on your own and dig it up? I sincerely hope that little plot isn't running through your mind.'

Moore glared at him, simple dislike showing where there should have been fear. 'Blow off the top of the island,' he said with a shrug, 'and see what it gets you. Level it to the waterline. You won't find an ounce of Huascar's treasure, not in a thousand years. Not without someone who knows the secrets of the markers.'

'He may be right,' Oxley said quietly. 'And if he's lying, we can return and excavate on our own. Either way, we win.'

Sarason smiled bleakly. He could read Henry Moore's thoughts. The anthropologist was playing for time, waiting and scheming to use the ultimate end of the search to somehow claim the riches for himself. But Sarason was a schemer too and he had considered every option. At the moment he could see no avenue open for Moore to make a miraculous escape with tons of gold. Certainly not unless Moore had a plan that he had not yet fathomed.

Leniency and patience, they were the watchwords for now, Sarason decided. He patted Moore on the back. 'Forgive my frustration. Let's get back to the plane and call it a day. I think we could all use a cool bath, a tall margarita, and a good supper.'

'Amen,' said Oxley. 'We'll take up tomorrow where we left off today.'

'I knew you'd see the light,' said Moore. 'I'll show you the way. All you boys have to do is keep the faith.'

When they arrived back at the aircraft, Sarason entered

first. On a hunch, he picked up Moore's discarded martini shaker and shook a few drops on to his tongue. Water, not gin.

Sarason silently cursed himself. He had not picked up on how dangerous Moore was. Why would Moore act the role of a drunk if not to lull everyone into thinking he was harmless? He slowly began to comprehend that Henry Moore was not entirely what he seemed. There was more to the famous and respected anthropologist than met the eye, much more.

As a man who could kill without the slightest remorse, Sarason should have recognized another killer when he saw one.

Micki Moore stepped out of the blue-tiled swimming pool below the hacienda and stretched out on a lounge chair. She was wearing a red bikini that did very little to conceal her thin form. The sun was warm and she did not dry herself, preferring to let the water drops cling to her body. She glanced up at the main house and motioned to one of the servants to bring her another rum collins. She acted as though she were the mistress of the manor, totally disregarding the armed guards who roamed the grounds. Her behaviour was hardly in keeping with someone who was being held hostage.

The hacienda was built around the pool and a large garden filled with a variety of tropical plants. All major rooms had balconies with dramatic views of the sea and the town of Guaymas. She was more than happy to relax around the pool or in her skylit bedroom with its own patio and Jacuzzi while the men flew up and down the Gulf in search of the treasure. She picked up her watch from a small table. Five o'clock. The conniving brothers and her husband would be returning soon. She sighed with pleasure at the thought of another fabulous dinner of local dishes.

After the servant girl brought the rum collins, Micki

drank it down to the ice cubes and settled back for a brief nap. Just before she drifted off, she thought she heard a car drive up the road from town and stop at the front gate of the hacienda.

When she awoke a short time later, her skin felt cool and she sensed that the sun had passed behind a cloud. But then she opened her eyes, and was startled to see a man standing over her, his shadow thrown across the upper half of her body.

The eyes that stared at her looked like stagnant black pools. There was no life to them. Even his face seemed incapable of expression. The stranger appeared emaciated, as if he been sick for a long time. Micki shivered as though an icy breeze suddenly swept over her. She thought it odd that he took no notice of her exposed body, but gazed directly into her eyes. She felt as if he were looking inside her.

'Who are you?' she asked. 'Do you work for Mr Zolar?'

He did not reply for several seconds. When he spoke, it was with an odd voice with no inflection. 'My name is Tupac Amaru.'

And then he turned and walked away.

34

Admiral Sandecker stood in front of his desk and held out his hand as Gaskill and Ragsdale were ushered into his office. He gave a friendly smile. 'Gentlemen, please take a seat and get comfortable.'

Gaskill looked down at the little man who stood slightly below his shoulders. 'Thank you for taking the time to see us.'

'NUMA has worked with Customs and the FBI in the past. Our relations were always based on cordial cooperation.'

'I hope you weren't apprehensive when we asked to meet with you,' said Ragsdale.

'Curious is more like it. Would you like some coffee?'

Gaskill nodded. 'Black for me, thank you.'

'Whatever artificial sweetener that's handy in mine,' said Ragsdale.

Sandecker spoke into his intercom, and then looked up and asked, 'Well, gentlemen, what can I do for you?'

Ragsdale came straight to the point. 'We'd like NUMA's help settling a thorny problem dealing with stolen artifacts.'

'A little out of our line,' said Sandecker. 'Our field is ocean science and engineering.'

Gaskill nodded. 'We understand, but it has come to Customs' attention that someone in your agency has smuggled a valuable artifact into the country illegally.'

'That someone was me,' Sandecker shot back without batting an eye.

Ragsdale and Gaskill glanced at each other and shifted uneasily in their chairs. This turn of events was not what they had expected.

'Are you aware, Admiral, that the United States prohibits the importing of stolen artifacts under a United Nations convention that seeks to protect antiquities worldwide?'

'I am.'

'And are you also aware, sir, that officials at the Ecuadorian embassy have filed a protest?'

'As a matter of fact, I instigated the protest.'

Gaskill sighed and visibly relaxed. 'I had a feeling in my bones there was more to this than a simple smuggling.'

'I think Mr Gaskill and I would both appreciate an explanation,' said Ragsdale.

Sandecker paused as his private secretary, Julie Wolff, entered with a tray of coffee cups and set them on the edge of his desk. 'Excuse me, Admiral, but Rudi Gunn called from San Felipe to report that he and Al Giordino have landed and are making final preparations for the project.'

'What is Dirk's status?'

'He's driving and should be somewhere in Texas about now.'

Sandecker turned back to the government agents after Julie had closed the door. 'Sorry for the interruption. Where were we?'

'You were going to tell us why you smuggled a stolen artifact into the United States,' said Ragsdale, his face serious.

The admiral casually opened a box of his cigars and offered them. The agents shook their heads. He leaned back in his desk chair, lit a cigar, and graciously blew a cloud of blue smoke over his shoulder towards an open window. Then he told them the story of Drake's *quipu*, beginning with the war between the Inca princes and ending with Hiram Yaeger's translation of the coiled strands and their knots.

'But surely, Admiral,' questioned Ragsdale, 'you and NUMA don't intend to get into the treasure hunting business?'

'We most certainly do.' Sandecker smiled.

'I wish you'd explain the Ecuadorian protest,' said Gaskill.

'As insurance. Ecuador is in bitter conflict with an army of peasant rebels in the mountains. Their government officials were not about to allow us to search for the *quipu* and then take it to the United States for decoding and preservation for fear their people would think they had sold a priceless national treasure to foreigners. By claiming we stole it, they're off the hook. So they agreed to loan the *quipu* to NUMA for a year. And when we return it with the proper ceremony, they'll be applauded as national heroes.'

'But why NUMA?' Ragsdale persisted. 'Why not the Smithsonian or *National Geographic*?'

'Because we don't have a proprietary interest. And we're in a better position to keep the search and discovery out of the public eye.'

'But you can't legally keep any of it.'

'Of course not. If it's discovered in the Sea of Cortez, where we believe it lies, Mexico will cry "finders keepers". Peru will claim original ownership, and the two countries will have to negotiate, thereby assuring the treasures will eventually be displayed in their national museums.'

'And our State Department will get credit for a public relations coup with our good neighbours to the south,' added Ragsdale.

'You said it, sir, not me.'

'Why didn't you notify Customs or the FBI about this?' inquired Gaskill.

'I informed the President,' Sandecker replied matter-of-factly. 'If he failed to filter the information from the White House to your agencies, then you'll just have to blame the White House.'

Ragsdale finished his coffee and set the cup on the tray. 'You've closed the door on one problem that concerned us all, Admiral. And believe me when I say we are extremely relieved at not having to put you through the hassle of an investigation. Unfortunately, or fortunately, depending on your viewpoint, you've opened the door to another dilemma.'

Gaskill looked at Ragsdale. 'The coincidence is nothing short of astonishing.'

'Coincidence?' Sandecker asked curiously.

'That after almost five hundred years, two vital clues to the mystery of Huascar's treasure surfaced from two different sources within five days of each other.'

Sandecker shrugged. 'I'm afraid I don't follow you.'

In turn, Gaskill filled the admiral in on the Golden Body Suit of Tiapollo. He finished by giving a brief summary of the case against Zolar International.

'Are you telling me that another party is searching for Huascar's treasure at this very minute?' Sandecker asked incredulously.

Ragsdale nodded. 'An international syndicate that deals in art theft, antiquity smuggling, and art forgery with annual profits running into untold millions of untaxed dollars.'

'I had no idea.'

'Regrettably, our government and news media have not seen the benefit in educating the general public on a criminal activity that is second only to the drug trade.'

'In one robbery alone,' explained Gaskill, 'the dollar estimate of the masterpieces stolen from the Gardner Museum in Boston in April 1990 came to two hundred million.'

'When you throw in the combined theft, smuggling, and forgery operations taking place in nearly every country of the world,' Ragsdale continued, 'you can understand why we're looking at a billion-dollar industry.'

'The list of art and antiquities stolen over the past hundred years would equal the number of names in the New York phone book,' Gaskill emphasized.

'Who buys such a staggering amount of illegal goods?' asked Sandecker.

'The demand far exceeds the supply,' answered Gaskill. 'Wealthy collectors are indirectly responsible for looting because they create a strong market demand. They stand in line to purchase historically significant hot goods from underground dealers. The list of clients reads like a celebrity register. Heads of state, high-level government officials, motion picture personalities, top business leaders, and even curators of major museums who look the other way while negotiating for black market goods to enhance their collections. If they have a buck, they'll buy it.'

'Drug dealers also buy untold amounts of illegal art and antiquities as a fast and easy way of laundering money while building an investment.'

'I can see why unrecorded artifacts are lost in the shuffle,' said Sandecker. 'But surely famous art paintings and sculptures turn up and are recovered.'

Ragsdale shook his head. 'Sometimes we get lucky, and a tip leads us to stolen property. Occasionally honest art dealers or museum curators will call us when they recognize pieces the thieves are trying to sell. All too often missing art remains lost from lack of leads.'

'A tremendous number of antiquities obtained by grave robbers are sold before archaeologists have a chance to study them,' Gaskill said. 'For example, during the desert war against Iraq in the early nineties, thousands of artifacts, including untranslated clay tablets, jewellery, textiles, glass, pottery, gold and silver coins, and cylinder seals, were plundered from both Kuwaiti and Iraqi museums by anti-Hussein opposition forces and Shiite and Kurdish rebels. Much of it had already passed through dealers and auction houses before any of the pieces could be catalogued as missing or stolen.'

'Hardly seems possible that a collector would pay big money for art he knows damn well belongs to someone else,' said Sandecker. 'He certainly can't put it on display without risking exposure or arrest. What does he do with it?'

'Call it a psychological warp,' replied Ragsdale. 'Gaskill and I can recite any number of cases involving collectors who stash their illegal acquisitions in a secret vault where they sit and view it once a day, or maybe once every ten years. Never mind that none of it is on public display. They get their high by possessing something no one else can own.'

Gaskill nodded in agreement. 'Collector addiction can make people carry out macabre schemes. It's bad enough to desecrate and despoil Indian graves by digging up and selling skulls and mummified bodies of women and children, but certain collectors of American Civil War memorabilia have gone so far as to dig up graves in national cemeteries just to retrieve Union and Confederate belt buckles.'

'A sad commentary on avarice,' mused Sandecker.

'The stories of grave plundering for artifacts are endless,' said Ragsdale. 'Bones of the dead from every culture, beginning with the Neanderthal, are smashed and scattered. The sanctity of the dead means little if there is a profit to be made.'

'Because of the many collectors' insatiable lust for antiquities,' said Gaskill, 'they're prime candidates for rip-offs. Their seemingly inexhaustible demand creates a lucrative trade in forgeries.'

Ragsdale nodded. 'Without proper archaeological study, copied artifacts can pass undetected. Many of the collections in respected museums display forged antiquities and no one realizes. Every curator or collector is unwilling to believe he has been screwed by a forger, and few scholars have the guts to state that the pieces they are examining are suspect.'

'Famous art is not exempt,' Gaskill further explained. 'Agent Ragsdale and I have both seen cases where an outstanding masterpiece was stolen, copied by experts, and the forgery returned through channels for the finder's fee and insurance. The gallery and its curator happily hang the fake, never realizing they've been had.'

'How are the stolen objects distributed and sold?' queried Sandecker.

'Tomb looters and art thieves sell through an underground network of crooked dealers who put up the money and supervise the sales from a distance, acting through agents without revealing their identity.'

'Can't they be traced through the network?'

Gaskill shook his head. 'Because the suppliers and their distributors also operate behind closed doors under a heavy veil of secrecy, it is next to impossible for us to penetrate any particular branch of the network with any prospect of following a trail to the top dealers.'

Ragsdale took over. 'It's not like tracing a drug user to his street-corner dealer, and then to his suppliers, and then up the ladder to the drug lords, who are mostly uneducated, seldom go to extremes to hide their identities, and are often drug users themselves. Instead, we find ourselves matching wits with men who are well educated and highly connected in the top levels of business and government. They're shrewd, and they're cunning. Except in rare cases, they never deal with their clients on a direct face-to-face basis. Whenever we get close, they pull into their shells and throw up a wall of expensive attorneys to block our investigations.'

'Have you had any luck at all?' asked Sandecker.

'We've picked off a few of the small dealers who operate on their own,' replied Ragsdale. 'And both our agencies have recovered substantial numbers of stolen goods. Some during shipment, some from buyers, who almost never do jail time because they claim they didn't know the pieces they bought were stolen. What we've recovered is only a trickle. Without solid evidence we can't stem the main flow of illegal objects.'

'Sounds to me like you fellows are outgunned and outclassed,' said Sandecker.

Ragsdale nodded. 'We'd be the first to admit it.'

Sandecker silently rocked back and forth in his swivel chair, mulling over the words of the government agents seated across the desk. At last he said, 'How can NUMA help you?'

Gaskill leaned across the desk. 'We think you cracked the door open by unknowingly synchronizing your search for Huascar's treasure with the world's largest dealer of hot art and antiquities.'

'Zolar International.'

'Yes, a family whose tentacles reach into every corner of the trade.'

'FBI and Customs agents,' said Ragsdale, 'have never before encountered a single group of art forgers, thieves, and artifact smugglers who have operated in so many countries for so many years and have involved such a diverse cast of wealthy celebrities, who have illegally bought literally billions of dollars worth of stolen art and antiques.'

'I'm listening,' said Sandecker.

'This is our chance to get in on the ground floor,' revealed Gaskill. 'Because of the possibility of finding fantastic riches, the Zolars have shed all caution and launched a search to locate the treasure and keep it for themselves. If they are successful, this presents us with a rare window of opportunity to observe their method of shipment and trail it back to their secret storehouse . . .'

'Where you nab them redhanded with the swag,' Sandecker finished.

Ragsdale grinned. 'We don't exactly use those terms anymore, Admiral, but yes, you're on the right track.

Sandecker was intrigued. 'You want me to call off my search team. Is that the message?'

Gaskill and Ragsdale looked at each other and nodded.

'Yes, sir,' said Gaskill. 'That's the message.'

'With your approval, of course,' Ragsdale hastily added.

'Have you boys cleared this with your superiors?'

Ragsdale nodded solemnly. 'Director Moran of the FBI and Director Thomas of the Customs Service have given their approval.'

'You don't mind if I give them a call and confirm?'

'Not at all,' said Gaskill. 'I apologize that Agent Ragsdale and I didn't go through the chain of command and request that they deal with you directly, but we felt it was best to present our case from firsthand knowledge and let the chips fall where they may.'

'I can appreciate that,' said Sandecker generously.

'Then you'll cooperate?' asked Ragsdale. 'And call off your search team?'

Sandecker stared idly at the smoke curling from his cigar for several moments. 'NUMA will play ball with the bureau and Customs, but I won't close down our search project.'

Gaskill stared at the admiral, not knowing if he was joking. 'I don't think I catch your drift, sir.'

'Have you people ever hunted for something that has been lost for almost five hundred years?'

Ragsdale glanced at his partner and shrugged. 'Speaking for the bureau, our search operations are generally confined to missing persons, fugitives, and bodies. Lost treasure is out of our domain.'

'I don't believe I have to explain what the Customs Service looks for,' said Gaskill.

'I'm quite familiar with your directives,' Sandecker said conversationally. 'But finding lost treasure is a million-to-one long shot. You can't interview people for leads who have been dead since the fifteen hundreds. All our *quipu* and your golden mummy have done is given vague references to a mysterious island in the Sea of Cortez. A clue that puts the proverbial needle somewhere within a hundred-and-sixty-thousand-square-kilometre haystack. I'm assuming the Zolars are amateurs at this kind of search game. So the chances of them finding the cavern containing Huascar's golden chain are ten metres this side of nil.'

'You think your people have a better chance?' asked Gaskill testily.

'My special projects director and his team are the best in the business. If you don't believe me, check our records.'

'How do you plan to play ball with us?' Ragsdale asked, his tone edged with disbelief.

Sandecker made his thrust. 'We conduct our search at the same time as the Zolars, but we hang in the shadows. They have no reason to suspect rivals and will assume any NUMA personnel or aircraft they sight are on an oceanographic research project. If the Zolars are successful in discovering the treasure, my team will simply melt away and return to Washington.'

'And should the Zolars strike out?' demanded Ragsdale.

'If NUMA can't find the treasure, it doesn't want to be found.'

'And if NUMA is successful?' Ragsdale pushed forward.

'We leave a trail of bread crumbs for the Zolars to follow, and let them think they discovered the hoard on their own.' Sandecker paused, his hard gaze moving from Ragsdale to Gaskill and back. 'From then on, gentlemen, the show belongs to you.'

35

'I keep imagining that Rudolph Valentino is going to ride over the next dune and carry me away to his tent,' said Loren sleepily. She was sitting on the front seat of the Pierce Arrow, her legs curled under her, staring at the ocean of sand dunes that dominated the landscape.

'Keep looking,' said Pitt. 'The Coachella Dunes, slightly north of here, are where Hollywood used to shoot many of their desert movies.'

Fifty kilometres (31 miles) after passing through Yuma, Arizona, across the Colorado River into California, Pitt swung the big Pierce Arrow left off Interstate Highway 8 and on to the narrow state road that led to the border towns of Calexico and Mexicali. Drivers and passengers in cars that passed, or those coming from the opposite direction, stared and gawked at the old classic auto and the trailer it pulled.

Loren had sweet-talked Pitt into driving the old auto crosscountry, camping in the trailer, and then joining a tour around southern Arizona sponsored by the Classic Car Club of America. The tour was scheduled to begin in two weeks. Pitt doubted that they could wrap up the treasure hunt in such a short time but went along with Loren because he enjoyed driving his old cars on extended tours.

'How much farther to the border?' Loren asked.

'Another forty-two kilometres will put us into Mexico,' he answered. 'Then a hundred and sixty-five klicks to San Felipe. We should arrive at the dock, where Al and Rudi have tied up the ferry, by dinnertime.'

'Speaking of edibles and liquids,' she said lazily, 'the

refrigerator is empty and the cupboards are bare. Except for breakfast cereal and coffee this morning, we cleaned out the food stock at that campground in Sedona last night.'

He took his right hand from the steering wheel, squeezed her knee and smiled. 'I suppose I have to keep the passengers happy by filling their bellies.'

'How about that truck stop up ahead?' She straightened and pointed through the flat, narrow windshield of the Pierce.

Pitt gazed over the ornate radiator cap, a crouched archer poised to fire an arrow. He saw a sign by the side of the road, dried and bleached by the desert sun, and on the verge of collapsing into the sand at any moment. The lettering was so old and faded he could hardly read the words.

Ice-cold beer and food a mother would love.
Only 2 more minutes to the Box Car Café.

He laughed. 'The cold beer sounds good, but I'm leery of the cuisine. When I was a boy, my mother loved to make dishes that turned me green.'

'Shame on you. Your mother is a good cook.'

'She is now, but twenty-five years ago, even the starving homeless wouldn't come near our doorstep.'

'You're terrible.' Loren turned the dial of the old tube-type radio, trying to tune in a Mexicali station. She finally found one, playing Mexican music, that came in clear. 'I don't care if the chef has the black plague, I'm starved.'

Take a woman on a long trip, Pitt mused miserably, and they're always hungry or demanding to stop at a bathroom.

'And besides,' she threw in, 'you need gas.'

Pitt glanced at the fuel gauge. The needle stood steady at a quarter tank. 'I guess it won't hurt to fill up before we cross the border.'

'It doesn't seem as if we've driven very far since the last gas stop.'

'A big car that was built sixty years ago, with a twelve-cylinder engine and pulling a house trailer, won't win any awards for fuel economy.'

The roadside restaurant and gas station came into view. All Pitt saw as they drove closer was a dilapidated pair of old railroad freight cars joined together, with two gas pumps out front and a neon EAT sign barely flickering in the shadow of the Box Car Café. A cluster of battered old house trailers was parked in the rear, abandoned and empty. Out front in the dirt parking lot, eighteen to twenty bikers were milling around a small fleet of Harley-Davidsons, drinking beer and enjoying a cool breeze that was blowing in from the Gulf.

'Boy, you sure can pick 'em,' said Pitt drolly.

'Maybe we'd better go on,' Loren murmured, having second thoughts.

'You afraid of the bikers? They're probably weary travellers just like you and me.'

'They certainly don't dress like us.' She nodded at the assembly, divided equally between men and women, all wearing black riding gear festooned with badges, patches, and embroidered messages touting America's most famous motorcycle.

Pitt turned the outsize steering wheel and the Pierce rolled off the blacktop up to the gas pumps. The big V-12 engine was so whisper-quiet it was hard to tell it had stopped when he turned off the ignition. He opened the suicide door that swung outward from the front, put a foot on the high running board and stepped down. 'Hi there,' he greeted the nearest biker, a bleached blond female with a ponytail, wearing black leather pants and jacket. 'How's the food here?'

'Not quite up to the standards of Spago's or Chasen's,' she said pleasantly. 'But if you're hungry, it's not half bad.'

A metal sign liberally peppered with bullet holes said

Self service, so Pitt inserted the nozzle of the gas pump inside the Pierce Arrow's tank filler and squeezed the handle. When he had the engine rebuilt, the machine shop modified the valves to burn unleaded gas without problems.

Loren warily hunched down in her seat as the bikers all walked over and admired the old car and trailer. After answering a barrage of questions, Pitt lifted the hood and showed them the engine. Then he pulled Loren from the car.

'I thought you'd like to meet these nice people,' he said. 'They all belong to a bike riding club from West Hollywood.'

She thought Pitt was joking and was embarrassed half to death as he made introductions. Then she was astounded to discover they were attorneys with their wives on a weekend ride around the Southern California desert. She was also impressed and flattered that they recognized her when Pitt gave them her name.

After a congenial conversation, the Hollywood barristers and their spouses bade goodbye, climbed aboard their beloved hogs and roared off, exhaust stacks reverberating in chorus, towards the Imperial Valley. Pitt and Loren waved, then turned and faced the freight cars.

The rails beneath the rusting wheel-trucks were buried in the sand. The weathered wooden walls had once been painted a reddish tan, and the lettering above the long row of crudely installed windows read Southern Pacific Lines. Thanks to the dry air, the body shells of the antique box cars had survived the ravages of constant exposure and appeared in relatively good condition.

Pitt owned a piece of railroad history, a Pullman car. It was part of the collection housed inside his hangar in Washington. The once-luxurious rail car had been pulled by the famed Manhattan Limited out of New York in the years prior to World War I. He judged these freight cars to have been built sometime around 1915.

He and Loren climbed a makeshift stairway and entered a door cut into the end of one car. The interior was time-worn but neat and clean. There were no tables, only a long counter with stools that stretched the length of the two attached cars. The open kitchen was situated on the opposite side of the counter and looked as if it was constructed from used lumber that had lain in the sun for several decades. Pictures on the walls showed early engines, smoke spouting from their stacks, pulling passenger and freight trains across the desert sands. The list of records on a Wurlitzer jukebox was a mix of favourite pop music from the forties and fifties and the sounds of steam locomotives. Two plays for twenty-five cents.

Pitt put a quarter in the slot and made his selections. One was Frankie Carle playing 'Sweet Lorraine'. The other was the clamour of a Norfolk & Western single expansion articulated steam locomotive leaving a station and coming to speed.

A tall man, in his early sixties, with grey hair and white beard, was wiping the oak counter top. He looked up and smiled, his blue-green eyes filled with warmth and congeniality. 'Greetings, folks. Welcome to the Box Car Café. Travel far?'

'Not far,' Pitt answered, throwing Loren a rakish grin. 'We didn't leave Sedona as early as I planned.'

'Don't blame me,' she said loftily. 'You're the one who woke up with carnal passions.'

'What can I get you?' said the man behind the bar. He was wearing cowboy boots, denim pants, and a plaid shirt that was badly faded from too many washings.

'Your advertised ice-cold beer would be nice,' replied Loren, opening a menu.

'Mexican or domestic?'

'Corona?'

'One Corona coming up. And you, sir?'

'What do you have on tap?' asked Pitt.

'Olympia, Coors, and Budweiser.'

'I'd like an Oly.'

'Anything to eat?' inquired the man behind the counter.

'Your mesquite chilliburger,' said Loren. 'And cole-slaw.'

'I'm not real hungry,' said Pitt. 'I'll just have the cole-slaw. Do you own this place?'

'Bought it from the original owner when I gave up prospecting.' He set their beer on the bar and turned to his stove.

'The box cars are interesting relics of railroad history. Were they moved here, or did the railroad run through at one time?'

'We're actually sitting on the siding of the old main line,' answered the diner's owner. 'The tracks used to run from Yuma to El Centro. The line was abandoned in 1947 for lack of business. The rise of truck lines did it in. These cars were bought by an old fella who used to be an engineer for the Southern Pacific. He and his wife made a restaurant and gas station out of them. With the main interstate going north of here and all, we don't see too much traffic anymore.'

The bartender/cook looked as if he might have been a fixture of the desert even before the rails were laid. He had the worn look of a man who had seen more than he should and heard a thousand stories that remained in his head, classified and indexed as drama, humour, or horror. There was also an unmistakable aura of style about him, a sophistication that said he didn't belong in a godforsaken roadside tavern on a remote and seldom-travelled road through the desert.

For a fleeting instant, Pitt thought the old cook looked vaguely familiar. On reflection, though, Pitt figured the man only resembled someone he couldn't quite place. 'I'll bet you can recite some pretty interesting tales about the dunes around here,' he said, making idle conversation.

'A lot of bones lie in them, remains of pioneers and miners who tried to cross four hundred kilometres of

367

desert from Yuma to Boriego Springs in the middle of summer.'

'Once they passed the Colorado River, there was no water?' asked Loren.

'Not a drop, not until Boriego. That was long before the valley was irrigated. Only after them old boys died from the sun did they learn their bodies lay not five metres from water. The trauma was so great they've all come back as ghosts to haunt the desert.'

Loren looked perplexed. 'I think I missed something.'

'There's no water on the surface,' the old fellow explained. 'But underground there's whole rivers of it, some as wide and deep as the Colorado.'

Pitt was curious. 'I've never heard of large bodies of water running under the desert.'

'There's two for sure. One, a really big sucker, runs from upper Nevada south into the Mojave Desert and then west, where it empties into the Pacific below Los Angeles. The other flows west under the Imperial Valley of California before curling south and spilling into the Sea of Cortez.'

'What proof do you have these rivers actually exist?' asked Loren. 'Has anyone seen them?'

'The underground stream that flows into the Pacific,' answered the cook, as he prepared Loren's chilliburger, 'was supposedly found by an engineer searching for oil. He alleged his geophysical instruments detected the river and tracked it across the Mojave and under the town of Laguna Beach into the ocean. So far nobody has proved or disproved his claim. The river travelling to the Sea of Cortez comes from an old story about a prospector who discovered a cave that led down into a deep cavern with a river running through it.'

Pitt tensed as Yaeger's translation of the *quipu* suddenly flashed through his mind. 'This prospector, how did he describe this underground river?'

The diner's owner talked without turning from his stove.

'His name was Leigh Hunt, and he was probably a very inventive liar. But he swore up and down that back in 1942 he discovered a cave in the Castle Dome Mountains not too far northeast of here. From the mouth of the cave, through a chain of caverns, he descended two kilometres deep into the earth until he encountered an underground river rushing through a vast canyon. It was there Hunt claims he found rich deposits of placer gold.'

'I think I saw the movie,' said Loren sceptically.

The old cook turned and waved a spatula in the air. 'People at the assay office stated that the sand Hunt carried back from the underground canyon assayed at three thousand dollars per ton. A mighty good recovery rate when you remember that gold was only twenty dollars and sixty-five cents an ounce back then.'

'Did Hunt ever return to the canyon and the river?' asked Pitt.

'He tried, but a whole army of scavengers followed him back to the mountain, hungering for a piece of the River of Gold, as it became known. He got mad and dynamited a narrow part of the passage about a hundred metres inside the entrance. Brought down half the mountain. Neither Hunt nor those who followed him were ever able to dig through the rubble or find another cave leading inside.'

'With today's mining technology,' said Pitt, 'reexcavating the passage should be a viable project.'

'Sure, if you want to spend about two million dollars,' snorted the cook. 'Nobody I ever heard about was willing to gamble that much money on a story that might be pure hokum.' He paused to set the chilliburger and coleslaw dishes on the counter. Then he drew a mug of beer from a tap, walked around the bar and sat down on a stool next to Pitt. 'They say old Hunt somehow made it back inside the mountain but never came out. He disappeared right after he blew the cave and was not seen again. There was talk that he found another way inside and died there. A

369

few people believe in a great river that flows through a canyon deep beneath the sands, but most think it's only another tall tale of the desert.'

'Such things do exist,' said Pitt. 'A few years ago I was on an expedition that found an underground stream.'

'Somewhere in the desert Southwest?' inquired the cook.

'No, the Sahara. It flowed under a hazardous waste plant and carried pollutants to the Niger River, and then into the Atlantic where it caused a proliferation of red tides.'

'The Mojave River north of here goes underground after running above the surface for a considerable distance. Nobody knows for certain where it ends up.'

Between bites of the chilliburger Loren asked, 'You seem convinced that Hunt's river flows into the Sea of Cortez. How do you know it doesn't enter the Pacific off California?'

'Because of Hunt's backpack and canteen. He lost them in the cave and they were found six months later, having drifted up on a beach in the Gulf.'

'Don't you think that's highly improbable? The pack and canteen could have belonged to anyone. Why would anyone believe they were his?' Loren questioned the cook as if she was sitting on a congressional investigation committee.

'I guess because his name was stencilled on them.'

The unexpected obstacle did not deter Loren. She simply sidestepped it. 'There could be a good twenty or more logical explanations for his effects being in the Gulf. They could have been lost or thrown there by someone who found or stole them from Hunt, or more likely he never died in the cave and dropped them from a boat himself.'

'Could be he lost them in the sea,' admitted the cook, 'but then how do you explain the other bodies?'

Pitt looked at him. 'What other bodies?'

'The fisherman who disappeared in Lake Cocopah,'

replied the cook in a hushed voice, as if he was afraid of being overheard. 'And the two divers that vanished into Satan's Sink. What was left of their bodies was found floating in the Gulf.'

'And the desert telegraph sends out another pair of tall tales,' suggested Loren drily.

The cook held up his right hand. 'God's truth. You can check the stories out with the sheriff's department.'

'Where are the sink and lake located?' asked Pitt.

'Lake Cocopah, the spot where the fisherman was lost, is southeast of Yuma. Satan's Sink lies in Mexico at the northern foot of the Sierra el Mayor Mountains. You can draw a line from Hunt's mountain through Lake Cocopah and then Satan's Sink right into the Sea of Cortez.'

Loren continued the interrogation. 'Who's to say they didn't drown while fishing and diving in the Gulf?'

'The fisherman and his wife were out on the lake for the better part of the day when she wanted to head back to their camper to start dinner. He rowed her ashore and then continued trolling around the lake. An hour later, when she looked for him, all she could see was his overturned boat. Three weeks later a water-skier spotted his body floating in the Gulf a hundred and fifty kilometres from the lake.'

'I'm more inclined to believe his wife did him in, dumped his remains in the sea and threw off suspicion by claiming he was sucked into an underground waterway.'

'What about the divers?' Pitt queried.

'Not much to tell. They dived into Satan's Sink, a flooded pool in an earthquake fault, and never came out. A month later, battered to a pulp, they were also pulled out of the Gulf.'

Pitt stabbed a fork at his coleslaw, but he was no longer hungry. His mind was shifting gears. 'Do you happen to know approximately where Hunt's gear and the bodies were found?'

'I haven't made a detailed study of the phenomena,'

answered the diner's owner, staring thoughtfully at the heavily scarred wooden floor. 'But as I recollect most of them were found in the waters off Punta el Macharro.'

'What part of the Gulf would that be?'

'On the western shore. Macharro Point, as we call it in English, is two or three kilometres above San Felipe.'

Loren looked at Pitt. 'Our destination.'

Pitt made a wry smile. 'Remind me to keep a sharp eye for dead bodies.'

The cook finished off his beer. 'You folks heading for San Felipe to do a little fishing?'

Pitt nodded. 'I guess you might call it a fishing expedition.'

'The scenery ain't much to look at once you drop below Mexicali. The desert seems desolate and barren to most folks, but it has countless paradoxes. There are more ghosts, skeletons, and myths per kilometre than any jungle or mountains on earth. Keep that in mind and you'll see them as sure as the Irish see leprechauns.'

'We'll keep that in mind,' Loren said, smiling, 'when we cross over Leigh Hunt's underground River of Gold.'

'Oh, you'll cross it all right,' said the cook. 'The sad fact is you won't know it.'

After Pitt paid for the gas and the meal, he went outside and checked the Pierce Arrow's oil and water. The old cook accompanied Loren on to the dining car's observation platform. He was carrying a bowl of carrots and lettuce. 'Have a good trip,' he said cheerfully.

'Thank you.' Loren nodded at the vegetables. 'Feeding a rabbit?'

'No, my burro. Mr Periwinkle is getting up there in age and can't graze too well on his own.'

Loren held out her hand. 'It's been fun listening to your stories, Mr . . .'

'Cussler, Clive Cussler. Mighty nice to have met you, ma'am.'

When they were on the road again, the Pierce Arrow and its trailer smoothly rolling towards the border crossing, Pitt turned to Loren. 'For a moment there, I thought the old geezer might have given me a clue to the treasure site.'

'You mean Yaeger's far-out translation about a river running under an island?'

'It still doesn't seem geologically possible.'

Loren turned the rearview mirror to reapply her lipstick. 'If the river flowed deep enough it might conceivably pass under the Gulf.'

'Maybe, but there's no way in hell to know for certain without drilling through several kilometres of hard rock.'

'You'll be lucky just to find your way to the treasure cavern without a major excavation.'

Pitt smiled as he stared at the road ahead. 'He could really spin the yarns, couldn't he?'

'The old cook? He certainly had an active imagination.'

'I'm sorry I didn't get his name.'

Loren settled back in the seat and gazed out her window as the dunes gave way to a tapestry of mesquite and cactus. 'He told me what it was.'

'And?'

'It was an odd name.' She paused, trying to remember. Then she shrugged in defeat. 'Funny thing . . . I've already forgotten it.'

36

Loren was driving when they reached San Felipe. Pitt had stretched out in the backseat and was snoring away, but she did not bother to wake him. She guided the dusty, bug-splattered Pierce Arrow around the town's traffic circle, making a wide turn so she didn't run one side of the trailer over the kerb, and turned south towards the town's breakwater-enclosed harbour. She did not expect to see such a proliferation of hotels and restaurants. The once sleepy fishing village was riding the crest of a tourist boom. Resorts appeared to be under construction up and down the beaches.

Five kilometres (3 miles) south of town she turned left on a road leading towards the waters of the Gulf. Loren thought it strange that an artificial, man-made harbour had been constructed on such an exposed piece of shoreline. She thought a more practical site would have been under the shelter of Macharro Point several kilometres to the north. Oh well, she decided. What did gringos know about Baja politics?

Loren stopped the Pierce alongside an antiquated ferryboat that looked like a ghost from a scrap yard. The impression was heightened by the low tide that had left the ferry's hull tipped drunkenly on an angle with its keel sunk into the harbour bottom's silt.

'Rise and shine, big boy,' she said, reaching over the seat and shaking Pitt.

He blinked and peered curiously through the side window at the old boat. 'I must have entered a time warp or I've fallen into the Twilight Zone. Which is it?'

'Neither. You're at the harbour in San Felipe, and you're

looking at your home for the next two weeks.'

'Good lord,' Pitt mumbled in amazement, 'an honest-to-God steamboat with a walking beam engine and side paddlewheels.'

'I must admit it does have an air of Mark Twain about it.'

'What do you want to bet it ferried Grant's troops across the Mississippi to Vicksburg?'

Gunn and Giordino spotted them and waved. They walked across a gangplank to the dock as Pitt and Loren climbed from the car and stood gazing at the boat.

'Have a good trip?' asked Gunn.

'Except for Dirk's snoring, it was marvellous,' said Loren.

Pitt looked at her indignantly. 'I don't snore.'

She rolled her eyes towards the heavens. 'I have tendinitis in my elbow from poking you.'

'What do you think of our work platform?' asked Giordino, gesturing grandly at the ferryboat. 'Built in 1923. She was one of the last walking beam steamboats to be built.'

Pitt lifted his sunglasses and studied the antique vessel.

When seen from a distance most ships tend to look smaller than they actually are. Only up close do they appear huge. This was true of the passenger/car ferries of the first half of the century. In her heyday the 70-metre (230-foot) vessel could carry five hundred passengers and sixty automobiles. The long black hull was topped with a two-storey white superstructure whose upper deck mounted one large smokestack and two pilothouses, one on each end. Like most car ferries, she could be loaded and offloaded from either bow or stern, depending on the direction the ferry was steaming at the time. Even when new, she would never have been called glamorous, but she had supplied an important and unforgettable service in the lives of millions of her former passengers.

The name painted across the centre of the superstructure

that housed the paddlewheels identified her as the *Alhambra*.

'Where did you steal that derelict?' asked Pitt. 'From a maritime museum?'

'To know her is to love her,' said Giordino without feeling.

'She was the only vessel I could find quickly that could land a helicopter,' Gunn explained. 'Besides, I kept Sandecker happy by obtaining her on the cheap.'

Loren smiled. 'At least this is one relic you can't get in your transportation collection.'

Pitt pointed to the walking beam mounted above the high A-frame that tilted up and down, one end driven by a connecting rod from the steam cylinder, the other driving the crank that turned the paddlewheel. 'I can't believe her boilers are still fired by coal.'

'They were converted to oil fifty years ago,' said Gunn. 'The engines are still in remarkable shape. Her cruising speed is twenty miles an hour.'

'Don't you mean knots or kilometres?' said Loren.

'Ferryboat speeds are measured in miles,' answered Gunn knowledgeably.

'Doesn't look like she's going anywhere,' said Pitt. 'Not unless you dig her keel out of the muck.'

'She'll be floating like a cork by midnight,' Gunn assured him. 'The tide runs four to five metres in this section of the Gulf.'

Though he made a show of disapproval, Pitt already felt great affection towards the old ferry. It was love at first sight. Antique automobiles, aircraft, or boats, anything mechanical that came from the past, fascinated him. Born too late, he often complained, born eighty years too late.

'And the crew?'

'An engineer with one assistant and two deckhands.' Gunn paused and gave a wide boyish smile. 'I get to man the helm while you and Al cavort around the Gulf in your flying machine.'

376

'Speaking of the helicopter, where have you hidden it?'

'Inside the auto deck,' replied Gunn. 'Makes it convenient to service it without worrying about the weather. We push it out on to the loading deck for flight operations.'

Pitt looked at Giordino. 'Have you planned a daily search pattern?'

The stocky Italian shook his head. 'I worked out the fuel range and flight times, but left the search pattern for you.'

'What sort of time frame are we looking at?'

'Should be able to cover the area in three days.'

'Before I forget,' said Gunn. 'The admiral wants you to contact him first thing in the morning. There's an Iridium phone in the forward pilothouse.'

'Why not call him now?' asked Pitt.

Gunn looked at his watch. 'We're three hours behind the East Coast. About now he's sitting in the Kennedy Centre watching a play.'

'Excuse me,' interrupted Loren. 'May I ask a few questions?'

The men paused and stared at her. Pitt bowed. 'You have the floor, Congresswoman.'

'The first is where do you plan to park the Pierce Arrow? It doesn't look safe enough around here to leave a hundred-thousand-dollar classic car sitting unattended on a fishing dock.'

Gunn looked surprised that she should ask. 'Didn't Dirk tell you? The Pierce and the trailer come on board the ferry. There's acres of room inside.'

'Is there a bath and shower?'

'As a matter of fact, there are four ladies' restrooms on the upper passenger deck and a shower in the crew's quarters.'

'No standing in line for the potty. I like that.'

Pitt laughed. 'You don't even have to unpack.'

'Make believe you're on a Carnival Lines cruise ship,' said Giordino humorously.

'And your final question?' inquired Gunn.

'I'm starved,' she announced regally. 'When do we eat?'

In autumn, the Baja sun has a peculiar radiance, spilling down through a sky of strange brilliant blue-white. This day, there wasn't a cloud to be seen from horizon to horizon. One of the most arid lands in the world, the Baja Peninsula protects the Sea of Cortez from the heavy swells that roll in from the dim reaches of the Pacific Ocean. Tropical storms with high winds are not unknown during the summer months, but near the end of October the prevailing winds turn east to west and generally spare the Gulf from high, choppy swells.

With the Pierce Arrow and its travel trailer safely tied down on the cavernous auto deck, Gunn at the wheel in the pilothouse, and Loren stretched on a lounge chair in a bikini, the ferry moved out of the breakwater harbour and made a wide turn to the south. The old boat presented an impressive sight as black smoke rose from her stack and her paddlewheels pounded the water. The walking beam, shaped like a flattened diamond, rocked up and down, transmitting the power from the engine's huge piston to the shaft that cranked the paddlewheels. There was a rhythm to its motion, almost hypnotic if you stared at it long enough.

While Giordino made a preflight inspection of the helicopter and topped off the fuel tank, Pitt was briefed on the latest developments by Sandecker in Washington over the Motorola Iridium satellite phone. Not until an hour later, as the ferry steamed off Point Estrella, did Pitt switch off the phone and descend to the improvised flight pad on the open forward deck of the ferry. As soon as Pitt was strapped in his seat, Giordino lifted the turquoise NUMA craft off the ferry and set a parallel course along the coastline.

'What did the old boy have to say before we left the *Alhambra*?' asked Giordino as he levelled the chopper off at 800 metres (2600 feet). 'Did Yaeger turn up any new clues?'

Pitt was sitting in the copilot's seat and acting as navigator. 'Yaeger had no startling revelations. The only information he could add was that he believes the statue of the demon sits directly over the entrance to the passageway leading to the treasure cavern.'

'What about the mysterious river?'

'He's still in the dark on that one.'

'And Sandecker?'

'The latest news is that we've been blindsided. Customs and the FBI dropped in out of the blue and informed him that a gang of art thieves is also on the trail of Huascar's treasure. He warned us to keep a sharp eye out for them.'

'We have competition?'

'A family that oversees a worldwide empire dealing in stolen and forged works of art.'

'What do they call themselves?' asked Giordino.

'Zolar International.'

Giordino looked blank for a moment, and then he laughed uncontrollably.

'What's so hilarious?'

'Zolar,' Giordino choked out. 'I remember a dumb kid in the eighth grade who did a corny magician act at school assemblies. He called himself the Great Zolar.'

'From what Sandecker told me,' said Pitt, 'the guy who heads the organization is nowhere close to dumb. Government agents estimate his annual illicit take in excess of eighty million dollars. A tidy sum when you consider the IRS is shut out of the profits.'

'Okay, so he isn't the nerdy kid I knew in school. How close do the Feds think Zolar is to the treasure?'

'They think he has better directions than we do.'

'I'm willing to bet my Thanksgiving turkey we find the site first.'

'Either way, you'd lose.'

Giordino turned and looked at him. 'Care to let your old buddy in on the rationale?'

'If we hit the jackpot ahead of them, we're supposed to fade into the landscape and let them scoop up the loot.'

'Give it up?' Giordino was incredulous.

'Those are the orders,' said Pitt, resentment written in his eyes.

'But why?' demanded Giordino. 'What great wisdom does our benevolent government see in making criminals rich?'

'So Customs and the FBI can trail and trap them into an indictment and eventual conviction for some pretty heavy crimes.'

'I can't say this sort of justice appeals to me. Will the taxpayers be notified of the windfall?'

'Probably not, any more than they were told about the Spanish gold the army removed from Victorio Peak in New Mexico after it was discovered by a group of civilians in the nineteen thirties.'

'We live in a sordid, unrelenting world,' Giordino observed poetically.

Pitt motioned towards the rising sun. 'Come around on an approximate heading of one-one-o degrees.'

Giordino took note of the eastern heading. 'You want to check out the other side of the Gulf on the first run?'

'Only four islands have the geological features similar to what we're looking for. But you know I like launching the search on the outer perimeters of our grid and then working back towards the more promising targets.'

Giordino grinned. 'Any sane man would begin in the centre.'

'Didn't you know?' Pitt came back. 'The village idiot has all the fun.'

37

It had been a long four days of searching. Oxley was discouraged, Sarason oddly complacent, while Moore was baffled. They had flown over every island in the Sea of Cortez that had the correct geological formations. Several displayed features on their peaks that suggested man-made rock carvings. But low altitude reconnaissance and strenuous climbs up steep palisades to verify the rock structures up close revealed configurations that appeared as sculpted beasts only in their imaginations.

Moore was no longer the arrogant academic. He was plainly baffled. The rock carving had to exist on an island in an inland sea. The pictographs on the golden mummy suit were distinct, and there was no mistaking the directions in his translation. For a man so cocksure of himself, the failure was maddening.

Moore was also puzzled by Sarason's sudden change in attitude. The bastard, Moore mused, no longer displayed animosity or anger. Those strange almost colourless eyes always seemed to be in a constant state of observation, never losing their intensity. Moore knew whenever he gazed into them that he was facing a man who was no stranger to death.

Moore was becoming increasingly uneasy. The balance of power had shifted. His edge was dulled now he was certain that Sarason saw beyond his credentials as an insolent schoolteacher. If he had recognized the killer instinct in Sarason, it stood to reason Sarason had identified it in him too.

But there was a small measure of satisfaction. Sarason was not clairvoyant. He could not have known, nor did any man alive know except the President of the United States, that Professor Henry Moore, respected anthropologist, and his equally respected archaeologist wife, Micki, were experts in carrying out assassinations of foreign terrorist leaders. With their academic credentials they easily travelled in and out of foreign countries as consultants on archaeological projects. Interestingly, the CIA was in total ignorance of their actions. Their assignments came directly from an obscure agency calling itself the Foreign Activities Council that operated out of a small basement room under the White House.

Moore shifted restlessly in his seat and studied a chart of the Gulf. Finally he said, 'Something is very, very wrong.'

Oxley looked at his watch. 'Five o'clock. I prefer to land in daylight. We might as well call it a day.'

Sarason's expressionless gaze rested on the empty horizon ahead. Untypically, he acted relaxed and quiet. He offered no comment.

'It's got to be here,' Moore said, examining the islands he had crossed out on his chart as if he had flunked a test.

'I have an unpleasant feeling we might have flown right by it,' said Oxley.

Now that he saw Moore in a different light, Sarason viewed him with the respect one adversary has for another. He also realized that despite his slim frame, the professor was strong and quick. Struggling up the rocky walls of promising islands, gasping from aggravated exhaustion and playing drunk, was nothing more than an act. On two occasions, Moore leapt over a fissure with the agility of a mountain goat. On another, with seemingly little effort, he cast aside a boulder blocking his path that easily equalled his weight.

Sarason said, 'Perhaps the Inca sculpture we're looking for was destroyed.'

In the rear seat of the seaplane Moore shook his head. 'No, I'd have recognized the pieces.'

'Suppose it was moved? It wouldn't be the first time an ancient sculpture was relocated to a museum for display.'

'If Mexican archaeologists had taken a massive rock carving and set it up for exhibit,' said Moore doggedly, 'I'd have known about it.'

'Then how do you explain that it is not where it is supposed to be?'

'I can't,' Moore admitted. 'As soon as we land back at the hacienda, I'll review my notes. There must be a seemingly insignificant clue that I missed in my translation of the golden suit.'

'I trust you will find it before tomorrow morning,' Sarason said drily.

Oxley fought the urge to doze off. He had been at the controls since nine o'clock in the morning and his neck was stiff with weariness. He held the control column between his knees and poured himself a cup of coffee from a thermos. He took a swallow and made a face. It was not only cold but tasted as strong as battery acid. Suddenly, his eye caught a flash of green from under a cloud. He pointed out the window to the right of the Baffin flying boat.

'Don't see many helicopters in this part of the Gulf,' he said casually.

Sarason didn't bother to look. 'Must be a Mexican navy patrol plane.'

'No doubt looking for a drunken fisherman with a broken engine,' added Moore.

Oxley shook his head. 'I can't ever recall seeing a turquoise military aircraft.'

Sarason looked up, startled. 'Turquoise? Can you make out its markings?'

Oxley lifted the binoculars and peered through the windscreen. 'American.'

'A Drug Enforcement Agency patrol working with Mexican authorities, probably.'

'No, it belongs to National Underwater and Marine Agency. I wonder what they're doing in the Gulf?'

'They conduct ocean surveys all over the world,' said Moore unconcernedly.

Sarason stiffened as though he'd been shot. 'Two scum from NUMA wrecked our operation in Peru.'

'Hardly seems likely there's a connection,' said Oxley.

'What operation did NUMA wreck in Peru?' asked Moore, sniffing the air.

'They stepped outside their jurisdiction,' answered Sarason vaguely.

'I'd like to hear about it sometime.'

'Not a subject that concerns you,' Sarason said, brushing him off. 'How many people in the craft?'

'Looks like a model that seats four,' replied Oxley, 'but I only see a pilot and one passenger.'

'Are they approaching or headed away?'

'The pilot has turned on to a converging course that will cross about two hundred metres above us.'

'Can you ascend and turn with him?' asked Sarason. 'I want a closer look.'

'Since aviation authorities can't take away a licence I never applied for' – Oxley smiled – 'I'll put you in the pilot's lap.'

'Is that safe?' Moore asked.

Oxley grinned. 'Depends on the other pilot.'

Sarason took the binoculars and peered at the turquoise helicopter. This was a different model from the one that had landed at the sacrificial well. That one had a shorter fuselage and landing skids. This one had retractable landing gear. But there was no mistaking the colour scheme and markings. He told himself it was ridiculous to think the men in the approaching helicopter could possibly be the same ones who appeared out of nowhere in the Andes.

He trained the binoculars on the helicopter's cockpit. In another few seconds he would be able to discern the faces inside. For some strange, inexplicable reason his calm began to crack and he felt his nerves tighten.

*

'What do you think?' asked Giordino. 'Could they be the ones?'

'They could be.' Pitt stared through a pair of naval glasses at the amphibian seaplane flying on a diagonal course below the helicopter. 'After watching the pilot circle Estanque Island for fifteen minutes as if he were looking for something on the peak, I think it's safe to say we've met up with our competition.'

'According to Sandecker, they launched their search two days ahead of us,' said Giordino. 'Since they're still taking in the sights, they can't have experienced any success either.'

Pitt smiled. 'Sort of gladdens the heart, doesn't it?'

'If they can't find it, and we can't find it, then the Incas must have sold us a wagon load of hocus pocus.'

'I don't think so. Stop and consider. There are two different search efforts in the same area, but as far as we know both teams are using two unrelated sets of instructions. We have the Inca *quipu* while they're following the engravings on a golden mummy suit. At the worst, our separate sets of clues would have led us to different locations. No, the ancients haven't misled us. The treasure is out there. We simply haven't looked in the right place.'

Giordino always marvelled that Pitt could sit for hours analysing charts, studying instruments, mentally recording every ship on the sea below, the geology of the offshore islands, and every variance of the wind without the slightest sign of fatigue, his concentration always focused. He had to suffer the same muscle aches, joint stiffness, and nervous stress that plagued Giordino, but he gave no indication of discomfort. In truth, Pitt felt every ache and pain, but he could shut it all from his mind and keep going as strongly as when he started in the morning.

'Between their coverage and ours,' said Giordino, 'we must have exhausted every island that comes anywhere close to the right geological features.'

'I agree,' said Pitt thoughtfully. 'But I'm convinced we're all on the right playing field.'

'Then where is it? Where in hell is that damned demon?'

Pitt motioned down at the sea. 'Sitting somewhere down there. Right where it's been for almost five hundred years. Thumbing its nose at us.'

Giordino pointed at the other aircraft. 'Our search buddies are climbing up to check us out. You want me to ditch them?'

'No point. Their airspeed is a good eighty kilometres per hour faster than ours. Maintain a steady course towards the ferry and act innocent.'

'Nice looking Baffin seaplane,' said Giordino. 'You don't see them except in the North Canadian lake country.'

'He's moving in a bit close for a passing stranger, wouldn't you say?'

'Either he's being neighbourly or he wants to read our name tags.'

Pitt stared through the binoculars at the cockpit of the plane that was now flying alongside the NUMA helicopter no more than 50 metres (164 feet) away.

'What do you see?' asked Giordino, minding his flying.

'Some guy staring back at me through binoculars,' replied Pitt with a grin.

'Maybe we should call them up and invite them over for a jar of Grey Poupon mustard.'

The passenger in the seaplane dropped his glasses for a moment to massage his eyes before resuming his inspection. Pitt pressed his elbows against his body to steady his view. When he lowered the binoculars, he was no longer smiling.

'An old friend from Peru,' he said in cold surprise.

Giordino turned and looked at Pitt curiously. 'Old friend?'

'Dr Steve Miller's imposter come back to haunt us.'

Pitt's smile returned, and it was hideously diabolic. Then he waved.

*

If Pitt was surprised at the unexpected confrontation, Sarason was stunned. 'You!' he gasped.

'What did you say?' asked Oxley.

His senses reeling at seeing the man who had caused him so much grief, uncertain if this was a trick of his mind, Sarason refocused the binoculars and examined the devil that was grinning fiendishly and waving slowly like a mourner at graveside bidding goodbye to the departed. A slight shift of the binoculars and all colour drained from his face as he recognized Giordino as the pilot.

'The men in that helicopter,' he said, his voice thick, 'are the same two who wreaked havoc on our operation in Peru.'

Oxley looked unconvinced. 'Think of the odds, brother. Are you certain?'

'It's them, there can be no others. Their faces are burned in my memory. They cost our family millions of dollars in artifacts that were later seized by Peruvian government archaeologists.'

Moore was listening intently. 'Why are they here?'

'The same purpose we are. Someone must have leaked information on our project.' He turned and glared at Moore. 'Perhaps the good professor has friends at NUMA?'

'My only connection with the government is on April fifteenth when I file my income tax return,' Moore said testily. 'Whoever they are, they're no friends of mine.'

Oxley remained dubious. 'Henry's right. Impossible for him to have made outside contact. Our security is too tight. Your assertion might make more sense to me if they were Customs officials, not scientists or engineers from an oceanographic research agency.'

'No. I swear it's the same men who appeared out of nowhere and rescued the archaeologist and photographer from the sacred well. Their names are Dirk Pitt and Al Giordino. Pitt is the most dangerous of the two. He was the one who killed my men and emasculated Tupac Amaru. We must follow them and find out where they're operating from.'

'I have only enough fuel to make it back to Guaymas,' said Oxley. 'We'll have to let them go.'

'Force them down, force them to crash,' Sarason demanded.

Oxley shook his head. 'If they're as dangerous as you suggest, they may well be armed, and we're not. Relax, brother, we'll meet up with them again.'

'They're scavengers, using NUMA as a cover to beat us to the treasure.'

'Think what you're saying,' snapped Moore. 'It is absolutely impossible for them to know where to search. My wife and I were the only ones ever to decode the images on the golden mummy suit. Either this has to be a coincidence or you're hallucinating.'

'As my brother can tell you,' said Sarason coldly, 'I am not one to hallucinate.'

'A couple of NUMA underwater freaks who roam the world fighting evil,' muttered Moore sharply. 'You'd better lay off the mescal.'

Sarason did not hear Moore. The thought of Amaru triggered something inside Sarason. He slowly regained control, the initial shock replaced by malevolence. He could not wait to unleash the mad dog from the Andes.

'This time,' he murmured nastily, 'they will be the ones who pay.'

Joseph Zolar had finally arrived in his jet and was waiting in the dining room of the hacienda with Micki Moore when the searchers entered wearily and sat down. 'I guess I don't have to ask if you've found anything. The look on your faces reflects defeat.'

'We'll find it,' said Oxley through a yawn. 'The demon has to be out there somewhere.'

'I'm not as confident,' muttered Moore, reaching for a glass of chilled chardonnay. 'We've almost run out of islands to search.'

Sarason came over and gave Zolar a brotherly pat on

both shoulders. 'We expected you three days ago.'

'I was delayed. A transaction that netted us one million two hundred thousand Swiss francs.'

'A dealer?'

'A collector. A Saudi sheik.'

'How did the Vincente deal go?'

'Sold him the entire lot, with the exception of those damned Indian ceremonial idols. For some inexplicable reason, they scared the hell out of him.'

Sarason laughed. 'Maybe it's the curse.'

Zolar shrugged impassively. 'If they come with a curse, it simply means the next potential buyer will have to pay a premium.'

'Did you bring the idols with you?' asked Oxley. 'I'd like to have a look at them.'

'They're in a packing crate inside the cargo hold of the aeroplane.' Zolar glanced admiringly at the quesadilla that was placed in front of him on a plate. 'I had hoped you would greet me with good news.'

'You can't say we haven't tried,' replied Moore. 'We've examined every rock that sticks out of the sea from the Colorado River south to Cabo San Lucas, and haven't seen anything remotely resembling a stone demon with wings and a serpent's head.'

'I hate to bring more grim tidings,' Sarason said to Zolar, 'but we met up with my friends who messed things up in Peru.'

Zolar looked at him, puzzled. 'Not those two devils from NUMA?'

'The same. As incredible as it sounds, I believe they're after Huascar's gold too.'

'I'm forced to agree,' said Oxley. 'Why else did they pop up in the same area?'

'Impossible for them to know something we don't,' said Zolar.

'Perhaps they've been following you,' said Micki, holding up her glass as Henry poured her wine.

Oxley shook his head. 'No, our amphibian has twice the fuel range of their helicopter.'

Moore turned to Zolar. 'My wife may have something. The odds are astronomical that it was a chance encounter.'

'How do we handle it?' Sarason asked no one in particular.

Zolar smiled. 'I think Mrs Moore has given us the answer.'

'Me?' wondered Micki. 'All I suggested was – '

'They might have been following us.'

'So?'

Zolar looked at her slyly. 'We'll begin by requesting our mercenary friends in local law enforcement to begin earning their money by launching an investigation to find our competitor's base of operations. Once found, we'll follow *them*.'

38

Darkness was only a half hour away when Giordino set the helicopter down neatly within the white circle painted on the loading deck of the *Alhambra*. The deckhands, who simply went by the names of Jesus and Gato, stood by to push the craft inside the cavernous auto deck and tie it down.

Loren and Gunn were standing outside the sweep of the rotor blades. When Giordino cut the ignition switch, they stepped forward. They were not alone. A man and a woman moved out of the shadow of the ferry's huge superstructure and joined them.

'Any luck?' Gunn shouted above the diminishing beat of the rotors at Giordino who was leaning out the open window of the cockpit.

Giordino replied with a thumbs-down.

Pitt stepped from the helicopter's passenger door and knitted his thick, black eyebrows in surprise. 'I didn't expect to see you two again, certainly not here.'

Dr Shannon Kelsey smiled, her manner coolly dignified, while Miles Rodgers pumped Pitt's hand in a genuine show of friendliness. 'Hope you don't mind us popping in like this,' said Rodgers.

'Not at all. I'm glad to see you. I assume you've all introduced yourselves to each other.'

'Yes, we've all become acquainted. Shannon and I certainly didn't expect to be greeted by a congresswoman and the assistant director of NUMA.'

'Dr Kelsey has regaled me with her adventures in Peru,' said Loren in a voice that was low and throaty. 'She's led an interesting life.'

Giordino exited the helicopter and stared at the newcomers with interest. 'Hail, hail, the gang's all here,' he said in greeting. 'Is this a reunion or an old mummy hunter's convention?'

'Yes, what brings you to our humble ferry in the Sea of Cortez?' asked Pitt.

'Government agents requested Miles and me to drop everything in Peru and fly here to assist your search,' answered Shannon.

Pitt looked at Gunn. 'Government agents?'

Gunn made a know-nothing shrug and held up a piece of paper. 'The fax informing us of their arrival came an hour after they showed up in a chartered boat. They insisted on waiting to reveal the purpose of their visit until you returned.'

'They were Customs agents,' Miles enlightened Pitt. 'They appeared in the Pueblo de los Muertos with a high-level State Department official and played on our patriotism.'

'Miles and I were asked to identify and photograph Huascar's treasure after you found it,' explained Shannon. 'They came to us because of my expertise in Andean culture and artifacts, Miles's reputation as a photographer, and mostly because of our recent involvement with you and NUMA.'

'And you volunteered,' Pitt surmised.

Rodgers replied. 'When the Customs agents informed us the gang of smugglers we met in the Andes are connected with the family of underground art dealers who are also searching for the treasure, we started packing.'

'The Zolars?'

Rodgers nodded. 'The possibility we might be of help in trapping Doc Miller's murderer quickly overcame any reluctance to become involved.'

'Wait a minute,' said Giordino. 'The Zolars are involved with Amaru and the *Solpemachaco*?'

Rodgers nodded again. 'You weren't told? No one

informed you that the *Solpemachaco* and the Zolar family are one and the same?'

'I guess someone forgot,' Giordino said caustically. He and Pitt looked at each other as understanding dawned. Each read the other's mind and they silently agreed not to mention their unexpected run-in with Doc Miller's imposter.

'Were you briefed on the instructions we deciphered on the *quipu*?' Pitt asked Shannon, changing the subject.

Shannon nodded. 'I was given a full translation.'

'By whom?'

'The courier who hand-delivered it was an FBI agent.'

Pitt stared at Gunn and then Giordino with deceptive calm. 'The plot thickens. I'm surprised Washington didn't issue press kits about the search to the news media and sell the movie rights to Hollywood.'

'If word leaks out,' said Giordino, 'every treasure hunter between here and the polar icecaps will swarm into the Gulf like fleas after a haemophiliac St Bernard.'

Fatigue began to tighten its grip on Pitt. He was stiff and numb and his back ached. His body demanded to lie down and rest. He had every right to be tired and discouraged. What the hell, he thought, why not share the despair? No good reason why he should bear the cross by himself.

'I hate to say it,' he said slowly, staring at Shannon, 'but it looks as if you and Miles made a wasted trip.'

Shannon looked at him in surprise. 'You haven't found the treasure site?'

'Did someone tell you we had?'

'We were led to believe you had pinned down the location,' said Shannon.

'Wishful thinking,' said Pitt. 'We haven't seen a trace of a stone carving.'

'Are you familiar with the symbol marker described by the *quipu*?' Gunn asked Shannon.

'Yes,' she replied without hesitation. '*The Demonio del Muertos*.'

Pitt sighed. 'The demon of the dead. Dr Ortiz told us. I go to the back of the class for not making the connection.'

'I remember,' said Gunn. 'Dr Ortiz was excavating a large grotesque rock sculpture with fangs and described it as a Chachapoyan god of the underworld.'

Pitt repeated Dr Ortiz's exact words. 'Part jaguar, part condor, part snake, he sank his fangs into whoever disturbed the dead.'

'The body and wings have the scales of a lizard,' Shannon added to the description.

'Now that you know exactly what you're looking for,' Loren said with renewed enthusiasm, 'the search should go easier.'

'So we know the ID of the beast that guards the hoard,' said Giordino, bringing the conversation back to earth. 'So what? Dirk and I have examined every island that falls within the pattern and we've come up empty. We've exhausted our search area, and what we might have missed our competitors have likely checked off their list too.'

'Al's right,' Pitt admitted. 'We have no place left to search.'

'You're sure you've seen no trace of the demon?' asked Rodgers.

Giordino shook his head. 'Not so much as a scale or a fang.'

Shannon scowled in defeat. 'Then the myth is simply that . . . a myth.'

'The treasure that never was,' murmured Gunn. He collapsed dejectedly on an old wooden passenger's bench. 'It's over,' he said slowly. 'I'll call the admiral and tell him we're closing down the project.'

'Our rivals in the seaplane should be cutting bait and flying off into the sunset too,' said Giordino.

'To regroup and try again,' said Pitt. 'They're not the type to fly away from a billion dollars in treasure.'

Gunn looked up at him, surprised. 'You've seen them?'

394

'We waved in passing,' answered Pitt without going into detail.

'A great disappointment not to catch Doc's killer,' Rodgers said sadly. 'I also had high hopes of being the first to photograph the treasures and Huascar's golden chain.'

'A washout,' murmured Gunn. 'A damned washout.'

Shannon nodded at Rodgers. 'We'd better make arrangements to return to Peru.'

Loren sank next to Gunn. 'A shame after everyone worked so hard.'

Pitt suddenly returned to life, shrugging off the exhaustion and becoming his old cheerful self again. 'I can't speak for the rest of you pitiful purveyors of doom, but I'm going to take a bath, mix myself a tequila on the rocks with lime, grill a steak, get a good night's sleep, and go out in the morning and find that ugly critter guarding the treasure.'

They all stared at him as if he had suffered a mental breakdown, all that is except Giordino. He didn't need a third eye to know Pitt was scenting a trail. 'You have the look of a born-again Christian. Why the about-face?'

'Do you remember when a NUMA search team found that hundred-and-fifty-year-old steamship that belonged to the Republic of Texas navy?'

'Back in 1987, wasn't it? The ship was the *Zavala*.'

'The same. And do you recall *where* it was found?'

'Under a parking lot in Galveston.'

'Get the picture?'

'I certainly don't,' snapped Shannon. 'What are you driving at?'

'Whose turn is it to cook dinner?' Pitt inquired, ignoring her.

Gunn raised a hand. 'My night in the galley. Why ask?'

'Because, after we've all enjoyed a good meal and a cocktail or two, I'll lay out Dirk's master plan.'

'Which island have you selected?' Shannon asked cynically. 'Bali Ha'i or Atlantis?'

'There is no island,' Pitt answered mysteriously. 'No island at all. The treasure that never was, but is, sits on dry land.'

An hour and a half later, with Giordino standing at the helm, the old ferry reversed course as her paddlewheels drove her northward back towards San Felipe. While Gunn, assisted by Rodgers, prepared dinner in the ferry's galley, Loren searched for Pitt and finally found him sitting on a folding chair down in the engine room, chatting with the chief engineer as he soaked up the sounds, smells, and motion of the *Alhambra*'s monstrous engines. He wore the expression of a man in the throes of undisguised euphoria. She carried a small bottle of blanco tequila and a glass of ice as she crept up behind him.

Gordo Padilla smoked the stub of a cigar while wiping a clean cloth over a pair of brass steam gauges. He wore scuffed cowboy boots, a T-shirt covered with bright illustrations of tropical birds, and a pair of pants cut off at the knees. His sleek, well-oiled hair was as thick as marsh grass, and the brown eyes in his round face wandered over the engines with the same ardour they would display if beholding the full-figured body of a model in a bikini.

Most ship's engineers are thought to be big ebullient men with hairy chests and thick forearms illustrated with colourful tattoos. Padilla was devoid of body hair and tattoos. He looked like an ant crawling on his great walking beam engines. Diminutive, his height and weight would have easily qualified him to ride a race horse.

'Rosa, my wife,' he said between swallows of Tecate beer, 'she thinks I love these engines more than her. I tell her they better than a mistress. Much cheaper and I never have to sneak around alleys to see them.'

'Women have never understood the affection a man can have for a machine,' Pitt agreed.

'Women can't feel passionate about greasy gears and pistons,' said Loren, slipping a hand down the front of

Pitt's aloha shirt, 'because they don't love back.'

'Ah, but pretty lady,' said Padilla, 'you can't imagine the satisfaction we feel after seducing an engine into running smoothly.'

Loren laughed. 'No, and I don't want to.' She looked up at the huge A-frame that supported the walking beams, and then to the great cylinders, steam condensers, and boilers. 'But I must admit, it's an impressive apparatus.'

'Apparatus?' Pitt squeezed her around the waist. 'In light of modern diesel turbines, walking beam engines seem antiquated. But when you look back on the engineering and manufacturing techniques that were state-of-the-art during their era, they are monuments to the genius of our forefathers.'

She passed him the little bottle of tequila and the glass of icc. 'Enough of this masculine crap about smelly old engines. Swill this down. Dinner will be ready in ten minutes.'

'You have no respect for the finer things in life,' said Pitt, nuzzling her hand.

'Make your choice. The engines or me?'

He looked up at the piston rod as it pumped the walking beam up and down. 'I can't deny having an obsession with the stroke of an engine.' He smiled slyly. 'But I freely confess there's a lot to be said for stroking something that's soft and cuddly.'

'Now there's a comforting thought for all the women of the world.'

Jesus dropped down the ladder from the car deck and said something in Spanish to Padilla. He listened, nodded, and looked at Pitt. 'Jesus says the lights of a plane have been circling the ferry for the past half hour.'

Pitt stared for a moment at the giant crank that turned the paddlewheels. Then he gave Loren a squeeze and said briefly, 'A good sign.'

'A sign of what?' she asked curiously.

'The guys on the other side,' he said in a cheery voice. 'They've failed and now they hope to follow us to the mother lode. That gives an advantage to our team.'

After a hearty dinner on one of the thirty tables in the yawning, unobstructed passengers' section of the ferry, the table was cleared and Pitt spread out a nautical chart and two geological land survey maps. Pitt spoke to them distinctly and precisely, laying out his thoughts so clearly they might have been their own.

'The landscape is not the same. There have been great changes in the past almost five hundred years.' He paused and pieced together the three maps, depicting an uninterrupted view of the desert terrain from the upper shore of the Gulf north to the Coachella Valley of California.

'Thousands of years ago the Sea of Cortez used to stretch over the present-day Colorado desert and Imperial Valley above the Salton Sea. Through the centuries, the Colorado River flooded and carried enormous amounts of silt into the sea, eventually forming a delta and diking in the northern area of the sea. This buildup of silt left behind a large body of water that was later known as Lake Cahuilla, named, I believe, after the Indians who lived on its banks. As you travel around the foothills that rim the basin, you can still see the ancient waterline and find seashells scattered throughout the desert.'

'When did it dry up?' asked Shannon.

'Between 1100 and 1200 A.D.'

'Then where did the Salton Sea come from?'

'In an attempt to irrigate the desert, a canal was built to carry water from the Colorado River. In 1905, after unseasonably heavy rains and much silting, the river burst the banks of the canal and water poured into the lowest part of the desert's basin. A desperate dam operation stopped the flow, but not before enough water had flowed through to form the Salton Sea, with a surface eighty meters below sea level. Actually, it's a large lake that will eventually go the way of Lake Cahuilla, despite irrigation drainage that has temporarily stabilized its present size.'

Gunn produced a bottle of Mexican brandy. 'A short intermission for spirits to rejuvenate the bloodstream.' Lacking the proper snifter goblets, he poured the brandy into plastic cups. Then he raised his. 'A toast to success.'

'Hear, hear,' said Giordino. 'Amazing how a good meal and a little brandy changes one's attitude.'

'We're all hoping Dirk has discovered a new solution,' said Loren.

'Interesting to see if he makes sense.' Shannon made an impatient gesture. 'Let's hear where all this is going.'

Pitt said nothing but leaned over the maps and drew a circular line through the desert with a red felt-tip pen. 'This is approximately where the Gulf extended in the late fourteen hundreds, before the river's silt buildup worked south.'

'Less than a kilometre from the present border between the United States and Mexico,' observed Rodgers.

'An area now mostly covered by wetlands and mudflats known as the Laguna Salada.'

'How does this swamp fit into the picture?' asked Gunn.

Pitt's face glowed like a corporate executive officer about to announce a fat dividend to his stockholders. 'The island where the Incas and the Chachapoyas buried Huascar's golden chain is no longer an island.'

Then he sat down and sipped his brandy, allowing the revelation to penetrate and blossom.

As if responding to a drill sergeant's command, everyone leaned over the charts and studied the markings Pitt had made indicating the ancient shoreline. Shannon pointed to a small snake Pitt had drawn that coiled around a high rock outcropping halfway between the marsh and the foothills of the Las Tinajas Mountains.

'What does the snake signify?'

'A kind of "X marks the spot",' answered Pitt.

Gunn closely examined the geological survey map. 'You've designated a small mountain that, according to the contour elevations, tops out at slightly less than five hundred metres.'

'Or about sixteen hundred feet,' Giordino tallied.

'What is it called?' Loren wondered.

'Cerro el Capirote,' Pitt answered. 'Capirote in English means a tall, pointed ceremonial hat, or what we used to call a dunce cap.'

'So you think this high pinnacle in the middle of nowhere is our treasure site?' Rodgers asked Pitt.

'If you study the maps closely, you'll find several other small mounts with sharp summits rising from the desert floor beside the swamp. Any one of them matches the general description. But I'm laying my money on Cerro el Capirote.'

'What brings you to such an uncompromising decision?' Shannon queried.

'I put myself in the Incas' shoes, or sandals as it were, and selected the best spot to hide what was at the time the world's greatest treasure. If I were General Naymlap, I'd look for the most imposing island at the upper end of a sea as far away from the hated Spanish conquerors as I could find. Cerro el Capirote was about as far as he could go in the early fifteen hundreds, and its height makes it the most imposing.'

The mood on the passenger deck of the ferry was definitely on the upswing. New hope had been injected into a project that had come within a hair of being written off as a failure. Pitt's unshakable confidence had infected everyone. Even Shannon was belting down the brandy and grinning like a Dodge City saloon hostess. It was as if all doubt had been thrown overboard. Suddenly, they all took finding the demon perched on the peak of Cerro el Capirote for granted.

If they had the slightest hint that Pitt had reservations, the party would have died a quick death. He felt secure in his conclusions, but he was too pragmatic not to harbour a few small doubts.

And then there was the dark side of the coin. He and Giordino had not mentioned that they had identified Doc Miller's killer as one of the other searchers. They both quietly realized that the Zolars or the *Solpemachaco*, whatever devious name they went under in this part of the world, were not aware that the treasure was in Pitt's sights.

Pitt began to picture Tupac Amaru in his mind, the cold, lifeless eyes, and he knew the hunt was about to become ugly and downright dirty.

39

They sailed the *Alhambra* north of Punta San Felipe and heaved to when her paddlewheels churned up a wake of red silt. A few kilometres ahead, the mouth of the Colorado River, wide and shallow, gaped on the horizon. Spread on either side of the murky, salt-laden water were barren mudflats, totally devoid of vegetation. Few planets in the universe could have looked as wretched and dead.

Pitt gazed at the grim landscape through the windscreen of the helicopter as he adjusted his safety harness. Shannon was strapped in the copilot's seat and Giordino and Rodgers sat in the rear passenger section of the cabin. He waved at Gunn, who replied with a V for victory sign, and Loren, who appropriately blew him a kiss.

His hands danced over the cyclic and collective pitch sticks as the rotors turned, gathering speed until the whole fuselage shuddered. And then the *Alhambra* was falling away, and he slipped the helicopter sideways across the water like a leaf blown by the wind. Once safely free of the ferry, he gently slipped the cyclic forward and the aircraft began a diagonal climb on a northerly course. At 500 metres (1640 feet) Pitt adjusted the controls and straightened out in level flight.

He flew above the drab waters of the upper Gulf for ten minutes before crossing into the marshlands of the Laguna Salada. A vast section of the flats was flooded from recent rains, and the dead limbs of mesquite rose above the heavily salted water like skeletal arms reaching for salvation.

The giant slough was soon left behind as Pitt banked the

helicopter across the sand dunes that marched from the mountains to the edge of the Laguna Salada. Now the landscape took on the characteristics of a faded brown moon, more substance than colour. The uneven, rocky terrain looked fearsome. Beautiful to the eye but deadly to the body that struggled to survive its horror during the blazing heat of summer.

'There's a blacktop road,' announced Shannon, motioning downward.

'Highway Five,' said Pitt. 'It runs from San Felipe to Mexicali.'

'Is this part of the Colorado Desert?' asked Rodgers.

'The desert north of the border is called that because of the Colorado River. In fact this is all part of the Sonoran Desert.'

'Not very hospitable country. I wouldn't want to walk through it.'

'Those who are intolerant of the desert die in it,' said Pitt thoughtfully. 'Those who respect it find it a compelling place to live.'

'People actually live down there?' Shannon asked in surprise.

'Mostly Indians,' replied Pitt. 'The Sonoran Desert is perhaps the most beautiful of all the world's deserts, even though the citizens of central Mexico think of it as their Ozarks.'

Giordino leaned out a side window for a better view and peered into the distance through the trusty binoculars. He patted Pitt on the shoulder. 'Your hot spot is coming up off to port.'

Pitt nodded, made a slight course change and peered at a solitary mountain rising from the desert floor directly ahead. Cerro el Capirote was aptly named. Though not exactly conical in shape, there was a slight resemblance to a dunce cap with the tip flattened.

'I think I can make out an animal-like sculpture on the summit,' observed Giordino.

'I'll descend and hover over it,' Pitt acknowledged.

He cut his airspeed, dropped, and swung around the top of the mountain. He approached and circled cautiously, on the watch for sudden downdraughts. Then he hovered the helicopter almost nose-to-nose with the grotesque stone effigy. Mouth agape, it seemed to stare back with the truculent expression of a hungry junkyard dog.

'Step right up, folks,' hawked Pitt as if he were a carnival barker, 'and view the astounding demon of the under-world who shuffles cards with his nose and deals 'em with his toes.'

'It exists,' cried Shannon, flushed with excitement, as they all were. 'It truly exists.'

'Looks like a timeworn gargoyle,' said Giordino, success-fully controlling his emotions.

'You've got to land,' demanded Rodgers. 'We must get a closer look.'

'Too many high rocks around the sculpture,' said Pitt. 'I have to find a flat spot to set down.'

'There's a small clearing free of boulders about forty metres beyond the demon,' Giordino said, pointing through the windscreen over Pitt's shoulder.

Pitt nodded and banked around the towering rock carving so he could make his approach into the wind blowing across the mountain from the west. He reduced speed, eased back the cyclic stick. The turquoise heli-copter hovered a moment, flared out, and then settled on to the only open space on the stone summit of Cerro el Capirote.

Giordino was first out, carrying tie-down lines that he attached to the helicopter and wrapped around rock outcroppings. When he completed the operation, he moved in front of the cockpit and drew his hand across his throat. Pitt shut off the engine and the rotor blades wound down.

Rodgers jumped down and offered a hand to Shannon. She hit the ground and took off at a run over the uneven terrain towards the stone effigy. Pitt stepped from the helicopter last, but did not follow the others. He casually raised the binoculars and scanned the sky in the direction of the faint sound of an aircraft engine. The seaplane was only a silver speck against a dome of blue. The pilot had maintained an altitude of 2000 metres (6500 feet) in an attempt to remain unseen. But Pitt was not fooled. His intuition told him he was being tailed the instant he lifted off from the *Alhambra*. Spotting the enemy only confirmed his suspicions.

Before he joined the others already gathered around the stone beast, he took a moment and stepped to the edge of the craggy wall and stared down, thankful that he did not have to make the ascent. The unobstructed panorama of the desert was breathtaking. The October sun tinted the rocks and sand in vivid colours that turned drab during the hot summer. The waters of the Gulf sparkled to the south and the mountain ranges on both sides of the marshlands of the Laguna Salada rose majestically through a slight haze.

Satisfaction swelled within him. He had made a good call. The ancients had indeed selected an imposing spot to hide their treasure.

When he finally approached the huge stone beast, Shannon was making detailed measurements of the jaguar body while Rodgers busied himself shooting roll after roll of photos. Giordino appeared intent on searching around the pedestal for a trace of the entrance to the passageway leading down into the mountain.

'Does he have the proper pedigree?' Pitt asked.

'Definitely Chachapoyan influence,' Shannon said, her face flushed with fervour. 'An extraordinary example of their art.' She stood back as if admiring a painting hanging in a gallery. 'See how the motifs on the scales are exactingly duplicated. They're a perfect match for those on the sculpted beasts in the Pueblo de los Muertos.'

'The technique is the same?'

'Almost identical.'

'Then perhaps the same sculptor had a hand in carving this one.'

'It's possible.' Shannon raised her hand as high as she could reach and stroked the lower part of the serpent's scaled neck. 'It wasn't uncommon for the Incas to recruit Chachapoyan stone carvers.'

'The ancients must have had a strange sense of humour to create a god whose looks could sour milk.'

'The legend is vague but it contends that a condor laid an egg that was eaten and vomited by a jaguar. A snake was hatched from the regurgitated egg and slithered into the sea where it grew fish scales. The rest of the mythological account says that because the beast was so ugly and shunned by the other gods who thrived in the sun, it lived underground where it eventually became the guardian of the dead.'

'The original ugly duckling fairy tale.'

'He's hideous,' Shannon said solemnly, 'and yet I can't help feeling a deep sadness for him. I don't know if I can explain it properly, but the stone seems to have a life of its own.'

'I understand. I sense something more than cold stone too.' Pitt stared down at one of the wings that had dropped off the body and shattered into several pieces. 'Poor old guy. He looks like he's fallen on hard times.'

Shannon nodded sadly at the graffiti and the gouges from bullet holes. 'The pity is that local archaeologists never recognized the beast for what it is, a remarkable piece of artwork by two cultures that thrived thousands of kilometres from here – '

Pitt interrupted her by abruptly raising a hand for silence. 'You hear something, a strange sound like someone crying?'

She cocked an ear and listened, then shook her head. 'I only hear the shutter and automatic winding mechanism on Miles's camera.'

The eerie sound Pitt thought he heard was gone. He grinned. 'Probably the wind.'

'Or those the *Demonio del Muertos* is guarding.'

'I thought he guaranteed they rest in eternal peace.'

Shannon smiled. 'We know very little about Inca and Chachapoyan religious rites. Our stone friend here may not have been as benevolent as we assume.'

Pitt left Shannon and Miles to their work and walked over to Giordino, who was tapping the rock around the beast's pedestal with a miner's pick. 'See any hint of a passage?' Pitt asked.

'Not unless the ancients discovered a method for fusing rock,' answered Giordino. 'This big gargoyle is carved from an immense slab of solid granite that forms the core of the mountain. I can't find a telltale crack anywhere around the statue's base. If there's a passage, it has to be somewhere else on the mountain.'

Pitt tilted his head, listening. 'There it is again.'

'You mean that banshee wail?'

'You heard it?' Pitt asked in surprise.

'I figured it was just wind whistling through the rocks.'

'There isn't a whisper of wind.'

A curious look crossed Giordino's face as he wetted one index finger with his tongue and tested the air. 'You're right. Nary a stir.'

'It's not a steady sound,' said Pitt. 'I only notice it at intervals.'

'I picked up on that too. It comes like a puff of breath for about ten seconds and then fades for nearly a minute.'

Pitt nodded happily. 'Could it be we're describing a vent to a cavern?'

'Let's see if we can find it,' Giordino suggested eagerly.

'Better it come to us.' Pitt found a rock that seemed moulded to his buttocks and settled in. He leisurely wiped a smudge from one lens of his sunglasses, dabbed his brow with a bandanna that hung from his pocket, then cupped his ears and began turning his head like a radar antenna.

Like clockwork, the strange wail came and went. Pitt waited until he heard three sequences. Then he motioned for Giordino to move along the north side of the peak. No reply was necessary, no words passed between them. They had been close friends since they were children and had maintained close contact during their years together in the Air Force. When Pitt joined NUMA at Admiral Sandecker's request twelve years ago, Giordino went with him. Over time they learned to respond to each other without needless talk.

Giordino moved down a steep slope for about 20 metres (65 feet) before stopping. He paused and listened while awaiting Pitt's next gesture. The dismal wail came stronger to him than it did to Pitt. But he knew that the sound reverberated off the boulders and was distorted. He didn't hesitate when Pitt motioned him away from where it sounded loudest and pointed to a spot where the side of the peak suddenly dropped off in a narrow chute 10 metres (33 feet) deep.

While Giordini was lying on his stomach surveying a way down to the bottom of the chute, Pitt came over, crouched beside him, and held out a hand, palm down.

The wail came again and Pitt nodded, his lips parting in a tight smile. 'I can feel a draught. Something deep inside the mountain is causing air to be expelled from a vent.'

'I'll get the rope and flashlight from the chopper,' said Giordino, rising to his feet and trotting towards the aircraft. In two minutes he was back with Shannon and Miles.

Her eyes fairly sparkled with anticipation. 'Al says you found a way inside the mountain.'

Pitt nodded. 'We'll know shortly.'

Giordino tied one end of a nylon line around a large rock. 'Who gets the honour?'

'I'll toss you for it,' said Pitt.

'Heads.'

408

Pitt flipped a quarter and watched as it clinked and spun to a stop on a small, flat surface between two massive boulders. 'Tails, you lose.'

Giordino shrugged without complaint, knotted a loop and passed it over and then under Pitt's shoulders. 'Never mind bedazzling me with mountain climbing tricks. I'll let you down, and I'll pull you up.'

Pitt accepted the fact his friend's strength was greater than his own. Giordino's body may have been short but his shoulders were as broad as any man's, and his muscled arms were a match for a professional wrestler. Anyone who tried to throw Giordino, including karate black belt experts, felt as if they were caught up in the gears of an unyielding piece of machinery.

'Mind you don't get rope burn,' Pitt cautioned him.

'Mind you don't break a leg, or I'll leave you for the gargoyle,' said Giordino handing Pitt the flashlight. Then he slowly paid out the line, lowering Pitt between the walls of the narrow chute.

When Pitt's feet touched the bottom, he looked up. 'Okay, I'm down.'

'What do you see?'

'A small cleft in the rock wall just large enough to crawl through. I'm going in.'

'Don't remove the rope. There could be a sharp drop just inside the entrance.'

Pitt lay on his stomach and wormed through the narrow fissure. It was a tight squeeze for 3 metres (10 feet) before the entryway widened enough so he could stand. He switched on the flashlight and swung its beam along the walls. The light showed he was at the head of a passageway that appeared to lead down into the bowels of the mountain. The floor was smooth with steps hewn into the rock every few paces.

A rush of dank air rushed past him like the steamy breath of a giant. He moved his fingertips over the rock walls. They came away wet with moisture. Driven by curiosity, Pitt moved along the passageway until the nylon became taut and he was stopped from venturing further. He aimed the light ahead into the darkness. The cold hand of fear gripped him around the neck as a pair of eyes flashed back at him.

There, upon a pedestal of black rock, seemingly sculpted by the same hand as the demon on the mountain peak above, glaring towards the entrance to the passage, was another, smaller *Demonio del Muertos*. This one was inlaid with turquoise stone and had white, polished quartz for teeth and red gemstones for eyes.

Pitt thought seriously of casting off the rope and exploring further. But he felt it wouldn't be fair to the others. They should all be in on the discovery of the treasure chamber together. Reluctantly, he returned to the crack in the wall and squirmed back into daylight.

When Giordino helped him over the edge of the chute, Shannon and Rodgers were waiting in hushed expectation.

'What did you see?' Shannon blurted, unable to contain her excitement. 'Tell us what you found!'

Pitt stared at her without expression for a moment, then broke into an elated grin. 'The entrance to the treasure is guarded by another demon, but otherwise the way looks clear.'

Everyone shouted in elation. Shannon and Rodgers hugged and kissed. Giordino slapped Pitt on the back so hard it jarred his molars. Intense curiosity seized them as they peered over the edge of the chute at the small opening leading inside the mountain. None saw a black tunnel leading downward. They gazed through the rock as if it were transparent and saw the golden treasure far below.

At least that's what they thought they saw. But not Pitt. His eyes were sweeping the sky. Foresighted, intuitive, maybe just superstitious, he had a sudden vision of the seaplane that had followed them to the demon, attacking the *Alhambra*. For a moment he could see it as clearly as if he were watching television. It was not a pretty sight.

Shannon noticed that Pitt was quiet, his face contemplative. 'What's wrong? You look like you've just lost your best girl.'

'I may have,' Pitt said darkly. 'I very well may have.'

40

Giordino returned to the helicopter and retrieved another coil of rope, a second flashlight, and a Coleman lantern from a storage locker. The rope he slung over his shoulder. He gave the flashlight to Shannon and handed the Coleman to Rodgers along with a box of wooden matches.

'The tank is full of gas, so we should have light for three hours or more.'

Shannon airily took the extra flashlight. 'I think it best if I lead the way.'

Giordino shrugged. 'Suits me. As long as somebody other than me sets off the Incas' booby traps down in the cave of doom.'

Shannon made a sour face. 'That's a cheery thought.'

Pitt laughed. 'He overdoses on Indiana Jones movies.'

'Give me a hard time,' said Giordino sadly. 'You'll be sorry some day.'

'I hope it's not soon.'

'How wide is the opening?' asked Rodgers.

'Dr Kelsey might make it through on her hands and knees, but we boys will have to snake our way in.'

Shannon peered over the edge at the bottom of the fissure. 'The Chachapoyas and the Incas could never have hauled several tons of gold up steep cliffs and then lowered it through a rathole. They must have found a larger passage somewhere around the base of the mountain above the ancient waterline.'

'You could waste years looking for it,' said Rodgers. 'It must be buried under landslides and the erosion of almost five centuries.'

'I'll bet the Incas sealed it off by causing a cave-in,' Pitt ventured.

Shannon was not about to allow the men to go first. Scrambling over rocks and slinking into dark recesses was her speciality. She eagerly slipped down the rope as smoothly as if she did it twice a day and crawled into the narrow aperture in the rock. Rodgers went next followed by Giordino, with Pitt bringing up the rear.

Giordino turned to Pitt. 'If I get caught in a cave-in, you will dig me out.'

'Not before I dial nine-one-one.'

Shannon and Rodgers had already moved out of sight down the stone steps and were examining the second *Demonio del Muertos* when Pitt and Giordino caught up to them.

Shannon was peering at the motifs embedded in the fish scales. 'The images on this sculpture are better preserved than those on the first demon.'

'Can you interpret them?' asked Rodgers.

'If I had more time. They appear to have been chiselled in a hurry.'

Rodgers stared at the protruding fangs in the jaws of the serpent's head. 'I'm not surprised the ancients were frightened of the underworld. This thing is ugly enough to induce diarrhoea. Notice how the eyes seem to follow our movements.'

'It's enough to make you sober,' said Giordino.

Shannon brushed away the dust from around the red gemstone eyes. 'Burgundy topaz. Probably mined east of the Andes, in the Amazon.'

Rodgers set the Coleman lantern on the floor, pumped up the fuel pressure and held a lit match against the mantle. The Coleman bathed the passage in a bright light for 10 metres (33 feet) in both directions. Then he held up the lantern to inspect the sculpture. 'Why a second demon?' he asked, fascinated by the fact that the well-preserved beast looked as if it had been carved only yesterday.

Pitt patted the serpent on the head. 'Insurance in case intruders got past the first one.'

Shannon licked a corner of a handkerchief and cleaned the dust from the topaz eyes. 'What is amazing is that so many ancient cultures, geographically separated and totally unrelated, came up with the same myths. In the legends of India, for example, cobras were considered to be semidivine guardians of a subterranean kingdom filled with astounding riches.'

'I see nothing unusual about that,' said Giordino. 'Forty-nine out of fifty people are deathly afraid of snakes.'

They finished their brief examination of the remarkable relic of antiquity and continued along the passageway. The damp air that came up from below drew the sweat through their pores. Despite the humidity they had to be careful they didn't step too heavily or their footsteps raised clouds of choking dust.

'They must have taken years to carve this tunnel,' said Rodgers.

Pitt reached up and ran his fingers lightly over the limestone roof. 'I doubt they excavated it from scratch. They probably hollowed out an existing fissure. Whoever they were, they weren't short.'

'How can you tell?'

'The roof. We don't have to stoop. It's a good foot above our heads.'

Rodgers gestured at a large plate set on an angle in a wall niche. 'This is the third one of these things I've seen since we entered. What do you suppose their purpose was?'

Shannon rubbed away the centuries-old coating of dust and saw her reflection on a shining surface. 'Highly polished silver reflectors,' she explained. 'The same system used by the ancient Egyptians for lighting interior galleries. The sun striking a reflector at the entrance bounced from reflector to reflector throughout the chambers and illuminated them without the smoke and soot given off by oil lamps.'

'I wonder if they knew they were paving the way for environmentally friendly technology?' murmured Pitt randomly.

The echoing sound of their footsteps spread ahead and behind them like ripples on a pond. It was an eerie, claustrophobic sensation, knowing they were entering the dead heart of the mountain. The stagnant air became so thick and heavy with moisture it dampened the dust on their clothing. Fifty metres (164 feet) later they entered a small cavern with a long gallery.

The chamber was nothing less than a catacomb, honeycombed with crypts hewn into the walls. The mummies of twenty men, wrapped tightly in beautifully embroidered woollen mantles, lay head to toe. They were the mortal remains of the guards who faithfully guarded the treasure, even after death, waiting for the return of their countrymen from an empire that no longer existed.

'These people were huge,' said Pitt. 'They must have stood two hundred and eight centimetres or six foot ten inches tall.'

'A pity they aren't around to play in the NBA,' muttered Giordino.

Shannon closely examined the design on the mantles. 'Legends claim the Chachapoyas were as tall as trees.'

Pitt scanned the chamber. 'One missing.'

Rodgers looked at him. 'Who?'

'The last man, the one who tended to the burial of the guardians who went before.'

Beyond the gallery of death they came to a larger chamber that Shannon quickly identified as the living quarters of the guardians before they died. A wide, circular stone table with a surrounding bench rose out of the floor that formed their base. The table had evidently been used to eat on. The bones of a large bird still rested on a silver platter that sat on the smoothly polished stone surface along with ceramic drinking vessels. Beds had been chiselled into the walls, some still with woollen covers neatly folded in the middle. Rodgers caught sight of something bright lying on the floor. He picked it up and held it under the light of the Coleman.

'What is it?' asked Shannon.

'A massive gold ring, plain, with no engravings.'

'An encouraging sign,' said Pitt. 'We must be getting close to the main vault.'

Shannon's breath was coming in short pants as the excitement mounted. She hurried off ahead of the men through another portal at the far end of the guardians' living quarters that led into a cramped tunnel with an arched ceiling, similar to an ancient cistern wide enough for only one person to pass through at a time. This passageway seemed to wind down through the mountain for an eternity.

'How far do you think we've come?' asked Giordino.

'My feet feel like ten kilometres,' Shannon answered, suddenly weary.

Pitt had paced the distance they'd travelled down the stone steps since leaving the crypts. 'The peak of Cerro el Capirote is only five hundred metres above sea level. I'd guess we've reached the desert floor and dropped twenty or thirty metres below it.'

'Damn!' Shannon gasped. 'Something fluttered against my face.'

'Me too,' said Giordino with obvious disgust. 'I think I've just been garnished with bat vomit.'

'Be happy he wasn't of the vampire variety,' joked Pitt.

They descended along the tunnel another ten minutes when Shannon suddenly stopped and held up a hand. 'Listen!' she commanded. 'I hear something.'

After a few moments, Giordino said, 'Sounds like someone left a tap on.'

'A rushing stream or a river,' Pitt said softly, recalling the old bartender's words.

As they moved closer, the sound of the moving water increased and reverberated within the confined space. The air had cooled considerably and smelled pure and less stifling. They rushed forward, anxiously hoping each bend in the passage was the last. And then the walls abruptly spread into the darkness and they rushed headlong into what seemed like a vast cathedral that revealed the mountain as incredibly hollow.

Shannon screamed a full-fledged shriek that echoed through the chamber as if intensified by huge rock concert amplifiers. She clutched the first body that was handy, in this case, Pitt's.

Giordino, not one to scare easily, looked as if he'd seen a ghost.

Rodgers stood petrified, his outstretched arm frozen like an iron support, holding the Coleman lantern. 'Oh, good God,' he finally gasped, hypnotized by the ghostly apparition that rose in front of them and glistened under the bright light. 'What is it?'

Pitt's heart pumped a good five litres (a gallon) of adrenaline through his system, but he remained calm and clinically surveyed the towering figure that looked like a monstrosity out of a science fiction horror movie.

The huge spectre was a ghastly sight. Standing straight, its grinning teeth, the grisly features on the face, its sunken eye sockets wide open, the apparition towered above them. Pitt judged the horror to be a good head taller than him. High above one shoulder, as though poised in the act of bashing out an intruder's brains, a bony hand held an ornate battle club with a notched edge. The Coleman's light gleamed off the gruesome figure that looked as if it were encased in yellowish amber or fibreglass resin. Then Pitt determined what it was.

The last guardian of Huascar's treasure had been frozen for all time into a stalagmite.

'How did he get like that?' Rodgers asked in awe.

Pitt pointed to the roof of the cavern. 'Ground water dripping from the limestone ceiling released carbon dioxide that splattered on the guardian and eventually covered him with a thick coating of calcite crystals. In time, he was encased like a scorpion inside a cheap gift shop acrylic resin paperweight.'

'But how in the world could he die and remain in an upright position?' queried Shannon, coming out of her initial fright.

Pitt ran his hand lightly over the crystallized mantle. 'We'll never know unless we chisel him out of his transparent tomb. It seems incredible, but knowing he was dying he must have constructed a support to prop him in a standing position with his arm raised, and then he took his life, probably by poison.'

'These guys took their jobs seriously,' muttered Giordino.

As if drawn by some mysterious force, Shannon moved within a few centimetres of the hideous wonder and stared up into the distorted face beneath the crystals. 'The height, the blond hair. He was Chachapoya, one of the Cloud People.'

'He's a long way from home,' said Pitt. He held up his wrist and checked the time. 'Two and a half hours to go before the Coleman runs out of gas. We'd better keep moving.'

Though it didn't seem possible, the immense grotto spread into the distance until their light beams barely revealed the great arched ceiling, far larger than any conceived or built by man. Giant stalactites that came down from the roof met and joined stalagmites rising from the floor, merging and becoming gigantic columns. Some of the stalagmites had formed in the shapes of strange beasts that seemed frozen in an alien landscape. Crystals gleamed from the walls like glittering teeth. The overpowering beauty and grandeur that sparkled and glittered under the rays of their lights made it seem they were in the centre of a laser light show.

Then the formations stopped abruptly, as the floor of the cavern ended on the bank of a river over 30 metres wide (100 feet). Under their lights, the black, forbidding water turned a dark emerald green. Pitt calculated the speed of the current at a rapid nine knots. The babbling brook sound they had heard further back in the passageway they now saw was the rush of water around the rockbound banks of a long, low island that protruded from the middle of the river.

But it was not the discovery of an extraordinary unknown river flowing far beneath the floor of the desert that captivated and enthralled them. It was a dazzling sight no ordinary imagination could ever conceive. There, stacked neatly on the level top of the island rose a mountain of golden artifacts.

The effect of the two flashlights and the Coleman lantern on the golden hoard left the explorers speechless. Overcome, they could only stand immobile and absorb the magnificent spectacle.

Here was Huascar's golden chain coiled in a great spiral 10 metres (33 feet) in height. Here also was the great gold disc from the Temple of the Sun, beautifully crafted and set with hundreds of precious stones. There were golden plants, water lilies and corn, and solid gold sculptures of kings and gods, women, llamas, and dozens upon dozens of ceremonial objects, beautifully formed and inlaid with huge emeralds. Here also, stacked as if inside a moving van, were tons of golden statues, furniture, tables, chairs, and beds, all handsomely engraved. The centrepiece was a huge throne made from solid gold inlaid with silver flowers.

Nor was this all. Arranged row after row, standing like phantoms, their mummies encased in golden shells, were twelve generations of Inca royalty. Beside each one lay his armour and headdresses and exquisitely woven clothing.

'In my wildest dreams,' Shannon murmured softly, 'I never envisioned a collection this vast.'

Giordino and Rodgers were both paralysed with astonishment. No words came from either one of them. They could only gape.

'Remarkable they could transport half the wealth of the Americas thousands of kilometres across an ocean on balsa and reed rafts,' said Pitt in admiration.

Shannon slowly shook her head, the awed look in her eyes turning to sadness. 'Try to imagine, if you can. What we see here is only a tiny part of the riches belonging to the last of the magnificent pre-Columbian civilizations. We can only make a rough assessment of the enormous number of objects the Spanish took and melted down into bullion.'

Giordino's face beamed almost as brightly as all the gold. 'Warms the cockles of your heart, knowing the gluttonous Spaniards missed the cream of the crop.'

'Any chance we can get over to the island so I can study the artifacts?' asked Shannon.

'And I'll need to get closeups,' added Rodgers.

'Not unless you can walk across thirty metres of rushing water,' said Giordino.

Pitt scanned the cavern by sweeping his light along the barren floor. 'Looks like the Chachapoyas and the Incas took their bridge with them. You'll have to do your study and shoot your pictures of the treasure from here.'

'I'll use my telephoto and pray my flash carries that far,' said Rodgers hopefully.

'What do you suppose all this is worth?' asked Giordino.

'You'd have to weigh it,' said Pitt, 'figure in the current market price of gold, and then triple your total for the value as rare artifacts.'

'I'm certain the treasure is worth double what the experts estimated,' said Shannon.

Giordino looked at her. 'That would be as high as three hundred million dollars?'

Shannon nodded. 'Maybe even more.'

'It isn't worth a good baseball card,' remarked Pitt, 'until it's brought to the surface. Not an easy job to barge the larger pieces, including the chain, off an island surrounded by a rushing flow of water, and then haul them up a narrow passageway to the top of the mountain. From there, you'll need a heavy transport helicopter just to carry the golden chain.'

'You're talking a major operation,' said Rodgers.

Pitt held his light on the great coiled chain. 'Nobody said it was going to be easy. Besides, bringing out the treasure isn't our problem.'

Shannon gave him a questioning stare, 'Oh, no? Then who do you expect to do it?'

Pitt stared back. 'Have you forgotten? We're suppose to stand aside and hand it over to our old pals from the *Solpemachaco*.'

The repulsive thought had slipped her mind after gazing enthralled at the wealth of golden artifacts. 'An outrage,' Shannon said furiously, her self-esteem blossoming once more, 'a damned outrage. The archaeological discovery of the century, and I can't direct the recovery programme.'

'Why don't you lodge a complaint?' said Pitt.

She glared at him, puzzled. 'What are you talking about?'

'Let the competition know how you feel.'

'How?'

'Leave them a message.'

'You're crazy.'

'That observation has been cropping up quite a bit lately,' said Giordino.

Pitt took the rope slung over Giordino's shoulder and made a loop. Then he twirled the rope like a lariat and threw the loop across the water, smiling triumphantly as it settled over the head of a small golden monkey on a pedestal.

'Ah, ha!' he uttered proudly. 'Will Rogers had nothing on me.'

41

Pitt's worst fears were confirmed when he hovered the helicopter above the *Alhambra*. No one stood on the deck to greet the craft and its passengers. The ferry looked deserted. The auto deck was empty, as was the wheel-house. The boat was not riding at anchor, nor was she drifting. Her hull was resting lightly in the water only two metres above the silt of the shallow bottom. To all appearances, she looked like a ship that had been abandoned by her crew.

The sea was calm and there was no pitch or roll. Pitt lowered the helicopter on to the wood deck and shut down the engines as soon as the tyres touched down. He sat there as the sound of the turbine and rotor blades slowly died into a morbid silence. He waited a full minute but no one appeared. He opened the entry door and dropped to the deck. Then he stood there waiting for something to happen.

Finally, a man stepped from behind a stairwell and approached, coming to a halt about 5 metres (16 feet) from the chopper. Even without the phony white hair and beard, Pitt easily recognized the man who had imperson-ated Dr Steven Miller in Peru. He was smiling as if he'd caught a record fish.

'A little off your beat, aren't you?' said Pitt, unruffled.

'You seem to be my never-ending nemesis, Mr Pitt.'

'A quality that thrills me no end. What name are you going under today?'

'Not that it's of use to you, but I am Cyrus Sarason.'

'I can't say I'm pleased to see you again.'

Sarason moved closer, peering over Pitt's shoulder at

the interior of the helicopter. His face lost the gloating smile and twisted into tense concern. 'You are alone? Where are the others?'

'What others?' Pitt asked innocently.

'Dr Kelsey, Miles Rodgers, and your friend, Albert Giordino.'

'Since you have the passenger list memorized, you tell me.'

'Please, Mr Pitt, you would do well not to toy with me,' Sarason warned him.

'They were hungry, so I dropped them off at a seafood restaurant in San Felipe.'

'You're lying.'

Pitt didn't take his gaze off Sarason to scan the decks of the ferry. Guns were trained on him. That was a certainty he knew without question. He stood his ground and faced Miller's killer as if he didn't have a care in the world.

'So sue me,' Pitt retorted, and laughed.

'You're hardly in a position to be contemptuous,' Sarason said coldly. 'Perhaps you don't realize the seriousness of your situation.'

'I think I do,' said Pitt, still smiling. 'You want Huascar's treasure, and you'd murder half the good citizens of Mexico to get it.'

'Fortunately, that won't be necessary. I do admit, however, two-thirds of a billion dollars makes an enticing incentive.'

'Aren't you interested in knowing how and why we were conducting our search at the same time as yours?' asked Pitt.

It was Sarason's turn to laugh. 'After a little persuasion, Mr Gunn and Congresswoman Smith were most cooperative in telling me about Drake's *quipu*.'

'Not very smart, torturing a United States legislator and the deputy director of a national science agency.'

'But effective, nonetheless.'

'Where are my friends and the ferry's crew?'

'I wondered when you'd get around to that question.'

'Do you want to work out a deal?' Pitt didn't miss the predator's eyes staring unblinkingly in an attempt to intimidate. He stared back piercingly. 'Or do you want to strike up the music and dance?'

Sarason shook his head. 'I see no reason why I should bargain. You have nothing to trade. You're obviously not a man I can trust. And I have all the chips. In short, Mr Pitt, you have lost the game before you draw your cards.'

'Then you can afford to be a magnanimous winner and produce my friends.'

Sarason made a thoughtful shrug, raised his hand, and made a beckoning gesture. 'The least I can do before I hang some heavy weights on you and drop you over the side.'

Four burly dark-skinned men, who looked like bouncers hired from local cantinas, prodded the captives from the passageway with automatic rifles, and lined them up on the deck behind Sarason.

Gordo Padilla came first, followed by Jesus, Gato, and the assistant engineer whose name Pitt could not recall ever hearing. The bruises and dried blood on their faces showed that they had been knocked around but were not hurt seriously. Gunn had not got off so lightly. He had to be half dragged from the passageway. He had been badly beaten, and Pitt could see the blotches of blood on his shirt and the crude rags wrapped around his hands. Then Loren was standing there, her face drawn and her lips and cheeks swollen and puffed up as though stung by bees. Her hair was dishevelled and purplish bruises showed on her arms and legs. Yet she still held her head proudly and shook off the guards' hands as they roughly pushed her forward. Her expression was one of defiance until she saw Pitt standing there. Then it turned to cruel disappointment, and she moaned in despair.

'Oh, no, Dirk!' she exclaimed. 'They've got you too.'

Gunn painfully raised his head and muttered through

lips that were split and bleeding. 'I tried to warn you, but
. . .' His voice went too soft to be understood.

Sarason smiled unfeelingly. 'I think what Mr Gunn
means to say is that he and your crew were overpowered
by my men after they kindly allowed us to board your
ferry from a chartered fishing boat after begging to borrow
your radio.'

Pitt's anger came within a millimetre of driving him to
inflict pain on those who had brutalized his friends. He
took a deep breath to regain control. He swore under his
breath that the man standing in front of him would pay.
Not now. But the time would surely come if he didn't try
anything foolish.

He glanced casually towards the nearest railing, gauging
its distance and height. Then he turned back to Sarason.

'I don't like big, tough men who beat up defenceless
women,' he said conversationally. 'And for what purpose?
The location of the treasure is no secret to you.'

'Then it's true,' Sarason said with a pleased expression.
'You found the beast that guards the gold on the top of
Cerro el Capirote.'

'If you had dropped for a closer look instead of playing
peekaboo in the clouds, you'd have seen the beast for
yourself.'

Pitt's last words brought a flicker of curiosity to the
beady eyes.

'You were aware you were being followed?' asked
Sarason.

'It goes without saying that you would have searched
for our helicopter after our chance meeting in the air
yesterday. My guess is you checked out landing fields on
both sides of the Gulf last night and asked questions until
someone in San Felipe innocently pointed the way to our
ferry.'

'You're very astute.'

'Not really. I made the mistake of overestimating you. I
didn't think you'd act like a reckless amateur and begin

425

mutilating the competition. An act that was completely unwarranted.'

Puzzlement filled Sarason's eyes. 'What goes on here, Pitt?'

'All part of the plan,' answered Pitt almost jovially. 'I purposely led you to the jackpot.'

'A barefaced lie.'

'You've been set up, pal. Get wise. Why do you think I let off Dr Kelsey, Rodgers, and Giordino before I returned to the ferry? To keep them out of your dirty hands, that's why.'

Sarason said slowly. 'You couldn't have known we were going to capture your boat before you came back.'

'Not with any certainty. Let's say my intuition was working overtime. That and the fact my radio calls to the ferry went unanswered.'

A shrewd hyenalike look slowly spread across Sarason's face. 'Nice try, Pitt. You'd make an excellent writer of children's stories.'

'You don't believe me?' Pitt asked, as if surprised.

'Not a word.'

'What are you going to do with us?'

Sarason looked disgustingly cheerful. 'You're more naïve than I gave you credit for. You know full well what's going to happen to you.'

'Crowding your luck, aren't you, Sarason? Murdering Congresswoman Smith will bring half the United States law enforcement officers down around your neck.'

'Nobody will know she was murdered,' he said impassively. 'Your ferryboat will simply go to the bottom with all hands. An unfortunate accident that is never fully solved.'

'There is still Kelsey, Giordino, and Rodgers. They're safe and sound in California, ready to spill the story to Customs and FBI agents.'

'We're not in the United States. We're in the sovereign nation of Mexico. The local authorities will conduct an extensive investigation but will turn up no evidence of

426

foul play despite unfounded accusations from your friends.'

'With close to a billion dollars at stake, I should have known you'd be generous in buying the cooperation of local officials.'

'They couldn't wait to sign on board after we promised them a share of the treasure,' Sarason boasted.

'Considering how much there is to go around,' said Pitt, 'you could afford to play Santa Claus.'

Sarason looked at the setting sun. 'It's getting late in the day. I think we've chatted long enough.' He turned and spoke a name that sent a shiver through Pitt. 'Tupac. Come and say hello to the man who made you impotent.'

Tupac Amaru stepped from behind one of the guards and stood in front of Pitt, his teeth set and grinning like a skull on a pirate's Jolly Roger flag. He had the joyful but clinical look of a butcher sizing up a slab of prime, specially aged beef.

'I told you I would make you suffer as you made me,' Amaru said ominously.

Pitt studied the evil face with a strangely paralysed intensity. He didn't need a football coach to diagram what was in store for him. He braced his body to begin the scheme he had formed in the back of his mind right after he had stepped out of the helicopter. He moved towards Loren, but stepped slightly sideways and inconspicuously began to hyperventilate.

'If you are the one who harmed Congresswoman Smith, you will die as surely as you stand there with that stupid look on your face.'

Sarason laughed. 'No, no. You, Mr Pitt, are not going to kill anybody.'

'Neither are you. Even in Mexico you'd hang if there was a witness to your executions.'

'I'd be the first to admit it.' Sarason surveyed Pitt inquiringly. 'But what witness are you talking about?' He paused to sweep an arm around the empty sea. 'As you can see, the nearest land is empty desert twenty kilometres away, and the only vessel in sight is our fishing boat standing off the starboard bow.'

Pitt tilted his head up and stared at the wheelhouse. 'What about the ferryboat's pilot?'

All the heads turned as one, all that is except Gunn's. He nodded unobserved at Pitt and then raised a hand, pointing at the empty pilothouse. 'Hide, Pedro!' he cried loudly. 'Run and hide.'

Three seconds were all Pitt needed. Three seconds to run four steps and leap over the railing into the sea.

Two of the guards caught the sudden movement from the edge of their vision, whirled and fired one quick burst from their automatic rifles on reflex. But they fired high, and they fired late. Pitt had struck the water and vanished into the murky depths.

42

Pitt hit the water stroking and kicking with the fervour of a possessed demon. An Olympic committee of judges would have been impressed; he must have set a new world record for the underwater dash. The water was warm but the visibility below the surface was less than a metre due to the murk caused by silt flowing in from the Colorado River. The blast of the gunfire was magnified by the density of the water and sounded like an artillery barrage to Pitt's ears.

The bullets struck and penetrated the sea with the unlikely sound of a zipper being closed. Pitt levelled out when his hands scoured the bottom, causing an eruption of fine silt. He recalled learning during his US Air Force days that a bullet's velocity was spent after travelling a metre and a half (5 feet) through water. Beyond that depth, it sank harmlessly to the seafloor.

When the light above the surface went dark, he knew he had passed under the port side of the *Alhambra*'s hull. His timing was lucky. It was approaching high tide and the ferryboat was now riding two metres off the bottom. He swam slowly and steadily, exhaling a small amount of air from his lungs, angling on a course astern that he hoped would bring him up on the starboard side near the big paddlewheels. His oxygen intake was nearly exhausted, and he began to see a darkening fuzziness creeping around the borders of his vision, when the shadow of the ferry abruptly ended and he could see a bright surface again.

He broke into air 2 metres (6.5 feet) abaft of the sheltered interior of the starboard paddlewheel. There was no question of his risking exposure. It was that or drown.

The question was whether Sarason's goons had predicted what his game plan would be and run over from the opposite side of the vessel. He could still hear sporadic gunfire striking the water on the port side, and his hopes rose. They weren't on to him, at least not yet.

Pitt sucked in hurried breaths of pure air while getting his bearings. And then he was diving under the temporary safety of the ferry's huge paddlewheels. After gauging the distance, he raised a hand above his head and slowly kicked upward. His hand made contact with an unyielding wood beam. He clutched it and lifted his head above the water. He felt as if he had entered a vast barn with support beams running every which way.

He looked up at the great circular power train that drove the big ferry through the water. It was a radial type similar in construction and action to the old picturesque water-wheels used to power flour- and sawmills. Strong cast-iron hubs mounted on the driveshaft had sockets attached to wooden arms that extended outward to a diameter of 10 metres (33 feet). The ends of the arms were then bolted into long horizontal planks called floats that swung around and around, dipping into the water, pushing backward while driving the ferry forward. The entire unit, and its mate on the opposite side, were housed in giant hoods set inside the ferry's hull.

Pitt hung on to one of the floats and waited as a small school of nosy spotted sand bass circled around his legs. He was not completely out of the woods yet. There was an access door for crewmen to perform maintenance on the paddlewheel. He decided to remain in the water. A sane mind dictated that it would be a big mistake to be caught in the act of climbing up the wooden arms by some tough customer who burst through the access door with an itchy trigger finger. Better to be in a position to duck under the water at the first sound of entry.

He could hear footsteps running on the auto deck above, accented by an occasional burst of gunfire. Pitt couldn't see anything, but he didn't need a lecture to know what Sarason's men were doing. They were roving around the open decks above, shooting at anything that vaguely resembled a body under the water. He could hear voices shouting, but the words came muffled. No large fish within a radius of 50 metres (164 feet) survived the bombardment.

The click of the lock on the access door came as he had expected. He slipped deeper into the water until only half his head was exposed but he was still hidden to anyone above by one of the huge boats.

He could not see the unshaven face that peered downward through the paddlewheel at the water, but this time he heard a voice loud and clear from behind the intruder at the door, a voice he had come to know too well. He could feel the hairs stiffen on the nape of his neck at hearing the words spoken by Amaru.

'See any sign of him?'

'Nothing down here but fish,' grunted the searcher in the access door, catching sight of the spotted sand bass.

'He didn't surface away from the ship. If he's not dead, he must be hiding somewhere underneath the ship.'

'Nobody hiding down here. A waste of energy to bother looking. We put enough lead into him to use his corpse for an anchor.'

'I won't feel satisfied until I see the body,' said Amaru in a businesslike tone.

'You want a body,' said the gunman, pulling back through the access door, 'then drag a grappling hook through the silt. That's the only way you'll ever see him again.'

'Back to the forward boarding ramp,' Amaru ordered. 'The fishing boat is returning.'

Pitt could hear the diesel throb and feel the beat of the fishing boat's propellers through the water as it pulled alongside to take off Sarason and his mercenary scum. Pitt wondered vaguely what his friends would say to him for

431

running out on them even though it was a desperate measure to save *their* lives.

Nothing was going according to plan. Sarason was two steps ahead of Pitt.

Already Pitt had allowed Loren and Gunn to suffer at the hands of the art thieves. Already he'd stupidly done nothing while the crew and ferryboat were captured. Already he'd given away the secret to Huascar's treasure. The way he was handling events, Pitt wouldn't have been surprised if Sarason and his cronies elected him chairman of the board of *Solpemachaco*.

Nearly an hour passed before he sensed the sounds of the fishing boat die in the distance. This was followed by the beating rotor of a helicopter lifting off the ferry, indisputably the NUMA helicopter. Pitt cursed. Another gift to the criminals.

Darkness had fallen and no lights reflected on the water. Pitt wondered why the men on the upper decks had taken so long to evacuate the vessel. His absolute conviction was that one or more would be left behind to take care of him in the event the dead came back to life. Amaru and Sarason could not kill the others unless they knew with cold certainty that Pitt was dead and could tell no tales to the authorities, especially the news media.

Pitt could feel apprehension in his chest like a stone tied to his heart. He was at a distinct disadvantage. If Loren and Rudi had been removed from the *Alhambra*, he had to get ashore somehow and inform Giordino and the Customs officials in the US border town of Calexico of the situation. And what of the crew? Caution dictated that he must be certain Amaru and his friends were no longer on board. If one of them stayed behind to see if he was only playing dead, they could wait him out. They had all the time in the world. He had practically none.

He pushed away from the float, curled over and dived under the hull. The bottom silt seemed closer to the keel than he remembered from his earlier dive. It didn't seem logical until he passed under a bilge exhaust pipe and felt a strong pull of suction. Pitt didn't have to be told that the seacocks in the bilge had been opened; Amaru was scuttling the *Alhambra*.

He turned and swam slowly towards the end of the ferryboat where he had left the helicopter. He took the risk of being seen by surfacing briefly alongside the hull beneath the deck overhang to take another breath. After nearly an hour and a half's immersion, he felt waterlogged. His skin looked like that of a shrivelled old man of ninety-five. He did not feel overly fatigued, but he sensed his strength was reduced by a good 20 per cent. He slipped under the hull again and made for the shallow rudders fitted on the end. They soon loomed out of the murky water. He reached out and gripped one and slowly raised his face out of the water.

No leering face stared back, no guns aimed between his eyes. He hung on to the rudder and floated, relaxing and building back his strength. He listened, but no sound came from the auto deck above.

Finally, he pulled himself up far enough to lift his eyes over the raised edge of the entry/exit ramp. The *Alhambra* was in complete darkness with neither interior nor exterior lights showing. Her decks appeared still and lifeless. As he suspected, the NUMA helicopter was gone. The tingling fear of the unknown travelled up his spine. Like an old fort on the western frontier before a surprise attack by the Apaches, it was far too quiet.

This wasn't one of his better days, Pitt thought. His friends were captured and held hostage. They might be dead. A thought he refused to dwell on. He'd lost another NUMA aircraft. Stolen by the very criminals he was supposed to entice into a trap. The ferryboat was sinking beneath him and he was dead certain one or more killers were lurking somewhere on board to exact a terrible revenge. All in all he'd rather have been in East St Louis.

How long he hung on the rudder he couldn't be sure.

Maybe five minutes, maybe fifteen. His eyes were accustomed to the dark, but all he could see inside the big auto deck was the dim reflection of the chrome bumpers and radiator grill of the Pierce Arrow. He hung there waiting to see a movement or hear the faint sound of stealth. The deck that stretched into the gaping cavern looked frightening. But he had to enter it if he wanted a weapon, he thought nervously, any weapon to protect himself from men who intended to turn him into sushi.

Unless Amaru's men had made a professional search of the old Travelodge, they wouldn't have found inventor John Browning's dependable Colt .45 automatic where Pitt kept it in the vegetable drawer of the refrigerator.

He gripped the deck overhang and heaved himself on board. It took Pitt all of five seconds to run across the deck, sweep the door of the trailer against its stops, and leap inside. In a clockwork motion, he tore open the door to the refrigerator and pulled open the vegetable drawer. The Colt automatic lay where he'd left it. For a brief instant relief washed over him like a waterfall as he gripped the trusty weapon in his hand.

His feeling of deliverance was short-lived. The Colt felt light in his hand, too light. He pulled back the slide and ejected the magazine. It and the firing chamber were empty. With mushrooming despair and desperation he checked the drawer beside the stove that held the kitchen knives. They were gone, along with all the silverware. The only weapon in the trailer was the seemingly useless Colt automatic.

Cat and mouse.

They were out there all right. Pitt now knew Amaru was going to take his time and toy with his prey before dismembering him and throwing the pieces over the side. Pitt treated himself to a few moments for strategy. He sat down in the dark on the trailer's bed and calmly began planning his next moves.

If any of the killers were haunting the auto deck, they

could easily have shot, knifed, or bashed Pitt with a club during his dash to the trailer. For that matter, there was nothing stopping them from breaking in and ending it here. Amaru was a sly hombre, Pitt grudgingly admitted to himself. The South American had guessed Pitt was still alive and would head for any available weapon at the first opportunity. Searching the trailer and finding the gun was shrewd. Removing the bullets but leaving the gun in its place was downright sadistic. That was merely the first step in a game of torment and misery before the final deathblow. Amaru intended to make Pitt twist in the wind before he killed him.

First things first, Pitt decided. Ghouls were lurking in the dark all right, ghouls who wanted to murder him. They thought he was as defenceless as a baby, and he was on a sinking ship with nowhere to go. And that was precisely what he wanted them to think.

If Amaru was in no rush, neither was he.

Pitt leisurely removed his wet clothes and soggy shoes and towelled himself dry. Next he donned a dark grey pair of pants, a black cotton sweatshirt, and a pair of sneakers. Then he made and calmly ate a peanut butter sandwich and drank two glasses of Crystal Light. Feeling rejuvenated, he pulled open a small drawer beneath the bed and checked the contents of a leather gun pouch. The spare magazine was gone, just as he knew it would be. But a small flashlight was there, and in one corner of the drawer he found a small plastic bottle with a label advertising its contents as vitamin supplement A, C, and beta carotene. He shook the bottle and grinned like a happy camper when it rattled.

He unscrewed the lid and poured eight .45-calibre bullets into his hand. Things are looking up, he thought. Amaru's cunning fell a notch below perfection. Pitt fed seven bullets into the magazine and one in the firing chamber. Now Pitt could shoot back, and the good old *Alhambra* was not about to sink above her lower deck overhang once her keel settled into the shallow bottom.

Just one more manifestation of Pitt's law, he thought: 'Every villain has a plan with at least one flaw.'

Pitt glanced at his watch. Nearly twenty minutes had passed since he entered the trailer. He rummaged through a clothing drawer until he found a dark blue ski mask and slipped it over his head. Next he found his Swiss army knife in the pocket of a pair of pants thrown over a chair.

He pulled a small ring in the floor and raised a trapdoor he'd built into the trailer for additional storage space. He lifted out the storage box, set it aside and squirmed through the narrow opening left in the floor. Lying on the deck beneath the trailer, he peered into the darkness and listened. Not a sound. His unseen hunters were patient men.

Coldly and deliberately, like a methodical man with a decisive purpose, who was in no doubt as to the outcome of his intended actions, Pitt rolled from under the trailer and moved like a phantom through a nearby open hatch down a companion ladder into the engine room.

He moved cautiously, careful not to make sudden movements or undue sound.

Amaru would not cut him any slack.

With no one to tend them, the boilers that created heat to make the steam that powered the walking beam engines had cooled to such a degree that Pitt could lay the palm of his bare hand against their thick riveted sides without blistering his skin. He levelled the gun with his right hand and held the flashlight as far to his left as his outstretched arm could allow. Only the unwary aim a beam in front of them. If a cornered man is going to shoot at the person shining a light into his eyes, they unerringly point their weapon where the body is expected to be, directly behind the light.

The engine room looked deserted, but then he tensed. There was a soft mumbling sound like somebody trying to talk through a gag. Pitt swung the beam of the flashlight up into the giant A-frames that supported the walking beam. Someone was up there. Four of them were up there.

Gordo Padilla, his assistant engineer, a man whose name Pitt had not learned, and the two deckhands, Jesus and Gato, all hung upside down, tightly bound and gagged with duct tape, their eyes pleading. Pitt prised open the largest blade of the Swiss army knife and quickly cut them down, freeing their hands and allowing them to pull the tape from their mouths.

'*Muchas gracias, amigo,*' Padilla gasped as the tape tore out a dozen hairs of his moustache. 'Blessed be the Virgin Mary you came when you did. They were going to cut our throats like sheep.'

'When did you see them last?' asked Pitt softly.

'No more than ten minutes ago. They could return at any second.'

'You've got to get away from the boat.'

'I can't remember when we dropped the lifeboats.' Padilla shrugged with a *mañana* display of indifference. 'The davits and motors are probably rusted solid and the boats are rotted.'

'Can't you swim?' Pitt asked desperately.

Padilla shook his head. 'Not very well. Jesus can't swim at all. Sailors do not like to go in the water.' Then his face lit up under the beam of the flashlight. 'There is a small six-man raft tied to the railing near the galley.'

'You'd better hope it still floats.' He handed Padilla his knife. 'Take this to cut away the raft.'

'What about you? Aren't you coming with us?'

'Give me ten minutes to conduct a quick search of the ship for the others. If I've found no sign of them by then, you and your crew get free in the raft while I create a diversion.'

Padilla embraced Pitt. 'Luck be with you.'

It was time to move on.

Before he travelled to the upper decks, Pitt dropped into

the water that was rapidly filling the bilges and turned off the valves of the seacocks. He decided against climbing back up the companion ladder or using a stairway. He had the uneasy feeling that somehow Amaru was following his every move. He climbed up the engine to the top of the steam cylinder and then took a Jacob's ladder to the top of the A-frame before stepping off on to the top deck of the ferry just aft of its twin smokestacks.

Pitt felt no fear of Amaru. Pitt had won the first round in Peru because Amaru wrote him off as a dead man after dropping the safety line into the sacred pool. The South American killer was not infallible. He would err again because his mind was clouded with hate and revenge.

Pitt worked his way down after searching both pilot-houses. He found no sign of Loren or Rudi in the vast passenger seating section, the galley, or the crew's quarters. The search went quickly.

Never knowing who or what he might encounter in the dark, or when, Pitt investigated most of the ship on his hands and knees, scurrying from nook to cranny like a crab, using whatever cover was available. The ship seemed as deserted as a cemetery, but by no stretch of his imagination did he believe for a moment the killers had abandoned the ship.

The rules had not changed. Loren and Rudi Gunn had been removed from the ferry alive because Sarason had a reasonably good hunch Pitt was still alive. The mistake was trusting the murder to a man fired with vengeance. Amaru was too sick with hate to take Pitt out cleanly. There was too much satisfaction in making the man who took away his manhood suffer the tortures of the damned. Loren and Rudi Gunn had a sword hanging over their heads, but it wouldn't fall until the word went out that Pitt was absolutely and convincingly terminated.

The ten minutes were up. There was nothing left for him but to cause a distraction so Padilla and his crew could paddle the raft into the darkness. Once he was certain they were away Pitt would try to swim to shore.

What saved him in the two seconds after he detected the soft sounds of bare feet padding across the deck was a lightning fall to his hands and knees. It was an obsolete football tackle that no longer worked with more sophisticated training. The movement was pure reflex. If he had swung around, flicked on the flashlight and squeezed the trigger at the dark mass that burst out of the night, he would have lost both hands and his head under the blade of a machete that sliced the air like an aircraft propeller.

The man that tore out of the dark could not halt his forward momentum. His knees struck Pitt's crouching body and he flew forward out of control as if launched by a huge spring and crashed heavily on to the deck, the machete spinning over the side. Rolling to one side, Pitt beamed the light on his assailant and pulled the trigger of the Colt. The report was deafening, the bullet entering the killer's chest just under the armpit. It was a killing shot. A short gasp and the body on the deck shrivelled and went still.

'A nice piece of work, gringo,' Amaru's voice boomed through a loudspeaker. 'Manuel was one of my best men.'

Pitt did not waste his breath on a reply. His mind rapidly turned over the situation. It suddenly became clear to him that Amaru had followed his movements once he reached the open decks. The need for stealth was finished. They knew where he was, but he couldn't see them. The game was over. He could only hope Padilla and his men were going over the side unnoticed.

For effect, he fired three more shots in the general direction Amaru's voice came from.

'You missed.' Amaru laughed. 'Not even close.'

Pitt stalled by firing one shot every few seconds until the gun was empty. He had run out of delaying tactics and could do no more. His situation was made even more desperate when Amaru, or one of his men, turned on the ferryboat's navigation and deck lights, leaving him as exposed as an actor on an empty stage under a spotlight. He pressed his back against a bulkhead and stared at the railing outside the galley. The raft was gone – the lines were cut and dangling. Padilla and the rest had slipped into the darkness before the lights came on.

'I'll make you a deal you don't deserve,' said Amaru in a congenial tone. 'Give up now and you can die quickly. Resist and your death will come very slowly.'

Pitt didn't require the services of a mediator to explain the depth of Amaru's intent. His options were somewhat limited. Amaru's tone reminded him of the Mexican bandit who tried to coax Walter Huston, Humphrey Bogart, and Tim Holt from their gold diggings in the motion picture *Treasure of the Sierra Madre*.

'Do not waste our time making up your mind. We have other – '

Pitt wasn't in the mood to hear more. He was as certain as he could ever be that Amaru was trying to hold his attention while another of the murderers crept close enough to stick a knife somewhere it would hurt. He did not have the slightest intention of waiting to be made sport of by a gang of sadists. He sprinted across the deck and leapt over the side of the ferry for the second time that evening.

A gold-medal diver would have gracefully soared into the air and performed any number of jackknifes, twists, and somersaults before cleanly entering the water 15 metres (50 feet) below. He'd have also broken his neck and several vertebrae after crashing into the bottom silt only two metres below the surface. Pitt had no aspirations of ever trying out for the US diving team. He went over the side feet first before doubling up and striking the water like a cannonball.

Amaru and his remaining two men ran to the edge of the top deck and looked down.

'Can you see him?' asked Amaru, peering into the dark water.

'No, Tupac, he must have gone under the hull.'

'The water is turning dirty,' exclaimed another voice. 'He must have buried himself in the bottom mud.'

'This time we're not taking any chances. Juan, the case of concussion grenades we brought from Guaymas. We'll crush him to pulp. Throw them about five metres from the hull, especially in the water around the paddlewheels.'

Pitt made a crater in the seafloor. He didn't impact hard enough to cause any physical damage, but enough to stir up a huge cloud of silt. He uncoiled and swam away from the *Alhambra*, unseen from above.

He was afraid that once he cleared the cover of murk he might still be seen by the killers. This was not to be. A freshening breeze from the south turned the water surface into a light chop that caused a refraction the lights from the ferryboat could not penetrate.

He swam underwater as far as he could until his lungs began to burn. When he came to the surface, he broke it lightly, trusting in the ski mask to keep his head invisible in the black water. A hundred metres (328 feet) and he was beyond the reach of the lights illuminating the ferry. He could barely distinguish the dark figures moving about on the upper deck. He wondered why they weren't shooting into the water. Then he heard a dull thud, saw the white water rise in a towering splash and felt a surge of pressure that squeezed the air out of him.

Underwater explosives! They were trying to kill him with the concussion from underwater explosives. Four more detonations followed in quick succession. Fortunately, they came from the area amidships, near the paddlewheels. By swimming away from one end of the boat, Pitt had distanced himself from the main force of the detonations.

He doubled over with his knees in front of his chest to absorb the worst of the impact. Thirty metres closer and he would have been pounded into unconsciousness. Sixty metres (200 feet) and he would have been crushed to putty. Pitt increased the gap between himself and the ferry until the eruptions came with the same sensual squeeze as from a strong woman.

He looked up at a clear sky and checked the north star for his approximate bearings. At 14 kilometres (8.7 miles) away, the desolate west coast of the Gulf was the closest land. He tore off the ski mask and rolled over. Face towards the carpet of stars across the sky, he began a comfortable backstroke towards the west.

Pitt was in no condition to try out for the swimming team either. After two hours, his arms felt as if they were lifting twenty-pound weights with each stroke. After six hours, his muscles protested with aches he didn't believe possible. And then finally, and most thankfully, fatigue began to dull the pain. He used the old Boy Scout trick of removing his pants, tying the ankles into knots and swinging them over his head to catch the air, making a reasonably efficient float for rest stops that became more numerous as the night wore on.

There was never any question of stopping and letting himself drift in the hope of being spotted by a fishing boat in daylight. The vision of Loren and Rudi in the hands of Sarason was more than an ample stimulus to drive him on.

The stars in the eastern sky were beginning to fade and blink out when his feet hit bottom, and he staggered out of the water on to a sandy beach where he collapsed and immediately fell asleep.

43

Ragsdale, wearing an armoured body suit beneath a pair of workman's coveralls, casually walked up to the side door of a small warehouse with a For Lease sign in the front window. He laid the empty toolbox he carried on the ground, took a key from his pocket, and opened the door.

Inside, a combined team of twenty FBI and eight Customs agents had assembled and were making last-minute preparations for the raid on the Zolar International building directly across the street. Advance teams had alerted local law enforcement to the operation and scouted the entire industrial complex for unusual activity.

Most of the men and the four women wore assault suits and carried automatic weapons, while several professional experts in the art and antiquities field wore street clothes. The latter were burdened with suitcases crammed with catalogues and photographs of known missing art objects targeted for seizure.

The plan called for the agents to split off into specific assignments once they entered the building. The first team was to secure the building and round up the employees, the second was to search out any stolen cache, while the third was to investigate the administration offices for any paper trail that led to theft operations or illegal purchases. Working separately, a commercial business team specializing in art handling was standing by to crate, remove and store the seized goods. The US Attorney's Office, working on the case for both the FBI and Customs, had insisted the raid be carried out in a faultless manner and that confiscated objects be treated with a velvet touch.

Agent Gaskill was standing at an operations board in the centre of the command post. He turned at Ragsdale's approach and smiled. 'Still quiet?'

The FBI agent sat down in a canvas chair. 'All clear except for the gardener trimming the hedge around the building. The rest of the grounds are as quiet as a churchyard.'

'Damned clever of the Zolars to use a gardener as a security guard,' said Gaskill. 'If he hadn't mowed the lawn four times this week, we might have ignored him.'

'That and the fact our surveillance identified his Walkman headset as a radio transmitter,' added Ragsdale.

'A good sign. If they have nothing to hide, why the wily tactics?'

'Don't get your hopes up. The Zolar warehouse operations may look suspicious, but when the FBI walked in with a search warrant two years ago, we didn't find so much as a stolen ballpoint pen.'

'Same with Customs when we talked agents at Internal Revenue into conducting a series of tax audits. Zolar and his family surfaced as pure as the driven snow.'

Ragsdale nodded a 'thank you' as one of his agents handed him a cup of coffee. 'All we've got going for us this time around is the element of surprise. Our last raid failed after a local cop, who was on Zolar's payroll, tipped him off.'

'We should be thankful we're not walking into a high-security armed fortress.'

'Anything from your undercover informant?' asked Gaskill.

Ragsdale shook his head. 'He's beginning to think we've put him in the wrong operation. He hasn't turned up the slightest hint of unlawful activities.'

'No one in or out of the building except bona fide employees. No illegal goods received or shipped in the past four days. Do you get the feeling we're waiting for it to snow in Galveston?'

'It seems that way.'

Gaskill stared at him. 'Do you want to rethink this thing and call off the raid?'

Ragsdale stared back. 'The Zolars aren't perfect. There has to be a flaw in their system somewhere, and I'm staking my career that it's across the street in that building.'

Gaskill laughed. 'I'm with you, buddy, right on down to forced early retirement.'

Ragsdale held up a thumb. 'Then the show goes on in eight minutes as planned.'

'I don't see any reason to call a halt, do you?'

'With Zolar and two of his brothers running around Baja looking for treasure, and the rest of his family in Europe, we'll never have a better opportunity to explore the premises before their army of attorneys gets wind of the operation and swoops in to cut us off at the pass.'

Two agents driving a pickup truck borrowed from the Galveston Sanitation Department pulled up at the kerb opposite the gardener who was cultivating a flower bed beside the Zolar building. The man in the passenger seat rolled down the window and called out, 'Excuse me.'

The gardener turned and stared questioningly at the truck.

The agent made a friendly smile. 'Can you tell me if your driveway gutters backed up during the last rain?'

Curious, the gardener stepped out of the flower bed and approached the truck. 'I don't recall seeing any backup,' he replied.

The agent held a city street map out the window. 'Do you know if any of the surrounding streets had drainage problems?'

As the gardener leaned down to study the map, the agent's arm suddenly lashed out and tore the transmitter from the gardener's head and jerked the cable leading from the microphone and headphones from its socket in the battery pack. 'Federal agents,' snapped the agent. 'Stand still and don't wink an eye.'

The agent behind the wheel then spoke into a portable radio. 'Go ahead, it's all clear.'

The Federal agents did not smash into the Zolar International building with the lightning speed of a drug bust, nor did they launch a massive assault like the disaster that occurred years before in the compound in Waco, Texas. This was no high-security, armed fortress. One team quietly surrounded the building's exits while the main group calmly entered through the main entrance.

The office help and corporate administrators showed no sign of fear or anxiety. They appeared confused and puzzled. The agents politely but firmly herded them out on to the main floor of the warehouse where they were joined by the workers in the storage and shipping section and the artisans from the artifact preservation department. Two buses were driven through the shipping doors and loaded with the Zolar International personnel, who were then taken to FBI headquarters in nearby Houston for questioning. The entire roundup operation took less than four minutes.

The paperwork team, made up mostly of FBI agents trained in accounting methods and led by Ragsdale, went to work immediately, searching through desks, examining files, and scrutinizing every recorded transaction. Gaskill, along with his Customs people and professional art experts, began cataloguing and photographing the thousands of art and antique objects stored throughout the building. The work was tedious and time-consuming and produced no concrete evidence of stolen goods.

Shortly after one o'clock in the afternoon, Gaskill and Ragsdale sat down in Joseph Zolar's luxurious office to compare notes amid incredibly costly art objects. The FBI's chief agent did not look happy.

'This is beginning to have the look of a big embarrassment followed by a storm of nasty publicity and a gigantic lawsuit,' Ragsdale said dejectedly.

'No sign of criminal activity in the records'?' asked Gaskill.

'Nothing that stands out. We'll need a good month for an audit to know for certain if we have a case. What did you dig up on your end?'

'So far every object we've studied checks clean. No stolen goods anywhere.'

'Then we've performed another abortion.'

Gaskill sighed. 'I hate to say it, but it appears the Zolars are a hell of a lot smarter than the best combined investigative teams the United States government can field.'

A few moments later, the two Customs agents who had worked with Gaskill on the Rummel raid in Chicago, Beverly Swain and Winfried Pottle, stepped into the office. Their manner was official and businesslike, but there was no hiding the slight upward curl of their lips. Ragsdale and Gaskill had been so absorbed in their private conversation that they hadn't noticed the two younger Customs agents had not entered through the office door, but from the adjoining, private bathroom.

'Got a minute, boss?' Beverly Swain asked Gaskill.

'What is it?'

'I think our instruments have detected some sort of shaft leading under the building,' answered Winfried Pottle.

'What did you say?' Gaskill demanded quickly.

Ragsdale looked up. 'Instruments?'

'The ground-penetrating sonic/radar detector we borrowed from the Colorado School of Mines,' explained Pottle. 'Its recording unit shows a narrow space beneath the warehouse floor leading into the earth.'

A faint ray of hope suddenly passed between Ragsdale and Gaskill. They both came to their feet. 'How did you know where to look?' asked Ragsdale.

Pottle and Swain could not contain their smiles of

triumph. Swain nodded at Pottle who answered, 'We figured that any passageway leading to a secret chamber had to start or end at Zolar's private office, a connective tunnel he could enter at his convenience without being observed.'

'His personal bathroom,' Gaskill guessed wonderingly.

'A handy location,' Swain confirmed.

Ragsdale took a deep breath. 'Show us.'

Pottle and Swain led them into a large bathroom with a marble floor and an antique sink, commode, and fixtures, with teak decking from an old yacht covering the walls. They motioned to a modern sunken tub with a Jacuzzi that seemed oddly out of place with the more ancient decor.

'The shaft drops under the bathtub,' said Swain, pointing.

'Are you sure about this?' asked Ragsdale sceptically. 'The shower stall strikes me as a more practical setup for an elevator.'

'Our first thought too,' answered Pottle, 'but our instrument showed solid concrete and ground beneath the shower floor.'

Pottle lifted a long tubular probe that was attached by an electrical cable to a compact computer with a paper printout. He switched on the unit and waved the end of the probe around the bottom of the tub. Lights on the computer blinked for a few seconds and then a sheet of paper rolled through a slot on the top. When the recording paper stopped flowing, Pottle tore it off and held it up for everyone to see.

In the centre of an otherwise blank sheet of paper, a black column extended from end to end.

'No doubt about it,' announced Pottle, 'a shaft with the same dimensions as the bathtub that falls underground.'

'And you're sure your electronic marvel is accurate?' said Ragsdale.

'The same type of unit found previously unknown passages and chambers in the Pyramids of Giza last year.'

Gaskill said nothing as he stepped into the tub. He fiddled with the nozzle, but it simply adjusted for spray and direction. Then he sat down on a seat large enough to hold four people. He turned the gold-plated hot and cold faucets, but no water flowed through the spout.

He looked up with a big smile. 'I think we're making progress.'

Next he wiggled the lever that raised and lowered the plug. Nothing happened.

'Try twisting the spout,' suggested Swain.

Gaskill took the gold-plated spout in one of his massive hands and gave it a slight turn. To his surprise it moved and the tub began to slowly sink beneath the bathroom floor. A reverse turn of the spout and the tub returned to its former position. He knew, he *knew*, this simple little water spout and this stupid bathtub were the keys that could topple the entire Zolar organization and shut them down for good. He gave a come-hither motion to the others and said gleefully, 'Going down?'

The unusual elevator descended for nearly thirty seconds before coming to a stop in another bathroom. Pottle judged the drop to be about 20 metres (65 feet). They stepped from the bathroom into an office that was almost an exact copy of the one above. The lights were on but no one was present. With Ragsdale in the lead, the little group of agents cracked open the door of the office and peered out on to the floor of an immense storehouse of stolen art and antiquities. They were all stunned by the size of the chamber and the enormous inventory of the objects. Gaskill made a wild guess of at least ten thousand pieces as Ragsdale slipped into the storeroom and made a fast recon. He was back in five minutes.

'Four men working with a forklift,' he reported, 'lowering a bronze sculpture of a Roman legionnaire into a wooden crate about halfway down the fourth aisle. Across on the other side, in a closed-off area, I counted six men and women working in what looked to be the artifact forgery section. A tunnel leads through the south wall, I'd guess to a nearby building that acts as a front for the shipping and receiving of the stolen property.'

'It must also be used for the covert employees to enter and exit,' suggested Pottle.

'My God,' murmured Gaskill. 'We've hit the jackpot. I can recognize four works of stolen art from here.'

'We'd better stay put,' said Ragsdale softly, 'until we can shuttle reinforcements from above.'

'I volunteer to operate the ferry service,' said Swain with a foxy grin. 'What woman can pass up the opportunity to sit in a fancy bathtub that moves from floor to floor?'

As soon as she left, Pottle stood guard at the door to the storage area while Gaskill and Ragsdale searched Zolar's underground office. The desk produced little of value so they turned their attention to searching for a storeroom. They quickly found what they were looking for behind a tall sideboard bookcase that swivelled out from the wall on small castors. Pushed aside, it revealed a long, narrow chamber lined with antique wooden cabinets, standing floor to ceiling. Each cabinet held file folders in alphabetical order containing acquisition and sales records of the Zolar family operations as far back as 1929.

'It's here,' muttered Gaskill in wonder. 'It's all here.' He began pulling files from a cabinet.

'Incredible,' Ragsdale agreed, studying files from another cabinet that stood in the middle of the storeroom. 'For sixty-nine years they kept a record of every piece of art they stole, smuggled, and forged, including financial and personal data on the buyers.'

'Oh, Jesus,' Gaskill groaned, 'take a look at this one.'

Ragsdale took the offered file and scanned the first two pages. When he looked up his face was marked with disbelief. 'If this is true, Michelangelo's statue of King Solomon in the Eisenstein Museum of Renaissance Aid in Boston is a fake.'

'And a damned good one, judging by the number of experts who authenticated it.'

'But the former curator knew.'

'Of course,' said Gaskill. 'The Zolars made him an offer he couldn't refuse. According to this report, ten extremely rare Etruscan sculptures excavated illegally in northern Italy, and smuggled into the United States, were exchanged along with the forged King Solomon for the genuine article. Since the fake was too good to be caught, the curator became a big hero with the trustees and patrons by claiming he had enhanced the museum's collection by persuading an anonymous moneybags to donate the objects.'

'I wonder how many other cases of museum fraud we'll find,' mused Ragsdale.

'I suspect this may only be the tip of the iceberg. These files represent thousands upon thousands of illegal deals to buyers who turned a blind eye in the direction the objects came from.'

Ragsdale smiled. 'I'd like to be a mouse hiding in the wall when the US Attorney's Office finds out we've laid about ten years worth of legal work on them.'

'You don't know federal prosecutors,' said Gaskill. 'When they get a load of all the wealthy businessmen, politicians, sports and entertainment celebrities who wilfully purchased hot art, they'll think they've died and gone to heaven.'

'Maybe we'd better rethink all the exposure,' cautioned Ragsdale.

'What've you got cooking?'

'We know that Joseph Zolar and his brothers, Charles Oxley and Cyrus Sarason, are in Mexico where we can't arrest and take them into custody without a lot of legal hassle. Right?'

'I follow.'

'So we throw a blanket on this part of the raid,' explained Ragsdale. 'From all indications, the employees on the legitimate side of the operation have no idea what's going on in the basement. Let them go back to work tomorrow as if the raid turned up nothing. Business as usual. Otherwise, if they get wind that we've shut down their operation and federal prosecutors are building an airtight case, they'll go undercover in some country where we can't grab them.'

Gaskill rubbed his chin thoughtfully. 'Won't be easy keeping them in the dark. Like all businessmen on the road, they probably keep in daily communication with their operations.'

'We'll use every underhanded trick in the book and fake it.' Ragsdale laughed. 'Set up operators to claim construction work severed the fibre optic lines. Send out phony memos over their fax lines. Keep the workers we've taken into custody on ice. With luck we can blindside the Zolars for forty-eight hours while we figure a scam to entice them over the border.'

Gaskill looked at Ragsdale. 'You like to play long shots, don't you, my man?'

'I'll bet my wife and kids on a three-legged horse if there is the tiniest chance of putting these scum away for good.'

'I like your odds.' Gaskill grinned. 'Let's shoot the works.'

44

Many of Billy Yuma's village clan of one hundred seventy-six people survived by raising squash, corn, and beans, others cut juniper and manzanita to sell for fence posts and firewood. A new source of income was the revival of interest in their ancient art of making pottery. Several of the Montolo women still created elegant pottery that had recently come into demand by collectors, hungry for Indian art.

After hiring out as a cowboy to a large ranchero for fifteen years, Yuma finally saved enough money to start a small spread of his own. He and his wife, Polly, managed a good living compared to most of the native people of northern Baja, she firing her pots, and he raising livestock.

After his midday meal, as he did every day, Yuma saddled his horse, a buckskin mare, and rode out to inspect his herd for sickness or injury. The harsh and inhospitable landscape with its bounty of jagged rocks, cactus, and steep-sided arroyos could easily maim an unwary steer.

He was searching for a stray calf when he saw the stranger approaching on the narrow trail leading to his village.

The man who walked through the desert seemed out of place. Unlike hikers or hunters, this man wore only the clothes on his back — no canteen, no backpack; he didn't even wear a hat to shade his head from the afternoon sun. There was a tired, worn-to-the-bones look about him, and yet he walked in purposeful, rapid strides as if he was in a hurry to get somewhere. Curious, Billy temporarily suspended his hunt for the calf and rode through a creek bed towards the trail.

Pitt had hiked 14 kilometres (almost 9 miles) across the desert after coming out of an exhausted sleep. He might still be dead to the world if a strange sensation hadn't awakened him. He blinked open his eyes to see a small rock lizard crouching on his arm staring back. He shook off the little intruder and checked his Doxa dive watch for the time. He was shocked to see that he had slept away half the morning.

The sun was already pouring down on the desert when he awoke, but the temperature was a bearable thirty degrees Celsius (86 degrees Fahrenheit). The sweat dried quickly on his body, and he felt the first longing for water. He licked his lips and tasted salt from his swim through the sea. Despite the warmth, a cold self-anger crept through him, knowing he had slept away four precious hours. An eternity, he feared, to his friends enduring whatever misery Sarason and his sadists felt like inflicting on them this day. The core of his existence was to rescue them.

After a quick dive in the water to refresh himself, he cut west across the desert towards Mexico Highway 5, twenty, maybe thirty kilometres away. Once he reached the pavement, he could flag a ride into Mexicali, and then make his way across the border into Calexico. That was the plan, unless the local Baja telephone company had thoughtfully and conveniently installed a pay phone in the shade of a handy mesquite tree.

He gazed out over the Sea of Cortez and took one final look at the *Alhambra* in the distance. The old ferryboat looked to have settled in the water up to her deck overhang and was resting in the silt at a slight list. Otherwise she seemed sound.

She also looked deserted. There were no search boats or helicopters in sight, launched by an anxious Giordino and

US Customs agents north of the border. Not that it mattered. Any search team flying a reconnaissance over the boat, he figured, wouldn't expect to look for anyone on land. He elected to walk out.

He maintained a steady 7-kilometre (4.3-mile) -an-hour pace across the isolated environment. It reminded him of his trek across the Sahara Desert of Northern Mali with Giordino two years before. They had come within minutes of dying under the fiery hell of scorching temperatures with no water. Only by finding a mysterious plane wreck did they manage to construct a land yacht and sail across the sands to eventual rescue. Next to that ordeal, this was a jaunt in the park.

Two hours into his journey, he came to a dusty footpath and followed it. Thirty minutes later he spotted a man sitting astride a horse beside the trail. Pitt walked up to the man and held up a hand in greeting. The rider gazed back through eyes worn and tired from the sun. His stern face looked like weathered sandstone.

Pitt studied the stranger, who wore a straw cowboy hat with a large brim turned up on the sides, a long-sleeved cotton shirt, worn denim pants, and scuffed cowboy boots. The black hair under the hat showed no tendency towards grey. He was small and lean and could have been any-where between fifty and seventy. His skin was burnt bronze with a washboard of wrinkles. The hands that held the reins were leathery and creased with many years of labour. This was a hardy soul, Pitt observed, who survived in an intolerant land with incredible tenacity.

'Good afternoon,' Pitt said pleasantly.

Like most of his people Billy was bilingual, speaking native Montolan among his friends and family and Spanish to outsiders. But he knew a fair amount of English, picked up from his frequent trips over the border to sell his cattle and purchase supplies. 'You know you trespass on private Indian land?' he replied stoically.

'No, sorry. I was cast ashore on the Gulf. I'm trying to

reach the highway and a telephone.'

'You lose your boat?'

'Yes,' Pitt acknowledged. 'You could say that.'

'We have telephone at our meeting house. Glad to take you there.'

'I'd be most grateful.'

Billy reached down a hand. 'My village not far. You can ride on back of my horse.'

Pitt hesitated. He definitely preferred mechanical means of transportation. To his way of thinking four wheels were better than four hooves any day. The only useful purpose for horses was as background in Western movies. But he wasn't about to look one with a gift in the mouth. He took Billy's hand and was amazed at the strength displayed by the wiry little man as he hoisted Pitt's 82 kilograms (181 pounds) up behind him without the slightest grunt of exertion.

'By the way, my name is Dirk Pitt.'

'Billy Yuma,' said the horseman without offering his hand.

They rode in silence for half an hour before cresting a butte overgrown with yucca. They dropped into a small valley with a shallow stream running through it and passed the ruins of a Spanish mission, destroyed by religion-resistant Indians three centuries ago. Crumbling adobe walls and a small graveyard were all that remained. The graves of the old Spaniards near the top of a knoll were long since grown over and forgotten. Lower down were the more recent burials of the townspeople. One tombstone in particular caught Pitt's eye. He slipped to the ground over the rump of the horse and walked over to it.

The carved letters on the weathered stone were distinct and quite readable.

Patty Lou Cutting
2/11/24–2/3/34
The sun be warm and kind to you.

The darkest night some star shines through.
The dullest morn a radiance brew.
And where dusk comes, God's hand to you.

'Who was she'?' asked Pitt.

Billy Yuma shook his head. 'The old ones do not know. They say the grave was made by strangers in the night.'

Pitt stood and looked over the sweeping vista of the Sonoran Desert. A light breeze gently caressed the back of his neck. A red-tailed hawk circled the sky, surveying its domain. The land of mountains and sand, jackrabbits, coyotes, and canyons could intimidate as well as inspire. This is the place to die and be buried, he thought. Finally, he turned from Patty Lou's last resting place and waved Yuma on. 'I'll walk the rest of the way.'

Yuma nodded silently and rode ahead, the hooves of the buckskin kicking up little clouds of dust.

Pitt followed down the hill to a modest farming and ranching community. They travelled along the streambed where three young girls were washing clothes under the shade of a cottonwood tree. They stopped and stared at him with adolescent curiosity. He waved, but they ignored the greeting and, almost solemnly it seemed to Pitt, returned to their wash.

The heart of the Montolo community consisted of several houses and buildings. Some were built from mesquite branches that were coated with mud, one or two from wood, but most were constructed of cement blocks. The only apparent influence of modern living was weathered poles supporting electrical and phone lines, a few battered pickup trucks that looked as if they'd barely escaped a salvage yard crusher, and one satellite dish.

Yuma reined in his horse in front of a small building that was open on three sides. 'Our meeting house,' he said. 'A phone inside. You have to pay.'

Pitt smiled, investigated his still soggy wallet, and produced an AT&T card. 'No problem.'

Yuma nodded and led him into a small office equipped with a wooden table and four folding chairs. The telephone sat on a very thin phone book that was lying on the tile floor.

The operator answered after seventeen rings. '*Sí, por favor?*'

'I wish to make a credit card call.'

'Yes, sir, your card number and the number you're calling,' the operator replied in fluent English.

'At least my day hasn't been all bad,' Pitt sighed at hearing an understanding voice.

The Mexican operator connected him to an American operator. She transferred him to information to obtain the number for the Customs' offices in Calexico and then put his call through. A male voice answered.

'Customs Service, how can I help you?'

'I'm trying to reach Albert Giordino of the National Underwater and Marine Agency.'

'One moment, I'll transfer you. He's in Agent Starger's office.'

Two clicks and a voice that seemed to come from a basement said, 'Starger here.'

'This is Dirk Pitt. Is Al Giordino handy?'

'Pitt, is that you?' Curtis Starger said incredulously. 'Where have you been? We've been going through hell trying to get the Mexican navy to search for you.'

'Don't bother, their local commandant was probably bought off by the Zolars.'

'One moment. Giordino is standing right here. I'll put him on an extension.'

'Al,' said Pitt, 'are you there?'

'Good to hear your voice, pal. I take it something went wrong.'

'In a nutshell, our friends from Peru have Loren and Rudi. I helped the crew escape on a life raft. I managed to swim to shore. I'm calling from an Indian village in the desert north of San Felipe and about thirty kilometres west of where the *Alhambra* lies half-sunk in the muck.'

'I'll dispatch one of our helicopters,' said Starger. 'I'll need the name of the village for the pilot.'

Pitt turned to Billy Yuma. 'What do you call your community?'

Yuma nodded. 'Canyon Ometepec.'

Pitt repeated the name, gave a more in-depth report on the events of the last eighteen hours and hung up. 'My friends are coming after me,' he said to Yuma.

'By car?'

'Helicopter.'

'You be an important man?'

Pitt laughed. 'No more than the mayor of your village.'

'No mayor. Our elders meet and talk on tribal business.'

Two men walked past, leading a burro that was buried under a load of manzanita limbs. The men and Yuma merely exchanged brief stares. There were no salutations, no smiles.

'You look tired and thirsty,' said Yuma to Pitt. 'Come to my house. My wife make you something to eat while you wait for friends.'

It was the best offer Pitt had had all day and he gratefully accepted.

Billy Yuma's wife, Polly, was a large woman who carried her weight better than any man. Her face was round and wrinkled with enormous dark brown eyes. Despite being middle aged, her hair was as black as raven's feathers. She hustled around a wood stove that sat under a ramada next to their cement brick house. The Indians of the Southwest deserts preferred the shade and openness of a ramada for their kitchen and dining areas to the confining and draftless interior of their houses. Pitt noticed that the ramada's roof was constructed from the skeletal ribs of the saguaro cactus tree and was supported by mesquite poles surrounded by a wall of standing barbed ocotillo stems.

After he drank five cups of water from a big olla, or pot, whose porous walls let it sweat and keep its contents cool, Polly fed him shredded pork and refried beans with fried cholla buds that reminded him of okra. The tortillas were made from mesquite beans she had pounded into a sweet-tasting flour. The late lunch was accompanied by wine fermented from fruit of the saguaro.

Pitt couldn't recall eating a more delightful meal.

Polly seldom spoke, and when she did utter a few words they were addressed to Billy in Spanish. Pitt thought he detected a hint of humour in her big brown eyes, but she acted serious and remote.

'I do not see a happy community,' said Pitt, making conversation.

Yuma shook his head sadly. 'Sorrow fell over my people and the people of our other tribal villages when our most sacred religious idols were stolen. Without them our sons and daughters cannot go through the initiation of adult-hood. Since their disappearance, we have suffered much misfortune.'

'Good God,' Pitt breathed. 'Not the Zolars.'

'What, señor?'

'An international family of thieves who have stolen half the ancient artifacts ever discovered.'

'Mexican police told us our idols were stolen by Ameri-can pothunters who search sacred Indian grounds for our heritage to sell for profit.'

'Very possible,' said Pitt. 'What do your sacred idols look like?'

Yuma stretched out his hand and held it about a metre above the floor. 'They stand about this high and their faces were carved many centuries ago by my ancestors from the roots of cottonwood trees.'

'The chances are better than good that your idols were bought from the pothunters by the Zolars for peanuts, and then resold to a wealthy collector for a fat price.'

'These people are called Zolars?'

460

'Their family name. They operate under a shadowy organization called *Solpemachaco*.'

'I do not know the word,' said Yuma. 'What does it mean?'

'A mythical Inca serpent with several heads that takes up housekeeping in a cave.'

'Never heard of him.'

'I think he may be related to another legendary monster the Peruvians called the *Demonio del Muertos*, who guards their underworld.'

Yuma gazed thoughtfully at his work-worn hands. 'We too have a legendary demon of the underworld who keeps the dead from escaping and the living from entering. He also passes judgment on our dead, allowing the good to pass and devouring the bad.'

'A Judgment Day demon,' said Pitt.

Yuma nodded solemnly. 'He lives on a mountain not far from here.'

'Cerro el Capirote,' Pitt said softly.

'How could a stranger know that?' Yuma asked, looking deeply into Pitt's green eyes.

'I've been to the peak. I have seen the winged jaguar with the serpent's head, and I guarantee you he wasn't put there to secure the underworld or judge the dead.'

'You seem to know much about this land.'

'No, actually very little. But I'd be most interested in hearing any other legends about the demon.'

'There is one other,' Yuma conceded. 'Enrique Juarez, our oldest tribal elder, is one of the few remaining Montolos who remember the old stories and ancient ways. He tells of golden gods who came from the south on great birds with white wings that moved over the surface of the water. They rested on an island in the old sea for a long time. When the gods finally sailed away, they left behind the stone demon. A few of our brave and curious ancestors went across the water to the island and never returned. The old people were frightened and believed the mountain was sacred and all intruders would be devoured by the demon.' Yuma paused and gazed into the desert. 'The story has been told and retold from the days of my ancestors. Our younger children, who are schooled in modern ways, think of it simply as an old people's fairy tale.'

'A fairy tale mixed with historical fact,' Pitt assured Yuma. 'Believe me when I tell you a vast hoard of gold lies inside Cerro el Capirote. Put there not by golden gods from the south, but Incas from Peru, who played on your ancestors' reverence of the supernatural by carving the stone monster to instil fear and keep them off the island. As added insurance, they left a few guards behind to kill the curious until the Spanish were driven from their homeland, and they could come back and reclaim the treasure for their new king. It goes without saying, history took a different turn. The Spaniards were there to stay and no one ever returned.'

Billy Yuma was not a man given to extreme emotion. His wrinkled face remained fixed, only his dark eyes widened. 'A great treasure lies under Cerro el Capirote?'

Pitt nodded. 'Very soon men with evil intentions are coming to force their way inside the mountain to steal the Inca riches.'

'They cannot do that,' Yuma protested. 'Cerro el Capirote is magic. It is on our land, Montolo land. The dead who did not pass judgment live outside its walls.'

'That won't stop these men, believe me,' said Pitt seriously.

'My people will make a protest to our local police authorities.'

'If the Zolars run true to form, they've already bribed your law enforcement officials.'

'These evil men you speak of. They are the same ones who sold our sacred idols?'

'As I suggested, it's very possible.'

Billy Yuma studied him for a moment. 'Then we do not

have to trouble ourselves with their trespass on to our sacred ground.'

Pitt did not understand. 'May I ask why?'

Reality slowly faded from Billy's face and he seemed to enter a dreamlike state. 'Because those who have taken the idols of the sun, moon, earth, and water are cursed and will suffer a terrible death.'

'You really believe that, don't you?'

'I do,' Yuma answered sombrely. 'In my dreams I see the thieves drowning.'

'Drowning?'

'Yes, in the water that will make the desert into the garden it was for my ancestors.'

Pitt considered making a contrary reply. He was not one to deposit his money in the bank of dreams. He was a confirmed sceptic of the metaphysical. But the intractable gaze in Yuma's eyes, the case-hardened tone of his voice, moved something inside Pitt.

He began to feel glad that he wasn't related to the Zolars.

45

Amaru stepped down into the main *sala* of the hacienda. One wall of the great room was filled by a large stone fireplace removed from an old Jesuit mission. The high ceiling was decorated with intricate precast plaster panels. 'Please excuse me for keeping you waiting, gentlemen.'

'Quite all right,' said Zolar. 'Now that the fools from NUMA have led us directly to Huascar's gold, we made good use of your tardiness by discussing methods of bringing it to the surface.'

Amaru nodded and looked around the room. There were four men there besides himself. Seated on sofas around the fireplace were Zolar, Oxley, Sarason, and Moore. Their faces were expressionless, but there was no concealing the feeling of triumph in the air.

'Any word of Dr Kelsey, the photographer Rodgers, and Albert Giordino?' Sarason inquired.

'My contacts over the border believe Pitt told you the truth on the ferry when he said he dropped them off at the US Customs compound in Calexico,' answered Amaru.

'He must have smelled a trap,' said Moore.

'That was obvious when he returned to the ferryboat alone,' Sarason said sharply to Amaru. 'You had him in your hands and you let him escape.'

'Not forgetting the crew,' added Oxley.

'I promise you, Pitt did not escape. He was killed when my men and I threw concussion grenades into the water around him. As to the ferryboat's crew, the Mexican police officials you've paid to cooperate will ensure their silence for as long as necessary.'

'Still not good,' said Oxley. 'With Pitt, Gunn, and Congresswoman Smith gone missing, every federal agent between San Diego and Denver will come nosing around.'

Zolar shook his head. 'They have no legal authority down here. And our friends in the local government would never permit their entry.'

Sarason looked angrily at Amaru. 'You say Pitt's dead. Then where is the body?'

Amaru stared back nastily. 'Pitt is feeding the fishes. Take my word for it.'

'Forgive me if I'm not convinced.'

'There is no way he could have survived the underwater detonations.'

'The man has survived far worse.' Sarason walked across the room to a bar and poured himself a drink. 'I won't be satisfied until I see the remains.'

'You also botched the scuttling of the ferryboat,' Oxley said to Amaru. 'You should have sailed her into deep water before opening the seacocks.'

'Or better yet, set her on fire, along with Congresswoman Smith and the deputy director of NUMA,' said Zolar, lighting a cigar.

'Police Comandante Cortina will conduct an investigation and announce that the ferryboat along with Congresswoman Smith and Rudi Gunn was lost in an unfortunate accident,' said Sarason.

Zolar glared at him. 'That won't solve the problem of interference from American law enforcement officials. Their Justice Department will demand more than a local investigation if Pitt survives to expose the blundering actions of your friend here.'

'Forget Pitt,' Amaru said flatly. 'Nobody had a stronger reason for seeing him dead than me.'

Oxley glanced from Amaru to Zolar. 'We can't gamble on speculation. No way Cortina can hold off a joint investigation by the Mexican and American governments for more than a few days.'

Sarason shrugged. 'Time enough to remove the treasure and be gone.'

'Even if Pitt walks out of the sea to tell the truth,' said Henry Moore, 'it's your word against his. He can't prove your connection with the torture and disappearance of Smith and Gunn. Who would believe a family of respected art dealers was involved with such things? You might arrange for Cortina to accuse Pitt of committing these crimes so he could grab the treasure for himself.'

'I approve of the professor's concept,' said Zolar. 'Our influential friends in the police and military can easily be persuaded to arrest Pitt if he shows his face in Mexico.'

'So far so good,' said Sarason. 'But what about our prisoners? Do we eliminate them now or later?'

'Why not throw them in the river that runs through the treasure cavern?' suggested Amaru. 'Eventually, what's left of their bodies will probably turn up in the Gulf. By the time the fish get through with them, about all a coroner will be able to determine is that they died from drowning.'

Zolar looked around the room at his brothers and then to Moore who looked oddly uneasy. After a moment he turned to Amaru. 'A brilliant scenario. Simple, but brilliant nonetheless. Any objections?'

There were none.

'I'll contact Comandante Cortina and brief him on his assignment,' Sarason volunteered.

Zolar waved his cigar and flashed his teeth in a broad smile. 'Then it's settled. While Cyrus and Cortina lay a smoke screen for American investigators, the rest of us will pack up and move from the hacienda to Cerro el Capirote and begin retrieving the gold at first light tomorrow.'

One of the hacienda's servants entered and handed Zolar a portable telephone. He listened without replying to the caller. Then he switched off the phone and laughed.

'Good news, brother?' asked Oxley.

'Federal agents raided our warehouse facilities again.'

'That's funny?' asked a puzzled Moore.

'A common occurrence,' explained Zolar. 'As usual, they came up dry and stood around like idiots with no place to go.'

Sarason finished his drink. 'So it's business as usual, and the treasure excavation goes on as scheduled.'

The great room went silent as each man conjured up his own thoughts of what incredible riches they would find under Cerro el Capirote. All except Sarason. His mind turned back to the meeting with Pitt on the ferry. He knew it was ridiculous, but it gnawed at his mind that Pitt had claimed to have led him and his brothers to the jackpot. And what did he mean when he said they had been set up?

Was Pitt merely lying or trying to tell him something, or was it sheer bravado from a man who thought he was going to die? The answers, Sarason decided, were not worth his time to ponder. The warning bells should have been clanging away in the back of his head, but there were more important issues at hand. He swept Pitt from his thoughts.

He never made a bigger mistake.

Micki Moore stepped carefully down the steep steps into the cellar beneath the hacienda as she balanced a tray. At the bottom, she approached one of Amaru's thugs who was guarding the door of a small storeroom that held the captives. 'Open the door,' she demanded.

'No one is allowed in,' muttered the guard unpleasantly.

'Step aside, you stupid cretin,' Micki snarled, 'or I'll cut your balls off.'

The guard was startled by the abusive coarseness from an elegant woman. He stepped back a pace. 'I have my orders from Tupac Amaru.'

'All I have is food, you idiot. Let me in or I'll scream and swear to Joseph Zolar you raped me and the woman inside.'

He peered at the tray and then gave in, unlocking the door and stepping aside. 'You do not tell Tupac of this.'

'Don't worry,' Micki snapped over her shoulder as she entered the dark and stuffy cubicle. It took a moment for her eyes to adjust to the dim light. Gunn was lying on the stone floor. He struggled to a sitting position. Loren was standing as if to protect him.

'Well, well,' murmured Loren testily. 'This time they sent a woman to do their filthy work.'

Micki pushed the tray into Loren's hands. 'Here is some food. Fruit and sandwiches, and four bottles of beer. Take it!' Then she turned and slammed the door shut in the guard's face. When she refaced Loren, her eyes had become more accustomed to the dark. She was stunned at Loren's appearance. She could make out puffy bruises on her lips and around the eyes. Most of Loren's clothing had been torn away and she had knotted what little remained to cover her torso. Micki also saw livid red welts across the top of her breasts and discolorations on her arms and legs. 'The bastards!' she hissed. 'The no-good sadistic bastards. I'm sorry, if I had known you'd been beaten, I would have brought medical supplies.'

Loren knelt and set the tray on the floor. She gave one of the bottles of beer to Gunn, but his injured hands could not twist off the cap. She removed it for him.

'Who is our Florence Nightingale?' asked Gunn.

'I'm Micki Moore. My husband is an anthropologist, and I'm an archaeologist hired by the Zolars.'

'To help them find Huascar's golden treasure?' Gunn rightly guessed.

'Yes, we deciphered the images – '

'On the Golden Body Suit of Tiapollo,' finished Gunn. 'We know all about it.'

Loren didn't speak for a few moments while she ravenously consumed one of the sandwiches and downed a beer. Finally, feeling almost as if she had been reborn, she stared at Micki curiously. 'Why are you doing this? To build up our spirits before they come back and use us for punching bags again?'

'We're not part of your ordeal,' Micki replied honestly. 'The truth is, Zolar and his brothers are planning to kill my husband and me as soon as they've recovered the treasure.'

'How could you know that?'

'We've been around people like these before. We have a feel for what's going on.'

'What do they plan on doing with us?' asked Gunn.

'The Zolars and their bribed cronies with the Mexican police and military intend to make it look as if you drowned while attempting to escape your sinking ferryboat. Their plan is to throw you in the underground river the ancients mentioned that runs through the treasure chamber and empties into the sea. By the time your bodies surface, there won't be enough left to prove otherwise.'

'Sounds feasible,' Loren muttered angrily. 'I give them credit for that.'

'My God,' said Gunn. 'They just can't murder a representative of the United States Congress in cold blood.'

'Believe me,' said Micki, 'these men have no scruples and even less conscience.'

'How come they haven't killed us before now?' asked Loren.

'Their fear was that your friend Pitt might somehow expose your kidnapping. Now they no longer care. They figure their charade is strong enough to stand against one man's accusations.'

'What about the ferryboat's crew?' asked Loren. 'They were witnesses to the piracy.'

'They'll be kept from raising the alarm by local police.' Micki hesitated. 'I'm sorry to have to tell you why they are no longer concerned about Pitt. Tupac Amaru swears that after you were transported to the hacienda, he and his men crushed Pitt to jelly by throwing concussion grenades at him in the water.'

469

Loren's violet eyes were grief-stricken. Until now she had harboured a hope Pitt had somehow escaped. Now her heart felt as though it had fallen into the crevasse of a glacier. She sagged against one wall of the stone room and covered her face with her hands.

Gunn pushed himself to his feet. There was no grief in his eyes, only iron-hard conviction. 'Dirk dead? Scum like Amaru could never kill a man like Dirk Pitt.'

Micki was startled by the fiery spirit of a man so sorely tortured. 'I only know what my husband told me,' she said as if apologizing. 'Amaru *did* admit he failed to retrieve Pitt's body, but there was little doubt in his mind that Pitt could not have survived.'

'You say you and your husband are also on Zolar's death list?' asked Loren.

Micki shrugged. 'Yes, we're to be silenced too.'

'If you'll pardon me for saying so,' said Gunn, 'you seem pretty damned indifferent.'

'My husband also has plans.'

'To escape?'

'No, Henry and I can break out any time it's convenient. We intend to take a share of the treasure for ourselves.'

Gunn stared at Micki incredulously. Then he said cynically, 'Your husband must be one tough anthropologist.'

'Perhaps you might better understand if I told you we met and fell in love when working on an assignment together for the Foreign Activities Council.'

'Never heard of it,' said Gunn.

Loren gave Micki a bemused stare. 'I have. FAC is rumoured to be an obscure and highly secret organization that works behind the scenes in the White House. No one in Congress has ever been able to come up with solid proof of its existence or its financing.'

'What is its function?' asked Gunn.

'To carry out covert activities under the direct supervision of the President outside the nation's other intelligence services without their knowledge,' replied Micki.

470

'What kind of activities?'

'Dirty tricks on foreign nations considered hostile to the United States,' replied Loren, studying Micki for some kind of sign. But her expression was aloof and remote. 'As a mere member of Congress I'm not privy to their operations and can only speculate. I have a suspicion their primary directive is to carry out assassinations.'

Micki's eyes turned hard and cold. 'I freely admit that for twelve years, until we retired from service to devote our time to archaeology, Henry and I had few peers.'

'I'm not surprised,' Loren said sarcastically. 'By passing yourselves off as scientists, you were never suspected of being the President's hired killers.'

'For your information, Congresswoman Smith, our academic credentials are not counterfeit. Henry has his doctorate from the University of Pennsylvania and I have mine from Stanford. We have no misgivings about the duties we performed under three former Presidents. By eliminating certain heads of foreign terrorist organizations, Henry and I saved more American lives than you can imagine.'

'Who are you working for now?'

'Ourselves. As I said, we retired. We felt it was time to cash in our expertise. Our government service is a thing of the past. Though we were well paid for our services, we weren't considered for a pension.'

'Tigers aren't known for changing stripes,' mocked Gunn. 'You can never achieve your objective without killing off Amaru and the Zolars.'

Micki smiled faintly. 'We may very well have to do unto them before they can do unto us. But only after enough of Huascar's gold is brought to the surface for us to carry out.'

'So the trail will be littered with bodies.'

Micki passed a weary hand over her face. 'Your involvement in the treasure hunt came as a complete surprise to everybody. Stupidly, the Zolars overreacted when they discovered another party was on the trail to the gold. They ran amok, murdering or abducting everyone their greed-crazed minds saw as an obstacle. Consider yourselves lucky they didn't murder you on the ferryboat like your friend Pitt. Keeping you alive temporarily is the hallmark of rank amateurs.'

'You and your husband,' murmured Loren caustically, 'you would have – '

'Shot you and burned the boat down around your bodies?' Micki shook her head. 'Not our style. Henry and I have only terminated those foreign nationals who have indiscriminately gunned down unfortunate women and children or blew them to pieces without blinking an eye or shedding a tear. We have never harmed a fellow American, and we don't intend to start now. Despite the fact your presence has hamstrung our operation, we will do everything in our power to help you escape this affair in one piece.'

'The Zolars are Americans,' Loren reminded her.

Micki shrugged. 'A mere technicality. They represent what is perhaps the largest art theft and smuggling ring in history. The Zolars are world-class sharks. Why should I have to tell you? You've experienced their brutality first-hand. By leaving their bones to bleach in the Sonoran Desert, Henry and I figure to save the American taxpayers millions of dollars that would be spent on a complicated and time-consuming investigation into their criminal activities. And then there are the court and prison costs if they're caught and convicted.'

'And once a portion of the treasure is in your hands?' asked Gunn. 'What then?'

Micki smiled like a wily shrew. 'I'll send you a postcard from whatever part of the world we're in at the time and let you know how we're spending it.'

46

A small army of soldiers set up a command post and sealed off the desert for two miles around the base of Cerro el Capirote. No one was allowed in or out. The mountain's peak had become a staging area with all treasure recovery operations conducted from the air. Pitt's stolen NUMA helicopter, repainted with Zolar International colours, lifted into a clear sky and dipped on a course back to the hacienda. A few minutes later, a heavy Mexican army transport helicopter hovered and settled down. A detachment of military engineers in desert combat fatigues jumped to the ground, opened the rear cargo door and began unloading a small forklift, coils of cable, and a large winch.

Officials of the state of Sonora who were on the Zolars' payroll had approved all the necessary licences and permits within twenty-four hours, a process that would normally have taken months and perhaps years. The Zolars had promised to fund new schools, roads, and a hospital. Their cash had greased the palms of the local bureaucracy and eliminated the usual rivers of red tape. Full cooperation was given by an unwitting Mexican government misled by corrupt bureaucrats. Joseph Zolar's request for a contingent of engineers from a military base on the Baja Peninsula was quickly approved. Under the terms of a swiftly drawn up contract with the Ministry of the Treasury, the Zolars were entitled to 25 per cent of the treasure. The rest was to be deposited with the national court in Mexico City.

The only problem with the agreement was that the Zolars had no intention of keeping their end of the bargain.

They weren't about to split the treasure with anyone.

Once the golden chain and the bulk of the treasure had been hauled to the top of the mountain, a covert operation was created to move the hoard under cover of darkness to a remote military airstrip near the great sand dunes of the Altar Desert just south of the Arizona border. There, it would be loaded aboard a commercial jet transport, painted with the markings and colours of a major airline company, and then flown to a secret distribution facility owned by the Zolars in the small city of Nador on the north coast of Morocco.

Everyone had been ferried from the hacienda to the mountaintop as soon as it became daylight. No personal effects were left behind. Only Zolar's jetliner remained, parked on the hacienda's airstrip, ready for takeoff on a moment's notice.

Loren and Rudi were released from their prison and sent over later the same morning. Ignoring Sarason's orders not to communicate with the hostages, Micki Moore had compassionately tended to their cuts and bruises and made sure they were fed a decent meal. Since there was little chance they could escape by climbing down the rocky walls of the mountain, no one guarded them and they were left on their own to wander about as they pleased.

Oxley quickly discovered the small aperture leading inside the mountain and wasted no time in directing a military work crew to enlarge it. He stayed behind to oversee the equipment staging while Zolar, Sarason, and the Moores set off down the passageway followed by a squad of engineers, who carried portable fluorescent lights.

When they reached the second demon, Micki lovingly touched its eyes, just as Shannon Kelsey had done before her. She sighed. 'A marvellous piece of work.'

'Beautifully preserved,' Henry Moore agreed.

'It will have to be destroyed,' said Sarason indifferently.

'What are you talking about?' demanded Moore.

'We can't move it. The ugly beast fills up most of the tunnel. There is no way we can drag Huascar's chain over, around, or between its legs.'

Micki's face went tense with shock. 'You can't destroy a masterwork of antiquity.'

'We can and we will,' Zolar said, backing his brother. 'I agree it's unfortunate. But we don't have time for archaeological zealotry. The sculpture has to go.'

Moore's pained expression slowly turned hard, and he looked at his wife and nodded. 'Sacrifices must be made.'

Micki understood. If they were to seize enough of the golden riches to keep them in luxury for the rest of their lives, they would have to close their eyes to the demolition of the demon.

They pushed on as Sarason lagged behind and ordered the engineers to place a charge of explosives under the demon. 'Be careful,' he warned them in Spanish. 'Use a small charge. We don't want to cause a cave-in.'

Zolar was amazed at the Moores' vast energy and enthusiasm after they encountered the crypt of the treasure guardians. If left on their own, they would have spent a week studying the mummies and the burial ornaments before pushing on to the treasure chamber.

'Let's keep going,' said Zolar impatiently. 'You can nose around the dead later.'

Reluctantly, the Moores continued into the guardians' living quarters, lingering only a few minutes before Sarason rejoined his brother and urged them onward.

The sudden sight of the guardian encased in calcite crystals shocked and stunned all of them, as it had Pitt and his group. Henry Moore peered intently through the translucent sarcophagus.

'An ancient Chachapoya,' he murmured as if standing before a crucifix. 'Preserved as he died. This is an unbelievable discovery.'

'He must have been a noble warrior of very high status,' said Micki in awe.

'A logical conclusion, my dear. This man had to be very powerful to bear the responsibility of guarding an immense royal treasure.'

'What do you think he's worth?' asked Sarason.

Moore turned and scowled at him. 'You can't set a price on such an extraordinary object. As a window to the past, he is priceless.'

'I know a collector who would give five million dollars for him,' said Zolar, as if he were appraising a Ming vase.

'The Chachapoya warrior belongs to science,' Moore lashed back, his anger choking him. 'He is a visible link to the past and belongs in a museum, not in the living room of some morally corrupt gatherer of stolen artifacts.'

Zolar threw Moore an insidious look. 'All right, Professor, he's yours for your share of the gold.'

Moore looked agonized. His professional training as a scientist fought a war with his greed. He felt dirtied and ashamed now that he realized that Huascar's legacy went beyond mere wealth. He was overcome with regret that he was dealing with unscrupulous scum. He gripped his wife's hand, knowing without doubt she felt the same. 'If that's what it takes. You've got yourself a deal.'

Zolar laughed. 'Now that's settled. Can we please proceed and find what we came here for?'

A few minutes later, they stood in a shoulder-to-shoulder line on the edge of the subterranean riverbank and stared mesmerized at the array of gold, highlighted by the portable fluorescent lamps carried by the military engineers. All they saw was the treasure. The sight of a river flowing through the bowels of the earth seemed insignificant.

'Spectacular,' whispered Zolar. 'I can't believe I'm looking at so much gold.'

'This easily exceeds the treasures of King Tut's tomb,' said Moore.

'How magnificent,' said Micki, clutching her husband's arm. 'This has to be the richest cache in all the Americas.'

476

Sarason's amazement quickly wore off. 'Very clever of those ancient bastards,' he charged. 'Storing the treasure on an island surrounded by a strong current makes recovery doubly complicated.'

'Yes, but we've got cables and winches,' said Moore. 'Think of the difficulty they had in moving all that gold over there with nothing but hemp rope and muscle.'

Micki spied a golden monkey crouched on a pedestal. 'That's odd.'

Zolar looked at her. 'What's odd?'

She stepped closer to the monkey and its pedestal which was lying on its side. 'Why would this piece still be on this bank of the river?'

'Yes, it does seem strange this object wasn't placed with the others,' said Moore. 'It almost looks as if it was thrown here.'

Sarason pointed to gouges in the sand and calcium crystals beside the riverbank. 'I'd say it was dragged off the island.'

'It has writing scratched on it,' said Moore.

'Can you decipher anything?' asked Zolar.

'Doesn't need deciphering. The markings are in English.'

Sarason and Zolar stared at him with the expressions of Wall Street bankers walking along the sidewalk and being asked by a homeless derelict if they could spare fifty thousand dollars. 'No jokes, Professor,' said Zolar.

'I'm dead serious. Somebody engraved a message into the soft gold on the bottom of the pedestal, quite recently by the looks of it.'

'What does it say?'

Moore motioned for an engineer to aim his lamp at the monkey's pedestal, adjusted his glasses and began reading aloud.

Welcome members of the **Solpemachaco**
to the underground thieves' and plunderers'
annual convention.

*If you have any ambitions in life other than
the acquisition of stolen loot, you have
come to the right place.
Be our guests and take only the objects
you can use.*

Your congenial sponsors,
*Dr Shannon Kelsey, Miles Rodgers, Al Giordino,
& Dirk Pitt.*

There was a moment of sober realization, and then Zolar snarled at his brother. 'What in hell is going on here? What kind of foolish trick is this?'

Sarason's mouth was pinched in a bitter line. 'Pitt admitted leading us to the demon,' he answered reluctantly, 'but he said nothing of entering the mountain and laying eyes on the treasure.'

'Generous with his information, wasn't he? Why didn't you tell me this?'

Sarason shrugged. 'He's dead. I didn't think it mattered.'

Micki turned to her husband. 'I know Dr Kelsey. I met her at an archaeology conference in San Antonio. She has a splendid reputation as an expert on Andean cultures.'

Moore nodded. 'Yes, I'm familiar with her work.' He stared at Sarason. 'You led us to believe Congresswoman Smith and the men from NUMA were merely on a treasure hunt. You said nothing of involvement by professional archaeologists.'

'Does it make any difference?'

'Something is going on beyond your control,' warned Moore. He looked as if he was enjoying the Zolars' confusion. 'If I were you, I'd get the gold out of here as fast as possible.'

His words were punctuated by a muffled explosion far up into the passageway.

'We have nothing to fear so long as Pitt is dead,' Sarason kept insisting. 'What you see here was done before Amaru put a stop to him.' But he was damp with cold sweat. Pitt's mocking words rang in his ears: 'You've been set up, pal.'

Zolar's features slowly altered. The mouth tightened and the set of the jaw seemed to recede, the eyes became apprehensive. 'Nobody discovers a treasure on the magnitude of this one, leaves behind a ridiculous message, and then walks away from it. These people have a method to their madness, and I for one would like to know their plan.'

'Any man who stands in our way before the treasure is safely off the mountain will be destroyed,' Sarason shouted at his brother. 'That is a promise.'

The words came forcefully, with the ring of a bullet-resistant threat. They all believed him. Except Micki Moore.

She was the only one standing close enough to see his lips quiver.

47

Bureaucrats from around the world looked the same, Pitt thought. The fabricated meaningless smile betrayed by the patronizing look in the eyes. They must have all gone to the same school and memorized the same canned speech of evasive phrases. This one was bald, wore thick horn-rimmed glasses, and had a black moustache with each bristle exactingly trimmed.

A tall, complacent man, whose profile and haughtiness reminded the Americans seated around the conference room of a Spanish conquistador, Fernando Matos was the very essence of a condescending, fence-and-dodge bureaucrat. He stared at the Americans in the Customs building less than 100 metres (328 feet) from the international border.

Admiral James Sandecker, who had arrived from Washington shortly after Gaskill and Ragsdale flew in from Galveston, stared back and said nothing. Shannon, Rodgers, and Giordino were relegated to chairs against one wall while Pitt sat at Sandecker's right. They left the talking to the chief Customs agent of the region, Curtis Starger.

A veteran of sixteen years with the service, Starger had been around the horn enough times to have seen it all. He was a trim, handsome man with sharp features and blond hair. He looked more like an ageing lifeguard on a San Diego beach than a hardened agent who gazed at Matos with an expression that could scorch asbestos. After the introductions were made, he launched his attack.

'I'll skip the niceties, Mr Matos. On matters such as this I'm used to dealing with your élite law enforcement agents, especially Inspector Granados and the chief of your

Northern Mexico Investigative Division, Señor Rojas. I wish you would explain, sir, why a midlevel official from an obscure office of the National Affairs Department was sent to brief us on the situation. I get the feeling that your national government in Mexico City is as much in the dark as we are.'

Matos made a helpless gesture with his hands. His eyes never blinked, and his smile remained fixed. If he felt insulted, it didn't show. 'Inspector Granados is working on a case in Hermosillo and Señor Rojas was taken ill.'

'Sorry to hear it,' Starger grunted insincerely.

'If they were not indisposed or on duties elsewhere, I'm certain they would have been happy to consult with you. I share your frustration. But I assure you, my government will do everything in its power to cooperate on this matter.'

'The United States Attorney's office has reason to believe that three men going under the names of Joseph Zolar, Charles Oxley, and Cyrus Sarason, all brothers, are conducting a massive international operation dealing in stolen art, smuggled artifacts, and art forgery. We also have reason to believe they have abducted one of our respected congressional legislators and an official of our most prestigious marine science agency.'

Matos smiled blandly behind his bureaucratic defences. 'Utterly ridiculous. As you very well know, gentlemen, after your fruitless raid on the Zolars' facilities in Texas, their reputation remains untarnished.'

Gaskill smiled wryly at Ragsdale. 'News travels fast.'

'These men you seem intent on persecuting have violated no laws in Mexico. We have no legal cause to investigate them.'

'What are you doing about securing the release of Congresswoman Smith and Deputy Director Gunn?'

'Our finest investigative police teams are working on the case,' Matos assured him. 'My superiors have already made arrangements to pay the ransom demands. And I

481

can guarantee it is only a question of a few hours before the bandits responsible for this travesty are captured and your people rescued unharmed.'

'Our sources claim the Zolars are the criminals who are responsible.'

Matos shook his head. 'No, no, the evidence proves a gang of thieving bandits is behind the abduction.'

Pitt joined in the fray. 'Speaking of abductions, what about the crew of the ferryboat? Where did they disappear to?'

Matos gazed at Pitt contemptuously. 'That is of no importance here. As a matter of record, our police officials have four signed statements naming you as the instigator of this plot.'

Resentment surged through Pitt. The Zolars had cunningly planned every contingency, but they had either ignored the fact the crew of the *Alhambra* were not dead or Amaru had botched the job and lied. Padilla and his men must have made shore and been put under wraps by the local police.

'Were your investigators as thoughtful in providing me with a motive?' asked Pitt.

'Motives do not concern me, Mr Pitt. I rely on evidence. But since you brought it up, the crew claims you killed Congresswoman Smith and Rudi Gunn to gain the location of the treasure.'

'Your police officials have Alzheimer's disease if they swallow that,' snapped Giordino.

'Evidence is evidence,' Matos said smoothly. 'As an official of the government I must operate within strict legal parameters.'

Pitt took the ridiculous accusation in stride and sneaked in from the side. 'Tell me, Señor Matos, what percentage of the gold will you take as your share?'

'Five – ' Matos caught himself too late.

'Were you about to say five per cent, sir?' Starger asked softly.

Matos tilted his head and shrugged. 'I was about to say nothing of the sort.'

'I'd say your superiors have turned a blind eye to a deep conspiracy,' said Sandecker.

'There is no conspiracy, Admiral. I'll take an oath on it.'

'What you're broadcasting,' said Gaskill, leaning across the table, 'is that officials of the Sonoran State government have struck a deal with the Zolars to keep the Peruvian treasure.'

Matos lifted a hand. 'The Peruvians have no legal claim. All artifacts found on Mexican soil belong to our people – '

'They belong to the people of Peru,' Shannon interrupted, her face flushed with anger. 'If your government had any sense of decency, they would invite the Peruvians to at least share in it.'

'Affairs between nations do not work that way, Dr Kelsey,' replied Matos.

'How would you like it if Montezuma's lost golden treasure turned up in the Andes?'

'I'm not in a position to judge outlandish events,' Matos answered imperviously. 'Besides, rumours of the treasure are greatly exaggerated. Its true value is really of little consequence.'

Shannon looked flabbergasted. 'What are you saying? I saw Huascar's treasure with my own eyes. If anything, it's far more substantial than anyone thought. I put its potential value at just under a billion dollars.'

'The Zolars are respected dealers who have a worldwide reputation for accurately appraising art and antiquities. Their evaluation of the treasure does not exceed thirty million.'

'Mister,' Shannon snapped in cold fury, 'I'll match my credentials against theirs any day of the week in appraising artifacts of ancient Peruvian cultures. I'll put it to you in plain language. The Zolars are full of crap.'

'Your word against theirs,' Matos said calmly.

'For a small treasure trove,' said Ragsdale, 'they appear to be mounting a massive recovery effort.'

'Five or ten labourers to carry the gold out of the cavern. No more.'

'Would you like to see reconnaissance satellite photos that show the top of Cerro el Capirote looking like an anthill with an army of men and helicopters crawling all over it?'

Matos sat silently, as if he hadn't heard a word.

'And the Zolars' payoff?' asked Starger. 'Are you allowing them to remove artifacts from the country?'

'Their efforts on behalf of the people of Sonora will not go unappreciated. They will be compensated.'

It was an obvious fish story and nobody in the room bought it.

Admiral Sandecker was the highest American official in the room. He stared at Matos and gave him a disarming smile. 'I will be meeting with our nation's President tomorrow morning. At that time I will brief him on the alarming events occurring in our neighbour to the south, and inform him that your law enforcement officials are dragging their feet on the investigation and throwing up a smoke screen on the kidnapping of our high-level representatives. I need not remind you, Señor Matos, the free trade agreement is coming up for review by Congress. When our representatives are informed of your callous treatment of one of their colleagues, and how you cooperate with criminals dealing in stolen and smuggled art, they may find it difficult to continue our mutual trade relations. In short, señor, your President will have a major scandal on his hands.'

Matos's eyes behind the glasses were suddenly stricken. 'There is no need for so strong a response over a minor disagreement between our two countries.'

Pitt noticed thin beads of perspiration on the Mexican official's head. He turned to his boss from NUMA. 'I'm hardly an expert on executive politics, Admiral, but what do you want to bet the President of Mexico and his cabinet have not been informed of the true situation?'

'I suspect you'd win,' said Sandecker. 'That would explain why we're not talking to a major player.'

The colour had drained from Matos's face, and he looked positively sick. 'You misunderstand, my nation stands ready to cooperate in every way possible.'

'You tell your superiors in the National Affairs Department,' said Pitt, 'or whoever you really work for, that they aren't as smart as they thought.'

'The meeting is over,' said Starger. 'We'll consider our options and inform your government of our actions this time tomorrow.'

Matos tried to retrieve a shred of dignity. He stared balefully and when he spoke his voice was quieter,. 'I must warn you of any attempt to send your Special Forces into Mexico – '

Sandecker cut him off. 'I'll give you twenty-four hours to send Congresswoman Smith and my deputy director, Rudi Gunn, over the border crossing between Mexicali and Calexico unharmed. One minute later and a lot of people will get hurt.'

'You do not have the authority to make threats.'

'Once I tell my President your security forces are torturing Smith and Gunn for state secrets, there is no telling how he will react.'

Matos looked horrified. 'But that is a total lie, an absurd fabrication.'

Sandecker smiled icily. 'See, I know how to invent situations too.'

'I give you my word – '

'That will be all, Señor Matos,' said Starger. 'Please keep my office apprised of any further incidents.'

When the Mexican official left the conference room, he looked like a man who had stood by and watched as his wife ran off with the plumber and his dog was run over by a milk truck. As soon as he was gone, Ragsdale, who had sat back and quietly absorbed the conversation, turned to Gaskill.

'Well, if nothing else, they don't know we knocked over their illegal storage facility.'

'Let's hope they remain in the dark for another two days.'

'Did you take an inventory of the stolen goods?' asked Pitt.

'The quantity was so great, it will take weeks to thoroughly itemize every object.'

'Do you recall seeing any Southwestern Indian religious idols, carved from cottonwood?'

Gaskill shook his head. 'No, nothing like that.'

'Please let me know if you do. I have an Indian friend who would like them back.'

Ragsdale nodded at Sandecker. 'How do you read the situation, Admiral?' he asked.

'The Zolars have promised the moon,' Sandecker said. 'I'm beginning to believe that if they were arrested, half the citizenry of the state of Sonora would rise up and break them out of jail.'

'They'll never allow Loren and Rudi to go free and talk,' said Pitt.

'I hate to be the one to mention it,' Ragsdale said quietly, 'but they could already be dead.'

Pitt shook his head. 'I won't let myself believe that.'

Sandecker rose and began working off his frustration by pacing the floor. 'Even if the President approves a clandestine entry, our special response team has no intelligence to guide them to the location where Loren and Rudi are held captive.'

'I have an idea the Zolars are holding them on the mountain,' said Giordino.

Starger nodded in agreement. 'You might be right. The hacienda they used as a headquarters to conduct the treasure search appears deserted.'

Ragsdale sighed. 'If Smith and Gunn are still alive, I fear it won't be for long.'

'We can do nothing but look helplessly through the fence,' said Starger in frustration.

Ragsdale stared out the window across the border. 'The FBI can't launch a raid on to Mexican soil.'

'Nor Customs,' said Gaskill.

Pitt looked at the federal agents for a moment. Then he addressed himself directly to Sandecker. 'They can't, but NUMA can.'

They all looked at him, uncomprehending.

'We can what?' asked Sandecker.

'Go into Mexico and rescue Loren and Rudi without creating an international incident.'

'Sure you will.' Gaskill laughed. 'Getting across the border is no trick, but the Zolars have the Sonoran police and military on their side. Satellite photos show heavy security on top and around the base of Cerro el Capirote. You couldn't get within ten kilometres without getting shot.'

'I wasn't planning on driving or hiking to the mountain,' said Pitt.

Starger looked at him and grinned. 'What can the National Underwater and Marine Agency do that Customs and the FBI can't? Swim over the desert?'

'No, not over,' said Pitt in a deadly earnest voice. 'Under.'

PART FOUR

Nightmare Passage

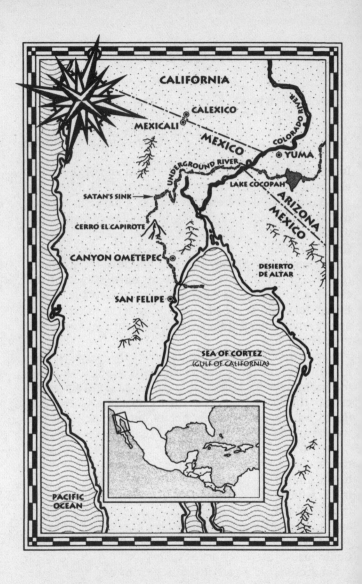

48

In the parched foothills on the northern end of the Sierra el Mayor Mountains, almost 50 kilometres (31 miles) due south of Mexicali, there is a borehole, a naturally formed tunnel, in the side of a cliff. Carved millions of years ago by the turbulent action of an ancient sea, the corridor slopes downward to the bottom of a small cavern, sculpted from the volcanic rock by Pliocene epoch water and more recently by windblown sand. There on the floor of the cavern a pool of water emerges from beneath the desert. Except for a tint of cobalt blue, the water is so clear as to appear invisible and from ground level the sinkhole looks to be bottomless.

Satan's Sink was shaped nothing like the sacrificial pool in Peru, Pitt thought, as he gazed at the yellow nylon line trailing into the transparent depths. He sat on a rock at the edge of the water, his eyes shaded with a look of concern, hands lightly grasping the nylon line whose end was wound around the drum of a compact reel.

Outside, 80 metres (262 feet) above the bottom of the tubular borehole, Admiral Sandecker sat in a lawn chair beside a ravaged and rusting 1951 Chevy half-ton pickup truck with a faded camper in the bed that looked as though it should have been recycled years ago. Another automobile was parked behind it, a very tired and worn 1968 Plymouth Belvedere station wagon. Both had Baja California Norte licence plates.

Sandecker held a can of Coors beer in one hand as he

lifted a pair of binoculars to his eyes with the other and scrutinized the surrounding landscape. He was dressed to complement the old truck, having the appearance of any one of thousands of retired American vagabonds who travel and camp around the Baja Peninsula on the cheap.

He was surprised to find so many flowering plants in the Sonoran Desert, despite scant water and a climate that runs from subfreezing nights in the winter to a summer heat that produces furnace temperatures. Far off in the distance he watched a small herd of horses grazing on bunchgrass.

Satisfied the only life within his immediate area was a red diamondback rattler sunning itself on a rock and a blacktailed jackrabbit that hopped up to him, took one look, and leapt away, he rose from his lawn chair and ambled down the slope of the borehole to the pool.

'Any sign of the law?' asked Pitt at the admiral's approach.

'Nothing around here but snakes and rabbits,' grunted Sandecker. He nodded towards the water. 'How long have they been down?'

Pitt glanced at his watch. 'Thirty-eight minutes.'

'I'd feel a whole lot better if they were using professional equipment instead of old dive gear borrowed from local Customs agents.'

'Every minute counts if we're to save Loren and Rudi. By doing an exploratory survey now to see if my plan has the slightest chance of succeeding, we save six hours. The same time it takes for our state-of-the-art equipment to arrive in Calexico from Washington.'

'Sheer madness to attempt such a dangerous operation,' said Sandecker in a tired voice.

'Do we have an alternative?'

'None that comes to mind.'

'Then we must give it a try,' said Pitt firmly.

'You don't even know yet if you have the slightest prospect of – '

'They've signalled,' Pitt interrupted the admiral as the line tautened in his hands. 'They're on their way up.'

Together, Pitt pulling in on the line, Sandecker holding the reel between his knees and turning the crank, they began hauling in the two divers who were somewhere deep inside the sinkhole on the other end of the 200-metre (656-foot) line. A long fifteen minutes later, breathing heavily, they brought in the red knot that signified the third fifty-metre mark.

'Only fifty meters to go,' Sandecker commented heavily. He pulled on the reel as he cranked, trying to ease the strain on Pitt who did the major share of the work. The admiral was a health enthusiast, jogged several miles a day, and occasionally worked out in the NUMA head-quarters health spa, but the exertion of pulling dead weight without a time-out pushed his heart rate close to the red line. 'I see them,' he panted thankfully.

Gratefully, Pitt let go of the line and sagged to a sitting position to catch his breath. 'They can ascend on their own from there.'

Giordino was the first of the two divers to surface. He removed his twin air tanks and hoisted them to Sandecker. Then he offered a hand to Pitt who leaned back and heaved him out of the water. The next man up was Dr Peter Duncan, a US Geological Survey hydrologist, who had arrived in Calexico by chartered jet only an hour after Sandecker contacted him in San Diego. At first he thought the admiral was joking about an underground river, but curiosity overcame his scepticism and he dropped everything to join in the exploratory dive. He spat out the mouthpiece to his air regulator.

'I never envisioned a water source that extensive,' he said between deep breaths.

'You found an access to the river,' Pitt stated, not asked, happily.

'The sinkhole drops about sixty metres before it meets a horizontal feeding stream that runs a hundred and twenty metres through a series of narrow fissures to the river,' explained Giordino.

'Can we gain passage for the float equipment?' Pitt queried.

'It gets a little tight in places, but I think we can squeeze it through.'

'The water temperature?'

'A cool but bearable twenty degrees Celsius, about sixty-eight degrees Fahrenheit.'

Duncan pulled off his hood, revealing the great bush of a red beard. He made no effort to climb from the pool. He rested his arms on the bank and babbled in excitement. 'I didn't believe it when you described a wide river with a current of nine knots under the Sonoran desert. Now that I've seen it with my own eyes, I still don't believe it. I'd guess anywhere from ten to fifteen million acre-foot of water a year is flowing down there.'

'Do you think it's the same underground stream that flows under Cerro el Capirote?' asked Sandecker.

'No doubt about it,' answered Duncan. 'Now that I've seen the river exists with my own eyes, I'd be willing to gamble it's the same stream that Leigh Hunt claimed runs beneath the Castle Dome Mountains.'

'So Hunt's canyon of gold probably exists.' Pitt smiled.

'You know about that legend?'

'No legend now.'

A delighted look crossed Duncan's face. 'No, I guess not, I'm happy to say.'

'Good thing we were tied to a fixed guideline,' said Giordino.

Duncan nodded. 'I couldn't agree more. Without it, we would have been swept away by the river when we emerged from the feeder stream.'

'And joined those two divers who ended up in the Gulf.'

'I can't help but wonder where the source is,' mused Sandecker.

Giordino rubbed a hand through his curly mop. 'The

latest in geophysical ground-penetrating instruments should have no problem tracking the course.'

'There is no predicting what a discovery of this magnitude means to the drought-plagued Southwest,' said Duncan still aroused by what he'd seen. 'The benefits could result in thousands of jobs, millions of acres brought under cultivation, pasture for livestock. We might even see the desert turned into a Garden of Eden.'

'The thieves will drown in the water that makes the desert into a garden,' Pitt said, staring into the crystal blue pool and remembering Billy Yuma's words.

'What was that you said?' asked Giordino curiously.

Pitt shook his head and smiled. 'An old Indian proverb.'

After carrying the dive equipment up to the surface entrance of the borehole, Giordino and Duncan stripped off their suits while Sandecker loaded their gear into the Plymouth station wagon. The admiral came over as Pitt drove alongside in the old pickup and stopped.

'I'll meet you back here in two hours,' he notified Sandecker.

'Mind telling us where you're going?'

'I have to see a man about raising an army.'

'Anybody I know?'

'No, but if things go half as well as I hope, you'll be shaking his hand and pinning a medal on him by the time the sun goes down.'

Gaskill and Ragsdale were waiting at the small airport west of Calexico on the United States side of the border when the NUMA plane landed and taxied up to a large Customs Service van. They had begun transferring the underwater survival equipment to the van from the cargo hatch of the plane when Sandecker and Giordino arrived in the station wagon.

The pilot came over and shook their hands. 'We had to hustle to assemble your shopping list, but we managed to scrounge every piece of gear you requested.'

'Were our engineers able to lower the profile of the Hovercraft as Pitt requested?' asked Giordino.

'A miraculous crash job.' The pilot smiled. 'But the admiral's mechanical whiz kids said to tell you they modified the *Wallowing Windbag* down to a maximum height of sixty-one centimetres.'

'I'll thank everyone personally when I return to Washington,' said Sandecker warmly.

'Would you like me to head back?' the pilot asked the admiral. 'Or stand by here?'

'Stick by your aircraft in case we need you.'

They had just finished loading the van and were closing the rear cargo doors when Curtis Starger came racing across the airstrip in a grey Customs vehicle. He braked to a stop and came from behind the wheel as if shot out of a cannon.

'We got problems,' he announced.

'What kind of problems?' Gaskill demanded.

'Mexican Border Police just closed down their side of the border to all US traffic entering Mexico.'

'What about commercial traffic?'

'That too. They also added insult to injury by putting up a flock of military helicopters with orders to force down all intruding aircraft and stop any vehicle that looks suspicious.'

Ragsdale looked at Sandecker. 'They must be on to your fishing expedition.'

'I don't think so. No one saw us enter or leave the borehole.'

Starger laughed. 'What do you want to bet that after Señor Matos ran back and reported our hard stand to the Zolars, they frothed at the mouth and coerced their buddies in the government to raise the drawbridge.'

'That would be my guess,' agreed Ragsdale. 'They were afraid we'd come charging in like the Light Brigade.'

Gaskill looked around. 'Where's Pitt?'

'He's safe on the other side,' replied Giordino.

Sandecker struck the side of the aircraft with his fist. 'To come this close,' he muttered angrily. 'A bust, a god-damned bust.'

'There must be some way we can get these people and their gear back to Satan's Sink,' said Ragsdale to his fellow federal agents.

Starger and Gaskill matched crafty grins. 'Oh, I think the Customs Service can save the day,' said Starger.

'You two got something up your sleeves?'

'The Escobar affair,' Starger revealed. 'Familiar with it?'

Ragsdale nodded. 'The underground drug smuggling operation.'

'Juan Escobar lived just across the border in Mexico,' Starger explained to Sandecker and Giordino, 'but oper-ated a truck repair garage on this side. He smuggled in a number of large narcotics shipments before the Drug Enforcement Agency got wise to him. In a cooperative investigation our agents discovered a tunnel running a hundred and fifty metres from his house under the border fence to his repair shop. We were too late for an arrest. Escobar somehow got antsy, shut down his operation before we could nail him, and disappeared along with his family.'

'One of our agents,' added Gaskill, 'a Hispanic who was born and raised in East Los Angeles, lives in Escobar's former house and commutes through the border crossing, posing as the new owner of Escobar's truck repair shop.'

Starger smiled with pride. 'The DEA and Customs have made over twenty arrests on information that came to him from other drug traffickers wanting to use the tunnel.'

'Are you saying it's still open?' asked Sandecker.

'You'd be surprised how often it comes in handy for the good guys,' answered Starger.

Giordino looked like a man offered salvation. 'Can we get our stuff through to the other side?'

Starger nodded. 'We simply drive the van into the repair shop. I'll get some men to help us carry your equipment under the border to Escobar's house, then load it into our undercover agent's parts truck out of sight in the garage. The vehicle is well known over there, so there is no reason why you'd be stopped.'

Sandecker looked at Giordino. 'Well,' he said solemnly, 'are you ready to write your obituary?'

49

The stone demon stoically ignored the activity around him as if biding his time. He did not feel, nor could he turn his head and see, the recent gouges and craters in his body and remaining wing, shot there by laughing Mexican soldiers who used him for target practice when their officers had disappeared into the mountain. Something within the carved stone sensed that its menacing eyes would still be surveying the ageless desert centuries after the intruding humans had died and passed beyond memory into the afterworld.

A shadow passed over the demon for the fifth time that morning as a sleek craft dropped from the sky and settled on to the only open space large enough for it to land, a narrow slot between two army helicopters and the big winch with its equally large auxiliary power unit.

In the rear passenger seat of the blue and green police helicopter, Police Comandante of Baja Norte Rafael Cortina stared thoughtfully out the window at the turmoil on the mountaintop. His eyes wandered to the malevolent expression of the stone demon. It seemed to stare back at him.

Aged sixty-five, he contemplated his coming retirement without joy. He did not look forward to a life of boredom in a small house overlooking the bay at Ensenada, existing on a pension that would permit few luxuries. His square, brown-skinned face reflected a solid career that went back forty-five years. Cortina had never been popular with his fellow officers. Hardworking, straight as an arrow, he had prided himself on never taking a bribe. Not one peso in all his years on the force. Though he never faulted others for accepting graft under the table from known criminals or shady businessmen seeking to sidestep investigations, neither did he condone it. He had gone his own way, never informing, never voicing complaints or personal moral judgements.

Bitterly he recalled how he had been passed over for promotion more times than he could remember. But whenever his superiors slipped too far and were discovered in scandal, the civilian commissioners always turned to Cortina, a man they resented for his honesty but needed because he could be trusted.

There was a reason Cortina could never be bought in a land where corruption and kickbacks were commonplace. Every man, and woman too, has a price. Resentfully but patiently Cortina had waited until his price was met. If he was to sell out, he wouldn't come cheap. And the ten million dollars the Zolars offered for his cooperation, above and beyond the official approval for the treasure removal, was enough to ensure that his wife, four sons and their wives, and eight grandchildren would enjoy life in the new and rejuvenated Mexico spawned under the North American Free Trade Agreement.

At the same time, he knew the old days of looking the other way while holding out an open palm were dying out. The last two presidents of Mexico had waged all-out war against bureaucratic corruption. And the legalization and price regulation of certain drugs had dealt the drug dealers a blow that had cut their profits by 80 per cent and their death-dealing volume by two-thirds.

Cortina stepped from the helicopter and was met by one of Amaru's men. He remembered arresting him for armed robbery in La Paz and helping obtain a conviction and a five-year prison term. If the freed criminal recognized Cortina, there was no indication. He was ushered by the ex-convict into an aluminium house trailer that had been airlifted from Yuma to be used as an office for the treasure recovery project on top of the mountain.

He was surprised to see modern oil paintings by some of the Southwest's finest artists adorning the walls. Inside the richly panelled trailer, seated around an antique French Second Empire table, were Joseph Zolar, his two brothers, Fernando Matos from the National Affairs Department, and Colonel Roberto Campos, commander of northern Mexico's military forces on the Baja Peninsula.

Cortina gave a nod and a slight bow and was motioned to a chair. His eyes widened slightly as a very attractive serving lady brought him a glass of champagne and a plate of smoked sturgeon topped by a small mound of caviar. Zolar pointed to a cutaway illustration of the passageway leading to the interior caverns.

'Not an easy job, let me tell you. Bringing all that gold across a river deep below the floor of the desert, and then transporting it up a narrow tunnel to the top of the mountain.'

'It goes well?' asked Cortina.

'Too early to throw confetti,' replied Zolar. 'The hardest part, dragging out Huascar's chain, is under way. Once it reaches the surface' – he paused to read the dial of his watch – 'in about half an hour from now, we will cut it into sections for easier loading and unloading during shipping. After it is safe inside our storage facilities in Morocco, it will be reconnected.'

'Why Morocco?' inquired Fernando Matos. 'Why not your warehouse in Galveston or your estate in Douglas, Arizona?'

'Protection. This is one collection of artifacts we don't want to risk storing in the United States. We have an arrangement with the military commander in Morocco who protects our shipments. The country also makes a convenient distribution centre to ship the artifacts throughout Europe, South America, and the Far East.'

'How do you plan to bring out the rest of the antiquities?' asked Campos.

'After they are floated across the underground river on

rafts, they will be drawn up the passageway on a train of narrow platforms with ski runners.'

'Then the winch I requisitioned has proven useful?'

'A godsend, Colonel,' replied Oxley. 'By six o'clock this evening your men should be loading the last of the golden artifacts on to the helicopters you so graciously provided.'

Cortina held his glass of champagne but didn't taste it. 'Is there any way of measuring the weight of the treasure?'

'Professor Henry Moore and his wife have given me an estimate of sixty tons.'

'Good God,' murmured Colonel Campos, an imposing figure of a man with a great mass of grey hair. 'I had no idea it was so vast.'

'Historical records failed to give a full inventory,' said Oxley.

'And the value?' asked Cortina.

'Our original estimate,' Oxley lectured, 'was two hundred and fifty million American dollars. But I think it's safe to say it's worth closer to three hundred million.'

Oxley's amount was a total fabrication. The market price of the gold alone had risen close to seven hundred million dollars after the Moores' inventory. Incredibly, the added value as antiquities easily pushed the price well over one billion dollars on the underground market.

Zolar faced Cortina and Campos, a broad smile on his face. 'What this means, gentlemen, is that we can raise the ante considerably for the people of Baja California Norte.'

'There will be more than enough for the public works your government administrators have envisioned,' added Sarason.

Cortina glanced sideways at Campos, and wondered how much the colonel was collecting to look the other way while the Zolars made off with the bulk of the treasure, including the massive golden chain. And Matos was an enigma. He couldn't figure out how the snivelling government official fitted into the scheme of things. 'In light of the increased estimated valuation, I believe a bonus should be forthcoming.'

An opportunist, Campos instantly picked up on Cortina's drift. 'Yes, yes, I agree with my good friend Rafael. For me, it was not an easy matter to seal off the border.'

It amused Cortina to hear Campos use his Christian name for the first time in the ten years they had occasionally met to discuss mutual police and military business. He knew how much it would irritate Campos if he did the same, so he said, 'Roberto is quite right. Local businessmen and politicians are already complaining about the loss of tourist revenue and the halting of commercial traffic. Both of us will have to do some heavy explaining to our superiors.'

'Won't they understand when you tell them it was to keep American federal agents from making an unauthorized border crossing to confiscate the treasure?' asked Oxley.

'I assure you the National Affairs Department will cooperate in every way to back your position,' said Matos.

'Perhaps.' Cortina shrugged. 'Who can say for certain whether our government will buy the story or order Colonel Campos and me tried in court for overstepping our authority.'

'Your bonus.' Zolar put it to Cortina. 'What did you have in mind?'

Without batting an eye, Cortina replied, 'An additional ten million dollars in cash.'

Campos was visibly stunned for an instant, but he jumped right in beside Cortina. 'Police Comandante Cortina speaks for both of us. Considering our risk and the added value of the treasure, ten million cash above our original agreement is not too much to ask.'

Sarason entered into the negotiations. 'You realize, of course, that the estimated value is nowhere near the price that we will eventually receive. Comandante Cortina knows that stolen jewels are rarely fenced for more than twenty per cent of their true worth.'

Zolar and Oxley maintained serious expressions, all the while knowing there were over a thousand collectors on their client list who were eagerly waiting to purchase portions of the golden artifacts at premium prices.

'Ten million,' Cortina repeated stubbornly.

Sarason kept up the pretence of hard bargaining. 'That's a lot of money,' he protested.

'Protecting you from American and Mexican law enforcement agents is only half our involvement,' Cortina reminded him. 'Without Colonel Campos's heavy transport helicopters to haul the gold to your transfer site in the Altar Desert, you would end up with nothing.'

'And without our involvement in the discovery, you would too,' said Sarason.

Cortina spread his hands indifferently. 'I cannot deny that we need each other. But I strongly believe it would be in your best interests to be generous.'

Sarason looked at his brbthers. Zolar gave a barely perceptible nod. After a moment, Sarason turned to Cortina and Campos and gestured in apparent defeat. 'We know when we have a losing hand. Consider yourselves another ten million dollars richer.'

The maximum load the winch could tow was five tons, so Huascar's chain was to be cut in the middle and dragged out in two pieces. The soldiers of the Mexican engineering battalion would then fashion a raft from boards requisitioned from the nearest lumber yard to ferry the main mass of the treasure across the subterranean river. Only the golden throne proved too heavy for the raft. Once Huascar's chain was pulled to the mountain peak, the winch cable was to be carried back down and attached to a harness wrapped around the throne. After sending a signal topside, it would be winched across the river bottom until it reached dry ground. From there the engineers, aided by Amaru's men, planned to muscle it on to a sled for the final journey from the heart of the mountain. Once out of the mountain, all of the artifacts would be loaded aboard vessels the Inca artisans who created the golden masterworks could never have visualized: birds that flew without wings, known in modern times as helicopters.

On the island of treasure, Micki Moore busily catalogued and recorded descriptions of the pieces while Henry measured and photographed them. They had to work quickly. Amaru was driving the military engineers to remove everything in a hurry, an effort that reduced the small mountain of golden antiquities at an incredible rate. What had taken the Incas and Chachapoyas six days to cache inside the mountain, modern equipment was about to remove in ten hours.

She moved close to her husband and whispered, 'I can't do this.'

He looked at her.

Her eyes seemed to reflect the gold that gleamed under the bright lights brought in by the engineers. 'I don't want any of the gold.'

'Why not?' he asked her softly.

'I can't explain,' she said. 'I feel dirty enough as it is. I know you must have come to feel the same. We must do something to keep it out of Zolar's hands.'

'Wasn't that our original intent, to terminate the Zolars and hijack the treasure after it was loaded aboard the aircraft in the Altar Desert?'

'That was before we saw how vast and magnificent it is. Let it go, Henry, we've bitten off more than we can chew.'

Moore turned thoughtful. 'This is one hell of time to get a conscience.'

'Conscience has nothing to do with it. It's ridiculous to think we could unload tons of antiquities. We have to face facts. You and I don't have the facilities or the contacts to dispose of so large a hoard on the underground market.'

'Selling Huascar's chain would not be all that difficult.'

Micki looked up into his eyes for a long time. 'You're a very good anthropologist, and I'm a very good archaeologist. We're also very good at jumping out of aeroplanes at night into strange countries and murdering people. Stealing priceless ancient art is not what we do best. Besides, we hate these people. I say we work together in keeping the treasure in one piece. Not scattered inside the vaults of a bunch of scavengers hungry for possessions no one else can own or ever view.'

'I have to admit,' he said wearily, 'I've had my reservations too. What do you suggest we do?'

'The right thing,' she replied huskily.

For the first time Moore noticed the compassion in her eyes. There was a beauty he had never seen before. She put her arms around him and gazed into his eyes. 'We don't have to kill anymore. This time we won't have to crawl back under a rock when our operation is finished.'

He took her head between his hands and kissed her. 'I'm proud of you, old girl.'

She pushed him back, her eyes widening as if she remembered something. 'The hostages. I promised them we would rescue them if we could.'

'Where are they?'

'If they're still alive, they should be on the surface.'

Moore looked around the cavern and saw that Amaru was overseeing the removal of the mummies of the guardians from inside the crypt. The Zolars were leaving the caverns as bare as when the Incas found them. Nothing of value was to be left.

'We've got a detailed inventory,' he said to Micki. 'Let's be on our way.'

The Moores hitched a ride on a sled stacked with golden animals being towed up to the staging area. When they came into daylight, they searched the summit, but Loren Smith and Rudi Gunn were nowhere to be found.

506

By then, it was too late for the Moores to reenter the mountain.

Loren shivered. Tattered clothing was no protection against the cool dampness of the cavern. Gunn put his arm around her to provide what body warmth he had to give. The tiny cell-like chamber that was their prison was little more than a wide crack in the limestone. There was no room to stand up, and whenever they tried to move about to find a comfortable position or to keep warm, the guard shoved his gun butt at them through the opening.

After the two sections of the golden chain had been brought through the passageway, Amaru forced them from the mountain crest down to the little cavity behind the guardian's crypt. Unknown to the Moores, Loren and Rudi had been imprisoned before the scientists made their way out of the treasure cavern.

'We would appreciate a drink of water,' Loren told the guard.

He turned and looked at her blankly. He was an appalling figure, enormous, with an entirely repulsive face, thick lips, flat nose, and one eye. The empty socket he left exposed, giving him the brutal ugliness of Quasimodo.

This time when Loren shivered it wasn't from the cold. It was the fear that coursed throughout her half-naked body. She knew that to show audacity might invite pain, but she no longer cared. 'Water, you drooling imbecile. Do you understand, *agua?*'

He gave her a cruel look and slowly vanished from their narrow line of vision. In a few minutes he returned and tossed a military canteen of water into the cave.

'I think you've made a friend,' said Gunn.

'If he thinks he's getting a kiss on the first date,' said Loren, twisting off the cap of the canteen, 'he's got another think coming.'

She offered Gunn a drink, but he shook his head. 'Ladies first.'

Loren drank sparingly and passed the canteen to Gunn. 'I wonder what happened to the Moores?'

'They may not know we were moved from the summit down to this hellhole.'

'I fear the Zolars intend to bury us alive in here,' Loren said. The tears came to her eyes for the first time as her defences began to crack. She had endured the beatings and the abuse, but now that it seemed she and Gunn were abandoned, the faint hope that had kept her going was all but extinguished.

'There is still Dirk,' Gunn said gently.

She shook her head as if embarrassed at being seen wiping away the tears. 'Please stop. Even if he were still alive, Dirk couldn't fight his way into this rotten mountain with a division of Marines and reach us in time.'

'If I know our man, he wouldn't need a division of Marines.'

'He's only human. He would be the last one to think of himself as a miracle worker.'

'As long as we're still alive,' said Gunn, 'and there is a chance, that's all that matters.'

'But for how long?' She shook her head sadly. 'A few more minutes, a couple of hours? The truth is, we're already as good as dead.'

When the first section of chain was dragged into daylight, everyone on the summit stood and admired it. The sheer mass of so much gold in one place took their breath away. Despite the dust and calcite drippings from centuries underground, the great mass of yellow gold gleamed blindingly under the noon sun.

In all the years the Zolars had been practising the theft of antiquities, they had never seen such a masterwork of art so rich in splendour from the past. No treasured object known to history could match it. Fewer than four collectors throughout the world could have afforded the entire piece. The sight was doubly grand when the second section of chain was pulled from the passage opening and laid beside the first.

'Mother of heaven!' gasped Colonel Campos. 'The links are as large as a man's wrist.'

'Difficult to believe the Incas had mastered such highly technical skills in metallurgy,' murmured Zolar.

Sarason knelt down and studied the links. 'Their artistry and sophistication is phenomenal. Each link is perfect. There isn't a flaw anywhere.'

Cortina walked over to one of the end links and lifted it with considerable effort. 'They must weigh fifty kilos each.'

'This is truly light-years ahead of any other discovery,' said Oxley, trembling at the incredible sight.

Sarason tore his gaze away and gestured to Amaru. 'Get it loaded on board the helicopter, quickly.'

The evil-eyed killer nodded silently and began giving orders to his men and a squad of soldiers. Even Cortina, Campos, and Matos pitched in. With help from a straining forklift and plenty of sweat, the two sections of chain were manhandled aboard two army helicopters and sent on their way to the desert airstrip.

Zolar watched as the two aircraft became tiny specks in the sky. 'Nothing can stop us now,' he said cheerfully to his brothers. 'A few more hours and we're home free, with the largest treasure known to man.'

50

To Sandecker, the audacious plan to come in through the back door of Cerro el Capirote in a wild attempt to save Loren Smith and Rudi Gunn was nothing less than suicidal. He knew the reasons Pitt had for risking his life: rescuing a loved one and a close friend from death, evening the score with a pair of murderers, and snatching a wondrous treasure from the hands of thieves. Those were grounds for justification of other men. Not Pitt. His motivation went much deeper. To challenge the unknown, laugh at the devil, and dare the odds. Those were his stimulants.

As for Giordino, Pitt's friend since childhood, Sandecker never doubted for an instant the rugged Italian would follow Pitt into a molten sea of lava.

Sandecker could have stopped them. But he hadn't built what was thought of by many as the finest, most productive, and budget efficient agency in the government without taking his fair share of risky gambles. His fondness for marching out of step with official Washington made him a source of respect as well as envy. The other directors of national bureaus would never consider hands-on control of a hazardous project in the field that might run the risk of censure from Congress and force resignation by presidential order. Sandecker's only regret was that this was one adventure he couldn't lead himself.

He paused after carrying a load of dive gear from the old Chevy down the tubular bore and looked at Peter Duncan, who sat beside the sinkhole, busily overlaying a transparency of a topographical map on to a hydrographic survey of known underground water systems.

The two charts were enlarged to the same scale, enabling Duncan to trace the approximate course of the subterranean river. Around him, the others were setting out the dive gear and float equipment. 'As the crow flies,' Duncan said to no one specifically, 'the distance between Satan's Sinkhole and Cerro el Capirote works out to roughly thirty kilometres.'

Sandecker looked down into the water of the sinkhole. 'What quirk of nature formed the river channel?'

'About sixty million years ago,' answered Duncan, 'a shift in the earth caused a fault in the limestone, allowing water to seep in and carve out a series of connecting caverns.'

The admiral turned to Pitt. 'How long do you think it will take you to get there?'

'Running with a current of nine knots,' said Pitt, 'we should make the treasure cavern in three hours.'

Duncan looked doubtful. 'I've never seen a river that didn't meander. If I were you I'd add another two hours to my estimated time of arrival.'

'The *Wallowing Windbag* will make up the time,' Giordino said confidently as he stripped off his clothes.

'Only if you have clear sailing all the way. You're entering the unknown. There is no second guessing the difficulties you might encounter. Submerged passages extending ten kilometres or more, cascades that fall the height of a ten-storey building, or unnavigable rapids through rocks. White water rafters have a saying – if there is a rock, you'll strike it. If there is an eddy, you'll get caught in it.'

'Anything else?' Giordino grinned, unshaken by Duncan's dire forecast. 'Like vampires or gluttonous monsters with six jaws of barracuda teeth lurking in the dark to have us for lunch?'

'I'm only trying to prepare you for the unexpected,' Duncan said. 'The best theory I can offer that might give you a small sense of security is that I believe the main section of the river system flows through a fault in the earth. If I'm right, the channel will travel in an erratic path but with a reasonably level depth.'

Pitt patted him on the shoulder. 'We understand and we're grateful. But at this stage, all Al and I can do is hope for the best, expect the worst, and settle for anything in between.'

'When you swam out of the sinkhole's feeder stream into the river,' Sandecker asked Duncan, 'was there an air pocket?'

'Yes, the rock ceiling rose a good ten metres above the surface of the river.'

'How far did it extend?'

'We were hanging on to the fixed guideline for dear life against the current and only got a brief look. A quick sweep of my light failed to reveal the end of the gallery.'

'With luck, they'll have an air passage the entire trip.'

'A lot of luck,' said Duncan sceptically, his eyes still drawn to the chart overlays. 'As underground rivers go, this one is enormous. In sheer length, it must be the longest unexplored subterranean water course through a field of karst.'

Giordino hesitated in strapping on a small console containing pressure gauges, a compass, and a depth meter to his arm. 'What do you mean by karst?'

'Karst is the term for a limestone belt that is penetrated by a system of streams, passages, and caverns.'

'It makes one wonder how many other unknown rivers are flowing under the earth,' said Pitt.

'Leigh Hunt and his river canyon of gold, another source of jokes by California and Nevada state hydrologists, now bear heavy investigation,' admitted Duncan. 'Because of what you discovered here, I'll guarantee that closed minds will take a second look.'

'Maybe I can do my bit for the cause,' said Pitt, holding up a small waterproof computer before strapping it to his forearm. 'I'll try to program a survey, and plot data on the river's course as we go.'

'I'll be grateful for all the scientific data you can bring back,' acknowledged Duncan. 'Finding a golden treasure under Cerro el Capirote may fire the imagination, but in reality it's incidental to the discovery of a water source that can turn millions of acres of desert into productive farm and ranch land.'

'Perhaps the gold can fund the pumping systems and pipelines for such a project,' said Pitt.

'Certainly a dream to consider,' added Sandecker.

Giordino held up an underwater camera. 'I'll bring back some pictures for you.'

'Thank you,' said Duncan gratefully. 'I'd also appreciate another favour.'

Pitt smiled. 'Name it.'

He handed Pitt a plastic packet in the shape of a basketball but half the size. 'A dye tracer called Fluorescein Yellow with Optical Brightener. I'll buy you the best Mexican dinner in the Southwest if you'll throw it into the river when you reach the treasure chamber. That's all. As it floats along the river the container will automatically release the dye over regular intervals.'

'You want to record where the river outlet emerges into the Gulf.'

Duncan nodded. 'That will give us an important hydrologic link.

He was also going to ask if Pitt and Giordino might take water samples, but thought better of it. He had already pushed them as far as he dared. If they were successful in navigating the river as far as the hollow interior of Cerro el Capirote, then he and his fellow scientists could mount subsequent scientific expeditions based on the data acquired by Pitt and Giordino.

Over the next ten minutes, Pitt and Giordino geared up and went over the plans for their journey. They had made countless dives together under a hundred different water and weather conditions, but none of this distance through the depths of the earth. Like doctors discussing a delicate brain operation, no detail was left to chance. Their survival depended on it.

Communication signals were agreed upon, buddy-breathing strategies in case of air loss, the drill for inflating and deflating the *Wallowing Windbag*, who was in control of what equipment – all procedures were deliberated and jointly approved.

'I see you're not wearing a pressurized drysuit,' observed Sandecker as Pitt pulled on his wet suit.

'The water temperature is a few degrees on the cool side, but warm enough so we don't have to worry about hypothermia. A wet suit gives us more freedom of movement than a drysuit that is pressurized by air tanks. This will prove a dire necessity if we find ourselves struggling in the water to right the Wallowing Windbag after it is flipped over by raging rapids.'

Instead of the standard backpack, Pitt attached his air tanks to a harness around his hips for easier access through narrow passages. He was also festooned with breathing regulators, air lines leading to dual valve manifolds, pressure gauges, and a small backup bottle filled with pure oxygen for decompression. Then came weight belts and buoyancy compensators.

'No mixed gas?' queried Sandecker.

'We'll breathe air,' Pitt replied as he checked his regulators.

'What about the danger of nitrogen narcosis?'

'Once we're clear of the bottom of the sinkhole and the lower part of the feeder stream before it upslopes to the river, we'll avoid any further deep diving like the plague.'

'Just see that you stay well above the threshold,' Sandecker warned him, 'and don't go below thirty metres. And once you're afloat keep a sharp eye for submerged boulders.'

Those were the words the admiral spoke. What he didn't say was, 'If something goes wrong and you need immediate help, you might as well be on the third ring of Saturn.' In other words, there could be no rescue or evacuation.

Pitt and Giordino made a final predive check of each other's equipment by the side of the pool and tested their quick-release buckles and snaps to ensure their smooth removal in an emergency. Instead of divers' hoods, they strapped construction workers' hardhats to their heads with dual-sealed miners' lamps on the front. Then they poised on the edge of the sinkhole and slipped into the water.

Sandecker and Duncan hoisted a long, pressure-sealed aluminium canister and struggled to lower one end into the sinkhole. The canister, measuring one metre in width by four in length, was articulated in the middle for easier manoeuvring through tight spaces. Heavy and cumbersome on land from the lead ballast required to give it neutral buoyancy, it was easily moved by a diver under water.

Giordino bit on his mouthpiece, adjusted his mask, and took hold of a handgrip on the forward end of the canister. He threw a final wave as he and the canister slowly sank together below the water surface. Pitt looked up from the water and shook hands with Duncan.

'Whatever you do,' Duncan warned him, 'mind you don't let the current sweep you past the treasure chamber. From that position to where the river emerges into the gulf has to be over a hundred and twenty kilometres.'

'Don't worry, we won't spend any more time down there than we have to.'

'May God dive with you,' said Duncan.

'All heavenly company will be warmly welcomed,' said Pitt sincerely. Then he gripped Sandecker's hand. 'Keep a tequila on ice for me, Admiral.'

'I wish there was another way into the mountain.'

Pitt shook his head. 'It can only be done with a dive-raft operation.'

'Bring Loren and Rudi back,' replied Sandecker, fighting off a surge of emotion.

'You'll see them soon,' Pitt promised.

And then he was gone.

51

The voice of his radio operator roused Captain Juan Diego from his reverie, and he turned from gazing out his command tent at the cone-shaped mountain. There was an indescribable ugliness about Cerro el Capirote and the bleak desert that surrounded it, he thought. This was a wasteland compared to the beauty of his native state of Durango.

'Yes, what is it, Sergeant?'

The radio operator had his back to him and Diego couldn't see the puzzled look on the soldier's face. 'I called the security posts for their hourly status reports and received no response from Posts Four and Six.'

Diego sighed. He didn't need unexpected predicaments. Colonel Campos had commanded him to set up a security perimeter around the mountain and he had followed orders. No reason was given, none was asked. Consumed with curiosity, Diego could only watch the helicopters arrive and depart and wonder what was going on up there.

'Contact Corporal Francisco at Post Five and have him send a man to check Four and Six.' Diego sat down at his field desk and duly noted the lack of response in his daily report as a probable breakdown in communications equipment. The possibility there was a real problem never entered his mind.

'I can't raise Francisco at Post Five either,' the radioman informed him.

Diego finally turned. 'Are you certain your equipment is working properly?'

'Yes, sir. The transmitter is sending and receiving perfectly.'

'Try Post One.'

The radioman adjusted his headphones and signalled the post. A few moments later, he turned and shrugged. 'I'm sorry, Captain, Post One is silent too.'

'I'll see to this myself,' Diego said irritably. He picked up a portable radio and headed from the tent towards his command vehicle. Suddenly, he stopped in his tracks and stared dumbly.

The army command vehicle was sitting with the left front end jacked up, the wheel and the spare tyre both nowhere to be seen. 'What in hell is going on?' he muttered to himself. Is this some sort of prank, he wondered, or could Colonel Campos be testing him?

He spun around on his heel and started for the tent but took only two steps. As if conjured up out of nothingness by a spell, three men blocked his way. All held rifles pointed at his chest. The first question that ran through his mind was why were Indians, dressed as if they were on a cattle drive, sabotaging his equipment?

'This is a military zone,' he blurted. 'You are not permitted here.'

'Do as you're told, soldier boy,' said Billy Yuma, 'and none of your men will get hurt.'

Diego suddenly guessed what had happened to his security posts. And yet he was confused. There was no way a few Indians could capture forty trained soldiers without firing a shot. He addressed his words to Yuma, whom he took to be the leader.

'Drop your weapons before my men arrive or you will be placed under military arrest.'

'I'm sorry to inform you, soldier boy,' Yuma said, taking delight in intimidating the officer in his neatly pressed field uniform and brightly shined combat boots, 'but your entire force has been disarmed and is now under guard.'

'Impossible!' snapped Diego haughtily. 'No mob of sand rats can stand up against trained troops.'

Yuma shrugged indifferently and turned to one of the

men beside him. 'Fix the radio inside the tent so it won't work.'

'You're crazy. You can't destroy government property.'

'You have trespassed on our land,' said Yuma in a low voice. 'You have no authority here.'

'I order you to put those guns down,' commanded Diego, reaching for his sidearm.

Yuma stepped forward, his weathered face expressionless, and rammed the muzzle of his old Winchester rifle deep into Captain Diego's stomach. 'Do not resist us. If I pull the trigger, your body will silence the gunfire to those on the mountain.'

The sudden, jolting pain convinced Diego these men were not playing games. They knew the desert and could move through the terrain like ghosts. His orders were to prevent possible encroachment by wandering hunters or prospectors. Nothing was mentioned about an armed force of local Indians who lay in ambush. Slowly, he handed over his automatic pistol to one of Yuma's men, who stuffed the barrel down the waist of his denim pants.

'Your radio too, please.'

Diego reluctantly passed over the radio. 'Why are you doing this?' he asked. 'Don't you know you are breaking the law?'

'If you soldier boys are working with the men who are defiling our sacred mountain, it is you who are breaking the law, our law. Now, no more talk. You will come with us.'

In silence, Captain Diego and his radioman were escorted half a kilometre (a third of a mile) to a large overhanging rock protruding from the mountain. There, out of sight of anyone on the peak, Diego found his entire company of men sitting nervously in a tight group while several Indians covered them with their own weapons.

They scrambled to their feet and came to attention, their faces reflecting relief at seeing their commanding officer. Two lieutenants and a sergeant came up and saluted.

'Is there no one who escaped?' asked Diego.

One of the lieutenants shook his head. 'No, sir. They were on us before we could resist.'

Diego looked around at the Indians guarding his men. Including Yuma, he counted only sixteen. 'Is this all of you?' he asked unbelievingly.

Yuma nodded. 'We did not need more.'

'What are you going to do with us?'

'Nothing, soldier boy. My neighbours and I have been careful not to harm anyone. You and your men will enjoy a nice siesta for a few hours, and then you'll be free to leave our land.'

'And if we attempt to escape?'

Yuma shrugged indifferently. 'Then you will be shot. Something you should think about, since my people can hit a running rabbit at fifty metres.'

Yuma had said all he had to say. He turned his back on Captain Diego and began climbing an almost unrecognizable trail between a fissure on the south wall of the mountain. No words were spoken between the Montolos. As if on silent command, ten men followed Billy Yuma while five remained behind to guard the prisoners.

The ascent went faster than the last time. He profited from his mistakes and ignored the wrong turns he had taken that curved into blind chutes. He remembered the good handholds and avoided the ones that were badly eroded. But it was still tough going on a trail no self-respecting pack mule would be caught dead on.

He would have preferred more men to support his assault, but the ten men struggling behind him were the only ones who were not afraid of the mountain. Or that was what they claimed. Yuma was not blind to the apprehension in their eyes.

After he reached a flat ledge, he stopped to catch his breath. His heart was beginning to pound, but his body was tensed with the nervous energy of a racehorse ready to burst from the gate. He pulled an old pocket watch from his pants pocket and checked the time. He nodded to himself in satisfaction and held the watch face for the others to see. They were twenty minutes ahead of schedule.

High above, on the mountain's summit, the helicopters hovered like bees around a hive. They were loaded with as much of the treasure as they could lift before struggling into the sky and setting a course for the airstrip in the Altar Desert.

Colonel Campos's officers and men were working so fast, and were so awed by the golden hoard, none thought to check the security forces stationed around the base of the mountain. The radio operator on the peak was too busy coordinating the comings and goings of the helicopters to ask for a report from Captain Diego. No one took the time to look over the edge at the deserted encampment below. Nor did they notice the small band of men who were slowly climbing ever closer to the mountaintop.

Police Comandante Cortina was not a man who missed much. As his police helicopter rose from Cerro el Capirote for the return trip to his headquarters, he stared down at the stone beast and caught something that was missed by all the others. A pragmatic man, he closed his eyes and put it off as a trick of sunlight and shadows, or perhaps the angle of his view. But when he refocused his eyes on the ancient sculpture, he could have sworn the vicious expression had altered. The menacing look was gone.

To Cortina, just before it slipped out of view of his window, the fang-filled jaws on the guardian of the dead were frozen in a smile.

THE WALLOWING WINDBAG

52

Pitt felt as though he were free-falling down a mammoth soda straw filled with cobalt blue mist. The sides of the vertical shaft of the sinkhole were round and smooth, almost as if they had been polished. If he hadn't been able to see his diving partner through the transparent water a short distance below, the shaft would have seemed bottomless. He cleared his ears as he descended, finning easily until he caught up with Giordino, who was towing their dry transport container past the elbow bend at the bottom of the shaft. Pitt helped by pushing his end through, and then followed in its wake.

He glanced at his depth-gauge needle. It was holding steady just shy of the 60-metre mark (197 feet). From here on, as the feeder stream sloped up towards the river, the water pressure would decrease, relieving any fear of depth blackout.

This was nothing like the dive into the sacrificial pool on the jungled slopes of the Andes. There, he had used a strong safety line with communications equipment. And except for the brief foray into the side cavern to rescue Shannon and Miles, he was never out of sight of the surface. This trip, they'd be entering an underworld of perpetual blackness no man or animal had ever seen.

As they moved their bulky canister through the twists and turns of the feeder stream leading to the river, Pitt recalled that cave diving is one of the most dangerous sports in the world. There was the Stygian blackness, the claustrophobic sensation of knowing you're far beneath the solid rock, the maddening silence, and the constant threat of disorientation if silt is stirred into impenetrable clouds. All this could lead to panic, which had killed scores of divers who were trained and equipped to deal with the perils, and made cave diving a morbid fascination that could not be learned from a book.

What was it his instructor from the National Speleological Society had told him before his first dive into a saltwater cave in the Bahamas? 'Anyone can die at any time on a cave dive.' In that peculiar way a particular fact learned in youth can stick in your mind forever, Pitt remembered that during the year 1974, twenty-six divers had lost their lives in Florida's underwater caves alone, and that the world total of deaths must have been three times that figure.

Pitt had never suffered from claustrophobia and fear seldom distracted him, but under hazardous conditions he experienced just enough uneasiness to sharpen his senses to unexpected dangers.

As it was, he didn't look forward to diving without a fixed guide or safety line. He well knew this operation could quickly turn into an exercise in self-destruction, especially once they became uncontrollably caught up in the river's current. Then there would be no escape until they reached the treasure chamber.

The horizontal fissure leading to the river expanded and tapered in a series of hourglass shapes. At 100 metres (328 feet) from the sinkhole they lost 90 per cent of the outside light. They switched on the lamps attached to their hard-hats. Another quick glance at his depth gauge told Pitt they had slowly ascended to within 20 metres (66 feet) of the water surface.

Giordino ceased his forward movement, turned, and waved with one hand. They had reached the outlet into the river system. Pitt answered with the hand signal for OK. Then he slipped his arm through the strap attached to the transport canister so it wouldn't be torn from him by unforeseen turbulence.

Giordino kicked his fins powerfully and angled upstream

in a vigorous effort to pull the canister broadside into the river as far as possible before the main flow of the current swung him downstream before Pitt could exit the feeder stream. His timing was near perfect. Just as he lost his momentum and the current caught him in its grip, thrusting him around, Pitt and his end of the canister popped out of the side gallery.

As previously planned, they calmly inflated their buoyancy compensators, released the lead weights on the canister to make it buoyant, and calmly drifted upward while being carried downriver. After travelling close to 50 metres (164 feet), they broke surface, their lights revealing a large open gallery. The ceiling was covered by a strange black rock that was not limestone. Only when Pitt steadied his light did he recognize it as volcanic. Fortunately, the river's flow was smooth and uninterrupted by rocks, but the walls of the passage rose steeply out of the water, offering them no place to land.

He spat out his regulator mouthpiece and called to Giordino. 'Be ready to cut to the side when you see an open spot on the bank.'

'Will do,' Giordino said over his shoulder.

They quickly passed from the volcanic intrusion back into limestone that was covered by an odd grey coating that absorbed their light beams and gave the impression the batteries were giving out on their lamps. A steady, thunderous sound grew and echoed through the passage. Their worst fears — being swept through unnavigable rapids or going over a waterfall before making a landing — suddenly loomed in the darkness ahead.

'Keep a tight grip,' Giordino shouted. 'It looks like we're in for a tumble.'

Pitt angled his head downward so the lights on his hardhat pointed directly to the front. It was a wasted motion. The passage was soon filled with a mist that rose out of the water like steam. Pitt had a sudden vision of going over Niagara Falls without a barrel. The roar was deafening now, magnified by the acoustics of the rocky cavern. And then Giordino passed into the mist and vanished.

Pitt could only hold on to the canister and watch with strangely paralysed fascination as he was enveloped by the spray. He braced himself for an endless fall. But the endless fall never came. The thunder came not from the river plunging downward, but from a furious torrent that crashed down from above.

He was pummelled by a surging deluge that burst in a great plume from the limestone roof of the cavern. The huge torrent of water barrelled down a tributary that fed into the subterranean river from another source. Pitt was baffled by the sight of so much water rushing under an arid and thirsty desert no farther away than the distance a good outfielder could throw a baseball. He decided that it must feed into the river by great pressure from a system of underground aquifers.

Once through the curtain of mist, he could see the walls had spread and the roof sloped upward into a chamber of vast size and proportion. It was a bizarrely decorated cavern filled with grotesquely shaped helictites, a family of stalactites that ignores gravity and grows in eccentric directions. Mineral deposits had also formed beautifully sculpted mushrooms over a metre tall and delicate gypsum flowers with graceful plumes. The spectacular formations would have been described by veteran spelunkers as a showcase grotto.

Pitt couldn't but wonder how many other subterranean worlds sprawled through the earth in eternal darkness, waiting to be discovered and explored. It was easy to let the mind run amok and imagine a long-dead and lost race who had lived down here and carved the magnificent calcite sculptures.

Not Giordino. The beauty was lost on him. He turned, gazed back at Pitt with a big I'm-glad-to-be-alive smile and said, 'Looks like a hangout for the Phantom of the Opera.'

'I doubt if we'll find Lon Chaney playing the pipe organ down here.'

'We have a landing thirty metres ahead to the left,' Giordino said, his spirits lifting considerably.

'Right. Start your turn into shallow water and swim like hell to get out of the main current.'

Giordino needed no urging. He cut his angle sharply, pulling the canister behind him and kicking his fins furiously. Pitt released his grip on the big aluminium tube, swam strongly alongside until he was at its midpoint, and then, using his body as a drag, he heaved it after Giordino.

The approach worked as Pitt had hoped. Giordino broke free of the current and swam into calmer water. When his fins touched the bottom, he climbed ashore, dragging the canister with him.

Now unhampered, Pitt easily stroked into the shallows, landing ten metres below Giordino. He crawled out of the water, sat down, removed his fins and goggles, and carefully walked back upstream across the smoothly textured rocks as he removed his air tanks.

Giordino did the same before he began dismantling the canister. He looked up at Pitt with a look of profound accomplishment. 'Nice place you've got here.'

'Sorry for the mess,' muttered Pitt, 'but the seven dwarfs are on a break.'

'Does it feel as good to you as it does to me that we've come this far?'

'I'm not sad to be alive, if that's what you mean.'

'How far *have* we come?'

Pitt tapped in a command on the computer strapped to his arm. 'According to my faithful wonder of technology, we have travelled two kilometres through damnation and dropped another two metres towards hell.'

'Twenty-eight to go.'

'Yes,' Pitt said, smiling like a magician about to bedazzle an audience. 'But from here on, we go in style.'

*

Five minutes later the eight air chambers of the *Wallowing Windbag* were filled and the hull fully inflated, deployed, and ready to do battle with the river. Known as a water rescue response vehicle, the ungainly Hovercraft could ride on a cushion of air effortlessly over boiling rapids, quicksand, thin ice, and polluted quagmires. Vehicles in use by police and fire departments around the country had saved countless victims from death by drowning. Now this one was going on an endurance trial its builders never conceived.

Three metres (10 feet) in length and 1.5 metres (5 feet) wide, the compact craft mounted a four-cycle, 50-horsepower engine that could propel her over a flat surface at 64 kilometres (40 miles) an hour.

'Our engineers did a fine job of modifying the height,' said Giordino.

'Adopting a horizontal engine and fan was a stroke of genius,' Pitt agreed.

'Amazing how much equipment they crammed inside the canister.'

Before they cast off, they stowed and tied down ten reserve air tanks, extra air bottles to reinflate the Hovercraft, a battery of lights including two aircraft landing lights built into waterproof housings, spare batteries, first aid equipment, and three additional breathing regulators.

From a watertight container Pitt retrieved his battered, old .45 Colt automatic and two ammo clips. He smiled as he also found a thermos of coffee and four bologna sandwiches. Admiral Sandecker never forgot the details that make for a successful operation. Pitt put the thermos and sandwiches back in the container. There was no time for a picnic. They had to push on if they were to reach the treasure chamber before it was too late to save Loren and Rudi. He inserted the gun and extra ammo clips into a plastic bag and sealed the opening. Then he unzipped the front of his wet suit and slipped the bag inside next to his stomach.

He stared for a moment at the black collapsible Hover-craft. 'Oh, Circe, who will guide us on this journey,' he quoted. 'To Hades no man ever went in a black ship.'

Giordino looked up from coupling a pair of steering oars to their locks. 'Where did you hear that?'

'The *Odyssey* by Homer.'

'Verily among the Trojans too there be men that dive,' Giordino recited glibly. 'The *Iliad*. I can quote Homer too.'

'You never cease to amaze me.'

'It's nothing really.'

Pitt climbed aboard. 'Gear stashed?'

'All buttoned down.'

'Ready to shove off?'

'Start her up.'

Pitt crouched in the stern just ahead of the engine fan. He engaged the starter and the air-cooled engine sputtered to life. The small engine was well muffled and the exhaust sounded only as a muted throb.

Giordino took his position in the bow of the craft and turned on one of the landing lights, illuminating the cavern as bright as daylight. He looked back at Pitt and laughed. 'I hope no one fines us for polluting a virgin environment.'

Pitt laughed too. 'A losing proposition for the local sheriff. I forgot my wallet.'

The Hovercraft moved off the shoreline, suspended on its self-produced 20-centimetre (8-inch) cushion of air into the mainstream of the river. Pitt held the vertical grips of the control bar in each hand and easily steered an arrow-straight course over the flowing current.

It seemed strange to be skimming over the water surface without a sensation of contact. From the bow, Giordino could look down into the remarkably transparent water that had turned from the cobalt blue of the sinkhole to a deep aqua green and see startled albino salamanders and small schools of blind cave fish darting amid the spherical boulders that carpeted the river bottom like fallen ornaments. He kept busy reporting the river conditions ahead and snapping photos as Pitt manoeuvred and recorded data on his computer for Peter Duncan.

Even with their rapid motion through the large corridors, their sweat and the extreme humidity combined to form a halolike mist around their heads. They ignored the phenomena and the darkness behind them, never looking back as they continued deeper into the river-carved canyon.

For the first 8 kilometres (5 miles) it was clear sailing and they made good time. They skimmed over bottomless pools and past forbidding galleries that extended deep into the walls of the caverns. The ceilings in the string of river chambers varied from a high of 30 metres (98 feet) to barely enough room to squeeze the Hovercraft through. They bounced over several small, shallow cascades without difficulty and entered a narrow channel where it took all their concentration to avoid the ever-present rocks. Then they travelled through one enormous gallery that stretched almost 3 kilometres (slightly over 2 miles) and was filled with stunning crystals that glinted and sparkled beneath the aircraft light.

On two different occasions, the passage became flooded when the ceiling merged with the water surface. Then they went through the routine of deflating the *Wallowing Windbag* until it achieved neutral buoyancy, returned to breathing from their air tanks, and drifted with the current through the sunken passage, dragging the flattened Hovercraft and its equipment behind them until they emerged into an open cavern and reinflated it again. There were no complaints over the additional effort. Neither man expected a smooth cruise down a placid river.

To relieve the stress they began giving nonsensical names to the galleries and prominent features. The Fun House, the Wax Museum, Giordino's Gymnasium. A small spout from a cavern wall was labelled Postnasal Drip. The river itself they called the Old Sot.

After travelling through a second submerged passage and reinflating their boat, Pitt observed that the current's pace had quickened by two knots and the river gradient began dropping at a faster rate. Like leaves through a gutter drain, they rushed into the eternal land of gloom, never knowing what dangers lurked around the next bend.

The rapids increased frighteningly as the Hovercraft was suddenly swept into a raging cataract. The emerald water turned a boiling white as it cascaded through a passage strewn with boulders. Now the *Wallowing Windbag* was rearing up like a rodeo bronco as it surged between the rocks and plunged sickeningly into the next trough. Every time Pitt told himself the rapids couldn't possibly get more violent, the next stretch of river slammed the Hovercraft into a seething frenzy that buried it completely on more than one occasion. But the faithful little craft always shook off the froth and fought back to the surface.

Pitt struggled like a madman to keep the boat on a straight course. If they swung halfway around broadside to the tumult, all chances for survival would have been lost. Giordino grabbed the emergency oars and put his back into keeping the boat steady. They swept around a sharp curve in the river over massive rocks, some partly submerged and kicking up great waves shaped like rooster tails, others rising above the turbulence like menacing monoliths. Several boulders were skinned by the little vessel. Then one rose out of the trough that seemed certain to crush the boat and its occupants. But the outer hull sideswiped the unyielding stone without a puncture and was carried past.

Their ordeals never ceased. They were caught in a swirling eddy like a cork being sucked down a drain. Pitt braced his back against an air-filled support cell to stay upright and pushed the throttle to its stop. The howl of the racing engine was lost in the roar of the rapids. All his will and concentration were focused on keeping the

Hovercraft from twisting broadside from the force of the speeding current as Giordino assisted by pulling mightily on the oars.

Lost when Giordino took up the oars, the landing lights had fallen overboard into the froth. Now the only light came from the lamps on their hardhats. It seemed a lifetime had passed before they finally broke clear of the whirlpool and were hurled back into the rapids.

Pitt eased back on the throttle and relaxed his hands on the grips of the control bar. There was no point in fighting the river now. The *Wallowing Windbag* would go where the surging water threw it.

Giordino peered into the black unknown ahead, hoping to see calmer water. What he saw was a fork in the river that divided the mainstream into two different galleries. He shouted above the tumult, 'We're coming to a junction!'

'Can you tell which is the main conduit?' Pitt yelled back.

'The one on the left looks the largest!'

'Okay, pull to port!'

The Hovercraft came terrifyingly close to being smashed against the great mass of rock that split the river and only missed turning turtle by a hair as it was overwhelmed by a giant backwash. The little vessel dug into the turbulence and lurched forward sickeningly, burying its bow under a wall of water. Somehow it regained a level keel before being thrown forward by the relentless current.

For an instant Pitt thought he'd lost Giordino, but then the burly little man rose out of the deep pool filling the inside of the boat and shook his head to clear the dizziness brought on by being spun around like a ball in a roulette wheel. Incredibly, he cracked a smile and pointed to his ears.

Pitt understood. The continuous roar of the rapids seemed to be slackening. The Hovercraft responded to his control again, but sluggishly, because it was half-full of water. The excess weight was making it impossible to maintain an air-cushion. He increased the throttle and yelled to Giordino.

'Start bailing!'

The boat designers had thought of everything. Giordino inserted a lever into a small pump and began shoving it back and forth, causing a gush of water to shoot through a pipe over the side.

Pitt leaned over and studied the depths under his headlamps. The channel seemed more constricted, and although the rocks were no longer churning up the water, the river seemed to be moving at a horrifying speed. Suddenly, he noticed that Giordino had stopped bailing and was listening with an apocalyptic look on his face. And then Pitt heard it too.

A deep rumble boomed from the black void downriver.

Giordino stared at him. 'I think we just bought the farm!' he shouted.

The vision of going over Niagara Falls returned. This was no spout from above they were approaching. The sound that reverberated through the cavern was that of an enormous volume of water rushing over an immense cascade.

'Hit the inflator on your buoyancy compensator!' Pitt roared above the chaos.

The water was sweeping them along at a good twenty knots and appeared to be funnelling into a concentrated surge. A million litres of water sucked them towards the unseen precipice. They rounded the next bend and sailed into a maelstrom of mist. The thunderous rumble became deafening.

There was no fear, no sense of helplessness, no feeling of despair. All Pitt felt was a strange numbness as if all power of intelligent thought had abruptly evaporated. It seemed to him that he was entering a nightmare where nothing had any shape or form. His final moment of clarity came when the Wallowing Windbag hung suspended for a moment before soaring into the mist.

With no point of reference, there was no sensation of falling; rather, it seemed as if they were flying through a cloud. Then his hold on the control bar was lost and he was hurled out of the Hovercraft. He thought he heard Giordino shout something, but the voice was lost in the roar of the falls. The drop through the vortex seemed to take forever. And then came the impact. He struck a deep pool at the base of the falls like a meteor. The air was driven from his lungs and he thought at first that he was smashed to bloody pulp on rocks, but then he felt the comforting squeeze of water all around him.

Instinctively holding his breath, he fought to reach the surface. Aided by his inflated buoyancy compensator, he quickly broke clear and was immediately swept away by the torrent. Rocks reached out for him like shrouded predators of the underworld. He was flung down a spill of rapids, colliding, he'd have sworn, with every boulder that protruded from the river. The contact rasped and shredded his wet suit, stripping skin from his legs and outspread arms. He suffered a blow to his chest and then his head struck something hard and ungiving. But for the protection of the hardhat that absorbed 80 per cent of the blow, he'd have cracked his skull open.

Incredibly, his buoyancy compensator stayed inflated and he floated half-unconscious through a short spill of rapids. One of the lights on his helmet was smashed by the impact and the other one seemed to cast an indistinct red beam. Gratefully, he felt loose stone beneath his feet and saw he was being spun towards shallows leading to a small open space along the shoreline. He swam until his knees scraped the coarse gravel, struggling to loosen the grip of the murderous current. He extended his hands to pull himself over the slippery stones on to the dry shelf. A groan of pain escaped his lips as one of his wrists exploded in agony. At some point after going over the falls, he had broken something there. His wrist was not all that was broken. He'd also cracked two or more ribs on his left side.

The rumbling thunder of the falls sounded far in the distance. Slowly his mind came back on track and he wondered how far he'd been swept by the ungodly torrent. Then, as more of the cobwebs cleared, he remembered Giordino. In desperation he shouted Al's name, his voice echoing through the air chamber, hoping but never really expecting to hear a reply.

'Over here.'

The answer didn't come much louder than a whisper, but Pitt heard it as if it came out of a loudspeaker. He rose unsteadily to his feet trying to get a fix. 'Say again.'

'I'm only six metres upstream of you,' said Giordino. 'Can't you see me?'

A red haze seemed to block Pitt's field of vision. He rubbed his eyes and found he could focus them again. He also realized the red haze that had been clouding his sight came from blood that was spilling from a gash in his forehead. Now he could clearly discern Giordino lying on his back a short distance away, half out of the water.

He staggered over to his friend, clutching the left side of his chest in a vain attempt to contain the pain. He knelt stiffly beside Giordino. 'Am I ever glad to see you. I thought you and the *Windbag* had sailed off without me.'

'The remains of our trusty boat were swept downstream.'

'Are you badly injured?' Pitt asked.

Giordino smiled gamely, held up his hands and wiggled his fingers. 'At least I can still play Carnegie Hall.'

'Play what? You can't even carry a tune.' Then Pitt's eyes filled with concern. 'Is it your back?'

Giordino weakly shook his head. 'I stayed with the *Windbag* and my feet were caught in the lines holding the equipment when she struck bottom. Then she went one way, and I went the other. I think both legs are broken below the knees.' He explained his injuries as calmly as if he were describing a pair of flat tyres.

Pitt gently felt Giordino's calves as his friend clenched

his fists. 'Lucky you. Simple breaks, no compound fractures.'

Giordino stared up at Pitt. 'You look like you went through the spin cycle in a washing machine.'

'A few scrapes and bruises,' Pitt lied.

'Then why are you talking through clenched teeth?'

Pitt didn't answer. He tried to call up a program on the computer on his arm, but it had been knocked against a rock and was broken. He unbuckled the straps and threw it in the river. 'So much for Duncan's data.'

'I lost the camera too.'

'Tough break. Nobody will be coming this way again soon, certainly not over those falls.'

'Any idea how far to the treasure cavern?' asked Giordino.

'A rough guess? Maybe two kilometres.'

Giordino looked at him. 'You'll have to go it alone.'

'You're talking crazy.'

'I'll only be a burden.' He was no longer smiling. 'Forget about me. Get to the treasure cavern.'

'I can't leave you here.'

'Busted bones or not, I can still float. I'll follow you later.'

'Take care when you get there,' said Pitt grimly. 'You may drift, but you can't escape the current. Mind you stay close to shore out of the mainstream or you'll be swept beyond recovery.'

'No big deal if I am. Our air tanks went with the *Wallowing Windbag*. If we meet a flooded gallery between here and the treasure chamber longer than we can hold our breath, we'll drown anyway.'

'You're supposed to look on the bright side.'

Giordino removed a spare flashlight from a belt around one thigh. 'You'll need this. Your head lamp looks like it lost a fight with a rock. Come to think of it, your face is a mess too. You're bleeding all over the shredded remains of your nice clean wet suit.'

'Another dip in the river will fix that,' said Pitt, attaching the flashlight around the forearm above his broken left wrist where the computer used to be. He dropped his weight belt. 'I won't be needing this any longer.'

'Aren't you taking your air tank?'

'I don't want to be hindered any more than I have to.'

'What if you come to a flooded chamber?'

'I'll have to free dive through as far as I can on my lungs.'

'One last favour,' said Giordino, holding up the empty harness straps that once supported his air tanks. 'Wrap my legs together to keep them from flopping around.'

Pitt cinched the straps as tight as he dared, conscious of his broken wrist and the need to be gentle. Except for a sharp intake of breath, Giordino uttered no sound. 'Rest up for at least an hour before you follow,' Pitt ordered.

'Just get a move on and do what you can to save Loren and Rudi. I'll be along as soon as I'm able.'

'I'll keep a watch for you.'

'Better find a big net.'

Pitt gave Giordino's arm a farewell grip. Then he waded into the river until the current swept him off his feet and carried him into the next cavern.

Giordino watched until Pitt's light vanished around the next bend in the canyon and was lost in the darkness. Two kilometres (1.2 miles), he mused. He hoped to God the final leg of the journey was in air-filled chambers.

53

Zolar drew a long, relieved breath. Things had gone well, better than he'd expected. The project was winding down. The trailer used for the operations office, the forklift, and the winch had been airlifted away along with most of Colonel Campos's men. Only a small squad of army engineers remained behind to load the final lot on to the army transport helicopter that was parked beside the stolen NUMA craft.

Zolar looked down at the remaining pieces of the golden treasure, which stood in a neat row. He studied the brilliantly gleaming antiquities with an eye towards their ultimate sale price. The artistry and magnificence of the metalwork of the twenty-eight golden statues of Inca warriors was indescribable. They each stood one metre high and provided a rare glimpse into the creative mastery of Inca artisans.

'A few more and you'd have yourself a chess set,' said Oxley, admiring the golden display.

'A pity I won't keep them,' replied Zolar sadly. 'But I'm afraid I'll have to be content with using the profits from my share of their sale to buy legitimate artifacts for my personal collection.'

Fernando Matos hungrily devoured the sight of the golden army with his eyes while he mentally estimated his 2 per cent cut of the spoils. 'We have nothing that can touch this in our National Museum of Anthropology in Mexico City.'

'You can always donate your share,' said Oxley sarcastically.

Matos shot him a barbed look and started to say something but was cut off by the approach of Colonel Campos. 'Lieutenant Ramos reports from the cavern that no objects remain inside the mountain. As soon as he and his men arrive from below, they will load the objects. Then I will be on my way to the airstrip to oversee the transshipment.'

'Thank you, Colonel,' Zolar said politely. He didn't trust Campos as far as he could throw the stone demon. 'If you have no objections, the rest of us will join you.'

'But of course.' Campos looked around the nearly vacated summit. 'And your other people?'

Zolar's deepset eyes took on a cold look. 'My brother Cyrus and his crew will follow in our helicopter as soon as they tie up a pair of loose ends.'

Campos understood. He smiled cynically. 'It makes me sick to think about all the bandits running loose to rob and murder foreign visitors.'

While they waited for Lieutenant Ramos and his squad to exit the passageway and load the artifacts, Matos walked over and inspected the stone demon. He reached out and laid his hand on the neck and was surprised at the coolness of the stone after it had been absorbing the sun's rays all day. Abruptly, he jerked his hand back. It felt as if the cold stone had suddenly turned pliant and slimy like the scaly skin of a fish.

He stepped back, startled, and half spun around to hurry away. At that instant he saw a human head rising over the edge of the sharp drop in front of the demon. As a man who grew up in a family of university instructors, he did not believe in superstition and folklore. Matos stood frozen more out of curiosity than fright.

The head rose and was seen to be attached to the body of a man who wearily climbed on to the surface of the summit. Then the intruder stood unsteadily for a moment and aimed an old rifle at Matos.

Yuma had lain on a ledge for nearly a full minute, catching his breath and waiting for his heart to slow. When he lifted his head over the rim, he saw a strange-looking little man with a bald head and huge glasses, incongruously dressed in a business suit with shirt and tie, staring back at him. To Yuma, the man reminded him of the government officials who passed through the Montolo village once a year, promising aid in the form of fertilizer, feed and grain, and money, but went on their way and never delivered. After climbing over the rim of the slope he also spotted a group of men standing by the army helicopter 30 metres (100 feet) away. They did not notice him. He had planned the climb to terminate behind the great stone demon out of sight of anyone. Except Matos, who unfortunately happened to be standing nearby.

He pointed his worn and scarred old Winchester at the man and spoke softly. 'Do not make a sound or you die.'

Yuma did not have to look back to confirm that the first of his neighbours and relatives were scrambling on to the mountaintop. He realized that he desperately needed another minute for all of his tiny force to reach high ground. If the man in front of him gave the alarm, all surprise would be lost and the rest of his people would be caught in an exposed position on the mountainside. He had to stall somehow.

Matters were made even worse by the sudden appearance of an officer and a squad of army engineers who walked from a deep fissure in the rock. They looked neither left nor right and headed straight towards what appeared to Yuma as a staggered row of short, golden men.

At seeing the approaching engineers, the helicopter pilot started up his engines and set them on idle and engaged the twin rotors of the big transport.

Beside the stone demon, Matos slowly raised his hands.

'Put your hands down!' Yuma hissed.

Matos did as he was ordered. 'How did you get through our security?' he demanded. 'What are you doing here?'

'This is my people's sacred ground,' Yuma answered

540

quietly. 'You are defiling it with your greed.'

For every few seconds gained, two more Montolos climbed over the rim of the ledge behind Yuma and formed a group out of sight behind the demon. They had come this far without causing injury or death, and Yuma hated to start now.

'Walk back towards me,' he ordered Matos. 'Stand next to the demon.'

There was a wild, crazed look in Matos's eyes. His lust for golden wealth slowly began to short-circuit his fear. His share would make him rich beyond his wildest dreams. He couldn't give it up because of a band of superstitious Indians. He glanced nervously over his shoulder at the engineers closing with the helicopter. Dread of losing his dreams created an agonizing knot in his stomach.

Yuma could see it coming. He was losing the man in the suit. 'You want gold?' said Yuma. 'Take it and leave our mountain.'

As he saw more men materializing behind Yuma, Matos finally snapped. He turned and began to run, shouting, 'Intruders! Shoot them!'

Without lifting his gun and aiming, Yuma fired from the hip, his shot striking Matos in the knee. The bureaucrat jerked sideways, his glasses flew off his head, and he sprawled heavily on his chest. He rolled over on his back, raising his leg and clutching his knee with both hands.

Yuma's relatives and neighbours, guns at the ready, fanned out like ghosts in a cemetery as they encircled the helicopter. Lieutenant Ramos, no fool he, instantly took in the situation. His men were engineers and not infantrymen and carried no weapons. He immediately raised his hands in surrender and shouted to his small squad to do likewise.

Zolar swore loudly. 'Where in hell did these Indians come from?'

'No time to reason why,' snapped Oxley. 'We're pulling out.'

He jumped through the cargo hatch and pulled Zolar in after him.

'The gold warriors!' Zolar protested. 'They're not loaded.'

'Forget them.'

'No!' Zolar resisted.

'You damn fool. Can't you see, those men are armed. The army engineers can't help us.' He turned and yelled to the pilot of the helicopter. 'Lift off! *Andale, andale!*'

Colonel Campos was slower than the others to react. He stupidly ordered Lieutenant Ramos and his men to resist. 'Attack them!' he cried.

Ramos stared at him. 'With what, Colonel, our bare hands?'

Yuma and his tribal members were only 10 metres (33 feet) from the helicopter now. So far only one shot had been fired. The sight of the sun glinting off the golden warriors momentarily stunned the Montolos. The only pure gold object any of them had ever seen was a small chalice on the altar of the little mission church in the nearby village of Ilano Colorado.

Dust began to swirl as the pilot applied the throttles and the rotor blades of the helicopter furiously beat the air. The wheels were lifting off the mountain's summit when Campos finally realized discretion was the better part of greed. He ran four steps and leapt towards the cargo door at the urging of Charles Oxley who reached out for him.

At that instant the helicopter lurched sharply upward. Campos's upraised hands caught empty air. His momentum carried him under the helicopter and off the edge of the cliff as if he'd taken a running dive into water. Oxley watched the colonel's body grow smaller and smaller as it turned end over end before smashing on to the rocks far below.

'Good Christ,' gasped Oxley.

Zolar, grimly hanging on to a strap inside the cargo bay, did not witness Campos's plunge to the base of the mountain. His concerns were elsewhere. 'Cyrus is still down in the cavern.'

'He's with Amaru and his men. Not to worry. Their automatic weapons are more than a match for a few Indians carrying hunting rifles and shotguns. They'll leave in the last helicopter still on the mountain.'

Only then did it occur to Zolar that someone was missing. 'Where's Matos and the colonel?'

'The Indians shot Matos and Campos made his move too late.'

'He stayed on Cerro el Capirote?'

'No, he fell *off* Cerro el Capirote. He's dead.'

Zolar's reaction was a psychiatrist's dream. His expression went thoughtful for a moment, and then he broke out laughing. 'Matos shot and the good colonel dead. More profits for the family.'

Yuma's prearranged plan with Pitt was accomplished. He and his people had secured the summit and forced the evil ones from the sacred mountain of the dead. He watched as two of his nephews led Lieutenant Ramos and his army engineers down the steep trail to the desert floor below.

There was no way to carry Matos. His knee was tightly bandaged and he was forced to hobble along as best he could, assisted by a pair of engineers.

Curiosity drew Yuma to the enlarged opening to the interior passageway. He had a nagging ache to explore the cavern and see with his own eyes the river described by Pitt. The water he saw in his dreams. But the older men were too frightened to enter the bowels of the sacred mountain, and the gold created a problem with the younger men. They wanted to drop everything and carry it off before armed troops returned.

'This is our mountain,' said one young man, the son of Yuma's neighbouring rancher. 'The little golden people belong to us.'

'First we must see the river inside the mountain,' countered Yuma.

'It is forbidden for the living to enter the land of the dead,' warned Yuma's older brother.

A nephew stared at Yuma doubtfully. 'There is no river that runs beneath the desert.'

'I believe the man who told me.'

'You cannot trust the gringo, no more than those with Spanish blood in their veins.'

Yuma shook his head and pointed to the gold. 'This proves he did not lie.'

'The soldiers will come back and kill us if we do not leave,' protested another villager.

'The golden people are too heavy to carry down the steep trail,' the young man argued. 'They must be lowered by rope down the rock walls. That will take time.'

'Let us offer prayers to the demon and be on our way,' said the brother.

The young man persisted. 'Not until the golden people are safely below.'

Yuma reluctantly gave in. 'So it is, my family, my friends. I will keep my promise and enter the mountain alone. Take the men of gold, but hurry. You do not have much daylight left.'

As he turned and walked through the enlarged opening leading to the passageway, Yuma felt little fear.

Good had come from the climb to the top of the mountain. The evil men were cast down. The demon was at peace again. Now, with the blessing of the demon, Billy Yuma felt confident he could safely enter the land of the dead. And maybe find a trail leading to the lost sacred idols of his people.

54

Loren sat huddled in the cramped rock cell sinking into the quicksand of self-pity. She had no more fight left in her. The hours had merged until time lost all sense of meaning. She could not remember when she had last eaten. She tried to recall what it felt like to be warm and dry, but that memory seemed like an event that occurred ages ago.

Her self-confidence, the independence, the satisfaction of being a respected legislator in the world's only super-power, meant nothing in that damp little cave. Standing on the floor of the House of Representatives seemed a million light-years away. She had come to the end, and she had fought as long as she could. Now she accepted the end. Better to die and get it over with.

She looked over at Rudi Gunn. He had hardly moved at all in the last hour. She didn't have to be a doctor to see that he had slipped badly in that time. Tupac Amaru, in a storm of sadistic wrath, had broken several of Gunn's fingers by stomping them. Amaru had also injured Gunn severely by kicking him repeatedly in the stomach and head. If Rudi didn't receive medical attention very soon, he might die.

Loren's mind turned to Pitt. Every conceivable road to freedom was blocked unless he could ride to their rescue at the head of the US Cavalry. Not a likely prospect.

She recalled the other times he had saved her. The first was on board the Russian cruise ship where she was held captive by agents of the old Soviet government. Pitt had shown up and rescued her from a savage beating. The second time was when she was held hostage by the fanatic

Hideki Suma in his underwater city off the coast of Japan. Pitt and Giordino had risked their lives to free her and a fellow congressman.

She had no right to give up. But Pitt was dead, crushed by concussion grenades in the sea. If her countrymen could have sent a group of Special Forces over the border to save her, they would have done so by now.

She had watched through the cave opening as the golden treasure was hauled past her cell and through the guardians' chamber up to the peak of the hollow mountain. When all the gold was gone, she knew it would be time for her and Rudi to die.

They did not have to wait long. One of Amaru's foul-smelling henchman walked up to their guard and gave him an order. The ugly slug turned and motioned them out of the cave. '*Salga, salga*,' he commanded them.

Loren shook Gunn awake and helped him rise to his feet. 'They want to move us,' she told him softly.

Gunn looked at her dazedly, and then incredibly, he forced a tight smile. 'About time they upgraded us to a better room.'

With Gunn shuffling alongside Loren, her arm around his waist, his over her shoulders, they were led to a flat area between the stalagmites near the shoreline of the river. Amaru was joking with four of his men who were grouped around him. Another man she recognized from the ferryboat as Cyrus Sarason. The Latin Americans appeared cool and relaxed, but Sarason was sweating heavily and his shirt beneath his armpits was stained.

Their one-eyed guard pushed them roughly forward and moved slightly apart from the others. Sarason reminded Loren of a high school coach who was pressed into service as a chaperon at a prom, seeing out a dull and boring duty.

In contrast, Amaru looked as if he were bursting at the seams with nervous energy. Excitement gleamed in his eyes. He stared at Loren with the same intensity as a man crawling through the desert who suddenly sights a saloon advertising cold beer. He came over and roughly cupped Loren's chin with one hand.

'Are you ready to entertain us?'

'Leave her be,' said Sarason. 'There is no need to prolong ·r stay here.'

Something cold and slimy moved through Loren's stomach. Not this, she thought, God not this. 'If you're going to kill us, get it over with.'

'You'll get your wish soon enough.' Amaru laughed sadistically. 'But not before you pleasure my men. When they are finished, and if they are satisfied, perhaps they will give you a thumbs up and let you live. If not, then a thumbs down like the Romans judging a gladiator in the arena. I suggest you make them happy.'

'This is crazy!' snapped Sarason.

'Use your imagination, *amigo*. My men and I have worked hard helping to transport your gold from the mountain. The least you can do is allow us a small reward for our services before we leave this hellish place.'

'You're all getting well paid for your services.'

'What is the term you use in your country?' said Amaru, breathing heavily. 'Fringe benefits?'

'I don't have time for prolonged sex games,' Sarason said.

'You will make the time,' Amaru hissed, baring his teeth like a coiled snake about to strike. 'Or my men will become most unhappy. And then I may not be able to control them.'

One look at the five toughs backing up the Peruvian killer and Sarason shrugged. 'She is of no interest to me.' He stared at Loren for a moment. 'Do with her what you will, but get it over with. We still have work to do and I don't want to keep my brothers waiting.'

Loren was on the verge of throwing up. She looked at Sarason, her eyes imploring. 'You're not one of them. You know who I am, whom I represent. How can you stand by and allow this to happen?'

'Barbaric cruelty is a fact of life where they come from,' Sarason replied indifferently. 'Every one of these vicious misfits would cut a child's throat as casually as you or I would slice a filet mignon.'

'So you'll do nothing while they do their perverted work?'

Sarason gave a detached shrug. 'It might be rather entertaining.'

'You're no better than they are.'

Amaru leered. 'I find great enjoyment in bringing haughty women like you to their knees.'

That was the signal to end the talk. Amaru made a gesture to one of his men. 'You may have the honour of going first, Julio.'

The others looked disappointed at not being chosen. The lucky one stepped forward, his mouth stretched in a lustful grin, and grabbed Loren by the arm.

Little Rudi Gunn, grievously injured and barely able to stand, suddenly crouched, launched himself forward, and rammed his head into the belly of the man about to assault Loren. His charge had all the impact of a broomstick against the gate of a fortress. The big Peruvian barely grunted before delivering a passionless backhand that sent Gunn sprawling across the floor of the cavern.

'Throw the little bastard in the river,' ordered Amaru.

'No!' Loren cried. 'For God's sake, don't kill him.'

One of Amaru's men took Gunn by the ankle and began dragging him towards the water.

'You may be making a mistake,' cautioned Sarason.

Amaru looked at him queerly. 'Why?'

'This river probably enters the Gulf. Instead of providing a floating body for identification, perhaps it might be wiser if they disappear forever.'

Amaru paused thoughtfully for a moment. Then he laughed. 'An underground river that carries them into the Sea of Cortez. I like that. American investigators will never suspect that they were killed a hundred kilometres away from where they're found. The idea appeals to me.' He made a motion to the man holding Gunn to continue. 'Heave him as far as you can into the current.'

'No, please,' Loren begged. 'Let him live and I'll do whatever you demand.'

'You'll do that anyway,' Amaru said impassively.

The guard hurled Gunn into the river with the ease of an athlete throwing the shotput. There was a splash, and Gunn vanished beneath the black water without a word.

Amaru turned back to Loren and nodded at Julio. 'Let the show begin.'

Loren screamed and moved like a cat. She sprang at the man who gripped her arm and rammed the long nails of her thumbs deeply into his eyes.

An agonized cry echoed through the treasure cavern. The man given the go-ahead to ravage Loren clutched his hands to his eyes and squealed like a stuck pig. Amaru and Sarason and the other men were momentarily paralysed with surprise as they saw blood flow through his fingers.

'Oh, Mother of Christ!' Julio cried. 'The bitch has blinded me!'

Amaru walked up to Loren and slapped her hard across the face. She staggered back but did not fall. 'You will pay for that,' he said with icy calm. 'When you have served your purpose, you shall receive the same treatment before you die.'

The fear in Loren's eyes had been replaced with raging anger. If she'd had the strength, she would have fought them tooth and nail like a tiger before being overpowered. But the days of ill-treatment and starvation had left her too weak. She kicked out at Amaru. He took the blows as if they were no more annoying than an attack by a mosquito.

He caught her flailing hands and twisted them behind her. Thinking he had her helpless, he tried to kiss her. But she spat in his face.

Infuriated, he punched her in her soft belly.

Loren doubled up, choking in agony and at the same time gasping for breath. She sank to her knees and slowly fell on her side, still doubled up and clutching her stomach with her arms.

'Since Julio is no longer able to function,' said Amaru, 'the rest of you help yourselves.'

The outstretched arms of his men, thick and strong, with their fingers hooked like claws, reached out and seized her. They rolled her over on her back and pinned down her arms and legs. Held down in a spread-eagled position by the combined strength of three men, including One-Eye, Loren cried out in defenceless terror.

The tattered remains of her clothing were torn away. The smooth, creamy skin shone under the artificial lights left by the army engineers. The sight of her exposed body aroused the attackers' level of excitement even higher.

The one-eyed Quasimodo knelt down and leaned over her, his breath coming in short pants, his lips drawn back from his teeth in a grimace of animal lust. He pressed his mouth against hers. Her screams were suddenly muffled as he bit her lower lip and she could taste the blood. Loren felt as if she were suffocating in a nightmare. He pulled back and moved rough callused hands over her breasts. They felt like sandpaper to her sensitive skin. Her deep violet eyes were sick with abhorrence. She screamed again.

'Fight me!' the hulk whispered huskily. 'I like a woman who fights me.'

Loren plunged into the depths of humiliation and horror as One-Eye lowered himself on to her. Her screams of terror turned into a shriek of pain.

Then abruptly, her hands were free and she clawed her attacker across the face. He sat back stunned, parallel streaks of red blooming on both cheeks, and stared dumbly at two men who had suddenly released her arms and hands. 'You idiots, what are you doing?' he hissed.

The men who were facing the river, fell backward in open-mouthed shock. They crossed themselves as if warding off the devil. Their eyes were not on the rapist or Loren. They were staring into the river beyond. Confused, Amaru turned and peered into the dark waters. What he saw was enough to turn a sane man mad. His mouth dropped open in shock at the sight of an eerie light moving under the water towards him. They all gaped as if hypnotized as the light surfaced and became part of a helmeted head.

Like some hideous wraith rising from the murky abyss of a watery hell, a human form slowly arose from the black depths of the river and moved towards the shore. The apparition, with black seaweedlike shreds hanging from its body, looked like something that belonged not to this world but to the deepest reaches of an alien planet. The effect was made even more shocking by the reappearance of the dead.

Clenched under the right arm, as a father might carry his child, was the inert body of Rudi Gunn.

55

Sarason's face looked like a white plaster death mask. Sweat poured down his forehead. For a man who did not excite easily, his eyes were near-crazed with shock. He stood silent, as the monstrosity left him too stunned to speak.

Amaru leapt to his feet and tried to speak, but only a whispered croak came out. His lips quivered as he rasped, 'Go back, *diablo*, go back to *infierno*.'

The phantom gently lowered Gunn to the ground. He removed his helmet with one hand. Then he unzipped the front of his wet suit and reached inside. The green eyes could be seen now, cast on Loren's exposed position on the cold, hard rock. They glinted under the artificial lights with a terrible anger.

The two men who were still pinning Loren's legs stared dumbly as the Colt thundered once, twice in the cavern. Their faces went wildly distorted as their heads snapped back and exploded. They collapsed and fell across Loren's knees.

The others bolted away from Loren as if she had suddenly acquired the black plague. Julio moaned in a far corner unable to see, his hands still over his injured eyes.

Loren was beyond screaming. She stared at the man from the river, recognizing him but convinced she was seeing a hallucination.

The shock of disbelief, then horror at the realization of who the apparition was, made Amaru's heart turn cold. 'You!' he gasped in a strangled voice.

'You seem surprised to see me, Tupac,' said Pitt easily. 'Cyrus looks a little green around the gills too.'

'You're dead. I killed you.'

'Do a sloppy job, get sloppy results.' Pitt cycled the Colt from man to man and spoke to Loren without looking at her. 'Are you badly hurt?'

For a moment she was too stunned to answer. Then finally, she stammered, 'Dirk . . . is it really you?'

'If there's another one, I hope they catch him before he signs our name to a lot of cheques. I'm sorry I didn't get here sooner.'

She nodded gamely. 'Thanks to you I'll survive to see these beasts pay.'

'You won't have to wait long,' Pitt said with a voice of stone. 'Are you strong enough to make it up the passageway?'

'Yes, yes,' Loren murmured as the reality of her salvation began to sink in. She shuddered as she pushed the dead men away from her and rose unsteadily to her feet, indifferent to her nakedness. She pointed down at Gunn. 'Rudi is in a bad way.'

'These sadistic scum did this to the two of you?'

Loren nodded silently.

Pitt's teeth were bared, murder glaring out of his opaline green eyes. 'Cyrus here just volunteered to carry Rudi topside.' Pitt casually waved the gun in the direction of Sarason. 'Give her your shirt.'

Loren shook her head. 'I'd rather go nude than wear his sweaty old shirt.'

Sarason knew he could expect a bullet, and fright was slowly replaced by self-preservation. His scheming mind began to focus on a plan to save himself. He sagged to the rock floor as if overcome with shock, his right hand resting on a knee only centimetres away from a .38-calibre derringer strapped to his leg just inside his boot. 'How did you get here?' he asked, stalling.

Pitt was not taken in by the mundane question. 'We came on an underground cruise ship.'

'We?'

'The rest of the team should be surfacing at any moment,' Pitt bluffed.

Amaru suddenly shouted at his two sound, remaining men. 'Rush him!'

They were hardened killers but they had no wish to die. They made no effort to reach for the automatic rifles they had laid aside during the attempt to rape Loren. One look down the barrel of Pitt's .45 beneath the burning eyes was enough to deter anyone who did not cherish suicidal tendencies.

'You yellow dogs!' Amaru snarled.

'Still ordering others to do your dirty work, I see,' said Pitt. 'It appears I made a mistake not killing you in Peru.'

'I vowed then you would suffer as you made me.'

'Don't bet your *Solpemachaco* pension on it.'

'You intend to murder us in cold blood,' said Sarason flatly.

'Not at all. Cold-blooded murder is what you did to Dr Miller and God only knows how many other innocent people who stood in your path. As their avenging angel, I'm here to execute you.'

'Without the decency of a fair trial,' protested Sarason as his hand crept past his knee towards the concealed derringer. Only then did he notice that Pitt's injuries went beyond the bloody gash across the forehead. There was a fatigued droop to the shoulders, an unsteadiness to his stance. The skewed left hand was pressed against his chest. Broken wrist and ribs, Sarason surmised. His hopes rose as he realized that Pitt was on the thin edge of collapse.

'You're hardly one to demand justice,' said Pitt, biting scorn in his tone. 'A pity our great American court system doesn't hand out the same punishment to killers they gave to their victims.'

'And you are not one to judge my actions. If not for my brothers and me, thousands of artifacts would be rotting away in the basements of museums around the world. We preserved the antiquities and redistributed them to people who appreciate their value.'

Pitt stopped his roving gaze and focused on Sarason. 'You call that an excuse? You justify theft and murder on a grand scale so you and your criminal relatives can make fat profits. The magic words for you, pal, are charlatan and hypocrite.'

'Shooting me won't put my family out of business.'

'Haven't you heard?' Pitt grimly smiled. 'Zolar International just went down the toilet. Federal agents raided your facilities in Galveston. They found enough loot to fill a hundred galleries.'

Sarason tilted his head back and laughed. 'Our headquarters in Galveston is a legitimate operation. All merchandise is lawfully bought and sold.'

'I'm talking about the second facility,' Pitt said casually.

A flicker of apprehension showed in Sarason's tan face. 'There is only *one* building.'

'No, there are two. The storage warehouse separated by a tunnel to transport illegal goods to the Zolar building with a subterranean basement housing smuggled antiquities, an art forgery operation, and a vast collection of stolen art.'

Sarason looked as if he'd been struck across the face with a club. 'Damn you to hell, Pitt. How could you know any of this?'

'A pair of federal agents, one from Customs, the other from the FBI described the raid to me in vivid terms. I should also mention that they'll be waiting with open arms when you attempt to smuggle Huascar's treasure into the United States.'

Sarason's fingers were a centimetre (less than half an inch) away from the little twin-barrelled gun. 'Then the joke's on them,' he said, resurrecting his blasé façade. 'The gold isn't going to the United States.'

'No matter,' Pitt said with quiet reserve. 'You won't be around to spend it.'

Hidden by a knee crossed over one leg, Sarason's fingers met and cautiously began slipping the two-shot derringer from his boot. He reckoned that Pitt's injuries would slow any reaction time by a split second, but decided against attempting a snap, wildly aimed shot. If he missed with the first bullet, Sarason well knew that despite Pitt's painful injuries there wouldn't be a chance to fire the second. He hesitated as his mind engineered a diversion. He looked over at Amaru and the two men eyeing Pitt with implacable black anger. Julio was of no use to him.

'You are the one who doesn't have long to live,' he said. 'The Mexican military who assisted us in removing the treasure will have heard your shots and will come bursting in here any minute to cut you down.'

Pitt shrugged. 'They must be on siesta or they'd have been here by now.'

'If we all attacked him at the same time,' Sarason said as conversationally as if they were all seated around a dining table, 'he might kill two or even three of us before the survivor killed him.'

Pitt's expression turned cold and remote. 'The question is, who will be the survivor?'

Amaru did not care who would live or die. His dark mind saw no future without his manhood. He had nothing to lose. His hatred for the man who emasculated him triggered a rage fuelled by the memory of pain and mental agony. Without a word, he launched himself at Pitt.

In a muscled flash of speed, Amaru closed like a snarling dog, reaching out for Pitt's gun hand. The shot took the Peruvian in the chest and through a lung, the report coming like a booming crack. The impact would have stopped the average man, but Amaru was a force beyond himself, driven like a maddened pit bull. He gave an audible grunt as the air was forced from his lungs, and then he crashed into Pitt, sending him reeling backwards towards the river.

A groan burst from Pitt's lips as his cracked ribs protested the collision in a burst of pain. He desperately spun around, throwing off Amaru's encircling grip around his gun hand and hurling him aside. He brought the butt of the Colt down on his assailant's head, but stopped short of a second blow when he spotted the two healthy guards going for their weapons at the edge of his vision.

Through his pain, Pitt's hand instinctively held steady on the Colt. His next bullet dropped the grotesque one-eyed guard with a quick shot to the neck. He ignored the blind Julio and shot the remaining henchman in the centre of his chest.

Pitt heard Loren's scream of warning as if it were far off in the distance. Too late he saw Sarason pointing the derringer at him. His body lagged behind his mind and moved a fraction slowly.

He saw the fire from the muzzle and felt a terrible hammer blow in his left shoulder before he heard the blast. It flung him around, and he went down sprawling in the water with Amaru crawling after him like a wounded bear intent on shredding a disabled fox. The current caught him in its grasp and pulled him from shore. He grabbed desperately at the bottom stones to impede the surge.

Sarason slowly walked to the water's edge and stared at the struggle going on in the river. Amaru had clenched his arms around Pitt's waist and was trying to drag him under the surface. With a callous grin, Sarason took careful aim at Pitt's head. 'A commendable effort, Mr Pitt. You are a very durable man. Odd as it sounds, I will miss you.'

But the *coup de grace* never came. Like black tentacles, a pair of arms circled around Sarason's legs and gripped his ankles. He looked down wildly at the unspeakable thing that was gripping him and began frantically beating at the head that rose between the arms.

Giordino had followed Pitt, drifting down the river. The current had not been as strong as he'd expected upstream from the treasure island and he had been able to painfully drag himself into the shallows unnoticed. He had cursed his helplessness at not being physically able to assist Pitt in fighting off Amaru, but when Sarason unknowingly stepped within reach, Giordino made his move and snagged him.

He ignored the brutal blows to his head. He looked up at Sarason and spoke in a voice that was thick and deep. 'Greetings from hell, butthead.'

Sarason recovered quickly at the sight of Giordino and jerked one foot free to maintain his balance. Because Giordino made no attempt to rise to his feet, Sarason immediately perceived that his enemy was somehow badly injured from the hips down. He viciously kicked Giordino, hitting one thigh. He was rewarded by a sharp groan as Giordino's body jumped in a tormented spasm and he released Sarason's other ankle.

'From past experience,' Sarason said, regaining his composure. 'I should have known you'd be close by.'

He stared briefly at the derringer, knowing he had only one bullet left, but aware there were four or five automatic weapons lying nearby. Then he glanced at Pitt and Amaru who were locked in a death struggle. No need to waste the bullet on Pitt. The river had taken the deadly enemies in its grip and was relentlessly sweeping them downstream. If Pitt somehow survived and staggered from the water, Sarason had an arsenal to deal with him.

Sarason made his choice. He stooped down and aimed the gun's twin barrels between Giordino's eyes.

Loren threw herself at Sarason's back, flinging her arms around him, trying to stop him. Sarason broke her grip as if it were string and shoved her aside without so much as a glance.

She fell heavily on one of the weapons that had been cast aside, lifted it and pulled the trigger. Nothing happened. She didn't know enough about guns to remove the safety. She gave a weak yelp as Sarason reached over and cracked her on the head with the butt of the derringer.

Suddenly he spun around. Gunn, remarkably come to life, had tossed a river stone at Sarason that bounced off his hip with the feeble force of a weakly hit tennis ball.

Sarason shook his head in wonder at the fortitude and courage of people who resisted with such fervour. He almost felt sorry they would all have to die. He turned back to Giordino.

'It seems your reprieve was only temporary,' he said with a sneer, as he held the gun at arm's length straight at Giordino's face.

In spite of the agony of his broken legs and the spectre of death staring him in the face, Giordino looked up at Sarason and grinned venomously. 'Screw you.'

The shot came like a blast from a cannon inside the cavern, followed by the thump sound of lead bursting through living flesh. Giordino's expression went blank as Sarason's eyes gazed at him with a strange confused look. Then Sarason turned and mechanically took two steps on to shore, slowly pitched forward and struck the stone floor in a lifeless heap.

Giordino couldn't believe he was still alive. He looked up and gaped at a little man, dressed like a ranch hand and casually holding a Winchester rifle, who walked into the circle of light.

'Who are you?' asked Giordino.

'Billy Yuma. I came to help my friend.'

Loren, a hand held against her bleeding head, stared at him. 'Friend?'

'The man called Pitt.'

At the mention of his name, Loren pushed herself to her feet and ran unsteadily to the river's edge. 'I don't see him!' she cried fearfully.

Giordino suddenly felt his heart squeeze. He shouted Pitt's name but his voice only echoed in the cavern. 'Oh, God, no,' he muttered fearfully. 'He's gone.'

Gunn grimaced as he sat up and peered downriver into the ominous blackness. Like the others who had calmly faced death only minutes before, he was stricken to find that his old friend had been carried away to his death. 'Maybe Dirk can swim back,' he said hopefully.

Giordino shook his head. 'He can't return. The current is too strong.'

'Where does the river go?' demanded Loren with rising panic.

Giordino pounded his fist in futility and despair against the solid rock. 'The Gulf. Dirk has been swept towards the Sea of Cortez a hundred kilometres away.'

Loren sagged to the limestone floor of the cavern, her hands covering her face as she unashamedly wept. 'He saved me only to die.'

Billy Yuma knelt beside Loren and gently patted her bare shoulder. 'If no one else can, perhaps God will help.'

Giordino was heartsick. No longer feeling his own injuries, he stared into the darkness, his eyes unseeing. 'A hundred kilometres,' he repeated slowly. 'Even God can't keep a man alive with a broken wrist, cracked ribs, and a bullet hole in the shoulder through a hundred kilometres of raging water in total darkness.'

After making everyone as comfortable as he could, Yuma hurried back up to the summit where he told his story. It shamed his relatives into entering the mountain. They fabricated stretchers out of material left by the army engineers and tenderly carried Gunn and Giordino from the river cavern up the passageway. An older man kindly offered a grateful Loren a blanket woven by his wife.

On Giordino's instructions, Gunn and his stretcher were strapped down in the narrow cargo compartment of the stolen NUMA helicopter abandoned by the Zolars. Loren climbed into the copilot's seat as Giordino, his face contorted in torment, was lifted and manoeuvred behind the pilot's controls.

'We'll have to fly this eggbeater together,' Giordino told Loren as the pain in his legs subsided from sheer agony to a throbbing ache. 'You'll have to work the pedals that control the tail rotors.'

'I hope I can do it,' Loren replied nervously.

'Use a gentle touch with your bare feet and we'll be okay.'

Over the helicopter's radio, they alerted Sandecker, who was pacing Starger's office in the Customs Service headquarters, that they were on their way. Giordino and Loren expressed their gratitude to Billy Yuma, his family, and friends, and bade them a warm goodbye. Then Giordino started the turbine engine and let it warm for a minute while he scanned the instruments. With the cyclic stick in neutral, he eased the collective pitch stick to full down and curled the throttle as he gently pushed the stick forward. Then he turned to Loren.

'As soon as we begin to rise in the air, the torque effect will cause our tail to swing left and our nose to the right. Lightly press the left foot pedal to compensate.'

Loren nodded gamely. 'I'll do my best, but I wish I didn't have to do this.'

'We have no choice but to fly out. Rudi would be dead before he could be manhandled down the side of the mountain.'

The helicopter rose very slowly less than a metre off the ground. Giordino let it hang there while Loren learned the feel of the tail rotor control pedals. At first she had a tendency to overcontrol, but she soon got the hang of it and nodded.

'I think I'm ready.'

'Then we're off,' acknowledged Giordino.

Twenty minutes later, working in unison, they made a perfect landing beside the Customs' headquarters building in Calexico where Admiral Sandecker was standing beside a waiting ambulance, anxiously puffing a cigar.

In that first moment when Amaru forced him beneath the water and he could feel the jaws of the current surround

561

his wrecked body, Pitt knew instantly that there was no returning to the treasure cavern. He was doubly trapped – by a killer who hung on to him like a vice and a river determined to carry him to hell.

Even if both men had been uninjured, it would have been no contest. Cutthroat killer that he was, Amaru was no match for Pitt's experience under water. Pitt took a deep breath before the river closed over his head, wrapped his good right arm around his chest to protect his fractured ribs and relaxed amid the pain without wasting his strength in fighting off his attacker.

Amazingly, he still kept his grip on the gun, although to fire it under water would probably have shattered every bone in his hand. He felt Amaru's encircling hold slide from his waist to his hips. The murderer was strong as iron. He clawed at Pitt furiously, still trying for the gun as they spun around in the current like toy dolls caught in a whirlpool.

Neither man could see the other as they swirled into utter darkness. Without the slightest suggestion of light, Pitt felt as though he was submerged in ink.

Amaru's wrath was all that kept him alive in the next forty-five seconds. It did not sink into his crazed mind that he was drowning twice – his bullet-punctured lung was filling with blood while at the same time he was sucking in water. The last of his strength was fading when his thrashing feet made contact with a shoal that was built up from sand accumulating on the outer curve of the river. He came up choking blood and water in a small open gallery and made a blind lunge for Pitt's neck.

But Amaru had nothing left. All fight had ebbed away. Once out of the water he could feel the blood pumping from the wound in his chest.

Pitt found he was able, by a slight effort, to shove Amaru back into the mainstream of the current. He could not see the Peruvian drift away in the pitch blackness, observe the face drained of colour, the eyes glazed in hate and approaching death. But he heard the malevolent voice slowly moving into the distance away from him.

'I said you would suffer,' came the words slightly above a hoarse murmur. 'Now you will languish and die in tormented black solitude.'

'Nothing like being swept up in an orgy of poetic grandeur,' said Pitt icily. 'Enjoy your trip to the Gulf.'

His reply was a cough and a gurgling sound and finally silence.

The pain returned to Pitt with a vengeance. The fire spread from his broken wrist to the bullet wound in his shoulder to his cracked ribs. He was not sure he had the strength left to fight it. Exhaustion slightly softened the agony. He felt more tired than he had ever felt in his life. He crawled on to a dry area of the shoal and slowly crumpled face forward into the soft sand and fell unconscious.

56

'I don't like leaving without Cyrus,' said Oxley as he scanned the desert sky to the southwest.

'Our brother has been in tougher scrapes before,' said Zolar impassively. 'A few Indians from a local village shouldn't present much of a threat to Amaru's hired killers.'

'I expected him long before now.'

'Not to worry. Cyrus will probably show up in Morocco with a girl on each arm.'

They stood on the end of a narrow asphalt airstrip that had been grooved between the countless dunes of the Altar Desert so Mexican Air Force pilots could hold training exercises under primitive conditions. Behind them, with its tail section jutting over the edge of the sandswept strip, a Boeing 747-400 jetliner, painted in the colours of a large national air carrier, sat poised for takeoff.

Zolar moved under the shade of the starboard wing and checked off the artifacts inventoried by Henry and Micki Moore as the Mexican army engineers loaded the final piece on board the aircraft. He nodded at the golden sculpture of a monkey that was being hoisted by a large forklift into the cargo hatch nearly 7 metres (23 feet) from the ground. 'That's the last of it.'

Oxley stared at the barrenness surrounding the airstrip. 'You couldn't have picked a more isolated spot to transship the treasure.'

'We can thank the late Colonel Campos for suggesting it.'

'Any problem with Campos's men since his untimely death?' Oxley asked with more cynicism than sense of loss.

Zolar laughed. 'Certainly not after I gave each of them a one-hundred-ounce bar of gold.'

'You were generous.'

'Hard not to be with so much wealth sitting around.'

'A pity Matos will miss spending his share,' said Oxley.

'Yes, I cried all the way from Cerro el Capirote.'

Zolar's pilot approached and gave an informal salute. 'My crew and I are ready when you are, gentlemen. We would like to take off before it's dark.'

'Is the cargo fastened down securely?' asked Zolar.

The pilot nodded. 'Not the neatest job I've seen. But considering we're not using cargo containers, it should hold until we land at Nador in Morocco, providing we don't hit extreme turbulence.'

'Do you expect any?'

'No, sir. The weather pattern indicates calm skies all the way.'

'Good. We can enjoy a smooth flight,' said Zolar, pleased. 'Remember, at no time are we to cross over the border into the United States.'

'I've laid a course that takes us safely south of Laredo and Brownsville into the Gulf of Mexico below Key West before heading out over the Atlantic.'

'How soon before we touch down in Morocco?' Oxley asked the pilot.

'Our flight plan calls for ten hours and fifty-five minutes. Loaded to the maximum, and then some, with several hundred extra pounds of cargo and a full fuel load, plus the detour south of Texas and Florida, we've added slightly over an hour to our flight time, which I hope to pick up with a tail wind.'

Zolar looked at the last rays of the sun. 'With time changes that should put us in Nador during early afternoon tomorrow.'

The pilot nodded. 'As soon as you are seated aboard, we will get in the air.' He returned to the aircraft and climbed a boarding ladder propped against the forward entry door.

Zolar gestured towards the ladder. 'Unless you've taken a fancy to this sand pit, I see no reason to stand around here any longer.'

Oxley bowed jovially. 'After you.' As they passed through the entry door, he paused and took one last look to the southwest. 'I still don't feel right not waiting.'

'If our positions were reversed, Cyrus wouldn't hesitate to depart. Too much is at stake to delay any longer. Our brother is a survivor. Stop worrying.'

They gave a wave to the Mexican army engineers who stood back from the plane and cheered their benefactors. Then the flight engineer closed and secured the door.

A few minutes later the turbines screamed and the big 747-400 rose above the rolling sand dunes, dipped its starboard wing and banked slightly south of east. Zolar and Oxley sat in a small passenger compartment on the upper deck just behind the cockpit.

'I wonder what happened to the Moores,' mused Oxley, peering through a window at the Sea of Cortez as it receded in the distance. 'The last I saw of them was in the cavern as the last of the treasure was being loaded on a sled.'

'I'll wager Cyrus handled that little problem in concert with Congresswoman Smith and Rudi Gunn,' said Zolar, relaxing for the first time in days. He looked up and smiled at his personal serving lady as she offered two glasses of wine on a tray.

'I know it sounds strange, but I had an uneasy feeling they wouldn't be easy to get rid of.'

'I have to tell you. The same thing crossed Cyrus's mind too. In fact, he thought they were a pair of killers.'

Oxley turned to him. 'The wife too? You're joking.'

'No, I do believe he was serious.' Zolar took a sip of the wine and made an expression of approval and nodded. 'Excellent. A California cabernet from Chateau Montelena. You must try it.'

Oxley took the glass and stared at it. 'I won't feel like

celebrating until the treasure is safely stored in Morocco and we learn that Cyrus has left Mexico.'

Shortly after the aircraft had reached what the brothers believed was cruising altitude, they released their seat belts and stepped into the cargo bay where they began closely examining the incredible golden collection of antiquities. Hardly an hour had passed when Zolar stiffened and looked at his brother queerly.

'Does it feel to you like we're descending?'

Oxley was admiring a golden butterfly that was attached to a golden flower. 'I don't feel anything.'

Zolar was not satisfied. He leaned down and stared through a window at the ground less than 1000 metres (less than 3300 feet) below.

'We're too low!' he said sharply. 'Something is wrong.'

Oxley's eyes narrowed. He looked through an adjoining window. 'You're right. The flaps are down. It looks like we're coming in for a landing. The pilot must have an emergency.'

'Why didn't he alert us?'

At that moment they heard the landing gear drop. The ground was rising to meet them faster now. They flashed past houses and railroad tracks, and then the aircraft was over the end of the runway. The wheels thumped on to concrete and the engines howled in reverse thrust. The pilot stood on the brakes and soon eased off on the throttles as he turned the huge craft on to a taxiway.

A sign on the terminal read Welcome to El Paso.

Oxley stared speechless as Zolar blurted, 'My God, we've come down in the United States!'

He ran forward and began beating frantically on the cockpit door. There was no reply until the huge plane came to a halt outside an Air National Guard hangar at the opposite end of the field. Only then did the cockpit door slowly crack open.

'What in hell are you doing? I'm ordering you to get

back in the air immediately – ' Zolar's words froze in his throat as he found himself staring down the muzzle of a gun pointed between his eyes.

The pilot was still seated in his seat, as were the copilot and flight engineer. Henry Moore stood in the doorway gripping a strange nine-millimetre automatic of his own design, while inside the cockpit Micki Moore was talking over the aircraft radio as she calmly aimed a Lilliputian .25-calibre automatic at the pilot's neck.

'Forgive the unscheduled stop, my former friends,' said Moore in a commanding voice neither Zolar nor Oxley had heard before, 'but as you can see there's been a change of plan.'

Zolar squinted down the gun barrel, and his face twisted from shock to menacing anger. 'You idiot, you blind idiot, do you have any idea what you've done?'

'Why, yes,' Moore answered matter-of-factly. 'Micki and I have hijacked your aircraft and its cargo of golden artifacts. I believe you're aware of the old maxim: There is no honour among thieves.'

'If you don't get this plane in the air quickly,' Oxley pleaded, 'Customs agents will be swarming all over it.'

'Now that you mention it, Micki and I did entertain the idea of turning the artifacts over to the authorities.'

'You can't know what you're saying.'

'Oh, I most certainly do, Charley, old pal. As it turns out, federal agents are more interested in you and your brother than Huascar's treasure.'

'Where did you come from?' Zolar demanded.

'We merely caught a ride in one of the helicopters transporting the gold. The army engineers were used to our presence and paid no attention as we climbed aboard the plane. We hid out in one of the restrooms until the pilot left to confer with you and Charles on the airstrip. Then we seized the cockpit.'

'Why would federal agents take your word for anything?' asked Oxley.

'In a manner of speaking, Micki and I were once agents ourselves,' Moore briefly explained. 'After we took over the cockpit, Micki radioed some old friends in Washington who arranged your reception.'

Zolar looked as if he were about to tear Moore's lungs out whether he got shot in the attempt or not. 'You and your lying wife made a deal for a share of the antiquities. Am I right?' He waited for a reply, but when Moore remained silent he went on. 'What percentage did they offer you? Ten, twenty, maybe as high as fifty per cent?'

'We made no deals with the government,' Moore said slowly. 'We knew you had no intention of honouring our agreement, and that you planned to kill us. We had planned to steal the treasure for ourselves, but as you can see, we had a change of heart.'

'The way they act familiar with guns,' said Oxley, 'Cyrus was right. They *are* a pair of killers.'

Moore nodded in agreement. 'Your brother has an inner eye. It takes an assassin to know one.'

A pounding came from outside the forward passenger door on the deck below. Moore gestured down the stair-well with his gun. 'Go down and open it,' he ordered Zolar and Oxley.

Sullenly, they did as they were told.

When the pressurized door was swung open, two men entered from a stairway that had been pushed up against the aircraft. Both wore business suits. One was a huge black man who looked as if he might have played professional football. The other was a nattily dressed white man. Zolar immediately sensed they were federal agents.

'Joseph Zolar and Charles Oxley, I am Agent David Gaskill with the Customs Service and this is Agent Francis Ragsdale of the FBI. You gentlemen are under arrest for smuggling illegal artifacts into the United States and for the theft of countless art objects from private and public museums, not excluding the unlawful forgery and sale of antiquities.'

'What are you talking about?' Zolar demanded.

Gaskill ignored him and looked at Ragsdale with a big toothy smile. 'Would you like to do the honours?'

Ragsdale nodded like a kid who had just been given a new disc player. 'Yes, indeed, thank you.'

As Gaskill cuffed Zolar and Oxley, Ragsdale read them their rights.

'You made good time,' said Moore. 'We were told you were in Calexico.'

'We were on our way aboard a military jet fifteen minutes after word came down from FBI headquarters in Washington,' replied Ragsdale.

Oxley looked at Gaskill, a look for the first time empty of fear and shock, a sudden look of shrewdness. 'You'll never find enough evidence to convict us in a hundred years.'

Ragsdale tilted his head towards the golden cargo. 'What do you call that?'

'We're merely passengers,' said Zolar, regaining his composure. 'We were invited along for the ride by Professor Moore and his wife.'

'I see. And suppose you tell me where all the stolen art and antiquities in your facility in Galveston came from?'

Oxley sneered. 'Our Galveston warehouse is perfectly legitimate. You've raided it before and never found a thing.'

'If that's the case,' said Ragsdale craftily, 'how do you explain the tunnel leading from the Logan Storage Company to Zolar International's subterranean warehouse of stolen goods?'

The brothers stared at each other, their faces abruptly grey. 'You're making this up,' said Zolar fearfully.

'Am I? Would you like me to describe your tunnel in detail and provide a brief rundown on the stolen masterworks we found?'

'The tunnel – you couldn't have found the tunnel.'

'As of thirty-six hours ago,' said Gaskill, 'Zolar International and your clandestine operation known as *Solpe-machaco* are permanently out of business.'

Ragsdale added. 'A pity your dad, Mansfield Zolar, aka the Spectre, isn't still alive or we could bust him too.'

Zolar looked as if he were in the throes of cardiac arrest. Oxley appeared too paralysed to move.

'By the time you two and the rest of your family, partners, associates, and buyers get out of prison, you'll be as old as the artifacts you stole.'

Federal agents began filling the aircraft. The FBI took charge of the air crew and Zolar's serving lady while the Customs people unbuckled the tiedown straps securing the golden artifacts. Ragsdale nodded to his team.

'Take them downtown to the US Attorney's office.'

As soon as the shattered and thoroughly broken art thieves were led into two different cars, the agents turned to the Moores.

'I can't tell you how grateful we are for your cooperation,' said Gaskill. 'Nailing the Zolar family will put a huge dent in the art theft and artifact smuggling trade.'

'We're not entirely benevolent,' said Micki happily relieved. 'Henry feels certain the Peruvian government will post a reward.'

Gaskill nodded. 'I think you've got a sure bet.'

'The prestige of being the first to catalogue and photograph the treasure will go a long way towards enhancing our scientific reputations,' Henry Moore explained as he holstered his gun.

'Customs would also like a detailed report on the objects, if you don't mind?' asked Gaskill.

Moore nodded vigorously. 'Micki and I will be happy to work with you. We've already inventoried the treasure. We'll have a report for you before it's formally returned to Peru.'

'Where will you store it all until then?' asked Micki.

'In a government warehouse whose location we can't reveal,' answered Gaskill.

'Is there any news on Congresswoman Smith and the little man with NUMA?'

Gaskill nodded. 'Minutes before you landed we received word they were rescued by a local tribe of Indians and are on their way to a local hospital.'

Micki sank down into a passenger seat and sighed. 'Then it's over.'

Henry sat on an armrest and took her hand in his. 'It is for us,' he said gently. 'From now on we'll live the rest of our lives together as a pair of old teachers in a university with vine-covered walls.'

She looked up at him. 'Is that so terrible?'

'No,' he said, kissing her lightly on the forehead, 'I think we can handle it.'

57

Slowly climbing from the depths of a dead stupor, Pitt felt as if he were struggling up a mud-slick slope, only to slip back every time he reached out and touched consciousness. He tried to retain a grip on these brief moments of awareness, only to fall back into a void. If he could open his eyes, he thought vaguely, he might return to reality. Finally, with a mighty effort, he forced open his eyelids.

Seeing only grave-cold blackness, he shook his head in despair, thinking he had fallen back into the void. And then the pain came rushing back like a burst of fire, and he came fully awake. Rolling sideways and then forward into a sitting position, he swung his head from side to side, trying to shade off the fog that clung to the alcoves of his mind. He renewed his fight with the pounding ache in his shoulder, the stiff hurt in his chest, and the sting from his wrist. Tenderly he felt the gash on his forehead.

'A hell of a fine specimen of manhood you are,' he muttered.

Pitt was surprised to find that he didn't feel overly weak from loss of blood. He unclipped from his forearm the flashlight that Giordino had given him after their drop over the falls, switched it on, and propped it in the sand so the beam was aimed at his upper torso. He unzipped his wet suit jacket and tenderly probed the wound in his shoulder. The bullet had passed through the flesh and out his back without striking the scapula or the clavicle. The neoprene rubber on his shredded but still nearly skintight wet suit had helped seal the opening and restrict the flow of blood. Relieved that he did not feel as drained as he thought he would, he relaxed and took stock of his situation. His chances of survival were somewhere beyond impossible. With 100 kilometres (62 miles) of unknown rapids, sharp cascades, and extensive river passages that passed through caverns completely immersed with water, he did not need a palmist to tell him that the life line running across his hand would halt long before he reached senior citizenship. Even if he had air passages the entire way, there was still the distance from the opening of the subterranean channel to the surface of the Gulf.

Most other men who found themselves in a Hades of darkness deep within the earth with no hope of escape would have panicked and died tearing their fingers to the bone in a vain attempt to claw their way to the surface. But Pitt was not afraid. He was curiously content and at peace with himself.

If he was going to die, he thought, he might as well get comfortable. With his good hand he dug indentations in the sand to accommodate his body contour. He was surprised when the flashlight beam reflected from a thousand golden specks in the black sand. He held up a handful under the light.

'This place is loaded with placer gold,' he said to himself.

He shone the light around the cavern. The walls were cut with ledges of white quartz streaked with tiny veins of gold. Pitt began laughing as he saw humour in the implausibility of it all.

'A gold mine,' he proclaimed to the silent cave. 'I've made a fabulously rich gold strike and nobody will ever know it.'

He sat back and contemplated his discovery. Someone must be telling him something, he thought. Just because he wasn't afraid of the old man with the scythe didn't mean he had to give up and wait for him. A stubborn resolve sparked within him.

Better to enter the great beyond after an audacious attempt at staying alive than to throw in the towel and go out like a dishrag, he concluded. Perhaps other adventurous explorers would give up everything they owned for the honour of entering this mineralogical sanctum sanctorum, but all Pitt wanted now was to get out. He rose to his feet, inflated the buoyancy compensator with his breath and walked into the water until he was adrift in the current that carried him along.

Just take it one cavern at a time, he told himself, flashing the light on the water ahead. There was no relying on eternal vigilance. He was too weak to fight rapids and fend off rocks; he could only be calm and go wherever the current took him. He soon felt as if he had been cruising from one gallery to another for a lifetime.

The roof of the caverns and galleries rose and fell with monotonous regularity for the next 10 kilometres (12.4 miles). Then he heard the dreaded rumble of approaching rapids. Thankfully, the first chute Pitt encountered was of medium roughness. The water crashed against his face and he went under churning froth several times before reaching placid water again.

He was granted a comfortable reprieve as the river turned smooth and ran through one long canyon in an immense gallery. When he reached the end nearly an hour later, the roof gradually sloped down until it touched the water. He filled his lungs to the last crowded millimetre and dived. Able to use only one arm and missing his swim fins, the going was slow. He aimed the flashlight at the jagged rock roof and swam on his back. His lungs began to protest the lack of oxygen, but he swam on. At last the light revealed an air pocket. He shot to the surface and mightily inhaled the pure, unpolluted air that had been trapped deep beneath the earth millions of years ago.

The small cave widened into a large cavern whose ceiling arched beyond the beam of the flashlight. The river made a sweeping turn where it had formed a reef of polished gravel. Pitt crawled painfully on to the dry area to rest. He turned off the light to prolong the life of the batteries.

Abruptly, he flicked the flash on again. Something had caught his eye in the shadows before the light blinked out. Something was there, not 5 metres (16 feet) away, a black form that revealed a straight line aberrant to natural geometrics.

Pitt's spirits soared as he recognized the battered remains of the *Wallowing Windbag*. Incredibly, the Hovercraft had come through the horrific fall over the cataract and had been cast up here after drifting nearly 40 kilometres. At last a gleam of hope. He stumbled across the gravel beach to the rubber hull and examined it under his light.

The engine and fan had been torn from their mountings and were missing. Two of the air chambers were punctured and deflated, but the remaining six still held firm. Some of the equipment was swept away, but four air tanks, the first-aid kit, Duncan's plastic ball of coloured water dye tracer, one of Giordino's paddles, two extra flashlights, and the waterproof container with Admiral Sandecker's thermos of coffee and four bologna sandwiches had miraculously survived.

'It seems my state of affairs has considerably improved,' Pitt said happily to nobody but the empty cavern.

He began with the first-aid kit. After liberally soaking the shoulder wound with disinfectant, he awkwardly applied a crude bandage on it inside his tattered wet suit. Knowing it was useless to bind fractured ribs, he gritted his teeth, set his wrist and taped it.

The coffee had retained most of its heat inside the thermos, and he downed half of it before attacking the sandwiches. No medium-rare porterhouse steak, doused and flamed in cognac, tasted better than this bologna, Pitt decided. Then and there he vowed never to complain or make jokes about bologna sandwiches ever again.

After a brief rest, a goodly measure of his strength returned and he felt refreshed enough to resecure the equipment and break open Duncan's plastic dye container. He scattered Fluorescein Yellow with Optical Brightener

576

into the water. Under the beam of his flashlight he watched until the dye stained the river with a vivid yellow luminescence. He stood and watched until the current swept it out of sight.

'That should tell them I'm coming,' he thought aloud.

He pushed the remains of the Hovercraft out of the shallows. Favouring his injuries, he awkwardly climbed aboard and paddled one-handed into the mainstream.

As the partially deflated *Wallowing Windbag* caught the current and drifted downriver, Pitt leaned back comfortably and began humming the tune to 'Up a Lazy River in the Noonday Sun.'

58

Informed of up-to-the-minute events from California by Admiral Sandecker and agents Gaskill and Ragsdale in El Paso, the secretary of state decided to sidestep diplomatic protocol and personally call the President of Mexico. He briefed him on the far-reaching theft and smuggling conspiracy engineered by the Zolars.

'An incredible story,' said Mexico's President.

'But true,' the secretary of state assured him.

'I can only regret the incident occurred, and I promise my government's full cooperation with the investigation.'

'If you'll forgive me, Mr President, I *do* have a wish list of requests.'

'Let's hear them.'

Within two hours the border between Mexico and California was reopened. The government officials who were suckered by the Zolars into jeopardizing their positions by false promises of incredible riches were rounded up.

Fernando Matos and Police Comandante Rafael Cortina were among the first to be arrested by Mexican Justice investigators.

At the same time, vessels of the Mexican navy attached to the Sea of Cortez were alerted and ordered to sea.

Lieutenant Carlos Hidalgo peered up at a squawking gull before turning his attention back to the straight line of the sea across the horizon. 'Are we searching for anything special, or just searching?' he casually asked his ship's captain.

'Looking for bodies,' Commander Miguel Maderas

replied. He lowered his binoculars, revealing a round, friendly face under long, thick black hair. His teeth were large and very white and almost always set in a Burt Lancaster smile. He was short and heavy and solid as a rock.

Hidalgo was a sharp contrast to Maderas. Tall and lean with a narrow face, he looked like a well-tanned cadaver. 'Victims of a boating accident?'

'No, divers who drowned in an underground river.'

Hidalgo's eyes narrowed sceptically. 'Not another gringo folktale about fishermen and divers being swept under the desert and disgorged into the Gulf?'

'Who is to say?' Maderas replied with a shrug. 'All I know is that orders from our fleet headquarters in Ensenada directed our ship and crew to patrol the waters on the northern end of the Gulf between San Felipe and Puerto Penasco for any sign of bodies.'

'A large area for only one ship to cover.'

'We'll be joined by two Class P patrol boats out of Santa Rosalía, and all fishing boats in the area have been alerted to report any sighting of human remains.'

'If the sharks get them,' Hildago muttered pessimistically, 'there won't be anything left to find.'

Maderas leaned back against the railing of the bridge wing, lit a cigarette, and gazed towards the stern of his patrol vessel. It had been modified from a 67-metre (220-foot) US Navy minesweeper and had no official name other than the big G-21 painted on the bow. But the crew unaffectionately called her *El Porquería* ('piece of trash') because she once broke down at sea and was towed to port by a fishing boat – a humiliation the crew never forgave her for.

But she was a sturdy ship, quick to answer the helm, and stable in heavy seas. The crews of more than one fishing boat and private yacht owed their lives to Maderas and *El Porquería*.

As executive officer of the ship, Hidalgo had the duty of

plotting a search grid. When he was finished poring over a large nautical chart of the northern Gulf, he gave the coordinates to the helmsman. Then the dreary part of the voyage began, ploughing down one lane and then reversing course as if mowing a lawn.

The first line was run at eight o'clock in the morning. At two o'clock in the afternoon a lookout on the bow yelled out.

'Object in the water!'

'Whereaway?' shouted Hildago.

'A hundred and fifty metres off the port bow.'

Maderas lifted his binoculars and peered over the blue-green water. He easily spotted a body floating face down as it rose on the crest of a wave. 'I have it.' He stepped to the wheelhouse door and nodded at the helmsman. 'Bring us alongside and have a crew stand by to retrieve.' Then he turned to Hildago. 'Stop engines when we close to fifty metres.'

The foaming bow wave faded to a gentle ripple, the heavy throb of the twin diesels died to a muted rumble as the patrol vessel slipped alongside the body rolling in the waves. From his view on the bridge wing, Maderas could see the bloated and distorted features had been battered to pulp. Small wonder the sharks didn't find it appetizing, he thought.

He stared at Hidalgo and smiled. 'We didn't need a week after all.'

'We got lucky,' Hidalgo mumbled.

With no hint of reverence for the dead, two crewmen jabbed a boat hook into the floating corpse and pulled it towards a stretcher, constructed from wire mesh, that was lowered into the water. The body was guided into the stretcher and raised on to the deck. The ghastly, mangled flesh barely resembled what had once been a human being. Maderas could hear more than one of his crew retching into the sea before the corpse was zipped into a body bag.

'Well, at least whoever he was did us a favour,' said Hidalgo.

Maderas looked at him. 'Oh, and what was that?'

Hidalgo grinned unfeelingly. 'He wasn't in the water long enough to smell.'

Three hours later, the patrol vessel entered the breakwater of San Felipe and tied up alongside the *Alhambra*.

As Pitt had suspected, after reaching shore in the life raft, Gordo Padilla and his crew had gone home to their wives and girlfriends and celebrated their narrow escape by taking a three-day siesta. Then, under the watchful eye of Cortina's police, Padilla rounded everyone up and hitched a ride on a fishing boat back to the ferry. Once on board they raised steam in the engines and pumped out the water taken on when Amaru opened the seacocks. When her keel was unlocked by the silt and her engines were fired to life, Padilla and his crew sailed the *Alhambra* back to San Felipe and tied her to the dock.

To Maderas and Hidalgo, looking down from their bridge, the forward car deck of the ferry looked like the accident ward of a hospital.

Loren Smith was comfortably dressed in shorts and halter top and exhibited her bruises and a liberal assortment of small bandages over her bare shoulders, midriff, and legs Giordino sat in a wheelchair with both legs propped ahead of him in plaster casts

Missing was Rudi Gunn, who was in stable condition in the El Centro Regional Medical Centre just north of Calexico, after having survived a badly bruised stomach, six broken fingers, and a hairline fracture of the skull.

Admiral Sandecker and Peter Duncan, the hydrologist, also stood on the deck of the ferryboat, along with Shannon Kelsey, Miles Rodgers, and a contingent of local police and the Baja California Norte state coroner. Their faces were grim as the crew of the navy patrol ship lowered the stretcher containing the body on to the *Alhambra*'s deck.

Before the coroner and his assistant could lift the body bag on to a gurney, Giordino pushed his wheelchair up to the stretcher. 'I would like to see the body,' he said grimly.

'He is not a pretty sight, señor,' Hidalgo warned him from the deck of his ship.

The coroner hesitated, not sure if under the law he could permit foreigners to view a dead body.

Giordino stared coldly at the coroner. 'Do you want an identification or not?'

The coroner, a little man with bleary eyes and a great bush of grey hair, barely knew enough English to understand Giordino, but he nodded silently to his assistant who pulled down the zipper.

Loren paled and turned away, but Sandecker moved close beside Giordino.

'Is it . . .'

Giordino shook his head. 'No, it's not Dirk. It's that psycho creep, Tupac Amaru.'

'Good lord, he looks as if he was churned through an empty cement mixer.'

'Almost as bad,' said Duncan, shuddering at the ghastly sight. 'The rapids must have beat him against every rock between here and Cerro el Capirote.'

'Couldn't happen to a nicer guy,' Giordino muttered acidly.

'Somewhere between the treasure cavern and the Gulf,' said Duncan, 'the river must erupt into a rampage.'

'No sign of another body?' Sandecker asked Hidalgo.

'Nothing, señor. This is the only one we found, but we have orders to continue the search for the second man.'

Sandecker turned away from Amaru. 'If Dirk hasn't been cast out into the Gulf by now, he must still be underground.'

'Maybe he was washed up on a beach or a sandbank,' offered Shannon hopefully. 'He might still be alive.'

'Can't you launch an expedition down the subterranean river to find him?' Rodgers asked the admiral.

Sandecker shook his head slowly. 'I won't send a team of men to certain death.'

'The admiral is right,' said Giordino. 'There could be a dozen cascades like the one Pitt and I went over. Even with a Hovercraft like the *Wallowing Windbag*, it's extremely doubtful anyone can gain safe passage through a hundred kilometres of water peppered with rapids and rocks.'

'If that isn't enough,' added Duncan, 'there's the submerged caverns to get through before surfacing in the Gulf. Without an ample air supply, drowning would be inescapable.'

'How far do you think he might drift?' Sandecker asked him.

'From the treasure chamber?'

'Yes.'

Duncan thought a moment. 'Pitt might have a chance if he managed to reach a dry shore within five hundred metres. We could tie a man on a guideline and safely send him downstream that far, and then pull them back against the current.'

'And if no sign of Pitt is found before the guideline runs out?' asked Giordino.

Duncan shrugged solemnly. 'Then if his body doesn't surface in the Gulf, we'll never find him.'

'Is there any hope for Dirk?' Loren pleaded. 'Any hope at all?'

Duncan looked from Giordino to Sandecker before answering. All eyes reflected abject hopelessness and their faces were etched with despair. He turned back to Loren and said gently, 'I can't lie to you, Miss Smith.' The words appeared to cause him great discomfort. 'Dirk's chances are as good as any badly injured man's of reaching Lake Mead outside of Las Vegas after being cast adrift in the Colorado River at the entrance to the Grand Canyon.'

The words came like a physical blow to Loren. She began to sway on her feet. Giordino reached out and grabbed her arm. It seemed that her heart stopped, and she whispered, 'To me, Dirk Pitt will never die.'

'The fish are a little shy today,' said Joe Hagen to his wife, Claire.

She was lying on her belly on the roof of the boat's main cabin, barely wearing a purple bikini with the halter untied, reading a magazine. She pushed her sunglasses on top of her head and laughed. 'You couldn't catch a fish if it jumped up and landed in the boat.'

He laughed. 'Just wait and see.'

'The only fish you'll find this far north in the Gulf is shrimp,' she nagged.

The Hagens were in their early sixties and in reasonably good shape. As with most women her age, Claire's bottom had spread and her waist carried a little flab, but her face was fairly free of wrinkles and her breasts were still large and firm. Joe was a big man who fought a losing battle with a paunch that had grown into a well-rounded stomach. Together they ran a family auto dealership in Anaheim specializing in clean, low-mileage used cars.

After Joe bought a 15-metre (50-foot) oceangoing ketch, and named it *The First Attempt*, out of Newport Beach, California, they began leaving the management of their business to their two sons. They liked to sail down the coast and around Cabo San Lucas into the Sea of Cortez, spending the fall months cruising back and forth between picturesque ports nestled on the shores.

This was the first time they had sailed this far north. As he lazily trolled for whatever fish took a fancy to his bait, Joe kept half an eye on the fathometer as he idled along on the engine with the sails furled. The tides at this end of the Gulf could vary as much as 7 metres (23 feet) and he didn't want to run on an uncharted sandbar.

He relaxed as the stylus showed a depression under the keel to be over 50 metres (164 feet) deep. A puzzling feature, he thought. The seafloor on the north end of the

Gulf was uniformly shallow, seldom going below 10 metres at high tide. The bottom was usually a mixture of silt and sand. The fathometer read the underwater depression as uneven hard rock.

'Aha, they laughed at all the great geniuses,' said Joe as he felt a tug on his trolling line. He reeled it in and discovered a California corbina about the length of his arm on the hook.

Claire shaded her eyes with one hand. 'He's too pretty to keep. Throw the poor thing back.'

'That's odd.'

'What's odd?'

'All the other corbinas I've ever caught had dark spots on a white body. This sucker is coloured like a fluorescent canary.'

She adjusted her halter and came astern to have a closer look at his catch.

'Now this is really weird,' said Joe, holding up one hand and displaying palm and fingers that were stained a bright yellow. 'If I weren't a sane man, I'd say somebody dyed this fish.'

'He sparkles under the sun as if his scales were spangles,' said Claire.

Joe peered over the side of the boat. 'The water in this one particular area looks like it was squeezed out of a lemon.'

'Could be a good fishing hole.'

'You may be right, old girl.' Joe moved past her to the bow and threw out the anchor. 'This looks as good a place as any to spend the afternoon angling for a big one.'

59

There was no rest for the weary. Pitt went over four more cataracts. Providentially, none had a steep, yawning drop like the one that almost killed him and Giordino. The steepest drop he encountered was 2 metres (6.5 feet). The partially deflated *Wallowing Windbag* bravely plunged over the sharp ledge and successfully ran an obstacle course through rocks hiding under roaring sheets of froth and spray before continuing her voyage to oblivion.

It was the boiling stretches of rapids that proved brutal. Only after they extracted their toll in battering torment could Pitt relax for a short time in the forgiving, unobstructed stretches of calm water that followed. The bruising punishment made his wounds feel as if they were being stabbed by little men with pitchforks. But the pain served a worthy purpose by sharpening his senses. He cursed the river, certain it was saving the worst for last before smashing his desperate gamble to escape.

The paddle was torn from his hand, but it proved a small loss. With 50 kilograms (110 pounds) of equipment in a collapsing boat in addition to him, it was useless to attempt a sharp course change to dodge rocks that loomed up in the dark, especially while trying to paddle with one arm. He was too weak to do little more than feebly grasp the support straps attached to the interior of the hull and let the current take him where it might.

Two more float cells were ruptured after colliding with sharp rocks that sliced through the thin skin of the hull, and Pitt found himself lying half-covered with water in what had become little more than a collapsed air bag. Surprisingly, he kept a death grip on the flashlight with his right hand. But he had completely drained three of the air tanks and most of the fourth while dragging the sagging little vessel through several fully submerged galleries before reaching open caverns on the other side and reinflating the remaining float cells.

Pitt never suffered from claustrophobia but it would have come easy for most people in the black never-ending void. He avoided any thoughts of panic by singing and talking to himself during his wild ride through the unfriendly water. He shone the light on his hands and feet. They were shrivelled like prunes after the long hours of immersion.

'With all this water, dehydration is the least of my problems,' he muttered to the dank, uncaring rock.

He floated over transparent pools that dropped down shafts of solid rock so deep the beam of his lamp could not touch bottom. He toyed with the thought of tourists coming through this place. A pity people can't take the tour and view these crystallized Gothic caverns, he thought. Perhaps now that the river was known to exist, a tunnel might be excavated to bring in visitors to study the geological marvels.

He had tried to conserve his three flashlights, but one by one their batteries gave out and he dropped them over the side. He estimated that only twenty minutes of light remained in his last lamp before the Stygian gloom returned for good.

Running rapids in a raft under the sun and blue sky is called white-water rafting, his exhausted mind deliberated. Down here they could call it black-water rafting. The idea sounded very funny and for some reason he laughed. His laughter carried into a vast side chamber, echoing in a hundred eerie sounds. If he hadn't known it came from him, it would have curdled his blood.

It no longer seemed possible that there could be any place but this nightmare maze of caverns creeping tortuously end on end through such an alien environment.

He had lost all sense of direction. 'Bearings' was only a word from a dictionary. His compass was made useless by an abundance of iron ore in the rock. He felt so disoriented and removed from the surface world above that he wondered if he had finally crossed the threshold into lunacy. The only breath of sanity was fuelled by the stupendous sights revealed by the light from his lamp.

He forced himself to regain control by playing mind games. He tried to memorize details of each new cavern and gallery, of each bend and turn of the river, so he could describe them to others after he escaped to sunlight. But there were so many of them his numbed mind found it impossible to retain more than a few vivid images. Not only that, he found he had to concentrate on keeping the *Windbag* afloat. Another float cell was hissing its buoyancy away through a puncture.

How far have I come? he wondered dully. How much farther to the end? His fogged mind was wandering. He had to get a grip on himself. He was beyond hunger; no thoughts of thick steaks or prime rib with a bottle of beer flooded through his mind. His battered and spent body had given far more than he expected from it.

The shrunken hull of the Hovercraft struck the cavern's roof which arched downward into the water. The craft revolved in circles, bumping against the rock until it worked off to one side of the mainstream of the river and gently grounded on a shoal. Pitt lay in the pool that half-filled the interior, his legs dangling over the sides, too played out to don the last air tank, deflate the craft, and convey it through the flooded gallery ahead.

He couldn't pass out. Not now. He had too far to go. He took several deep breaths and drank a small amount of water. He groped for the thermos, untied it from a hook and finished the last of the coffee. The caffeine helped revive him a bit. He flipped the thermos into the river and watched it float against the rock, too buoyant to drift through to the other side.

The lamp was so weak it barely threw a beam. He switched it off to save what little juice was left in the batteries, lay back, and stared into the suffocating blackness.

Nothing hurt anymore. His nerve endings had shut down and his body was numb. He must have been almost two pints low on blood, he figured. He hated to face the thought of failure. For a few minutes he refused to believe he couldn't make it back to the world above. The faithful *Wallowing Windbag* had taken him this far, but if it lost one more float cell he would have to abandon it and carry on alone. He began concentrating his waning energies on the effort that still lay ahead.

Something jogged his memory. He smelled something. What was it they said about smells? They can trigger past events in your mind. He breathed in deeply, trying not to let the scent get away before he could recall why it was so familiar. He licked his lips and recognized a taste that hadn't been there before. Salt. And then it washed over him.

The smell of the sea.

He had finally reached the end of the subterranean river system that climaxed in the Gulf.

Pitt popped open his eyes and raised his hand until it almost touched the tip of his nose. He couldn't distinguish detail, but there was a vague shadow that shouldn't have been there in the eternal dark of his subterranean world. He stared down into the water and detected a murky reflection. Light was seeping in from the passage ahead.

The discovery that daylight was within reach raised immensely his hopes of surviving.

He climbed out of the *Wallowing Windbag* and considered the two worst hazards he now faced – length of dive to the surface and decompression. He checked the pressure gauge that ran from the manifold of the air tank. Eight hundred fifty pounds per square inch. Enough air for a run of maybe 300 metres (984 feet), providing he stayed calm, breathed easily, and didn't exert himself. If surface air was much beyond that, he wouldn't have to worry about the other problem, decompression. He'd drown long before acquiring the notorious bends.

Periodic checks of his depth gauge during his long journey had told him the pressure inside most of the air-filled caverns ran only slightly higher than the outside atmospheric pressure. A concern but not a great fear. And he had seldom exceeded 30 metres of depth when diving under a flooded overhang that divided two open galleries. If faced with the same situation, he would have to be careful to make a controlled 18-metre- (60-foot-) per-minute ascent to avoid decompression sickness.

Whatever the obstacles, he could neither go back nor stay where he was. He had to go on. There was no other decision to make. This would be the final test of what little strength and resolve was still left in him.

He wasn't dead yet. Not until he breathed the last tiny bit of oxygen in his air tank. And then he would go on until his lungs burst.

He checked to see that the manifold valves were open and the low-pressure hose was connected to his buoyancy compensator. Next, he strapped on his tank and buckled the quick-release snaps. A quick breath to be sure his regulator was functioning properly and he was ready.

Without his lost dive mask, his vision would be blurred, but all he had to do was swim towards the light. He clamped his teeth on the mouthpiece of his breathing regulator, gathered his nerve, and counted to three.

It was time to go, and he dived into the river for the last time.

As he gently kicked his bare feet he'd have given his soul for his lost fins. Down, down the overhang sloped ahead of him. He passed thirty metres, then forty. He began to worry after he passed fifty metres. When diving on compressed air, there is an invisible barrier between sixty and eighty metres. Beyond that a diver begins to feel like a drunk and loses control of his mental faculties.

His air tank made an unearthly screeching sound as it scraped against the rock above him. Because he had dropped his weight belt after his near-death experience over the great waterfall, and because of the neoprene in his shredded wet suit, he was diving with positive buoyancy. He doubled over and dived deeper to avoid the contact.

Pitt thought the plunging rock would never end. His depth gauge read 75 metres (246 feet) before the current carried him beneath and around the tip of the overhang. Now the upward slope was gradual. Not the ideal situation. He'd have preferred a direct ascent to the surface to cut the distance and save his dwindling air supply.

The light grew steadily brighter until he could read the numbers of his dive watch without the aid of the dying beam from the lamp. The hands on the orange dial read ten minutes after five o'clock. Was it early morning or afternoon? How long since he dived into the river? He couldn't remember if it was ten minutes or fifty. His mind sluggishly puzzled over the answers.

The clear, transparent emerald green of the river water turned more blue and opaque. The current was fading and his ascent slowed. There was a distant shimmer above him. At last the surface itself appeared.

He was in the Gulf. He had exited the river passage and was swimming in the Sea of Cortez. Pitt looked up and saw a shadow looming far in the distance. One final check of his air pressure gauge. The needle quivered on zero. His air was almost gone.

Rather than suck in a huge gulp, he used what little was left to partially inflate his buoyancy compensator so it would gently lift him to the surface if he blacked out from lack of oxygen.

One last inhalation that barely puffed out his lungs and he relaxed, exhaling small breaths to compensate for the declining pressure as he rose from the depths. The hiss of his air bubbles leaving the regulator diminished as his lungs ran dry.

The surface appeared so close he could reach out and touch it when his lungs began to burn. It was a spiteful illusion. The waves were still 20 metres (66 feet) away.

He put some strength into his kick as a huge elastic band seemed to tighten around his chest. Soon, the desire for air became his only world as darkness started seeping around the edges of his eyes.

Pitt became entangled in something that hindered his ascent. His vision, blurred without a dive mask, failed to distinguish what was binding him. Instinctively, he thrashed clumsily in an attempt to free himself. A great roaring sound came from inside his brain as it screamed in protest. But in that instant before blackness shut down his mind, he sensed that his body was being pulled towards the surface.

'I've hooked a big one!' shouted Joe Hagen joyously.

'You got a marlin?' Claire asked excitedly, seeing her husband's fishing pole bent like a question mark.

'He's not giving much fight for a marlin,' Joe panted as he feverishly turned the crank on his reel. 'Feels more like a dead weight.'

'Maybe you dragged him to death.'

'Get the gaff. He's almost to the surface.'

Claire snatched a long-handled gaff from two hooks and pointed it over the side of the yacht like a spear. 'I see something,' she cried. 'It looks big and black.'

Then she screamed in horror.

Pitt was a millimetre away from unconsciousness when his head broke into a trough between the waves. He spat out his regulator and drew in a deep breath. The sun's reflection on the water blinded eyes that hadn't seen light in almost two days. He squinted rapturously at the sudden kaleidoscope of colours.

Relief, joy of living, fulfilment of a great accomplishment – they flooded together.

A woman's scream pierced his ears and he looked up, startled to see the Capri-blue hull of a yacht rising beside him and two people staring over the side, their faces pale as death. It was then that he realized he was entangled in fishing line. Something slapped against his leg. He gripped the line and pulled a small skipjack tuna, no longer than his foot, out of the water. The poor thing had a huge hook protruding from its mouth.

Pitt gently gripped the fish under one armpit and eased out the hook with his good hand. Then he stared into the little fish's beady eyes.

'Look, Toto,' he said jubilantly, 'we're back in Kansas!'

60

Commander Maderas and his crew had moved out of San Felipe and resumed their search pattern when the call came through from the Hagens.

'Sir,' said his radioman, 'I just received an urgent message from the yacht *The First Attempt.*'

'What does it say?'

'The skipper, an American by the name of Joseph Hagen, reports picking up a man he caught while fishing.'

Maderas frowned. 'He must mean he snagged a dead body while trolling.'

'No, sir, he was quite definite. The man he caught is alive.'

Maderas was puzzled. 'Can't be the one we're searching for. Not after viewing the other one. Have any boats in the area reported a crew member lost overboard?'

The radioman shook his head. 'I've heard nothing.'

'What is *The First Attempt*'s position?'

'Twelve nautical miles to the northwest of us.'

Maderas stepped into the wheelhouse and nodded at Hidalgo. 'Set a course to the northwest and watch for an American yacht.' Then he turned to his radioman. 'Call this Joseph Hagen for more details on the man they pulled from the water and tell him to remain at his present position. We'll rendezvous in approximately thirty-five minutes.'

Hidalgo looked at him across the chart table. 'What do you think?'

Maderas smiled. 'As a good Catholic, I must believe what the church tells me about miracles. But this is one I have to see for myself.'

*

The fleet of yachts and the many boats of the Mexican fishing fleets that ply the Sea of Cortez have their own broadcast network. There is considerable bantering among the brotherhood of boat owners, similar to the old neighbourhood telephone party lines. The chatter includes weather reports, invitations to seaboard social parties, the latest news from home ports, and even a rundown of items for sale or swap.

The word went up and down the Gulf about the owners of *The First Attempt* catching a human on a fishing line. Interest was fuelled by those who embellished the story before passing it on through the Baja net. Yacht owners who tuned in late heard a wild tale about the Hagens catching a killer whale and finding a live man inside.

Some of the larger oceangoing vessels were equipped with radios capable of reaching stations in the United States. Soon reports were rippling out from Baja to as far away as Washington.

The Hagen broadcast was picked up by a Mexican navy radio station in La Paz. The radio operator on duty asked for confirmation, but Hagen was too busy jabbering away with other yacht owners and failed to reply. Thinking it was another of the wild parties in the boating social swing, he noted it in his log and concentrated on official navy signals.

When he went off duty twenty minutes later, he casually mentioned it to the officer in charge of the station.

'It sounded pretty loco,' he explained. 'The report came in English. Probably an intoxicated gringo playing games over his radio.'

'Better send a patrol boat to make an inspection,' said the officer. 'I'll inform the Northern District Fleet Headquarters and see who we have in the area.'

Fleet headquarters did not have to be informed. Maderas had already alerted them that he was heading at full speed towards *The First Attempt*. Headquarters had also received an unexpected signal from the Mexican chief of naval operations, ordering the commanding officer to rush the search and extend every effort for a successful rescue operation.

Admiral Ricardo Alvarez was having lunch with his wife at the officers' club when an aide hurried to his table with both signals.

'A man caught by a fisherman.' Alverez snorted. 'What kind of nonsense is this?'

'That was the message relayed by Commander Maderas of the G-21,' replied the aide.

'How soon before Maderas comes in contact with the yacht?'

'He should rendezvous at any moment.'

'I wonder why Naval Operations is so involved with an ordinary tourist lost at sea?'

'Word has come down that the President himself is interested in the rescue,' said the aide.

Admiral Alvarez gave his wife a sour look. 'I knew that damned North American Free Trade Agreement was a mistake. Now we have to kiss up to the Americans every time one of them falls in the Gulf.'

So it was that there were more questions than answers when Pitt was transferred from *The First Attempt* soon after the patrol vessel came alongside. He stood on the deck, partially supported by Hagen, who had stripped off the torn wet suit and lent Pitt a golf shirt and a pair of shorts. Claire had replaced the bandage on his shoulder and taped one over the nasty cut on his forehead.

He shook hands with Joseph Hagen. 'I guess I'm the biggest fish you ever caught.'

Hagen laughed. 'Sure something to tell the grandkids.'

Pitt then kissed Claire on the cheek. 'Don't forget to send me your recipe for fish chowder. I've never tasted any so good.'

'You must have liked it. You put away at least a gallon.'

'I'll always be in your debt for saving my life. Thank you.'

Pitt turned and was helped into a small launch that ferried him to the patrol boat. As soon as he stepped on to the deck, he was greeted by Maderas and Hidalgo before being escorted to the sick bay by the ship's medical corpsman. Prior to ducking through a hatch, Pitt turned and gave a final wave to the Hagens.

Joe and Claire stood with their arms around each other's waist. Joe turned and looked at his wife with a puzzled expression and said, 'I've never caught five fish in my entire life and you can't cook worth sour grapes. What did he mean by your great-tasting fish chowder?'

Claire sighed. 'The poor man. He was so hurt and hungry I didn't have the heart to tell him I fed him canned soup doused with brandy.'

Curtis Starger got the word in Guaymas that Pitt had been found alive. He was searching the hacienda used by the Zolars. The call came in over his Motorola Iridium satellite phone from his office in Calexico. In an unusual display of teamwork, the Mexican investigative agencies had allowed Starger and his Customs people to probe the buildings and grounds for additional evidence to help convict the family dynasty of art thieves.

Starger and his agents had arrived to find the grounds and airstrip empty of all life. The hacienda was vacant and the pilot of Joseph Zolar's private plane had decided now was a good time to resign. He simply walked through the front gate, took a bus into town, and caught a flight to his home in Houston, Texas.

A search of the hacienda turned up nothing concrete. The rooms had been cleaned of any incriminating evidence. The abandoned plane parked on the airstrip was another matter. Inside, Starger found four crudely carved wooden effigies with childlike faces painted on them.

597

'What do you make of these?' Starger asked one of the agents, who was an expert in ancient Southwest artifacts.

'They look like some kind of Indian religious symbols.'

'Are they made from cottonwood?'

The agent lifted his sunglasses and examined the idols close up. 'Yes, I think I can safely say they're carved out of cottonwood.'

Starger ran his hand gently over one of the idols. 'I have a suspicion these are the sacred idols Pitt was looking for.'

Rudi Gunn was told while he was lying in a hospital bed. A nurse entered his room followed by one of Starger's agents.

'Mr Gunn. I'm Agent Anthony Di Maggio with the Customs Service. I thought you'd like to know that Dirk Pitt was picked up alive in the Gulf about half an hour ago.'

Gunn closed his eyes and sighed with heavy relief. 'I knew he'd make it.'

'Quite a feat of courage, I hear, swimming over a hundred kilometres through an underground river.'

'No one else could have done it.'

'I hope the good news will inspire you to become more cooperative,' said the nurse, who talked sweetly while carrying a long rectal thermometer.

'Isn't he a good patient?' asked Di Maggio.

'I've tended better.'

'I wish to hell you'd give me a pair of pyjamas,' Gunn said nastily, 'instead of this peekaboo, lace-up-the-rear, shorty nightshirt.'

'Hospital gowns are designed that way for a purpose,' the nurse replied smartly.

'I wish to God you'd tell me what it is.'

'I'd better go now and leave you alone,' said Di Maggio beating a retreat. 'Good luck on a speedy recovery.'

'Thank you for giving me the word on Pitt,' Gunn said sincerely.

'Not at all.'

'You rest now,' ordered the nurse. 'I'll be back in an hour with your medication.'

True to her word, the nurse returned in one hour on the dot. But the bed was empty. Gunn had fled, wearing nothing but the skimpy little gown and a blanket.

Strangely, those on board the *Alhambra* were the last to know.

Loren and Sandecker were meeting with Mexican Internal Police investigators beside the Pierce Arrow when news of Pitt's rescue came from the owner of a luxurious powerboat that was tied up at the nearby fuel station. He shouted across the water separating the two vessels.

'Ahoy the ferry!'

Miles Rodgers was standing on the deck by the wheelhouse talking with Shannon and Duncan. He leaned over the railing and shouted back. 'What is it?'

'They found your boy!'

The words carried inside the auto deck and Sandecker rushed out on to the open deck. 'Say again!' he yelled.

'The owners of a sailing ketch fished a fellow out of the water,' the yacht skipper replied. 'The Mexican navy reports say it's the guy they were looking for.'

Everyone was on an outside deck now. All afraid to ask the question that might have an answer they dreaded to hear.

Giordino accelerated his wheelchair up to the loading ramp as if it were a super fuel dragster. He apprehensively yelled over to the powerboat. 'Was he alive?'

'The Mexicans said he was in pretty poor shape, but came around after the boat owner's wife pumped some soup into him.'

'Pitt's alive!' gasped Shannon.

Duncan shook his head in disbelief. 'I can't believe he made it through to the Gulf!'

'I do,' murmured Loren, her face in her hands, the tears

flowing. The dignity and the poise seemed to crumble. She leaned down and hugged Giordino, her cheeks wet and flushed red beneath a new tan. 'I knew he couldn't die.'

Suddenly, the Mexican investigators were forgotten as if they were miles away and everyone was shouting and hugging each other. Sandecker, normally taciturn and reserved, let out a resounding whoop and rushed to the wheelhouse, snatched up the Iridium phone and excitedly called the Mexican Navy Fleet Command for more information.

Duncan frantically began poring over his hydrographic charts of the desert water tables, impatient to learn what data Pitt had managed to accumulate during the incredible passage through the underwater river system.

Shannon and Miles celebrated by breaking out a bottle of cheap champagne they had found in the back of the galley's refrigerator, and passing out glasses. Miles reflected genuine joy at the news, but Shannon's eyes seemed unusually thoughtful. She stared openly at Loren, as a curious envy bloomed inside her that she couldn't believe existed. She slowly became aware that perhaps she had made a mistake by not displaying more compassion towards Pitt.

'That damned guy is like the bad penny that always turns up,' said Giordino, fighting to control his emotions.

Loren looked at him steadily. 'Did Dirk tell you he asked me to marry him?'

'No, but I'm not surprised. He thinks a lot of you.'

'But you don't think it's a good idea, do you?'

Giordino slowly shook his head. 'Forgive me if I say a union between you two would not be made in heaven.'

'We're too headstrong and independent for one another. Is that what you mean?'

'There's that, all right. You and he are like express trains racing along parallel tracks, occasionally meeting in stations but eventually heading for different destinations.'

She squeezed his hand. 'I thank you for being candid.'

'What do I know about relationships?' He laughed. 'I never last with a woman more than two weeks.'

Loren looked into Giordino's eyes. 'There is something you're not telling me.'

Giordino stared down at the deck planking. 'Women seem to be intuitive about such things.'

'Who was she?' Loren asked hesitantly.

'Her name was Summer,' replied Giordino honestly. 'She died fifteen years ago in the sea off Hawaii.'

'The Pacific Vortex affair, I remember him telling me about it.'

'He went crazy trying to save her, but she was lost.'

'And he still carries her in his memory,' said Loren.

Giordino nodded. 'He never talks about her, but he often gets a faraway look in his eyes when he sees a woman who resembles her.'

'I've seen that look on more than one occasion,' Loren said, her voice melancholy.

'He can't go on forever longing for a ghost,' said Giordino earnestly. 'We all have an image of a lost love who has to be put to rest someday.'

Loren had never seen the wisecracking Giordino this wistful before. 'Do you have a ghost?'

He looked at her and smiled. 'One summer, when I was nineteen, I saw a girl riding a bicycle along a sidewalk on Balboa Island in Southern California. She wore brief white shorts and a soft green blouse tied around her midriff. Her honey-blond hair was in a long ponytail. Her legs and arms were tanned mahogany. I wasn't close enough to see the colour of her eyes, but I somehow knew they had to be blue. She had the look of a free spirit with a warm sense of humour. There isn't a day that goes by I don't recall her image.'

'You didn't go after her?' Loren asked in mild surprise.

'Believe it or not, I was very shy in those days. I walked the same sidewalk every day for a month, hoping to spot her again. But she never showed. She was probably vacationing with her parents and left for home soon after our paths crossed.'

'That's sad,' said Loren.

'Oh, I don't know.' Giordino laughed suddenly. 'We might have married, had ten kids and found we hated each other.'

'To me, Pitt is like your lost love. An illusion I can never quite hold on to.'

'He'll change,' Giordino said sympathetically. 'All men mellow with age.'

Loren smiled faintly and shook her head. 'Not the Dirk Pitts of this world. They're driven by an inner desire to solve mysteries and challenge the unknown. The last thing any of them wants is to grow old with the wife and kids and die in a nursing home.'

61

The small port of San Felipe wore a festive air. The dock was crowded with people. Everywhere there was an atmosphere of excitement as the patrol boat neared the entrance to the breakwaters forming the harbour.

Maderas turned to Pitt. 'Quite a reception.'

Pitt's eyes narrowed against the sun. 'Is it some sort of local holiday?'

'News of your remarkable journey through the earth has drawn them.'

'You've got to be kidding,' said Pitt in honest surprise.

'No, señor. Because of your discovery of the river flowing below the desert, you've become a hero to every farmer and rancher from here to Arizona who struggles to survive in a harsh wasteland.' He nodded at two vans with technicians unloading television camera equipment. 'That's why you've become big news.'

'Oh, God.' Pitt groaned. 'All I want is a soft bed to sleep in for three days.'

Pitt's mental and physical condition had improved considerably upon receiving word over the ship's radio from Admiral Sandecker that Loren, Rudi, and Al were alive, if slightly the worse for wear. Sandecker also brought him up to date on Cyrus Sarason's death at the hands of Billy Yuma and the capture of Zolar and Oxley, along with Huascar's treasure, by Gaskill and Ragsdale with the help of Henry and Micki Moore.

There was hope for the little people after all, Pitt thought stoically.

It seemed like an hour, though it was only a few minutes before the *Porquería* tied up to the *Alhambra* for the second time that day. A large paper sign was unfolded across the upper passenger deck of the ferryboat, the letters still dripping fresh paint. It read, WELCOME BACK FROM THE DEAD.

On the auto deck a Mexican mariachi street band was lined up, playing and singing a tune that seemed familiar. Pitt leaned over the railing of the patrol boat, cocked an ear, and threw back his head in laughter. He then doubled over with pain as his merriment caused a burst of fire inside his rib cage. Giordino had pulled off the ultimate coup.

'Do you know the song they're playing?' asked Maderas, mildly alarmed at Pitt's strange display of mirth and agony.

'I recognize the tune, but not the words,' Pitt gasped through the hurt. 'They're singing in Spanish.'

Míralos andando
Véalos andando
Lleva a tu novia favorita, tu compañero real
Bájate a la represa, dije la represa
Júntate con ese gentío andando, oiga la música y la canción
Es simplemente magnífico camarada, esperando en la represa
Esperando por el Roberto E. Lee.

'*Míralos andando*,' repeated Maderas, confused. 'What do they mean, "go to the dam"?'

'Levee,' Pitt guessed. 'The opening words of the song are, "go down to the levee".'

As the trumpets blared, the guitars strummed, and the seven throats of the band warbled out a mariachi version of 'Waiting for the Robert E. Lee,' Loren stood among the throng that had mobbed on board the ferry and waved wildly. She could see Pitt search the crowd until he found her and happily waved back.

She saw the dressing wrapped around his head, the left arm in a sling, and the cast on one wrist. In his borrowed shorts and golf shirt he looked out of place among the uniformed crew of the Mexican navy. At first glance, he appeared amazingly fit for a man who had survived a journey through hell, purgatory, and a black abyss. But Loren knew Pitt was a master at covering up exhaustion and pain. She could see them in his eyes.

Pitt spotted Admiral Sandecker standing behind Giordino in his wheelchair. His wandering eyes also picked out Gordo Padilla with his arm around his wife, Rosa. Jesus, Gato, and the engineer, whose name he could never remember, stood nearby brandishing bottles in the air. Then the gangplank was down, and Pitt shook hands with Maderas and Hidalgo.

'Thank you, gentlemen, and thank your corpsman for me. He did a first-rate job of patching me up.'

'It is we who are in your debt, Señor Pitt,' said Hidalgo. 'My mother and father own a small ranch not far from here and will reap the benefits when wells are sunk into your river.'

'Please make me one promise,' said Pitt.

'If it's within our power,' replied Maderas.

Pitt grinned. 'Don't ever let anyone name that damned river after me.'

He turned and walked across to the auto deck of the ferry and into a sea of bodies. Loren rushed up to him, stopped, and slowly put her arms around his neck so she would not press her body against his injuries. Her lips were trembling as she kissed him.

She pulled back as the tears flowed, smiled and said, 'Welcome home, sailor.'

Then the rush was on. Newsmen and TV cameramen from both sides of the border swarmed around as Pitt greeted Sandecker and Giordino.

'I thought sure you'd bought a tombstone this time,' said Giordino, beaming like a neon sign on the Las Vegas strip.

Pitt smiled. 'If I hadn't found the *Wallowing Windbag*, I wouldn't be here.'

'I hope you realize,' said Sandecker, faking a frown, 'that you're getting too old for swimming around in caves.'

Pitt held up his good hand as if taking an oath. 'So help me, Admiral, if I ever so much as look at another underground cavern, shoot me in the foot.'

Then Shannon came up and planted a long kiss on his lips that had Loren fuming. When she released him, she said, 'I missed you.'

Before he could reply, Miles Rodgers and Peter Duncan were pumping his uninjured hand. 'You're one tough character,' said Rodgers.

'I busted the computer and lost your data,' Pitt said to Duncan. 'I'm genuinely sorry.'

'No problem,' Duncan replied with a broad smile. 'Now that you've proven the river runs from Satan's Sinkhole under Cerro el Capirote and shown where it resurges into the Gulf, we can trace its path with floating sonic geophysical imaging systems along with transmitting instrument packages.'

At that moment, unnoticed by most of the mob, a dilapidated Mexicali taxi smoked to a stop. A man jumped out and hurried across the dock and on to the auto deck wearing only a blanket. He put his head down and barrelled his way through the mass of people until he reached Pitt.

'Rudi!' Pitt roared as he wrapped his free arm around the little man's shoulder. 'Where did you fall from?'

As if he'd timed it, Gunn's splinted fingers lost their grip on the blanket and it fell to the deck, leaving him standing in only the hospital smock. 'I escaped the clutches of the nurse from hell to come here and greet you,' he said, without any sign of embarrassment.

'Are you mending okay?'

'I'll be back at my desk at NUMA before you.'

Pitt turned and hailed Rodgers. 'Miles, you got your camera?'

'No good photographer is ever without his cameras,'

Rodgers shouted over the noise of the crowd.

'Take a picture of the three battered bastards of Cerro el Capirote.'

'And one battered bitch,' added Loren, squeezing into the lineup.

Rodgers got off three shots before the reporters took over.

'Mr Pitt!' One of the TV interviewers pushed a microphone in front of his face. 'What can you tell us about the subterranean river?'

'Only that it exists,' he answered smoothly, 'and that it's very wet.'

'How large would you say it is?'

He had to think a moment as he slipped his arm around Loren and squeezed her hip. 'I'd guess about two-thirds the size of the Rio Grande.'

'That big?'

'Easily.'

'How do you feel after swimming through underground caverns for over a hundred kilometres?'

Pitt was always irritated when a reporter asked how a mother or father felt after their house burned down with all their children inside, or how a witness felt who watched someone fall from an aeroplane without a parachute.

'Feel?' stated Pitt. 'Right now I feel that my bladder will burst if I don't get to a bathroom.'

EPILOGUE

Homecoming

62

November 4, 1998
San Felipe, Baja California

Two days later, after everyone gave detailed statements to the Mexican investigators, they were free to leave the country. They assembled on the dock to bid their farewells.

Dr Peter Duncan was the first to leave. The hydrologist slipped away early in the morning and was gone before anyone missed him. He had a busy year ahead of him as director of the Sonoran Water Project, as it was to be called. The water from the river was to prove a godsend to the drought-plagued Southwest. Water, the lifeblood of civilization, would create jobs for the people of the desert. Construction of aqueducts and pipelines would channel the water into towns and cities and would turn a dry lake into a recreational reservoir the size of Lake Powell.

Soon to follow would be projects to mine the mineral riches Pitt had discovered on his underground odyssey and to build a tourist centre beneath the earth.

Dr Shannon Kelsey was invited back to Peru to continue her excavations of the ruins in the Chachapoyan cities. Where she went, Miles Rodgers followed.

'I hope we meet again,' said Rodgers, shaking Pitt's hand.

'Only if you promise to stay out of sacred sinkholes,' Pitt said warmly.

Rodgers laughed. 'Count on it.'

Pitt looked down into Shannon's eyes. The determination and boldness burned as bright as ever. 'I wish you all the best.'

She saw in him the only man she had ever met whom she couldn't have or control. She felt an undercurrent of affection towards him she couldn't explain. Just to spite Loren again, Shannon kissed Pitt long and hard.

'So long, big guy. Don't forget me.'

Pitt nodded and said simply, 'I couldn't if I tried.'

Shortly after Shannon and Miles left in their rented car for the airport in San Diego, a NUMA helicopter dropped out of the sun and touched down on the deck of the *Alhambra*. The pilot left the engine idling as he jumped down from the cargo hatch. He looked around a moment and then, recognizing Sandecker, approached him.

'Good morning, Admiral. Ready to leave, or should I shut down the engine?'

'Keep it running,' answered Sandecker. 'What's the status of my NUMA passenger jet?'

'Waiting on the ground at the Yuma Marine Corps Air Station to fly you and the others back to Washington.'

'Okay, we're set to board.' Sandecker turned to Pitt. 'So, you're going on sick leave?'

'Loren and I thought we'd join a Classic Car Club of America tour through Arizona.'

'I'll expect you in one week.' He turned to Loren and gave her a brief kiss on the cheek. 'You're a member of Congress. Don't take any crap from him and see that he gets back in one piece, fit for work.'

Loren smiled. 'Don't worry, Admiral. My constituents want me back on the job in fighting shape too.'

'What about me?' said Giordino. 'Don't I get time off to recuperate?'

'You can sit behind a desk just as easily in a wheelchair.' Then Sandecker smiled fiendishly. 'Now, Rudi, he's a different case. I think I'll send him to Bermuda for a month.'

'Whatta guy,' said Gunn, trying desperately to keep a straight face.

It was a charade. Pitt and Giordino were like sons to Sandecker. Nothing went on between them that wasn't marked with a high degree of respect. The admiral knew with dead certainty that as soon as they were sound and able, they'd be in his office pressuring him for an ocean project to direct.

Two dockhands lifted Giordino into the helicopter. One seat had to be removed to accommodate his outstretched legs.

Pitt leaned in the doorway and tweaked one of the toes that protruded from the cast. 'Try not to lose this helicopter like all the others.'

'No big deal,' Giordino came back. 'I get one of these things every time I buy ten gallons of gas.'

Gunn placed his hand on Pitt's shoulder. 'It's been fun,' he said lightly. 'We must do it again sometime.'

Pitt made a horrified face. 'Not on your life.'

Sandecker gave Pitt a light hug. 'You rest up and take it easy,' he said softly so the others couldn't hear above the beat of the rotor blades. 'I'll see you when I see you.'

'I'll make it soon.'

Loren and Pitt stood on the deck of the ferryboat and waved until the helicopter turned northeast over the waters of the Gulf. He turned to her. 'Well, that just leaves us.'

She smiled teasingly. 'I'm starved. Why don't we head into Mexicali and find us a good Mexican restaurant?'

'Now that you've broached the subject, I have a sudden craving for huevos rancheros.'

'I guess I'll have to do the driving.'

Pitt lifted his hand. 'I still have one good arm.'

Loren wouldn't hear of it. Pitt stood on the dock and guided her as she competently drove the big Pierce Arrow and its trailer up the ramp from the auto deck of the ferryboat on to the dock.

Pitt took one last, longing look at the walking beams of the old paddlesteamer and wished he could have sailed it through the Panama Canal and up the Potomac River to Washington. But it was not meant to be. He gave a forlorn sigh and was slipping into the passenger seat when a car pulled up alongside. Curtis Starger climbed out.

He hailed them. 'Glad I caught you before you left. Dave Gaskill said to make sure you got this.'

He handed Pitt something wrapped in an Indian blanket. Unable to take it with both hands, he looked helplessly at Loren. She took the blanket and spread it open.

Four faces painted on clublike prayer sticks stared back at them. 'The sacred idols of the Montolos,' Pitt said quietly. 'Where did you find them?'

'We recovered them inside Joseph Zolar's private plane in Guaymas.'

'I'd guessed the idols were in his dirty hands.'

'They were positively identified as the missing Montolo effigies from a collector's data sheet we found with them,' explained Starger.

'This will make the Montolos very happy.'

Starger looked at him with a crooked smile. 'I think we can trust you to deliver them.'

Pitt chuckled and tilted his head towards the Travelodge. 'They're not nearly as valuable as all the gold inside the trailer.'

Starger threw Pitt a you-can't-fool-me look. 'Very funny. All the golden artifacts are accounted for.'

'I promise to drop the idols off in the Montolo village on our way to the border.'

'Dave Gaskill and I never nourished a doubt.'

'How are the Zolars?' Pitt asked.

'In jail with every charge from theft and illegal smuggling to murder hanging over their heads. You'll be happy to learn the judge denied them bail, dead certain they would flee the country.'

'You people do nice work.'

'Thanks to your help, Mr Pitt. If the Customs Service can ever do you a favour, short of smuggling illegal goods into the country, of course, don't hesitate to give us a call.'

'I'll remember that, thank you.'

Billy Yuma was unsaddling his horse after making the daily rounds of his small herd. He paused to look over the rugged landscape of cactus, mesquite, and tamarisk scattered through the rock outcroppings making up his part of the Sonoran Desert. He saw a dust cloud approaching that slowly materialized into what looked to him to be a very old automobile pulling a trailer, both vehicles painted in the same shade of dark, almost black, blue.

His curiosity rose even higher when the car and trailer stopped in front of his house. He walked from the corral as the passenger door opened and Pitt stepped out.

'A warm sun to you, my friend,' Yuma greeted him.

'And clear skies to you,' Pitt replied.

Yuma shook Pitt's right hand vigorously. 'I'm real glad to see you. They told me you died in the darkness.'

'Almost, but not quite,' said Pitt nodding at the arm held by the sling. 'I wanted to thank you for entering the mountain and saving the lives of my friends.'

'Evil men are meant to die,' said Yuma philosophically. 'I'm happy I came in time.'

Pitt handed Yuma the blanket-wrapped idols. 'I've brought something for you and your tribe.'

Yuma pulled back the top half of the blanket tenderly, as if peeking at a baby. He stared mutely for several moments into the faces of the four deities. Then tears brimmed in his eyes. 'You have returned the soul of my people, our dreams, our religion. Now our children can be initiated and become men and women.'

'I was told those who stole them experienced strange sounds like children wailing.'

'They were crying to come home.'

'I thought Indians never cried.'

Yuma smiled as the joyous impact of what he held in

his hands washed over him. 'Don't you believe it. We just don't like to let anyone see us.'

Pitt introduced Loren to Billy and his wife, Polly, who insisted they stay for dinner, and would not take no for an answer. Loren let it slip that Pitt had a taste for huevos rancheros, so Polly made him enough to feed five ranch hands.

During the meal, Yuma's friends and family came to the house and reverently looked upon the cottonwood idols. The men shook Pitt's hand while the women presented small handcrafted gifts to Loren. It was a very moving scene and Loren wept unashamedly.

Pitt and Yuma saw in each other two men who were basically very much alike. Neither had any illusions left. Pitt smiled at him. 'It is an honour to have you as a friend, Billy.'

'You are always welcome here.'

'When the water is brought to the surface,' said Pitt, 'I will see that your village is at the top of the list to receive it.'

Yuma removed an amulet on a leather thong from around his neck and gave it to Pitt. 'Something to remember your friend by.'

Pitt studied the amulet. It was a copper image of the *Demonio del Muertos* of Cerro el Capirote inlaid with turquoise. 'It is too valuable. I cannot take it.'

Yuma shook his head. 'I swore to wear it until our sacred idols came home. Now it is yours for good luck.'

'Thank you.'

Before they left Canyon Ometepec, Pitt walked Loren up to Patty Lou Cutting's grave. She knelt and read the inscription on the tombstone.

'What beautiful words,' she said softly. 'Is there a story behind them?'

'No one seems to know. The Indians say she was buried by unknown people during the night.'

'She was so young. Only ten years old.'

Pitt nodded. 'She rests in a lonely place for a ten-year-old.'

'When we get back to Washington, let's try to find if she exists in any records.'

The desert wildflowers had bloomed and died so Loren made a wreath from creosote bush branches and laid it over the grave. They stood there for a while looking over the desert. The colours fired by the setting sun were vivid and extraordinary, enhanced by the clear November air.

The whole village lined the road to wish them *adiós* as Loren steered the Pierce Arrow towards the main highway. As she shifted through the gears, Loren looked over at Pitt wistfully.

'Strange as you might think it sounds, that little village would be an idyllic place to spend a quiet honeymoon.'

'Are you reminding me that I once asked you to marry me?' said Pitt, squeezing one of her hands on the steering wheel.

'I'm willing to write it off as a moment of madness on your part.'

He looked at her. 'You're turning me down?'

'Don't act crushed. One of us has to keep a level head. You're too scrupulous to back out.'

'I was serious.'

She turned her eyes from the road and gave him a warm smile. 'I know you were, but let's face reality. Our problem is that we're great pals, but we don't need each other. If you and I lived in a little house with a picket fence, the furniture would only gather dust because neither of us would ever be home. Oil and water don't mix. Your life is the sea, mine is Congress. We could never have a close, loving relationship. Don't you agree?'

'I can't deny you make a strong case.'

'I vote we continue just the way we have. Any objections?'

Pitt did not immediately answer. He hid his relief remarkably well, Loren thought. He stared through the windshield at the road ahead for a long time. Finally, he said, 'You know what, Congresswoman Smith?'

'No, what?'

'For a politician, you're an incredibly honest and sexy woman.'

'And for a marine engineer,' she said huskily, 'you're so easy to love.'

Pitt smiled slyly and his green eyes twinkled. 'How far to Washington?'

'About five thousand kilometres. Why?'

He pulled the sling off his arm, threw it in the backseat and slid his arm around her shoulder. 'Just think, we've got five thousand kilometres to find out just how lovable I am.'

Postscript

The walls in the waiting room outside Sandecker's private office in the NUMA headquarters building are covered with a rogues' gallery of photographs taken of the admiral hobnobbing with the rich and famous. The subjects include five Presidents, numerous military leaders and heads of state, congressmen, noted scientists, and a sprinkling of motion picture stars, all staring at the camera, lips stretched in predictable smiles.

All have simple black frames. All except one that hangs in the exact centre of the others. This one has a gold frame.

In this photograph Sandecker is standing amid a strange group of people who look as if they have just been in some kind of spectacular accident. One short, curly-headed man sits in a wheelchair, his legs in plaster casts, jutting towards the cameraman. Beside him is a small man wearing hornrimmed glasses, with his head encased in a bandage and splints on several of his fingers, wearing what appears to be a flimsy untied hospital smock. Then there is an attractive woman in shorts and a haltertop who looks as if she belongs in a safe house for battered wives. Next to her stands a tall man with a bandage on his forehead and one arm in a sling. His eyes have a devil-may-care look and his head is tilted back in robust laughter.

If, after being ushered into the admiral's office, you casually ask about the unusual characters in the photograph with the gold frame, be prepared to sit and listen attentively for the next hour.

It is a long story, and Sandecker loves to tell how the *Río Pitt* got its name.

Sahara
Clive Cussler

HIS SPECTACULAR INTERNATIONAL
NO.1 BESTSELLER

Clive Cussler's peerless hero Dirk Pitt in his most gripping
and action-packed adventure yet.

Deep in the African desert, Pitt discovers that a top-secret
scientific installation is leaking a lethal chemical into the
rivers, threatening to kill thousands of people – and to
destroy all life in the world's seas.

To warn the world of the catastrophe, Pitt must escape
capture and death at the hands of a ruthless West African
dictator and French industrialist, and undertake a long,
perilous journey across the merciless Sahara . . .

'The ultimate Dirk Pitt tale. Nobody does it better than
Clive Cussler, America's finest adventure writer.'
    STEPHEN COONTS, author of *Under Siege*

'A cram course in rip-roaring action . . . a sizzling yet
thoughtful thriller.'   *Chicago Tribune*

'Amazing feats of derring-do . . . non-stop action . . .
refreshing escapist entertainment.'   *Washington Post*

ISBN 0 586 21766 5

Dragon
Clive Cussler

A NUCLEAR PEARL HARBOR

Buried in the depths of the Pacific Ocean, off the coast of Japan, lies one of the greatest drowned secrets of World War II – a crashed B-29 bomber that was carrying a third atomic bomb to Japan in 1945.

Its deadly cargo, lost in the sea for nearly fifty years, is at the heart of this latest Dirk Pitt adventure thriller, in which a small group of Japanese nationalist fanatics, dreaming of a new Nipponese Empire, set out to neutralise and black-mail the USA – with nuclear weapons planted strategically in the country's major cities. . .

'Clive Cussler and Dirk Pitt are the first names in adventure. In *Dragon* they're tightly wound to their heart-stopping best.'
STEPHEN COONTS

'A page-turning romp that achieves a level of fast-paced action and derring-do . . . solidly entertaining.'
Publishers Weekly

ISBN 0 00 720560-0

Treasure
Clive Cussler

THE HIGH EXPLOSIVE
SECRET OF THE AGES

AD 391: Fanatics destroy the greatest storehouse of knowledge and treasure in the ancient world – the great library and museum of Alexandria. But a few conspirators secretly remove the most precious items and ship them to a distant, desolate land, hiding them deep in a specially excavated stronghold. . .

AD 1991: A UN plane, with the Secretary General aboard, crashes in the icy wastes of Greenland, brought down by a monstrously cunning terrorist conspiracy. Troubleshooter supreme Dirk Pitt, in the area on an undercover search mission for a crippled Soviet submarine, finds himself caught up in an even more dangerous vortex of complex intrigue. And with a beautiful, sensual female archaeologist who has found an ancient gold coin nearby – far further north than it should be. . .

Dirk Pitt's quest for the Alexandrian treasure combines with his battle against the forces of murderous international terrorism in an outstanding story of razor's-edge suspense, hair-trigger international intrigue and all-out action and excitement.

'If you like your action fast, your prose faster and your plot unexpected, then Mr Cussler is the man for you.'

Manchester Evening News

'Clive Cussler is the guy *I* read.'   TOM CLANCY

ISBN 0 00 720559-7